C000154483

HAROLD ROBBINS

By Harold Robbins

Never Love a Stranger
The Dream Merchants
A Stone for Danny Fisher
Never Leave Me
79 Park Avenue
Stiletto
The Carpetbaggers
Where Love Has Gone
The Adventurers
The Inheritors
The Betsy
The Pirate
The Lonely Lady
Dreams Die First
Memories of Another Day
Goodbye, Janette
Spellbinder
Descent From Xanadu
The Storyteller
The Piranhas

STILETTO

THE LONELY LADY

DREAMS DIE FIRST

Harold Robbins

Hodder & Stoughton
LONDON SYDNEY AUCKLAND

Stiletto first published in Great Britain
by Mayflower Books

The Lonely Lady first published in Great Britain in 1976
by New English Library

Dreams Die First first published in Great Britain in 1977
by New English Library

This collected volume first published in Great Britain in 1994
by Hodder and Stoughton Limited
a division of Hodder Headline PLC

10 9 8 7 6 5 4 3 2 1

British Library Cataloguing in Publication Data

A CIP catalogue record for this title is available from
the British Library

ISBN 0 340 62327 6

Printed and bound in Great Britain by
Mackays of Chatham PLC, Chatham, Kent

Hodder and Stoughton Ltd
A division of Hodder Headline PLC
338 Euston Road
London NW1 3BH

ONE

It was after ten o'clock and there were only three men at the bar and one man at a table in the rear when the hustler came in. A blast of the cold night air came in with her.

She climbed up on a stool and let her thin winter coat fall from her shoulders. 'Gimme a beer,' she said.

Silently the bartender drew a glass of beer and placed it in front of her. He picked up the quarter and rang it up.

'Any action tonight, Jimmy?' she asked, her eyes searching the men at the bar for a response to her question.

The bartender shook his head. 'Not tonight, Maria. It's Sunday night and all the *touristas* are home in their beds.' He walked away and began to polish some glasses under the bar. He watched her sip at her beer. Maria.

He called them all Maria. The little Puerto Rican girls with their bright shiny black eyes and their hard little breasts and buttocks. He wondered when she had had her last shot.

The hustler gave up on the men at the bar. She turned to look at the man seated at the table. She could only see his back but she could tell from the cut of his clothing that he wasn't local. She looked questioningly at the bartender. He shrugged his shoulders and she slid off her stool and started back to the table.

The man was looking down at his whisky glass when she stopped beside him. 'Lonesome, señor?' she asked.

She knew the moment he lifted his head to look at her what his answer would be. The dark ice-blue eyes and tanned face and hungry mouth. Men such as he never bought their pleasures, they took them.

'No, thank you,' Cesare said politely.

The hustler smiled vaguely, nodded her head and went back to the bar. She climbed up on the stool again and took out a cigarette.

The stocky little bartender held a match for her. 'Like I said,' he whispered, smiling, 'it's Sunday night.'

The girl dragged deep on the cigarette and let the smoke out slowly. 'I know,' she said tonelessly, the first faint sign of worry appearing on her face. 'But I gotta keep workin'. It's an expensive habit.'

The telephone in the booth beside the bar began to ring and the bartender left her to answer it. He came out of the booth and walked over to Cesare's table. '*Para usted*, señor.'

'*Mil gracias*,' Cesare answered, going to the telephone. 'Hello,' he said as he closed the door of the booth.

The woman's voice was almost a whisper. She spoke in Italian. 'It will have to be in the morning,' she said, 'before he appears in court.'

Cesare answered in the same language. 'There is no other place?'

'No,' she said, her voice very clear in the receiver despite its softness. 'We have not been able to learn where he is coming from. We only know that he will appear at court at eleven o'clock.'

'And the others?' Cesare asked. 'Are they still in the same place?'

'Yes,' she answered. 'In Las Vegas and Miami. Are your plans made?'

'I have everything in readines,' Cesare replied.

The woman's voice grew harsh. 'The man must die before he sits in the witness chair. The others too.'

Cesare laughed shortly. 'Tell Don Emilio not to worry. They are all as good as dead right now.'

He put down the telephone and walked out into the dark Spanish Harlem night. He turned his collar up against the cold winter wind and began to walk. Two blocks away on Park Avenue he caught a lone cruising taxi. He climbed into it. 'El Morocco,' he said to the driver.

He sank back into his seat and lit a cigarette, an excitement beginning inside him. It was real now. For the first time since the war it was real again. He remembered how it was the first time. The first girl and the first death. Strange how they always seemed to come together. The reality of living was never greater than when you held death clutched tightly in your hands.

It seemed a long time ago. He was fifteen years old and the year was 1935. There had been a parade in the little Sicilian village at the foot of the mountain that day. The Fascisti were always having parades. There were banners and pictures of Il Duce everywhere. His scowling face and angry clenched fist and piglike bulging eyes. Live Dangerously. Be Italian. Italy Means Strength.

It had been evening when Cesare reached the foot of the mountain on his way home. He looked up. The castle stood there on the edge of a promontory near the peak. Ornate and ugly. As it had been for almost six hundred years. Since some long-gone ancestor, the first Count Cardinali, took to wife a daughter of the family Borgia.

He had started up the mountain past Gandolfo's vineyard and the heavy smell of the black grapes came out to him. He could still remember the drums beating and the excitement inside him that night. His mind was filled with the old recruiting sergeant's lewd stories of the orgies that took place in Il Duce's palace.

'*Collones*! ' the old soldier had chortled. 'There never was such *collones* in all the history of Italy! Five different girls he had in one night. I know for it was my duty to bring each one of them to him. And each girl left bowlegged, as if she had been mounted by a bull. While he, he was up at six o'clock in the morning, strong and fresh, leading us in two hours of drill.' The spittle ran down his cheeks. 'I tell you, young fellows, if it's women you want, the uniform of the Italian Army will get them for you. It makes every girl think she's getting a piece of Il Duce!'

It was then that Cesare had seen the girl. She had come from in back of the Gandolfo house. He had seen her before but never when his senses had been so aflame. She was a tall, strong, full-breasted animal, this daughter of the wine-maker, and she was carrying a skin of wine from the cooling house in the back field near the stream. She paused when she saw him.

He stopped and looked at her. The heat of the day was still heavy in him and he wiped the beads of sweat from his face with the back of his arm.

Her voice was very soft and respectful. 'Perhaps the signor would like a drink of cooling wine?'

He nodded, not speaking, and walked toward her. He held the skin high and the red wine ran down his throat, spilling over his chin. He felt the grape bite into him and warm him inside and cool him at the same time. He gave the skin back to her and they stood there looking at each other.

Slowly a redness crept up from her throat and bosom into her face and her eyes fell. He could see the sudden thrusting of her nipples against the thin peasant blouse and the swell of her breasts over the top of it.

He turned away from her and began to walk into the woods. From the generations of knowledge deep inside him came the command that had no doubt about its ability to possess.

'Come!'

Obediently, almost as if she were an automaton, the

girl followed him. Deep into the woods where the trees were so thick one could hardly see the sky above. She sank to the ground beside him and never said a word while his fingers stripped the clothing from her body.

He knelt there for a moment, studying the strong muscular lines of her body, the full plum-tipped breasts, the flat muscular belly that rose and fell, her heavy strong legs. He felt a torrent rise inside him and he threw himself across her.

It was the first time for him but not for her. Twice he screamed in an agony as she locked him tightly to her, then spent, he rolled away and lay breathing heavily on the moist ground beside her.

She turned towards him silently, her fingers and mouth exploring, probing. At first he pushed her away, then his hands touched her breasts and froze there. Involuntarily he squeezed and she cried out in pain.

For the first time now he looked into her face. Her eyes were wide and moisture was full in them. He squeezed again. Again she cried out. But this time her eyes were closed. There were tears in their corners but her mouth was open in a gasping ecstasy as if she sought to gulp strength from the air.

A sense of power he had never known before came up in him. Cruelly now, he tightened his fingers. This time her scream of pain sent the birds shrilling from the perches in the trees. Her eyes flew open and she stared at him, then worshipfully she bent her head to his suddenly reawakened body.

It was dark when he began to walk away from her. He felt strong and complete and the grass was like carpet beneath his feet. He was almost at the edge of the small clearing when her voice stopped him.

'Signor!'

He turned around. She was on her feet now and her nude body gleamed in the dark as if it sprang from the very earth itself. Her eyes were luminous pools in her face. She half smiled to herself, a pride and satisfaction deep within her. The others would be jealous when she told them of this. This was no labourer, no itinerant crop worker. This was the blood, the true blood, the future Count Cardinali.

'*Grazia!*' she said sincerely.

He nodded curtly and plunged into the woods and was gone from her sight before she could bend to pick up her clothing.

It was six weeks later at the fencing school down in the village that Cesare next heard of her. The Maestro had long since given up teaching Cesare who was far superior to his aging skills and only attended classes to keep in practice. The door had opened and a young soldier entered.

He came into the small gymnasium and looked around, his modern Il Duce's guard uniform oddly out of place in this ancient atmosphere of swords. His voice was tense. 'Which one of you is known by the name of Cesare Cardinali?'

There was a sudden silence in the room. The two young men who were fencing put down their foils and turned to the newcomer. Cesare came slowly from the wall where he had been practicing with the weights.

He stopped in front of the soldier. 'I am,' he said.

The soldier stared at him. 'I am the affianced of my cousin, Rosa,' he said tightly.

Cesare looked at him. He knew no one by that name. 'And who is she?' he asked politely.

'Rosa Gandolfo!' The name tore angrily from the soldier's lips. 'And I am called from my post in Rome to marry her because you have made her with child!'

Cesare stared at him for a moment as the understanding came to him. Then he relaxed slightly. 'Is that all?' he asked, a strange feeling of pride beginning to come up inside him. 'I will speak to my father, the Count, about some money for you.'

He turned and started to walk away. The soldier spun him around again. 'Money?' he shouted. 'Is that all you think I want? Money? No!'

Cesare looked at him coldly. 'As you wish. Then I will not speak with my father.'

The soldier's hand slashed across his face. 'I demand satisfaction!'

The handprint stood out clearly on Cesare's suddenly white face. He stared at the soldier without fear. 'The Cardinalis find no honour in fighting with a commoner.'

The soldier spat forth the words venomously: 'The Cardinalis are cowards, pimps and despoilers of women! And you, the bastard son, are more like them than they are themselves! Il Duce was right when he said that the aristocrats of Italy are sick and decadent and that they must give way to the strength of the paisanos!'

Cesare's hand moved faster than light and, though the soldier weighed a good twenty pounds more than he, the soldier sprawled on the floor. Cesare looked down at him. A strange look began to come into his face, his eyes grew dark, so dark one could not see the blue of them. He looked up at the Maestro. It had been a long time since anyone had dared refer to his illegitimate birth.

'Give him a sword,' he said quietly. 'I will fight him.'

'No, Signor Cesare, no!' The Maestro was frightened. 'The Count, your father, will not—'

Cesare interrupted him. His voice was quiet but there was no mistaking the authority in it. 'Give him a sword. My father will not like this slur on our name to go unanswered!'

The soldier was on his feet now. He smiled and looked at Cesare. 'In the army of Italy we are trained in the tradition. A sword in the right hand, a stiletto in the left.'

Cesare nodded. 'So be it.'

The soldier began to take off his jacket, his muscular arms and shoulders came into view. He stared confidently at Cesare. 'Send for a priest, my young rapist,' he said, 'for you are already a dead man.'

Cesare did not answer, but deep in his eyes an unholy joy began to grow. He threw his shirt on the floor. 'Ready?'

The soldier nodded. The Maestro called position. Cesare's white frame looked thin beside the heavy brown body of the soldier.

'En garde!'

The crossed swords gleamed over their heads. The Maestro struck them up. The soldier's sword flashed down in a powerful thrust.

Cesare parried and the sword slipped past his side. He laughed aloud. The soldier cursed and slashed heavily.

Lightly Cesare slid the blow away from him and bent to the attack. Quickly he circled his foil, the swords locked and he tore the soldier's sword from his grasp. It fell clattering to the floor.

Cesare placed his sword's point against the soldier's breast. 'Your honor, sir?'

The soldier cursed and struck it away with his stiletto. He circled to one side trying to get to his sword but Cesare was in front of him.

The soldier stared at him and cursed. Cesare laughed again. There was a joy in him now that none there had ever seen. Cesare threw his sword into the corner beside the other.

Before its clatter ceased the soldier sprang at him, the stiletto flashing downward toward Cesare's face. Cesare moved slightly and the stiletto slashed the empty air.

Cesare was crouching, the stiletto held lightly, point out, in the palm of his hand. The soldier, too, was crouching now. Warily he reached out. Cesare easily parried.

Cesare thrust forward; the soldier stepped back then, seeing an opening, sprang again. This time the two bodies locked in a grotesque embrace. Cesare seemed all but lost as the soldier's arms wrapped themselves around him. They stood there for a moment, swaying back and forth as if in some obscene embrace, then slowly the soldier's arms began to fall.

His stiletto fell from his nerveless fingers and he sank to his knees on the floor, his hands clutching at Cesare's hips. Cesare stepped back.

It was then they could see the stiletto in Cesare's hand.

The soldier fell face down on the floor and the Maestro hurriedly rushed forward. 'Call a doctor! ' he said anxiously, kneeling beside the soldier.

Cesare turned from picking up his shirt. 'Don't bother,' he said quietly, starting for the door. 'He's dead.'

Unthinking, he dropped the stiletto in his jacket as he went out the door into the night.

The girl was waiting for him on the hill where the road made its last turn toward the castle. He stopped when he saw her. They stared at each other silently. Then Cesare turned and walked off the road into the woods. Obediently the girl followed him.

When they could no longer see the road, Cesare turned to her. Her eyes were wide and luminous as she stepped toward him. He ripped down her blouse and seized her naked breasts cruelly in his hands.

'Ai-ee!' she screamed, half fainting.

Then the pain tore through him, from his swollen testes to his vitals. Frantically he ripped his clothing from him, his seed already spilling wildly on the ground.

The bright Sicilian moon was already high over their heads when he sat up in the darkness and reached for his clothing.

'Signor,' she whispered.

He didn't answer. His hands found his trousers and he got up and stepped into them.

'Signor, I have come to warn you. My cousin—'

'I know,' he interrupted, looking down at her.

Her voice was frightened. 'But he said he was going to kill you.'

He laughed almost silently. 'I am here.'

'But, signor, he may find you any moment. Even here. He is very jealous and very proud.'

'Not any more,' Cesare said flatly. 'He is dead.'

'Dead?' The girl's voice was almost a scream. She leaped to her feet. 'You killed him?'

Cesare was buttoning his shirt. '*Si*,' he said shortly.

She came at him like a tigress, her hands scratching and striking at him. She was half crying, half screaming. 'You fiend! Lie with me when his blood is still fresh on your hands? Lower than animals, you! Who am I to marry now? What am I going to do with this thing you put in my belly?'

A sudden knowledge came to him as he gripped her hands and held them tight. 'You wanted it there or it wouldn't be there,' he said.

She stared up into his eyes knowing now that he knew. She drew her head back and spat up into his face. 'I don't want it now!' she shouted. 'It will be a monster, a bastard like its father!'

He brought his knee up sharply into the softness of her belly. The pain choked in her throat and she fell, writhing and vomiting against the earth.

He looked down at her, his hand involuntarily going into his jacket pocket and finding the stiletto still there. He took it out.

She looked up at him, a fear beginning to grow in her eyes.

His lips pulled back in a cold smile. 'If you don't want it then, cut it out of yourself with this.' He threw the stiletto to the ground beside her. 'It will purify you. His blood is still on it.'

He turned and walked away.

In the morning they found the girl dead. She was lying there with the stiletto grasped in her two hands, her thighs already caked with the drying blood that had soaked into the earth beneath her.

Two days later Cesare left for school in England. He was not to return to Italy until the war began almost five years later.

In the meantime the Gandolfos built a new winery with the ten thousand lire Count Cardinali gave them.

The taxi pulled to a stop before El Morocco and the giant doorman opened the door. He saw Cesare and smiled. 'Ah, Count Cardinali,' he said warmly. 'Good evening. I was beginning to think we weren't going to see you tonight.'

Cesare paid the driver and got out of the taxi, looking at his watch. It was eleven-thirty. He smiled to himself. The thought of the woman waiting inside the restaurant for him was part of the excitement too. Her warm lovely body also held the reality of living.

TWO

SPECIAL Agent George Baker began to turn off the lights in his office. When he reached the door he hesitated a moment, then went back to his desk and picked up the telephone. It was a direct line to Captain Strang at Police Headquarters. 'How does it look?' Baker asked.

Strang's heavy voice boomed through the wire. 'Haven't you gone home yet? It's after eleven o'clock.'

'I know,' Baker replied. 'I had some things to clean up. I thought I'd check with you before I left.'

'There's nothing to worry about,' the policeman boomed confidently. 'We got the place covered. The area around the courthouse is clear and I put men in every building and on every corner all around the place. They will stay there all night and through the morning until we get the witness into court. Believe me, nobody will get within ten feet of him until he enters the courthouse.'

'Good,' Baker said. 'I'll go right out to the airport in the morning and meet the plane. I'll see you at the courthouse at eleven o'clock.'

'Okay. Stop worrying now and get some sleep,' Strang said. 'Everything's under control here.'

But when Baker got back to his hotel room, he couldn't sleep. He sat up in bed and thought of calling his wife, then put the thought out of his mind. She would be too upset at the telephone call in the middle of the night. He got out of bed and sat in a chair.

Idly he took his gun from the holster draped over the back of the chair and checked it. He spun the cylinder and thrust it back in the holster. I'm edgy, he thought. I've been on this thing too long.

For the past six years there had been nothing else for him. Only this one case. 'Break the back of the Mafia, the Society, the Syndicate, or whatever the name of the organization is that has a stranglehold on America's underworld,' the chief had said to him.

He was a young man then, at least it seemed so because he felt like an old man now. When he had started on this case, his son had been a junior in high school; this year the boy was graduating from college.

Time went by; the years had passed frustratingly as every lead petered out. There was no way to get to the top, to the Dons. Sure, the small fry kept falling into their traps with almost statistical regularity; but the big ones always got away.

Then the break had come. A man had talked about

the murder of two federal narcotics agents aboard a small ship just coming into New York. Painstakingly the lead had been followed and now for the first time in the history of organized crime, four of its top leaders were on trial. For murder and conspiracy to murder.

In his mind's eye he could see the I.D. file on each defendant. George 'Big Dutch' Wehrman, age 57, 21 arrests, no convictions, present occupation union official; Allie 'The Fixer' Fargo, age 56, 1 arrest, 1 conviction, 1 suspended sentence, present occupation contractor; Nicholas 'Dandy Nick' Pappas, age 54, 32 arrests, 9 for murder, 2 convictions, 20 days in jail, present occupation none, known gambler; Emilio 'The Judge' Matteo, age 61, 11 arrests, 1 conviction, 5 years in jail, deported, present occupation retired.

The thought of the last man brought a bitter smile to his lips. Retired, the report had said. Retired from what? From murder, from narcotics, from participation in almost any form of illegal activity conceived by the mind of man? Not the Judge, not Don Emilio as he was sometimes called by his associates.

Deportation to Italy along with Luciano and Adonis after the war had resulted only in giving him a license to steal. No matter what aid Matteo had given the government in planning the invasion of Italy during the war, they should not have agreed to let him out of jail. Once they had a man like that locked up, the only sensible thing to do was to throw away the key.

Baker remembered the countless times he had gone flying around the country on the tip that Matteo had come back; but he was never there. Still there were all the signs that he had been there. The narcotics and the dead. Mute evidence. But this time it was different. This time they had evidence that would talk, if only to save their own lives. And because of that evidence, Matteo had been brought back from Italy.

It had taken a long time but now they had them. Three witnesses, whose testimony corroborated each other. The testimony that almost certainly meant death for the defendants. There was only one problem remaining now. That was to bring each man to the witness chair in the courtroom – alive.

Restlessly Baker got out of the chair and walked over to the window and stared out at the darkened city. Knowing Matteo as he did, he was certain that somewhere in the city, an assassin or assassins were waiting.

The big questions were how, what, when, where and who?

The maitre d' with the mustache bowed obsequiously before her. 'Miss Lang,' he murmured, 'Count Cardinali is already here. If you will follow me, please.'

He turned and she followed him with her slow, graceful, model's walk, her long red tresses shimmering against her shoulders. She walked slowly, savoring the turning heads, the appreciative looks following her. She heard one of the dowagers whispering.

'That's the "Smoke and Flame" girl, Barbara Lang. You know, my dear. From the cosmetic ads.'

The captain led her down along the zebra-striped banquette to where Cesare sat at a table. Cesare rose as he saw her. He smiled and kissed her hand as the captain held the table away. She sat down and let her coat slip back on the banquette.

'Champagne?' Cesare asked.

She nodded as she looked around the restaurant. The soft lights, the elaborately jeweled women and the men with the round, well-fed, yet hungry faces. This was the heights. This was El Morocco. And she was here with a real Count. Not with a phony, half-slobbering promoter who sat with one hand holding in his fat little gut and the other hand under the table trying to creep up inside her dress.

She turned to look at him as she lifted the glass to her lips. Cesare, Count Cardinali, who could trace his family back six hundred years to the time of the Borgias, who drove racing cars all over the world, who had his name in the society columns every day.

'Will you be ready in the morning?' he asked, smiling.

She returned his smile. 'I'm very efficient,' she said. 'My bags are already packed.'

'Good,' he nodded, lifting his glass. 'To you.'

'To our holiday.' She smiled. She sipped her champagne reflectively. It hadn't always been like this. It wasn't too long ago that the only 'sparkling' drink she had tasted was beer. It seemed only the day before yesterday that the model school she had attended while working as a clerk in the store back home in Buffalo had called her. This was a chance for her to get some work and experience doing some publicity on a motion picture that was having its première locally.

She had taken the afternoon off and gone up to the hotel

for an interview. Nervously she stood in the corridor outside the largest suite in the hotel and heard the raucous shouts of laughter coming from inside the suite. Quickly, before she lost her nerve, she pressed the buzzer. The door opened and a tall young man stood there.

She took a deep breath and the words tumbled out. 'I'm Barbara Lang,' she said. 'The agency sent me over. They said you needed a girl for publicity work.'

The young man stood there for a moment and looked at her. Then he smiled. It was a pleasant smile and gave his rather pale face a nice, gentle look. He stepped back and opened the door wide. 'I'm Jed Goliath,' he said. 'I handle the publicity. Come on in, I'll introduce you around.'

She had entered the room, hoping her nervousness wouldn't show. She felt the moisture breaking out on her upper lip the way it always did and silently she cursed to herself. There were three other men in the living room of the suite and a table set up in the corner held the makings of a cocktail lounge.

Goliath led her over to the man seated on a chair near the open window. Despite his smile, his face had a tortured, worried look. This was Mendel Bayliss, the writer-producer of the picture, and the worried look came from having his own money in the picture. 'Hi,' he said. 'It's hot. Have a drink?'

The second man was one she recognized right away. He was the second banana on a weekly television show. The pratfall kid they called him. He had just stopped by to visit the producer for whom he had worked in an unsuccessful show some years before.

The third man was Johnny Gleason. He was the local manager of the motion-picture company. He was tall, red-faced and very drunk. He stood up and bowed when they were introduced and almost fell over the coffee table in front of him.

Jed smiled at Barbara encouragingly as he pushed the manager safely back on the couch. 'We've been drinking since eight o'clock this morning,' he explained.

She managed a smile as if to imply that things like this happened every day in her life. 'The agency said there was some publicity work to do on a movie,' she said, trying to get some note of business back into the meeting.

'That's right,' Jed answered. 'We need a Never-Never girl.'

'A what?' she gasped.

'A Never-Never girl,' he explained. 'That's the name of our picture: "Never, Never".'

'You're tall,' Bayliss said.

'Five-nine,' she answered.

'Take off your shoes,' he answered, standing up.

She took off her shoes and stood there holding them in her hand while he walked over and stood next to her.

'I'm five-eleven,' he said proudly. 'We can't have a girl taller than me in all the newspaper pictures. You'll have to wear low heels.'

'Yes, sir,' she said.

He walked back to his chair and sat down, his eyes going over her figure appraisingly. 'Bring a bathing suit with you?' he asked.

She nodded. It was standard equipment in the model's

hatbox she carried with her everywhere she went.

'Put it on,' he said curtly. 'Let's see what you got.'

The pratfall kid picked it right up. He weaved his way over to her and peered up into her face. He leered happily. 'We won't mind if you show us without the bathing suit either, baby,' he whispered loudly.

She could feel her face flushing and she looked helplessly at Jed. He smiled again reassuringly and led her to a bedroom. 'You can change in here,' he said, closing the door behind her.

She changed swiftly, pausing only for a moment to check herself in the bathroom mirror. For once she was grateful for the golden tan that clung to her since the summer. She took a Kleenex and patted the moisture from her upper lip and went back into the living room.

All eyes turned to her as she opened the door. For a moment she felt self-conscious, then with her model's walk she glided to the center of the room and slowly turned around.

'She's got a good clean figure,' the producer said.

'Not enough tits for me,' the pratfall kid chortled. 'I'm a T-man, myself.'

The producer was still watching her. 'What d'yuh expect from a high-fashion model? The clothes fall better on them without 'em. She's got more than most.' He looked up at her face. 'Thirty-five?' he asked.

She nodded.

The producer got to his feet, smiling. 'I got the best eye in Hollywood,' he said. 'Haven't guessed wrong in twenty years.' He turned to Jed. 'She'll do.'

The pratfall kid came over and leered up at her

breasts. 'Thanks for the mammaries,' he sang in an off-key voice.

Bayliss laughed. 'Cut the clownin',' he said. 'Come on, it's time we got something to eat.' He started for the door.

The pratfall kid and the film manager staggered after him to the door. At the door Bayliss turned back and spoke to Jed. 'Tell her what she's gotta do and have her at the press conference at five o'clock.'

The door closed behind them and she and Jed looked at each other. He smiled. 'Maybe you'd like to sit down for a moment and catch your breath?'

Her legs felt suddenly weak. She smiled gratefully and sank into the chair the producer had vacated. It was still warm from his body.

Jed filled a glass with ice cubes and poured a bottle of Coke into it. He took it over and handed it to her.

'Thanks,' she said, taking it from him and sipping it.

'They're crazy,' he said, still smiling, looking down at her white bathing suit and her long tan legs.

'Are they always like that?' she asked.

Jed was still smiling but she thought she detected a faint note of bitterness in his voice. 'Always,' he answered. 'They're big men. They're always proving something.'

For the next week she was the best-known girl in Buffalo. Not a day passed that her picture wasn't in the papers. Twice that week she was in the Niagara Falls paper. She was on every local radio and television show and met every important newspaperman and person in the area.

Jed was always near. Unobtrusively he set up pictures for her and the producer, together and alone. Somewhere in the picture was always a plug for the movie. That first night she didn't get home until three o'clock in the morning. The next night she didn't get home at all. She spent the night in Jed's room.

It was a giddy, supercharged week and when it was over, everything seemed flat and meaningless. Of all the people she had met that week, no one seemed to remember her, not even the matrons who attended the weekly fashion show at the department store where she worked.

She remembered what Jed had said to her the last night. 'You got too much for this hick town, Barbara. You come down to New York. That's the place for a girl like you.'

He had given her his card and the card of a photographer he knew. Six months later she went to New York. The manager of Jed's building said that he had moved to California but the photographer was still there. The funny thing about it all was that Jed had been right. New York *was* the place for her. Within two weeks she had an assignment for a *Vogue* cover. Within a year she was one of the most sought-after high-fashion models in New York. Her fee was sixty dollars an hour and she earned almost twenty thousand a year.

She worked very hard and went out very little. The camera was too harsh and revealing when she did not get enough rest. On the weekends she flew home to Buffalo and lounged around the front yard of the new house she had bought for her mother.

Then one afternoon she had been modeling some new

suits in front of the Plaza Hotel. One of the props they were using was a bright red Alfa Romeo sports car. As she posed opening the door of the car, the agency executive came up to her. With him was a tall, lean, foreign-looking man. The man had a handsome, savage look about him and when he smiled his teeth were strong and white.

'Barbara,' the agency executive said, 'I'd like you to meet Count Cardinali. He was kind enough to loan us this car for these shots.'

Barbara looked up at him. She knew the name. Count Cardinali. It was one of those names you read in the papers. Almost a legend. Like De Portago and Pignatari, somehow you never expected them to be quite real. Cesare took her hand and kissed it. 'So pleased to meet you.' He smiled.

She smiled and nodded and he went away and she went back to work. That evening she was lounging in her slacks, watching television, when the phone rang. She picked it up. 'Hello,' she said.

'Barbara?' Somehow his accent was slightly stronger when it came through the telephone. 'This is Cesare Cardinali. How would you like to have some supper with me tonight?'

'I – I don't know,' she answered, unexpectedly flustered. 'I was just lounging around.'

His voice was very sure. 'That's all right. I won't pick you up until eleven o'clock. We'll go to El Morocco.'

He put down the phone before she could answer and she went into the bathroom and began drawing a tub of water. It wasn't until she was in the steaming tub that she realized she was really going to see him that night.

Later, when they were seated in the restaurant, he lifted his glass of champagne toward her. 'Barbara,' he said in a serious voice. 'There is a great deal of talk around town that you are planning to become a promiscuous woman. I like that. And I would like it even more if you would allow me to be of some help in that matter.'

'What?' she gasped, looking at him startled.

But he was smiling and she knew that he was mocking her. She began to smile and picked up her glass. He had a lot to learn about American girls.

Now Cesare's voice brought her back from her reverie. 'I'll pick you up about nine-thirty,' he was saying. 'That will give me time to go down to the courthouse and get my papers before we drive to the airport.'

'Fine,' she said. 'I'll be ready.'

THREE

CESARE pulled the red Alfa Romeo into a parking place outside the building reserved for official cars only. He grinned at Barbara. 'You don't mind waiting a few minutes while I run inside and pick up the papers, do you?'

She shook her head. But with a typical middle-class fear of official signs and orders, she said, 'Hurry, I don't want them to chase me out of here.'

'They won't,' Cesare said confidently, getting out of the car. He walked toward the building, his Alpine fedora sitting jauntily on his head.

She looked after him as he went into the entrance. He walked under the sign that read *U.S. Dept. of Immigration and Naturalization* and disappeared into the building. In some ways he was like a small boy.

That was how it had been when he called her up last

week. He had just returned from Europe, he had said, and had visited his home. Now his mind was made up. He was going to become an American citizen. And to celebrate it, when he picked up the papers, would she join him on a week's vacation some place where the sun was shining?

She had agreed to go without even thinking about it but when she put down the telephone she began to smile to herself. Maybe this time he was serious about a girl. Of course she had heard about the others but a whole week – a lot could happen in a week.

There was a noise from around the corner and she looked up. There seemed to be a crowd of people gathering there. A policeman came by. He stopped at the side of the car and looked at her. 'Will you be here long, miss?' he asked.

'Not long, officer,' she said quickly. 'My friend just went inside to pick up his first papers.'

The policeman nodded and started to walk away. A roar came from around the corner. She called after him. 'What's going on around the corner, officer?'

He glanced toward the corner and then back at her. 'That's Foley Square, miss. They're starting the big trial of them gangsters this morning. It seems like everybody in New York wants to get into that courtroom.'

Cesare went into the first reception room. The clerk at the counter looked up at him. 'I'm Cesare Cardinali,' he said. 'I've come to pick up my papers.'

The clerk nodded. 'First papers?'

'Yes,' Cesare answered.

The clerk checked a tab file on the counter. He pulled out a small card and looked up. 'If you'll just take a seat, Mr Cardinali, I'll have them ready for you in about ten minutes.'

Cesare smiled. 'That will be fine.' He hesitated a moment then asked, 'Is there a lavatory around here?'

The clerk smiled and pointed out the door. 'Down the hall to your left,' he said.

'Thank you,' Cesare answered, already on his way to the door. 'I'll be right back.'

He walked out the door and down the hall. He stopped in front of the men's room and looked around. There was no one watching. He walked quickly past it and opened a door marked *stairs*. The door closed behind him and he began to go up the steps two at a time.

The black limousine pulled to a stop in front of the court-house and the crowd pressed around it. Baker looked out from his seat next to the witness then turned back to him. 'You're a big draw,' he said.

Dinky Adams, the witness, a long horse-faced man, shrank back in his seat and pulled his hat down over his face. 'Big deal,' he snarled humorlessly. 'My life ain't goin' to be worth two cents once they know who I am.'

'Nobody's going to bother you,' Baker said reassuringly. 'We told you you would be protected and we've done all right so far.'

A flying squad of police cleared the area around the car. Captain Strang stuck his head down near the window. 'Okay, let's go.'

Baker got out first, followed by three other agents.

They stood there for a moment looking around, then Baker nodded and the witness began to get out.

A roar of recognition came from the crowd. The agents and police crowded in around him as they started to move through the mass. Photographers and reporters were yelling questions at them but they kept moving on up the steps, entered the courthouse and moved down the corridor.

'This way,' Strang said. 'We've got an elevator waiting.'

They followed the police captain into an empty elevator. The doors were promptly closed and the car started up. Intangibly the tension seemed to disappear. Baker looked at Strang. 'Well, we made it,' he said, smiling.

The policeman nodded and smiled back at him. 'The worst is over. All we got to get through upstairs is the reporters.'

Dinky looked at them. His face was white and still frightened. 'I got time the rest of my life to congratulate you guys. If I live long enough.'

The smile disappeared from Baker's face. The detectives looked at one another and then turned seriously towards the door as it began to open.

Cesare came out of the stairway on the third floor and turned and pushed his way quickly toward the elevators. He looked across the crowd to the courtroom doors. There were two policemen standing there. He pulled his right hand up into the sleeve of his lined car coat and felt the cold metal of the stiletto tingle against his fingers. A strange smile began to come to his lips.

He could feel his heart beginning to thump inside his chest. It was the way he felt when he took a car into a tight curve and didn't know whether he had enough traction to make it. He took a deep breath and the smile became fixed on his face.

The elevator door opened and the crowd surged toward it. Cesare didn't move. He knew they wouldn't be on that car. His information was complete. It was just too bad that he hadn't more time to prepare. He leaned back against the wall between the second and third elevators.

The next door opened and the detectives came out in a phalanx around the witness. Cesare stepped in quickly behind them and let the crowd push him along. There was no chance for him here, a detective was between him and the witness. The reporters were screaming unanswered questions. Flashbulbs were going off as the photographers jumped up and down trying to get a picture of the witness. He could only hope for a break. Once the man got into the courtroom it would be too late.

They were near the door now and the stiletto was cold in Cesare's hand. He had stopped breathing a long time ago. His lungs were filled to bursting with oxygen that would never be needed. There was a heavy pressure in his ears and everyone seemed to be moving in a sort of slow motion.

The group stopped for a moment before the closed door. The detective behind the witness moved slightly. The air spilled from Cesare's lungs in a gasp. The crowd pushed against his back, thrusting him forward. Now! Now was the time!

Cesare never even felt his hand move. It was almost as if it weren't even a part of him. The stiletto slid into the witness's heart as easily as a warm knife into butter. Cesare felt the blade snap back into his sleeve, pulled by the coiled wire attached to its hilt, as he opened his palm.

The witness stumbled slightly as the two policemen moved to open the door to the courtroom. Cesare began to walk toward the stairway. A flashbulb went off almost in his face, momentarily blinding him, but then his vision cleared and he kept on walking.

There was a hush in the courtroom. From outside in the corridor they could hear some noise growing. The sound of voices grew louder.

Matteo looked at the other defendants. Big Dutch was playing nervously with his tie clasp, Allie Fargo was tearing at his nails with his fingers, even Dandy Nick was doodling on the yellow pad before him. The noise grew louder.

Big Dutch leaned over toward him. 'I wonder who they bringin' in,' he said.

Dandy Nick grinned. It was an unhealthy grin of fear. 'You'll find out soon enough,' he said.

Matteo shut them up with a gesture, his eyes watching the courtroom door. The others turned to look.

First a couple of detectives appeared in the doorway, then the witness. He stumbled for a moment and a cop put out a hand to steady him.

Big Dutch leaped to his feet with an angry roar. 'It's Dinky Adams, the son of a bitch!'

The judge's gavel rapped on the desk. The witness took several more steps into the courtroom. His face seemed to be glazed with fear. He stumbled again. He looked down the courtroom toward the defendants' table. He opened his mouth as if to speak but no sound came out. Only a tiny dribble of blood appeared in the corner of his lips. A tortured look came into his eyes and he stumbled again and began to fall. His hands clutched at Baker's coat. But he couldn't get a grip and slid down to the floor.

Pandemonium that the judge's gavel could not control broke out in the courtroom.

'Lock the doors!' Strang shouted.

Big Dutch leaned over to say something to Matteo. 'Shut up!' Matteo snapped, his dark eyes glittering in his impassive face.

The clerk looked up and smiled as Cesare appeared in the doorway. 'I have the papers ready for you, Mr Cardinali, if you'll just sign here.'

Cesare took the pen from his fingers, scrawled his name on the papers and gave the pen back to the clerk. 'Thank you,' he said, picked up the papers and walked out.

The tight feeling was still in his chest as he stepped out into the bright sunlight. He blinked his eyes. Barbara waved to him from the car. He smiled and waved back to her, the papers in his hand flashing whitely.

Barbara smiled up at him mischievously as he crossed

the curb to the car. 'Congratulations, Count Cardinali.'

He laughed as he walked around the car and got into it. 'You haven't read the papers, my dear. It is no longer Count Cardinali. It is just plain Mr Cesare Cardinali.'

She laughed aloud as he started the motor. 'Just plain Cesare. I like that. I think it has a nice homespun quality.'

Cesare looked at her as he moved the car out into traffic. 'You know, I think you're teasing me.'

'No, I'm not,' she said quickly. 'I'm really very proud of you.'

The tension was gone from his stomach now as they turned the corner away from the building. 'Light a cigarette for me, will you, darling?' he asked. There was a heat growing in his loins, he could feel a pulse beating in his thighs.

She placed the cigarette between his lips. 'I wonder what my mother would think,' she said lightly. 'Going off for a week with a man. Not married to him. Not even engaged.'

He saw her smile out of the corner of his eye. 'What your mother don't know won't hurt her.'

Barbara was still smiling. 'Of course, she might understand it if I were going with a Count. Europeans are different that way. But with just a plain mister—'

Cesare interrupted her. 'You know what I think?'

She looked at him, her eyes wide. 'No. What?'

The pain in his loins was growing unbearable. He reached for her hand and put it on the hard muscle of his thigh. The smile suddenly vanished from her face as she felt the tension in him. He turned his face toward her and for a moment she could see hundreds of years into his eyes. Then a veil dropped over them.

'I think your mother is a snob,' he said.

She laughed and they fell silent as he turned the car into the Mid-Town Tunnel and the parkways to the airport. He drove by reflex, automatically, as his mind went back to Sicily, to his home. He had been there just a few weeks ago. But already it seemed as if years had passed.

What was it that Don Emilio had once called his uncle? A shylock. He laughed to himself. He wondered what Don Emilio thought of him now.

The man who lay dead behind him represented merely the principal payment on his debt. The two to come would be the interest, the accumulated interest for twelve years. Three lives for one. That should mean payment in any man's book.

He remembered how it was the night Don Emilio had presented his note.

FOUR

THE courtyard of the Castle Cardinali had been empty as Cesare pulled the car to a stop in front of the house. He turned off the motor as the door opened and an old man peeked out. When he saw Cesare his face broke into a wide happy smile. He hurried creakingly down the steps.

'Don Cesare, Don Cesare!' he cried in an ancient voice.

Cesare turned to him with a smile. 'Gio!' he exclaimed.

The old man bobbed up and down before him. 'You should have let us know you were coming, Don Cesare,' he said. 'We would have had the house ready for you.'

Cesare smiled wryly. 'It is an unexpected visit, Gio. I can only remain overnight. Tomorrow I must be on my way home.'

A frown crossed the old man's face. 'Home, Don Cesare? This is home.'

Cesare started up the steps toward the house. 'Yes,' he said gently. 'I keep forgetting. But now I live in America.'

Gio pulled the valise from the back seat of the car and hurried after Cesare. 'What happened in the race, Don Cesare? Did you win?'

Cesare shook his head. 'No, Gio. My generator burned out. I had to stop. That is how I had time to come here.'

He crossed the big chilly entrance hall and came to a stop under the portrait of his father. For a moment he stared up at the thin patrician face that looked down at him from the portrait. The war had broken him. Spiritually and physically. He had spoken out against the Germans and Il Duce ordered the lands confiscated. The old man had died soon after.

'I am sorry about your car, Don Cesare.' Gio's voice came from behind him.

'The car, oh, yes.' Cesare turned from the portrait and walked to the library. He hadn't been thinking about the car, not even about his father. He had just been realizing how changed it all was.

He had come back after the war and everything was gone. His uncle had come to own everything then. The bank, the lands. Everything except the castle and the title. His uncle had never forgiven his brother for legitimizing Cesare, thus depriving him of succession to the title.

No word was ever spoken aloud about it but everyone

knew how the miserly little man who owned the exchange bank felt. Cesare remembered bitterly how he hade gone to see his uncle.

'Signor Raimondi,' he had said arrogantly, 'I have been told that my father had some monies deposited with you.'

Raimondi had peered at him shrewdly across the dirty black desk. 'You have heard incorrectly, my nephew,' he had said in his thin reedy voice. 'It is, in truth, the other way round. The late Count, my good brother, unfortunately died owing me vast sums. I have here in my desk mortgages on the castle and all its lands.'

It had been the truth. Everything was proper and in order. Leave it to Raimondi Cardinali to do that. For three years after the war Cesare had to live under the old man's thumb. Dependent upon him for his very existence, he came to hate him. He even had to come to his office to get money for the fare to his beloved fencing matches.

It was one such afternoon that Cesare had first met Emilio Matteo. He had been in his uncle's office in the bank when there was a great commotion outside. He turned and looked out the glass-framed door.

A handsomely dressed gray-haired man was walking toward it. There was much bowing and scraping as he walked along. 'Who is that?' Cesare asked.

'Emilio Matteo,' Raimondi had answered, already getting to his feet in greeting.

Cesare raised an inquiring eyebrow. He had never heard of the man.

'Matteo,' his uncle explained impatiently. 'One of the

Dons of the Society. He has just come back from America.'

Cesare smiled. The Society, they called it. The Mafia. Grown men playing like boys, spilling their blood together, calling each other Uncle and Nephew and Cousin.

'Do not smile,' his uncle had snapped. 'In America the Society is very important. Matteo is the richest man in all Sicily.'

The door opened and Matteo came in. '*Bon giorno*, Signor Cardinali,' he spoke with a heavy American accent.

'I am honored by your visit, Signor Matteo.' Raimondi bowed. 'How can I serve you today?'

Matteo looked inquiringly at Cesare. Raimondi hastened forward. 'Allow me to present my nephew, Count Cardinali.' He turned to Cesare. 'Signor Matteo from America.'

Matteo looked at him with a calculating eye. 'Major Cardinali?'

Cesare nodded. 'That was during the war.'

'I have heard of you,' Matteo said.

It was Cesare's turn to look at him. There were very few people that had heard of him during the war. Only those who had very special information. He wondered how much the man knew. 'I am honored, sir,' he said.

Raimondi wanted to get down to business. Peremptorily he dismissed Cesare. 'Come back tomorrow,' he said importantly, 'and I will see if we can spare you the money to go to your petty fencing match.'

Cesare's lips tightened, his blue eyes grew dark and cold. For a moment his body tensed. Someday the old man would go too far. Already he took upon himself too many liberties. He could feel Matteo's eyes upon him as he went to the door.

He heard Raimondi's voice as he closed it. 'A fine boy but an expense. He is a relic of the past, trained for nothing, he can do no work . . .' The door closed, shutting off the patronizing voice.

Gio had started a fire in the library and Cesare stood in front of it, holding a glass of brandy in his hand.

'I will have dinner ready in half an hour,' the old man said.

Cesare nodded. He crossed the room to the desk and picked up the photograph of his mother that still stood on it. He remembered her eyes. They were blue like his own but soft and warm and kind. He remembered the day she came upon him in the garden. He was only eight years old then.

He had been absorbed watching the big green fly he had impaled on a pin in the wood struggling to get away.

'Cesare! What on earth are you doing?'

He turned and saw his mother standing there. He smiled happily and pointed. Her eyes followed his finger.

Her face had paled, then grew angry. 'Cesare, stop that! Release him immediately. That's cruel.'

Cesare pulled the pin from the wood but the fly still stuck to it. He looked up at his mother curiously, then down at the fly. Quickly he pulled the wings from it and dropped it on the floor and stepped on it.

His mother stared at him angrily. 'Cesare, why did you do that?'

His face turned serious for a moment as he thought,

then it wrinkled in a winning smile. 'I like to kill,' he said.

His mother had stared at him for another moment, then turned and went back into the house. A year later she was dead of the fever and after that the Count took him to the castle to live and there was a succession of teachers and tutors but no one that dared speak to him with impunity.

He put the photograph down. He was getting restless. There were too many memories here. The castle reeked of the past. What he should do was sell it and become an American citizen. That was the only way to deal with the past. Cut it cleanly as if with a knife so that no trace of it remained anywhere inside you.

He thought of the message that summoned him here. The message that took him from the race, that kept him from meeting Ileana on the Riviera. He smiled to himself when he thought of Ileana. There was something about those Rumanian women, especially the demimondaines with the titles. By now she was probably on her way to California with that rich Texan.

Gio opened the library door. 'Dinner is ready, Your Excellency,' he said.

FIVE

THE napery was white and soft; the candles, gold and glowing; the silver, polished and gleaming. Gio had done him proud. There was cold sliced eel, flecked with sparkling ice and hot steaming *scampi* in the warmer on the sideboard.

Gio had changed to his purple and green butler's uniform and stood proudly, holding the chair at the head of the long, white empty table for Cesare.

Cesare sat down and reached for a napkin. 'My compliments, Gio. You are indeed a genius.'

Gio bobbed proudly. 'I try, Your Excellency.' He began to open a bottle of white Orvieto. 'It is not like the old days, when the board was crowded for dinner every night. It has been a long time.'

Cesare tasted the wine and nodded. It had been a long time. But the world had moved on. Time would not stand still, even for Gio. He looked down the table.

It had not been like this after the war. Then they were lucky if there was food on the table, much less cloth. He remembered the night that Matteo had come to see him. It had been the same day that he had met him in his uncle's office. He had been seated at this same table then, eating cheese and bread and apple from the naked wooden board.

There had been the sound of a car outside and Gio had gone to the door. A moment later he was back. 'Signor Matteo to see Your Excellency,' he had said.

Cesare told Gio to bring him in. Matteo had come into the room, his quick appraising eyes seeing everything at once. The naked board, the poor food, the steel cutlery. His face told Cesare nothing.

Cesare waved him to a seat and invited him to share the food. Matteo sat down and shook his head. He had already eaten. Cesare couldn't care less. He was of the class to whom poverty wasn't important. It was a point of annoyance, not of embarrassment. He was secure in his position.

The amenities over, Gio cleared the table and Cesare leaned back in his chair, his strong white teeth biting into the apple.

Matteo looked at him. He saw the lean rakish face, the dark, almost black, ice-blue eyes and strong jaw of the young man opposite him. He also saw the savage strength in the wrist and hands that held the apple. 'Do you speak English, Major?' he asked in that language.

Cesare nodded. 'I was educated in England before the war,' he answered in the same language.

'Good,' Matteo answered. 'If you don't mind we'll speak in that language then. My Italian . . . well . . . I left here when I was a child of three.'

'I don't mind,' Cesare answered.

'I suppose you are wondering why I am here?' Matteo had asked.

Cesare nodded silently.

Matteo waved his hand, indicating the castle. 'My father used to tell me of the wonders of the Castolo Cardinali. How they used to look up from the village and see it all gay and sparkling with light.'

Cesare put the core of the apple on the table and shrugged his shoulders. 'It is the fortunes of war.'

Matteo answered quickly. 'Or the good fortune of your uncle.'

'That moneylender,' Cesare said contemptuously. 'He owns everything now.'

Matteo looked directly into Cesare's eyes. 'While he lives,' he said.

'That kind is too stingy to die,' Cesare said.

Matteo smiled. 'In America we have a name for that kind of man. Shylock. After the usurer in the play.'

Cesare smiled back. 'America has a way of expressing things very pithily. Shylock. It is very good.'

Matteo continued as if there hadn't been the minor diversion. 'Your uncle is alone, he has no family, no other relative but you. And he has a bank with two hundred million lire.'

Cesare looked at him. He recognized himself in the older man. 'I have thought about it many times. The pig does not deserve to live. But if I were to kill him it would do me no good.'

Matteo shook his head seriously. 'True. But if he were to die, say while you are at the fencing match one hundred fifty meters away from here, you would be a rich man again.'

Cesare looked at him for a moment then got to his feet. 'Gio!' he called. 'Bring that bottle of Napoleon brandy. We are going into the library.'

When Gio had closed the door behind him and they were alone in front of the leaping fire, Cesare turned to Matteo. 'Why did you come here?' he asked directly.

Matteo smiled and picked up his brandy. 'I had heard about you, Major.'

'Heard what?'

'You remember of course that part of the war just before the Allies invaded Italy?' He didn't wait for Cesare to answer. 'An associate of mine, who is at present in Naples, and I gave the American government a list of people to contact in preparation for that invasion. These people were members of an underground that had existed long before the war, before even the first war. The Mafioso.'

Cesare didn't speak.

'I learned that you were one of the Italian officers assigned to co-operate with the O.S.S. by the Italian High Command. You were assigned to contact nine men and secure their co-operation. You murdered five of them.'

'They would not co-operate,' Cesare said quickly. 'That was explained in my report.'

Matteo smiled. 'The official explanation does not concern me. I have made enough of them myself to have no faith in their veracity. But you and I know better. You see, the officials never saw the bodies of the men you killed. My friends did.'

Matteo put down his glass of brandy and looked across at Cesare. 'That's why I do not understand about your uncle, my friend. When death comes so joyously and easily to your hand, how you could let him live?'

Cesare looked down at him. 'That was different then. It was war.'

Matteo smiled. 'War was only the excuse for you. There were others. The soldier down in the village when you were still a boy, the young Englishman you ran off the road in your car the last year you were in school, the German mistress of your commanding officer in Rome when she threatened to expose you to him.' He looked up into Casare's face. 'You see, I have much better sources of information than the authorities.'

Cesare sank into the chair opposite. He took a drink of his brandy and smiled. 'So you have the information. It is of no use to you, so what can you do with it?'

Matteo shrugged his shoulders. 'I don't intend to do anything with it. I have told you just to let you know that I am interested in you. You see, we can be of much mutual help to one another.'

'So?'

Matteo nodded. 'Circumstances have forced me to return to the land of my birth, but I am an American, not an Italian, in my heart. And also in my business interests. Unfortunately I cannot return to America for some time. Legally, that is. Of course I can go back for short periods but that is very dangerous and I cannot remain too long. Also I foresee a time when I will need an ally there, someone like yourself, someone that no one would connect me with, someone who could be of help when necessary.'

Cesare stared at him. 'What about your associates? Your friends in the Society? Surely you have many allies there?'

Matteo nodded. 'True. But they are all known. To each other and to the police. Sooner or later there are no secrets among them.'

Matteo got to his feet and walked over to the open hearth. He turned his back on the fire and looked over at Cesare. 'You must be bored with the poverty of your existence by now. It is dull and drab and not at all in keeping with your nature. What would you do if you were free of all this?'

Cesare looked up. 'I don't know. Travel, maybe. I would get some cars and race them. Le Mans, Turino, Sebring. There is much excitement there.'

Matteo laughed. 'I mean how would you make a living? Money does not last forever, you know.'

Cesare shook his head. 'I never thought of that. I never liked business.'

Matteo took out a cigar and lit it. 'Ah, the young, the thoughtless young.' His voice was pleasantly tolerant. 'I have an interest in an automobile company recently acquired through some legitimate associates. In several years they plan to go into the American market. If by that time you had a reputation in the racing cars, you could conceivably become the head of the American company. Would you like something like that?'

'What is there about it not to like?' Cesare answered. 'But what am I expected to do in return?'

Matteo looked at him. 'A favor now and then.'

'What kind of favor? I want no part of your stupid business, the petty gambling, the dope . . .'

Matteo interrupted. 'Even if it should bring you undreamed-of wealth?'

Cesare laughed. 'Wealth? Who needs it? All I desire is enough to do what I like to do.'

Matteo laughed with him. 'Good. You are not ambitious then. Another point in your favor. There is no one who need be afraid of you.'

Cesare picked up his glass again. 'You still have not told me what kind of favor you will ask.'

Matteo stared at him. Their eyes met and locked. 'Only to return the favor I will do you when your uncle dies tomorrow night while you are at the fencing match.'

A long moment passed, then Cesare smiled. 'Good. It is done and we are agreed.'

Matteo's face was serious. 'You will take the oath?'

'I will swear on it.'

'Have you a knife?' Matteo asked.

A stiletto suddenly appeared in Cesare's hand. Matteo stared at it. Cesare smiled and turned it over in his hand and extended it to him, hilt forward. 'This is my brother,' he said. 'We are always together.'

Matteo took it. 'Give me your hand,' he said.

Cesare held out his hand. Matteo placed his left hand flat on Cesare's palm. With a quick motion he pierced each index finger with the stiletto. The blood from each man's finger bubbled up and then ran together into their palms.

Matteo looked at him. 'Our blood has mingled and now we are of one family.'

Cesare nodded.

'I will die for you,' Matteo said.

'I will die for you,' Cesare repeated.

Matteo released his hand and gave him back the stiletto. He looked up into Cesare's face. He stuck his finger into his mouth and sucked on it to stop the bleeding. 'From this time on, my nephew,' he said, 'we will not meet except at my wish.'

Cesare nodded. 'Yes, my uncle.'

'Should you find it necessary to communicate with me, send a message to the postmaster in the village. I will get in touch with you.'

'I understand, my uncle.'

That had been almost twelve years ago. True to Matteo's word, Raimondi had died the next night while Cesare was at the fencing match. The next five years had gone quickly. The races and the motor cars. The gala balls and romances. Then in 1953, just as Emilio had said, the offer came for him to head up the American agency of the automobile company. Much was made of his appointment in the press. His wild living and dangerous driving had made him an international figure of glamour. Twice he had fought duels over women. To America he was a man from another world.

Only once in all the twelve years had he seen Matteo.

Last year, he had gone in response to a telephone message to a room in a boarding house over a bar in Spanish Harlem where they had merely exchanged good wishes and Matteo had told him of his pleasure in Cesare's success. He did not stay long as a plane was waiting to take Matteo to Cuba from where he would return to Sicily. They had parted and not until a slip of paper telling him to go at once to the castle was thrust into his hand just before the start of the race did he hear from Matteo again.

The chicken cacciatore had been light and delicious, the lobster fra diavolo had been tangy and spicy and he was just putting down his napkin when a car came into the courtyard.

He could not help but watch for Gio to return from the door. A moment later Gio was back. He held an envelope in his hand.

'It was the postmaster from the village. He said he had this special letter to deliver to you.'

Cesare took it from him and ripped it open. It was two pages of closely typewritten instructions. He read it quickly, then read it again. Slowly he put the letter down on the table and reached for the espresso.

Twelve years had passed. And Don Emilio had presented his note for payment. With interest.

SIX

LAS VEGAS is a night town. Outside the hotels are the pools, clear, filtered and aquamarine, but no one sits around them except the tourists and the hustlers who work the hotels and keep their tans as a kind of pancake makeup of their trade. Inside the lobbies it is always night.

Someone once said never let them see the daylight. There is something about the harsh white light of day that interferes with the gambler's sense of reality. The reality of the spinning roulette wheel, the dull thumping of dice on hard felt-covered tables, the reality of the fever to win, the reality of the shifting desert sands on which the town was built.

Here is the prize, the great adventure, the promise of all the tomorrows. Free money. And everything else runs second to it. Sex, business, laughter. Free money. Pull the handle on the slot machines. It may be your turn at the jackpot.

They came out of the dining-room-theater, still laughing at the comedy of one of the world's greatest entertainers. They paused, looking down into the lobby of the gambling casino.

It was ten o'clock at night and the tables at the Maharajah were crowded with the people who had come from the dinner show. Cesare's eyes searched the room.

'You didn't hear what I asked,' Barbara said.

Cesare turned and looked down at her. His eyes were glowing with a strange excitement. 'No, I didn't, my dear. What was it?'

Barbara looked up at him. Another man would have apologized or protested that he had heard. He merely said that he hadn't. 'Dice or roulette, I asked.'

He smiled suddenly. 'Roulette, I have given enough to those crazy little cubes of ivory. I will never understand them.'

They began to walk down toward the roulette tables. 'Too bad they don't play baccarat here. Now there is a game for the civilized human being. For that some skill is needed, merely having luck is not enough.'

Barbara turned toward a table. He held her arm. 'Not this one. It is too crowded. Over here.'

It was the table opposite the one she had been going to but he had been right: it was less crowded. He pulled out a stool for her and she sat down. She smiled up at him. 'Feel lucky tonight?'

He nodded his head and smiled back at her. 'Very lucky,' he said, placing a pile of chips in front of her.

In New York the telephone on Baker's desk began to ring. He put down the container of coffee and picked it up.

'Jordan calling from Las Vegas,' the operator said.

'Put him on,' he answered.

Ted Jordan came on the wire. 'Hello, George, how we doin'?'

'No good,' Baker answered wearily. 'We're up the creek. We still can't figure out how Dinky Adams was killed. How's your boy holding up?'

Jordan laughed. 'Just great. Right now he's out at the roulette wheel betting like there's no tomorrow.'

'Is he covered?' Baker asked anxiously.

'I got a man on each side of him and one standing right behind him. Nobody can get anywhere near him.'

'I'm still nervous. We thought we had Adams covered too and look what happened.'

'If you're that worried, George,' Jordan said, 'why don't we just lock him up. We can keep him away from everybody in there.'

'You know the deal,' Baker replied. 'If we do that, the defense will know who the witnesses are before we get them into court. And if they know, the witnesses won't talk and there goes our case.'

'Matteo must be laughing like hell right this minute,' Jordan said.

'He won't when we get back into court,' Baker promised.

'My boy is giving twenty to one that he never gets into that courtroom,' Jordan said.

Baker's voice was incredulous. 'You mean to say he really believes that he'll be killed? And he's still going out to the casinos?'

'Yeah,' Jordan answered laconically. 'He says there's nothing anybody can do about it so he might as well live it up while he can.'

Baker put down the telephone and picked up the container of coffee again. There was the one thing he could never understand about them. They were cowards, pimps and murderers but there was still something in them that gave them a fatalistic approach to life. Or was it death? He just didn't know.

The Twister sat at the roulette table, his gaze concentrated on the wheel. It stopped and the ball bounced into the red twenty. He made another note on the small sheet of paper. Quickly he added up the columns. He was right. The wheel was running toward the black tonight. Time for him to make his move. He pushed a small pile of chips onto the black.

He heard Jordan come up behind him. He didn't turn around. The bodyguard behind him spoke. 'Could you spell me for a few minutes, Ted? I gotta get to the john before I bust.'

He didn't hear Jordan's reply. The ball bounced into the red. He lost. He looked down and pushed another pile of chips on the black.

Cesare turned around and looked at the Twister while Barbara concentrated on the spinning wheel. Matteo's note had been very specific. For almost three days now, Cesare had been watching the Twister.

The bodyguards were there. They were always there. One on each side of him and one standing back to back with him, his eyes constantly alert. Now the last one went away but another took his place. Cesare turned away just as the man's gaze began to sweep toward him. He had seen enough. With a little bit of luck . . . He smiled to himself as the phrase jumped through his mind. Everybody used it out here. With a little bit of luck he would complete his business here tonight.

He tapped Barbara on the shoulder. 'I'll get you a drink,' he said.

She looked up at him and smiled and then turned back, absorbed in the game. He began to walk toward the lounge. He walked around the Twister's table and glanced back.

He could see the Twister's face now, a look of concentration on it. Opposite the Twister sat a big blonde girl. Cesare stared for a moment. The girl leaned forward and he could see her full breasts pull against the two thin straps that held up her dress. Suddenly he began to smile. He knew how he would do it now. It was all because of a joke. A very old joke that was told to everyone who came to Las Vegas.

Jordan looked around him wearily. He wished the job was over. When he came to the F.B.I. fresh from law school and filled with the propaganda, he envisioned an exciting life filled with chasing criminals and spies. He never thought he would spend three months playing chief nursemaid to a cheap hood.

He looked at the table opposite him. That couple was there again. A good-looking couple. He remembered noticing them the first night. There was something familiar about them. As if he had seen them before. With his usual thoroughness he had checked on them.

The girl was one of the best-known models in America. Barbara Lang, the 'Smoke and Flame' girl whose face he had seen in a thousand cosmetic ads and the man was Cesare Cardinali. Count Cardinali, the society racing-car driver.

He saw Cesare say something to the girl and begin to walk away. Some of the things he had read about the man came to mind. There was a guy who really lived. Leave it to those rich Europeans. They didn't give a damn for anybody. They had a ball everywhere they went. Here he was with one of the most beautiful dames in America and just as cool as you could be. He looked at the girl again. All the promise the advertisements held was right. Some guys had all the luck.

Cesare waited until the blonde sat up straight on her stool. Petulantly she turned to her escort, a fat little man. He gave her some bills from a big roll and she turned back to the table. Cesare started down from the lounge, holding a drink in his left hand.

He walked down the aisle behind the blonde and hesitated for a moment. The croupier turned the wheel and dropped the ball. Cesare's hand moved quickly behind the blonde's back and he started to walk around the table toward his own.

He could feel the throbbing begin in his temples and the pain. It was always like this. The pain would start there, and then, step by step, move down into his body.

He knew the pain now and had a long time ago ceased to fear it. It was the pain of excitement, of danger, of looking into the abyss of time, the hell of oblivion.

He was behind the Twister who was resting his chin in his hands, supported by his elbows on the table edge. The bodyguard was just starting to turn toward him when the scream came.

The bodyguard whirled, his hand streaking toward his shoulder holster. Cesare moved quickly. Across the table, the blonde fought to hold her dress over her bosom. It was a losing battle. There was too much of her.

Cesare let go of the stiletto and felt the knife spring back into his sleeve. The Twister still sat quietly on his stool, not moving. The bodyguard turned back. Cesare could see him smiling as Barbara took her drink.

The blonde was passing their table now, the fat little man hurrying after her. Her high-pitched voice floated back to them. 'They didn't break I tell you, they didn't! They were cut! Somebody—'

'Ssh! Please, baby! Everybody's looking!' the little man pleaded.

'I don't give a damn!' the blonde retorted as they hurried up the steps toward the lounge.

Cesare and Barbara laughed and she turned back to the table to make another bet.

Jordan turned around and looked down at the Twister. He was sitting there not moving, his chin in his hands. The wheel stopped. It was on the black. The croupier pushed a pile of chips to join the others on the table. The Twister didn't move.

The wheel started to spin again. Jordan looked at one of the other bodyguards. The man shrugged his shoulders.

'Get your bets down, ladies and gentlemen,' the croupier called in his soft monotone. A few more bets came down and the croupier threw the ball into the wheel. The pile in front of the Twister grew. It was black again. He didn't move.

The pain bound Cesare's chest now, making it difficult for him to breathe. He looked down at Barbara. 'This is no way to spend our last night in Las Vegas,' he said. 'In this crowded place with all these stupid people.'

She looked up at him. A faint smile lurked in the corners of her mouth. 'Just what do you have in mind?' she asked.

Cesare forced himself to smile. 'Just the two of us. Alone.'

Excitement began to grow in her eyes. She could feel the current flowing out of him but couldn't resist a tease. 'It was the blonde that did it. There was too much for any man.'

'That's not true,' he answered quickly. He reached for her hand.

His palm was warm and moist as if he had a fever. She looked up at him quickly. 'Are you all right?'

'I'm fine,' he answered. 'I'm just bored with this, bored with all these people who think of nothing but money. I want to be with you. I want to feel the life inside you.'

Her lips were suddenly dry. She could feel a heat

suddenly surging inside her. Inside her mind there was a flashing image of his muscular thrusting body. She held his hand tightly and looked up into his face.

There was an intensity that had not been there a moment before. 'We'll have cold champagne for before,' he said. 'And warm brandy for after.'

She moved off the seat as if in a haze. Her legs felt curiously weak. She tried to smile up at him. 'And then cold champagne again?' she whispered.

Jordan looked down at the Twister. This was the fourth time that black had won. The chips in front of the Twister amounted to almost nine thousand dollars now. 'Don't press your luck, Jake. Better pick up some of that loot.' He smiled, tapping the witness on the shoulder.

Grotesquely the witness slid forward, face down on the table, his hands knocking the chips away from him, his face coming to rest on a pile of them.

A woman screamed. Jordan lifted the Twister's head. His eyes were open, expressionless. Jordan dropped his hand. 'Help me get him out of here!' he snapped.

The bodyguards moved quickly. They lifted the Twister expertly and stared toward the assistant manager's office. There was a brief moment of hysteria. But only a moment.

The calm monotonous voices of the house men spoke up, quietly reassuring. 'It's all right, folks. The man just fainted. It's all right.'

Such is the promise of Las Vegas – the free money, the dream of tomorrow – that in a moment the wheel began to turn again and the man was all but forgotten by those who had sat at the table with him.

That is by all but the croupier who was fired the next morning for stealing five thousand dollars from the pile of chips that had lain in front of the Twister.

They turned to look as the men hurried past them carrying the Twister. Barbara looked up into Cesare's face.

His eyes were cold and shining, his mouth was slightly open as if in a twisted smile. He turned to look after them then back to her.

A shiver ran through her. 'Why do you look like that?'

His face softened suddenly and his lips turned to a real smile. 'I was just thinking that they have everything figured here. No matter what you do you can't win.'

He took a deep breath. The pain was in his guts now. He could hardly keep from crying out with it. 'Come,' he said. 'There is nothing for us here.'

The telephone on Baker's desk began to ring again just as he started to leave the office. He walked back and picked it up.

It was Jordan. His voice crackled excitedly through the telephone. 'They just killed the Twister!'

Slowly Baker sank into his seat. 'Killed? How?'

'Stiletto! The same way they got Adams.' Jordan's voice almost broke. 'I'm sorry, George. We were on him every minute. I don't know how they did it. There were over a thousand people in that casino tonight.'

Baker's mind suddenly cleared. 'Look,' he said. 'Call me back in an hour. I want to call Miami and make sure that Vanicola is okay.'

He pressed down the button on the phone then let it come up again. The operator came on. 'Get me Special Agent Stanley in Miami Beach,' he said.

They know the witnesses, he thought to himself while the call was going through. They know. All the secrecy, all the preparation would be for nothing.

They know.

Baker's mind suddenly cleared. "Look," he said. "Call me back in an hour. I want to call Miami and make sure that [illegible] is okay."

He pressed down the button on the phone then let it come up again. The operator came on. "Get me Special Agent Stanley in Miami Beach," he said.

They know the witnesses, he thought to himself while the call was going through. They know. All the secrecy, all the preparation would be for nothing.

They know.

THE room was silent except for the soft whisper of her breath. He stared up at the ceiling, his eyes wide. It was many years ago, he had almost forgotten.

The fear. There was nothing like it anywhere. Everything else was a substitute. A substitute for death. The [illegible] danger, the [illegible] the feeling of [illegible] that [illegible] through your body with the knowledge of the death-force [illegible] coming your way, bringing you close to your own destiny.

He smiled slowly into the dark, a feeling of well-being permeating his body. He reached for a cigarette on the night table. The package was empty.

He slid silently out of the bed and crossed the room to the dresser, took a cigarette from the package there and lit it. Through the terrace door the first gray streaks of dawn were lifting the horizon.

SEVEN

THE room was silent except for the soft whisper of her sleep. He stared up at the ceiling, his eyes wide. It was so many years ago he had almost forgotten.

The war. There had been nothing like it since. Everything else was a substitute. A substitute for death. The great danger, the great excitement, the feeling of power that ran through your body with the knowledge of the death-force inside you tearing its way out, bringing you closer to your own destiny.

He smiled slowly into the dark, a feeling of well-being permeating his body. He reached for a cigarette on the night table. The package was empty.

He slid silently out of the bed and crossed the room to the dresser, took a cigarette from the package there and lit it. Through the terrace doors the first gray streaks of dawn were lifting the horizon.

'Cesare.' Her voice was a whisper from the bed.

He turned toward her. He could not see her in the dark. 'Yes?'

'Open the second bottle of champagne.' Her voice was husky with sleep.

'We already did,' he said.

'But I'm still thirsty,' she said in a small girl's voice.

Cesare laughed almost inaudibly. 'You are an insatiable woman.'

He heard the rustle of the sheets as she sat up. 'I can't help it if I'm still thirsty, can I?'

He laughed again. 'I guess you can't,' he answered and went out onto the terrace.

The night was still and in the distance he could hear the sound of the crickets and the faint dry whisper of the desert wind. The dark blue of the sky was lightening with the thrust of morning. He leaned against the railing looking out into the desert.

She came out onto the terrace behind him. He didn't turn around. She came up close behind him and slipped her arms around his chest and leaned her head against his naked back.

'It will soon be morning,' she said.

'I know,' he answered.

She pressed her lips to his shoulder. 'Your skin is smooth and clean and soft. Sometimes I wonder where all the fierce driving strength comes from. I didn't know a man could be like you.'

He laughed, turning around. 'It must be the wines I drank when I was a boy. The wines of Sicily are supposed to be good for your blood and your skin.'

She looked up into his face. There were some things

about him she would never understand. 'When you make love to me, why do you always say you are dying?' she asked in a wondering tone. 'What a strange thing to say at a time like that.'

He smiled down at her. 'That is what we Italians call it. The little death.'

'Why?' she asked. 'When everything inside you is bursting open and being born, why should you say it is like dying?'

The smile faded from his lips. 'Is it not? Is not each birth the beginning of death? Do you not feel the pain of it?'

She shook her head. 'No. Only the lifting joy of it.' She looked up into his eyes. 'Maybe that's the difference between us. Maybe that's why I feel even when you're closest to me that there's a part of you that's far away in a world I know nothing about.'

'That's silly,' he said.

'No, it's not,' she said quickly. 'Like the way you looked when they carried that man past us. One moment it was like I could feel you inside me, right in that room with all those people. The next moment they came by and you were gone. He was dead, wasn't he?'

He stared down at her. 'What makes you say that?'

'He was dead,' she whispered. 'I could tell from the expression on your face. You knew. Nobody else knew. But you knew.'

'That's a foolish thing to say,' he said lightly. 'How would I know?'

She shook her head. 'I don't know. But it was the same expression you had on your face when you came out of the building the day we started on our trip. Then when we opened the newspapers on the plane we read about that man being killed in the court around the corner from where we were.'

She placed her head against his chest and did not see the slowly tightening expression of his face. 'I don't have to read tomorrow's papers to know that the man downstairs was killed. I can feel it. I wonder what it will be like in Miami?'

He wondered if she could feel his heart beginning to thump through his naked flesh. He forced his voice to be light. 'Like it always is. Sunny and warm.'

She looked up into his eyes. 'That's not what I meant, darling. I mean will someone die there too?'

The veil was gone from his eyes and she was looking deep into them. 'People die everywhere, every day,' he said.

She felt almost hypnotized. 'You're not the Angel of Death, are you, darling?'

He laughed suddenly and the veil was back. 'Now that is a crazy thing to say.'

'It's not really,' she spoke slowly. 'I read in a story once about a girl who fell in love with the Angel of Death.'

His hand caught the back of her head and held her close to his chest. 'What happened to her?' he asked.

He could feel her lips move against his breast. 'She died. When he knew that she knew who he was, he had to take her with him.'

She looked up at him suddenly. 'Will you take me with you, Cesare?'

His hand tightened in the long hair that hung down

her shoulders, pulling her head back so that her face turned up toward him. 'I will take you with me,' he said, placing his mouth brutally on her lips.

He could hear her gasp of pain as his free hand took her breast. She turned her face from him and cried aloud, 'Cesare! You're hurting me!'

He ground her face to his naked chest and moved her head slowly in a widening circle, never stopping the pressure of his hand on her breast. He heard her moan softly and a torrent began to rise inside him. The circle became wider, she was moaning steadily now as she sank slowly to her knees.

She cried aloud at his growing strength. 'Cesare! Stop, please stop! The pain, I can't stand the pain!'

He was smiling now. There was power inside him. And life. And death. His voice seemed to come from some distant place outside him. 'It is time you learned, my dear, how exquisite the pleasure of pain can be.'

'Don't, Cesare, don't!' Her body began to shiver in a wild convulsion. 'I can't stand the pain! I am dying!'

He looked down at her and let go suddenly. She almost fell, then her hands caught his hips and she clung to him, sobbing, 'Cesare, I love you! I love you!'

EIGHT

MIAMI Beach is a sun town built on a sterile strip of sand along the Florida coast. Each year by an artificial insemination of capital it gives birth to a new hotel. The St Tropez is this year's new hotel.

Not far from the Fontainebleu and Eden Roc, the St Tropez rises eleven stories into the ocean sky in an architectural style vaguely reminiscent of a Picasso impression of the palace at Monte Carlo. The Floridians, who judge beauty by the amount of rental per room in season, call it the most beautiful hotel ever built. The rental per room is eighty dollars a day.

It has a ten-foot-wide beach fronting on the ocean on which no one is ever seen except the tourists in off season. It also has a cloverleaf pool that has been proclaimed as the largest pool ever built. It is completely surrounded by four tiers of cabanas, stepped back so they resemble bleachers in a ball park and do not obstruct the sun. Each cabana is complete with private bath and telephone, card table, chairs and small refrigerator.

By three o'clock in the afternoon each cabana has a gin game going full blast, the players generally sitting in their shorts and swim suits, shielded from the sun they waste at the going rate per diem. Around the pool on long wooden lounge chairs are the sun worshippers, their bodies glistening with oil and lotions, trying to make the most of their already overburdened pocketbooks.

Sam Vanicola was standing at the window of the suite in the St Tropez, looking down at the pool. He was a big man. Even when he was a punk kid running errands for Lepke in Brooklyn, he was big. He weighed over two hundred pounds then, now he weighed two-forty on his five-eleven frame.

He gave a snort of disgust and came back into the room where three men were playing cards. He looked down at them. 'This is a lot of crap!' he announced.

Special Agent Stanley looked up at him. 'We got our orders, Sam,' he said genially.

'Orders, borders!' Vanicola snorted. 'Look, it didn't mean nuttin' when they kept Abe Reles locked up in his hotel room in the Half Moon in Brooklyn. They got to him anyway.'

Stanley smiled again. 'How do you know, Sam? He went out the window and they said it was suicide.'

'That's a horse laugh! ' Vanicola replied. 'I knew him. That boy was pushed. He'd never jump.'

'Besides,' Stanley persisted. 'That was twenty years ago. Things are different now.'

Vanicola laughed. 'They sure are,' he said derisively. 'Dinky Adams gets his on his way into court, Jake the Twister in a room with a thousand people – and you tell me things are different.'

Stanley fell silent. He exchanged glances with the other agents. They didn't speak.

Vanicola took a cigar out of his pocket, walked across the room and sat down on the couch. He bit the end off the cigar and spat it out on the rug. He lit it and leaned back, looking at them. His voice was less harsh now. 'Now look, you guys. I'm a taxpayer too. The guvviment is spending two Cs a day of my good money to keep me in a joint like this. What for they spending the dough if nobody gets any benefit out of it?'

Stanley got up from his chair. 'You'd rather sit in the pokey?' he asked.

Vanicola stared up at him. 'Don't make me laugh, Stanley. You do and I clam up. You ain't got no more chances left after me.'

'What's the matter with you anyway, Sam?' Stanley cried out in sheer frustration. 'What've you got against staying alive?'

Vanicola's eyes were suddenly serious. 'The way I look at it I was dead the day you picked me up. If I didn't talk you had me on a murder rap; if I did, it would only be a question of time before the boys got to me. Now I'm runnin' out of time real fast. So why don't you call up your boss and tell him all I wanna do is spend an hour or two down at that pool every afternoon? I'll go along with everything else you say.'

Stanley walked over to the window and looked down at the pool. There was the usual number of people down there. Vanicola's voice came from the couch.

'Nobody can get to me down there. You can cover every entrance. There are only two.'

Stanley turned and went into the next room and closed the door behind him. Vanicola looked over at the two agents seated at the card table. They began to play gin again. He sat there silently, puffing at his cigar.

A few minutes later Stanley came out. He crossed the room and stood in front of Vanicola. 'Okay, Sam, you get what you want. But, remember, if you see anything we don't, recognize anyone, let us know right away. We don't want anything to happen to you.'

Vanicola got out of the chair and walked over to the window. He looked down at the pool. 'Sure, sure,' he agreed quickly. 'I ain't that much in a hurry to croak.'

Stanley walked back to the card table and sat down. Vanicola turned and looked after him. He smiled but there was no humor in his eyes. 'At least I'll be sure of one thing,' Vanicola said.

One of the agents looked up at him. 'What's that, Sam?'

'Getting a pretty good tan,' he answered. 'Ain't nobody who'll come to see me when they lay me out won't be able to tell where I spent the winter.'

Barbara was standing on the balcony looking out at the ocean when she heard the telephone ringing in the room. She walked inside and picked it up.

'New York calling Count Cardinali,' the operator said.

She covered the mouthpiece with her hand. 'Cesare, there's a call for you,' she called into the bedroom.

He came into the room in his swimming shorts, the deep tan he had already acquired in the few days they had been here contrasting with the white trunks. He took the telephone from her hand. 'Cardinali speaking,' he said into it.

The operator's voice crackled through the receiver. 'All right,' Cesare said. 'Put her on.' He looked across at Barbara. 'It's Miss Martin, my secretary.'

Barbara nodded and went outside on the balcony again. She could hear faint snatches of his conversation. It had something to do with a car that was in Palm Beach. After a few minutes he put down the telephone. He didn't come out. When she turned around, he was seated at the desk making a few notes on a scratch pad. She went back inside.

He looked up at her and smiled. 'Forgive me,' he said. 'Business.'

She looked down at him and nodded slowly. This was the last day of the week they had planned together. 'I wish the week were only beginning,' she said.

'So do I,' he answered.

'I hate to think that tomorrow we'll be back in New York and it will be cold and bleak and we won't be warm like this until summer. I wish we could stay here forever.'

He smiled. 'That is always the trouble. Holidays must have an end.'

'Must ours?' she asked, not speaking of the holiday at all.

He knew what she meant. 'It must,' he said quietly. 'I have my business to go back to. You have your work.'

A kind of sadness was in her. She knew now that the only one she had been fooling when she agreed to start this week was herself. What had happened between them was no more than a holiday for him. 'Does anybody really know you, Cesare?'

A look of surprise leaped into his eyes. 'That's a funny question,' he answered.

Suddenly she wanted to touch him, to make him feel her reality. She turned away so that her hands would not reach for him. 'No, it's not,' she said. 'Most people think you're a playboy. I know you're not.'

Cesare walked around the desk to her. 'I have been very fortunate. It is good for my business to do what I like to do.'

She looked up into his eyes. 'Is that the reason for the girls like me? To build your reputation along with the fast cars? Because it's good for your business?'

He took her hand. 'There are no girls like you.'

'No?' she said, getting angry with herself for not being able to stop. 'What about that Baroness? De Bronczki or something? A month ago the papers were full of how you were chasing her all over Europe.'

'Ileana?' He chuckled. 'I've known her since she was a child. Our families were old friends. Besides she doesn't matter now. She's in California with a rich Texan. She has a taste for rich Texans.'

Her eyes fell. 'I'm sorry,' she said.

He put his hand under her chin and lifted her face up. 'I have an idea,' he said. 'There is a car my office wants me to look at in Palm Beach. Instead of flying back to New York tonight, let's pick up the car and drive back. I am bored with planes anyway and that way we can stretch our holiday.'

She began to smile. Maybe she had been wrong about him. Maybe it was not just a holiday. 'That will be wonderful!'

He looked down at his wristwatch. 'It's almost three o'clock,' he said. 'We have time for one more swim. We can have dinner in Palm Beach and be in Jacksonville before morning.'

Vanicola came out of the cabana bathroom. He had on his swimming trunks, of a bright Hawaiian pattern. He stood in the shadows of the cabana and looked down at the F.B.I. men. 'Okay if I get my ration of sunshine now?'

The agents exchanged glances and Stanley turned and checked the men at the exits. They caught his look and nodded. He got to his feet. 'I guess it's okay,' he said grudgingly.

The other two agents got to their feet. Vanicola started down toward the pool, picking his way carefully around the sunbathers stretched out on the lounge chairs. They stood around him as he took a plastic float from the rack and slid it into the water. He walked down the steps into the pool and clumsily stretched on the float.

Stanley was studying the people around them. The youngest agent looked at him. 'See anything, chief?'

Stanley shook his head. 'No, I guess it's safe enough. They aren't wearing enough clothes around here to conceal any weapons.'

The young man grinned, his eyes going over some of the girls lounging at poolside. 'Some of those babes aren't wearing enough to conceal their weapons either.'

Stanley didn't smile. Nothing was funny to him right now.

Vanicola spoke to them from the pool where he was stretched on his back on the raft. 'I told you guys there was nothing to worry about.' He grinned. 'This is the third day we been out and nothing's happened yet. Let me know when ten minutes are up and I'll turn over. I don't want to get fried.'

'Okay,' Stanley answered. He sat down on a chair near poolside. He would be glad when this job was over.

Vanicola floated away. As the agents idly watched the swimmers, their tension gradually began to ease off.

Cesare saw them from across the pool. He glanced at Barbara. She was lying on her stomach, her back to the sun, her eyes closed. He could feel his heart begin to pound. He looked across the pool again.

Vanicola was floating out toward the center of the cloverleaf where a group of youngsters were frolicking. Their voices came back to Cesare. Unconsciously his hand dropped to his waist. He could feel the stiletto in the concealed sheath beneath his trunks. He took his hand away quickly.

One of the bodyguards was getting up now. He called something to Vanicola. Vanicola sat up clumsily and almost fell into the water, then he turned around and stretched out face down on the float. The bodyguard sat down again.

Cesare glanced at Barbara. She was still lying quietly. He rose swiftly, took a deep breath and dove into the water. He went down deep, his eyes straining as he swam out to the center of the pool.

Barbara sat up when she heard the splash of his dive. 'Cesare,' she called.

But he was already gone, bubbles trailing in his wake. She blinked her eyes and smiled. In some ways he was like a small boy. For three days now he had been practicing swimming underwater across the pool and back. She glanced up at the clock on the cabana wall. It was twenty minutes to four. She began to gather up her things. It was getting late and they would have to leave soon.

She had just finished retouching her lickstick when his head came up over the edge of the pool near her. His mouth was open in a strange grin as he gulped air into his lungs. He stared at her as if she were far away.

'Did you make it this time?' she asked, smiling.

'I made it,' he answered as he pulled himself out of the pool.

Her voice was shocked. 'Cesare!'

A flash of fear leaped into his eyes. His hand felt for the stiletto. It was there, back in the sheath. He looked at her, then followed her gaze back down to himself. He caught the robe she flung at him and wrapped it around himself. She was laughing now as he walked toward her. 'Cesare, you are like a little boy. The minute you get excited, it shows,' she teased.

He grinned at her without embarrassment. He took her hand and pulled her to her feet. 'Didn't I tell you that we Sicilians are very basic people?' He laughed.

She picked up her beach bag and, still laughing, they walked back into the hotel.

The telephone in the cabana began to ring. Stanley got to his feet. 'Keep an eye on him while I get the phone,' he said to the other agents.

They nodded and he walked back into the cabana. The youngest agent looked around and then spoke to the other man. 'I'd like to come back here sometime when I'm not working.'

The other man grinned. 'You couldn't afford it. Everything comes high in this place.'

Stanley came back. For the first time in several days, he was smiling. 'Come on,' he said to them. 'Let's get him out of there. We're going to New York tonight.'

The other men got to their feet and they all turned toward the pool. Stanley's voice carried over to the raft. 'Okay, Sam. Come on in. Your ten minutes are up.'

But more than ten minutes were up for Sam. Sam Vanicola was lying there dead on the slowly sinking raft, his face pressed close to the plexiglass shield, looking into the water. And even the last memory was gone from his mind now. The sight of Cesare's grinning face coming up at him from the bottom of the pool just before his heart exploded in a pain he never knew he could feel.

NINE

THE Sunshine State Parkway runs north from Miami to Fort Pierce, past the swamps and marshes and citrus groves that dot the Florida Atlantic Coast. And many times at night in the early winter the fog rolls in from the suddenly cooling seas and, mixed with the smoke from the smudge pots, forms a shroudlike mist that clings to the roadway like a down quilt on a feather bed.

The powerful engine in the Ghia convertible throbbed as Barbara reached over and turned on the radio. The music filled the car and she peered over the wheel, the powerful headlights biting through the first mist. 'The fog's coming in,' she said.

Cesare nodded. 'Want me to put the top up?' he asked.

'Let it go for a while,' she answered. 'I'm comfortable.'

They drove along in silence for a few minutes then the announcer's voice broke into the music. 'And now, the eleven o'clock news from Miami.'

Cesare looked at her. She was driving with a fierce concentration on the road before her. The newscaster came on.

'With the murder of Sam Vanicola in the swimming pool of the St Tropez Hotel here in Miami Beach this afternoon, the government announced tonight in New York the complete collapse of its case against the four alleged leaders of the Syndicate. It was disclosed also that the murder weapon used in each case was a stiletto. The stiletto is a weapon of vengeance that originated in Italy about the time of the Borgias. It was a great favorite of assassins of that period due to the fact that its peculiar shape caused internal hemorrhaging while the surface wound itself closed after the weapon was withdrawn from the victim. The police and the F.B.I. attach a great deal of significance to this fact and are pressing every means at their disposal to discover clues that would lead them to the identity of the killer or killers. Meanwhile in Washington—'

Cesare reached over and turned off the radio. 'News is so dull these days,' he said with a short laugh. 'Murder and crime all the time. Can't they find anything else to talk about?'

Barbara didn't answer. Her eyes seemed fastened to the road.

He laughed again. 'Wake up, sleepy one. You're driving.'

'I'm awake,' she said.

'That's good to know.' He smiled. 'I feel better.'

Her voice was thoughtful. 'I was just thinking.'

'About what?' he asked.

'About the man that died in the pool. I wonder which one he was. If I saw him or he saw me.'

'That's a strange thought,' he said. 'Why do you think it?'

Her eyes still were on the road. 'Maybe if we had spoken to each other I might have warned him. I don't know.'

He laughed shortly. 'What would you have warned him about? You did not know what was to happen.'

She glanced at him. Her eyes were deep and troubled. 'I could have told him about the Angel of Death. And how it followed us from New York to Las Vegas and then to Miami.' She shivered slightly. 'Do you think he is still following us, Cesare?'

'Now you are being silly,' he said. 'You better pull over here and let me drive. You're letting all this nonsense upset you.'

Silently she put on the right turn indicator and began to slow up. She pulled the car off on a shoulder of the road and came to a stop. She turned to look at him.

'It is just as well,' he said. 'I know the road up ahead. There is a very narrow bridge and the fog is beginning to thicken.'

'I'm not arguing,' she said. 'You drive. But be careful.'

'I'll be careful.' He laughed and pulled her to him. He kissed her.

Her lips were cold and they clung to his mouth. 'I

don't care if you are the Angel of Death,' she whispered. 'Being with you has made me happier than I've ever been in my whole life.'

He couldn't suppress the question that rose to his lips. 'What would you do if I were?'

She looked up at him questioningly. 'Now *you're* being silly,' she said.

Something inside was driving him on. Maybe if she knew, if she could understand, it wouldn't all seem so empty. Why did he have to be the only one that felt as he did? 'I could have been the killer,' he said slowly. 'After all we were each place where a murder happened.'

She stared up at him, then she began to smile. 'So were hundreds of others. Sometimes, Cesare, I think that you're as crazy as I am.'

He laughed and got out of the car. He walked around to her side of the car and looked down at her. She had taken out her lipstick and was beginning to apply it.

'Be a dear, will you, and give me some light?' she said without looking up. 'I'm afraid I'll make a mess of this.'

He flicked on his lighter and looked down at her. He could feel his lips tightening across his teeth.

She looked up at him. 'What are you staring at?' she asked curiously.

'You,' he answered tightly. 'You're very beautiful.'

She smiled. 'That deserves another kiss before I put the lipstick on.'

He bent over the side of the car and kissed her. Her lips were warmer now, they moved against his. 'Cesare,' she whispered. 'I'm afraid I'm beginning to love you so very much that it doesn't really matter any more whether you killed those men or not.'

He straightened up and she turned to begin to apply the lipstick again. He looked down. There was the white flesh of her neck, just below where the short curls turned into ringlets. He raised his right hand, palm out and flat. There was nothing else he could do. Already she had put too many facts together. Death led to death and murder was like concentric ripples in a pool that spread out and out until they reached farther and farther away from the victim and the violator. He brought his hand down sharply in a vicious judo chop.

The lipstick shot from her hand like a bullet and smashed into the dashboard and then fell tinkling to the floor of the car. He stared down at her, his heart bursting inside him.

She lay slumped across the wheel, one hand still closed on it, her head in an odd position. He was glad he could not see her eyes. He looked around quickly. There were no cars coming. He ran around to the other side of the car and got into it on the seat beside her. He reached over and turned the key, starting the motor. It caught with a roar.

He looked around again. The road was still empty. He reached into his sleeve and took out the stiletto and the hook spring to which it was attached. With a quick motion of his hand he flung it far into the darkness and heard it sink into the watery marsh on the other side of the shoulder. He put the car into gear and, steering from his side, moved it out into the road.

He jammed his foot down on the accelerator. The bridge should be less than a mile from here. In a moment the car was doing eighty. He peered through the fog. Barbara slumped toward him.

There was the bridge. With a muttered curse, he shoved her back under the wheel. He took his foot from the accelerator and pulled both feet up under him. He held the wheel steady, driving the car right at the concrete abutment at the side of the bridge.

He sprang high into the air in an arcing dive at almost the moment of impact. The speed of the car pushed him forward and he tumbled awkwardly through the air toward the water.

The sound of the crash came to his ears at almost the same moment he hit the water. It was cold and black and murky and he gasped for breath. He was going down and down, his lungs were bursting, he would never come up. Frantically his arms flailed the water. The reeds clung to him, trying to keep him down. Then he saw the sky above him again.

He pulled himself toward the shore. There was a pain inside him now, racing all through his body. He felt his feet touch the land and stumbled to his knees. He crawled out of the water slowly and then sprawled out on the ground. His mouth felt filled with dirt and his face scratched and burning.

The ground was moist and clammy and its chill raced through him. He began to shudder convulsively, digging his fingers into the earth, clinging to it. Then he closed his eyes and the night came up and over him.

*

Baker leaned back in his chair and stared out the window. The white winter sun formed sharp patterns on the buildings. Three days had passed since Vanicola had died and they were exactly nowhere. He looked down the desk at the men seated opposite. There was Captain Strang of the New York Police, Jordan in from Las Vegas and Stanley up from Miami.

He spread his hands on the desk in a gesture of defeat. 'That's the story. I'm not blaming any one of you, the responsibility was mine and I accept it. Tomorrow morning I'm due in Washington to see the chief. Senator Bratton is on the Bureau's back and the chief wants a personal report.'

'What are you going to tell him, George?' Stanley asked.

'What can I tell him?' Baker answered rhetorically. 'I don't know any more than he does.' He picked up an envelope from the desk. 'My resignation's in here. I'm turning it in tomorrow.'

'Wait a minute,' Jordan said. 'The chief hasn't asked for your scalp.'

Baker smiled wryly. 'Come on, Ted, don't be naïve. You know the chief as well as I do. He doesn't like failure.'

As they fell silent Baker absently pressed the button on the slide projector on his desk. It jumped to life and threw a picture on the wall. It was a scene of the crowd inside the corridor of the courthouse.

'What've you got there?' Jordan asked.

Baker pressed the button idly. 'Pictures of the corridor taken by newspaper photographers as Dinky Adams was going into the courtroom.' He pressed another button and the scene changed. 'I've looked at them a thousand times. You'd think with all the pictures they took, we'd find something. Not one of them took the picture at the time we needed it.'

He hit the button and the scene changed again. 'I forgot you fellows didn't see it yet.'

He stared for a moment then pressed the button again.

'Wait a minute,' Stanley said, an excitement rising in his voice. 'Can you go back to the picture you had on before this one?'

Baker hit the button. Stanley got up and walked over to the wall and looked closely at the picture. He put a finger out and pointed to a man. 'Have you got a doohickey on that machine that will enlarge the picture of this guy in the green alpine hat?'

Baker laughed disgustedly. Another blank. 'That hat isn't green. It's the wall paint.'

Captain Strang interrupted. 'It was green, George. I remember noticing it in the crowd.'

Swiftly Baker fiddled with the lens. Now there was only one man's face on the screen. There was only a side angle of the face but there was no mistaking the hat.

'I've seen that hat before,' Stanley said.

'There are lots of hats like that,' Baker said.

'But not faces like that,' Jordan said suddenly. 'I know that one.'

They turned to him. 'That's Count Cardinali,' he said. 'The racing-car driver. He was at the table next to us in Vegas. He was there with the girl who models for all those "Smoke and Flame" cosmetic ads, Barbara Lang.'

Stanley jumped to his feet, almost sputtering. 'They were at the St Tropez too. That's where I saw the hat. I was in the lobby when they checked in and he was wearing it!'

Baker stared at them. Maybe it wasn't over yet. He picked up the telephone and spoke into it. 'I want a complete I.D. file on Count Cardinali. The works, from the day he was born until yesterday!'

He put down the telephone, still looking at them. 'Do you have any idea where he may be right now?'

'I do,' Captain Strang answered. He took a newspaper out of his pocket and opened it on the desk. He pointed to the top corner of the page.

Baker looked down at it. There was a picture of Cardinali over the story. The headline read, *Famous Sportsman Out of Hospital Tomorrow*. There was a brief story beneath about the accident on the Sunshine State Parkway in which the girl was killed.

Baker lifted his eyes from the paper and whistled. 'If this guy is the Stiletto,' he said in a sober voice, 'he's goin' to be a tough one to nail down. He doesn't believe in leaving any witnesses around. Either his own or someone else's!'

Stanley jumped to his feet, almost screaming. "They were at the St. Tropez too. That's where I saw the hat. I was in the lobby when they checked in and he was wearing it!"

Baker stared at them. Maybe it wasn't over yet. He picked up the telephone and spoke into it. "I want a complete FBI file on Count Cardinali. The works, from the day he was born until yesterday."

He put down the telephone, still looking at them. "Do you have any idea where he may be right now?"

"I do," Stanley answered. He took a newspaper out of his pocket and opened it on the desk. He pointed to the top corner of the page.

Baker looked down at it. There was a picture of Cardinali over the story. The headline read, [illegible]

TEN

BAKER stood in front of the automobile showroom on Park Avenue. Through the windows, the sleek foreign cars shone with their highly polished newness. Lettered simply in small gold [illegible] letters on the glass entrance [illegible] Cardinali [illegible] He opened the door [illegible] walked in. There were several customers looking at cars and he stood around for a few minutes. One of the customers [illegible] and the salesman came toward him.

He was a tall silver-haired man and wore a morning coat and a small flower in his buttonhole. He looked more like a stockbroker than an automobile salesman. "Can I help you, sir?" His voice was impeccably polite yet somehow aloof.

Baker smiled to himself as he thought of the diffe-

TEN

BAKER stood in front of the automobile showroom on Park Avenue. Through the windows the sleek foreign cars shone with their highly polished newness. Lettered simply in small silver block letters on the glass entrance doors were the words: *Cesare Cardinali, Imported Automobiles.*

He opened the door to the showroom and walked in. There were several customers looking at cars and he stood around for a few minutes. One of the customers left and the salesman came toward him.

He was a tall silver-haired man and wore a morning coat and a small flower in his buttonhole. He looked more like a stockbroker than an automobile salesman. 'Can I help you, sir?' His voice was inquiringly polite yet somehow aloof.

Baker smiled to himself as he thought of the difference in the approach to a customer here and at the Smiling Irishman where he had bought his car. He shook his head slightly. 'I would like to see Mr Cardinali.' He asked, 'Is he around?'

A disapproving look came over the salesman's face. 'Mr Cardinali never comes into the showroom,' he said haughtily.

'No?' Baker smiled. 'Then where can I find him?'

'I'm sure I don't know,' the salesman answered. 'But you might try the office.'

'Where is that?' Baker asked gently. He had long since learned not to be annoyed by snobs. Too many of them proved empty shells once their props were removed.

'On the fifteenth floor. You can get the elevator in the lobby through that door.' The salesman indicated an entrance on the side.

'Thank you,' Baker said.

'Not at all,' the salesman replied, walking politely toward another prospect who had just entered the showroom.

Baker walked into the lobby and waited for an elevator. This was one of the new buildings on Park Avenue. Everything was automatic, even the elevators had music piped into them. Cardinali was for real, he thought. He had it made. What could it be that tied a man like this to the Syndicate?

He remembered the incredulous expression on Strang's face when they had gone over the I.D. report.

'I don't get it,' the captain had said. 'This guy's got everything. Title. Money. War hero. Fame. Where does he fit in with the mob?'

That was the question that bothered them all. And there were the soft points that bothered him. The soft edges around the hard facts that reached out toward something that could not be explained factually. For example there was the war record. Cardinali had co-operated with the Allies in the undercover job prior to the invasion of Italy and had received a medal for it. Still he had killed five of his contacts on that mission while all the others on the same mission, and there were more than twenty agents, found it necessary to eliminate only four people among them. Then there was the matter of Cardinali's uncle who had been murdered. Of course, Cardinali had been far away but soon after, though he had been broke at the end of the war, he began to make it big. There were the fast cars and the races, and in almost no time at all Cardinali had become a figure in international society. True, there were others like him. De Portago who was killed in that race. Cesare had been in that race too. He had been set down for unnecessarily reckless driving. There had been other races too where he had been set down. Twice the implication had been that he was responsible for the deaths of other contestants. But nowhere was there any clue that pointed to a connection with the underworld.

The elevator doors opened and Baker came out into a softly lit reception room around whose walls were prints of famous automobiles. The receptionist sat at a small desk in the far corner.

'Can I be of help, sir?' she asked.

Baker nodded. 'I would like to see Mr Cardinali.'

'Do you have an appointment?' the girl asked.

Baker shook his head.

'May I have the nature of your business?' the girl asked.

'It's personal,' Baker answered.

Disapprovingly the girl picked up the telephone. 'I will see if Count Cardinali is in,' she said haughtily. 'Your name, please?'

'George Baker,' he replied.

He stood there waiting while the girl whispered into the telephone. After a moment she looked up at him. 'If you will be kind enough to take a seat, Miss Martin, Count Cardinali's secretary, will be out to speak with you in a few minutes.'

He walked over to a comfortable couch and sat down. The table in front of him was covered with sports car magazines in every language and from every country. Idly he picked one up and began to glance through it. He looked up when a girl came through a door and stood in front of him.

'I'm Miss Martin,' the girl said, smiling politely, 'Count Cardinali's secretary. He doesn't see anyone except by appointment. Can I be of help to you?'

He got to his feet slowly, aware of the curious gaze of the receptionist. Silently he reached into his pocket and took out his identification. He gave it to Miss Martin.

She glanced down at it and then up at him, a puzzled expression crossing her face.

'I'm sorry to trouble the Count,' he said reassuringly, 'but there are some matters in which he may be able to assist us.'

Miss Martin gave him back the small identification case and he put it in his pocket. 'If you'll be kind enough to wait a moment more, I will see if an appointment can be arranged for you.'

She disappeared through the door and he sat down again. A few minutes later she reappeared. 'Follow me, please.'

He followed her into a large working office. There were several girls and men working at desks there. The usual business office. Through that he entered another office. There was only one desk there. She led him past the desk into another office. This belonged to Cardinali.

Baker's eyes widened as he took in the furnishings. The antiques were authentic, the lamps of genuine statuary. Even the artificial fireplace was of fine Italian marble. On the mantelpiece over the fireplace were some awards and gold cups that were the only concession to commercialism in the entire office. Cardinali did not sit at a desk. There was no desk anywhere in the office.

He rose from a comfortable lounge chair next to a small telephone table with a note pad beside the telephone. He held out his hand to Baker. His grip was firm.

'How can I be of help to you, Mr Baker?' he inquired, waving him to the seat opposite him.

Baker waited until the secretary left the office and then sat down. He studied the man opposite him for a few moments.

Cardinali took the scrutiny well. His expression remained even, a smile faintly on his lips. He seemed no more than politely curious over the reason for the visit. That fitted too, Baker found himself thinking. Any man who had done what the Stiletto had needed nerves of ice. He smiled slowly.

'You are smiling?' Cesare asked.

Baker nodded. The thought had just jumped through his mind. Everyone had approached him since he had come here with a stock phrase: *Can I be of help to you?* Even Cardinali. And it had been his experience when there was so much overt helpfulness offered, there would be very little actually given.

'I was just thinking, Mr Cardinali,' he said, 'how much more comfortable your office is than many I have been in. It seems almost too comfortable to be an inducement to work.'

Cesare smiled. 'Actually that is true,' he admitted. 'But in my line of work I do not find it necessary to disturb myself with the mechanics of business. So I keep my office as little like one as I possibly can. Mainly because I am a very selfish creature who is rather fond of his comforts.'

Baker nodded. Everything this man said and did was exactly right. There would be no point in beating around the bush with him. Cardinali could keep this up all day. He leaned forward in his chair. 'I trust you are well recovered from the effects of your recent accident?'

Cesare nodded. 'I am quite well, thank you.'

'It must have been a shattering experience,' Baker prompted.

'It was more than that,' Cesare said with a strange sort of earnestness as if he were seeking words in English to describe it. 'It was tragic. I shall never stop blaming myself for allowing it to happen.'

'You could have prevented it?' Baker asked quickly.

He thought he caught a glimpse of mockery deep in Cesare's eyes. 'I think so,' Cesare answered. 'I should never have let her drive. The car was too much for her.'

It was at that moment that Baker knew he had it, the answer to a great many questions. He had wanted Cesare to bait him into a direct probe and had succeeded, without revealing any of his own suspicions.

'I'm glad you're over it,' Baker said quietly. 'Now if we may get down to business?'

Cesare nodded. 'By all means.'

'As a result of the accident,' Baker said, 'it has come to our attention through the newspapers that during the past week you spent some time at the Maharajah in Las Vegas and the St Tropez in Miami Beach.'

'That's true,' Cesare confirmed.

'And that also on Monday of last week you were in the Federal Courthouse in Foley Square here in New York?'

'Your people are very thorough,' Cesare said. 'That is also true.'

'Do you have any idea why I'm referring to these places?' Baker asked.

Cesare smiled. 'I would be a fool if I pretended ignorance, wouldn't I?' he asked. 'I read the newspapers also.'

'You are aware then of the murders of the witnesses in the trial of the criminal syndicate?'

Cesare nodded. 'I am. But what I do not see is how I can be of help to you in connection with them.'

Baker looked at him. 'What were you doing in the courthouse that day?'

Cesare met his gaze. 'You do not know?' He laughed shortly. 'I went there to get my first citizenship papers.'

'Immigration is on the ground floor,' Baker said. 'Yet you were observed on the third-floor corridor outside the courtroom.'

Cesare laughed again. 'That is simple enough too. You see the lavatory on the ground floor was occupied. I was told there was one on the third floor so I went up the staircase to it. When I saw the crowds I came downstairs again.'

'You didn't notice anything unusual while you were on the third floor?' Baker asked.

'The whole thing was unusual to me,' Cesare answered. 'If you refer to anything particular, an incident, no. There was just the crowd and the men coming off the elevator and my trying to push my way through them to get back to the staircase.'

'What reason did you have for going to these hotels particularly? Why not any of the others in Vegas or Miami?'

Cesare looked at him. 'Hotels, Mr Baker, are a matter of fashion. And in my business I have to be aware of such things.' He took a cigarette from a box on the table next to him. 'It would seem to me more relevant to ask the same question of the one responsible for allowing those witnesses to stay in those hotels.'

'You never saw any of them?' Baker asked.

Cesare lit the cigarette and shook his head. 'Not to my knowledge. Besides if I had seen them I would not have recognized them. I did not even know what they looked like.' He hesitated a moment. 'Perhaps in Vegas I saw one of them. I do not know. But as Miss Lang and I were leaving the casino, a man was carried out, past us.'

'That was one of the witnesses,' Baker said.

'It was?' Cesare asked politely. 'Too bad I did not know then. I would have perhaps looked more closely.'

'Is there anything at all that comes to your mind that might be of help to us? Other people that you may have noticed?'

Cesare shook his head. 'I'm sory, Mr Baker,' he said regretfully, 'there is nothing I can think of. You see, I was on a holiday with a very beautiful woman and I'm afraid I wasn't very interested in anything else.'

Baker recognized the end of the road. The interview was over and nothing had been learned. And it wouldn't do any good to try to sweat it out of this man either. He wasn't the type. Baker got to his feet. As he did he saw a pair of crossed daggers mounted on the wall behind Cesare. 'What are those?' he asked.

Cesare didn't turn around. 'They are stilettos,' he answered.

Baker walked over to the wall and looked at them. They were dull with patina. 'Stilettos,' he said. 'The witnesses were killed with that sort of weapon.'

'So I have read,' Cesare said imperturbably.

'Have you had them long?' Baker asked.

'They are family heirlooms,' Cesare answered. 'I have quite a collection of them, here in New York in my apartment and at home in Italy. The stiletto was a favorite weapon of the Borgias who are listed among my ancestors.'

'I see,' Baker said. 'I suppose you are an expert in their use.'

Cesare got up smiling. 'I suppose I am,' he answered. 'But there is not much room in our society to become really proficient at it. Weapons, like many other things, also are subject to the whims of fashion.' He came over to Baker and took one of the stilettos down from the wall. He looked at it for a moment then handed it to Baker.

'Those little toys we market downstairs in the showroom kill more people in a month than all the stilettos made since they were first adapted from the Florentine.'

Baker looked down at the delicate blade in his hand, then up at Cesare. A vague memory ran through his mind. 'Are you the same Cardinali who was once fencing champion of Italy?'

Cesare nodded. 'Another of the ancient sports I enjoy. Do you fence?'

'I did,' Baker replied. 'I was on the team at college.' He put the stiletto down on the telephone table gently. 'I must be going now,' he said. 'Thank you very much for your co-operation, Count Cardinali.'

'I'm sorry I couldn't have been of more help,' Cesare replied politely.

The stiletto was still on the small telephone table when Miss Martin came in to the office after Baker had left. She looked down at the stiletto then up at Cesare. 'What did he want?' she asked with a familiarity born of long association.

Cesare picked up the stiletto and replaced it on the wall. He turned to her, smiling. 'It seems I was very unwise in choosing the route for my holiday,' he said.

Baker leaned back in his chair. 'I didn't learn a damn thing,' he admitted.

Strang smiled. 'You didn't think you would, did you?'

Baker shook his head. 'I guess I didn't. The only thing I did was convince myself. That guy is the Stiletto. I know it.'

'Knowing it and proving it are two different things,' Strang said.

Baker leaned over his desk and came up with several photographs of a wrecked car. He pushed them over to Strang. 'Look at them. They were sent up from Florida.'

Strang looked down at them. 'Well?'

'See how the girl is wedged in behind the wheel?

'See how the motor was pushed back almost to the front seat through the dashboard? Well, if Cardinali was asleep like he said he was when the crash happened, where in hell were his feet? Not on the floor under the dash like you would think they were, or he never would have gotten out of that car. His legs would have been crushed when the front end came in on him.'

'I've seen enough automobile accidents to know anything is possible,' Strang said.

'Maybe,' Baker admitted. 'But I'm willing to bet my shirt right now that Cardinali had his feet on the seat under him until almost the moment the car hit and then he jumped.'

'But what about the girl?' Strang asked. 'She was driving.'

Baker looked at him. 'The only thing we're sure of is that she was behind the wheel.'

'You still can't prove anything,' Strang said.

'Right now I can't,' Baker said. 'But I have some ideas.'

'Going to put a tail on him?' Strang asked.

Baker shook his head. 'It would be wasted. In the circles in which that guy moves anyone we could put on him would stick out like a sore thumb. Besides it would make too much of a stink. You know how careful the chief is with important people.'

'Then what are you going to do?' Strang asked.

Baker smiled. 'The first thing is to leak to the newspapers that he was questioned. The next thing to do is to find someone that will stick close enough to him to maybe learn something and be of real help to us.'

'Like who?' Strang asked.

'Like a dame,' Baker said. 'He's quite a ladies' man. Well, we're on to one that will fit right in. Society. Racing cars. The works.'

'If he is the Stiletto, it might be dangerous for her,' Strang said.

'She says she can handle him,' Baker answered. 'And I've had a look at her record and, believe me, if she can't, then nobody can.'

ELEVEN

THE party was in full swing when Cesare entered the stateroom. He stood in the doorway, his eyes searching for the hostess. She saw him at almost the same time as he saw her and came hurrying forward, her hand outstretched.

'Cesare, my dear boy,' she said, as he kissed her hand. 'I'm so glad you could come.'

'I would sooner die than miss Madame's sailing.' He smiled.

She smiled, her somber eyes glowing under the rich gray hair. Her voice lowered and assumed a tone that was much like the voice Cesare had heard on the telephone just a few weeks ago. 'This stateroom is next to his,' she whispered. 'There is a connecting door between the two bathrooms. He should be aboard in about ten minutes.'

He didn't speak and she raised her voice as another guest approached. 'And thank you for the lovely flowers.'

'It is a pleasure, Madame,' he answered.

He watched her turn to the other guest and move away. Once she had been a very beautiful woman, one of the most famous in international society. Her name still conjured up visions of glamorous ballrooms and princes. But now, she belonged to Don Emilio.

He moved toward the bathroom door slowly. He heard her laughter as he opened the door. How many more like her were there who walked the borderline of the two worlds? For that matter how many more were there like himself?

Emilio Matteo put his coat up against the wind that blew in from the chilly Hudson River as he got out of the taxicab in front of the pier. He looked up at the ship morosely as the detectives got out beside him. Without speaking, he gave one of them a bill for the driver.

'This way,' the detective said and started for the pier.

'I know the way,' Emilio said sourly. They walked onto the pier and over to the gangplank.

The little steward led them down a corridor on the first-class deck. Sounds of merriment came from behind the doors where bon voyage parties were almost at their height. The *Italia* was due to leave in less than an hour. The steward opened a door.

'This way, signore.' He bowed.

Emilio entered the suite and the detectives followed

him. There was a small bar set up in the corner of the room.

The steward came in after them. 'Is everything to the signor's satisfaction?' he asked Emilio.

Emilio gave him a bill. 'Fine,' he said.

The steward bowed again and left. The two detectives looked around. The oldest turned to Emilio. 'This is prety snazzy, Matteo,' he said.

Emilio smiled at him. 'Nothing but the best,' he said, crossing to the bar. 'You didn't think I would stay in one of those lousy cabins the government pays for, did you?'

The detective grinned. 'I guess not.'

Emilio opened a bottle and poured himself a drink. He threw it down his throat. 'Ah,' he said, 'that's good whisky. It warms you up a little after that cold wind on the docks.' He turned to the detectives. 'Have a drink?'

The detectives looked at each other and smiled. 'Don't mind if we do,' the oldest said, walking over to the bar.

'Help yourself.' Emilio pushed the bottle toward him. He took off his overcoat and threw it on a chair. 'I guess I'm getting old all right, my kidneys ain't what they used to be. I'm going to the john.'

He opened the bathroom door. The younger detective was at his side. Emilio stepped back. 'Age before beauty,' he said sarcastically. 'Maybe you'd better have a look first.'

The detective looked inside the bathroom. He turned back, a sheepish expression on his face. 'Okay,' he said.

'Thank you,' Emilio said with formality. He stepped

into the bathroom and began to close the door. 'For some things a man must have a little privacy.'

The door closed behind him and a burst of noise came into the stateroom from the cabin next door. 'Sounds like a wild party,' the younger detective said, pouring himself a drink.

'All it takes is money,' the other said. He held his drink up in the air. 'Shalanta.'

'Shalanta,' the other man replied. They swallowed their drinks. 'This is good whisky,' he added.

The other detective looked at him. 'Like Matteo says,' he said in a bitter voice, 'nothing but the best.'

The younger man stared at him. 'Yeah,' he said sarcastically. 'Crime doesn't pay.'

Emilio walked over to the sink and turned on the tap. He waited for a moment and listened. He could hear the faint murmur of the detectives' voices from his room. Quickly he crossed to the far end of the bathroom. There was a door there that connected with the next suite. It was locked.

He ran his fingernails against the door, making a scraping sound. 'Cesare!' he whispered.

A scraping sound came back to him. Quickly he turned and opened the medicine cabinet. On the top shelf was a key. He put it in the door and turned it. The tumbler on his side clicked. A moment later he could hear the tumbler fall on the other side.

The door opened slightly and Cesare slipped into the room quickly and shut the door behind him.

Emilio smiled. 'Don Cesare! My nephew!'

Cesare smiled also. 'Don Emilio! My uncle!'

The two men embraced. 'It has been a long time,' Emilio said.

'A long time indeed,' Cesare answered formally.

'You have done well, my nephew,' Emilio whispered. 'I am proud.'

'I have kept the oath, Don Emilio,' Cesare replied.

'You have, and the family will be pleased when I tell them of you. It is time now that you take a place in our councils.'

Cesare shook his head. 'I am content only to keep my agreement with you, Don Emilio. I seek nothing from the Brotherhood.'

An expression of surprise came into Emilio's face. 'You will have riches you never dreamed possible!'

'I do not need the riches,' Cesare replied. 'I have more than enough for my needs now.'

Emilio shook his head. 'The Dons will take this as an affront.'

'It is not intended as such,' Cesare said quickly. 'You will explain this to them. I will repay my debt as I am called upon to do so, but no more.'

'Already the other three men who were with me in the trial have petitioned the council for your death!' Emilio said. 'They feel that you are a danger to them as long as you are free. And they have read in the papers that you have been questioned by the authorities.'

'They are old women,' Cesare said scornfully. 'The police have learned nothing.'

'But they are still worried.'

'Explain to the council there is nothing to fear. There is nothing I want from any of them.'

Emilio shook his head. 'I will do as you ask, my nephew. But until you hear from me, be careful. They are dangerous men.'

'I will be careful, Don Emilio.' Cesare smiled. 'For their own sakes I trust they too will be careful.'

'I will get word to them,' Emilio said.

Cesare nodded. 'Good. And when will I hear from you?'

'Next month,' Emilio answered. 'I will bring word to you of the council's decision at the Gran Mexico sports car races. You will enter your Ferrari. Your mechanic will be detained in Italy and when you arrive in Mexico City the day before the race, you will receive a telegram that he is ill. You will hire one that I will send you. Then you will receive further instructions.'

Cesare nodded again. 'If there are any changes in my plans I will leave word for you at the restaurant of the Quarter Moon in Harlem as before.'

Emilio smiled. 'It is understood.' He embraced Cesare again and then took his hand. 'I will die for you,' he said.

Cesare stared at him for a moment, then he replied, 'I will die for you.' Swiftly he turned and slipped out the door.

Emilio heard the tumbler click. He turned the key on his own side and put it back into the medicine cabinet. Then he turned off the tap and started back to his room, shaking his head. Cesare had signed his own death warrant by refusing further alliance with the Brotherhood. Now, he too must seek Cesare's death. Too bad he did not have the time to let the others know of his change of heart.

*

There is a restaurant in Manhattan on Lexington Avenue where the steaks are reputed to be the finest obtainable anywhere in the world and the spaghetti better even than in the old country. It is only natural in such a fine restaurant that the prices are so high that someone wandering in from the street could ill afford to have even bread and butter served to him. It is also only natural that the only customers who can afford such a restaurant either live on an expense account or have cash in such sufficient amounts that if necessary they could use the crisp new bills they love to carry in the large green salads served to them with spicy dressings.

Big Dutch stuffed a large piece of rare steak into his mouth and chewed on it. A tiny dribble of gravy slipped out of the corner. He swabbed at it with a piece of bread and pushed the bread into his mouth along with the meat. He chewed a moment more then looked over at his two companions. 'I don't care what any of youse guys say,' he mumbled, 'I say we should hit him.'

Allie Fargo stared at him. 'But we ain't even sure he's the right guy. Emilio never came right out and told us.'

Big Dutch swallowed his mouthful. His knife began to cut another piece of steak. 'What difference does it make?' he demanded. 'We ain't got time to check him out. The newspapers already said the F.B.I. has questioned the guy. Then what happens to us if he starts to sing?'

Dandy Nick looked down at his plate with distaste. This much food was wasted on him. He didn't eat very much anyway. 'I don't like it,' he said. 'Emilio said we should sit tight and wait word from Italy. He's takin' it up with Lucky and Joe.'

'Emilio says, Emilio says,' Big Dutch burst out angrily, his mouth still filled with food. He swallowed quickly and went on. 'I'm getting tired of what Emilio says. Them guineas sit over there on their fat asses while we stay here stickin' our necks out! They think just because they started the business they still own it!'

Almost unconsciously, Dandy Nick looked around the restaurant to see if they had been overheard. His voice dropped to a whisper. 'Take it easy! That kind of talk will only wind up getting you measured.'

Big Dutch stared at him balefully. 'How do you guys know that they ain't settin' us up? Maybe they're figgerin' for this guy to take over? You know how them guineas stick together.'

Dandy Nick was silent. He looked at Allie. Allie was eating stolidly, his eyes on his plate. After a moment, Allie looked up. He put his knife and fork down carefully. 'It'll make an awful big stink,' he said softly. 'This ain't no dock walloper in one of your phony unions, Big Dutch. This is a pretty important geister.'

'Yeah,' Dandy Nick added. 'And if he ain't the Stiletto, we'll still be in the same boat. And we'll have to explain to Emilio anyway.'

Big Dutch kept on eating. It was time they made the move anyway. The Italians had had it long enough. The organization was here anyway; all the work, all the money was here. It was time they cut loose from the Mafia. What could they do from three thousand miles away if nobody wanted to work with them?

'I say we don't wait. We hit him.' He didn't look up. He kept on eating. In a way it was too bad that he was in jail when they turned Roger Touhy loose. Big Dutch had already arranged a meet. The boys would have gone with Roger against the Mafia.

Dandy Nick's appetite was completely gone now. He pushed his plate away from him. He knew what Big Dutch was thinking. He glanced over at Allie. From the way Allie was eating he could tell that he knew too. This was more than just hitting one guy. This could be the beginning of a revolution. And he felt too old to go through another war just now. 'What would we tell Emilio?' he asked, hoping to stall the decision.

Big Dutch's eyes flashed up at him for a moment, then down at the food again. 'We'll think of something,' he said.

Allie came right out with it. 'I don't know,' he said. 'Look what they did to Touhy. Twenty-five years they waited for him.'

Big Dutch's voice was scornful. 'Touhy went soft in the clink. He should've gone right to work. Things would've been different then. They were afraid of him. Remember how he had Capone buffaloed?'

'But they got him, didn't they?' Dandy Nick asked.

'Sure, but look how they did it,' Big Dutch retorted. 'With a couple of punk amateurs. The kids were so excited they even left the cop alive. All they can count on now is the punks who go for the reputation. Even this Stiletto guy. He don't belong. We got a business to protect. There ain't a top man in the country who won't go with us.'

He put down his knife and fork and picked up the

steak bone in his fingers. He waved it at them. It was time they got off the fence. 'I say we hit,' he said emphatically.

Allie looked at Dandy Nick, then back to Big Dutch. There was no room nor time left for stalling. 'Okay, we hit,' he said.

They turned to Dandy Nick. His mind was already made up. The percentage was with the house, it was heads you lose, tails they win and all anybody could do was hope to stay on his feet until it was over. 'Hit,' he said.

Big Dutch smiled. It was only the first step but he had made it and they had gone with him. The Stiletto was only a symbol, it was the Mafia that was important. It was time they returned the country to the Americans to whom it belonged. Already his mind was busy redividing the take. The sums made his head spin. He got to his feet and looked down at them.

'I don't know about you guys,' he said, 'but this is the first night the old lady let me out of the house since I got back from the can and I'm going to Jenny's and get laid.'

They didn't answer and he turned and started out of the restaurant. When he was gone they looked at each other. 'Coffee,' Dandy Nick told the waiter.

He turned back to Allie when the waiter had gone. Now was the time for them to take out an insurance policy. They had to get a message through to Emilio.

TWELVE

THE weekly session of the Fencing Club was in full swing on the third floor of the New York Athletic Club on Central Park South. Through the small gymnasium that they used echoed the clash of foil upon foil as the white-shirted men danced back and forth, their grotesque black masks hiding their faces.

Cesare's foil flashed down in the white light and arced in past his opponent's guard, coming to a stop on the little red heart emblazoned on the white shirt.

'*Touché!*' his opponent said, stepping back and lifting his foil.

Cesare flipped up his mask. He smiled. 'You did very well, Hank. You still must watch your wrist though. It is too loose.'

The opponent lifted his mask. He was breathing heavily. He smiled back at Cesare. 'Are you going to enter the tournament next month, Cesare?' he asked.

Cesare shook his head. 'I don't think so. I have entered the Gran Mexico races and probably will not be back in time. But, after all, it is for business, no?'

The man nodded. 'Too bad though. We won't have much of a chance without you. Thanks for the lesson anyway.'

Cesare nodded. 'You are quite welcome.' He turned to the small group of onlookers and grinned. 'Who is to be my next, how do you call it, pigeon?' he teased.

They laughed a little self-consciously and looked at each other. 'I guess you'll have to wait until Fortini gets here. You're out of our class,' one of them said, referring to the fencing coach.

'All right, then,' Cesare said. He began to take off his mask.

A voice came from the doorway. 'How about giving me a chance?'

Cesare turned. Baker was standing there, in uniform, smiling. 'Ah, Mr Baker,' Cesare said, no surprise in his voice, 'of course.'

Baker walked toward him, picking up a foil from the rack. He flicked it through the air, loosening his wrist. He transferred the foil to his left hand and held out his right hand. Cesare took it. Baker's grip was firm. 'Count Cardinali,' he said, 'when I learned you were a member here, I could not resist the temptation – the chance to cross swords with one of the truly great fencers of our time.'

Cesare smiled slowly. 'I am honored. You are very kind. Would you like a few minutes to warm up?'

Baker nodded. 'Thank you, no. I am about as good

as I ever will be. I only hope to give you a few interesting moments.'

'I'm sure you will.' Cesare smiled again. They moved out into the open space and took up positions. 'I did not know you were a member here.'

Baker smiled back at him. 'I'm afraid I don't have very much time to spend. My work usually keeps me pretty occupied.' He flipped down his mask. 'Ready?' Cesare nodded. He closed his mask. The foils crossed in mid-air. '*En garde!*' Baker called.

Baker lunged forward and Cesare deflected the thrust and stepped back. He knew at once that Baker was no ordinary amateur. He smiled beneath his mask. He waited for Baker to lead again. There might be some fun in this encounter after all.

People began to drift across the gymnasium. There was a curious kind of tension that was immediately felt in the room. Baker pressed forward with a furious kind of concentration. Cesare's foil flashed as he parried attack after attack. Slowly, step by step, he began to fall back. The onlookers began to sense an upset. A low murmur began to fill the room.

Baker still kept pressing forward. He was beginning to feel confident. Cardinali didn't seem to be anywhere near as good as his reputation. He slashed in and Cesare locked foils with him. Baker tried to free his foil but Cesare held him easily. Baker pushed with all his strength at the man in front of him. Cesare didn't move. It seemed to Baker as if he were pushing against a steel coil. Suddenly he realized that Cardinali had only been toying with him.

At the same moment Cesare pushed him away. Baker

fell back a few steps and recovered in time to block a simple thrust. He lunged forward in a feint, then turned his foil quickly. Cesare was waiting for him.

Cesare laughed. 'Very good,' his voice came patronizingly from beneath the mask. 'Maestro Antonelli?'

'Yes,' Baker answered, watching Cardinali carefully. 'Rome, 1951.'

'My compliments,' Cesare said, beginning his attack. 'Signor Antonelli is very careful about his pupils. He accepts only the best.'

Baker was busy defending himself now. There was no time left for him to launch an attack. 'Apparently I didn't spend enough time with him,' he managed to say wryly.

Cesare laughed again. 'The sword is a very demanding master. And in our time, as I said before, there are other weapons much more in fashion.'

Cesare's foil seemed to suddenly have a life of its own. Baker could feel himself running out of breath. His own foil seemed to weigh a ton in his hand. Cesare seemed to sense his weariness and slowed down his attack.

Baker could feel the perspiration running down his face inside his mask. Each breath began to come more labored to his throat. Every motion was an effort now and still Cesare was moving gracefully, breathing easily. There were a dozen times he felt Cesare could have scored and each time Cesare purposely turned his foil away. A little more of this and he would fall exhausted to the floor.

His rising anger brought a wave of strength back to

his arms. He summoned all his reserves for a last attack. He deflected Cesare's foil and thrust forward.

'*Touché*,' the sound came from the spectators.

Baker stopped suddenly and looked down. Cesare's foil was resting on his heart. It had come so quickly that he hadn't even seen it.

He lowered his foil and opened his mask. 'You're much too good for me, Count Cardinali,' he said, breathing heavily.

Cesare saluted him with his foil. 'I am lucky that you do not have more time for practice,' he said smiling.

Baker forced a smile to his lips. 'Now, *you* are being kind.'

'Perhaps you will join me in a drink, Mr Baker?' Cesare asked.

'Thanks,' Baker said quickly. 'I could use one right now. I've had it.'

They sat in front of an open fire in the lounge. Cesare's long legs were stretched out in front of him. He looked at Baker sitting opposite him and lifted his drink. 'You did not come here merely to fence, Mr Baker.'

Baker looked at him. In some ways Cardinali wasn't very European at all. In this, for example, he came right out and spoke his mind. 'That's true, Count Cardinali,' he said. 'Actually I've come to warn you and offer our help.'

Cesare lifted an eyebrow. 'That's very kind of you, but for what reason do I need warning?'

'We've had word downtown that your life is being threatened,' Baker said.

Cesare laughed. 'How very melodramatic!'

'It's not funny,' Baker said. 'Certain men want you killed.'

'Me? What men?'

Baker looked at him. 'Big Dutch, Allie Fargo, Dandy Nick.'

Cesare's face was impassive. 'Who are they?'

'The defendants in the trial where the witnesses were killed. You see, they think you're the Stiletto.'

Cesare's laugh was genuine and clear. 'In that case why should they want to kill me? If I am the one who saved their miserable lives?'

Baker leaned forward. 'That's just it. They are afraid of you. They think you might turn against them.'

'They are stupid,' Cesare said, taking a sip of his drink.

'But they are dangerous,' Baker said earnestly. 'There is no protection against a bullet in the back.'

Cesare got to his feet. 'I can look after myself,' he said shortly. 'I have survived worse dangers in the war than those men. You must know that by now. I hear your office is very thorough.'

Baker nodded. 'Yes, but we would still like to be of help.'

Cesare's voice grew cold. 'Your office has been of all the help to me I want. Perhaps if you were not so eager to obtain publicity in the newspapers, these men would not even know of me.'

Baker stood up. 'We're sorry about that, Count Cardinali. I don't know how the newspapers got wind of our conversation, but if you should have any trouble don't hesitate to call on us.' He held out his hand.

Cesare took it. 'Thank you, Mr Baker. But I don't think it will be necessary.'

Cesare opened the door and entered the small foyer of his apartment. He began to take off his topcoat. 'Tonio!' he called.

He stood there for a moment, then dropped his coat into a chair. He crossed to the kitchen door and opened it. 'Tonio,' he called again. There was no answer.

Shaking his head, he crossed back into the living room and walked toward his bedroom. He would have to do something about that boy, whether or not he was Gio's nephew. A servant should go only so far. Too often Tonio was not around when he arrived home. America had spoiled him.

He opened the door and walked into the bedroom. He turned on the light and started for the bathroom. The sound of running water came from it. He stopped. 'Tonio!' he called again.

There was no answer. He started for the bathroom quickly, then stopped. Baker's warning flashed through his mind. He moved his hand and the stiletto appeared in it. Silently he stepped to the door and flung it open.

A girl was just stepping from the shower, a towel held in her hand. She stared up at him, a startled expression on her face. 'Cesare! '

'Ileana!' His voice was an echo of her surprise. 'What are you doing here? I thought you were in California!'

Ileana raised the towel to her bosom. 'I am taking a

shower,' she said. Her eyes fell to the stiletto in his hand. 'What are you doing with that knife? Who did you think would be in your bathroom?'

Cesare let go of the stiletto and it disappeared into his sleeve. Ileana ran to him, threw a moist arm around him and kissed him, holding the towel with her other hand. 'Oh, Cesare, I need your help!'

Cesare looked down at her skeptically. It wasn't Ileana who usually needed help. 'What happened to your rich Texan?' he asked.

Ileana looked up at him. 'You are angry with me,' she said. 'I can tell. Because I did not wait for you in Monte Carlo.'

Cesare began to smile. 'Ileana, you didn't answer my question,' he said softly.

She turned away from him and went over to the dressing table and sat down before it. She looked up at his reflection in the mirror. 'Be kind to me, Cesare,' she said in a small voice. 'I have gone through a terrible experience.' She took a small towel from the rack and held it back toward him. 'Please dry my back, I can never reach it.'

He took the towel from her. 'The Texan, Ileana. What about him?'

Her eyes were wide. 'I don't want to talk about it. It was too horrible. Do you think I've lost weight, Cesare?'

He was smiling now. He began to pat her back with the towel. 'You look all right. What happened?'

Ileana closed her eyes for a moment. 'I am relieved,' she said. 'I was sure I had lost weight.' She opened her eyes and turned toward him. 'The Texan, he was married.'

'You knew that.' Cesare smiled.

'Of course,' Ileana retorted. 'I am not a child. But his wife was a horrible woman. Not very understanding. Really very provincial. She even reported me to the Department of Immigration. Do you know, Cesare, they are very stupid men?'

Cesare shook his head silently, still smiling.

'They could not understand,' she continued quickly, 'how I could live in this country eight years without money and without working. They said if I did not have a job or a source of income they would deport me on the grounds of moral turpitude.'

Cesare put down the towel. 'And what did you tell them?'

'What else could I tell them?' She shrugged. 'I told them I was working for you. They did not believe it when I told them that I did not need a job in order to live. Cesare, would you give me a job?'

Cesare looked down at her. 'I don't know,' He smiled. 'What can you do? You can't take dictation, you can't type. What will I use you for?'

She rose from the chair and turned toward him. She still held the towel precariously in front of her. Her eyes looked into his. 'You are in the automobile business, no?'

Cesare nodded.

She moved very close to him. 'There must be something I can do. I once owned a Rolls Royce.'

He began to laugh. He held out his arms to her and

she came into them and he kissed her. 'All right, we'll see what we can do.'

'You will, Cesare?' Her voice was excited. 'You're wonderful!' She put her hands up to stroke his cheek. 'I won't be any trouble to you, Cesare. I promise. I only have to work long enough to get a social security number, I think they call it. That's all they need to convince them that I'm legitimate.'

His arms tightened around her. 'You're legitimate all right.' He laughed. 'You can always tell them I knew your parents.'

She glanced up at him quickly to see if there were any hidden meanings in his words but his eyes were laughing. Something caught in her throat and for the first time in a long while, even as he kissed her, she thought of her parents.

She remembered the expression on her father's face the night he opened the door of her bedroom and saw them all in bed together. Her mother. Herself. And the rich American.

THIRTEEN

HER mother was English and only seventeen when she had married the dashing young Rumanian, Baron de Bronczki. The tabloids at the time had called it a storybook romance. Less than a year later Ileana had been born, there had been a revolution and the storybook was ended. Life has a way of dealing with romance.

Actually she never had much of a chance to know her parents while she was a child. She had a vague idea that her mother had been a very beautiful girl and her father a very handsome man, but she had spent most of her life in schools away from them.

First there had been that school in England. She had gone there when she was almost five years old when the war had begun. Her father had gone into the British Army and her mother was wrapped up in the wartime social frenzy and had no time for her.

Then when the war was over they had moved to

Paris and she had been sent to a school in Switzerland. The excuse then was that her father, almost a cripple now from his wounds, would be too occupied with his struggle to regain his lands and former wealth to let them settle permanently in any one place. It never occurred to her to question her mother on her feelings about it. Her mother was always too busy with her friends and social activities. Besides there was something about her mother that made Ileana feel too awkward and out of place to dare speak with her.

Ileana was almost fourteen then and the school in Switzerland was different from the one in England. In England the emphasis had been on the academic, in Switzerland the emphasis was on the social. The school was filled with rich young ladies who had been sent from England and America to have superimposed on their youthful freshness a finishing polish that was available nowhere else in the world. Ileana learned to ski and swim and ride. She also learned how to dress and dance and make small talk.

When Ileana was sixteen, she had already begun to fulfill the promise of her beauty. Her complexion and eyes were English, her figure and grace came from her father. And right across the lake from her school was a similar school for young men. Close contact was kept between the two schools for they needed each other to complement their work.

There had been an outing that summer when she turned sixteen. Her partner had been a tall dark young man who was heir to some throne in the Middle East. He had a long name that no one could remember so they called him Ab, short for Abdul. He was a year older than she, and darkly aquiline, blue-eyed and handsome. Their canoe had taken them to a small island away from the others and now they lay, stretched out in their swimming suits on the sand, soaking up the bright midday sun.

He rolled over on his side and looked at her for a moment. She looked into his eyes and smiled. His face was serious, then he leaned over and kissed her.

She closed her eyes and put an arm around his shoulder and held him closely to her. She felt good. The sand and the sun and the warmth of his mouth. She felt him open the straps of her thin bathing suit, then his fingers on her naked breast. A pleasurable excitement began to grow inside her. A bubble of happy laughter rose into her throat.

He raised his head and looked at her, still serious. The young strong breasts and awakened nipples. Slowly he traced them with his fingers and kissed them.

She smiled at him. 'I like that,' she said softly.

His eyes were unwinking as he looked at her. 'You're still a virgin?'

She couldn't tell whether he was making a statement or asking her. She nodded silently.

'Why?' he asked. 'Has it something to do with your religion?'

'No,' she answered. 'I don't know why.'

'They call you "the cold one" in my school,' he said. 'None of the others in your class are virgins.'

'That's silly,' she said. She could feel her heart beginning to pound inside her.

He stared at her for another moment. 'I think, then, it's about time, don't you?'

She nodded silently.

He got to his feet. 'I will be right back,' he said and walked down to the canoe.

She watched him go down the beach to the water's edge and reach into the canoe. She put her hands up under her bathing suit and pushed it down her legs and kicked it off. The sun felt good on her body. She turned her head to see what he was doing.

He had taken something from the pocket of his trousers and was walking up the beach toward her. He stopped when he saw her. He held something in his hand.

'What's that?' she asked.

He opened his hand so that she could see what he held in it. 'So you won't become pregnant,' he answered.

'Oh,' she said, without surprise. Everything had been very carefully explained to them in school. It was part of the curriculum, one of the important finishing touches so their young ladies would be completely equipped to venture forth in the world. She turned her face away as he slipped out of his trunks.

He knelt in the sand beside her and she turned back to him. She stared at him for a moment. Her voice filled with wonder. 'You're beautiful,' she said reaching for him. 'Beautiful and strong. I never knew a man could be so beautiful.'

'Men are naturally more beautiful than women,' he said matter-of-factly. He bent to kiss her. 'But you're very beautiful too.'

She pulled him closer to her, a sudden demanding fever leaping in her veins. Unexplainably she began to tremble.

He raised his head, thinking she might be frightened. 'I'll try not to hurt you,' he said.

'You won't hurt me,' she said hoarsely, aware now and knowing of the capacity for delight within her. 'I'm strong too!'

And she was. Much stronger than she thought. It took a doctor in Lausanne to complete her defloration on the surgical table.

She was eighteen when she appeared at the door of the de Bronczki apartment in Paris. Her education had been as complete as any girl in the school and in many ways she had surpassed most of the students because she was more beautiful and her capacities were greater. She pressed the bell and waited for the door to open.

Her mother opened the door and looked at her without recognition. 'Yes?' she asked, in the tone of voice she kept for servants and inferiors.

Ileana half smiled to herself. She didn't expect much more from her mother. 'Hello, Mother,' she said in Rumanian.

A look of surprise came over her mother's face. 'It's you,' she said in a shocked voice.

'That's right, Mother,' Ileana said. 'May I come in?'

Flustered, her mother stepped back from the door. 'We didn't expect you until next week.'

Ileana picked up her suitcase and walked into the apartment. 'I sent you a telegram last week.' She asked, 'Didn't you get it?'

Her mother closed the door. 'The telegram. Oh, yes,' she said vaguely. 'Your father did mention something about it before he left on a business trip.'

For the first time Ileana felt a sense of disappointment. 'Daddy's away?'

'He'll be back in a few days,' her mother said quickly. 'Something came up with his estate claims.' For the first time she really looked at Ileana. 'Why, you're taller than I am,' she said in surprise.

'I'm all grown up, Mother,' she said. 'I'm not a little child any more.'

Her mother's voice grew petulant. 'For God's sake, Ileana, speak French instead of that horrible language. You know I never could understand it.'

'Of course, Mother,' Ileana replied in French.

'That's better,' her mother said. 'Now let me take a look at you.'

Ileana stood very still while her mother walked around her slowly. She felt like a horse on the auction block.

'Aren't you dressed rather too old for your years, dear?' her mother asked.

'I'm eighteen, Mother. What did you expect me to wear? A middy blouse and skirt?'

'Don't be fresh, Ileana. I'm trying hard enough to get used to the idea of having a grown-up daughter. Why I don't look that much older than you that we can't be mistaken for sisters.'

Ileana looked at her mother. In some ways, she was right. Somehow she had managed to keep an air of youthfulness about her. She didn't look her thirty-six years. 'Yes, Mother,' she said quietly.

'And stop calling me "Mother," ' the older woman snapped. 'It's old-fashioned anyway. If you must call me something call me by name. Or better still "Dearest," as your father does. Everyone calls me that now.'

'Yes, Moth—Dearest,' Ileana said.

Her mother smiled. 'Now that wasn't so bad, was it? Come, let me show you your room.'

Ileana followed her mother down the long corridor to a small room on the far side of the kitchen. No one had to tell her it was a servant's room. The furnishings did that very clearly.

'It will be quite nice when we fix it up,' Dearest said. She looked up at Ileana. Ileana's face was impassive. 'What's the matter?' she asked sharply. 'You don't like it?'

'It's small,' Ileana said. Her closet at school seemed larger than this.

'Well, you'll have to make do with it,' Dearest snapped. 'Your father isn't one of the wealthiest men in the world, you know. And its difficult enough to manage on the money we have as it is.'

She started to leave the room and at that moment the doorbell rang. She stopped, then turned back to Ileana, a startled expression on her face. 'Oh, I almost forgot. I have a cocktail date with an American friend of ours. Be a dear, will you, and get the door for me. Tell him I'll be ready in a moment.'

She hurried back through the corridor, Ileana following her. At the door to her room, Dearest stopped and looked at Ileana. 'And do me another favor, darling. Don't introduce yourself as my daughter this time.

Tell him you're my sister and down for a visit. I don't feel quite up to involved explanations just now.'

Dearest shut her door quickly before Ileana could answer. Ileana walked down the hall and through the living room slowly. She didn't need anyone to draw a diagram for her. The school in Switzerland was very thorough.

When her father came home the following week, Ileana was shocked at the change in his appearance. The once tall figure was bent and stiff with the pain from his almost immobilized legs. He moved slowly with his canes and dropped into his wheelchair as soon as he was inside the door. He looked at her and smiled as she knelt beside him. He reached out his hand and drew her toward him.

'Ileana,' he said. 'I'm glad you're home at last.'

In spite of his infirmity, the Baron had to spend a great deal of time away from home. There was the matter of his estate to be settled, a negotiation was pending with the present regime that would allow some sort of compensation for their losses to the former holders of property. Return was impossible for now the country was firmly in the Soviet bloc.

During the times her father was away, Ileana busied herself with friends. She kept out of the apartment as much as possible and very often used the back door when she heard voices in the living room.

It was more than a year later that she received a letter from a school friend inviting her to spend the summer with them in Monte Carlo. The Baron was away again and she hurried to her mother's room with the letter. Excitedly, she gave the letter to her mother.

She spoke while her mother was reading the letter. 'It will be so wonderful, just to get away from Paris in the blistering heat. The beach and the water. I just can't wait!'

Dearest folded the letter and put it down on the table. 'You can't go,' she said. 'We can't afford it.'

'I can't?' Ileana's voice was incredulous. 'But I won't need any money. I'll be their guest.'

Dearest looked up at her. 'You'll need clothes,' she said. 'You can't go looking like a ragpicker.'

'I have clothes,' Ileana flared up. 'Everything I had from school still looks well on me.'

'But the styles have changed and they're dated,' Dearest said. 'And everyone will know you couldn't afford a proper wardrobe. Drop her a note and explain that unfortunately you've made other arrangements. You can use my stationery if you like.'

'Save your crested stationery!' Ileana said, close to tears. 'I have my own.' She stamped out of the room.

While she was still in the corridor, the front doorbell rang. Dearest's voice floated after her. 'Get the front door for me, darling. I'll be out in a minute.'

Clenching her teeth, Ileana went to the front door. It was another one of Dearest's American friends. He was already slightly drunk. Ileana introduced herself as Dearest's sister.

He came into the apartment and sat down on the couch. He looked up at her. 'The Baroness never told me she had such a beautiful sister.'

Ileana laughed at his typically American attempt at

gallantry. 'My sister never told me she had such an attractive friend.'

He laughed, pleased with himself. 'It's too bad I have to go back home tonight. Otherwise we might have become better acquainted.'

Dearest's voice came from the doorway. 'You have to return, John? Oh, I'm so sorry.'

She came into the room and John struggled to his feet. 'I was called back,' he said sadly. 'An emergency in the factory.'

'That is too bad,' Dearest said, taking his hand.

'It is too bad,' he said earnestly, looking into her eyes. 'Three times we had cocktails and dinner together and each time I said to myself it would be the next time. And now I have to go back and there will never be a next time.'

'You will come back to Paris,' Dearest said.

'Yes,' he answered. 'But who knows when?' He sat down on the couch again. He looked up at Dearest. 'I stopped in the bar downstairs and had three whiskies before I came up.'

Dearest laughed, her false tinkling laughter that Ileana knew so well. 'What on earth for?' she asked.

His face became very serious. 'I have something very important to ask you.'

Dearest looked at Ileana. 'Will you get some ice from the fridge, darling? John likes lots of ice with his whisky.'

Ileana turned and left the room. She pulled the ice cubes from the tray and put them into a small serving bowl. When she came back into the room, John and her mother were both silent. She began to place the bowl on the small coffee table in front of the couch when she saw the pile of bills stacked on it. It was American money.

She glanced at John quickly. He didn't speak. He still held his wallet in his hand. She looked at her mother questioningly.

John saw the look. He spoke to Dearest. 'I'll make it twenty-five hundred dollars if she joins in the party.'

Suddenly she knew what he meant. She fled from the room, her face flaming, and closed the door of her room behind her.

A few moments later Dearest came into the room. Her face was cold and she looked down at her daughter. 'Why did you run from the room like that?' she asked angrily. 'It was absolutely infantile.'

Ileana stared up at her mother. 'But you know what he was asking, Mother. It was disgusting. He wanted us to go to bed with him.'

'You don't have to explain it to me,' Dearest snapped.

'You're not going to bed with him?' Ileana's voice was incredulous. 'With that drunk?'

'I am,' Dearest said calmly. 'And so are you!'

Ileana sprang to her feet. 'I will not! And you cannot make me!'

'Do you know how much money twenty-five hundred American dollars is? One and a half million francs on the black market. How do you think we have been living anyway? On the thirty-two pounds a month disability pension that your father gets from the army? How do you think we can afford the medicine and doctors for him? From the estates he will never see again? What kind of a life do you think it is for me to spend my days with a cripple who cannot walk and is no good for anything a man is supposed to be good for?'Dearest shook Ileana angrily. 'With this money you can go to Nice to your friends, we can live for six months, your father can have that operation he has postponed so many times.'

Ileana sank back into her chair. 'I won't do it. I can't. The whole idea makes me sick to my stomach.'

Dearest laughed scornfully. 'What are you talking about? Don't make me laugh. You're no innocent little virgin. I know what went on at that precious school of yours. You'll do as I say or I leave right now and you can explain to your father why I won't live with him any more. See if he appreciates your actions then – or even if he believes you!' She turned and swept out of the room.

Ileana sat for a moment, then got up slowly and walked out into the corridor. She stumbled against a table in the dark hallway. Her mother's voice came from the living room.

'Is that you, Ileana?'

'Yes,' she answered.

'Be a dear, will you, and fetch us some more ice?'

'Yes, Dearest,' Ileana replied. Her mother's tinkling laughter followed her into the kitchen.

A faint sound made her bolt upright in the bed. She cast a quick glance at her mother. Dearest was sleeping, an arm thrown over her eyes to shield them from the light. The American lay next to her on his stomach, breathing stertorously.

There was the sound again. A faint squeak as if from the wheel of a rolling chair. A cold fear clutched at her heart. She reached out and touched her mother quickly.

Dearest sat up. She rubbed her eyes. 'What, what?'

'Hurry, Mother,' she whispered, 'into the next room! Hurry!'

Dearest was wide awake now, her eyes frightened. She began to get out of bed then stopped. It was too late. The door was opening.

The Baron sat there in his wheelchair, looking at them. His face was white and impassive, his eyes were cold.

The American got out of bed, reaching for his trousers with trembling hands. 'I – I can explain,' he stammered.

The Baron's lips scarcely moved. 'Get out!'

Frightened, the man ran from the room. A moment later they heard the front door slam behind him.

The Baron sat there in his chair, looking at them. They stared back at him, Dearest shrinking back against the bed, Ileana, leaning forward and holding a sheet to her bosom. At last, her father spoke.

His eyes tore at his wife. 'It is not enough for you that I looked away from what you are, because I loved you once and somehow felt responsible for you. But do you hate me so much that you have to turn your own daughter into a whore?'

Ileana spoke. 'Father, it was I who—'

Her father looked at her. His eyes were the saddest

she had ever seen. 'Put something on, Ileana,' he said gently, 'and go to your room.'

Silently, she slipped into her robe and started through the doorway. He rolled back his chair slightly to let her pass and his hand brushed her arm. His hand was cold as ice.

She went out into the corridor and he rolled his chair into the room and closed the door behind him. She was almost at the door of her room when she heard the shots. She ran back and opened the door. She screamed. Her mother lay dead across the bed, her father in his chair, the gun still smoking on the floor near his outstretched fingers.

Her father left her no money but her mother left an estate of more than sixty thousand dollars. Ileana took the money and went to Monte Carlo and lost it all in a week. She felt better when the money was gone. Cleaner. Then she went to Nice and visited with her friend.

It was there she first met Cesare. He had placed second in the annual race. It was also there she found a new way to live. Like her mother, there was always some rich man who was willing to help her. And somehow when she realized how like her mother she had become nothing much mattered any more.

The only thing that mattered was today. And how much living she could squeeze out of it – or into it.

FOURTEEN

CESARE walked back into the living room. 'Tonio!' he called.

Tonio appeared in the dining-room archway, a bag of groceries still in his arms. 'Excellency! ' he cried. 'You are home early!' He lowered his voice to a conspiratorial whisper and looked meaningfully toward the bedroom. 'The Baroness de Bronczki is—'

'I know,' Cesare interrupted him. 'I've already seen her. Where have you been?'

Ileana's voice came from the bedroom door. 'I sent him out to get some things in for dinner. I thought it would be nice if we had dinner in tonight.'

Cesare turned to look at her. She was wearing black-velvet toreador pants that clung to her body, a gold lamé blouse and gold shoes. 'You did, eh?' he asked. 'What made you think I want to eat in? How did you know that I didn't have plans to dine at El Morocco?'

She laughed, shaking her head. Her long black hair shone in the light as she came into the room. 'Oh, no, Cesare. We couldn't do that. Not tonight.'

'Why not?'

She looked up into his face. 'I could not go to El Morocco in these clothes. And they are all I brought with me.'

He stared at her. 'All? Where are rest of them?'

She put her arms up to his face and kissed his cheek. Then she crossed to the couch and sat down.

'Tonio, bring us some cocktails,' Cesare said.

Tonio bowed, shaking his entire frame. 'Yes, Excellency.' He went back into the kitchen.

Cesare looked down at her. 'What happened to the rest of your clothes?'

'They are in California,' she said simply. 'All I have with me are these – and the mink coat. The hotel manager was not very understanding either. He locked me out of my room when my credit was cut off by that woman. Fortunately I still had the return ticket to New York in my purse. So I came to the airport and here I am.' She smiled up at him. 'Wasn't I lucky?'

Before he could answer, Tonio was back in the room. 'Cocktails, signor,' he announced.

Tonio placed the silver coffee pot and the tiny cups on the small table in front of the couch and, bowing, went back into the dining room. Cesare heard him clearing away the dishes.

Ileana leaned forward and poured the coffee. He watched her. In some unfathomable manner, he felt good. He was relaxed. That was a good thing about her. There was no need for pretenses between them. They understood each other. That was one advantage of being European.

She held the coffee cup toward him. 'Sugar?'

He shook his head and took it. He sipped at his coffee slowly. The slightly bitter espresso tasted good in his mouth.

'You are very quiet tonight, *mon cher*,' she said in French.

'I am tired,' he answered in the same language. 'I have been very busy.'

She came over and sat down next to him. She stroked his temples gently. 'See,' she said softly. 'It is a good thing I decided that we should eat in, no?'

He nodded, soothed by the light touch of her fingers.

'We shall retire early,' she continued. 'I shall see that you rest well. I will take care not to disturb you. I will be very small in the bed.'

He opened his eyes and looked at her. 'Tomorrow, we shall make arrangements to get you a room in the hotel.'

'That will not be necessary,' she said quickly, still stroking his temples. 'This apartment is comfortable. There is room enough.'

He smiled. 'Americans are different, Ileana. You know that. It will be better if we get you a room.'

She kissed him lightly. 'All right. Anything you say.'

He sipped at his coffee. Tonio came back into the room. 'Will there be anything else, Excellency?' he asked.

'No, thank you, Tonio. Good night,' Cesare answered.

'Good night, Excellency.' He turned to Ileana. 'Good night, Baroness.' He bowed.

'Good night, Tonio.' She smiled and watched the little servant walk from the room. She turned back to Cesare and refilled his coffee cup. 'I have just been thinking,' she said. 'We cannot eat in every night.'

A smile began to come to his lips. He knew what was coming. His hand started for his pocket. 'Of course,' he said. 'How much will you need?'

Her face grew thoughtful for a moment. 'Since I will be working for you, it will be proper to get a small advance on my salary?'

He nodded, still smiling. 'Absolutely proper. It is done all the time.'

She smiled. 'Good. I am relieved. Let me have one thousand, no, better make it two thousand dollars. You can deduct it from my salary.'

'Two thousand dollars?' His voice was incredulous.

She nodded her head seriously. 'I will try to make that cover everything. I will be very careful.'

'What are you going to buy?' he exploded. 'The House of Dior?'

'Don't make jokes, Cesare,' she said. 'Surely you don't expect me to go out in these clothes?'

He began to laugh. It was completely ridiculous. She really had no conception of money. 'All right then. I'll give you a check,' he said.

He crossed to the small desk and wrote a check, then brought it back to her. 'This should do,' he said, holding it out to her.

She took it from him and placed it on the coffee table. It was for twenty-five hundred dollars. She looked up at him. Suddenly she felt very sorry for him. He was such a strange tortured man. She held out a hand to him and drew him down on the couch beside her.

'Thank you, Cesare,' she said softly.

His eyes were somber. 'It is nothing,' he replied. 'After all, we must stick together. We're the last remnants of a dying civilization.'

'Don't talk like that,' she said quickly. 'You make everything sound so hopeless.'

He looked at her and in his eyes she could see the emptiness of futility. The inexplicable sorrow welled up in her. She kissed him and her hand dropped to his thigh. Her fingers felt the quick response of his muscle to her touch. She tightened her grip.

'Come,' she said gently, a peculiar maternalism stirring inside her. He was tortured as her father was tortured. 'I'll help you to relax.'

Of this one thing she was sure. She knew everything that could make a man forget. And make herself forget too.

Big Dutch, looking back through the rear window of the limousine parked near the corner, saw them come out of El Morocco. 'Start your motor,' he said to the driver.

The tall doorman signaled for a cab. Big Dutch saw Ileana say something to Cesare. Cesare smiled and shook his head at the doorman. They turned and began to walk up the block away from him.

He swore angrily. Four nights they had cased the

job and every night they had taken a cab. 'They're walkin',' he said. 'Go up Fifty-Third. We'll try to pick them up on Lexington Avenue.'

But when they turned north on Lexington and sped toward the corner, they shot right past them. Ileana and Cesare were on the far side of the street and just turning up Fifty-Third toward Park Avenue. Big Dutch caught a glimpse of them as they turned. 'Damn it! We missed them!' He swore. 'Get over to Fifty-Fifth and come down Park. We'll try to pick 'em up there.'

The driver turned a white anxious face back toward him. 'I don't like this, boss,' he said nervously. 'Maybe we better hit 'em another night.' He turned forward just in time to miss colliding with a milk truck. The big limousine swerved up Fifty-Fifth Street.

'You keep your eyes on the road,' Big Dutch snarled. 'I said it's gonna be tonight.'

He stared down the street impatiently as they waited for the traffic light on Park Avenue. It had to be tonight. His wife was blowing a fuse. He had been out every night casing this job and he didn't know if she would stand for another.

The light changed and the car began to move. 'There they are,' he said. They were just crossing the pavilion in front of the Seagram Building. They stopped to look at the light playing on the fountain.

'Turn at Fifty-Second,' Big Dutch said, reaching for the tommy gun on the seat beside him. 'We'll hit him when he comes down the steps!'

The big car turned and stopped near the east corner. Big Dutch looked around. The street was deserted. He looked up at the pavilion. Cesare and Ileana were just strolling casually toward the near fountain.

He picked up the gun and lined them up in his sights. It would be a cinch. He smiled. If you wanted a job well done, you had to do it yourself. There was no use in trusting the punk kids nowadays. They were always horsing around, never paying enough attention to business. Another moment and the couple would be just where he wanted them.

Cesare and Ileana reached the top of the steps next to the fountain. He had Cesare squarely in his sights. 'Now!' he shouted and squeezed the trigger.

The driver stepped on the accelerator and the motor roared together with the gun. The submachine gun fired twice and jammed. He saw Cesare's face turn toward him in the lights from the building; at the same time, the car began to move.

Frantically he tried to clear the jammed gun. He stole a quick glance at the building in time to see Cesare pushing Ileana into the fountain and diving behind the small wall. He cursed, pulling the clear lever. It was no use.

By this time they were turning the corner at Lexington Avenue. Through the rear window, he saw Cesare pull the girl out of the fountain. Then they were hidden behind the buildings as the car raced down the street. Angrily he threw the useless tommy gun on the seat beside him.

The driver turned the car down another street. 'Yuh get him, boss?' he asked over his shoulder.

'Nah!' Big Dutch growled.

The driver turned the car into Third Avenue. 'Where to, now, boss?' he asked almost cheerfully.

'Downtown to the union office,' Big Dutch said. As he spoke there was a loud report and he grabbed for the gun in his pocket.

Almost immediately the big car began to bump and lurch. The driver pulled over to the curb. 'We got a flat,' he announced.

Big Dutch stared at him for a moment. 'So what else is new?' he snarled, getting out of the car. He flagged down a passing taxi.

'It was no use,' he thought, getting into the cab. There were some nights that nothing went right.

FIFTEEN

'ARE you all right?' Cesare asked, as he pulled her, dripping, from the fountain.

Her eyes were wide and frightened. 'Cesare, those men were shooting at you?' she asked.

He glanced around quickly. People were starting to come out of the building. 'Don't talk,' he said, quickly moving her down to the curb and into a cab.

'The Towers, driver,' he said. The taxi started and he turned to her. 'Are you all right?' he asked again.

She was still dazed. 'I'm all right,' she answered automatically. She looked down at herself. 'My new dress! It's ruined!'

He smiled grimly. 'Don't complain. You were lucky.'

She stared at him, a growing knowledge in her eyes. 'Those men were shooting at you!' she said.

'I don't know,' he answered sarcastically. 'I didn't have time to ask them.'

She began to shiver. He took off his coat and placed it around her shoulders. His eyes were cold and hard. 'I don't want anyone to know about this. Understand? Anyone,' he said harshly.

She nodded. 'I understand,' she said, trying to keep her teeth from chattering. Her hand sought his and a hint of sadness came into her voice. 'Maybe you're in more trouble than I am, my friend,' she said softly.

The taxi stopped in front of the hotel and they got out. The doorman looked curiously at Ileana as she walked into the building while Cesare paid the driver.

He held a twenty-dollar bill in his hand so that the driver could see it. 'You never brought us here,' he said.

The bill disappeared in the driver's hand. 'I never even picked you up,' he said cheerfully, driving off.

Cesare opened the door to her room. He stepped back to let her enter. 'Get into something dry,' he said.

She hesitated in the doorway. 'Maybe I'd better go upstairs with you,' she said. 'I'm afraid to be alone tonight.'

'No,' he said quickly. Then he looked at her. It might be a good idea to spend the night with her. 'Let me change my clothes too,' he said. 'Then I'll come back in a little while.'

Big Dutch sat in his empty office in the Union Hall and stared at the bottle of whisky on his desk. He picked it up and poured himself another drink. From downstairs came the faint sounds of the morning check-off. He picked up the glass and swallowed the liquor. It burned its way down his throat.

Maybe the others were right after all. He was too big a man to go out on jobs like these. It was better to leave them to the punk kids even if they weren't as good as he was. They had less to lose.

Nostalgically he thought about his youth. They were the good old days. Everything was wide open then. You called a spade a spade, and if somebody crossed you, you went after them. You didn't have to wait for no lousy council to have a meet first and then decide what to do.

He remembered the time that Lep called him and Sam Vanicola down to the little speakeasy in Brooklyn. 'I want you and Sam to take a little drive up to Monticello and burn Varsity Vic,' he had said. 'He's getting too big for himself.'

'Okay, Lep,' they answered and went over to the bar and got six bottles of whisky to keep them company on the long ride.

When they got outside, they had an argument over whose car to take. He didn't like Sam's Chevy and Sam didn't like his Jewett. So they compromised and heisted a big Pierce from in front of one of the mansions on Brooklyn Heights.

It was about a five-hour drive in those days and close to two o'clock in the morning when they pulled up in front of Varsity Vic's roadhouse. They had about three bottles of whisky left in the car.

They got out of the car and stretched. 'Take a whiff of this air,' Sam had said. 'It smells different than the city. Clean. Boy, this is the place to live.'

He still remembered the crickets chirping as they went inside. The place was fairly crowded and the last floor show was on. They stopped in the doorway and looked at the girls dancing a variation of the Black Bottom on the darkened dance floor. 'Hey! Look at that one!' he had chortled. 'The third from the end. That's for me. Them boobs bounce around like rubber balls! '

'We ain't got the time for that,' Sam had said, pulling him over to the bar. 'We're workin'. Let's get another drink.'

'Private stock,' Sam ordered.

The bartender put the bottle of whisky in front of them. 'What brings you guys up from the city?' he asked sourly.

'We were takin' a drive,' Big Dutch answered cheerfully. 'It was hot in town.'

'It was plenty hot up here too,' the bartender said.

'Gettin' plenty of action, I see,' Sam said, leaning on the bar.

'Good and bad,' the bartender said noncommittally.

'Is Vic around?' Sam asked casually.

'I ain't seen him tonight,' the bartender replied, equally casual.

The number was over and the girls picked their way past the bar as they went back to the dressing rooms. He leaned over and jiggled the breast of the girl as she passed him.

She turned quickly and looked at him. 'Fresh!' she said, smiling, and walked on.

'I can fix that for you,' the bartender said meaningfully.

'I'll take you up on that sometime,' he answered, looking after the girl.

He looked at Sam and nodded. Sam turned and started for the manager's office. The bartender bent over the button that flashed a signal into the room.

'I wouldn't touch that if I were you,' he said, smiling genially.

Slowly the bartender straightened up. He came down the bar, polishing the top with his cloth. 'It's none of my business anyway,' he said. 'I'm just the barkeep here.'

'That's right,' he agreed. 'Just leave it like that.' He walked off and joined Sam at the door to the office.

They went in. Varsity Vic was sitting behind his desk. He looked up. A smile crossed his face. 'Come in, fellas,' he said.

They closed the door behind them. 'We got a message from the Boss,' he said. 'He wants a meet.'

'Okay,' Varsity Vic answered. He looked across the room at his bodyguard, who promptly got to his feet. 'Just let me know. I'll come down whenever he wants.'

'He wants right now,' he said.

Varsity Vic stared up at him. 'Make it tomorrow. I can't come right now.'

They turned as if to start out. The bodyguard began to smile and put away his gun. Sam knocked him cold with one punch. They turned back to Varsity Vic.

'You know the Boss doesn't like to be kept waiting,' he said.

Varsity Vic's face had been white as they walked out of the roadhouse with him between them. The bartender sourly watched them go and kept polishing the same spot over and over with his rag.

He had gotten into the back seat with Varsity Vic

and Sam got into the front to drive. As soon as they had pulled away from the roadhouse, he picked up another bottle of whisky and pulled the cork with his teeth. He held the bottle toward Vic.

'Have a drink,' he offered. 'You look cold.'

Varsity Vic shook his head.

'Go ahead,' he urged. 'This is good stuff. Not like that crud you sell back there.'

Still Varsity Vic shook his head. When he finally spoke, his voice was thin and almost cracking. 'I'll give you guys a grand if you'll let me out of this car.'

Big Dutch had taken another swill from the bottle. He looked at him silently without answering.

'I'll make it two grand,' Vic said quickly. 'How much are you guys getting for this job anyway? A hundred? A hundred and fifty? Two grand's a lot of dough.'

'You hear him, Sam?' he called.

'I hear him,' came the reply.

'Got the dough on ya'?' he asked.

'Right here in my pocket,' Vic answered, touching his jacket.

'Okay,' he said. He looked around. They were out in the country now. There were no houses around. 'Pull off the road, Sam,' he called.

The car jounced to a stop on the soft ground. 'Gimme the dough,' he said.

Varsity Vic had taken his wallet out with trembling hands. Quickly he counted out the money on the seat. 'Two grand,' he said. 'You guys are lucky. That was all the dough I had on me.' He held up the empty wallet.

'Yeah,' he said, 'we're lucky. Now get out.'

Varsity Vic opened the door of the car and stepped out. He turned back to the car. 'Thanks, fellas,' he said. 'I won't forget this.'

'I'll bet you won't,' Sam laughed, squeezing the trigger of his automatic.

The heavy 45-caliber slugs threw Varsity Vic about ten feet back into the bushes. They got out of the car and walked over to look at him. The body twitched and then lay still.

'Siphon some gas out of the tank and douse him with it,' he said.

'What for?' Sam asked.

'Lep said, "Burn him," and when the Boss says something, he means what he says.'

Then they sat on the running board of the Pierce and drank the remaining bottles of whisky while they watched the fire. When they went to start the car, they found that Sam had taken all the gas from the tank and they had to walk three miles before they could steal another car and get back to the city.

Big Dutch leaned forward on the desk and sighed. He poured another drink. The good old days. They were gone all right. Lep and Sam were gone too. Lep had gone to the chair and Sam had caught the knife in the pool.

He picked up his drink and looked at it. Everything looked like gold through a whisky glass. It was the guineas' fault. He never believed that Sam really would talk. Not good old Sam. Sam was his pal. But they killed him anyway. They were like leeches: once they got on your back, they never let go. But this time it would be different. This time he would show them.

He swallowed the drink and reached for the telephone. Might as well call the old lady and let her know he was on his way home. She would be mad enough anyway.

He was busy dialing and he didn't see Cesare opening the door.

It was just before dawn that she heard his key turn the lock. 'Is that you, Cesare?' she asked.

His voice was flat and tense. 'Yes.'

Then he was at the side of her bed, stripping off his clothes in a violent kind of haste. He came into her bed, his body hard and trembling. He seized her breasts.

Pain and fear came up together inside her. 'Don't be in such a hurry, Cesare,' she managed to laugh. 'One would almost think you're an American!'

SIXTEEN

CESARE was raising his glass of orange juice to his lips when Tonio came bustling in. 'Mr Baker to see you, Excellency,' he announced.

Cesare nodded. 'Show him in,' he said. He drank his orange juice and got to his feet as Baker came into the dining room.

'Mr Baker,' he said. 'I did not expect to see you so soon again. Do sit down and have some coffee.'

Baker sat down and studied Cesare while Tonio filled a coffee cup and set it down before him. Cesare returned his gaze evenly. 'I see you had a little trouble last night,' Baker said.

'I did?' Cesare replied politely. 'What makes you say that?'

'The morning papers,' Baker said.

'I did not see them.'

Baker looked at the folded newspaper next to Cesare's cup. 'What's that?' he asked pointedly.

Cesare looked down at the table. He looked up again at Baker, a faint hint of a smile in his eyes. '*The Wall Street Journal*. It's the only paper I read. For business.'

Baker could feel his face flush. He reached in his overcoat pocket and took out a copy of the *Daily News*. He spread it on the table in front of Cesare silently.

Cesare looked down at it. The half-page headline seemed to leap up at him:

STILETTO STRIKES AGAIN!

BIG DUTCH MURDERED!

Cesare looked up at Baker. He shrugged his shoulders. 'I don't see what that has to do with me,' he said. 'I told you I didn't know the man.'

'On page five there's another story,' Baker said. 'A little after midnight a man and a woman were shot at on Park Avenue in front of the Seagram Building. The woman fell into the fountain. They hurried away before they were recognized.'

Cesare buttered some toast. 'So?' he asked.

'This Baroness you came in with last night. The doorman said her dress was soaking wet.'

'No one shot at me,' Cesare said, adding some jam to the butter on his toast.

Baker sipped at his coffee. 'That still doesn't explain how the lady got her dress wet.'

Ileana appeared in the doorway behind him. 'Why don't you ask the lady?' she said, coming into the room.

The men got to their feet. Cesare introduced them. 'Mr Baker is with the F.B.I.,' he added.

Ileana's eyes widened. 'Oh,' she said. She turned to Cesare. 'Are you in trouble?' she asked in a concerned voice.

Cesare smiled. 'I don't think so. But Mr Baker thinks some people are trying to kill me.'

'How perfectly horrible!' she exclaimed. She turned back to Baker. 'Is that why you want to know how my dress got wet?'

Baker nodded.

'It was very embarrassing,' Ileana explained with just the right amount of dignity. 'You see, we had been at El Morocco and I'm afraid I had a little too much champagne. That and the new shoes. I tripped and fell into a puddle. I had hoped no one saw me.'

'Are you sure you didn't fall into the fountain at the Seagram building?' Baker asked.

Ileana looked at him. Her voice became very haughty at the implication that he might doubt her word. 'Of that, I am most positive!'

'What did you do after that?' he asked.

'Count Cardinali took me to my room. It's in this hotel,' she said.

'What time did he leave you?'

She looked at Cesare. He reached over and patted her hand reassuringly. 'You don't have to answer that if you don't want to,' he said.

She turned back to Baker. 'Is it important?'

Baker nodded. 'It's important,' he said seriously.

She took a deep breath. 'About an hour ago. When he

left to breakfast here in his own suite,' she said, looking into Baker's eyes.

Cesare got to his feet. His voice was still low but it had gone cold. 'And now, Mr Baker, don't you think you've asked enough questions for one morning?'

Baker rose. He looked down at Ileana. 'I am sorry, Baroness, for any embarrassment I may have caused you but it is my job to ask these questions.'

Ileana kept her gaze down on the tablecloth. She did not look up at him. 'I understand, Mr Baker.'

He turned to Cesare. 'I would still keep my eyes open if I were you, Mr Cardinali. The rest of those men will be even more dangerous now.'

'I will, Mr Baker,' Cesare said, still standing.

Tonio came bustling in. 'Your new luggage will be ready in time, Excellency,' he said to Cesare. 'I will have it at the airport at four o'clock.'

Cesare nodded. 'Thank you, Tonio,' he said in an annoyed voice.

Baker looked at him. 'Going somewhere?'

'I have entered the Gran Mexico Road Race,' Cesare answered. 'It begins the day after tomorrow. My Ferrari is already there.'

'I am going too.' Ileana looked up. She was smiling. 'It will be very exciting.'

Baker looked from one to the other, then he smiled slowly. 'Good luck,' he said, starting for the door. 'Drive safely.'

Cesare waited until he heard the door close then turned and spoke angrily. 'Why did you tell him you were going with me?'

Ileana smiled up at him brightly. 'I was only trying to help, Cesare.' Tonio appeared again in the doorway. 'Just half a grapefruit, please,' she said to him.

Cesare waited until the servant had gone. 'If I wanted you to go with me, I would have asked you!' he snapped.

Her eyes widened. 'Oh! I did not understand. There is another woman. Forgive me, Cesare.'

Tonio returned with the grapefruit. He placed it before her and left again.

'There is not another woman! ' Cesare said angrily.

'In that case I will go with you then,' Ileana said practically. She spooned up some grapefruit and looked up at him. 'Besides I cannot afford to work for you. I spoke to your secretary just before I came up here this morning. She told me my salary was recorded at one hundred twenty-five dollars a week.'

Cesare was seething now. 'Just what did you expect to make? You cannot do anything.'

'I haven't the faintest idea.' She shrugged her shoulders prettily and looked down at her grapefruit. 'But I need at least that much money every day.' She put a spoonful of grapefruit in her mouth. 'This is delicious.'

He stared down at her, beginning to smile in spite of himself. That was what happened when you understood each other. She never said a word about lying to Baker for him. And she never would.

She looked up at him, smiling in the knowledge that she had made her point. 'Besides,' she added, 'there are some very rich Texans I know who will be in Mexico City for the race.'

SEVENTEEN

THE desk clerk at El Ciudad Hotel in Mexico City permitted himself a knowing smile. 'The Baroness has a lovely suite right next to your own, Count Cardinali.'

Cesare glanced at him as he finished signing the register. 'That will be fine. Thank you.'

'And we have been holding this telegram for you.' The clerk took an envelope from beneath the counter and held it out to him.

Cesare took it and opened it as he walked back to Ileana. He scarcely looked at it. It was the expected message. 'I have just received word,' he said to her, 'my mechanic is ill.'

'I'm sorry,' Ileana said. 'Is it serious?'

'It means I will have to find a new mechanic,' he answered. 'I'd better go right over to the garage and see what I can do.'

'All right,' Ileana said. 'Will you be long?'

'I don't know,' he answered. 'Better go upstairs and get settled. I may be a little while. I will join you for dinner.'

The garage hummed with activity as Cesare came into it. Men were everywhere, going over the cars in last-minute preparation for the race. He walked through to the small office in the back.

The little old man came out of the office when he saw him. 'Count Cardinali!' he exclaimed, a smile on his face. 'It's good to see you again.'

Cesare took his hand. 'It's always good to see you, Señor Esteban.'

'Your car is on the lower ramp, stall twelve,' Esteban said. 'I suppose you are anxious to have a look at it.'

'I am, Señor Esteban, but I have a serious problem,' Cesare answered. 'My mechanic was taken ill and I must find a replacement.'

A sober look replaced the smile on the old man's face. 'That will be difficult, Count Cardinali. All the Ferrari men are spoken for.'

'I know,' Cesare said. 'But we must do something. Otherwise I shall not be able to start in the race.'

'We must not allow that to happen,' Esteban said quickly. 'Let me start looking for one at once. I will call you the moment I have news.'

'*Mil gracias.*' Cesare smiled. 'In the meantime I will be at the car. I will do as much as possible to get it ready.'

He had been working on the white Ferrari about an hour when he saw the girl approaching. She was coming directly toward him. He straightened up, admiring the trim figure she made in the white coveralls.

She stopped in front of the car. 'Count Cardinali?' she asked. Her voice was low and pleasant.

He nodded, reaching for a cigarette in his jacket which was hung over the door of the Ferrari. 'Yes?'

'Señor Esteban says you're looking for a mechanic.' Her eyes were very blue.

'You know of one? Where can I meet him?' he said eagerly. He was already bored with the work. This was the part of racing that he did not like.

The girl smiled. 'I am one.'

His surprise showed in his voice. 'But a girl? This race is no place for a woman. It is fourteen hundred miles!'

The smile disappeared from her eyes. She looked right at him. 'I've driven that far when I've had to,' she said quietly. 'But we're not going that far.'

Cesare stared at her. 'No?'

She shook her head, the blond ringlets around her tanned face caught the light and sparkled. 'It will not be necessary.' She bent over the hood of the car and looked in at the engine. 'Don Emilio has other plans,' she whispered.

His eyes widened slightly. He had not expected a girl.

She straightened up, smiling again. She held out her hand man-fashion. 'I'm Luke Nichols,' she said.

They shook hands. Cesare studied her. 'But do you really know Ferraris?'

Her smile broadened. 'I should. I've raced them all over the world.' She saw Esteban approaching over Cesare's shoulder. 'Ask him.'

Cesare turned. Esteban smiled. 'I see you two have already met. That is good.'

'But a girl in the Gran Mexico Race,' Cesare said. 'Who ever heard of such a thing?'

'You are very lucky, Count Cardinali,' Esteban reassured him. 'Señorita Nichols had many offers but she had already decided not to enter this race until she heard of your predicament. Last year she drove her own Ferrari.'

Cesare turned back to her. 'Your own car?' he questioned. 'What happened to it?'

She shrugged her shoulders. 'I didn't win. It was hocked to the hubcaps so it's gone now. I had hoped to pick up something down here, but no luck.'

'All right,' Cesare said. 'You must be good if my friend, Señor Esteban, says so. Standard cut of the purse if we win. Five hundred if we don't.'

'It's a deal, Mr Cardinali.' She smiled.

He reached for his jacket and put it on. 'Tune her up and take her out for a road check. Have a full report for me at five o'clock. I'll be in the bar at El Ciudad.'

'Okay,' she said. She turned to Esteban. Her voice became very businesslike. 'Would you make arrangements for me to use the number two pit, Señor Esteban? The one with the new electrical timer. The first thing I want to do is go over the wiring.'

Esteban nodded and Cesare turned away and started up the ramp. When he reached the top of the ramp and looked back, she already had the car rolling toward the pit.

The light in the cocktail lounge of the El Ciudad came

from hidden recesses in the wall that not only hid the lamps but also the light that came from them. Cesare was happy that he could not see the drink on the table before him; there was no use looking at his watch to check the time, he was sure he couldn't see the dial.

The door opened and a shaft of sunlight split the gloom. Cesare looked toward it. Luke came in and stood there, her eyes adjusting to the dimness, trying to find him. He stood up and waved to her.

Smiling, she sat down opposite him in the booth. 'They ought to give you miners' lamps when you come in.' She laughed.

'It is dark,' he admitted. The waiter came up. 'Can we have a little more light before we go blind?' Cesare asked him.

'Of course, señor.' The waiter reached across the table and pressed a hidden button on the wall. Immediately a soft light came into the booth.

'That's better,' Cesare smiled. 'What will you have to drink?'

'A daiquiri, please,' she said.

The waiter went away. Cesare looked at her. 'What do you think of the car?'

Something almost like sadness came into her eyes. 'It's a wonderful car. Too bad. Under ordinary circumstances with a car like that, one could win this race.'

The waiter placed her drink before her and left. Cesare lifted his glass. '*Salud!*'

'Luck!'

They sipped at their drinks and put them down. 'There will be other races,' Cesare said.

Her voice was expressionless. 'I hope so.' She looked

around. There was no one near them. 'I have connected a timing mechanism to the speedometer,' she said in a low voice. 'Exactly one hundred fifteen miles from our starting point, it will blow, wrecking your generator. We will then be two hundred ninety miles from the next check point so it will be about five hours before they find us. There is a small deserted house about a half mile from the road. We will go there and wait for Don Emilio.' She picked up her drink again.

Cesare sipped at his own. 'Is that all?' he asked.

'That's all,' she answered.

Cesare studied her. She had changed into a light summer frock that left no doubt as to her femininity. It also served to make her look more like a young American coed than a woman involved with the illegal activities of the Mafia. He half smiled to himself. Don Emilio was full of surprises.

She began to feel uncomfortable under his scrutiny. He was different from the others she had met. Generally they were coarse men and overt in their manner. There was no question as to where they belonged. But she didn't quite fit him into the pattern.

'What are you staring at?' she finally asked. 'Haven't you seen a girl before?' Almost as soon as the words were out of her mouth she felt the fool.

He smiled slowly. 'I apologize for staring,' he said. 'I was just wondering why? A girl like you?'

'The money is good,' she said coldly. 'I told you I wanted a Ferrari. This is the quickest way for me to get it.' She took another sip of her cocktail. 'But what about you? You don't need the money.'

He laughed easily. 'There aren't enough races like

these. And life between them can become very dull if one does not keep occupied.'

He signaled the waiter and they were silent until the man had placed fresh drinks before them. Then Cesare picked up his glass and looked into it. 'It is too bad,' he said regretfully. 'This is one race I would like to win.'

Luke sipped at her drink. 'I know how you feel,' she said, her face suddenly lighting up. 'There's nothing quite like it. The speed, the danger, the excitement. You feel alive, everything inside you tingles, the whole world is churning inside your body.'

'That's it! That's just it,' Cesare said quickly. An almost boyish excitement crept into his voice. 'I didn't think anyone else felt like that. It is like having everything you want in the world. All the money, all the power, all the women!'

'Luke looked down at her glass. She felt almost shy. 'I didn't know anyone else could feel like that.'

He put his hands across the table on her own. She could feel the strength and power coming from them. She looked up into his face. It was intense and his eyes were glowing like a tiger's eyes in the night.

'It is as if I had never been with a woman before,' he said softly.

A sudden fright came up in her. Not of him, but of herself. She knew too well what a man like him could do to her. She took her hands away quickly. 'Let's keep it business, shall we?' she said as coldly as she could. 'We both know we cannot win.'

His voice was still soft. 'Why, Luke? We are here. Why must we keep it business?'

His eyes were deep magnets and she could feel herself beginning to swirl in their depths. The familiar fever began to rise in her loins, the familiar weakness seep down into her limbs. Why did it always have to be like this? Just when she had everything worked out. She felt the bitter resentment toward herself creep into her voice. 'Because with you I'm a loser. I've met guys like you before. It's always the same. First thing you know you can touch the stars. Then, like that—' She snapped her fingers.

'Must it always be like that?'

She met his look steadily. 'Always.'

'And you are content to go through life without living because you are afraid of losing?' he asked, almost gently.

She was angry because he had unerringly put his finger right on it. 'What do you want from me anyway?' she snapped. 'Are you one of those men who have to gobble up everything in sight? Possess every woman? You're here with a woman who can probably give you more sex in ten minutes than I can give you in ten days!'

The tears of anger were beginning to flood into her eyes and she got to her feet before he could see them. 'So let's keep it business!' she said angrily. 'See you at the starting line tomorrow!'

She turned and started out, almost knocking over Ileana who was on her way to the table. Ileana looked after her and then sat down in the seat she had vacated. She looked at Cesare. 'Who was that?' she asked curiously.

Cesare watched Luke go out the door. 'My mechanic,' he answered.

Ileana raised an eyebrow. 'Oh?' She turned to the waiter who just came up. 'Cinzano on the rocks, please.' The waiter left. 'Your mechanic,' she repeated.

Cesare looked at her. 'That's right!' he snapped.

Ileana smiled. 'You know I could not help overhearing her last few remarks. She is right, you know.'

Cesare didn't answer. The waiter placed her drink on the table and left. She picked up the drink and held it toward him in a sort of mock toast.

'Just the same, I do not think I will meet you in Cuernavaca as we had planned. I will wait right here for you in Mexico City,' she said. She sipped her drink. 'Not being American and therefore very understanding about such things, I think I shall give both of you the chance to find out for yourselves and prove each other right.'

EIGHTEEN

THE bright sunlight hurt her eyes after the dimness of the cocktail lounge. She put on her dark glasses and began to walk. At first she walked quickly, angry with herself. Then she noticed people were looking at her strangely. She slowed down. After all this was Mexico City. And nobody down here walked fast.

What was there about her that brought on things like this? Even when she had been a kid, it had been like that. Other girls had fellows at their houses for a study session and nothing ever happened to them. She had played it as straight as they did but something would always happen before the evening was over.

When the boy had gone, she used to sit and curse herself. Usually she never saw the boy again but there was always another. And it would start the same way. She had the highest resolves. Just the schoolbooks. She wouldn't even go near him, would sit on the other side of the table or across the room and they would throw each other questions. At least that was the way the evening would begin.

But before long she would feel the fever begin inside her. Her legs would grow weak and her speech begin to falter. She would find it more and more difficult to concentrate on the lessons. She would fight the fever inside her, fight so hard the perspiration would break out on her face and her arms so that even she would get the faint scent of musk that rose mixed with perfume from her body.

And then it would happen. The first few exploratory kisses. She would prove it to herself. Just those kisses and then she would stop. Nothing more after that. Then suddenly the fever would rise inside her and with it would come the frenzy. The frantic tearing of clothing that was constricting her, the wild desire to cause pain and to feel pain. The worship of the arrogant male and the need to subdue it inside her so she could be the master of its exploding strength.

She began to feel dizzy. Unconsciously she shook her head. She glanced up at the sun. It was still hot. Too hot. She had better go inside and sit down. She would feel better in the shade.

She looked around. She had walked almost back to the garage. That was good. She would go there and check the car again. There was something cold and masculine about a racing car that always made her feel better.

The garage felt cool after the heat outside. Most of the men had gone, it was near dinner time. She walked down the ramp.

Esteban came out of his little office and called after her. 'Hola, Señorita Nichols!'

She turned toward him, smiling. 'Hello, Señor Esteban.'

He hurried up to her. 'You have seen the Count?' he asked. 'He is satisfied?'

She nodded. 'I owe you many thanks, Señor Esteban.'

'*No hay de que*,' he said. 'I am glad to be of service to both of you.' He looked up at her shrewdly. 'An interesting man, this Count Cardinali, no?'

'*Si*,' she answered. 'Very interesting. But tell me this, is he good?'

He looked at her. 'He could be the best. But there is something missing.'

They started to walk down the ramp. 'Missing? I don't understand.' She asked, 'What is missing?'

'Fear,' he answered. 'A racer is like a matador. Neither are any good until they have tasted fear. Once they have done that, they develop their skill. They don't do foolish unnecessary things. They just drive to win.'

They came to a stop in front of the long white Ferrari. 'He doesn't care about winning?' she asked, walking over to the car and resting her hand on it.

'A beautiful automobile,' he said.

She looked down at it. Unconsciously she rubbed her hand across the fender. 'The best in the garage,' she said.

He smiled shrewdly. 'I think maybe this time I will bet my ten pesos on the Count.' He stared back up the ramp. 'Good luck, señorita.'

She watched him until he disappeared around the turn. Then she opened the door and sat down in the car.

The harsh mixed odor of oil and gasoline and the rubbed leather of the seat came up to her. She slid over behind the wheel and put her hands upon it. This was strength. Pure male strength.

She remembered sitting in her father's lap while he drove their car in to town to do their marketing. How big she had felt and how she had waved for everyone to see she was driving. Even Mr Saunders, the fat policeman who directed traffic on Main Street, came over to see if she had a license. She was only six years old then.

She knew how to drive before she was ten years old. Papa used to let her run the car on the back road behind the house. Mother used to shake her head.

'Half the time she doesn't act like a girl at all,' her mother used to say. 'Always hanging around the garage, fooling with cars and hearing all kinds of talk from the roughneck boys that hang around there too.'

'Aw, let her go, Ma,' her father used to say tolerantly. 'Time enough for her to grow up and learn to cook and sew. That ain't so important nowadays anyhow with everything coming in cans and frozen packages and dresses all readymade.' He was secretly pleased. He always wanted a son.

It was better when she was sixteen and got her license to drive. Somehow the boys didn't bother her so much then. She didn't feel the need to tear them down so much. Maybe it was because she took it out on them on the road and in the drag races they used to hold out on the Ocean Drive.

She knew what they thought the first time she came up to them in her own hot rod. Here comes 'Easy,' looking to get laid. She knew the stories that went around the school about her. That whenever a boy showed up in the locker room with scratches on his back, the other boys would laugh and begin to pitch nickels at him. It didn't stop them from clustering around her car when she drove up though.

Johnny Jordan, the leader of the boys, had swaggered up to the car. He leaned over the door, a cigarette drooping from his lips. 'Where'ja get the jalopy?' he asked.

'At Stan's,' she said, mentioning the name of the garage where all the boys picked up their second-hand cars.

He looked it up and down critically. 'I never seen it there,' he said.

'I did a little work on it myself,' she lied. It wasn't a little work. She had taken the car apart and rebuilt it by hand. It was a beat-up Pontiac convertible that had been in a wreck when she got it. She had taken out the motor and replaced it with a Cadillac engine, put in a new differential, repacked the bearings, widened the brake bands, cut down the body and fitted an old Cord frame over it, then poured lead into the doors to give it weight, and painted it shining silver and black. It had taken her six months.

'Does it go?' Johnny asked her.

'It goes,' she said.

'Move over,' he said, starting to get in.

She sat firmly behind the wheel. 'Uh-uh,' she said. 'Nobody gets to drive this until I take a few.'

He stared at her. 'Who yuh gonna get to drag yuh? Ain't nobody here gonna race a girl.'

She smiled. 'Chicken?' she asked.

His face flushed. 'Ain't that,' he said. 'Who ever heard

of a girl ridin' drag? It just ain't done.'

'Okay,' she said. She started the motor again. 'I'll tell 'em back in town that you're all afraid.' She started to back down the road from them.

Johnny started after her. 'Hey, wait a minute. You got no right to say that.'

She stopped the car and smiled at him. 'Oh, no? Then prove it.'

'Okay,' he said reluctantly. 'But don't blame me if you get hurt.'

He pulled his car up beside her. 'Drag up the road one mile,' he shouted over the noise of the engines. 'Then you hold up there an' I'll come back and we'll go "chicken".'

She nodded and watched the starter. The boy dropped his hand. She released the clutch and the car jumped forward. She double-clutched into high and looked over at Johnny. His car was even with her. She laughed excitedly and swung toward him. They were no more than a few inches apart now.

He hit the accelerator trying to inch in front of her. She laughed again and opened up the throttle. He didn't gain an inch. She moved the car in closer toward him. There was the sound of metal on metal and he moved away to give her room. He was riding half on the shoulder of the road now. She stepped on the accelerator and went away from him as if he were standing still.

She had the car already turned around as he swung past her and went back down the road. He glared balefully at her as he went by.

She watched for the starter's signal again. When it came, she was ready and the car leaped down the road.

Then they were coming at each other in the dead center of the pavement. She smiled and put her foot all the way down on the floor. The wheel was steady in her hands.

When she looked up, his car was almost upon her. Her smile became frozen on her face. She wouldn't turn the wheel. She wouldn't.

At the last possible moment she saw him turn his wheel. She watched his car in the mirror as she slowed down. It was swerving wildly but he brought it under control and came to a stop. She turned around and drove back to him.

He was out of his car and the boys were around him. They were staring at his left rear fender. It was half torn off. She didn't even know that she had hit the rear of his car as they passed.

He looked up at her. 'You're crazy! ' he said.

She smiled and slid over on the seat. 'Want to drive? ' she asked. 'It can do a hundred and twenty on the stretch.'

He walked around the car and got in beside her. He put the car into gear and they moved off. In a moment he had the car up to ninety miles per hour. He was her first steady.

It had been different with him. Not like the others. She felt easier, more sure of herself. They didn't have to go at it like cats and dogs. He respected her. He knew she was his equal. All the same it didn't keep him from making her pregnant.

She was in her last year in high school. She waited one week and then went to him. 'We're gonna have to get married,' she said.

'Why? ' he asked her.

'Why do you think, stupid?' she snapped.

He stared at her then he cursed. 'God damn!' he said. 'It's those lousy cheap rubbers I bought at the drive-in!'

'It wasn't the rubbers that did it,' she said. She began to get angry. 'It was that goddam thing of yours. You never stopped poking it at me.'

'You seemed to like it good enough,' he said. 'You never said no!' He glared at her. 'Besides how do I know it's even mine? I heard enough stories about you!'

She stared at him for a moment and all the dreams she had had about the two of them came tumbling down. Deep inside him, he was just like all the others. She turned on her heels and walked away from him.

The next Saturday she drew a hundred dollars from her savings account and drove up to Center City. There was a doctor there in Mex town who had taken care of some of the girls at school.

Silently she waited until all the other patients had gone, then she walked into the office. He was a fat little man with a shining bald head. He looked tired.

'Take off your dress and come over here,' he said.

She hung her dress on the wall hook and turned toward him.

'All your clothes,' he said.

She took off her brassière and panties and walked over to him. He got up from behind his desk and came around it toward her. He felt her breasts and her stomach and listened to her heart. He came up to about her shoulders. He led her over to a long narrow table. 'Put your hands on the edge and bend way over,' he said, putting a rubber finger on his right hand. 'Take a deep breath and let it out slowly,' he said.

She took a deep breath and let it slip past her open mouth while he did something inside her. Then he was finished and she straightened up and turned around.

He looked up into her face. 'About six weeks I figure,' he said.

She nodded. 'That's about right.'

He went back to his desk and sat down. 'It'll be a hundred dollars,' he said.

Silently she went over to her purse and took out the money. She counted it out on the desk before him.

'When do you want it done?' he asked.

'Right now,' she said.

'You can't stay here,' he said. 'You got anyone with you?'

She shook her head. 'I got my car outside.' The doctor looked at her skeptically. 'Don't worry about me,' she said. 'I'll get home all right.'

He picked up the hundred dollars and put it in his desk. He walked over to the sterilizer and took out a hypodermic. He fitted it into a small bottle and approached her as he drew the liquid up into the syringe.

'What's that?' she asked, for the first time feeling a little fear.

'Penicillin.' He smiled. 'Thank God for it. It kills every bug there is except the one you got inside you.'

He was deft and quick and competent. It was over in twenty minutes. He helped her down from the table and helped her dress. He gave her some pills in a small envelope that had no markings on it.

'The big ones are penicillin,' he said. 'Take one of them every four hours for the next two days. The small ones are pain killers. Take one of them every two hours after you get home. Get right into bed and stay there for at least two days. Don't worry if you bleed a lot, that's normal. If you feel you're losing too much blood after the first day, don't be a fool, call your doctor. If your mother asks any questions tell her you got a heavy curse. Remember all that?'

She nodded her head.

'All right, then,' he said gently. 'You can go. Get right home and into bed. In an hour you'll be in so much pain, you'll wish you'd never been born.'

He went back to his desk and sat down as she went to the door. She turned and looked back at him. 'Thank you, doctor,' she said.

He looked up at her. 'It's all right,' he said. 'But get smart now. I don't want to see you back here again.'

She made the forty miles to her home in less than a half hour. She was beginning to feel lightheaded and weak when she stopped the car in front of her house. She went right upstairs to her room, grateful that the house was empty. She gulped one of each of the pills quickly and crept under the sheets, beginning to shiver with the pain.

About a week later, she was pulling her car out of the parking lot behind the supermarket when Johnny came over and put his hands on the door.

'I been thinkin', Luke,' he said with that masculine sureness that was so irritating. 'We kin get married.'

'Drop dead, you chicken shit!' she said coldly and shot the car out of the lot, almost taking his arm off.

After that it was the car. By the time she entered college she had already achieved a certain amount of fame locally. Every week she entered the stock-car races at the Cow Pasture Track. She began to win with a regularity that made her a favorite with the townsfolk. They began to speak with pride of the little girl who drove even the professional drivers off the track.

It was during her first summer vacation that she got married. He was a racing-car driver of course. He was six-feet-three, with curly black hair and laughing brown eyes and the best driver at the meet. He came from West Texas and spoke with a drawl.

'I reckon you 'n' me ought to hook up, little one,' he said, looking down at her. 'Between the two of us we're the best on the road.'

'You mean you want to marry me?' she asked, feeling the fever start up inside her again.

'I reckon so,' he said. 'That's what I mean.'

Her parents were against it. They wanted her to finish school and become a teacher. There was plenty of time for her to get married. Besides, what kind of a life would she lead, traipsing all around the country to every cheap little auto track there was?

That was the wrong argument to use because that was exactly the kind of life she wanted to lead. It was only behind the wheel of a car that she really came alive. That made everything and everybody equal. And the strange thing about it was that they did pretty well at it too. Within a year she had managed to put almost fifteen thousand dollars in the bank.

Then the police came in and arrested her husband for bigamy. It seemed he had three wives before her that he had neglected to divorce. And two weeks after they took him off to jail, she discovered she was pregnant. This time she had the baby. It was a boy.

She took him home and left him with her parents. Then she bought a plane ticket to Europe and bought a Ferrari. In France she entered a race for women and won. The prize wasn't very much but now she had a Ferrari and two thousand dollars in the bank. And she was through with the cheap tracks. From now on it was nothing but the big ones.

It was in Monaco that she met the Irishman. He drove well and he laughed a lot. He had only one fault. He gambled. But the fever was inside her whenever she looked at him. This time she didn't marry him though she might just as well have. They went everywhere in the world together, drove madly in every country and he was always broke.

It was in Mexico just before the race last year that he came to her. For the first time she saw fear in his eyes. 'It's the gamblers, me darlin',' he said. 'They'll murder me if I don't pay them.' He broke down and began to cry.

'How much?' she asked.

He looked up at her, hope rising in his eyes like a whipped puppy. 'Ten thousand dollars,' he said.

'I have four in the bank,' she said. 'I can get six on the car.'

He had seized her hand and kissed it gratefully. 'I'll pay you back,' he swore. 'Ivery penny of it.'

The next day he came to the bank with her while she got the money. When she gave it to him, he said he would meet her back at the hotel for dinner. He never showed up. By ten o'clock that night the news was all over the garage. He had run away with the wife of another driver.

She lost the race and the bank took the car. She was sitting in the hotel room wondering how she was going to get the money to pay the bill when a knock came at the door.

She walked over and opened it. A neatly dressed man who had an oddly familiar-looking face stood there. 'Miss Nichols?' he asked.

She nodded.

'May I come in?' he asked.

She stepped back. He came into the room and she closed the door. He turned to face her. 'I have long been an admirer of yours,' he said. 'I have seen you race in many places. Italy, France, Monaco. I also have heard you have a little problem. I would like to help you.'

She opened the door again. 'Get out,' she said.

He held up his hand, smiling. 'Don't be so quick. It's nothing like that. You drive racing cars. I own one. I want you to drive it for me.'

She closed the door. 'Where is it?'

'In Acapulco,' he answered. 'The race is from there into California. I will settle up all your bills here and give you one thousand dollars when you deliver the car to the garage at the end of the race. You may keep whatever purse you win.'

'What's the catch?' she asked. 'The car weighted down with dope?'

He smiled again. 'All you have to do is drive the car. For that you will get paid.' He took out a thin Italian cigar and lit it. 'You don't have to know anything more than that.'

She stared at him. It was either take his offer or wire her parents for the money. It wasn't that they would refuse her but if she took their money she would have to return home. She would never get the chance to get another car then, she would never have enough money. She would be stuck there.

'I'll do it,' she said.

'Good.' He smiled. 'There will be a money order at the desk when you come downstairs in the morning.' He gave her a few more instructions and then left before she had a chance to ask him his name.

It wasn't until she was aboard the plane the next day that it came to her. She had seen him in Rome at a restaurant. Someone had pointed him out.

'That's Emilio Matteo,' he had said. 'One of the three most important men in the Mafia today. The U.S. kicked him out but it hasn't seemed to stop him very much. He gets around all right.'

Six times more during the next year she saw him. Each time it was to perform some errand for him. She had to be a fool not to know that she had become a messenger for the Mafia. And she was not a fool.

But each time there was another thousand dollars in the bank. There was eight thousand there now. Five more and she could get that Ferrari.

By this time she and Matteo were practically old friends. And she had read enough in the newspapers to know she was leading a man to his death. Not that it made any great difference to her. She had seen too many men die in the races. In tortured turning, twisting, burning wrecks. Everybody had to die sometime. That was the chance you took when you got behind the wheel.

At least that was the way she had felt before she met him. Before she felt the fever burning in her loins, the weakness in her legs. Before she felt the fire leap between them at his touch.

NINETEEN

CESARE had just finished dressing when she came into his room. He looked up in surprise. 'Ileana! What are you doing up at six o'clock in the morning?'

She finished tying the robe around her. 'I couldn't let you go without wishing you good luck in the race.'

He flashed a quick smile at her and bent to snap his boots. 'That's very kind of you. Thank you.' He straightened up and came over and kissed her cheek, then started for the door.

At the door he turned and looked back at her. 'See you at dinner tonight,' he said automatically.

'Dinner, tonight?' Her voice was puzzled. 'I thought the race was going to take two or three days.'

An annoyed look came to his face. 'That's right, I forgot,' he said quickly, realizing his inadvertent slip. He forced a smile to his lips. 'It is becoming a habit to see you every evening.'

A vague sense of warning began ticking in her mind. Cesare wasn't the kind of man who made mistakes like that. 'Good or bad habit?' she asked.

He grinned. 'You tell me when I get back,' he said. closing the door behind him.

She stood there for a moment then turned back to the bedroom. His valise lay open on the bed. Idly she went over and began to close it. A flap fell forward from the top of the case. She bent to straighten it before she closed the lid.

It was a peculiar triangle-shaped flap that took up a small diagonal corner of the valise. Inside it was a thin stitched sheath that was fastened to the flap. It had recently held a knife. She could tell that from the stretched appearance.

A picture of the stiletto that Cesare held in his hand the night he found her in his apartment flashed through her mind. Why would he need a knife like that in an automobile race?

The vague sense of warning that had troubled her when he had said he would see her at dinner came back. Maybe it was the truth even if he said it was a mistake afterward. Maybe those men were right in what they had said, even though she did not believe them at the time.

A feeling of panic began to rise inside her. Suddenly she knew why he had taken the knife. He was coming back tonight to kill her.

Luke looked across the car at Cesare. He was driving easily, his eyes hidden beneath the large black goggles, a faint smile on his lips. She leaned forward to check the dash.

The tach needle stood at 26,000 r.p.m., it checked out with speedometer. The temperature gauge was normal, the oil pressuure gauge was even, the generator and the battery were at normal discharge. She straightened up. They could go a million miles in this car if they wanted to.

They turned the corner and came upon two other contestants. Cesare looked at her. 'Can we have a little fun before we quit?' he shouted over the motor.

She glanced at the mileage indicator. They were about sixty miles from the starting point. She nodded.

Cesare grinned and hit the accelerator. He cut in behind the two cars. They were blocking his way through. He inched up until he was practically riding their rear bumpers.

She looked at him. His lips were drawn back across his teeth in a savage grin. Beneath the goggles his eyes seemed to shine with an unholy joy. The cars in front of him began to go into a curve.

He laughed aloud and picked up more speed. She looked down at the speedometer. They were doing one hundred and twenty now and the needle was climbing. She felt the drag on her body as the big Ferrari tore into the curve. She looked ahead nervously. If the cars in front didn't split now, they would all be dead. Before the thought had gone from her mind, the Ferrari had crept between the two cars. They had split.

Deliberately, Cesare sawed the Ferrari back and forth across the road. She could see the other drivers cursing and fighting to stay on the road. Then they came into the straightaway and now the Ferrari was a few feet ahead of them. Cesare laughed aloud again and opened the car up. The speedometer jumped to one-fifty and the Ferrari left the two cars behind them.

She looked back at them and laughed. Now she knew what Esteban had meant back in the garage. Here was a race that Cardinali knew he wasn't even going to finish and still he drove the same way he always did. But he could drive. Esteban was right. If he really wanted to he could be the best in the business.

She felt his hand come down on her own and she turned around. Unconsciously, she had moved closer to him in the excitement. He lifted her hand from the seat and moved it on to his thigh. She looked up at him. He turned his head and met her gaze, a mocking smile on his lips.

She could feel the heat coming up from his leg into her hand and running into her body. For a moment she was wild at what he could do to her, how he could make her feel. She dug her fingers into the muscles of his thigh, feeling her nails go through his clothing into his flesh. She wanted him to feel pain, to hurt and push her hand away.

He only laughed aloud at her. She felt a pulse begin to throb in the palm of her hand. Angrily she raked her nails back along his leg and took away her hand. She moved away from him. She closed her eyes at the sudden pain that came up inside her when she lost contact with his warmth. She shook her head to clear it. What was the matter with her anyway? There was no percentage in it. Did she always have to try to be a loser?

She looked down at the mileage indicator. They were a hundred miles from the starting point. She tapped him on the shoulder. 'Begin slowing down. We better let those cars behind us go by.'

Cesare nodded. The big Ferrari began to lose speed. They were down to sixty miles per hour and it felt as if they were standing still. Within a few minutes the two cars they had passed went by with much hooting of their horns.

He shook his head. 'The party's over,' he said.

'It never really began,' she replied, her eye on the mileage indicator.

The one-fifteen was creeping up on the dial. He seemed to be paying no attention to it. She looked at him. Sixty miles an hour was still too fast to be going if even a small bomb was going to blow up your generator but if he thought she was going to chicken, he was crazy.

The one-fifteen locked in the dial. He laughed and hit the accelerator. The big car began to leap forward. At the same moment, there was a faint explosion under the hood. The car shuddered and the motor stopped. They began to weave crazily on the road.

She could see the muscles on his forearms ridge as he fought to hold the wheel steady while he pumped the brake a little at a time to bring the speed down. At last they were rolling slowly. She let her breath out slowly. 'Now that you've had your fun, Mr Cardinali,' she said sarcastically, 'I guess it's safe to pull off the road now.'

'Okay,' he said. He turned the wheel toward the shoulder of the road. He smiled at her.

'Look out!' she yelled, seeing it first. 'A ditch!'

Cesare spun the wheel sharply but it was too late. The

two wheels on the right side of the car caught the ditch. Slowly the heavy car settled in the sandy earth and rolled over on its top.

Cesare slid out from under the car. He got to his feet and pulled off his helmet. Faint wisps of smoke began to come up from the engine. He turned back to the car. 'Luke! Are you all right?'

Her voice came faintly from beneath the other side of the car. 'I'm okay.'

He ran around the car and knelt beside it. He peered under the car. She had her hands on the back of the seat and was squirming around, trying to get out.

'What are you waiting for?' he yelled. 'Come on out. There are fifty gallons of gasoline back in the tank!'

She stopped squirming and stared at him balefully. 'What the hell do you think I'm trying to do? A snake dance?' she snapped, beginning to wriggle again. Suddenly she began to laugh. 'My coveralls are caught on something.'

He threw himself to the ground beneath her. 'Why didn't you say so?' he grinned. He put his hands under the coveralls and ripped them open. Then she felt his arms under her shoulders. 'Kick your shoes off,' he commanded.

Automatically she did as he told her. She felt herself slide forward, out of the coveralls onto the ground beside him. She was still laughing.

He looked at her, a faint smile beginning to twitch the corners of his mouth. 'Well, you said it was safe.'

'Show-off!' she retorted.

'Who is showing off now?' he asked, his eyes glancing down at her.

The laughter faded from her lips. She was suddenly aware of her near nudity. The thin brassière and panties didn't serve to cover very much. 'I'll get my coveralls,' she said, turning to reach for them.

His hand fell on her shoulder, pinning her to the ground. She lay there motionless feeling the warmth in his hand, staring up at him. She felt his other hand move and free one breast from her brassière. She looked down at herself then back up at him, oddly aroused at the sight of her white flesh against his darkly tanned hand.

'Stop it,' she said in a low voice, the fever beginning to work inside her. This time she wasn't going to be easy.

His eyes were glowing. She felt as if she were under a microscope, as if he could read every hidden thought, knew every emotion inside her. 'You don't want me to stop,' he said.

She felt his strong fingers suddenly crush her breast and the pain tore her from her lethargy. 'I'll make you stop!' she screamed, thrusting her hands inside his open shirt, her body writhing wildly. 'I'll tear your flesh into ribbons!'

But when her fingers felt the soft cool touch of his skin, the fever rose and took possession of her body and the strength drained from her limbs. She thrust her hands deeper into his shirt and closed her eyes. His arm held her away.

She opened her eyes, feeling the tears come to them. It was no use. She couldn't change, she would never change. 'Let me touch you, let me worship you,' she begged.

And when, after a while, he took her, she knew she

had been right from the moment she first saw him. Never had there been a man like him before that could fit and fill every hidden corner of her mind and body.

She closed her eyes and began to run softly through the forest toward the mountain. She knew the animal was there somewhere, his black and yellow stripes, stalking her in the brush. She was scrambling frantically up the mountain now, her heart pounding, her breath like a rasping fire inside her lungs. Then she was on the peak with the whole world spinning round below her, this time when the animal sprang she was ready for him. Locked in an embrace of death, they tumbled together, over and over down the face of the mountain.

She moaned softly. 'Tiger, tiger, tiger!'

Cesare kicked open the door of the shack. 'There is no one here,' he said.

She walked into the shack and he followed her. 'What do we do now?' he asked.

'We wait,' she said succinctly.

There were a few battered chairs and a table in the shack. He pulled one of the chairs toward her. She sat down. He lit two cigarettes and held one toward her. She took it without speaking.

'You are very silent,' he said.

She blew the smoke from her lungs, its acrid taste somehow cleansing. 'What is there to say?' she asked. 'You made your point.'

'Was that all there was to it?' he asked.

She stared at him. 'What difference does it make? It won't happen again.'

'Are you always that sure of everything? How do you know what will happen tomorrow?'

'Tomorrow I'll have enough money to buy a Ferrari,' she said almost bitterly. 'And we'll never see each other again.'

'Is that all it meant to you?' He laughed shortly. 'An automobile? A Ferrari can do many things but it cannot love you.'

'You speak of love?' she said cynically. 'You forget I know about you. To how many women have have you spoken of love? Ten, twenty, a hundred? More?'

His eyes were veiled. 'A man may live in many places and still not call them home.'

The sound of an automobile came from outside the shack. Luke got up from her chair and walked past him to the door. She turned and looked back at him. Her face was set and tense. 'It's over,' she said with finality. 'I said I was never going to be a loser again.'

'You changed your mind back there, under the automobile,' he said softly.

'I was paid for what I did,' she said harshly. 'I was told to keep you here.' She swung open the door.

Two men stood there, the guns in their hands pointed at Cesare.

She looked back at him over her shoulder. 'See what I mean?' she asked, stepping carefully behind them and out into the sunlight. 'We did not come to praise Cesare,' she said.

"Are you always this sure of everything? How do you know what will happen tomorrow?"

"Tomorrow I'll have enough money to buy a Ferrari," he said almost angrily. "And we'll never see each other again."

"Is that all it means to you?" He laughed shortly. "An automobile! A Ferrari can do everything but it cannot love you."

"You speak of love?" ... "You forget I know about you. To how many women have you spoken of love? Eight, twenty, a hundred? Many?"

His eyes were veiled. "A man may live in many places and still not call them home."

The sound of an automobile came from outside the steps. Julie got up from her chair and walked out into the door. She turned and looked back at him. Her

THE door closed behind them, cutting off the sunlight. He stood there, steady. "Come over," again.

"Where's Marco?" he asked.

Allie smiled. "He's coming."

Caesar felt his muscles tense. His saliva was suddenly dry. He wet them with his tongue. ... make ... Any of ... Marco ... had not ... him by ...

... one of them. "It has been a while," he said.

She ... stepped forward, motioning with the gun. ... face the wall and put your hands ... your head.

He felt Allie's hand check him down. "There is no gun," he said.

"I'm lookin' for a gun," Allie said ...

199

TWENTY

THE door closed behind them, cutting off the sunlight. They stood there, staring at Cesare.

'Where's Matteo?' he asked.

Allie smiled. 'He couldn't come. He sent us.'

Cesare felt his muscles tense. His lips were suddenly dry. He wet them with his tongue. It didn't make sense to him. Any of it. Matteo had nothing to gain by his death. None of them. 'It must be a mistake,' he said.

Allie shook his head. 'It's no mistake.' He stepped forward, motioning with the gun. 'Turn around and face the wall and put your hands on it. Over your head. Real slow.'

Cesare looked at him, then slowly did as he was told. He felt Allie's hand check him down. 'There is no gun,' he said.

'I ain't lookin' for a gun,' Allie said quickly.

The stiletto felt cold against Cesare's arm over his head. 'You won't find the knife either,' he said. 'I don't need it to drive a car.'

Allie stepped back. 'I guess not,' he admitted. 'Well, you won't need it any more.'

The gunman looked at him. 'Hit him now, Allie?' He began to raise his gun.

Allie stopped him with a gesture. 'No. I got my own plans. This guy needs something special.'

Cesare looked back over his shoulder. Allie was taking something out of his pocket. He saw Cesare watching him and grinned. 'Know what this is, baby?' he asked, holding it in the air.

Cesare didn't answer. He knew.

'It's an ice pick,' Allie was still grinning. 'It ain't got a fancy name like that pig sticker you use but it does a job. Big Dutch could have told you that.' Quickly he reversed the gun in his hand and swiped it viciously across the back of Cesare's head.

His mind reeling, Cesare went to his knees, his fingers trying to hold onto the wall. He heard Allie's harsh voice.

'Turn around, ya' bastard! I want ya' to see what's comin'!'

Slowly he turned around. He shook his head, his vision beginning to clear. He stared up at Allie.

Allie was smiling. He dropped the gun into his pocket and transferred the ice pick to his right hand. He put his face very close to Cesare. 'Yuh're gonna get this right in the gizzard!' he snarled.

Cesare watched him raise the ice pick. He threw himself desperately to the side as the ice pick came slashing down. The pick went into the rotten wood of the wall behind him and stuck there. He swung his hand in a vicious judo chop at Allie's throat.

Without waiting the result of the blow he flung himself across the room at the gunman. The gun flew from the man's hand as they sprawled to the floor. From the corner of his eye, Cesare saw Allie pick up the gun. He rolled over, clasping the gunman to him as a shield, just as Allie began to fire.

The man's body jerked with the impact of the bullets. He squirmed for a moment, trying to loosen himself then went limp in Cesare's grasp. He began to fall to the floor and Cesare tried to scramble for the door.

Allie laughed. 'No, ya' don't, ya' bastard!' He squeezed the trigger.

There was a click as the hammer fell on an empty chamber. He swore and threw the gun at Cesare. He turned, grabbing for the ice pick. He pulled it from the wall and turned just in time to see Cesare moving toward him slowly, the stiletto gleaming in his hand.

He held the ice pick out in front of him as he began to move along the wall. He remembered the gun he had dropped into his pocket. A smile began to come to his lips as he surreptitiously dropped his hand to get it. All he needed was a moment of time.

She sat in the front seat of the car behind the wheel absolutely motionless. Her hands gripped the wheel so hard that her knuckles were white and her eyes were focused on some distant point in space beyond the windshield. It wasn't until she felt the point of the stiletto touch her throat that she turned her head and saw him.

He leaned toward her, his lips drawn back in an animal-like snarl across his tense face. His blue eyes shone with a yellow light in the sun.

Her eyes widened for a moment with an expression he did not understand, then went blank and guarded. She did not speak.

'Why did you do it?' he asked, the stiletto steady in his hand.

She looked up at him. Her voice was as empty as her eyes. 'I told you before. It was my job. I didn't ask questions of Matteo. Did you?'

The yellow light seemed to flame up in his eyes. 'That was different. I kept my oath.'

'And so did I,' she said. 'The only difference was in the manner in which we were paid for what we did.'

'I ought to kill you!' he said harshly.

She felt the point of the stiletto press against her throat. She closed her eyes and leaned her head back against the top of the seat. 'Go ahead,' she said wearily. 'It really doesn't matter. Matteo will not tolerate my failure any more than he did your success.'

He did not speak and the silence that followed seemed interminable. She felt the fever rise suddenly within her, radiating through her body like a shock wave of heat. The image of the tiger leaped into her mind. In another moment, she would not be able to control the auto-orgiastic convulsions that were already taking possession of her loins. 'Go ahead! Get it over with!' she cried wildly. Death would still the tiger too.

Again he did not answer and she opened her eyes. His face was bathed in perspiration and she could feel the trembling of his body against the seat. A sudden recognition came to her and she saw herself deep inside him. 'Oh, God!' she cried faintly, reaching up to him. They were so alike.

She heard the stiletto drop to the floor of the car as she felt his lips seek her throat and cover the tiny bleeding wound left there by the knife. The danger and the excitement were over and they were the same for him as they were for her. They only served to whet the appetite of the tiger.

He stopped the car in front of her hotel. 'Get your things and meet me at the airport in two hours,' he said.

'You will be careful?' she asked, looking at him.

He nodded confidently. 'We will be on our way back to New York before anyone knows what happened. Somehow I must get in touch with Emilio. He will straighten this out.'

She pressed his hand and got out of the car. She watched him drive off and then went into her hotel.

He walked into the lobby of El Ciudad and over to the desk. 'My key, please,' he asked of the clerk who had his back toward him.

The clerk turned around. 'Count Cardinali!' he exclaimed, a note of surprise in his voice. He reached for the key behind him and placed it on the desk. 'The race—'

Cesare interrupted him. 'My generator burned out.'

'I am sorry, señor,' the clerk said. He brought up an

envelope and gave it to Cesare. 'The Baroness left this for you.'

Cesare opened the note. It was in Ileana's handwriting.

'Sorry, Darling, I could not wait for your return. Have left for New York with a rich Texan who insists that we do some holiday shopping. Love, Ileana.'

Cesare smiled to himself. He should have known that Ileana had a reason not to meet him in Cuernavaca. He looked up at the clerk. 'What time did the Baroness leave?' he asked.

'About eleven o'clock this morning,' the clerk replied with a knowing smirk.

Cesare nodded and started toward the elevator. He checked his watch. It was about seven o'clock. Ileana was probably in New York already.

TWENTY-ONE

BAKER leaned across his desk and stared at Ileana. 'Why did you come back? You were supposed to stay with him.'

'I was afraid, I told you.' Ileana looked at him nervously. 'I had a feeling that he was going to kill me. That he knew . . .'

'What made you feel like that?' Baker asked quickly. 'Was it something he said or did? Something you saw?' Ileana shook her head. 'It was nothing like that. It was just that flap on the suitcase that I told you about. When I touched it I had the feeling that death had taken possession of his soul. So I came back.'

'But you never saw a stiletto there,' Baker said. 'I have a flap like that in my valise. It's for my toothbrush holder and razor.' There was a knock at the door. 'Come in,' he called.

An agent entered, carrying a teletype. He put it on Baker's desk. 'This just came in from Mexico City,' he said. 'They found the bodies of Allie Fargo and some hood in a deserted hut on the desert about a half mile from where Cardinali's car went off the road.

Ileana rose excitedly. 'See! I was right!'

Baker looked up at her. 'Maybe if you had stayed, we would know more about this.'

'Maybe, also, I would be dead!' Ileana snapped. 'I don't like this at all.'

Baker looked up at the agent. 'Where is Cardinali now?' he asked.

'On his way back to New York. His plane is due at Idlewild in the morning,' the agent replied. 'He has a woman with him.'

Baker turned back to Ileana. 'A woman?' he asked. 'Is that why you came back?'

'Don't be silly!' Ileana snapped.

Baker began to smile. 'I'm beginning to get the picture. He found another girl friend and told you to beat it.'

Ileana rose to the bait. 'That's not true,' she retorted. 'I know the girl. She's his mechanic.'

'His mechanic?' Baker said skeptically.

She nodded. 'Her name is Luke something. His regular mechanic was ill and he hired her down there.'

Baker turned back to the agent. 'Wire down there and get me the rundown on her.'

'Yes, sir,' the agent said. 'Do you want Cardinali picked up when the plane lands?'

Baker shook his head. 'That won't do any good. We

have nothing to hold him on. Just have a car ready for me. I want to see where he goes when he lands.'

The agent left the room and Baker looked across the desk at Ileana. 'You better go back to the hotel and stay as close to him as you can.'

'I will not!' Ileana said quickly.

'He won't harm you as long as he doesn't know about us.' His voice hardened. 'Or would you prefer deportation?'

'Being deported is better than being dead,' she retorted.

'Moral turpitude is a pretty serious charge,' he continued. 'It means you will never be able to enter this country again. And it doesn't look pretty in the newspapers.'

She stared at him resentfully. 'In Europe they are much more understanding. They realize some women are not made for work.' She took out a cigarette and tapped it nervously on the desk.

Baker lit it for her and leaned back. He knew he had her now. 'I think we Americans know that too.' He smiled. 'It's just that we don't talk about it.'

She drew deeply on her cigarette. 'I am beginning to get the impression that sex is considered un-American!'

He stared at her for a moment then he leaned across the desk. When he spoke his voice was almost gentle. 'You're frightened, aren't you?'

She looked up into his eyes, then she nodded slowly. 'At first I thought it was all a big joke. But now I realize it is not. I am beginning to get very frightened.'

He got to his feet and walked around the desk to her.

'Try not to, Baroness,' he said slowly. 'We'll keep an eye on you. And I promise we'll get you out of there at the first sign of trouble.'

The young agent with Baker whistled as he saw Luke get into the taxi with Cesare in front of the airport. 'Say, that guy does pretty good with the dames, doesn't he, chief?'

Baker nodded. He watched the cab pull off. 'Better get started,' he said.

The agent pulled the car out into traffic. Another car cut in front of them. He looked over at Baker. 'Want me to jump in front of him?'

Baker shook his head. 'No, it's all right. Stay where you are. We can't lose him on the expressway.'

They rode along silently for about ten minutes until they had almost reached the curve at Jamaica Bay. Baker looked at the car in front of them curiously. It still kept its position between their car and Cesare's taxi. Now it began to pick up speed and swung into the left lane. A feeling that something was going wrong began to come over him.

He had been in this business too long to disregard hunches. He opened his coat and loosened the revolver in its holster. 'Stay with that car,' he told the younger man. 'I don't like it.'

Obediently the agent swung into the left lane. 'That car is acting peculiar,' he said. A sound of muffled explosions came back to them. 'They're shooting at him!' he shouted.

'Hit the gas!' Baker yelled back at him, whipping out his gun. He leaned out the window and fired at the car in front of them.

Cesare's taxi was going off the road on to the shoulder of grass as they sped past it. Baker couldn't tell whether anybody in it had been hurt. He fired his gun again.

A bullet hole appeared in the back window of the car directly behind the driver. The driver pitched forward across the wheel and the car plunged wildly off the road toward the bay. Just before it hit the water, Baker saw the door open and the man come tumbling out.

They were on the grass now and coming to a stop. Baker leaped from the car and took off after the running man. 'Stop!' he shouted, firing a warning shot in the air.

The man turned for a moment. Baker saw something glint in his hand. There was a ping as the bullet went by him, then the sound of the shot.

Baker flung himself to the ground. The man was running again. Baker aimed low, for the man's legs. He squeezed the trigger gently. He wanted this one alive, to talk. His first shot missed. He fired again.

This time the man tumbled headlong to the ground. He rolled over and over and down a slight crest of the ground.

The young agent came running up, his gun in his hand. He looked down at Baker. 'You okay?'

Baker began to get to his feet. 'I'm okay.'

'The one in the car is dead,' the agent said.

Baker looked at him. 'Go and look at the one over there. I tried to hit him in the legs.'

The agent ran off and bent over the fallen man. 'This one's dead too!' he yelled back.

Grimly Baker began to place his gun back in the holster. Cesare's voice came from behind him.

'You're a good shot, Mr Baker.' He was smiling.

Baker stared at him almost balefully. The man must have nerves of ice. He had just been shot at, two men had been killed and his voice was as calm as the day they met in his office. 'You can't tell me they weren't shooting at you this time, Mr Cardinali,' he said, trying to keep his voice as calm as the other's.

Cesare shrugged his shoulders. 'No, I can't, Mr Baker.' A kind of mocking challenge crept into his eyes. 'What I don't understand is – why?'

Baker's eyes grew cold. He felt the pretenses slip away from him now. 'And I suppose you don't know why Allie Fargo was killed in a shack not a half mile from where your car went off the road in Mexico either?'

Cesare smiled. 'I did not even know that he had been killed. You see I did not read the newspapers.'

'You can account for your time on the road?' Baker asked.

'Of course I can,' Cesare said. 'I was with my mechanic every moment. You can check with her. She is still in the taxi, repairing her makeup.'

'You're pretty good at coming up with women to alibi you,' Baker said sarcastically.

Cesare was still smiling. 'Most fortunate,' he agreed.

Baker stared at him for a moment as a police car came speeding up. 'Go ahead, Cardinali, have your fun,' he said angrily. 'Just remember, we won't be around all the time to protect you!'

The cab pulled over to the curb and Cesare got out. He

leaned back into the cab. 'Wait here,' he said to Luke. 'I have to run up to the office for a moment.'

The receptionist seemed surprised to see him. He went by her into the general office. There was a group of employees standing around the water cooler. They looked up as he approached and scattered to their desks. He nodded to them and went into his office.

'Come inside,' he said as he walked through Miss Martin's anteroom.

Inside his own office, he turned to her. 'What's going on out there? Why aren't they working?' he demanded.

Miss Martin looked at him. 'Are you all right?' she asked.

'Of course, I'm all right,' he snapped.

'We just heard over the radio that somebody took some shots at you on the way into the city,' she said.

'What excuse is that for them to be standing around doing nothing?' he asked angrily. 'They are being paid to do their jobs, not to gossip.'

'There is nothing for them to do,' Miss Martin said.

'What do you mean, nothing?' He was getting angrier. 'Why not?'

She picked up a telegram lying on his desk and gave it to him. 'Our franchises have been revoked. That's the last one. It just came in about an hour ago.'

He looked down at it and then picked up the other telegrams from his desk. They all read practically the same. The two Italian companies, the two English companies, the French company and the Swedish company. He looked up at her. 'When did this happen?' he asked.

'It began the morning you left for Mexico,' she said.

'I don't understand it. It was almost as if someone gave the signal.'

He looked down at the telegrams in his hand again. Angrily he threw them back on the desk. The Society was so sure of itself. So sure he would be dead that they didn't need to continue the franchises with his company. He would have to reach Matteo now. This business had gone far enough.

'I'm sorry, Mr Cardinali,' Miss Martin said sympathetically. 'I tried to reach you but you had already left the hotel for the race. I guess it was because of all that business in the newspapers.'

He didn't answer. He was thinking. Someone would have to get a message to the postmaster in his village in Sicily. He was sure that Matteo was in the country somewhere but he could spend the next twenty years and not find him. His secretary's voice cut into his thoughts.

'What are you going to do?' she asked.

He stared at her. 'What else is there to do?' He shrugged. 'Give everybody their severance pay and lay them off. Tell them we'll call them back as soon as the situation clears up.'

'Do you think it will?' she asked.

'I don't know,' he said, starting for the door. He stopped and looked back at her. 'And, frankly, I don't give a damn!'

TWENTY-TWO

CESARE turned the key in the lock. He swung open the door. 'Go on in,' he said to Luke.

She walked into the apartment and he followed her, closing the door behind him. Ileana's voice came from the bedroom.

'Is that you, Cesare?'

He looked at Luke for a moment. Her face was expressionless. Then he smiled. 'Yes, Ileana,' he called.

Her voice still came from the bedroom. 'I don't know what this world is coming to! All the rich Texans I meet are either married or phonies! This one actually wanted me to help him shop for his wife! '

He couldn't keep his smile from growing broader as the expression on Luke's face became more fixed. 'That's too bad, Ileana,' he said.

'I can't hear you,' she replied. 'But no matter. I've

had Tonio ice up some champagne for us. It's on the liquor cabinet. Be a dear, will you, and pour some for me. I'll be out in a minute!'

He walked over to the liquor cabinet. The champagne was there in an ice bucket with two glasses. Solemnly he took down another glass and stood it next to the others. Then he opened the bottle and began to pour the wine.

Ileana came to the doorway, tying the belt of her negligee. She was smiling. 'I couldn't wait for you—' Her smile faded as she saw Luke standing in the center of the room. She cast a questioning glance at Cesare.

He looked from one to the other, enjoying the situation. 'I believe you ladies have only met *en passant.*' He smiled. 'Allow me to introduce you.'

He performed the introduction and gave each of them a glass of wine. He raised his glass in a toast. 'To a happy friendship.' He smiled and drank.

Ileana looked at Luke coldly then she turned to Cesare, smiling sweetly. 'Though she is a little thin, don't you think your apartment is still too small for a *menage à trois?*' she asked in French.

Cesare answered in the same language. 'Don't be a cat, Ileana. She has unsuspected talents.'

'I don't doubt it,' Ileana said dryly. 'But if the hotel management objects to one, how do you think they will feel about two? Or have you told them you've turned Moslem?'

It was then the idea came to Cesare. He knew how to contact Matteo. The smile broadened on his lips. 'It does not matter to them at all,' he continued in French.

'You see I have already told them you are leaving for Italy tonight and that she will occupy your room until you return!'

Ileana stared at him. 'I will not do it!' she said angrily, still in French. 'I will not step aside while you roll in the hay with that *chienne!*' She flung the glass at him and went back into the bedroom, slamming the door behind her.

The glass smashed against the cabinet and shattered into tiny fragments. Cesare looked down at them, then up at Luke. 'Ileana has a rather quick temper,' he said in English.

'The important thing is, will she go?' Luke asked in perfect French.

He stared at her for a moment, then began to laugh. 'You understood?'

She was smiling now. 'Every word.' She nodded. 'But that doesn't answer my question.' The smile faded from her lips. 'Will she go?'

'Of course she will,' Cesare said confidently, still smiling. 'Ileana and I are old friends. She will do anything for me.'

Tonio put down the telephone and went back into the dining room. They looked up at him. 'It was the airlines, Excellency,' he said to Cesare. 'They confirmed the Baroness' reservation for tonight!'

'Thank you, Tonio,' Cesare said.

Ileana waited until Tonio had gone, then she turned to Cesare. 'I won't do it!' she said angrily. 'I don't care what you say. I won't do it!'

Cesare stared at her. Out of the corner of his eye he could see Luke looking at him with a knowing expression. He began to get angry. 'You will do as I say, Ileana!' he said, his voice going hard. 'Or would you like the immigration authorities to learn that you do not really work for me?'

Ileana looked over at Luke. Luke kept her eyes down on her plate. 'Why don't you send her?' Ileana asked resentfully.

'You know I can't,' Cesare snapped. 'She would stick out like a sore thumb. Now, finish eating and pack your things. The jet to Rome leaves at midnight.'

Angrily Ileana threw down her spoon and stormed from the table. They heard the door slam angrily behind her.

Luke looked up from her plate. There was a faint smile on her lips. 'Ileana will do anything for me,' she mimicked sarcastically.

Cesare stared at her, scowling. 'Shut up!' he snapped angrily. 'She's going, isn't she?'

Ileana came into her room and locked the door behind her. She crossed the room quickly and picked up the telephone and gave the operator a number. A voice answered. 'Mr Baker please,' she said.

He came on to the phone. 'Yes?'

'He is sending me to Sicily, Mr Baker,' she said quickly in a low voice. 'To his village. I'm to see the postmaster there and give him a message.'

Baker's voice picked up interest. 'What message?' he asked.

'It is this.' Ileana said quoting. ' "Tell my uncle that I must meet with him." Then I'm to wait in the hotel until the postmaster gives me an answer to bring back to him.'

'Good,' Baker said. 'Now we're beginning to get somewhere.'

Ileana could feel the fear rising inside her. 'Good. Is that all you have to say, Mr Baker? Maybe you don't know it but Cesare's uncle has been dead for almost twelve years! One does not carry messages to and from a dead man!'

'Don't worry,' he said soothingly. 'The uncle you are taking a message to is very much alive. In the Society each man's sponsor is addressed by him as "Uncle".'

Her voice was suddenly very low. 'If it is the Mafia I'm carrying a message to, Mr Baker, then I am really frightened. They would not hesitate to kill me!'

'I told you before not to worry,' he said still soothingly. 'There will be a man on the plane with you and every place you go. You will never be alone. You did say you preferred rich Texans, didn't you? Well, look for the one on the plane with you.'

Slowly she put down the telephone and lit a cigarette. She walked over to the french doors, opened them and walked out on the terrace in spite of the cold. She looked down at the city, its lights sparkling coldly in the winter night.

The sound of voices came floating up to her. Curiously, she looked over the parapet and down. The voices didn't come from the street but from the floor below her. Her balcony was set back from the one below.

There was a young man and a girl in a close embrace down there.

In the night she could see the girl's white face turn upward in a kiss. They seemed oblivious to the cold. She shivered slightly and started back inside. She closed the doors carefully behind her.

It had been a long time since she had felt like the girl down there. Vaguely she wondered if she ever would feel like that again. Suddenly she knew she never could. That was behind her, left in her mother's bedroom when she was nineteen years old.

For the first time in a long time she thought of her parents. Poor Daddy was lost. And Dearest, her mother, in her own way was lost. Strange that it should take so long for her to understand them.

It was only now, with no one to cling to and no one to love, that she could feel close to them. And lost like them. She felt the tears come welling up into her eyes. And cry for them.

TWENTY-THREE

BAKER leaned across his desk and looked at Captain Strang. 'Dan, I think we're getting our first break. Cardinali is asking his uncle for a meeting. If that meeting comes off and his uncle is who I think he is, we'll take the roof off this case!'

The policeman smiled. 'It's about time. But what if the mob gets to Cardinali first?'

Baker nodded thoughtfully. 'We can't let that happen. The stakes are too big.'

'You can't be behind him every time they start shooting,' Strang said quickly.

'I know,' Baker said. 'But I've got a plan.'

'Let's hear it,' Strang said.

Baker looked up at him, he lowered his voice to a confidential tone. 'This will have to be between us. The chief won't like it. It's not regulation.'

Strang smiled again. 'I'm beginning to like it already,' he said. 'And I haven't even heard it yet.'

'We'll frighten him into hiding,' Baker said. 'We'll start a campaign. Telephone calls every hour. Threats. We'll put the toughest-looking guys on his tail and let him spot them. He'll think it's the mob. He's got to break. If only to hide until the meeting is set.'

Strang looked at him thoughtfully. 'It might work.'

'It's got to work!' Baker said. 'Once we've got him pinned down, then we can set up a stake-out that will work both ways. Nobody gets out, nobody gets in without our knowledge.'

Strang stared at him. 'It means our jobs if we louse it up.'

Baker nodded. 'I know.'

'You got it real bad for that guy,' Strang said.

'Real bad,' Baker admitted. Emotion flooded through him so strongly that he rose from his chair and walked over to the window. When he spoke again, his voice was trembling. 'I can understand most of these guys. I've seen the places they came from, the nothing they started out with. I know why they went wrong and how. But this one I don't get at all.

'He started out with everything. As far as we can see, he doesn't want anything. Maybe he's doing it just for kicks, maybe he likes to kill. I don't know.

'I only know if we don't find a way to stop him, a lot more people will die. And I don't mean only gangsters but innocent people like that girl in Florida. No one can tell where a psychopath like him will draw the line!'

Strang drew in his breath slowly. He took out his pipe and knocked it against the ash tray. He stuck the empty pipe in his mouth and looked up at Baker. The smile in his eyes belied the grimness in his voice. 'I've already put in thirty years with the force,' he said. 'And I never really wanted a steady job!'

The telephone began to ring. Cesare walked over and picked it up. 'Cardinali speaking,' he said into it.

The voice was rough and harsh and one he had never heard before. 'Cardinali?' the voice said menacingly. 'The Stiletto has outlived its usefulness. We will get you sooner or later. Why don't you make it easy on yourself?'

The phone went dead in his hand. Impatiently Cesare jiggled the button. 'Hello. Who is this? Who is this?'

There was no answer. He put down the receiver and walked back to the couch where Luke was sitting. She looked up at him curiously. 'What was it?' she asked.

'A warning,' he answered. 'Probably from some cheap gangster.'

Luke nodded thoughtfully. 'That's how they begin. I've seen the pattern before. They'll try to wear you out.'

Cesare was angry. 'If they think they can panic me with their phone calls, they'll find out that I am different from the swine they are used to dealing with!' He started angrily for the door.

'Where are you going?' Luke asked.

He turned and looked back at her. 'Downstairs to see that Ileana gets to the plane. Want to come along?'

She shook her head. 'No, thanks,' she said. 'I can live without saying goodbye to your lady friend.' She reached for a drink as he went out the door.

•

He was smiling as he came out of the Italian Airlines Building and started for the parking lot where he had left his car. Ileana would do all right. He didn't have to worry about her. The message would be delivered.

Still there was something about her. Who else but Ileana would keep her eyes open for opportunity at a time like this? He almost laughed to himself at the way she found that young man. It was the white Stetson hat. Of course, he turned out to be a rich Texan. That young man would be a lot poorer before the flight was over.

He stepped into the parking lot and began to walk down the row of cars. It was late and there were not too many cars about. The sound of footsteps keeping time with his own came to him. He stopped for a moment and looked back.

There was no one there. He shrugged his shoulders and began to walk again. Again he heard the footsteps. He paused to light a cigarette. The footsteps stopped also. The cigarette lit, he began to walk again.

A moment later he heard the footsteps. They were heavy and deliberate. This time he was sure they were following him. He slowed his pace to see if the footsteps would keep time with him. They did.

He was almost at his car now. He let the stiletto slide into his hand. The cold feel of the metal was reassuring. He stepped between the two cars and whirled suddenly, the knife pointed outward in his hand.

'Who's there?' His voice echoed strangely in the empty parking lot.

There was no answer. He waited a moment. The lot was silent. It had been nothing but the echoes of his own footsteps that he had heard. He let the stiletto slide back into its sheath. He was letting that stupid telephone call disturb him. He laughed to himself, feeling the tension drain from him as he got into the car.

He switched on the motor. He felt the faint prickling in his loins as he always did after a moment of danger. He thought of Luke waiting in the apartment. He was glad she would be there tonight. He needed someone like her. She would help him to rest.

He put the Alfa Romeo into gear and started out of the lot. He knew the type of woman Luke was but she was not the kind who went with every man. She was motivated by identification. And when she found what she sought it was like a magic key to her own body and she could no longer control her desires.

Then would come the struggle to assert her superiority. First, sexually, by demands that would grow beyond the limits of fulfillment. He smiled to himself. That was the stage she was at right now. After that would come the others, the insistence upon acceptance as equal to the male in work and achievement, then superiority to the male by virtue of her femininity.

That she would never achieve. Not with him nor with anyone who would attract her, for she was not drawn to weaklings. For them she only had contempt. And the last stage in the pattern was her demand for rejection which came last. This she would always achieve.

For this was the stone on which she cleansed herself and absolved her conscience so that she might go forward and repeat the pattern of her life. So it would not be too difficult when this was over for him to do what he had to do. In a way it was of her own seeking. By that time he would be ready too. He would have had his fill and become bored with her.

And Ileana would be back by then. He thought of her with a smile. Maybe they would marry. It was time to think of carrying on the name. The blood lines would be good together and Ileana was European.

Europeans were much more honest than Americans, much more realistic. Compared with the complexities of Luke, Ileana seemed as simple and as direct as a schoolgirl.

TWENTY-FOUR

'WELL, it's been two days,' Strang said. 'How do you think we're doin'?'

Baker shrugged his shoulders. 'It's anybody's guess. He picks up the phone now and disconnects before we get halfway through.' He took out a cigarette and lit it. 'What do your men in the field have to say?'

'I've switched them about six times already,' Strang answered. 'They say he's beginning to get jumpy. The usual things. Looking back over his shoulder, checking doorways before he goes in and out of them.'

'And the girl?' Baker asked. 'What about her?'

'She seems in better shape than he is,' Strang said. 'She's always with him but maybe she doesn't know what's going on.'

'I've got the report on her,' Baker said. 'She seems pretty straight. She is a racing-car driver. Pretty good too, from what we can tell. Had some hard luck and lost her own car last year and she's saving up to get another one now.'

'That isn't much help,' Strang said. 'It doesn't explain her willingness to alibi him for what happened out in the Mexican desert.'

'She seems to want a car pretty bad,' Baker said. 'He's the boy who can give her one.'

'Not just now, he isn't,' Strang said. 'We just found out that his car franchises were canceled.'

'All of them?' Baker asked.

Strang nodded. 'All of them. I wonder if that means anything.'

'It might,' Baker answered. 'I'll have it checked out.' The telephone rang. He picked it up. 'It's for you,' he said, giving the telephone to Strang.

Strang took it and listened for a moment, then put down the phone. 'That was one of my men. Cardinali and the girl just went into the Pavillon on 57th Street for lunch.'

Baker smiled and picked up the telephone. 'It's about time for another call,' he said to Strang. 'Call Mr Cardinali at the Pavillon restaurant and play the recording for him again,' he said into it.

'I tell you I saw that man following us,' Cesare insisted. 'I recognized him. I saw him before.'

Luke looked at him. 'Are you sure, Cesare? I didn't see anyone.'

'He was around the corner on Park Avenue by that time. I am sure.' Cesare fell quiet as the waiter brought their drinks.

They sipped at their cocktails silently until the waiter

left. Luke put her hand on his arm. 'What you need is some rest,' she said softly. 'You didn't get any sleep at all last night.'

'Who can sleep with that telephone ringing?' Cesare said irritably. 'There were four calls before we finally left the receiver off the hook.'

'I'd have the phone shut off,' Luke said.

'And admit to them that they have upset me?' Cesare said. 'That is what they would like.'

The waiter came back to the table. He was carrying a telephone with him. 'There is a call for Count Cardinali.' He bowed.

Cesare looked at Luke. 'All right, I'll take it,' he said to the waiter.

The waiter bowed again and plugged it into a jack behind them on the banquette. Cesare took the phone from him. 'Cardinali speaking,' he said into it.

Luke could see his face harden as he listened. He put down the telephone silently. He nodded in answer to the question on her face.

'Again,' he said heavily, picking up his drink. 'You see, we were being followed. They knew just where to call me.'

The telephone began to ring just as they entered the apartment. Tonio hurried by them to pick it up. 'Count Cardinali's residence,' he said into it. He looked up at them. 'Just a moment I will see if he's in.'

He put down the telephone and came over to them. 'There is a call for you, Excellency, but the signor will not give his name. He says only that he has an important message for you.'

'I'll take it,' Cesare said, crossing to the phone. He listened silently as Tonio hurried from the room. Suddenly his face contorted with anger and he ripped the telephone from its socket and flung it across the room.

'Damned instrument of torture!' he snapped as it crashed into a vase. He flung himself down on the couch as Tonio came hurrying into the room, a look of fright on his round little face.

'Clean up that mess!' Cesare snapped at him.

'Yes, Excellency! Immediately, Excellency!' the little man answered and hurried from the room.

Cesare leaned forward and placed his head in his hands. Luke went around behind him and massaged the back of his neck sympathetically.

'Take it easy,' she said. 'That won't do any good. I'll fix you a drink.'

She walked over to the liquor cabinet and took down the gin and vermouth. Quickly she stirred a martini and poured it. She looked around for the bitters. Europeans liked a dash of bitters in their martinis.

It wasn't on any of the open shelves. She turned the key on the small door at the rear of the cabinet. A lone small dark bottle stood there. She took it out and turned toward him. 'A dash of bitters?' she asked.

He was staring at her hand. 'Where did you get that?' he snapped.

She gestured with her hand. 'From here. I know you like . . .'

'Put it back,' he said sharply. 'And stay out of locked doors.'

'You don't have to take my head off,' she retorted

angrily, putting the bottle back and closing the door.

He relaxed slightly. 'I'm sorry, darling,' he apologized. 'The bitters are on the shelf below the bar.'

'What's in that bottle anyway?' she asked, handing him the drink.

He sipped the drink and looked up at her. 'Poison. Unfortunately I can't hang it on the wall like the other weapons,' he said. 'I got it from a chemist in Florence who was doing research on the poisons Lucrezia Borgia used. A few drops and there's no antidote. He said their knowledge of chemistry was fantastic for their times.'

She looked over at the cabinet curiously. 'I wouldn't feel safe having it around.'

He finished the drink. 'It's safe enough there. Nobody ever opens that door, even to clean it.' He leaned his head back against the couch and closed his eyes. 'I'm so tired,' he said.

She stroked his forehead. 'I know, lover,' she said gently. 'If there were only some place we could go, some place where nobody could find us until Ileana got back.'

He turned around suddenly and looked up at her. The tension was disappearing from his face and he began to smile. 'That's it!' he exclaimed. 'Why didn't I think of it? I know just the place. They will never think of looking for us there!'

She smiled down at him. A warmth began to spread inside her. The time was only beginning, she thought proudly, when he would learn how necessary she was to him.

Detective Sergeant McGowan looked at his watch. It

was almost eleven o'clock. One more hour until his relief would show up. He stamped his feet in the cold night air. That was the only lousy thing about this job. He had been waiting outside the hotel since four this afternoon.

Still it wasn't too bad. At least they didn't have to try to remain invisible like they did on some jobs. That was one of the big jokes in the trade. On television one lone private eye shadowed a suspect right into his bedroom and was never spotted. In real life it was a little different. The captain had six men on this job. There was one man at every entrance to the big hotel and two men constantly circling the block in a car to maintain contact and lend a hand if they were needed.

The car had just turned the corner at Lexington away from him when he glanced back at the hotel entrance and they came out.

The girl was carrying a small valise, the man looked up and down the street quickly and, waving away a taxi, took her arm. They started walking rapidly toward Lexington.

McGowan started after them. Just his luck they would pick this time to make a break. Now he wouldn't get home before six in the morning.

They cut across the street at the corner and headed up toward 51st Street. He cut in behind them and saw the man look back. He didn't try to hide himself. He didn't have to on this job. They turned the corner and went down into the subway entrance.

He broke into a run now and reached the top of the subway steps just as the roar of an entering train came to him. He took the steps down two at a time. The captain wouldn't like it if he were to lose them.

He caught a glimpse of a shadow out of the corner of his eye as he darted around the corner at the bottom of the stairway. He half turned to see the flat upraised hand of the man coming down on him in a vicious judo chop. He tried to roll away from it when the pain exploded in his shoulder and he sank to his knees.

He wasn't all the way out but there were lights flashing in his eyes and ringing sounds in his brain. That was like it was on TV, he remembered thinking vaguely. He shook his head. His vision began to clear.

He put his hand against the wall and pushed himself to his feet. He stood there dizzily for a moment, his eyes peering down to the platform.

He saw them getting on the train and started toward the platform after them. Before he reached the turnstiles, the doors had closed and the train began to pull out. He saw the man's face through the window, looking back at him. He was smiling.

Wearily he turned and headed for the telephone booth. He sank into it and heard the dime go tinkling down the box. The captain wouldn't like to hear they had gotten away but the captain should have told him the guy could hit like that. He began to dial the number.

Strang put down the telephone. He stared at Baker. 'The plan worked all right,' he said grimly. 'But it worked too good. He cold-cocked McGowan on a subway platform and got away from him.'

'The girl too?' Baker asked.

Strang nodded. 'Yes.'

Baker reached for a cigarette. His fingers were trembling. 'Heaven help them if the mob finds them before we do,' he said.

'If they do, better have your resignation typed,' Strang said heavily. 'Mine's already in my top desk drawer!'

TWENTY-FIVE

THERE are few places in New York that are resisting the advance of modern low-cost housing aid as successfully as upper Park Avenue. One of the reasons is that this is the shopping mecca of Spanish Harlem. Here below the tracks of the New York Central that speeds the commuter safely to his tiny suburban comfort is one of the last open markets of the city.

The people who shop here are mostly of Puerto Rican descent and they thread their way in their gaily-colored clothing among the pushcarts and sidewalk displays, chattering as lightly and as happily, despite their poverty, as they did at home in their tropical island. There are hotels in this section of Park Avenue also. They do not much resemble the hotels farther downtown on the same avenue but they accomplish the same purpose. They are a place to sleep and eat and offer solace to a weary traveler. The main difference between the hotels in addition to the furnishings is the credit card. In Spanish Harlem the hotels are only interested in cash.

Cesare turned back from the window of the Del Rio Hotel as a train shot past them on the tracks outside. He looked at Luke who was seated in a chair, the morning newspapers in front of her. He lit a cigarette. 'Isn't there something else you can do beside read the damn newspapers all day?'

Luke looked up at him. The whole of the last week he had been on edge. Nervous and irritable. It had been more than two weeks since Ileana had left and they had remained cooped up in this room most of that time.

At first it had been fun. They had laughed at all the little inconveniences: the dripping faucet, the squeaking bed, the sagging chairs. Then bit by bit the tawdry room seemed to creep into them until one morning it was no longer fun.

She was aware of what was coming but he had not been. Women were much more adaptable than men. They had a great deal more patience. They were better equipped for waiting. All the way around, mentally as well as physically. She remembered that she had felt a twinge of pain that usually accompanied the onslaught of her period. But nothing had happened. Idly she wondered if she were pregnant. It was more than a week now and she was rarely that late.

'Why don't you lie down and get some rest?' she suggested patiently.

He turned on her savagely. 'Rest? That's all I've

been getting in this stinking hole! Eating greasy food and sleeping in that dirty bed! I'm sick of it!'

'It's better than being dead,' she said.

'Sometimes I wonder,' he snapped, walking back to the window and looking down at the street.

She turned back to the newspaper but his voice came to her from the window and she looked up at him. He was still looking out.

'I used to see people like those down there in the village in Italy when I was a little boy. Look at them. Smiling, shouting as they scratch around in the rubble for something to eat.'

She got out of her chair and joined him at the window. 'They seem perfectly happy to me,' she said, looking down.

Cesare's voice was wondering. 'That is what I never could understand. What makes them so happy all the time? What have they got that we have not? Don't they know this world is for the few who take? They must know this. And still they are content to smile and laugh and make babies. What is it they have, that we have not?'

She looked up at him. She remembered when she had been a little girl. The excitement of going into town on shopping days. Poor Cesare, there were so many things he had never had. 'Maybe they have hope,' she said.

He looked down at her. 'Hope?' He laughed. 'That is a word invented by dreamers.'

She wanted him to understand. 'Maybe they have faith.'

He laughed again. 'That is a word invented by priests.'

She couldn't keep her hand from his bare arm. Maybe the knowledge would flow from her touch into him. The way she felt. 'Maybe they have love,' she said softly.

He stared down at her, then turned, pulling his arm from her touch. 'That word is the biggest fraud of them all. It is a word invented by women to mask their biological needs and duties. Love, hah!'

She walked back to her chair and sat down. She picked up the newspapers but she did not really see them. There was a strangely familiar hurt aching inside her. 'Maybe I don't know then.'

He came over from the window and stared down at her. She didn't have to look up to know the cruel smile on his lips. She had seen it often enough in the last few days. Each time he turned from her, from the desperate need for him inside her.

'That is right,' he said. 'You don't know. The truth is that nobody knows. But I am the only one who admits it. There is nothing more to men than the desire to exist. And most of them don't really care how. Just exist. Day to day. Year to year. For nothing.'

She was just about to answer him when there was a knock at the door. When she looked up, there was a stiletto in his hand. 'Yes?' she called.

The porter's voice came through the door. 'I have the afternoon papers, ma'am.'

'Leave them at the door,' she called. 'I'll get them in a minute.'

'Yes, ma'am,' the voice called back. They waited a moment until they heard the footsteps go down the hall.

She got out of her chair and walked over to the door.

Quickly she opened it, pulled the papers inside and closed the door again. She took them back to her chair and sat down. She began to open one of them.

He knocked the paper viciously from her hand. 'Will you never stop reading those damn newspapers?' He walked back to the window.

Patiently she bent over to pick them up when she saw the picture. 'Cesare, Cesare!' she cried, holding the paper toward him. 'Look! She's back!'

There on the photo page of the *Journal-American* was a picture of Ileana, smiling and waving at the camera from the ramp of an airliner. The caption over the picture was simple: *Baroness Returns From Holiday Abroad.*

The group of men in Baker's office leaned forward tensely as Ileana's voice came through the speaker on his desk. 'Hello,' she said.

Cardinali's voice sounded strained and hurried. 'This is Cesare. Have you got the message?'

One of the agents picked up another phone and whispered into it.

'Cesare, where are you? Are you all right?' Ileana's voice came from the speaker.

Baker looked up at the agent on the telephone. 'She's stalling just as we told her. Are you on the trace?'

'We're moving as fast as we can, sir,' the agent replied.

'I have it,' Ileana said. 'But Cesare, I don't understand it!'

'That doesn't matter,' he snapped. 'Tell me!'

Her voice was hesitant. 'The moon will rise tonight.'

A click came through the speaker as Cesare hung up, then Ileana's voice again. 'Cesare! Cesare! Are you there?'

Baker looked up at the agent. 'Did you pin him?'

The agent shook his head. 'He went off too fast.'

Ileana's voice came through the speaker again. 'Cesare?'

Baker picked up the other telephone on his desk. 'He's off the line, Baroness.'

Her voice sounded frightened to him. 'Did I do all right, Mr Baker?' she asked. 'I held him as long as I could.'

'You did fine, Baroness,' he said with a confidence he did not feel. 'We've got everything under control.'

He put down the telephone and looked up at the agent. 'Thank you,' he said to him. 'You can knock off now.'

'Surely there's something we can do if he comes out of hiding tomorrow,' the agent said.

'What?' Baker asked.

'He did send the woman out of the country to get a message,' the younger man said.

Baker smiled. 'There's no law against that.'

The agent shook his head and walked out of the office. Baker turned to Captain Strang who sat opposite him. Strang looked at him. 'It was a good try, George,' he said quietly.

Baker smiled wearily. 'It wasn't good enough.'

'You did everything you could,' Strang said.

Baker got out of his chair. Failure tasted bitter in his

mouth. He looked down at Strang. 'Let's be honest about it, Dan,' he said. 'It's over.' He walked to the window and looked out. 'If Cardinali shows up tomorrow, it means the Stiletto will have gotten away with it. If he doesn't, well, we lose anyway. We're no closer to Matteo than we were before.'

He turned back to the policeman, his voice was bitter. 'They beat us, Dan. Either way, we lose.'

TWENTY-SIX

THEY left the hotel about ten o'clock at night. 'It's not far from here,' he told her as they began to walk. They turned off Park Avenue at 116th Street and headed for Madison. They made several turns more at different corners, then Cesare touched her arm.

'It's across the street,' he said.

She looked. It was one of those old brownstone tenements that had a bar and grill in the basement floor. A small neon sign blinked on and off over the door. *The Quarter Moon Bar and Grill* it read in white and green letters.

He led her past the saloon entrance and up the steps of the house. The door was open and they walked into the hallway. A single naked bulb hung overhead and cast a dim yellow light.

She looked up at him. 'Who are we going to see?' she asked.

He looked down at her. 'Matteo, of course,' he answered matter-of-factly.

'But I thought he couldn't enter this country,' she said in surprise.

He smiled at her. 'So do many others.' He took her arm again. 'Come.'

They walked up one flight of stairs to the next floor. Cesare stopped in front of a door. He knocked on it.

'Come in. The door is unlocked.' Matteo's voice came through it.

Cesare opened the door and they entered the room. She was surprised to see it was a comfortably furnished office. She did not expect it in a building such as this. Cesare closed the door behind him.

Matteo looked up at them from behind a desk. 'Don Cesare! And Miss Nichols too. I am surprised.'

Cesare left her standing at the door and walked over to the desk. He stood there looking down silently at Matteo.

Luke looked curiously around the room. It was just like a regular business office. There was another desk in the corner with a typewriter on it. Next to it was a file cabinet and next to that was a small curtained alcove that probably led to the lavatory. The only thing strange about the room was that there seemed to be no windows in it. Matteo's voice came to her and she looked back to them.

'You have asked for a meeting, my nephew,' he said.

Cesare nodded. 'I have come to talk to you about a misunderstanding between us.'

'Yes?' Emilio inclined his head.

'When we last met, you said to me that I have done

my work well. That the Society was pleased.' Cesare's voice was low.

Emilio nodded. 'That is true.'

'Then why is it they ask my death?' Cesare asked calmly.

Emilio folded his hands across his stomach and leaned back in the chair. He looked up at Cesare. 'You are young, my nephew, and there are many things you do not understand.'

'What things?' Cesare asked.

'The Society owes its existence to one simple rule,' Emilio said blandly. 'One simple rule that helped it survive many wars and many difficult times of strife and built it to the power it is today. And this rule is our strength. "No one man can exist who threatens the security of more than himself."'

'I have not broken this rule,' Cesare said quickly. 'Except at the request of the Society to protect certain of its members.'

Emilio's voice was still patient as if he were speaking to a child. 'It is regrettable, of course, but that knowledge is now a dagger at our throats. You see, already the police suspect you and if somehow your knowledge should become available to them—' He didn't finish his sentence.

'They will discover nothing from me,' Cesare said.

'I believe that,' Emilio agreed. 'But vast harm would be done if we both are in error. The others have not the same confidence as you and I.'

'Why not?' Cesare demanded. 'I have kept the oath. And I want nothing from them.'

'That's just it,' Emilio said quickly. 'That is what

concerns them. A man who wants nothing has nothing to protect. You are not like Dandy Nick, or Big Dutch and Allie whom you have already eliminated. They had reason to be loyal, they had something to protect, profits to contribute. While you, my nephew, bring us no profit, produce nothing. You are a dilettante, interested only in the excitement and danger like a little child.'

'So, because of Dandy Nick, they ask my death?' Cesare asked.

Emilio looked up at him. He held his hands apart expressively in a gesture of helplessness. 'For that reason you must keep your oath to the society.'

Luke saw a movement behind the curtain. 'Cesare! Look out!' she screamed in sudden terror.

Cesare whirled so quickly that her eye did not follow the stiletto flying from his hand. It plunged into the curtain and into the man hidden behind it in the alcove. The man's hands gripped the curtain and fell with it to the floor, ripping it from its hanger. A gun fell clattering to the floor near Luke.

Cesare knelt quickly by the man, pulling the curtain from his face. He looked back at Emilio. 'It is Dandy Nick!' he said harshly. 'Now according to the law there is no one I threaten!'

'There is still one, my nephew,' Emilio said softly.

Cesare stared up at him. 'Who is that, my uncle?'

The gun appeared in Emilio's hand. 'Me,' he said quietly. His finger began to tighten on the trigger. In a way, it was a shame, he thought almost regretfully. Cesare could have become one of the great ones, one of the Dons, but there was something missing.

He was so lost in his reverie that he did not see Luke

squeeze the trigger of the gun she had picked up from the floor. The impact of the bullet in his shoulder tumbled him backward from his chair, the gun flying from his hand.

In a moment, Cesare was upon him, the stiletto high in the air over his head. 'No! No!' Matteo screamed. 'I will speak to the council! They will listen to me!'

Cesare was laughing wildly now. 'It is too late, my uncle!' he shouted. 'Their own rules condemn you! With your death, I am free!'

Luke watched, frozen in horror, as the knife came down again and again into Emilio's body. 'Stop, Cesare!' she screamed. 'It's enough!'

Slowly Cesare rose from behind the desk. He turned toward her, the wild maniacal light beginning to fade from his eyes. He was smiling by the time he reached her. He took her arm and opened the door.

He looked back into the room and then down at her. 'You know,' he said softly with a laugh, 'he was beginning to believe he really was my uncle!'

He opened the door of his apartment and they went inside. He crossed to the desk and sat down. He pushed aside the stack of mail and took out a check book and began to write in it.

Luke came up behind him and gently began to massage the back of his neck. 'It's good to be home,' she said softly.

He finished writing the check and turned around, holding it up to her. 'Here!' he said harshly.

She stopped massaging his neck and stared down at him. 'What's that for?' she asked.

His voice was flat and his eyes were the eyes of a stranger. 'You said you wanted a Ferrari. Now you can pack your things and go!'

She stared at him, unbelieving. There was a sickness in her stomach, a nausea that was creeping up in her. It was happening again. The same thing was happening again! 'You think—' Her voice choked for a moment. She could taste the bitter bile from her stomach. 'You think that is why I stayed with you?'

He got out of the chair and walked roughly past her to the liquor cabinet. He poured himself a drink and swallowed it. He turned back to her. 'It doesn't matter what I think,' he said. 'We are finished!'

She had to tell him. Maybe if he knew she was pregnant, he wouldn't feel like that. It wasn't his fault. He had been through so much. 'Cesare, what am I going to do now? I am . . . I don't . . .'

He reached behind him in the cabinet, opened the little door and took out the small dark bottle. He placed it on the cabinet near the whisky. 'I don't care what you do,' he interrupted her. 'But you have a choice. You know what is in this bottle. A few drops and in three minutes – oblivion! Very painless. I give it to you!'

He walked past her to the door. She followed him. 'Cesare!' she cried. 'Where are you going? To her?'

He smiled slowly, his voice was cruelly soft. 'Yes. I am tired of you. I've had enough of lying with you on coarse bleach-smelling sheets, of your plebeian attempts at love-making! You were right in what you said the first time we met. She can give me more in ten minutes than you can in ten days. And you've just proved it!'

Her hand reached for his lapel. 'You don't want me any more?' she asked dully.

He brushed her hand away. 'That's not quite right,' he said coldly. 'I don't need you any more!'

The door closed behind him and she stood there for a moment staring at it. Then she turned and slowly walked back to the couch. It had happened again. She looked over at the vial of poison standing on the edge of the liquor cabinet. He was right. It was the only way for someone like her.

She got to her feet and started for it when the nausea came up in her. She ran to the bathroom wildly and bent over the sink, retching. Tears began to burn in her eyes. She retched again and then her stomach was empty. Slowly she sank to her knees and placed her head against the cool porcelain. The tears came rolling down her cheeks. There was no doubt about it now.

TWENTY-SEVEN

HE turned the key in Ileana's door and walked into the room. The lights were on and he could hear the sound of the water running in the shower. He smiled and walked over to the bathroom door and called to her. 'Ileana!'

He heard the water stop, then her voice. 'Cesare! Is that you?'

'Yes.' He laughed. 'I'm back.'

'Are you all right?' she asked.

'I'm fine,' he called. 'Hurry out. I have something important to tell you!'

He turned from the door. It was time for them. The time for adventure was over and the time for family had begun. He knew now what his father had meant when he said to him, 'Do not let the name die, my son. Take care not to waste all your seed.'

He heard her call through the door. 'Be a dear, will

you, and hand my makeup case in through the door to me? It will never do for you to see me without lipstick. It's on the night table.'

He laughed to himself, thinking of all the times he had seen her without lipstick. But he might as well get used to her little vanities. It would be a part of their life together.

He walked over to the night table and picked up the small case by the handle. The snaps were open and the case opened outward, the lower half spilling its contents on the floor. Still smiling, he knelt to pick them up. He tumbled the lipsticks and the compacts back into the case and began to pick up the cards and letters still on the floor.

Idly he looked at them. What junk a woman carried. Credit cards and charge plates. The last letter caught his eye. It was marked, *Official Business U.S. Government*. It was addressed to Ileana from the Department of Immigration. Automatically he began to read it.

'At the request of Mr George Baker of the Federal Bureau of Investigation we herewith advise you that your request for a visa as a permanent resident alien has been approved. Please bring this letter and your passport to our nearest office so that proper entry may be made accordingly.'

Slowly Cesare got to his feet, the letter still in his hand, the makeup case forgotten on the floor. He had opened the bathroom door before he fully understood what the letter meant. She had been working for Baker all the time. There could be no other reason for him to help her.

She was standing before the mirror tying her robe

around her. She looked up into it and saw him. She spun around swiftly at the expression on his face. 'Cesare! What is wrong?' she cried. Then she saw the letter in his hand. Her eyes widened.

He stood there in the doorway, his eyes cold and dead. 'Why, Ileana, why? You came to me as a friend for help and I helped you. Why?'

She stared up at him. 'I had to, Cesare. They gave me no choice!'

'I don't believe that, Ileana,' he said, walking toward her. 'You still could have told me. We could have fought this together.'

She watched him raise his hand slowly. Oddly enough she wasn't afraid now that it was happening. She wondered if the others had felt the same way. 'Don't do it, Cesare,' she said calmly. 'You can't get away with it now. They'll know it was you.'

He stared down at her, his hand hesitating.

'Don't, Cesare,' she said quickly, trying to take advantage of his hesitation. 'You're sick. Let me help you!'

'You've helped enough,' he said bitterly. 'I was even fool enough to think of marrying you!'

She tried to dart past him to the door and never saw the blow that tumbled her unconscious to the floor.

He stood there looking down at her, breathing heavily. His mind raced. He dare not use the stiletto. There had to be a way to make it look like an accident.

As he did with Barbara. He opened the bathroom door and looked out into the bedroom. He saw the french doors leading to the terrace. The idea crystallized in his mind. A suicide was even better.

He picked her up swiftly and caried her to the terrace doors. He opened them and looked out. The night was silent and the snow had started to fall in big white flakes. He stepped out onto the terrace and carried her to the parapet. He placed her limp body on it for a moment and looked at her.

Her face was white and still and small. Somewhere in his mind he could hear the sound of her tinkling laughter. She would have made a lovely bride for him. He touched her lightly and she rolled over and was gone.

He did not stop to look down after her. He turned and hurried back into the room and out into the hall.

He came back into his living room and walked toward the couch. He stopped as Luke came to the bedroom door. 'You still here?' he snapped.

She didn't answer.

He turned from her and sank into the couch. 'What are you waiting for?' he almost shouted. 'Get out!'

He leaned forward and placed his head in his hands. He rubbed his neck wearily. Luke walked over to the liquor cabinet and poured a drink into his glass.

She came around in front of him and held it out. 'Here,' she said.

He took it and swallowed the whisky in one gulp. He put the glass down on the table before him and looked up at her. 'Now get your things and go,' he said harshly.

Silently she turned and went into the bedroom. He leaned his head back against the couch wearily. He was so tired. Tomorrow he would go away somewhere and do nothing but lie in the sun. He closed his eyes. It had been such a long time since he had been in the sun. He started to get to his feet. He might as well go to bed.

He brought his head forward but something had gone wrong. It was as if his feet had gone to sleep. He pushed himself from the couch but that didn't help either, there was no strength in his arms.

Luke came out of the bedroom, carrying her valise. She walked by him without speaking.

He felt the perspiration break out on his forehead. 'Luke! Help me,' he called. 'I feel strange!'

She turned to look at him. 'I can't help you now, Cesare,' she said in a low voice.

He stared at her for a moment, then he looked at the empty liquor glass on the table before him. Suddenly comprehension came to him. 'You bitch! You've poisoned me!' he shouted. 'I should have killed you in the desert!'

'Maybe you should have,' she said unemotionally. 'I told you I never wanted to be a loser again.' She turned to the door and opened it.

Baker and several men stood there. They pushed her back into the room with them. Baker looked down at him. He turned to Luke. 'What's the matter with him?' he asked.

A vague memory stirred through Cesare's mind. He stared up at them, his face tightening.

'He's dying,' Luke said.

'Lucrezia!' Cesare suddenly screamed.

Baker sprang into action. 'Get a doctor up here!' he snapped to one of the men.

'It's too late for that.' Luke began to laugh. 'The only thing that will help him is a priest!'

'Get a doctor anyway,' Baker said quickly. 'And get her out of here!'

Strang came into the room as Luke and the agent went out. 'The Baroness will be okay,' he said. 'She'll have to stay in bed for a few days but there are no bones broken!'

Cesare looked up at them. 'But Ileana is dead!'

Baker shook his head. 'Her terrace was on a set-back. She only fell one flight. And that was broken by an awning.'

Cesare began to laugh.

Strang looked at Baker. 'What's the matter with him?' he asked.

'He's dying,' Baker said. 'He took poison!'

Cesare looked up at them. That was the biggest joke of all. The fools should know that the Borgias did not poison themselves. For a moment he almost told them what had really happened, then he kept it inside him. Let it be one more thing the stupid *carabinieri* would never find out. He laughed again.

Baker leaned over him. 'Where are Matteo and Dandy Nick?' he asked.

Cesare looked up at him. He was smiling. 'Dead. They are all dead.'

'Why did you do it, Cardinali? Why?' Baker asked quickly. 'You never wanted what they did. You had everything going for you.'

Cesare tried to focus his eyes on Baker's face. It was blurring in front of him. 'My father used to say that too, Mr Baker, but the only reason he took me into the house was to carry on the name. And I don't know whether you would understand it either. There are only two things in life that mean anything. Birth and death. Everything else in between – living – is nothing. Empty.'

He paused to catch his breath. 'It is only when you dip your hands into these that a man is really alive. That's why you go inside a woman. To be born again. That's why you stand there watching me die, sharing the excitement of my death. You feel more alive this moment than you ever felt before!' He leaned his head back against the couch, the perspiration running down his face in rivulets.

'The man's mad!' Strang said hoarsely, his face white. 'Stark, raving mad!'

Cesare raised his head to look at the policeman. It was taking all his strength just to see through the veil that was falling in front of him. In the distance he could hear the sound of an infant crying. Maybe the man was right. Maybe he was mad. What was a new-born baby doing, crying in a place like this? Suddenly the knowledge came to him. It was his child that was crying. That was what Luke had tried to tell him. She was carrying his child within her.

He called up all his strength to find his voice. He could feel his lips twist in an agony of effort. 'Isn't the . . . whole world . . . a little . . . mad?' he asked as the veil dropped down, taking them away from him.

two things in life that he knew [illegible]
He paused to catch his [illegible] slowly [illegible]
the your hands [illegible]
That's why you [illegible] nodded. The big Frenchman began to jog
That's why you [illegible]
the [illegible] of my death. You [illegible]
[illegible]
back against the couch [illegible]
Chance raised his head to look at the [illegible]
[illegible] all his [illegible]
that everything [illegible]
could not [illegible] bomb [illegible] going to blow up [illegible]
[illegible] he was
been very [illegible] He knew

THE LONELY LADY

This book is dedicated to the memory of
Jacqueline Susann and Cornelius Ryan,
Both of whom had not only the gift of life within them
But the courage to live it to the very end.
I miss you, my friends.

You get real cooled out if you're an achievement-oriented woman. No matter how high a price you pay, you're alone when you get anywhere – in a way that no man ever has to be.

Phyllis Chesler, *Women and Madness*

Book One
Small Town

CHAPTER ONE

SHE SAT at the top of the stairs and cried.

As she came out of the anesthesia, she saw the little girl weeping, her face covered by her hands and long golden hair. She had seen the image of herself thousands of times in that fractional moment between waking and sleeping – ever since the death of her father.

Her vision cleared and the doctor's face looked down at her, smiling. 'Everything's okay, JeriLee,' he said.

She glanced around the room. There were several women on rolling beds near her.

The doctor answered the question before she asked it. 'You're in the recovery room,' he said.

'What was it?' she asked. 'A boy or a girl?'

'Does it matter now?'

'It does to me.'

'It was too soon to tell,' he lied.

A hint of tears came into the corners of her eyes. 'It seems like an awful lot of trouble to have gone through and not know what it might have been.'

'It's better this way,' he said reassuringly. 'Now try and get some rest.'

'When can I get out of here?' she asked.

'This afternoon, as soon as I get the results of the tests.'

'What tests?'

'Routine,' he said. 'We think you may have an Rh problem. If so, we have a shot we can give you so that there will be no complications with your next pregnancy.'

She stared at him. 'Would there have been with this one?'

'There was a possibility.'

'Then maybe it was a good thing that I had the abortion.'

'Probably. But after this try to be more careful.'

'There won't be another abortion,' she said firmly. 'The next one I keep. I don't give a damn what anyone says. And if the father doesn't like it he can go fuck himself.'

'You have plans?' he asked in a shocked tone.

'No. But you won't give me the pill because of the clotting factor and I keep rejecting the I.U.D. I feel kind of stupid walking around with a diaphragm and a tube of Delfen in my handbag all the time.'

'You don't have to go to bed with every man you meet, Jeri-Lee,' the doctor said. 'It doesn't prove anything.'

'I don't go to bed with every man I meet,' she retorted. 'Only those I want to.'

The doctor shook his head. 'I don't understand you, JeriLee. You're too bright to let yourself in for something like this.'

She smiled suddenly. 'That's one of the hazards of being a woman. A man can ball all he likes and nothing happens to him. But a woman can get knocked up. She's the one who has to be careful. I thought the pill was going to even things up and it's just my luck I can't take it.'

The doctor gestured to a nurse. 'I've got one pill you can take,' he said, scribbling on his prescription pad. 'It will help you sleep for a while.'

'Will I be able to work tomorrow?' she asked.

'I'd rather you waited a few days,' he said. 'It won't hurt if you rest a bit longer. You may be bleeding rather heavily. The nurse will take you back to your room now. I'll see you later when I discharge you.'

The nurse took the prescription from him and began to roll the bed away. 'Wait a minute,' JeriLee said. The nurse stopped. 'Sam.'

The doctor turned back. 'Yes?'

'Thank you,' she said.

He nodded and the nurse pushed her through the swinging doors and down the corridor to the elevator. She pressed the call button and looked at JeriLee with a professional smile. 'Now, that wasn't too bad, was it, honey?'

JeriLee stared up at her. 'It was fucking hell,' she said, her eyes beginning to fill with tears. 'I've just killed my baby.'

'Why are you crying, JeriLee?' her aunt asked as she came out of her mother's room and found her sitting on the steps.

The child turned up her tear-stained face. 'Daddy's dead, isn't he?'

Her aunt did not answer.

'He won't be coming back like Mommy said?'

The woman bent down and picked her up, holding her close. 'No,' she said softly. 'He won't be coming back.'

The tears stopped. 'Mommy lied to me,' JeriLee said accusingly.

Her aunt's voice was soft. 'Your mother wanted to spare you, child. She didn't want to hurt you.'

'But that's not what she told me to do. She said I must always tell the truth no matter what.'

'Come, let me wash your face with cold water,' her aunt said. 'It will make you feel better.'

Obediently JeriLee followed her aunt into the bathroom. 'Will Mommy tell Robbie?' she asked as her face was being sponged.

'Your brother's only four years old. I don't think he's old enough to understand.'

'Shall I tell him?'

Her aunt met her questioning gaze. 'What do you think you should do, JeriLee?'

JeriLee saw the warm sympathy in her aunt's eye. 'I don't think I will,' she said thoughtfully. 'Maybe he is too young.'

Her aunt smiled and kissed her cheek. 'That's very wise, JeriLee. That's a very grown-up decision for an eight-year-old to make.'

JeriLee was pleased by the warmth of the approval. But in later years she was strangely regretful. It was her first adult decision and it had been a compromise.

Later that night when she was still lying awake, she heard her mother come up the steps and go into her room. She waited for the familiar sound of her father's footsteps to follow after he had turned out the lights downstairs. When they did not come, she knew she would never hear them again. Then she turned her face into the pillow and began to cry for him.

She had been just a little over three years old on that day when her mother dressed her carefully in a white bouffant cotton dress and brushed the golden-brown ringlet of curls around her face. 'Be very careful about your dress. I want you to look very pretty today,' her mother had said. 'We're meeting Daddy at the train. He's coming home.'

'Is the war over, Mommy?'

'No. But Daddy is out of the service now. He's been discharged.'

'Why, Mommy? Is he hurt?'

'A little bit. Nothing serious,' her mother answered. 'He hurt his leg and walks with a slight limp. But you mustn't say anything about it. Pretend you don't notice.'

'Okay,' JeriLee said. She turned and looked at herself in the mirror. 'Do you think Daddy will recognize me now that I'm all grown up?'

'I'm sure he will,' her mother said laughingly.

In a town the size of Port Clare the return of the first discharged veteran would not go unnoticed. The mayor, the town council and the high school band had all been mustered out for the occasion. Across the front of the small railroad station hung a large white banner imprinted with red and blue lettering:

WELCOME HOME, BOBBY

It was typical of Robert Gerraghty that he decided not to get off on the station side of the tracks but jumped off on the other side because it was nearer home.

Frantically the crowd searched the platform for the missing hero. 'You sure he's supposed to be on this train?' the mayor asked JeriLee's mother with mounting frustration.

Her mother was near tears. The train was beginning to roll out of the station. 'That's what he said in his letter.'

At that moment a shout came from the far end of the platform. 'There he is!'

Robert Gerraghty was almost half a block away, walking briskly in the other direction. When he heard the shout he put down his bag, took off his army cap and scratched his head.

The high school band broke into 'Hail the Conquering Hero', and the mayor, forgetting his dignity, scrambled across the tracks.

In the confusion, the crowd followed and the mayor, giving up all their elaborate plans, made his speech in the middle of the dusty street. 'We are gathered here to honor the return of one of Port Clare's own, a genuine hero, wounded in the service of his country, Private First Class Robert F. Gerraghty . . . ' The noise of the band was so great that he was forced to stop.

Her father held JeriLee in one arm, his other arm around her mother, JeriLee kept tugging at his sleeve. He turned to her, smiling. 'What is it, JeriLee?'

'Were you shot in the leg?' she whispered.

He laughed. 'No, darling.'

'But Mommy says you were hurt. That you walk with a limp.'

'That's true.' He nodded. 'But I wasn't wounded in action.' He saw the puzzled look on her face. 'I guess your daddy was stupid enough to let a truck run over him.'

'Then you're not a hero,' she said with disappointment.

He put his face close to hers and, smiling, held a silencing finger to his lips. 'I won't tell if you won't.'

She began to laugh. 'I won't tell anybody,' she promised. Then she thought for a moment. 'Can I tell Mommy?'

He grinned and kissed her cheek. 'I think Mommy already knows.' He looked into her face. 'Did anyone ever tell you that you look exactly like Shirley Temple?'

She smiled, forcing the dimples into her cheeks. 'Everybody says that, Daddy,' she said proudly. 'And Mommy says that I sing and dance better than she does.'

'Will you sing and dance for me when we get home?'

She threw her arms around his neck. 'Yes, Daddy.'

'Hold that!' a photographer called out. 'We want that one for the paper.'

JeriLee held her brightest Shirley Temple smile, but somehow the mayor got his face in front of hers and when the picture finally appeared on the front page of the Port Clare *Weekly Bulletin* all you could see of JeriLee was her arms around her father's neck.

JeriLee was dozing when the nurse came in with her lunch. For a moment she was startled. Yesterday had been so vivid in her thoughts that today seemed an intrusion. Her father had been a very special man, laughing at the world around him, the town of Port Clare and all its hypocrisies. 'Nothing makes sense anymore, JeriLee,' he had said to her. 'Someday they'll discover the war has really changed the world. Freedom is more than a word for nations, it's really a very personal thing.'

Then, she had not known what he meant. All she knew was that her mother was angry with him a great deal of the time and often took it out on her. Her brother, born less than a year after her father returned, escaped the brunt of it. But she was growing up and much too much like her father, her mother often said.

The nurse gave her a menu. 'The doctor said you can have

anything you like as long as you eat lightly.'

'I'm not hungry,' she said.

'You have to eat something,' the nurse insisted. 'Doctor's orders.'

She glanced briefly at the menu. 'Hot roast beef sandwich. No gravy. Jell-O and coffee.'

The nurse nodded. 'Good. Now roll over and let us give you this shot.'

JeriLee looked at the needle. 'What's that for?'

'Didn't the doctor tell you? It's for the Rh factor. In case you get pregnant again you won't have any trouble with the child.'

JeriLee turned on her side. The nurse was quick and efficient. She scarcely felt the needle. 'I don't intend to get pregnant again,' she said.

The nurse laughed, turning away. 'That's what they all say, honey. But they all come back.'

JeriLee watched her leave the room. Supercilious bitch. White uniforms make them think they know everything. She leaned back against the pillows. She felt tired but not as weak as she had expected. What was it she had heard them say about abortions? Today it was no worse than treating a cold. Maybe they were right.

She looked out the window. The Los Angeles morning smog had lifted and the day was bright and sunny. She wished she had thought of having a telephone in the room. But they had told her she would be there only a few hours. Instead the Rh thing was going to hold her up almost all day.

She wondered how the meeting was going. Her agent should be with the producer right now. She wanted very badly to do the screenplay of her book herself. The first writer they had hired had botched it up completely. Finally they had come to her.

Her agent was high. He was sure the producer was over a barrel and he wanted to sock it to him. He was thinking of asking a hundred thousand dollars. She thought he was crazy. That was more than they had paid for the book, and she would have been willing to write it for nothing.

'Leave it to me,' the old man had said soothingly. 'This is my business. I know how to handle it. Besides we can always come down.'

'Okay,' she had finally agreed reluctantly. 'But don't blow it.'

'I won't,' he'd promised, then looking at her, asked, 'Where will you be tomorrow afternoon in case I should have to get in touch with you?'

'Probably home.'

'And if not?'

'Cedars.'

He'd looked at her in surprise. 'What are you going there for?'

'A D. and C.'

'You?' he asked with shock in his voice.

'Why not?' she retorted. 'After all, I am a woman. Women sometimes get pregnant. Even in this day and age.'

He became very solicitous. 'Do you have everything you need? I can drive you – '

'You're sweet, Mike,' she interrupted. 'But it's all arranged. There's nothing to worry about.'

'Will you call me then? When it's over?'

'As soon as I get home.'

He got out of his chair and walked her to the door. 'You take care now.'

'I will,' she promised.

Freedom was a very personal thing, her father had said. She wondered what he would have thought if he'd known what she had done today.

Probably he would have only wanted to be sure she was doing what she wanted to do, that she was making her own choice. For him that had been what freedom was about.

But the world had not completely caught up with his way of thinking. Her mother was unchanged. She would have been appalled if she'd known. And so would many others. Even among some of her so-called liberated friends abortion was in many ways still a dirty word.

She looked down at the luncheon tray in front of her. The roast beef had a pale anemic hospital look about it. Tentatively she began to cut the rubbery meat, then put down her knife and fork in disgust. She really wasn't hungry anyway.

She looked out the window at the bright California day. It was not a bit like Port Clare in January. Remembering one snowy day with the freezing cold wind coming off the Sound as she walked down the road to catch the bus to school, she actually shivered. The snow had fallen the night before and felt crisp and clean under her galoshes as she made her way down the sidewalk. The plows had been out all night and the snow was banked neatly on the sides of the road. She climbed over a bank and came down on the road where the snow was turning brown and dirty from the passing cars. In the distance the bus came into view.

It seemed like such a long time ago. Almost another age. And in a way it was.

CHAPTER TWO

'YOU ALMOST always die,' the man said.

She turned from the bus window and looked at him. For the three months she had been taking this bus to Port Clare Central High the man had been in the seat next to her. This was the first time he had ever spoken. 'Yes,' she said, her eyes unexpectedly filling with tears.

He stared past her out the window. 'The snow. Why is it always the damn snow?' he said, speaking to no one.

'I'm going to die,' he went on matter-of-factly.

'My father died,' she said.

For the first time he focused on her. A shade of embarrassment crept into his voice. 'I'm sorry,' he apologized. 'I didn't realize I was talking aloud.'

'It's all right.'

'I didn't mean to make you cry.'

'I'm not crying,' she said defiantly.

'Of course,' he said quickly.

She felt a strange pain in her stomach. She realized with a sense of shame that she hadn't thought about her father for a long time. In a way it had been almost too easy for her stepfather to push him from her mind.

The man's face seemed thin and pinched. 'Do you go to Central?'

'Yes.'

'What term?'

'Sophomore.'

'You look older,' he said. 'I would have thought you were a senior.'

A faint flush came over his pale skin. 'I hope I – I mean – I don't want to offend. I just don't know too much about young girls.'

'That's okay,' she said. 'People are always taking me for older.'

He smiled, recognizing that he had pleased her. 'Forgive me anyway,' he said. 'I'm Walter Thornton.'

Her eyes widened. 'You're that – ?'

He didn't allow her to finish. 'I'm that Walter Thornton,' he said quickly.

'But' – she hesitated – 'you ride the bus every morning.'

He laughed. 'You know a better way to get to the station?'

'But you have two plays and a movie on Broadway at the same time.'

'I also don't drive.' He looked at her. 'How do you know so much about me?' he asked curiously.

'Everybody knows about you,' she said.

'Not high school kids. They know about actors, not writers.'

'I'm going to be a writer,' she said.

'Why not an actress?' He was curious. 'You're beautiful enough.'

She blushed. 'Why? Is it wrong for me to want to be a writer?'

'No,' he said. 'It's just unusual. Most girls want to go to Hollywood and become a movie star.'

'Maybe I'll do that too,' she said thoughtfully.

The bus began to slow down. They were at the railroad station. He got to his feet and smiled at her. 'I'll see you tomorrow. We'll talk some more.'

'Okay,' she said. Through the window she watched the tall thin figure in the flapping raincoat disappear into the waiting 8:07 New York express.

Her boy friend, Bernie Murphy, was waiting for her in front of the school. 'Do you know who I met on the bus today?' she asked excitedly. 'Walter Thornton! Imagine that? I've been sitting next to him every day for three months and I didn't even know who he was.'

'Who's Walter Thornton?' Bernie asked.

'Who's Mickey Mantle?' she retorted with disgust.

When JeriLee was ten years old two things happened that were to change her life. The first was that her mother remarried. The second was that she wrote a story which she then produced as a play on the final day of school.

She called it 'A Gory Fairy Tale'. And it was. For by the time the curtain fell everyone on stage had died.

As writer, producer and director, she cast herself in the only dual role, that of the cook who had been put to death by the king and then risen from the grave as a witch who came back for revenge.

JeriLee loved the feeling of power. During that brief period she was the most important girl in the fifth grade.

For the first time she could feel the impact she had on other people and instinctively she recognized that the words she had written were the source of the heady sense of power.

Later, clutching her award for creative writing, her face still smudged with the black soot makeup of the witch, she went to her mother and announced her decision.

'I'm going to be a writer, Mommy.'

Her mother, who was sitting with Mr Randall of the Farmer's Bank, smiled vaguely. She had scarcely watched the performance. She was too busy thinking about John Randall's proposal the previous night. 'That's nice, dear,' she said. 'But I thought you wanted to be an actress.'

'I did,' JeriLee answered. 'But I changed my mind.'

'I thought you looked beautiful on the stage,' her mother said. 'Didn't you, John?'

'She was the most beautiful girl there,' John Randall agreed heartily.

JeriLee stared at them. They had to be blind. The whole point of the makeup was to make her look like an ugly witch. 'My makeup was horrible,' she said.

Her mother smiled reassuringly. 'Don't you worry, dear,' she said. 'We thought you looked beautiful.'

Later they went to dinner at the Port Clare Inn, a candlelit restaurant which overlooked the Sound.

'We have something very important to tell you, dear,' her mother began over dessert.

JeriLee scarcely looked at her. She was too busy watching the drunken couple who were openly fondling each other at the corner table.

'JeriLee!' her mother said sharply.

JeriLee looked at her mother.

'I said we had something very important to tell you.'

She became the dutiful child. 'Yes, Mother.'

Her mother spoke awkwardly. 'Ever since your father died . . . well, you know how difficult it has been for me to take care of you and your brother while going to work in the bank every day.'

JeriLee was silent. She was beginning to understand. But she didn't know whether she liked what was coming.

Her mother glanced at Mr Randall for support. He nodded reassuringly. Under the table her hand sought his. 'We thought it would be nice if the two of you had a father again,' she said, then added quickly, 'Bobby is almost six years old now and a boy should have a father to do things with. You know, ball-games, fishing, things like that.'

JeriLee looked first at her mother, then at Mr Randall. 'You mean you want to marry him?' There was a note of disbelief in her voice. Mr Randall and her father were nothing alike. Her father had always been laughing and full of fun, while Mr Randall almost never smiled.

Her mother fell silent.

For the first time Mr Randall spoke. Soothingly, as if he were talking to a client of the bank who had been questioning an error on his monthly statement. 'I'd make a very good father to the two of you. You're a very lovely girl and I like your brother very much.'

'Don't you like me too?' she asked with a child's unerring logic.

'Of course, I do,' he answered quickly. 'I thought I made that quite clear.'

'You didn't say it.'

'JeriLee!' Her mother's voice was sharp again. 'You have no right to speak like that to Mr Randall.'

'It's all right, Veronica,' he said soothingly. 'I like you very much, JeriLee, and I would be proud if you would have me as your father.'

JeriLee looked into his eyes and for the first time saw the hidden warmth and kindness. She responded immediately but didn't know what to say.

'I know I can never take the place of your real father but I love your mother and will be very good to all of you,' he said earnestly.

JeriLee smiled suddenly. 'Can I be the flower girl at the wedding?'

John Randall laughed in relief. 'You can be anything you want,' he said, covering her mother's hand with his. 'Except the bride.'

A year after they were married, John Randall formally adopted the two children and her name became JeriLee Randall. A curious sadness came over her the first time she wrote her new name. Now there would be almost nothing left to remind her of her father. Bobby, who had never really known him, had already forgotten. And she wondered if, in time, she would too.

CHAPTER THREE

JOHN RANDALL looked over the top of his *New York Times* as his daughter came to the breakfast table. She came quickly around the table and kissed him on the cheek. He caught a quick scent of perfume as she went to her chair.

Her voice was bright with suppressed excitement. 'Good morning, Daddy.'

He smiled, looking at her. He was genuinely fond of her. None of the individual features that made up her face were beautiful. Her nose was perhaps a trifle too long, her mouth a bit too wide, her dark blue eyes over high cheekbones too large for the size of her face, but somehow together they had an incredible effect. Once you looked at her you could never forget. She was beautiful.

He could see that this morning she had taken extra care with her appearance. Her hair looked even silkier than usual and her skin was shining clean. He was glad that she didn't use makeup like so many of the girls did nowadays. 'Something must be happening,' he said.

She looked at him over the bottle of milk she was pouring on her cornflakes. 'What, Daddy?'

'I said something's going on.'

'Nothing special.'

'Come on now,' he said gently. 'Has a new boy come into the class?'

She laughed, shaking her head. 'Nothing like that.'

'Still Bernie?'

She blushed but didn't answer.

'There has to be something.'

'Daddy,' she said reproachfully, 'why does it always have to be a boy?'

'Because you're a girl.'

'It's nothing like that,' she said. 'But I did meet someone yesterday. On the bus.'

'On the bus?' he echoed, puzzled.

She nodded. 'He sat down yesterday right next to me. Imagine that, Daddy? For three months he's been sitting next to me and I never knew who he was.'

'He?' Now he was really puzzled. 'Who?'

'Walter Thornton,' she said. 'I always thought he was only here for the summer. I never knew he lived here all the time.'

'Walter Thornton?' he asked, a note of disapproval in his voice.

'Yes. America's greatest writer.'

The disapproval in his voice became more apparent. 'But he's a communist.'

'Who said so?' she challenged.

'Senator McCarthy, more than two years ago. He took the fifth before the committee. And everybody knows what that means. When the news came out, the bank seriously considered asking him to take his business somewhere else.'

'Why didn't you?'

'I don't know,' he answered. 'We felt sorry for him, I guess. After all, we are the only bank in town and it would be inconvenient to make him go out of town.'

JeriLee had heard enough talk about the banking business to absorb an idea of how it was run. 'Did he maintain heavy balances?' she asked shrewdly.

He flushed. She had put her finger on it. When all was said and done, the man probably had greater cash balances than any other client of the bank. The weekly income was fantastic. 'Yes,' he admitted.

Having made her point, she was silent.

He stared at her. She was not like other girls or even other women he had known. Certainly her mother did not have the same ability to cut through to the bone the way she did. In many ways she seemed to think like a man. Still there was nothing about her that was not female.

'What's he like?' he asked curiously.

'What's who like?' Veronica asked, bringing the eggs and bacon from the kitchen.

'Walter Thornton. JeriLee met him on the bus yesterday.'

'Oh him? I read in the papers he's going through a divorce.' She went to the dining-room door and called up the stairs, 'Bobby! You come right down and have your breakfast. Otherwise you'll be late for school.'

Bobby's voice echoed faintly through the door. 'It's not my fault, Mom. JeriLee was hogging the bathroom all morning.'

Veronica came back into the room and sat down at the table. 'I don't know what I'm going to do with him. Every day he comes up with another excuse.'

John looked across the table at his daughter and smiled. She was blushing. 'Don't get upset,' he said to his wife. 'Things like that happen sometimes. I can always drop him off on my way to the bank.'

Veronica turned to her daughter. 'What is he like?' she asked. 'Mr Smith at the market says that whenever Mrs Thornton came in she smelled of liquor. At times he even suspected she might be drunk. They all felt sorry for him.'

JeriLee shrugged her shoulders. 'He seems very nice. Quiet. You wouldn't think he is who he is.'

'Did you tell him you wanted to be a writer?' her mother asked.

JeriLee nodded.

'What did he say?'

'He thought it was nice. He was very polite.'

'Maybe he will look at some of your things. He could give you advice.'

'Oh, Mother!' JeriLee exclaimed. 'A man like that wouldn't bother reading the work of a schoolkid.'

'I don't know, you never – '

'I don't think she should trouble him,' John interrupted. 'JeriLee's right. The man is a professional. It would be very unfair to ask him. He's probably got more important things to worry about.'

'But – ' Veronica began.

Again he interrupted. 'Besides he's not exactly the kind of person JeriLee should be associated with. He's very different than us. He has different standards. Everyone knows that communists have very loose morals.'

'He's a communist?' Veronica asked.

John nodded. 'Mr Carson says that the bank has to be very careful in our dealings with him. We don't want anyone to get the wrong ideas about us.'

Mr Carson was president of the bank, the leading Republican and the most important man in Port Clare. For the past twenty years he had personally selected the mayor of the town, although he was too modest to want the office for himself.

Veronica was impressed. 'Well, if Mr Carson thinks so – '

'I think that's unfair!' JeriLee burst out. 'There are many

people who think that Senator McCarthy was worse than the communists.'

'Senator McCarthy is a real American. He was the only one standing between us and the communists. The way Truman was acting, we were lucky we didn't give the whole country away.' John's voice was positive.

'Your father is right, dear,' Veronica said. 'The less you have to do with him the better.'

Suddenly JeriLee found herself near tears. 'I'm not doing anything with him, Mother. He just sits in the seat next to me on the bus.'

'That's all right, JeriLee.' Her mother's voice was soothing. 'Just be careful you don't let people see you talking too much to him.'

Bobby came tearing into the room, pulled his chair to the table and began helping himself to eggs and bacon.

'What's the matter?' Veronica asked sharply. 'Have you forgotten your manners? Not even a "good morning"?'

'Good morning,' Bobby grumbled, his mouth full. He looked at JeriLee. 'It's all her fault anyway. If she didn't spend so much time in the bathroom I wouldn't be late.'

'Take it easy,' John said. 'I'll drop you off at school.'

Bobby smiled triumphantly at JeriLee. 'Gee, Dad, thanks.'

For a brief moment JeriLee had a twinge of hatred for her brother and the male kinship he had with their father. Maybe that was the way it was supposed to be. After all, she was a girl. But that did not make it right. It wasn't reason enough to make her feel isolated from their world.

She rose from the table. 'I'll be going now.'

'All right, dear,' her mother said, beginning to gather the dishes.

She went around the table and dutifully kissed her mother and father. Then she picked up her schoolbooks, went out into the street and began walking toward the bus stop.

Mr Thornton wasn't on the bus that morning, nor the following morning or the morning after that. A few days later she read that he had gone to Hollywood for the filming of his latest picture, and that he was then going on to London, where one of his plays was being produced. It wasn't until the following summer that, the day after she turned sixteen, she saw him again. By that time she was no longer a girl. She was a woman.

Physically she had matured long before. Her breasts had begun developing soon after she was eleven. By the time she was twelve she started having her periods. At fifteen there were still traces of baby fat in her face but during that winter it disappeared, leaving her cheeks with long interesting planes. She noticed the thickening of the hair under her arms and around her pubis. Like all the girls, she began shaving under her arms and using a deodorant. But she also became aware of other changes that had taken place within her.

It began in the spring, when as a member of the girls' cheerleading squad she came on the field where the baseball team was practicing. Like the other girls, she wore the loose sweatshirt with an orange and black PC emblazoned across the white shirt and the very short skirt that barely came to the top of her thighs.

They took up their position in front of the stands which ran from behind home plate down toward first and third base. Miss Carruthers, the phys. ed. teacher, lined them up, their backs to the players on the field. Since JeriLee had been on the squad the year before, Miss Carruthers had her standing next to her as she led them through the various cheers.

After about fifteen minutes Mr Loring, the baseball coach, came over to her. 'Miss Carruthers, may I talk to you for a moment please?'

'Of course, Mr Loring.' She stood waiting for him to continue.

He cleared his throat. 'Privately.'

She nodded and followed him to the front of the visitors' dugout. After looking around carefully to see that they were out of earshot he turned to her. 'Miss Carruthers,' he growled, 'what are you trying to do to my team?'

She was bewildered. 'I . . . I don't understand.'

'Can't you see?' he snapped. 'In the fifteen minutes you've been out there, my boys have missed two easy pop flies, the outfielder stepped into a pothole and the pitcher caught a line drive with his stomach.'

She still didn't understand. 'Mr Loring, what has that got to do with me?'

He almost exploded. 'You got to get those girls out of there or I won't have any team left by the time the season starts.'

'Mr Loring!' she exclaimed indignantly. 'My girls are in no

way interfering with your players. They are merely doing their jobs.'

'Their jobs are to cheer the team on,' Loring snarled. 'Not tease them out of their minds. Look at that one.' He pointed. 'Everything's sticking out on her.'

'You mean JeriLee?'

'That's the one!' he said angrily. 'Those aren't buttons on the front of her shirt!'

Miss Carruthers was silent for a moment as she watched Jeri-Lee. There was no doubt about her female animal quality. Her nipples were hard and clearly defined, even under the loose sweatshirt. 'I see what you mean,' she said thoughtfully.

'You'll have to do something about her,' he said. 'Make her wear a brassiere or something.'

'All my girls wear brassieres,' she retorted.

'Then get her one that fits!' he snapped.

Just then there was a loud crash from the far end of the field. An outfielder ran headlong into the fence and fell to the ground. Immediately the other players began to gather around him. The coach hurried down the field. By the time he got there, the boy was sitting up groggily.

'God damn it, Bernie!' the coach shouted angrily. 'What are you trying to do? Kill yourself?'

'No, sir. I was just trying to catch the ball but I lost it in the sun.'

Loring turned and looked up at the sky. 'Sun? What sun?' he shouted. 'The sky is covered with clouds.'

Then he looked down the field and saw JeriLee. Even at this distance he could see the motion of her breasts. Suddenly he couldn't take any more. 'Miss Carruthers!' he yelled. 'Get those girls off my field!'

Bernie was waiting for JeriLee after practice. He fell into step with her as they walked toward the bus stop.

'Did you hurt yourself, Bernie?' she asked.

He shook his head.

'You really hit that fence. You ought to look where you're going. What was on your mind?'

'I was watching you,' he admitted.

'That's silly. You're supposed to keep your eye on the ball.'

'I know. That's what the coach said.'

'Then why were you watching me?' she asked.

'You don't know?'

'No,' she said with annoyance. 'I don't know.'

'You grew since last year.'

'Of course I did, stupid. So did you.'

'I don't mean like that,' he said, raising his hand over his head. 'I mean like that.' He held his two hands out in front of his chest.

'You mean – ?'

He nodded. 'Just like Marilyn Monroe. That's what all the fellows say.'

She flushed and involuntarily glanced down at herself. 'They're stupid,' she said, but at the same time she felt her nipples harden and a warm feeling come over her.

CHAPTER FOUR

THE BEACH CLUB at the Point opened for the season in mid-May. The summer people began coming from New York, first for weekends, and later, when school closed, they moved out full time. By then the club would be crawling with children during the week, and on weekends their fathers would be stretched out, burning from the sun, exhausted by an overdose of tennis or golf. And every Saturday night there would be a big buffet dinner and dance for the members.

A job at the club was a plum for the local kids. It was Bernie who first gave JeriLee the idea that she should apply.

'I'm going to work at the club this summer,' he announced.

'Doing what?'

'Lifeguard.'

'But you're not a good swimmer. Even I can swim rings around you?'

He smiled at her. 'They know that.'

'And they still hired you?'

He nodded. 'They figure I'm big. The kids'll listen to me.'

She nodded. At seventeen he was already well over six feet tall, with broad shoulders and a muscular body.

'Besides they've already got two crackerjack swimmers guarding the beach. That's where they really need them. I'll be working the pool. That's easy.'

'That's where all the city girls hang out,' she said, feeling a strange twinge of jealousy. 'You'll really have it made.'

He blushed. 'Cut it out, JeriLee. You know I don't look at other girls.'

'Even when they come on with those two-piece suits – you know, the French ones they call bikinis?'

'They still won't be you,' he said awkwardly. After a pause, he asked, 'Why don't you get a job out there?'

'Doing what?'

'I heard Mr Corcoran telling somebody they were looking for waitresses. It's not a bad job. Just a few hours at lunch and dinner. In between, your time is your own. We could see a lot of each other then.'

'I don't know,' she said indecisively. 'I don't think my father would like it. You know how he feels about the summer people.'

'Why don't you ask him?'

'What makes you think I can get the job?'

'Mr Corcoran said many of the girls he interviewed weren't pretty enough. He said it's very important for the club to have good-looking people around.' He looked at her. 'You'd have no trouble.'

She smiled. 'You really think so?'

He nodded.

'Maybe I will ask my father then.'

Her father agreed that it was a good idea. He had noticed her development and the sudden interest the boys had taken in her and had been concerned that when school was out there wouldn't be enough to keep her occupied. Once he had given his approval and arranged the interview with Mr Corcoran, her employment was assured, since the bank held the first mortgage on the club.

Until school closed she worked weekends only. Middays she served lunch by the pool. On Saturday night she was at the club-house dining-room.

Lunch was not a problem, because the menu was simple – hamburgers and hot dogs mostly and a few other sandwiches with side orders of cole slaw, potato salad and french fries. Once lunch was over, about three-thirty, she was on her own until six o'clock, when she reported to the main dining-room to help set up the tables.

The three other girls with whom she worked in the main dining-room had already put in two seasons at the club and knew the ropes. As a result, JeriLee found herself stuck with all the dirtiest jobs. Dinner was also made more difficult by the fact that the maitre d' and the chef were Italian brothers who created an air of panic by screaming at each other in Italian and at everyone else in broken English.

After school closed and the summer families were in residence, there was a dance every Saturday night. Small orchestras were brought from the city, and when the dining-room closed JeriLee and the other girls would drift over to the bar where the dance floor had been set up and sit on the terrace listening to the music and watching the members dance. Bernie was one of the two boys who bused the small cocktail tables set up around the dance floor, and she would wait for him to take her home, usually around one o'clock in the morning.

His father had gone in with him on the purchase of a 1949 Plymouth Belvedere convertible, and the payments took up almost all of Bernie's salary. During that summer, between his responsibilities for the car and his job, Bernie seemed to acquire a maturity along with the dark summer tan and the sunbleached hair. He was no longer a boy.

The girl members at the club also had their effect on him. As lifeguard at the pool, he was one of the few boys that was always around and so it was inevitable that they would try to exercise their charms on Bernie.

JeriLee saw it when in the afternoons she would change into a swimsuit and go out to the pool to cool off. The girls were always sending him for Cokes or cigarettes or towels or asking him to help them with their strokes or dives. She felt a twinge of jealousy as she saw Bernie glow under the attention. But she never said anything that would indicate she had noticed.

Instead she would slip into the pool and begin to swim back and forth in strong steady laps until her arms were like lead. Then she would climb out of the pool at the far end, away from his lifeguard's chair, stretch out on a towel on the concrete edge of the pool and read a book. When it was time for her to return to work, she would gather up her towel and leave the pool without a backward look.

After a while Bernie began to notice and one night on the way home he asked, 'How come you don't talk to me when you come down to the pool in the afternoon?'

'Keep your eyes on the road,' she said, not answering his question.

'You mad at me about something?'

'No,' she said shortly. 'You know the rules. Mr Corcoran doesn't like the help to mix when the members are around.'

'Come on, nobody pays attention to that and you know it.'

'Besides, you're always too busy.' Her voice took on a New York tone. 'Bernie, is my stroke too short? Bernie, I would love a Coke. Bernie, would you get me a light?'

'You sound like you're jealous.'

'I am not!'

'It's part of my job,' he said defensively.

'Of course,' she said with a note of sarcasm.

Silently Bernie followed the road that led out to the Point. He pulled into the parking area overlooking the Sound and stopped the motor. There were only a few other cars parked, their motors off and the lights out. It was still early. When the clubs and bars closed after two o'clock, the area would be full. A faint sound of music came from one of the car radios.

He turned and reached for her. She brushed his hand away. 'I'm tired, Bernie. I want to go home.'

'You are jealous.'

'I just don't like them making a fool of you, that's all.'

'They're not making a fool of me,' he said quickly. 'I'm supposed to be nice to the members.'

'Sure.'

'Besides there's not one of them that can hold a candle to you, JeriLee. They're all so phony and artificial.'

'Do you mean that?'

He nodded.

'Even Marian Daley?' Seventeen and blonde, Marian Daley had always been indulged by her doting parents. She wore the briefest bikinis at the club and was said to be even wilder than the New York girls.

'She's the phoniest of them all,' he said. 'The boys know she's the biggest teaser around.'

Without knowing it, he had said exactly the right thing. She softened. 'I was beginning to wonder,' she said. 'She never lets you alone.'

'She never lets any guy alone,' he said, clinching his case. He reached for her again.

She slid next to him, lifting her face for his kiss. His mouth was warm and soft. After a moment she let her head fall on his shoulder. 'It's so quiet here,' she said softly.

'Yes,' he said, raising her face to his and kissing her again. This time his lips were harder and more demanding.

She felt his excitement and her own response. Her heart began to pound. She opened her mouth slightly and his tongue found its way inside. A warmth ran through her, leaving her peculiarly weak. She pressed herself harder against him.

His hands slipped from her shoulders, cupping her breasts. He felt her nipples hardening. 'Oh, Jesus!' he moaned softly, fumbling with the buttons of her blouse.

Her hand caught his, stopping him. 'No, Bernie,' she said softly. 'Don't spoil it.'

'You're making me crazy, JeriLee,' he whispered. 'I just want to touch them. Nothing else.'

'It's not good. You know it leads to other things.'

'Oh, Christ!' he swore, suddenly angry. He pulled his hands away. 'You're a worse tease than Marian Daley. At least she lets a guy feel her tits.'

'Then you did go with her,' she accused.

'I did not!' he retorted, lighting a cigarette.

'I thought you weren't supposed to smoke.'

'I'm not in training,' he snapped.

'Then how do you know about her if you didn't go with her?'

'I know some of the guys who did. And I could have too.'

'Then why didn't you? If that's what you want?'

'I don't want her. I want you. You're my girl. I don't want any other.'

She saw that his face was hurt and troubled. 'Bernie, we're much too young to feel like that,' she said gently.

But even then she knew that there were currents running inside her that were bringing her closer and closer to the brink of her own sexual awareness.

CHAPTER FIVE

'YOU'RE NEW AROUND HERE, aren't you?'

She was lying face down at the side of the pool and when she opened her eyes the first thing she saw were his white city feet. She rolled to one side and, squinting against the sun, looked up.

The boy was tall, not as tall or broad as Bernie but wiry with curly black hair. He smiled. 'I'll buy you a Coke.'

She sat up. 'No thank you,' she said politely.

'Come on,' he said. 'We're all friends here.'

She shook her head. 'I work here. It's against the rules.'

'Stupid rules.' He grinned and held out his hand. 'I'm Walt.'

'I'm JeriLee,' she said. She took his hand and found herself being pulled to her feet.

'I'll buy you the Coke anyway,' he said. 'I'd like to see them try and stop me.'

'No. Please. I don't want to make waves.'

She picked up her towel. 'Besides I have to set the tables for dinner.' She started to walk away.

'Maybe I'll see you at the dance later.'

'We're not allowed to do that either.'

'Then we can go to a juke joint.'

'It will be too late. I'll have to go home then.'

'Something tells me that you don't want to go out with me.'

Without answering, she hurried away, a strange feeling knotting the pit of her stomach and creating a trembling in her legs.

She saw him again with a group of boys and girls in the dining-room that evening. He was seated next to Marian Daley and seemed engrossed in her conversation. When he glanced up and saw her walking by, he nodded and smiled. She went through the swinging doors into the kitchen feeling once more that strange sensation of weakness. She was glad that he wasn't at one of her tables.

'Coming to the dance?' Lisa, one of the waitresses, asked as they were putting away the last of the dishes.

JeriLee finished drying her hands. 'I don't think so. I think I'll just go home.'

'They say the singer with the new orchestra is just like Sinatra.'

'I'm too tired. If you see Bernie tell him that I've gone straight home. I can still make the eleven-thirty bus.'

'Okay, see you tomorrow.'

'Right,' JeriLee replied. 'Have fun.'

She heard the faint sound of the music as she walked past the clubhouse. In her mind she pictured the dance floor.

He was dancing with Marian Daley, who was pressing herself tightly against him. Her full breasts swelled over the top of her dress and she was smiling wet-lipped into his face. He was looking down at her and dancing even closer than before. Then he was whispering something in her ear. She laughed and nodded and a moment later they were leaving the floor on the way outside to his car.

It all seemed so real that for a second she expected to meet them in the parking lot. She began to hurry as if to avoid seeing them, then she stopped abruptly.

JeriLee, she said to herself, what's the matter with you? You must be going crazy!

'Going to the bus, JeriLee?' said a voice from behind her.

She turned. It was Martin Finnegan, one of the beach boys who bused in the dining-room on Saturday nights. They all thought he was rather strange because he kept mostly to himself. 'Yes, Martin.'

'Mind if I walk with you?'

'Okay.'

Silently he fell into step with her. They had walked almost a block before he spoke. 'Did you and Bernie have a fight?'

'No. What makes you think that?'

'I never saw you take the bus before.'

'I was just too tired to stay for the dance tonight. You never stay for the dances, do you?' she asked.

'No.'

'Don't you like to dance?'

'Sure.'

'Then, why don't you stay?'

'I have to be up early to go to work.'

'You don't start on the beach until ten-thirty.'

'I work at Lassky's Sunday mornings and have to be at the station at five to pick up the New York papers.' He looked at her. 'During the week you get the *Herald Tribune* every morning, but on Sundays you get the *Times* as well.'

'How do you know that?'

'I make up the papers for the home routes. I know exactly what papers everyone reads.'

'That's interesting.'

'It sure is. It's amazing how much you can learn about people just from reading what papers they read. For example, your father's boss, Mr Carson. His favorite paper is the *Daily Mirror.*'

'The *Daily Mirror*? I wonder why.'

He smiled. 'I know why. It's the only paper that has complete race results from all the tracks in the country. I often wonder what people would think if they knew that the president of the only bank in town played the horses?'

'Do you really think he does?'

'Lassky calls it the closet horse player's *Green Sheet*. That's strictly a horse-racing paper.'

They were almost at the bus stop. 'Are you going steady with Bernie?' he asked.

'Bernie is a good friend.'

'He says you're his girl.'

'I like Bernie but he has no right to say that.'

'Would you go out with another guy if he asked you?'

'I might.'

'Would you go out with me?'

She didn't answer.

'I haven't got the money that Bernie's got an' I haven't got a car but I could spring for a movie and a Coke one night if you want.' There was a hesitant tone in his voice.

'Maybe we'll do that one night,' she said gently. 'But if we do, we go dutch.'

'You don't have to do that. I could afford that much, really I can.'

'I know but that's the way I do it with Bernie.'

'You do?'

'Yes.'

'All right then,' he said, smiling suddenly. 'Gee, that makes me feel good. I wanted to ask you out so many times but I was always afraid to.'

She laughed. 'It wasn't too difficult, was it?'

'No,' he said. 'One night next week?'

'Sure.'

The bus squeaked to a stop in front of them and the door

opened. He insisted on paying her fare, and since it was only a dime she let him.

'Gee, JeriLee,' he said, 'you really are very nice.'

'You're not so bad yourself, Mr Finnegan.' She noticed that he had been carrying a book. 'What's that you're reading?'

'*The Young Manhood of Studs Lonigan*, by James T. Farrell.'

'I never heard of it. Is it any good?'

'I think so. In some ways it reminds me of my own family. It's about an Irish family on the South Side of Chicago.'

'Will you lend it to me when you're finished?'

'I got it from the library. I'll renew it and give it to you next week.'

She looked out the window. They were nearly at her stop. 'I get off here.'

He got up with her. 'I'll walk you to your house.'

'You don't have to do that. I'll be all right.'

'It's almost midnight,' he said firmly. 'I'll walk you home.'

'But you'll have to wait a half hour for another bus.'

'That's okay.'

At her door she turned to him. 'Thank you very much, Martin.'

He shook her hand. 'Thank you, JeriLee. Don't forget you said we could go to a movie.'

'I won't forget.'

'And I won't forget to give you the book,' he said. 'Good night.'

'Good night, Martin.' She watched him go down the porch steps, then turned and went into the house.

Her parents were in the living room watching television. They looked up as she came in. 'I didn't hear Bernie's car,' her mother said.

'I took the bus. I didn't hang around for the dance.'

'Are you all right, dear?' Veronica asked.

'I'm okay, Mom. Just a little tired, that's all.'

'Did you come home alone?' John asked. 'I don't know whether I like that this late at night. Next time maybe you ought to call and I can come and get you.'

'I wasn't alone. Martin Finnegan saw me to the door.' She sensed a change in her father's expression. 'He really was very nice. Very polite.'

'He may be, but his family has a bad reputation. His father

hasn't worked in years and he and his wife spent all their time in bars. I don't know how they manage to get along.'

'Martin isn't like that. Do you know he works at Lassky's every morning as well as at the Beach Club?'

'That's very nice, but all the same I would be careful about seeing too much of him. I don't want people to think that I approve of a family like that.'

'I don't see what business it is who we see or don't.'

'When you're a banker, everything you do is your neighbor's business. How else do you think you can get them to place their faith in you?'

She thought of Mr Carson and what Martin had told her. For a moment she was tempted to mention it to her father but then she kept silent. 'I'm tired,' she said. 'I'm going to take a hot bath and go to bed.'

She kissed her parents good night and went up the stairs to her room. She started the water in the tub and began to undress. She thought first of Martin and then of Walt. Again the peculiar warmth flowed through her and her legs felt strangely weak.

She stared at her naked body in the mirror over the dresser. The whiteness of her breasts contrasted with the tan of the rest of her body. Her nipples hurt and seemed to be trying to burst from her breasts. Wonderingly, she touched them. An excitement radiated through her body, culminating in a flush of heat in her pubis. She put a hand on the dresser for support.

She lowered herself into the warm tub and leaned back. There was an aching in her groin and a prickly sensation in her breasts that she had never felt before. The warm water flowed around her soothingly. Slowly she began to lather herself with soap. Her hand moved down her body, increasing her painful pleasure. Almost as if in a dream, she touched her pubis, the soap turning to lather on her fur. She leaned back, closing her eyes as the warm excitement mounted in her. The movements of her hand became almost automatic.

As Walt's face appeared before her all the muscles in her groin expanded, then contracted in an exquisite, agonizing flash of white fire. She almost screamed aloud in the throes of her first orgasm. Then it passed, leaving her limp, contented, yet strangely empty.

Is this what love is really like? she wondered to herself. And even into the night, while she lay sleepless in her bed, she kept on wondering.

CHAPTER SIX

SUDDENLY IT WAS everywhere around her – in the magazines, newspapers and books she read, in the movies she saw, in the ads and commercials on television, in the conversation of her friends. And it all pointed to a growing awareness of her own inner sexuality.

It seemed as if Walt had triggered a reaction that was pulling her down a road she was not sure she wanted to travel. Unsure of these new feelings, she fought the impulse to explore without really knowing what it was she wanted to discover.

Her dreams were filled with sexual fantasies involving everyone she knew, even her parents and her brother. And in the morning she would awake tired from the struggle with sleep.

She began to masturbate regularly. At first only in her bath, then in bed. But in a little while even that was not enough. The day between waking and sleeping was much too long. By this time she had become so expert in self manipulation that she could take herself off almost in a matter of minutes. At work she would disappear into the rest room several times a day and carefully lock the door. Frantically she would hike up her dress and pull down her panties. Then she would lean back on the toilet seat and give herself up to the sweet sensations her fingers gave her. A few minutes later she would be back at work as if nothing had taken place.

During this time of inner turmoil her surface appearance seemed almost unchanged. Perhaps she was more rigid in her relations with boys than she had been before, because she did not trust herself. She began to avoid contact with boys, even Bernie, whenever possible. Now she no longer waited for him to take her home but left early so that she could retire to the safety of her own bed.

One day Bernie finally confronted her. 'What's the matter, JeriLee? Did I do something wrong?'

She flushed. 'I don't know what you're talking about. There's nothing the matter.'

'It's more than two weeks since we've been alone. You never

let me take you home anymore.'

'I'm just too tired to wait around for you to get through, that's all.'

'You sure?'

'I'm sure.'

'Will you wait for me tonight then?'

She hesitated a moment, then nodded. 'Okay.' With a choking feeling that brought her close to tears, she went into the dining-room to begin setting the tables for dinner.

He turned the car into the parking area at the Point. 'Don't stop, Bernie,' she said tensely. 'I'm really very tired.'

'I just want to talk to you, that's all,' he said, switching off the motor. The music from the car radio drifted into the night air. He took out a cigarette and lit it.

'You're still smoking.'

'Yeah.' He looked across the seat at her. She was sitting up against the door as far away from him as she could get. 'Don't you like me anymore, JeriLee?'

'I like you just as much as I always did.'

'Is there someone else?' he asked. 'I know you went to the movies with Martin a couple of weeks back.'

She shook her head.

'I don't understand it,' he said in a puzzled voice.

'Take me home, Bernie.'

'JeriLee, I love you.'

That broke the dam. Suddenly she was crying, her hands covering her face, her body shaking with sobs.

He reached across the seat and drew her to him. 'JeriLee,' he asked softly, 'what's the matter?'

'I don't know,' she said, her voice muffled against his shoulder. 'I think I'm going crazy. I think such crazy thoughts.'

'What thoughts?'

'I can't talk about them. It's too horrible.' She regained her self-control. 'I'm sorry.'

'There's nothing to be sorry about. I only wish I could help.'

'Nobody can help. It's something I have to do myself.'

He placed a hand under her chin and, turning her face up to him, kissed her gently. At first her lips were soft and quivering then suddenly her tongue forced its way into his mouth.

For a moment he felt surprise, then he responded to her excitement. Roughly he pulled her closer, crushing her breasts against him.

Tentatively he let one hand cup her breast. He heard her breath quicken but she did not push him away as she always had. Emboldened by her lack of resistance, he slipped his hand into her dress and under her brassiere. He felt the warm flesh of her breast and the nipple hardening against his fingers. As she moaned and began to shiver, he felt himself straining painfully against his tight trousers. 'JeriLee!' he groaned, pushing her back across the seat almost covering her with his body.

He fumbled with her dress and one breast sprang free. He put his face down and took the thrusting nipple into his mouth. Grinding against her, his hardness pressed into her mound even through the cloth of his pants.

The sensation was too exquisite. His orgasm took him by complete surprise. He shuddered spastically, his ejaculation flowing uncontrollably into his trousers. 'Oh, Jesus!' he said. And stopped.

For a moment she continued moving, her eyes closed tightly. Then she too stopped and opened her eyes.

He stared into them. There was something in her expression he had never seen before. It was as if she had discovered and confirmed something she had always known. He sat up and looked down at her. He had soaked through his trousers and onto her dress. 'I'm sorry,' he said.

'That's all right,' she said quietly.

'I lost my head. I stained your dress.'

She sat up slowly. 'Don't worry,' she said. Suddenly she appeared very calm.

'It won't happen again, I promise.'

'I know,' she said. 'Now will you take me home?'

'You're not angry with me, are you?'

'No, Bernie, I'm not angry with you,' she said softly. Then she smiled and kissed his cheek quickly. 'Thank you.'

'For what?'

'For helping me to understand.'

He drove her home without knowing what she meant.

Oddly enough it was easier after that. Having confirmed her own worst suspicions about herself, she began to accept her own sexuality. Unfortunately she had no one to talk to. Her mother would be the last person in whom she would confide.

Veronica was part of that prewar generation in which the

rules were strict and simple. Good girls didn't, bad girls were punished or made pregnant. In her own bed she was always reserved and proper. Even with her first husband, JeriLee's father, who had the capacity to arouse her to a point almost beyond her control, she managed to stop just before she came to orgasm. And she never felt the lack. A good woman had many other things to occupy her mind. Sex was incidental; the important things were to keep a good home and bring up a proper family. And she was fortunate that her second husband was as conservative as she was.

To his great disappointment, John Randall had not gone to war. He had volunteered but had always been turned down. And so while others left for the service he remained in his job at the bank and, as one of the few younger men, almost automatically gained promotions. Veronica Gerraghty had first come to work at the bank during the war while her husband was away. And even then he had been very impressed with her.

She was not like most of the young married girls who told you how much they missed their husbands while hinting at dates and promising other things. She was quiet and pleasant and smiled often, but it was a friendly smile, not an invitation. After her husband came home he did not see her except when she would come to the bank to make a deposit or a withdrawal. On those occasions she would always stop at his desk and ask how he was. And she was always nice.

Then tragedy had struck. Her husband had been killed in a car accident on the highway just out of town late one night. There were rumors about the accident. Bob had always been wild. And that night he had been drinking and was seen with a woman who was known to have a bad reputation. But none of these facts ever appeared in the newspaper account of the death of Port Clare's first war hero.

John Randall remembered checking into the file following his death. For a man as erratic as he had been, Bob Gerraghty's affairs were in remarkably good order. At the time, he thought that Mrs Gerraghty was probably responsible. There was about eleven thousand dollars in the joint savings account, and seven hundred in checking. The records indicated that she owned more than two thousand dollars in war savings bonds at maturity value. The mortgage the bank held on their home for twenty-five thousand dollars was completely paid off by the insurance clause, as was another small personal loan of one thousand dollars that he had made just the month before. There was G.I. insurance for ten thousand dollars which had been converted to a civilian policy. He had heard there were several other small policies the amount of which he did not know. In addition the widow would be eligible for service and social security pensions for herself and the children. All of which meant that she fared far better than most people thought.

John Randall had sent Veronica a note of condolence and received a polite reply thanking him. A few weeks after the funeral she came to the bank and he helped her rearrange the accounts under her own name. After that he had not seen her for almost two months, when she came to ask if there was a job for her. While there was no great pressure on her financially, she said she would feel better if she knew she was helping to provide for herself. He thought that she displayed a great deal of good sense. If only more women were like her, they would have fewer problems. Fortunately, a job had just opened up and she began work the following week as the teller at the savings account window.

She had been there for little more than three months when he asked her out.

She hesitated. 'I don't know. It may be a little too soon. People might not like it.'

He nodded in appreciation. He knew what she was thinking. Mr Carson, the bank president, was a strict Presbyterian and had his own ideas of how his employees should act. He was continually railing about the erosive influence of modern thinking on the moralities of the country. 'I'll wait a little longer,' Randall promised.

'Thank you,' she said.

Another three months went by before they had their first date – a movie and dinner. She was home by eleven o'clock and he said good night to her at the front door. He nodded to himself as he went down the walk to his car. It was a lovely little house – neat, well kept and in a good neighborhood. She would make a very good wife for some man, even a future bank president.

They went to Niagara Falls on their honeymoon. On the first night John stood at the window in his new pajamas and silk robe, the gift bottle of champagne the hotel gave each newlywed couple icing in the bucket near him. The literature had promised a view of the falls but had neglected to mention that only a tiny corner was visible between the two hotels facing them. As he squinted into the cloudy sky he heard Veronica come into the room behind him.

She was wearing a silk chiffon nightgown with lace inset over her breasts under a transparent peignoir. There was an almost frightened look on her face.

'Would you like some champagne?' he asked.

She nodded.

Awkwardly he opened the bottle. The cork popped and ricocheted from the ceiling. He laughed. 'That's the way a good champagne can be told from a bad one. If the cork pops.'

She laughed.

He filled the two glasses and handed one to her. 'A toast,' he said. 'To us.'

They sipped the wine. 'It is good,' she said.

'Come here and look out the window,' he invited.

She looked into his eyes for a moment, then shook her head. 'I think I'll go to bed. I'm a little bit tired from the long drive.'

He watched her place her peignoir on a chair, get into bed and close her eyes. 'Is there too much light for you, dear?' he asked.

She nodded without opening her eyes.

He pressed the wall switch and went around to the other side of the bed. He could hear her soft breathing. Tentatively he put out a hand and touched her shoulder.

She did not move.

He turned her face toward him. In the faint light he saw that her eyes were open. 'You'll have to help me,' he said embarrassedly. 'I've never . . . you know . . . ' His voice failed.

'You mean – ?' she began.

'Yes,' he answered. 'I could have, I suppose, but I knew I could never bring myself to do it with anyone but my wife.'

'I think that's beautiful,' she said. Her fear was suddenly gone. At least he would not be like Bob, always comparing her with other women and always insisting that it would never be good until she got something out of it. She had made the right choice. John Randall would be a good husband. 'John,' she whispered.

'Yes?'

She reached out her arms to him. 'The first thing you do is come here and kiss me.'

Slowly she led him through the mysteries of her body until the trembling eagerness in him was almost more than he could stand, then she closed her hand around his bursting shaft and guided him into her.

With an involuntary groan, he came almost immediately in a long shuddering orgasm. She slipped her hand between his legs as Bob had taught her and cupped his testicles, applying a slight pressure to make sure they were completely emptied. He moaned again at her touch. Then he was silent, breathing heavily. She moved out from under him.

He touched her face in wonder. 'I never felt anything like that before.'

She didn't answer.

'Was it good for you?'

'Very good.'

'I heard that if a man came too quickly the woman didn't get anything out of it.'

She smiled. 'That's not true. Maybe certain kinds of women. But not normal ones. This is everything I ever wanted.'

'You're not just saying that?' he asked anxiously.

'I mean it. I never had anything as good, even with Bob. I'm very satisfied.'

'I'm glad,' he whispered.

She bent forward and kissed him. 'I love you.'

'I love you.' A note of wonder came into his voice. 'You know . . . I think . . . I'm getting excited again.'

'Try not to think about it. More than once a night can cause serious strain. You might hurt yourself.'

'Touch me,' he said. 'I'm hard again.'

She let him put her hand on him. He seemed carved from rock. She was surprised. Even Bob had never recovered so rapidly.

'I think this once it won't do any harm,' he said. 'Put me inside you.'

Almost reluctantly she guided him into her again. This time he lasted slightly longer but still exploded in a few minutes. He groaned in a strange combination of pleasure and pain as his almost empty testicles strained to express the semen.

He rolled onto his side, looking at her. He was still breathing heavily. 'You know you may be right,' he said.

'I am right,' she said. She kissed his cheek. 'Now try to get some sleep,' she said gently. 'It will be all right tomorrow.'

And from that moment on that was the way it was.

CHAPTER SEVEN

WHEN HE SAW HER, Bernie came down from his lifeguard's perch at the deep end of the pool. He walked over to where she had spread out her towel. 'You're not angry about last night, JeriLee?' he asked.

She smiled at him. 'Should I be?'

'I didn't mean to – '

'It's okay,' she said quickly. 'Nothing really happened. Besides I liked it too.'

'JeriLee!'

'Is there anything wrong in that? Didn't you like it?'

He didn't answer.

'Why shouldn't I?' she asked. 'Boys aren't the only ones who have feelings.'

'But, JeriLee,' he protested, 'girls are supposed to be different.'

She laughed. 'If they are, there are an awful lot of girls doing something they don't like.'

'I don't understand you, JeriLee. One day you're one way, the next another.'

'At least I conform as far as that is concerned,' she said. 'Girls are said to be changeable.' She laughed. 'You ruined my dress. I told my mother I spilled something on it in the kitchen.'

'It's not funny. I felt guilty as hell about it all night.'

'Don't be. Next time just be more careful.'

'There won't be a next time, JeriLee. I won't lose my head again.'

She looked at him quizzically.

'I mean it. I respect you too much.'

'You mean you won't do it even if I want you to?'

'You don't want it, JeriLee,' he said with conviction.

'If that's what you think, why did I let you do it?'

'Because you lost your head too.'

'No, Bernie, that's not the reason. I let you do it because I wanted you to do it. Suddenly I discovered why I was feeling so strangely, why I was always nervous and upset. It's because I was trying to run away from the feelings inside me.'

'You don't know what you're saying, JeriLee.'

'I'm being honest, Bernie. I'm not pretending to myself that I didn't want it or like it. Maybe now I'll find a way to cope with it.'

'JeriLee, nice girls don't feel like that.' He was upset. 'Maybe you ought to talk to somebody.'

'Who? My mother?' JeriLee asked sarcastically. 'I can't talk to her. She would never understand.'

'Then what are you going to do?'

'The same thing you're doing. Maybe in time we'll know what it's all about.'

He walked back to his stand without answering. All that afternoon he watched her. Nothing was right anymore. He was sorry he had started the whole thing with her.

'Did you finish the book?' Martin asked when she returned it to him.

'Yes.'

'What did you think?'

'There were parts of it I didn't understand. Most of the time I felt sorry for all of them. They seemed so lost and unhappy no matter what they did.'

'What is it you didn't understand?'

'You said that it reminded you of your own family. You're nothing like Studs Lonigan.'

'I could be if I allowed myself to drink the way he did,' Martin said. 'And my parents are as hypocritical as his. They're always preaching at me but they don't live the way they say I should.'

'Did you ever make it with a girl the way he did?'

Martin blushed. 'No.'

'Do you do anything else?'

'I . . . I don't know what you mean,' he stammered.

'I think you do.'

He turned fiery red. 'Golly, JeriLee, people don't ask questions like that.'

'You're blushing,' she said. 'Do you like it?'

He didn't answer.

'How often do you do it?'

'That's not fair, JeriLee. How would you like it if I asked you a question like that?'

'Maybe you're right,' she said after a moment. 'I went over to the library myself and took out two more books by James Farrell. You know, I like him. At least he's honest.'

'He's a good writer,' Martin said. 'I tried to get my father to read him but he wouldn't. He said he'd heard all about him from Father Donlan in church, and that he had been excommunicated because of the dirty words in his book.'

JeriLee nodded. 'I know. When I took out the books, the librarian looked at me kind of funny. She said she thought I might be too young for James Farrell.'

He laughed. 'Sometimes I wonder what they think we are. Children?'

JeriLee stood on the terrace listening to the music through the open doors of the lounge. The colored orchestra had been playing at the club for the last several weeks. At first some members had objected. They said that the only reason Mr Corcoran had hired them was because they were cheaper than the white orchestras. But from the first night they played, all except the diehards admitted they were the best orchestra the Beach Club had ever had.

JeriLee and Lisa were sitting on the railing when the music stopped and the orchestra came out on the terrace. They moved off to one side, talking among themselves. After a few moments the boy singer walked over to the railing and stood looking out over the water.

'That last number was very beautiful,' JeriLee said to him. 'You sounded just like Nat King Cole.'

'Thank you.'

She had the vague feeling that he did not like her compliment. 'I bet everybody says that. You must get sick of hearing it.'

He turned to look at her. His eyes were appraising. 'That's whut folks want to hear,' he said in a soft accent.

She felt the faint antagonism. 'I'm sorry,' she said, 'I meant it as a compliment.'

He seemed to relax. 'We have to give the people whut they want.'

'There's nothing wrong in that.'

'I guess not,' he admitted.

'I'm JeriLee Randall,' she said. 'I work here.'

'I'm John Smith. I work here too.' Then he laughed.

She laughed with him. 'John Smith. Is that really your name?'

His eyes brightened. 'No. But my pappy always warned me. Never tell white folk your real name.'

'What is your name?'

'Fred Lafayette.'

'Fred, I'm pleased to meet you,' she said, holding out her hand.

He shook her hand, then looked into her face. 'JeriLee, I'm pleased to meet you.'

'And I really do like your singing,' she said.

'Thank you.' He was smiling now. The orchestra was filing back into the room. 'I got to go now. See you later.'

'He even looks like Nat King Cole,' Lisa whispered as he went inside.

'Yes,' JeriLee replied thoughtfully. She felt the warm excitement and her hand still tingled from his touch. She wondered if it would be like that with every boy she met or whether there had to be some special attraction. She turned to her friend. 'Lisa, will you answer an honest question?'

'Sure,' Lisa answered.

'Are you a virgin?'

'JeriLee! What kind of question is that?'

'Are you?'

'Of course,' she said indignantly.

'Then you wouldn't know.'

'What?'

'What it's like?'

'No,' Lisa said shortly.

'Don't you ever wonder?'

'Sometimes.'

'Did you ever ask anybody about it?'

'No,' Lisa answered. 'Who is there to ask?'

'I know what you mean.'

'I guess it's something every girl has to find out for herself,' Lisa said.

JeriLee thought her friend had, in her own way, just about summed it up.

CHAPTER EIGHT

THE SUN BEAT DOWN, spreading its warmth through her body. She dozed, her face resting on her arms, her eyes closed against the light. She knew the voice the moment he spoke even though she had heard it only once and that almost a month ago.

'Hi, JeriLee. I'm back and I still want to buy you a Coke.'

She looked at the feet first. They had now been bronzed by the sun. 'Where have you been?' she asked.

'In California, visiting my mother,' he said. 'They're divorced.' He paused. 'Are you still worried about the rules?'

She shook her head. As the season went on, the rules about fraternization between employees and members had been relaxed. She learned from Lisa that it was the same every year. She rose to her feet. He was taller than she remembered.

He took her arm casually as they walked toward the cabana bar. It seemed that an electric current ran through his hand, creating a tingling where he touched her. She felt a slight weakness in her legs and a knotting in her stomach. She wondered why it was stronger with him than with anyone else.

He gestured at one of the small tables under an umbrella. 'Sit here,' he said. 'It's cooler than at the bar. I'll bring the drinks.'

'I'll have a cherry Coke,' she said.

He returned in a moment with the Coke for her and a can of beer for himself. He sat down opposite her and smiled. 'Cheers,' he said and took a large swallow from the can.

She sipped at the Coke through the straw. He was older than she had thought. He had to be over eighteen to get a beer.

'Is it good?' he asked.

She nodded.

'Has it been good so far this summer?'

'Okay.'

'The weather, I mean.'

'I know.'

An awkward silence descended upon them. After a few minutes he spoke. 'You're the first person I looked for when I came in.'

Her gaze was direct. 'Why?'

He smiled. 'Maybe it's because you're so pretty.'

'There are prettier girls.' She was neither coquettish nor dissembling. It was merely a statement of fact.

'That's a matter of opinion,' he said, smiling. 'You see, I didn't forget your name. I bet you forgot mine.'

'Walt.'

'What's the rest of it?'

'You never told me the rest of it.'

'Walter Thornton Jr. What's the rest of your name?'

'Randall,' she answered. She looked at him. 'Is your father the – ?'

'Yes. Do you know him?'

'Not really. He just sat next to me on the bus every morning on his way to the station.'

He laughed. 'That's my father all right. He won't drive.'

'Is he here now?' she asked. 'I heard he had gone to Europe.'

'He came in yesterday. I flew in from Los Angeles to meet him.'

'I didn't know he was a member,' she said. 'I never saw him in the club.'

'He never comes to the club. I don't think he's ever been here. He bought the membership for my mother. She used to complain she had nothing to do while he was away.'

'Oh,' she said, disappointed. 'I thought I might be able to talk with him. I want to be a writer and I think he's really good.'

'I can get Dad to talk with you.'

'Thank you,' she said.

He smiled. 'Now maybe I can get you to talk to me.'

'I am talking to you.'

'Not really. Mostly you're just answering questions.'

'I don't know what to talk about.'

'That's honest.' He laughed. 'What are you interested in?'

'I told you. I want to be a writer.'

'Besides that. Do you like sports? Dancing?'

'Yes.'

'That's not much of an answer.'

'I'm afraid I'm not very interesting. I'm not like the girls you know.'

'How do you know that?'

'They know how to have a good time. I don't. Port Clare isn't a very interesting place to grow up in. Nothing much ever happens here.'

'Are you coming to the dance tonight?' he asked.

She nodded.

'Maybe I'll see you there?'

'Okay.' She got to her feet. 'Thanks for the Coke. I've got to go now.'

'See you later.' He watched her walk toward the clubhouse. She was right about one thing. She was not like the other girls he knew. In one way or another they were all cockteasers and, oddly enough, he had the feeling that was a game she would never play.

The muscles of her stomach relaxed as she walked back to the clubhouse. It was strange the effect he had on her. The sudden intense awareness of self, and the rising sexual heat. All the time she had been with him she was aware of the constant wetness between her legs.

She went into the locker room, stripped off her swimsuit and got under a cold shower. But it didn't seem to help. While soaping herself she touched her pubis and almost sank to her knees with the quick intensity of her orgasm.

After a moment she regained her self-control and leaned her head against the cold tile wall of the shower stall. There was something wrong with her. Very wrong. She was sure that none of the girls she knew were going through what she was.

'Looks like you goin' to lose youah little friend, Fred,' Jack, the drummer, said, gesturing with his stick at the dance floor.

JeriLee and Walt were moving by in a slow fox trot. He was holding her close, too close, Fred thought. There was an expression on her face he had never seen before, an intensity he could almost sense. Abruptly he segued into a fast Lindy. The orchestra stumbled for a moment, then caught up with him.

Jack grinned. 'Ain't goin' to he'p. You jes been playin' it too cool, man.'

'She's not like that,' Fred whispered fiercely. 'She's just a straight kid.'

'I ain't arguin'. She straight all right. But she also ready. That sweet li'l white pussy is ripe an' beggin' to be picked.'

'What makes you such an expert?' Fred asked angrily.

'Becuz I only got two things on my mind, man. Drums an'

pussy. If'n I ain't thinkin' about one, I'm thinkin' 'bout t'other.' He laughed. 'You better believe it.'

Fred looked back at the dance floor but JeriLee and Walt were gone.

The moment she came into his arms on the dance floor he had felt her breasts pressing against him through his thin shirt. She wasn't wearing a brassiere. He was sure of it. Instantly he felt himself growing hard and tried to move his hips slightly away from her so that she would not know. But she moved along with him, sighed slightly and rested her head on his shoulder.

'Hey,' he said.

She raised her face.

'Do you always dance like this?'

'I don't know. I just follow,' she said.

'Do you know what you're doing to me?' he asked. 'I'm getting very excited.'

Her eyes were level. 'I didn't know I was doing that. I thought you were doing it to me.'

'You mean you're excited too?'

'I think if you let go of me I'd fall. My legs feel so weak.'

He stared at her. He had been wrong. All the time he had thought she was just an innocent little girl. Abruptly the orchestra broke into a fast number. He stopped and looked down at her. 'JeriLee, let's get out of here.'

'Okay,' she said and followed him through the open terrace doors. They cut across the lawn toward the parking lot. She didn't speak until he held the door of his car open for her. 'Where are we going?'

'Some place we can be alone,' he said.

She nodded as if she had known that was what he would say and got into the car. In ten minutes they pulled into the driveway of a small house just off the beach.

He cut the motor and looked at her. 'There's no one at home. My father won't be in from New York until tomorrow and the housekeeper's gone home.'

She looked at him without comment.

'Don't you have anything to say?'

She looked down at her hands folded in her lap, then back at him. 'I'm a little frightened.'

'Of what?'

'I don't know.'

'Don't be,' he said, not knowing her real fears. 'No one will know you're here. The nearest neighbor is a half mile down the beach.'

She didn't answer.

'There's a heated pool out back,' he said. 'It's great to swim there at night. Would you like that?'

She nodded. 'But I don't have a swimsuit.'

He smiled. 'That's one of the nice things about swimming at night. It's dark.' He got out of the car and walked around to open the door. 'Coming?'

She suddenly laughed. 'Why not?'

'What are you laughing about?'

'I'm afraid you'd never understand.' For the first time in a month she was beginning to feel better. It was almost as if she had always known that this was the way it would happen.

They walked through the house and out the back door to the pool. He pointed to a small cabana. 'You can leave your things in there.'

'Okay,' she said, starting toward it. 'Where are you going?' she asked when she noticed he was heading back into the house.

'I'll be back in a minute,' he said. 'I just want to get a few cold drinks.'

Entering the cabana, JeriLee looked at herself in the large mirror over the vanity table. There was a calmness about her face that surprised her because it did not reflect the excitement seething within her. Quickly she unfastened her blouse and her breasts sprang free. The nipples were swollen and distended. Softly she touched them. They still ached but the touch was pleasant. Actually that was why she had not worn her brassiere. It had hurt her breasts too much. Gently she pressed her breasts again and felt the pleasure run down into her groin. She slipped out of her skirt. Her panties were moist and she could see the dark pubic hairs clearly in the wet nylon material. Slowly she stepped out of them and spread them neatly on the bench so that they could dry.

She wondered what he was thinking. She remembered how hard he had been when they were dancing, so hard that it hurt as he pressed against her mound. Twice she had almost stumbled and fallen as she climaxed during the dance. Each time she wondered if he had known what had happened, but there were no signs that he did.

She heard him call from outside. 'I'm back. Are you coming out?'

She pressed the light switch, plunging the cabana into darkness, and opened the door. He was spreading some towels on the large chaises near the far end of the pool. He was still dressed, his back toward her. Silently she slipped into the water. He was right, it was warm and soft.

He turned quickly. 'That's not fair,' he said. 'You got in before I could even see you.'

She laughed. 'You're the one that's not fair. You're not even undressed yet.'

He bent over the table and turned on the portable radio he had brought with him. The music drifted softly across the pool. With his back to her, he undressed quickly, dropping his clothes to the ground, then swiftly he turned and, almost before she could catch a glimpse of him, dove in. He came up on the other side of the pool.

'How do you like it?' he asked. 'Is the water warm enough?'

'I like it. This is the first time I've ever gone skinny dipping. It feels good. Better than when you have a suit on.'

'That's what my father says. He says that if nature meant for us to have clothes we would have been born with them.'

'Your father might be right,' she said. 'I just never thought about it.'

'My father has a lot of peculiar ideas. About everything. He says if people would only learn to be honest with themselves it would be the end of most of the problems in the world.'

'Are you honest with yourself?' she asked.

'I try to be.'

'Do you think you could be honest with me?'

'I think so.'

'Why did you bring me here?'

'I wanted to be alone with you. Why did you come?'

She didn't answer. Instead she swam away toward the deep end of the pool. He swam after her. Abruptly she turned under water and came up on the other side of him. He laughed and caught her at the shallow end.

He held her by the arm. 'You didn't answer my question?'

Her eyes looked into his. 'Because you weren't being honest with me.'

'Why do you think I brought you here?' he asked.

'Because I thought – ' she hesitated a moment and then, unable to think of another way to say exactly what she meant, she went on – 'you wanted to fuck me.'

He was startled. 'If you thought that why did you come?'

'Because I wanted you to fuck me.'

Abruptly he let go of her arm and climbed out of the pool. He picked up a towel and tied it around his waist and made himself a rum and Coke. He sipped it without speaking.

She rested her arms on the edge of the pool. 'Are you angry with me? Did I say anything wrong?'

He took another swallow of his drink. 'Christ, JeriLee, you sound cheap and vulgar.'

'I'm sorry. I was only trying to be honest. I felt you against me while we were dancing and I thought that was what you wanted.'

'But girls don't act like that,' he protested. 'You just don't make it with every guy that gets a hard-on for you.'

'I don't.'

'But the way you talk. What's a fellow supposed to think?'

'Is that what you think?'

'I don't know what to think. I never had a girl talk like that to me before.'

Suddenly the warm feeling left her and she was perilously close to tears. She was silent for a moment. When she spoke her voice was calm. 'It's getting late, Walt. I think you better take me home. My parents will be wondering what happened to me.'

He let her out of the car in front of her house, but made no move to get out of the car himself. 'Good night, Walt,' she said.

'Good night,' he said abruptly. Then he put the car into gear and drove off, leaving her on the sidewalk. Slowly she went into the house.

Her father looked up from the television set as she came in. She kissed his cheek. 'Where's Mom?'

'She was tired and went up to bed,' he said. 'You're home early. Who brought you?'

'A boy named Walt. He's one of the members.'

'Is he nice?'

'Yes.' She started from the room, then stopped. 'Dad.'

'Yes?'

'Is there such a thing as being too honest?'

'That's a strange question, darling. Why do you ask?'

'I don't know. It seems to me that whenever I answer a question truthfully my friends get upset with me.'

He looked at her thoughtfully. 'Sometimes people don't want to hear the truth. They would rather live with illusion.'

'Is it always like that?'

'In a way I guess it is. I try to be as honest as I can with people. But there are times when it's not always possible.'

'Are you honest with me?'

'I hope I am.'

'Do you love me?'

He reached over and turned off the television set. Then he turned and held out his arms to her. 'I think you know I do.'

She knelt in front of his chair and laid her head on his chest. He closed his arms around her and held her quietly against him. For a long while they did not speak.

Finally in a tight small voice of hurt she said, 'You know, Dad, it's not easy growing up to be a woman.'

He kissed her cheek and tasted the salty wetness of the tears on her cheeks. A curious sadness came over him. 'I know, darling,' he said gently. 'But then I think that it's not easy to grow up to be anything.'

CHAPTER NINE

IT WAS LIKE a storm that had passed. For weeks the pressure of having to know and understand the nature of her sexual being had been tearing her apart. Then one morning she awakened and the urgency was over.

She knew what she did not know. But she was no longer driven by the need to force the knowledge. The things she felt were part of her expanding consciousness and somehow she knew she would experience them all in their own time. She became more herself, more relaxed, more able to enjoy the simple exchange of being with other people.

Once again she and Bernie could be friends. Now when they parked and petted at the Point she was able to respond without having to push further and further into her desires. Sex no longer permeated her every thought. She knew that it would come in time. But it would come when she was equipped to deal with it as part of her total being.

And it was not with Bernie alone that she had dates. Martin too was a good friend. They would sit on her porch for hours talking about the books they had read and discussing different people in town. Often they shared laughter at the ridiculous postures that some people assumed in order to seem important. Once she even let Martin read a short story she had written.

It was about a mayor of a small town who during the war became depressed because all the towns around him had war heroes and his small town did not. So he made up his mind to make a hero out of the first returning veteran. It happened to be a man who had gotten a medical discharge and had never been near the front. Nevertheless he was given a welcoming ceremony at which everything went wrong. In a way it was very much like the story of her real father but with a twist. In the midst of the proceedings, two M.P.s appeared and took the hero away, because it seemed that he had faked his discharge from a psycho ward.

'It's great. JeriLee,' he told her enthusiastically after she'd finished it. 'I recognize almost everybody. You should send it away to a magazine.'

She shook her head. 'I'm not ready yet. I still feel there are too many things wrong with it. Besides I'm working on another I think might be better.'

'What's it about?'

'It's about a girl like me. About growing up in a town like this.'

'Can I read it when you're finished?'

'It may not be finished for a long time. There are too many things I have to learn before I can begin to write about them.'

'I understand that,' Martin said. 'Hemingway says the best writing comes from gut experience.'

'I don't like Hemingway. He knows nothing about women. He seems not to care about them at all.'

'Who do you like?'

'Fitzgerald. At least he feels for the women characters in his books as much as he does for the men.'

'To me, all of his men seem strange, weak sort of,' Martin said after a moment. 'They seem to be afraid of women.'

'Funny. I think that about Hemingway. His men always seem to me more afraid of women because they are always trying to prove themselves as men.'

'I have to think about that,' he said, getting to his feet. 'Now I'd better be getting home.'

'Everything all right there now?' she asked. They had long since dropped pretenses and she was openly inquiring about the problems he had with his parents.

'A little better,' he said. 'At least they're not drinking as much now that Dad's got that job at the gas station.'

'I'm glad.' She rose from the chair. 'Good night.'

Martin stood looking at her without moving.

She touched her cheek self-consciously. 'Is there anything wrong?'

'No.'

'Then what are you staring at?'

'You know I never realized it before. You really are very beautiful.'

Another time she might have smiled but there was a sincerity in his voice that moved her. 'Thank you,' she said simply.

'Very beautiful,' he repeated, then he smiled and ran down the steps. 'Good night, JeriLee,' he called.

Bit by bit JeriLee's popularity was growing. There was something in her that seemed to attract friends. Boys and girls alike. Maybe it was because she dealt with each of them on their own terms and within their own frame of reference. At the same time she was still a very private person. In the end they liked to talk to her because they all felt that she really listened.

Once the season was in full swing, the club stayed open every night for dinner and there was a dance on Wednesdays as well as on Fridays and Saturdays. Since it became impractical for the musicians to return to the city every night, Mr Corcoran put them up in a small cottage out in back of the tennis courts. The back of the cottage faced out on the parking lot, so they did not have to come through the club in order to get to the bandstand.

JeriLee, who now worked late on Wednesday nights, was on the terrace railing sipping a Coke and talking to Fred between sets when Walt came out the terrace doors.

'JeriLee,' he said, ignoring Fred completely.

It had been more than a month since that night at his house and this was the first time he had spoken to her. 'Yes?'

'I have some friends down from school and we're getting up a beach party. I thought you might like to join us.'

JeriLee looked at Fred. There was no expression on his face. She turned back to Walt. 'Do you know Fred?'

'Yes. Hello, Fred.'

'Waltuh.' Fred's voice was as expressionless as his face.

'It'll be fun,' Walt said. 'And if the Sound is too cold, there's always the pool at my house.'

'I don't think so,' she said. 'I have to be here early tomorrow. I'm working lunch.'

'Come on, JeriLee. We won't be too late. We'll just have a few drinks and a few laughs, that's all.'

'No, thank you,' she said politely. 'As a matter of fact I was thinking of leaving early. There's still time for me to catch the eleven-thirty bus.'

'You don't have to do that. We can drop you off at your house.'

'I don't want to trouble you. It's out of your way.'

'Not much. Besides it's no trouble.'

'Okay.'

'I'll get the guys,' Walt said and went back into the cocktail lounge.

Fred looked at her. 'You got a thing for that boy?'

JeriLee thought for a moment. 'I thought I did. But not now.'

'He's angry with you,' Fred said.

She was puzzled. 'How do you know?'

'I feel it. But I could be wrong. He also don't like me much. But that might be because he don't like black folk in general.'

'I hope you're wrong. He might be a little spoiled but I wouldn't want to think that about him.'

It was time for the orchestra to go back to work. Fred looked at her. 'See you on the weekend?'

'Sure.' She nodded. 'Sing pretty for the people.'

He smiled. 'I always do.'

'Good night, Fred.'

'Night, JeriLee.'

The sound of music began to drift through the doors just as Walt came out.

'Okay, JeriLee. Let's go.' He started down the terrace steps. 'We can cut across here to the parking lot.'

'What about your friends?'

'They already went to the car with Marian Daley.'

She followed him down the steps and they crossed the tennis courts to the parking lot. She could hear the laughter coming from his car. 'Sure I wouldn't be spoiling anything?' she asked. 'I can still make the bus. I don't mind.'

'I said it was okay, didn't I?' He sounded annoyed.

'Okay,' she said.

Silently they walked the rest of the way to the car. It was an open convertible. Marian and two boys were already in the back seat. 'What took you so long?' one of the boys called as they came up.

'I had to sign the bar check,' Walt said. He opened the door of the car. 'Fellows, this is JeriLee. JeriLee, Joe and Mike Herron. They're brothers. You know Marian.'

JeriLee nodded. 'Hi.'

Marian seemed cool, but both boys smiled and one of them held a bottle up to JeriLee. 'Join the party,' he said. 'Have a drink.'

'No, thank you.' JeriLee said.

'I'll have one,' Walt said. He took the bottle and held it to his mouth. He took a long swallow, then handed the bottle back to the boy. 'That's good rum.'

'It should be.' The boy laughed. 'Your father has nothing but the best.'

Walt closed the door and got in behind the wheel. He started the motor and gunned the car out of the parking lot. They turned down the highway in the direction that led away from her house.

JeriLee looked at him. 'We're going the wrong way.'

'I thought I'd drop them off first before I took you home,' he said.

She didn't answer. A sound of laughter came from the back seat. She turned around. Both boys were trying to unbutton Marian's blouse and she was giggling while slapping their hands away. 'Not fair.' She laughed. 'It's two against one.'

JeriLee turned back in the seat. She glanced at the speedometer. The needle was up around seventy. 'Better slow down,' she said. 'The highway patrol is on the road tonight.'

'I can handle them,' Walt said grimly.

There was no sound from the back seat now. She glanced into the rearview mirror. Marian seemed to have disappeared. Involuntarily she turned and looked into the back seat. Marian had her head in Joe's lap. It was a moment before she realized what the girl was doing. She was holding Joe's penis in her hand and taking it in her mouth.

She turned back quickly, a curiously sick feeling in the pit of her stomach. Somehow she knew this was not the way it should be. She knew what girls and boys did in cars but this was not at all what she had imagined. She couldn't wait until Walt dropped them off and took her home.

Walt pulled the car into the driveway and cut the motor. 'Okay,' he said. 'Everybody out.' He opened his door and came around to her side.

'You said you were going to take me home.'

'I will,' he said. 'What's the big deal? Last time you couldn't wait.'

'Last time was different. You were different.'

Marian and the two boys were out of the car. 'Come on.' Marian laughed. 'Don't be a party pooper.'

'Just one drink, then I'll take you home. I promise,' Walt said.

Reluctantly she got out of the car and followed them into the house. They went right through to the pool. With a loud whoop the boys dropped their clothes and dove into the water. 'It's great,' Mike shouted. 'Come on in.'

She turned, looking for Walt. She saw a light go on in the house as he went into the kitchen. A moment later music came from the portable radio on the table near the pool. Marian was dancing by herself to the music.

Walt came out with a tray of Cokes and a bucket of ice. He picked up the bottle of rum near the radio and quickly mixed the drinks. He held one toward Marian. She took it and began to drink it quickly. He held one out to JeriLee.

'No, thank you.'

'You're not much fun, are you?'

'I'm sorry. I told you I wanted to go right home.'

'Well, you can damn well wait until I have a drink,' he said angrily, raising his glass.

'Come on, JeriLee,' Marian said. 'Don't be a pill. You're among friends.'

'No, thank you,' she said again. She started toward the house.

Walt put a hand on her arm. 'Where do you think you're going?'

'I can get the bus on the highway,' she said levelly.

'I said I'd take you home,' he snapped. 'Isn't my word good enough for you?'

Before she could answer him, she felt a pair of hands grab her ankles and her feet went out from under her as she was dragged into the pool. She came up spluttering and angry and striking out at the boy nearest her.

'She wants to play,' she heard one of the boys say. Then two pairs of hands grabbed her shoulders and pushed her down into the water again. She tried to wriggle free and she felt her dress rip as their hands caught her. Then she went under again. She came up gasping and held on to the sides of the pool.

She looked up at Walt through eyes burning with tears. 'Please take me home,' she cried.

'I will,' he said, raising the glass to his lips. 'As soon as your clothes are dry.'

CHAPTER TEN

BERNIE CAME UP to Fred on the terrace. 'Is JeriLee out here?'
'No.'
'If you see her, tell her that her father called. He wants her to bring home a quart of ice cream.' Bernie started back.
Fred stopped him. 'When did he call?'
'Just now. I picked it up in the bar.'
'That's funny. How long does it take from here to her house?'
'About ten minutes by car, half hour by bus.'
'Then she should have been home by now. She left more than an hour ago.' A curious feeling of dread came over him. 'You know where the Thornton kid lives?'
'On the other side of the Point. Why?'
'He was supposed to drop her off home. But he was higher than a kite and so were his two friends. I saw them inside knocking back rum and Cokes like water. He wanted her to join him at a beach party but she said she wanted to go home.'
Bernie stared at him. 'I saw Marian Daley leave with those two boys. She was trying to get another girl to go with them but the girl wouldn't.'
'I don't like it, JeriLee should have been home by now.' He looked at Bernie. 'You got a car?'
The two boys stared at each other. 'I'll get the keys and meet you in the parking lot,' Bernie said.

She was crying, lying huddled and naked on the grass beside the pool, trying to cover herself. She sensed a movement and looked up.
Joe was bending over her. 'Stop bawling,' he said in an annoyed voice. 'It isn't as if you never did this before.'
'I never – '
'You did,' he said positively. 'Walt told us about the time you came here with him.'
'Nothing happened,' she cried. 'Honest, nothing happened.'
'You never stop lying, do you?' He turned and shouted at

Walt. 'You better get over here and do something about this cunt or I'm goin' to belt her.'

Walt came up. He still had a glass in his hand and was weaving. 'Come on, JeriLee,' he said in a placating voice. 'We just want to have a little fun. Take a drink of this. It'll make you feel better.'

'No.'

There was a sound from the other side of the pool. Joe turned around. 'Well, lookee over there.' He laughed.

She looked across the pool. Marian and his brother were coupled on the ground. She could see the frenzied movements of the boy, and the moaning sounds they made echoed in the night.

'Ain't that pretty?' Joe asked. 'They're makin' it. How about comin' off your high horse and we can have a real party?'

She didn't answer.

Joe got angry. 'Then what the hell did you come out here for, you fucking cockteaser?' he shouted.

'I didn't!' she cried, suddenly realizing that Walt had not told them she was going home, that he never intended to take her home. She turned to Walt. 'Tell them, please. I didn't – '

Joe knelt by her side and grabbed her hair. He forced her head back. 'Gimme the drink,' he snapped. He took the drink from Walt and, forcing her mouth open by bending her head back, poured the drink down her throat.

She began to choke and gasp. The sticky sweet liquid ran down her cheeks spilling across her shoulders and breasts. He didn't stop until the glass was empty. Then he threw it away. JeriLee heard it breaking against the concrete.

He put his face close to her. 'Now, you goin' to cooperate an' be nice or am I goin' to have to get rough with you?'

Her eyes widened. She tried to hold her breath. 'Please, let me go. Please.'

He moved suddenly, throwing his weight against her, pushing her flat on the ground with his body. His fingers sank into her breasts as he tried to kiss her.

She thrashed wildly, trying to turn her face to avoid him. Involuntarily she brought her knee up into his groin.

A grunt of pain escaped him. 'Bitch!' he yelled. Angrily he slapped her face with his open palm. 'You hold her,' he shouted up to Walt. 'No bitch is gonna try to knee my balls an' get away with it.'

Walt stood there indecisively.

'Hold her!' Joe snarled. 'Time she got what's comin' to her.'

Walt dropped to one knee, pinning her arms to the ground.

Suddenly she felt a sudden pain on her breast. She cried out.

Joe raised the lighted cigarette. He was smiling. 'You didn't like that, did you?'

She stared back at him, unable to speak. He moved swiftly. The scorching pain burned into her other breast. She screamed.

'Yell your head off. Ain't nobody to hear you.' Joe held the cigarette to his mouth and dragged on it.

'Walt, please, make him stop!' she implored.

'Maybe, we better – ' he began.

Joe cut him off. 'You stay out of it! This is between me an' her. When I get through she ain't gonna cocktease nobody.' He straddled her legs with his knees and brutally put his hand on her pubis. With his fingers he spread her open. A strange smile came to his face. 'Now, ain't that a pretty pink little pussy?'

He bent his face forward and bit her mound. She tried to move but couldn't. He straightened up and laughed. 'Not bad. A little pissy, but not bad.' Slowly he brought the cigarette down toward her. 'Now you'll get a taste of something real hot.'

Fascinated, as if she were watching a snake, she stared, her eyes following the glowing tip of the cigarette as it came toward her. Suddenly she felt its approaching heat and she shut her eyes tightly.

They heard her scream as their car stopped in the driveway and were out of the car running through the house almost before the engine had stopped.

Bernie was the first one through the sliding doors. He froze for a moment at the horror of what he saw – the two boys holding JeriLee down and her mouth still open in a scream. His mouth opened. 'What – ?'

Fred reacted with the reflexes of one used to street fighting. He took one step and kicked Joe in the side of his head, lifting him from the ground and tumbling him backward on to the concrete walk. Walt was trying to get to his feet, but Fred never gave him a chance. Slashing viciously with his fist, he caught Walt flush on the nose and mouth, and felt the crunch of bone and teeth against his knuckles. Walt fell back as if he had been hit by an ax.

Fred knelt beside JeriLee pillowing her head in his arms. She was crying in pain. 'Don't hurt me, please. Don't hurt me.' Her eyes were tightly shut.

'It's okay, honey,' he said softly. 'Nobody's gonna hurt you now.'

'Fred!' Bernie's voice was sharp.

He turned to see another boy coming toward him and started to get up. But Bernie caught the boy from behind in a tackle and they fell to the ground, rolling over and over. Joe was coming back toward him now and there was something in his hand that looked like a rock.

He rose quickly, his hand making a lightning move under his trouser leg. The knife came to his fingers and at the same time he pressed the switch and the blade flashed forward. He held the knife flat in his hand before him. 'One move, white boy,' he said quietly, 'an' I'll cut your balls off.'

Joe froze, staring at him, his hand still in the air. It wasn't a rock that had been in his hand, it was a portable radio.

Fred stepped back on catlike feet so that he could see them all. 'Get something to cover her up,' he said to Bernie. 'And let's get her out of here.'

He heard a sound from across the pool. Marian was coming around the walk, staggering drunkenly, a bottle of rum in her hand.

'What'sh happenin' to the party?' she asked.

'The party's over, honey,' he said, his voice filled with contempt.

They managed to cover JeriLee with the remnants of her dress and a towel and get her to the car. She sat between them shivering and crying and moaning in pain, her head against Fred's chest, while Bernie drove. She was still crying as the car pulled up in front of her house.

When Fred tried to help her out of the car, she wouldn't move. 'I'm afraid,' she whispered.

'There's nothing to be afraid of now, JeriLee,' he said soothingly. 'You're safe now. You're home.'

But an instinct told her that this was only the beginning of the horror. And she was right.

CHAPTER ELEVEN

THE LETTERS WERE scrawled in black crayon on the white picket fence:

JERILEE FUCKS. JERILEE SUCKS.

John stared silently at the words. Next to him, Bobby was still holding the wet bloody handkerchief against his nose, although the heavy bleeding had stopped. 'I saw them doing it when I came around the corner, Daddy.'

'Who was it?' John asked, a sick feeling inside him.

'They were big boys,' the twelve-year-old replied. 'I never saw them before. When I went to stop them, they hit me.'

John turned to his son. 'There's a can of white paint in the garage,' he said. 'Get it. Maybe we can paint it over before your mother and JeriLee get home from shopping.'

'Okay, Dad. But why do they say things like that about my sister?'

'Some people are just sick, Bobby. They're stupid.'

'It's an awful thing to do. I wanted to kill them.'

John looked at his son. The child's face was grim. 'Get the paint,' John said gently.

The boy ran across the lawn toward the garage and John turned to look down the street. There was no one in sight. He fished in his pocket for a cigarette. It had been less than a month since that night. The night he had opened the door to find the two boys holding a frightened beaten JeriLee between them.

The late show was almost over when the doorbell rang. He rose from the chair in front of the television set where he had been dozing and glanced at his wristwatch. It was one o'clock. 'It must be JeriLee,' he said. 'She probably forgot her key.'

Veronica was absorbed in the film. 'Tell her not to be so forgetful the next time. We might have been asleep.'

He went into the small hallway leading to the front door. The doorbell rang agan. 'I'm coming, honey,' he called, turning the lock.

The door swung open without his touch. For a moment he was transfixed by what he saw. JeriLee stood between the two boys, her clothes torn, blood running down one cheek almost to the top of an exposed breast. Bernie held one arm around her waist to keep her from falling.

There was a look of terror in her eyes as she raised her face to him. 'Daddy,' she said in a weak voice, taking a stumbling step toward him.

He caught her before she fell. His arms tightened around her, he could feel the frightened flutter of her heart pounding against his shirt. 'My God!' he exclaimed. 'What happened?'

The colored boy whom he had never seen before spoke first. 'We'll tell you what happened, Mr Randall,' he said, 'but you better get a doctor for JeriLee. She's been hurt bad.'

By this time Veronica was behind him. When she saw her daughter she let out a small scream. 'John!'

JeriLee turned her face to her mother. 'Mother, I –'

A tone of anger and fear came into her mother's voice. 'What trouble did you get yourself into this time, JeriLee?'

'Ronnie!' John said harshly. 'Get Dr Baker on the phone and tell him to come over right away!' Without waiting for a reply, he lifted JeriLee into his arms and carried her upstairs to her room. Gently he placed her on the bed.

She moaned softly. The remnant of the dress which clung to her breasts fell away, revealing the angry burns welting her flesh. 'I'm frightened, Daddy,' she cried.

'There's nothing to be afraid of now. You're home now. And safe.'

'But I hurt all over, Daddy.'

'It's okay,' he said softly. 'Dr Baker is on his way. He'll stop the pain.'

'He'll be right here,' Veronica said as she came into the room. She looked down at JeriLee. 'What happened?'

'Walt said he was going to take me home –'

Veronica didn't wait for her to finish. 'Walt?' she asked angrily. 'Who's Walt? That colored boy down there? You know better than to have anything to do with people like that!'

'No.' JeriLee shook her head weakly. 'He's not Walt. He's Fred. He came with Bernie to get me.'

Again Veronica interrupted. 'Get you? Where did you go? You were supposed to be at work.'

John saw the fear come into his daughter's eyes. 'Ronnie!' he said sharply. 'No more questions. Let's try to make her a little more comfortable until the doctor gets here. Get a washcloth and some warm water.

'It's okay, baby,' he said as Veronica left the room.

'I don't want to wake up Bobby,' she whispered. 'I don't want him to see me like this.'

'Don't worry,' he reassured her. 'Your kid brother can sleep through an earthquake.' The doorbell rang downstairs. 'That must be the doctor.' His hand brushed some hair away from her forehead. 'You're going to be all right now.'

'Mother is going to be angry with me.'

'No she won't. She's just upset.'

Dr Baker had been around a long time. After forty years of practice, he didn't wait for verbal explanations. Without speaking, he snapped open his black bag. Quickly he administered a shot. 'That will take away the pain, JeriLee,' he said. He straightened up and turned to her parents. 'You two go downstairs while I look after her.'

'Will she be all right?' John asked.

'She'll be all right,' the doctor said.

They went down the stairs and into the living room where Fred and Bernie were waiting. 'How is she?' Bernie asked.

'Dr Baker said she'll be okay,' he said. 'Now tell me what happened.'

'She was tired and wanted to go home early,' Bernie said. 'Walt said he would drop her off on his way home. He had some friends with him. When you called and she wasn't home yet, Fred figured something was wrong. That was when we went after her.'

'What made you think that?' John asked Fred.

'Walt and his friends were drinkin' pretty good. I thought they were acting mean.'

'Who is this boy Walt that you're talking about?' Veronica asked. 'I haven't heard JeriLee mention him before.'

'Walt Thornton,' Bernie said. 'He lives out at the house on the Point.'

'The writer's son?' John asked.

'Yes.'

'What happened when you got there?'

It was Fred who answered. 'Walt was holding her on the ground, the other boy was doin' things to her. She was screamin' so loud we could hear her on the other side of the house.'

John's face was tight. He picked up the telephone.

'What are you doing?' Veronica asked.

'I'm calling the police,' he answered in a tight voice.

'Wait a minute,' she said, taking the telephone from his hand and putting it down. 'We don't know if they did anything yet.'

John stared at her. 'You saw what they did. They were like animals. They tortured her. Isn't that enough?'

'Did you see them doing anything else?' she asked Fred in a calm voice.

The black boy's face was impassive. 'I don't know what you mean, ma'am.'

She flushed. 'Did you see them having intercourse with her?'

'No, ma'am.' Fred's voice was even. 'I don't think they got that far.'

'You see?' she asked, turning back to her husband. 'They didn't do anything.'

'They did enough,' John said angrily.

'You call the police and everybody in town will know what's happened,' she said. 'I don't think Mr Carson would like that.'

'I don't give a damn what Mr Carson would like.'

'Besides, we don't know what JeriLee might have done to provoke them.'

'You don't believe that?'

'That's the first thing people will think. I know this town and so do you.'

John was silent for a moment. 'Okay. I'll wait until the doctor comes down. We'll see what he has to say.' He turned back to the boys. 'I don't know how to thank you for what you've done. If it weren't for you . . . ' His voice trailed off.

The boys stood looking awkward.

'Would you like a cup of coffee or something?' Veronica asked.

Fred shook his head. 'No, thank you, ma'am. I have to be getting back to the club. They'll be wonderin' what happened to me. We'll just wait a minute to hear what the doctor says.'

'You don't have to wait,' Veronica said quickly. Suddenly she wanted them out of the house. If anything more had happened to JeriLee she did not want them to know about it. 'I'll call you first thing in the morning.'

Bernie hesitated. He glanced at Fred, then nodded. 'Okay,' he said reluctantly. They started moving toward the door.

Veronica cleared her throat. 'I'd appreciate it if you would keep this to yourself,' she said. 'This is a small town. You know how people will talk even if there's nothing to talk about.'

Bernie nodded. 'You don't have to worry about us, Mrs Randall. We won't say anything.'

The door closed behind them and John came back to his wife. 'The doctor's been up there a long time.'

'It's only fifteen minutes.' She glanced up the staircase, then back to him. 'I don't know how JeriLee could get herself into a position like that.'

'You heard what the boys said,' John replied. 'They were supposed to drop her off here.'

'Do you believe that?' she asked.

He met her eyes. 'Yes,' he said simply.

'I don't,' she said flatly. 'I know JeriLee. She's more like her father than I like to think. He never thought of consequences, neither does she. I think she knew exactly what she was doing.'

'You're not being fair to her,' he said angrily. 'JeriLee's a good girl.'

How naïve he was, she thought. 'We'll see what the doctor has to say,' she said noncommittally. 'I'll put some coffee on.'

She had just put the coffee on the table when the doctor came down.

'She's okay,' he said. 'She's sleeping. I gave her a shot.'

'Some coffee, Doctor?' Veronica asked.

He nodded wearily. 'Thank you.'

She filled a cup and gave it to him, then handed a cup to John and poured one for herself. 'Did they – ?' she asked.

The doctor looked at her. 'No,' he said.

'She's still a virgin?'

'If that's all you're worried about,' he answered edgily, 'yes, she's still a virgin.'

'Then nothing happened,' she said in a relieved tone.

'Nothing happened,' he said sarcastically. 'If you don't count the violent beating and almost third-degree burns on her breasts and pubis, besides a broken nose and teeth marks that look as if they'd been made by a wild animal.'

'I'm going to call the police,' John said. 'They can't be allowed to get away with it.'

'No,' Veronica said firmly. 'The best thing to do is to forget it. We still don't know what she did to provoke them. And even if she did nothing, you know what people will think. It's always the girl's fault.'

'Do you believe that, Dr Baker?' John asked.

The doctor hesitated. He knew how John felt. He would feel the same way if she were his daughter. But Veronica was right. The best thing was to sit on it. 'I'm afraid your wife is right, John,' he said. 'People are funny about these things.'

John's lips tightened. 'Then you'd let those boys get away with it completely.'

'Maybe you could discuss it confidentially with their parents,' the doctor suggested.

'What good would that do?' John asked. 'I'm sure the boys will find a way to blame it all on JeriLee.'

'That's exactly what I mean,' Veronica said quickly. 'Either way it will get all over the town. I say we just forget about it.'

John looked at his wife. It was as if he were seeing her for the first time. She was more frightened and more calculating than he had ever thought. His voice was heavy with pain. 'Maybe we can forget about it,' he said. 'But what about JeriLee? Do you think she will be able to forget?'

CHAPTER TWELVE

'YOU AN' YOUAH fuckin' college ways!' Jack muttered as he began to throw his clothing angrily into the battered valise.

Fred lit a cigarette without speaking.

Jack straightened up. 'Better git youah things together. The man gave us until noon to git out.'

Fred got to his feet. 'I'm goin' out,' he said. He blinked as the morning sun hit his eyes, the sky was clear. It was going to be a scorcher. He cut across the parking lot to the beach and looked out across the Sound.

The water shimmered blue-green, and small white-crested waves broke across the deserted sand. He took off his shoes, rolled up his trouser cuffs to his knees and, holding his shoes in one hand, began to walk along the water's edge. He took a deep breath of the sweet ocean air. Jack was right. It was a beautiful world – if you were white. It was nothing like this back in Harlem.

Less than a week had gone by since that night. The first day had been quiet. JeriLee had not come into work, and neither Walt nor his friends had shown up at the club. Even Marian Daley had not appeared. Then suddenly in the afternoon the rumors began to fly.

One of the boys that was visiting Walt Thornton had wound up in the hospital at Jefferson, about thirty miles from Port Clare. He had a broken cheekbone, a fractured jaw and several caved-in ribs. It had been reported as an accident, the result of a bad fall. Perhaps it would have escaped notice, except that Walt too had cuts and bruises. It was enough to raise questions.

Meanwhile, Marian Daley's mother had been checking around town among her daughter's friends. Marian had not come home that night. By morning she had begun to worry. She traced her to Walt's house and, when the telephone was not answered, decided to drive out there.

There had been no answer at the front door but when she discovered that it was unlocked she went inside. Finding no one on the main floor of the house, she went out the sliding doors to the pool. The whole area was a mess of overturned chaises and broken bottles. She stood for a moment, then went back into the house and picked up the telephone to call the police. It was then that she heard a sound coming from one of the bedrooms.

She had reached the top of the staircase just as Marian came out of the room. She was totally naked. As they stood there staring at each other in stunned surprise, a boy she did not know appeared in the doorway behind her daughter. He too was naked.

Mrs Daley was the first to find her voice. 'Get your clothes, Marian, and come with me.' Then she turned and went out to the car without waiting for an answer.

A few minutes later Marian came out and got into the car silently beside her mother. Without a word, her mother started the engine and pulled out of the driveway. It wasn't until they were on the street that she spoke. 'You've really done it this time, Marian. When your father finds out about it, there's no telling what he'll do.'

Marian began to cry. It took only two minutes for her to blurt out her version of what had happened. Her mother did not interrupt her. At the end she glanced at her daughter, 'You say JeriLee came with you?'

'Yes,' Marian said quickly. 'We were only going to go swimming. Then Bernie and Fred suddenly showed up. There was a terrible fight and they took JeriLee away with them.'

'Where's Walt and the other boy?' her mother asked.

'He was hurt so badly that Walt took him over to Jefferson to the hospital,' Marian said.

'Why was the nigger there?' Mrs Daley asked.

'I don't know,' Marian said quickly. 'But JeriLee is very friendly with him. They're always together around the club.'

Mrs Daley's lips tightened. 'I told Mr Corcoran when he hired them that you couldn't trust niggers. They have no respect for people.'

'What are you going to tell Daddy?' Marian asked in a small voice.

'I don't know yet,' her mother said. 'He'll go crazy if he finds out that a nigger was out there and saw you like that. First I better have a talk with JeriLee's mother and find out if she knows what her daughter's been doing. Then I'm going to have a talk with Corcoran. If he wants to keep his memberships he better find a way to get rid of those niggers.'

The telephone on his desk rang just as he returned from lunch. He picked it up. 'Randall speaking.'

'John?' Veronica was clearly upset.

A sudden fear clutched him. 'Is JeriLee all right?' he asked quickly.

'Yes, but I just had a call from Mrs Daley. She told me that boy is in the hospital at Jefferson, he was so badly beaten up.'

'Too bad,' John said sarcastically. 'If it had been me I would have killed him.'

'That's not it. She said that JeriLee was very friendly with the colored boy and that they had been running around together and that the reason they went out there was because he was jealous of her.'

'That's crazy.'

'She said Marian was there. That she said that Jerilee went with them. Nobody said anything about taking her home.'

'The Daley girl's a liar!' he exploded.

'She asked me if JeriLee got home all right.'

'What did you tell her?'

'I said she did. Then she wanted to know who brought her home. I told her. She told me that she was going out to the club to talk to Mr Corcoran about getting rid of the colored orchestra and that I ought to be more strict with JeriLee and not let her associate with people like that.'

'We can't let that happen,' John said. 'The boy deserves a medal for what he's done. You call her back and tell her exactly what happened.'

'I can't do that. She wouldn't believe me anyway. She thinks JeriLee went there with her daughter. And even if she does believe me, the story will spread all over town like wildfire.'

'Better that than having the boy lose his job for something he's not responsible for.'

'Nobody will believe that. They'll all think that it's JeriLee's fault. We won't be able to hold our heads up in this town. And you know how Mr Carson feels about bank employees. One bad word and they're finished.'

'He'll believe the truth if I tell him,' John said. 'I think I better go in and have a talk with him before this gets any further.'

'I think you ought to stay out of it.'

'I'm already in it. I can't let that boy suffer for saving my daughter from being raped.' He put down the phone and walked to the rear of the bank and knocked on the glass door that partitioned off Mr Carson's office.

The bank president's voice came through the door. 'Come in.'

He opened the door and took a half step into the office. 'Mr Carson,' he said in a polite voice, still standing half across the threshold, 'would you have a moment to spare?'

Mr Carson looked up. 'Of course, John,' he said in his nice-guy voice. 'Any time. My door is always open. You know that.'

John nodded, even though it wasn't true. He closed the door carefully behind him. 'It's a personal matter, Mr Carson,' he said.

'No raises,' Carson said quickly. 'You know our policy. We review once a year.'

'I know that, Mr Carson. It's not that. I'm perfectly satisfied with my compensation.'

Carson broke into a smile. 'I'm glad to hear that. People never seem to be satisfied anymore.' He waved a hand at the chair opposite the desk. 'Sit down, sit down. What is it you want to talk about?'

'It's very confidential.'

'You don't have to tell me, John. Anything said in here remains within these four walls.'

'Thank you, Mr Carson. It's about my daughter, JeriLee.'

Carson sighed. 'You don't have to tell me, John. I have children of my own. Problems, always problems.'

John lost his patience. 'She was beaten up and almost raped last night!' he blurted out.

'My God!' Carson's shock was genuine. 'Is she all right?'

'Yes. Dr Baker took care of her. He said she'll be fine.'

Carson took out his handkerchief and mopped at his forehead. 'Thank God. You're very fortunate.' He put the handkerchief down on the desk. 'I don't know what this world is coming to. I hope you've caught the fiend responsible for it.'

'That's just it,' John said. 'Veronica thinks we shouldn't say anything about it, that it would only expose JeriLee to further public shame.'

'There is something to what she says,' Carson agreed. 'But

you can't let a man like that walk around. There's no telling who he might pick on next time.'

'That's the way I feel. But now it's even worse than that. One of the boys who helped save JeriLee is going to lose his job because he tried to help her.'

Carson was not altogether stupid, and instinct told him that he had better learn more about what had happened. 'Suppose you tell me the whole story from the beginning.'

He listened quietly while John told him what had happened. 'I don't see how the Daley girl is involved,' he said at the end of John's story.

'Apparently she was there when it happened. JeriLee said she was still there when they left.'

'Did they do anything to her?'

'I don't know.'

'How did her mother hear about it?'

John shrugged his shoulders.

The banker fell silent. It would be a simple matter if John were not an officer of the bank. 'Did you talk to the police?' he asked.

'I was going to, but Veronica told me to wait. Perhaps I'd better do that now.'

'No,' Carson said quickly. 'I think things like this are better handled privately.'

'How do I do that?' John asked. 'I just can't go over to Mr Thornton and say, "Your son tried to rape my daughter," or to Mr Daley and tell him that his daughter is a liar.'

'No,' Carson said thoughtfully.

'Meanwhile that poor boy is going to lose his job.'

'Ordinarily I wouldn't say this but I think it might be better for all concerned if you followed Mrs Randall's advice and just let the matter slide. As an officer of the bank, you must realize that Mr Thornton maintains huge balances here and that Mr Daley, as a home builder, steers us a tremendous amount of business. Something like this could very well lead them to place their business elsewhere.'

'That would be stupid.'

'Of course it would,' Carson said smoothly. 'But you know customers. We've lost them for flimsier reasons. And these two are very important to us.'

'But what about the boy?'

'I'll have a quiet talk with Corcoran at the club and see what

I can do.' Carson got to his feet and came around the desk, placing his hand on John's shoulder. 'I know how you feel, but take my word for it. There are some things that are better left unspoken. The boy is only here for a few weeks anyway. But we have to continue to live in this town.'

John didn't answer.

Carson dropped his hand from John's shoulder. His voice took on a more businesslike tone. 'By the way, I've heard via the grapevine that the state bank examiners might be paying us a surprise visit. I'd like you to review all the accounts just to make sure that everything's in tiptop order.'

John got to his feet. 'I'll get on it right away, Mr Carson.'

'Good,' Carson said. 'The main thing is that your daughter is all right. Don't worry about anything else. Things have a way of working themselves out.'

'Thank you, Mr Carson,' John said. He went back to his desk and sat down, a strange futility in him. Carson would do nothing. He knew that. It had all been spelled out very clearly. The bank's business was the primary consideration. As usual.

It took Mrs Daley only four days to get Fred fired.

CHAPTER THIRTEEN

JeriLee was sitting on the porch when Dr Baker came up the walk. He thought as he looked at her that the healing powers of the young never ceased to amaze him. The swelling around her nose had almost gone, and the puffy black and blue under her eyes had vanished completely. 'I didn't expect to find you out here,' he said.

'I got tired of staying in my room.'

He came up the steps. 'How are you feeling?'

'Much better. Will I have any scars on my . . . ?' She didn't finish the question.

'No. You'll have white marks where you were burned for a while, but eventually they'll blend in and disappear.'

'Good,' she said in a relieved tone. 'I was beginning to worry. They looked so bad.'

'You are getting better.' He laughed. It was good to see her vanity returning. 'Come inside and let me have a look at you.'

They went up to her room. She undressed quickly without self-consciousness and wrapped a towel around her. He put his reflector on even though he really didn't need it. He felt somehow that it made his examination seem more professional. She stretched out on the bed while he removed the dressings. Carefully he wiped away the ointment and studied the burns. After a moment he nodded with satisfaction. 'You're doing okay. I think we can leave the dressings off now. Just don't wear anything that will be irritating.'

'You mean a brassiere?'

He nodded.

'I can't do that.'

'Why not? No one can see anything under your blouse.'

'That's not it,' she said. 'I bounce too much. It's embarrassing.'

He laughed. 'Walk slower, it will be all right.' He got to his feet. 'I don't have to come here anymore. Suppose you come down to my office in about a week and we'll see how you are getting on.'

'Okay,' she said, sitting up. 'Can I go back to work?'

'Do you want to?'

'Yes.'

'You might run into those boys out there.'

'I'm not afraid of them. They're not going to try anything again. Besides I can't hang around the house all the time.'

'You can go back if you want to,' he said. 'But don't push it. You still haven't got all your strength back.'

'I thought I'd wait over the weekend and go back on Monday. It's easier at the beginning of the week.'

'Okay,' he said, 'but don't hesitate to call me if there's anything you need.'

'Thank you, Doctor.' She watched the door close behind him, then got out of bed. She felt vaguely troubled. Bernie and Fred had been telephoning every morning but this morning there had been no calls. She slipped into a robe, went downstairs and on a hunch decided to call Bernie at home.

When he answered he said, 'I was just going to call you.'

She looked at her watch. It was after eleven o'clock. 'Why aren't you at work?' she asked.

'Corcoran fired us,' he answered.

'You and Fred?' Surprise raised her voice. 'What for?'

'I don't know. But Marian's mother has been making a big stink. God knows what kind of story Marian told her.'

'Where's Fred?'

'He's out at the club packing. They fired the whole group.'

'I have to see him,' she said. 'Will you run me out there?'

He hesitated a moment. 'He's pretty upset.'

'So am I,' she said. 'Will you?'

'Okay. When?'

'Right now. I'll be ready in ten minutes.'

'Fred! Fred!' Her voice floated on the wind across the dunes.

She was standing at the crest of the small hill that separated the beach from the clubhouse. He raised his hand and waved, then stood waiting as she ran down the hill. There was, he thought, something simple and animal-like about the way she moved. He came out of the water to join her on the beach.

Without speaking, she took his hand. He stood very still for a moment, feeling the warmth in her fingers. Then, still holding hands, they began to walk along the water's edge.

'It's not fair,' she said finally.

His eyes sought hers, his voice was soft. 'Nothing ever is, little girl.'

'Why do you call me that?'

'That's what you are. A little girl just growin' up. Trying being a woman on for size.'

'Maybe you're right. I feel like that sometimes.'

They were silent again for a few minutes and then she said, 'They can't do this to you.'

He smiled. 'They have done it.'

'They won't do it if they learn the truth,' she said. 'I don't know what Marian's mother said, but when I tell Mr Corcoran what happened he'll hire you back. You'll see.'

'You're not goin' to tell that queer bastard nothin'!' His voice was almost savage.

She looked up at him, startled by his tone.

He hadn't meant to frighten her. But she hadn't heard the stories that had been circulated by Mrs Daley and Mr Corcoran. Suddenly JeriLee had become the villain of the piece while Marian had grown an instant halo. 'I'll find another job,' he said more softly.

She stopped. 'But where will I find another friend like you?'

Her words seemed to reach into his heart and suddenly his eyes burned with tears. 'You're a lovely lady, JeriLee. You'll find many friends in your lifetime.' He turned and stared out over the water, fearing that if he looked at her, he would take her into his arms and lose something he never really had. 'It's beautiful here,' he said. 'So peaceful.'

She didn't speak.

'I guess that's what I'll miss. Walkin' on the beach barefoot in the mornin' before anyone's awake an' there's no people aroun' to spoil it.' He deliberately lapsed into black talk. 'Black folk got nothin' lak this back in Harlem.'

'Won't you ever come back to see me?'

He let go of her fingers. 'I got no business here. Besides I'll be busy. Workin' all summer an' back to school in September.'

'You're bound to have a day off sometime.'

There was an agony in his voice. 'JeriLee, leave me be!'

He saw the tears spring suddenly to her eyes but held himself away from her. 'I got to get back an' finish packin' or we goin' to miss the bus to New York.'

She nodded, regaining her self-control. 'I'll walk back with you.'

They didn't see the policemen until they crested the dune. The two uniformed men stopped in front of them. The bigger man looked at Fred. 'You Fred Lafayette?'

Fred glanced at JeriLee before he spoke. 'Yes.'

The policeman took a paper from his pocket. 'I have a warrant here for your arrest.'

Fred took the warrant without looking at it. 'What's it for?'

'Assault and battery with a deadly weapon against the person of one Joe Herron on the night of July tenth. Will you come quietly or do we have to put the cuffs on you?'

'I won't make any trouble,' Fred said.

'Good boy.' For the first time the policeman relaxed. 'Let's go.'

JeriLee found her voice. 'Where are you taking him?'

'County jail at Jefferson.'

'I know Chief Roberts,' she said. 'Can I talk to him?'

'You can talk to anyone you like, lady, but he's got nothin' to do with this case. We're out of the county sheriff's department.'

'Don't worry, Fred. I'll talk to my father. He'll get this straightened out.'

'You keep out of it, JeriLee, I'll make out okay.'

'How can I keep out of it?' she asked. 'I'm already in it.'

CHAPTER FOURTEEN

JUDGE WINSTED looked at the large old-fashioned gold pocket watch his father had given him fifty years ago when he had come into the law office. 'It's twelve-forty-five,' he announced, snapping the case shut and returning the watch to his pocket. 'First time since the war that Carson's been late.'

Arthur Daley nodded. 'Must be something important to hold him up.'

The monthly luncheon had become more than a ritual. On the third Friday of each month the three men would meet and review the concerns of the town. Together they formed the core of power that moved Port Clare. Nothing could be accomplished without their stamp of approval, and though none of them had ever been elected to office it was understood by everyone, even the politicians, that the only way to get things in Port Clare was through them.

'Another drink?' the judge asked.

'No thanks. I'm due out at the construction site at two. I want to have a clear head.'

'I'll have one.' The judge signaled the waiter. 'How's it going?'

'Okay. I should have the first ten houses ready by September.'

'That's not bad.'

'Still haven't got county approval on the water lines and sewers yet though.'

'Township approval okay?'

Daley nodded.

'No problem then,' the judge said. 'I'll have the state D.W.P. get on it.'

'That will be a help.'

'V.H.F. mortgages?' the judge asked.

'I don't know yet. I wanted to talk to Carson about it. Thirty thousand is a high price for V.H.F. If I price the houses cheaper we won't get the kind of people we want in there.'

'We can't have that. We have a responsibility to the community not to lower the standards.'

'Yeah,' Daley said dryly. They understood that one of the most effective ways of keeping out undesirables was to price them out of the market.

The judge looked up. 'Here he comes now.'

Carson was walking quickly toward them. His face was red and flushed. He dropped into his chair without apologies. 'I need a drink,' he said.

Wisely the others said nothing until after he had taken a good swallow of his scotch. He put his glass squarely on the table. 'We've got trouble,' he announced.

He didn't wait for them to ask questions. 'Your wife started the damned thing, Daley,' he said angrily. 'Why didn't you check with me before you let her go off half cocked?'

Daley was genuinely bewildered. 'I don't know what you're talking about?'

'That thing that happened out at the Thornton house last Sunday night.'

'What thing?'

'You don't know?'

Daley shook his head.

'Your daughter and JeriLee Randall went out there from the club. Apparently two of the boys tried to rape JeriLee and were beating her up when two of her friends showed up. Murphy's kid and a nigger from the club orchestra. The nigger put one of the boys in the Jefferson hospital.'

'I don't see what my wife had to do with it,' Daley said.

'Apparently your wife found out about it and went after the nigger's ass. She didn't stop until she got Corcoran to fire the Murphy kid and the nigger. If she had stopped there it wouldn't have been so bad. I could have still controlled it. I'd already talked Randall into not doing anything. But then your wife convinced the boy's parents to sign an assault charge against the nigger. The county police took him in this morning. Now JeriLee says she's going into court and file charges against the Thornton boy and his two friends. She also said she'd testify for the nigger. If she does that, Port Clare will get the kind of publicity we're not looking for. Nothing like a juicy attempted rape charge against the son of one of the country's most important writers to make headlines.'

'Any way of talking her out of it? Maybe her father – '

Carson interrupted the judge. 'None. He's just as upset as she is. He would have preferred charges the next day if I didn't talk him out of it. But he's heard the stories going around town making his daughter out to be a tramp and he's boiling about it.' He looked at Daley. 'You knew nothing about your daughter being out there?'

'No.' Daley's voice was flat. 'My wife never said anything to me.'

'Then you have to be the only man in town who hasn't heard about it.' He turned to the judge. 'You?'

'I heard some stories.'

'What do we do now?'

The judge thought for a moment. 'If the charges were dropped we could probably keep it quiet without too much trouble. But someone will have to talk to the boy's parents and to Randall.'

'I can take care of Randall,' Carson said. 'But someone's got to talk to the parents.' He turned to Daley. 'Your wife got us into it, maybe she can get us out of it.'

'I don't see how,' Daley protested. 'If the boy was really hurt – '

'You better find a way. Don't forget your daughter was involved in this too.'

'She had nothing to do with it.'

'How do you know?' Carson asked, his voice cold and blunt. 'She and the boys were drunk when they left the club that night. Your wife found her and one of the boys naked when she went looking for her the next morning.'

'Oh, Jesus!' Daley groaned. 'I keep telling Sally she was letting the kid get away with murder.'

Carson looked at him coldly. 'Maybe you're lucky after all. It could very well have come to that.'

Daley got to his feet. 'I'd better skip lunch and go right home and talk to Sally.'

Carson watched the builder walk out of the restaurant, then turned to the judge. 'You get on to the county prosecutor over in Jefferson and tell him to sit on it. That you have word that the charges are going to be withdrawn.'

'What if he already has impaneled a grand jury?'

'Tell him to stall then.'

'Okay,' the judge said.

'He'll listen,' Carson said confidently. 'Without Port Clare's votes he never would have been elected. He won't forget that.'

'Why the hell didn't you tell me what was going on?' he yelled. 'I felt like a damn fool. I was the only man in town that didn't know.'

'I didn't want to upset you, Arthur,' Sally said placatingly. 'You had enough on your mind with the new construction.'

'God damn it, woman, how many times do I have to tell you to check with me if there are any problems? Have I ever refused to talk with you?'

She was silent.

'Now we got a real mess on our hands. Bad enough our daughter was fucking her brains out with those boys, now it's going to be all over the papers.'

'Nobody will believe JeriLee's story,' she said. 'Who's going to take the word of JeriLee and a nigger against Marian and those three boys?'

'Enough people. Especially when they bring in Dr Baker to tell how badly JeriLee was beat up.'

'I didn't know about that until today.'

'Of course you didn't,' he said sarcastically. 'You should have had brains enough when you found Marian bare-assed with that boy to leave well enough alone. Why weren't you satisfied with getting the nigger canned? What made you push the kid's parents into signing a complaint?'

'I didn't push them,' she protested. 'What could I say to them when they called me to check on their son's story? Especially after I had been yelling at Corcoran to fire him for what he did.'

'But you said you would back their complaint.'

'I had no choice. It was either that or admit that I knew what Marian had done. I didn't think it would go this far.'

'That's the trouble. You didn't think. You never think. You're stupid.'

She began to cry.

'Stop bawling,' he snapped. 'That ain't going to solve anything.' He paused for a moment. 'Where are they now?'

'Who?' she sniffled.

'Who the hell do you think I'm talking about? That kid's parents. Where are they?'

'They're staying at the Thornton house.'

'Call them up and tell them we have to see them. It's important.'

'I can't do that. I don't know them well enough.'

'Oh, Jesus!' he groaned in despair. 'Tell them your daughter's been fucking one of their sons or maybe both. That makes us practically in-laws. That should be reason enough.'

'Why do you have to do everything Carson tells you? Can't you once do anything on your own?'

'Because I owe him two hundred and ninety thousand in building loans, that's why. If it weren't for him I'd still be a carpenter building one house at a time. Now get on that phone.' He walked to the door. 'I don't care what you say to them, but get an appointment.'

'Where are you going?'

'Upstairs to see that little cunt we call our daughter,' he said harshly. 'If she won't tell me the truth about that night, I'll beat it out of her.'

He slammed the door violently. She heard his heavy footsteps on the stairs as she reached for the telephone. She began to dial the number but stopped when she heard her daughter shout in pain. Her fingers froze on the dial. There were no more sounds from upstairs. Slowly she began to dial again.

As he pressed the doorbell, he automatically cast an appraising eye around the property. Prime beach-front land. At least forty thousand an acre. The house was worth a good seventy thousand too.

The door was opened by a slim tired-looking man of about fifty. 'I'm Walter Thornton,' he said. 'Come in.'

He put out his hand. 'Arthur Daley,' he said. 'My wife and my daughter, Marian.'

Thornton shook his hand and nodded at the other two. 'Mr and Mrs Herron are in the library.'

'I'm sorry to be bustin' in on you like this,' Daley said after having been introduced to the Herrons, 'but I feel we have something important to talk about. It concerns all of us here in this room.'

'I think everything has been taken care of,' Mr Herron said. 'The police have that boy in custody.'

'I'm not too sure we all did not act kind of hasty.'

'I'm not sure I understand you, Mr Daley,' Thornton said.

'What I mean . . . ' Daley hesitated a moment, embarrassment creeping into his voice. 'We did not get the true story of what happened that night.'

'My son was beaten severely,' Mrs Herron said. 'I don't need to know any more than that.'

'Mrs Herron, you might not like to hear what I have to tell you, but did you ever stop to think maybe your son brought it on himself? Maybe he was doin' something he shouldn't?'

The doorbell rang. Thornton looked surprised.

'That must be Judge Winsted and John Randall,' Daley said quickly. 'I took the liberty of asking them to join us. John maybe knows more about this than any of us, an' the judge is a good friend of mine. We may need his advice.'

Thornton went to the door and returned a moment later with the two men. 'Now, Mr Daley,' Thornton said, 'supposing you continue.'

'I asked John Randall to come because his daughter is involved in this.'

Mrs Herron's voice was cold. 'She certainly is. It was her friend that attacked my son.'

John slowly got to his feet. His voice was calm but he was shaking inside. 'I'm going to say this once and I'm not going to repeat it. Your son, Mrs Herron, and your son, Mr Thornton, attempted to rape my daughter. They beat her severely and savagely burned her breasts and body with a live cigarette after bringing her here under the pretense that they were going to take her home from work. We were persuaded by friends not to bring charges in view of good community relations but we cannot stand idly by and see the boy who saved my daughter go to jail. Despite the fact that none of us want public attention, my daughter and I are planning to file these charges against your sons first thing in the morning.'

Thornton was the first to break the heavy silence. 'Obviously you must believe this story, Daley, because you brought Mr Randall here. What I don't understand is why you are so convinced.'

Arthur cleared his throat. 'My daughter was there. She corroborates JeriLee's story.'

'They're both lying!' Mrs Herron burst out. 'What was she doing while it was going on? Standing idly by?'

'Tell her, Marian,' Arthur said harshly.

Marian began to cry.

'Tell her!' he repeated.

'Mike and I were makin' out on the other side of the pool while Joe and Walt were with JeriLee.' She sniffled.

'Didn't you see what was happening?' Thornton asked.

'We couldn't see in the dark too good. Besides we thought they were only fooling with her. Just before that they pulled her into the pool with her clothes on.'

'I still don't believe you,' Mrs Herron said stiffly. 'Neither of my boys would do things like that.'

'Sally,' Arthur said. 'Tell Mrs Herron what you found when you came the next morning to get Marian.'

'They both came out of the bedroom upstairs. They were naked,' she said in a hushed voice.

Thornton walked to the door that led to the back. 'Walt,' he called. 'Mike back there with you?' He didn't wait for an answer. 'Both of you come in here a minute.'

A moment later the boys came into the room, and stopped when they saw Marian and the others.

'You didn't tell me the whole story about what you tried to do to JeriLee that night, did you?' Thornton asked his son in a pained voice.

The boy looked at the floor. 'We didn't mean to hurt her, Dad.' His voice broke. 'It all started as a joke.'

'It seems a terrible mistake has been made,' he said. 'Now what can we do to make it right?'

'That's why I asked the judge to come along,' Daley said. 'He'll tell us what to do.'

CHAPTER FIFTEEN

JACK AND AN OLDER man Fred had never seen before were in the sheriff's office when the policeman brought him from the cell. 'You're being released, boy,' the sheriff said. 'The charges have been dropped.'

The sheriff took a heavy manila envelope out of the desk and pushed it toward him. 'Your things are in there. Would you please check them?'

He opened the envelope and took out the contents. His ten-dollar Timex was still there, so was the small gold ring his mother had given him when he graduated high school and the silver-plated I.D. chain bracelet with his name engraved on it that had been a gift from his sister. Two single crumpled dollar bills and seventy cents in small change made up the rest of the envelope's contents. He put the watch and bracelet on and the money in his pocket.

'Is it all there, boy?' the sheriff asked.

'Yes.'

The sheriff held a paper out to him. 'Sign that. It's a receipt for your property.'

Quickly he took the pen and signed the inventory sheet. 'Everything's okay now,' the sheriff said. 'You can go.'

Jack pumped his hand enthusiastically. 'I'm glad you're out. I jes' spoke to the agent. He got us a gig up in Westport.'

Jack saw Fred look questioningly at the older man with the white hair and mustache. 'This is Judge Winsted,' he said quickly. 'He got things straightened out fer us.'

The judge held out his hand. 'Glad to meet you, Fred.'

'Thank you, Judge.'

The judge turned to the sheriff. 'Peck, do you have a room where I can talk to my client?'

'Sure thing, Judge,' the sheriff said, pointing. 'Through that door there. The room is empty.'

Fred and Jack followed the judge into the other room. The judge pulled a chair up to the small table and sat down heavily.

'The older I get, the hotter it gets. I wonder if it's a sign of something.'

The judge gestured for them to sit down. 'In case you're wondering what I'm doing here,' he said, 'I'm representing JeriLee and her father.'

Fred nodded.

'When they came to me early this afternoon, I could see there might be a terrible miscarriage of justice. I couldn't permit a thing like that.'

'Lucky for me,' Fred said. 'They were going to throw the book at me.'

'Couldn't happen,' the judge said definitely. 'I must admit that things get fouled up sometimes but in the end justice manages to win out.'

Fred didn't believe the statement any more than he thought the judge believed it, but he didn't say anything.

'You have a real friend in JeriLee. You know that. Despite what it would do to her, she was ready to go into court to prove your case.'

'JeriLee's a very special lady.'

'She sure is,' the judge agreed. 'She's got much more sense than most girls her age. Anyway, soon's I heard her story I went right out and saw that boy's parents. It didn't take me long to convince them of their error. Then I went over to the club to see Corcoran but it was too late to get him to take you back. He had already hired another orchestra. I didn't think that was right, because you were still out the money you would have made if you had continued working there. I didn't think that was the way to reward a hero.'

'I'm glad to get out of jail,' Fred said. 'I don't care about the job. Or the money.'

'It still isn't right. Somebody ought to be made to pay for the anguish you went through.'

'Yeah,' Jack agreed. 'That po' boy went through a lot jes' for doin' right.'

'Exactly how I felt. I had another discussion with those concerned and they have agreed to reimburse you for the loss of employment. Figuring that you all lost five weeks' work at the club at two hundred dollars a week plus board, which was worth another two hundred, we came to a total of two thousand dollars.' He reached into his pocket and pulled out an envelope from which he removed a package of bank notes that he spread fanwise on the table in front of him.

Fred looked at the twenty hundred-dollar bills. 'I don't want their damn charity money!' he snapped.

'It's not charity, son. It's justice.'

'Man, the jedge is right,' Jack said. 'That's four hundred dollars fer each of us. Take it, boy. That's gravy money.'

'You knew about it?'

'Sure I did. That there money is for all of us. We all lost our jobs along with you.'

'You take it, son,' the judge advised. 'It's the right thing to do. After all, there's no reason why your friends should suffer because of what happened.'

Fred thought for a moment, then nodded. 'Okay,' he said.

The judge smiled. 'That's good thinking.' He took another paper from his pocket and put it on the table in front of Fred. 'This piece of paper is a release by which you and the people who pressed charges against you mutually agree that you won't hold each other in further liabilities. It's just a form thing. When you sign it the money is yours.'

Fred signed the paper without reading it.

'I have to be getting back to Port Clare,' the judge said as he placed the paper in his pocket. 'It's a pleasure to have met you. And I'm glad I was able to be of service to you.'

Fred shook his hand. 'Thank you, Judge. Don't think I don't appreciate what you've done. I'm very grateful.'

When the door closed behind the judge Fred turned to Jack. The drummer was grinning from ear to ear.

'What is it, Jack?'

'That judge is the shittiest character I ever met. He was goin' to try to get you to sign that piece of paper fer a hundred dollars. But I knew you had them by the short hairs.' He picked up the money and fingered it lovingly. 'Oh, baby, don' that look pretty? The easiest day's work any of us ever had.'

She was waiting at the foot of the steps when he came out of the building. And suddenly he realized that without knowing it he had been looking for her.

He stopped on the bottom step. 'JeriLee.' His voice was soft.

She looked into his eyes. 'Are you okay?'

'I'm fine. Actually they were very nice. One of the best jails I've ever been in.'

There was a startled expression on her face. 'Have you ever been in jail before?'

'No,' he laughed. 'I was jes' foolin'. You didn't have to come all the way over here. I would have called you.'

She looked at him skeptically.

'I mean it. I had to thank you for what you did.'

Jack tugged at his arm. 'It's goin' on seven o'clock, Fred. We better git a move on if'n we goin' to make the last bus to the city.'

'You got transportation back to Port Clare, JeriLee?'

'Yes. Bernie loaned me his car. He's working tonight.'

'Corcoran give him back his job?'

'Yes.'

'Are you going to go back to work there?'

'I was going to, but now I don't think so.'

'What are you going to do?'

'I don't know. Catch up on my reading. Maybe try to finish the story I've been writing.'

'Man, we better hurry,' Jack said.

'You go on ahead, Jack. I'll catch up to you.'

'You know where the bus station is?'

'I'll find it.'

'The bus leaves at seven-thirty.'

'I'll be there.'

They watched Jack hurry off. 'Where you parked, JeriLee? I'll walk you over.'

'Not far, just the next block.'

'What are you going to do?' she asked.

'Jack's got another job lined up in Westport.'

'I'm glad,' she said. 'Bernie asked me to give you his regards and wish you luck for him.'

'Your boy friend's okay.'

'He's not my boy friend really. We just sort of grew up together.'

'That'll do it every time.'

'Do you have a girl friend?'

'Yes,' he lied.

'Is she pretty?'

'I guess so.'

'What kind of an answer is that?'

'It's kind of hard for me to tell. You see, we just sort of grew up together.'

She looked at him quizzically for a moment. 'That'll do it every time,' she said finally with mock seriousness.

They both laughed. 'Here's the car,' she said. 'I'll drop you at the bus station.'

A few minutes later she pulled the car to the curb in front of the bus terminal and looked across the seat at him. 'I would like for us to be friends,' she said.

'We are.'

'I mean . . . to see each other again.'

'No, JeriLee,' he said after a moment of silence. He opened the door and started to get out.

She put a hand on his arm. 'Thank you, Fred,' she said gently. 'For everything.'

'JeriLee.'

'Yes?'

'I lied, JeriLee. I have no girl friend.'

She smiled. 'You didn't have to tell me. I knew that.'

'Goodbye, JeriLee.' He didn't wait for her reply but moved quickly into the bus terminal. He didn't turn to look back until he was inside the building. And by then she was gone.

CHAPTER SIXTEEN

SHE CAME OUT of the five-and-ten, walked to the corner and waited for the light to change. A car pulled up to the curb. 'Can I give you a lift, JeriLee?'

It was Dr Baker. 'I thought you were coming in to the office,' he said as she got into the car.

'I've been feeling all right. I didn't want to bother you.'

'It's no bother. I'm your doctor.'

When she didn't answer, he said, 'I thought you were going back to work.'

'I changed my mind,' she said shortly.

He stopped for a light and turned to her. 'What's wrong, JeriLee?'

'Nothing.'

The light changed and he put the car into gear. 'Cigarette?' he asked, holding the pack toward her after coming to a stop in front of her house.

She shook her head but made no move to get out of the car.

'You can talk to me,' he said, lighting a cigarette.

She turned away from him. He reached out, turned her face toward him and saw the tears in her eyes. 'You can talk to me,' he repeated gently. 'I've heard the stories too.'

She began to cry then. No sounds, just the tears running down her cheeks. He opened the glove compartment, took out a Kleenex and gave it to her. 'You don't know how they look at me.'

He dragged on his cigarette without speaking.

'There are times when I wish that I just let those boys do what they wanted. Then nobody would have said anything.'

'That's not true and you know it,' he said.

'Everybody believes that something happened,' she said. 'And that I wanted it.'

'No one who knows you, JeriLee, would believe that.'

She laughed bitterly. 'They wouldn't believe the truth if I told them. I don't understand it.' She looked at him. 'What do I do now, Doctor?'

'You pay no attention. It will pass. Tomorrow they will have something else to talk about.'

'I wish I could believe that.'

'You can believe me,' he said confidently. 'I know this town. It will happen.'

'Mother said that Daddy might lose his job if Mr Thornton takes his account away from the bank. She said that's why she didn't want me to do anything.'

'Has Mr Thornton said anything about it?'

'I don't know. I only heard that he hasn't come into the bank since.'

'That doesn't mean anything.'

'Daddy is worried,' she said. 'I can tell. His face is very drawn. And he's been working late every night.'

'Maybe there's another reason,' he said. 'Did you ask him?'

'No,' she answered. 'And if I did, he wouldn't tell me.'

'Put it out of your mind for tonight,' he said. 'And come into the office tomorrow. I want to check those burns. We can talk some more then.'

'Okay.' She opened the door. 'Thanks, Doc.'

He smiled. 'Tomorrow. Don't forget.'

'I won't.' He watched her walk toward the house before putting the car into gear. He drove off thoughtfully. The maliciousness and stupidity of people never ceased to amaze him. Given the choice of believing good or bad about others, they always chose the bad.

'How about a soda?' Martin asked as they came out of the movie.

'I don't feel like it,' she answered.

'Come on,' he urged. 'It'll be fun. The whole crowd will be there.'

'No.'

'What's the matter, JeriLee?' he asked. 'You're not the same.'

She didn't answer.

'Let's have a soda,' he said. 'I'll spring for it. We don't have to go dutch this time.'

A reluctant smile came to her lips. 'Be careful, Marty. You're becoming a big spender.'

He laughed. 'You don't know me. A dime here, twenty cents there.' He snapped his fingers.

She looked thoughtful for a moment. 'Okay,' she said finally.

Martin was right. Pop's ice cream parlor was jammed. The juke was blaring in the corner but they managed to spot a table in the back. She walked through the crowd, her eyes fixed straight ahead.

When they found that there was only one chair, Martin reached for a vacant chair at the crowded table next to them. 'Anyone using this?'

'No.' The boys glanced up at him, then at JeriLee. There was a long silence. Then one of the boys leaned over and whispered something to the others. They all laughed and turned to look at JeriLee.

She felt her face flushing under their stares and buried her face in the menu as the waiter came up. He was a pimply-faced boy she knew from school. 'What'll it be?' he asked, then he saw her. 'Hey, JeriLee,' he said. 'Haven't been around much lately, have you?'

She heard the burst of laughter at the next table and one of the boys remark raucously, 'Not much, she's been around.'

She looked at Marty. 'I really don't feel like anything.'

'Have something,' he urged. 'How about a chocolate pine-apple float?'

'No,' she answered. There was another shout of laughter from the next table. She didn't hear what they were saying but she was very conscious of their stares. 'I'd better go,' she said, suddenly standing up. 'I don't feel too well.' Without giving Martin a chance to reply she almost ran from the ice cream parlor.

He caught up to her halfway down the block and fell silently into step with her. They turned the corner before she spoke.

'I'm sorry, Martin.'

'It's okay,' he said. 'But you're not handling it right.'

'I . . . I don't know what you mean.'

He stopped under a streetlight and turned to her. 'I may not know much,' he said, 'But I'm the world's greatest expert on people talking about me. I grew up on it.'

She didn't speak.

'With parents like mine, people never stopped. It's not easy being the kid of the town drunks.' He stopped suddenly, his voice tightening.

'I'm sorry, Marty,' she said.

He shook his head, blinking his eyes. 'I learned when I was

very young how to deal with it. You know what you are and you have to hold your head up no matter what people say. That's what I always did. After a while it got so that they didn't matter anymore. I knew I was doing right.'

'It's different when you're a girl,' she said. 'No one comes right out with anything. You don't have a chance to fight back.'

'It's the same with me,' he said. 'Do you think anyone comes right out – Hey, your father's the town drunk? Nohow. Instead they whisper and look until you wish they would come out with it so that you could say something instead of having to sit there and pretend that nothing is going on.'

She nodded, remembering what her mother had said about his coming from the wrong kind of people the first time he had come to see her. 'I can't get used to it,' she said. 'I always have the feeling that they're looking right through my clothing. I just know what they're thinking.'

'But you know what you've done,' he said. 'That's more important.'

'I haven't done anything,' she said. 'That's what makes it so terrible.'

'No,' he said with knowledge beyond his years. 'That's what makes you right and all the others wrong. And when you know that, ain't nothing anybody can do to take it away from you.'

She turned the corner in front of the drugstore. The boys standing around the door suddenly fell silent but separated to let her pass. She could feel their eyes following her to the counter.

Doc Mayhew came from the back. 'Afternoon, JeriLee,' he said. 'What can I do for you?'

'Toothpaste, mouthwash, deodorant,' she said.

He nodded and quickly placed the packages in front of her. 'We have a one-cent sale on Love-Glo cosmetics,' he said. 'Buy one lipstick and get the second for only a penny.'

She shook her head. 'I don't think so.'

'It's very good,' he said. 'You ought to try it. Just as good as Revlon or Helena Rubinstein or those other fancy labels.'

'Maybe next time,' she said. She took out her list. 'Aspirin too, please.'

He picked up the bottle from the shelf behind him. 'Love-Glo has eye shadow and nail polish too. Same deal goes.'

'No, thank you, Doc.'

'Sale's on only till the end of the week.'

She nodded. 'I'll mention it to my mother. Maybe there's something she might want.'

'Do that,' he said pleasantly. 'Charge or cash?'

'Charge, please.' She walked over to the magazine rack while he was writing up the sales slip and picked up a Hollywood magazine. There was a picture of Clark Gable on the cover. Idly she leafed through it. Out of the corner of her eyes she could see the boys outside still watching her.

'All ready now, JeriLee,' the druggist said.

She put the magazine back on the rack and picked up the package from the counter. The boys parted again to let her go by. She acted as if she didn't even see them. She was almost at the corner when they caught up to her.

'JeriLee,' one of them said.

She stopped and looked at him coldly.

'How you doin', JeriLee?' he asked.

'Okay, Carl,' she answered shortly.

'Not workin' out at the club no more?'

'No.'

'Good.' He smiled. 'Now, maybe, you'll have some time to give a local guy a break.'

She didn't return his smile.

'Never could understand why the town girls all run after those city people.'

'I don't see anybody running after them,' she said.

'Come on, JeriLee. You know what I mean.'

Her eyes were steady. 'No, I don't.'

'They ain't the only ones who know how to have fun. We don't do so bad, do we, fellers?'

There was a general chorus of agreement from the other boys. He looked at them, smiling. Emboldened by their support, he turned back to her. 'What do you say, JeriLee? Suppose we take in a movie one night? Then maybe take a ride out to the Point? I got wheels.'

'No,' she said flatly.

He stared at her, suddenly deflated. 'Why not?'

'Because I don't like you, that's why,' she answered in a cold voice.

He grew angry. 'What's the matter, JeriLee? You like niggers better?'

Her slap took him by surprise. He caught her hand angrily

and held it so tightly she felt the pain shooting up her arm. 'You got no right to be so snooty, JeriLee. We know all about you.'

She stared into his eyes, her face white. 'Let me go!' she said through clenched lips.

He dropped her hand abruptly. 'You'll be sorry,' he said.

She pushed her way past them and managed to hold her head high until she turned the corner. Then she felt herself begin to tremble. She put a hand against the wall of the building to steady herself. A moment later she drew a very deep breath and began to walk again. But she could hardly see where she was going. She was almost blinded by her tears.

It was the next day that the graffiti began to appear on the fences and walls near her home: JERILEE FUCKS. JERILEE SUCKS.

CHAPTER SEVENTEEN

JERILEE AND HER MOTHER turned the car into the driveway just as her father and brother finished painting the fence. They got out of the car. Veronica looked at her husband. 'The fence didn't need another coat,' she said.

'Some boys painted dirty words on it, Ma,' Bobby said.

Veronica looked at John. He didn't speak. His eyes squinted against the sun. She heard JeriLee come up behind her. 'Let's go inside,' Veronica said quickly. 'I'll make some coffee.'

He nodded. 'Bobby, put the paint back in the garage,' he said. 'And don't forget to rinse out the brush.'

'Okay, Pop.' The boy picked up the can of paint and cut across the lawn to the garage.

'What happened?' JeriLee asked.

'Nothing,' John said.

She looked at the fence. The paint had not yet dried and the letters beneath the white were still faintly visible. Her face tightened.

'Come inside, dear,' her mother said.

JeriLee stared at the fence. 'Did you see who did it?' she asked tautly.

'No,' John answered. 'Lucky for them that I didn't.' He took her arm. 'A cup of coffee wouldn't do any of us harm.'

Silently she followed them into the house. 'I don't think I want any coffee,' she said. She looked at her father. 'Could I have the car for a while?'

He glanced at his wife. 'Sure,' he said.

'I left the keys in the dash,' Veronica said. 'Be careful. There's a lot of maniacs on the road today.'

'I will, Mother.' She went to the door. 'I just want to go out to the beach for a while.'

They heard the car pull out of the driveway. John looked up at his wife. 'They're crucifying her.'

Veronica did not answer. She put the coffee on the table and sat down opposite him.

'I don't know what to do anymore,' he said.

'There's nothing you can do,' she said. 'Nothing anyone can do. It will just have to pass.'

'If just once we could catch them at it. We could make an example of them.'

'Anything you do will only make it worse,' she said. 'We'll just have to be patient.'

'I can wait. You can wait. But what about JeriLee? How much more of this do you think she can take before she breaks down completely? Already she's stopped seeing her friends. She won't go out anymore, won't do anything. Bernie says she won't even go to the movies with him. School opens in four more weeks. What do you think will happen then?'

'By that time it should be over,' Veronica said.

'And if it's not?'

The question went unanswered as they both silently sipped their coffee.

She stopped the car at the far end of the Point overlooking the Sound and walked down to the beach. It was a deserted rocky section, much too rough for swimming. She sat down on a rock at the edge of the water and stared out at the sea.

A sailboat was tacking into the wind, its snow-white sail billowing against the blue of the water. Idly her eyes followed it until it disappeared around the Point.

'Beautiful, isn't it?'

The sound of the voice behind her made her jump. She turned around.

'I didn't mean to startle you,' the man said. He paused, staring at her. 'Do I know you? You look familiar.'

'We met once, Mr Thornton,' she said. 'On a bus.'

'Oh, yes.' He snapped his finger, remembering. 'You were the girl who wanted to be a writer.'

She smiled. He did remember.

'Do you still take the same bus?' he asked. 'I haven't seen you on it recently.'

'School's out,' she said. 'It's vacation time.'

'Of course.' He looked at her. 'How's the writing coming on?'

'I haven't been doing much lately.'

'Neither have I.' He smiled. He looked out at the water. 'Do you come out here often?'

'Sometimes. When I want to think.'

'It's a good place for thinking,' he said. 'There's usually no one around.' He fished in his pocket for a cigarette and took one without offering the pack to her. He lit the cigarette, inhaled deeply, then coughed and threw it away. 'I'm trying to give up smoking,' he said apologetically.

'That's a funny way to do it,' she said.

'I figure if I light one and inhale very deeply, I cough. That makes me realize what it's doing to me and I throw it away.'

She laughed. 'I'll have to tell my father to try that one.'

'Does he smoke much?'

'Too much,' she said.

'What does he do?' he asked.

'He works in a bank,' she answered.

He nodded absently, his eyes looking beyond her to the sea. She turned following his gaze. The sailboat was coming back.

'Walter!' The sound wafted down on the wind.

They looked back. There was a woman standing at the edge of the road on the crest of the hill overlooking the beach. She waved.

He waved back. 'My secretary,' he explained over his shoulder. 'What is it?' he yelled.

'London is calling,' the woman shouted back. 'I came out in the car to get you.'

'Okay.' He turned to JeriLee. 'I have to go. Will you be out here again?'

'Probably.'

'Maybe we'll see each other.'

'Maybe,' she answered.

He looked at her peculiarly. 'I hope so.' He hesitated a moment. 'I have a strange feeling that I intruded on your thoughts. That you wanted to be alone.'

'It's okay,' she said. 'I'm glad I saw you.'

He smiled and held out his hand. 'So long.'

His hand was firm and warm. 'So long, Mr Thornton,' she said.

He turned and started up the dunes toward the road, then stopped and looked back. 'You never told me your name,' he said.

She looked up at him. 'JeriLee. JeriLee Randall.'

He stood for a long moment registering the name. 'Tell them

I'll call back,' he shouted up the hill, then he turned and came back down on the beach.

'Why didn't you tell me who you were?' he asked.

'You didn't ask me.'

'I don't know what to say.'

'You don't have to say anything.'

'You're not angry with me?'

'No.'

'What my son did was unforgivable,' he said. 'I'm sorry.'

She didn't answer.

'If you don't want to speak to me,' he said, 'I'll understand.'

'You had nothing to do with it,' she said. 'Besides I like talking to you. You're the only real writer I know.'

He fished out a cigarette and lit it. 'You really want to become a writer?'

'Yes,' she said. She looked at him. 'This time you didn't throw it away.'

He looked at the cigarette. 'That's right. But this time I didn't cough.'

'It's not going to work,' she said. 'You won't give them up.'

He smiled suddenly. 'I know.' He sat down on the edge of a rock. 'You said you come out here to think. What about?'

'Things.'

'This time, I mean?'

She looked at him. 'About going away.'

'Where?'

'I don't know,' she said. She looked out at the sea. 'Anywhere. Just away from here.'

'Have you always felt like that?'

'No.'

'Only since . . . since it happened?'

She thought for a moment. 'Yes.' She looked into his eyes. 'Port Clare is a funny town. You wouldn't know unless you grew up here. You see, everybody makes up stories.'

'About you?'

She nodded. 'They think that I . . . ' She didn't finish.

He was silent for a moment. 'I am sorry,' he said.

She looked away but he could see the tears on her cheeks. He reached for her hand and held it. 'JeriLee.'

She raised her head.

'I want to be your friend,' he said. 'You can talk to me.'

The tears were flowing freely. 'No,' she said. 'I can't talk to anyone. There's nothing they can do to help.'

'I can try,' he said earnestly. 'At least I owe you that for what my son did.'

'You don't owe me anything.'

'Talk to me, JeriLee. Maybe it will help.'

She shook her head silently.

Still holding her hand, he rose to his feet and drew her close to him. 'Come here, child,' he said gently, placing her head against his chest. He felt the sobs shaking her body. For a long time he stood there holding her. After a while the tears stopped.

She drew back and looked into his face. 'You're a very nice man,' she said.

Without answering, he took out his pack of cigarettes. This time he offered one to her. She took it and he lit their cigarettes. He inhaled with pleasure. 'I really like smoking,' he said. 'I think I'll give up giving it up.'

She laughed. 'You are funny.'

He smiled at her. 'Not really. I'm just being realistic.'

'Do you really want to help me?' she asked.

He nodded. 'I said I did.'

'Would you read something I wrote if I gave it to you?'

'Yes.'

'And you'll tell me the truth about it? If it's bad, I mean. You won't be polite.'

'I respect writing too much to be phony about it. If it stinks I'll tell you. But if it's good I'll say so.'

She was silent for a moment. 'There's something else you can do.'

'What's that?'

'If you have time, that is,' she said hesitantly. 'It would be nice if you went into the bank and let them know that you're not angry with them because of my father.'

'Is that what they think?' he asked, the surprise plain in his voice.

She nodded.

'That's really stupid!'

'I told you that you don't know this town unless you grew up here,' she said. 'That's exactly how they think. My mother is worried that Dad will lose his job if you take your account away. That's why she didn't want to do anything about what happened to me. Dad was angry. He wanted to press charges, but she talked him out of it.'

'Then what made him speak up finally?'

'We couldn't let Fred go to jail for something that wasn't his fault,' she said.

He nodded soberly. He was beginning to realize that she was right about this being the kind of town you didn't understand unless you grew up in it. 'Is your father from here?'

She shook her head. 'No.'

He nodded. It made sense. 'I'll make time to go down to the bank,' he said.

Her face brightened. 'Thank you.'

Suddenly he wanted to meet her father again. 'I'd like to have lunch with him if that's all right with you.'

'That's up to you. Just going there will be enough.'

'I'd like to know him,' he said. 'He sounds like a nice man.'

She looked into his eyes. The words came from a feeling deep inside her. 'He's the gentlest, kindest man in the whole world.'

CHAPTER EIGHTEEN

BEFORE THE SUMMER was over, Port Clare had a new topic of conversation. JeriLee and Walter Thornton. At first they met at the beach, where they'd sit and talk for hours. He was fascinated by her curiosity and insights into people. Her instincts led her to a subtle understanding of motivations that was far beyond her years.

When the weather grew too cool for the beach she began to drive to his house once or twice a week. He read her work and made some suggestions. She rewrote and he explained to her what worked and what did not. Then one day he gave her a copy of the play he was writing.

She asked if she could read it somewhere alone, and he allowed her to take it with her when she left. He didn't hear from her for three days. Then late one afternoon after school she appeared with the play under her arm.

She gave him the script without comment.

'What did you think?' he asked. Suddenly it was important to him that she liked it.

'I don't know,' she said slowly. 'I read it twice but I don't think I understand it.'

'In what way?'

'Mainly the young girl. She doesn't work. I think you tried to make her like me but she's not. I'm not that smart. And she's too smart to be that naïve.'

Hearing those words from her, he felt a new respect. The one thing he had not surmised was her awareness of her own naïveté.

'But if she doesn't maneuver the people around her we don't have the story,' he said.

'Maybe there isn't any,' she said bluntly. 'I don't see how a man as bright as Jackson could fall in love with a girl less than a third his age. There's nothing really there to attract him outside of her youth.'

'And you don't think that's enough?'

'Not just physical attraction,' she said. 'And certainly not cunning. That would repel him. It would have to be something more. Now, if she were a woman, a real woman, I could understand it. But she's not.'

'What do you think it would take to make her a real woman?' he asked.

She looked at him. 'Time. Time and experience. That's the only way people grow up. And that's the way I'll grow up.'

'Do you think he might have fallen in love with what she could be?'

'I hadn't considered that,' she said. 'Let me think about it.' She was silent for a few minutes, then she nodded. 'It's possible. But there would have to be more of a hint of what she could be, something that would let the audience feel there is more to her than they now see.'

'You've made your point,' he said. 'I'll take another look at it.'

'I feel silly. I'm like a child trying to teach an adult how to walk.'

'We can learn a great deal from children,' he said. 'If we would only listen.'

'You're not angry at me for what I said?'

'No. I'm grateful. You made me look at something that could very well have made the whole play invalid.'

She smiled, suddenly happy. 'I've really been of help?'

'Yes,' he said, smiling. 'Really.' He reached for his cigarettes. 'Tonight's the cook's night off. Do you think your parents would object if I took you out to dinner?'

She was suddenly silent, and there was a troubled expression on her face.

'What is it?' he asked.

'I don't think my parents would object. Dad likes and respects you. But do you think it's wise?'

'You mean – ?'

She nodded. 'This is still Port Clare. People will talk.'

He looked at her. 'You're right. I don't want to cause any more unhappiness for you.'

She met his gaze. 'I'm not thinking about myself,' she said quickly. 'I'm thinking about you. The way they think, there's only one reason a man like you would go out with a girl like me.'

He smiled. 'That's very flattering. I didn't know they thought that way about me.'

'You're a stranger,' she said. 'You're rich. You're divorced. You go to Hollywood and Europe and all those wild places. Only heaven knows what goes on there and what you do.'

He laughed. 'I only wish they knew how dull it really is. I go there just to work, that's all.'

'That may be the truth,' she said. 'But you'll never get them to believe it.'

'If you're up to it,' he said, 'I'd like to take that chance.'

She looked at him for a long moment, then she nodded. 'Okay,' she said. 'Let me check home first.'

They went to dinner at the Port Clare Inn. The next morning, just as JeriLee had predicted, the news was all over town. And for the first time since they were children she and Bernie had a bitter quarrel.

It was Bernie's night off from work and they had gone to a movie. Afterwards they had gotten in his car and driven out to the parking place at the Point.

He switched on the radio and music filled the car. He turned and reached for her.

She drew back, pushing his hands away. 'No, Bernie, I'm not in the mood right now.'

He looked at her. She was staring out the window at the sea which shimmered in the moonlight. He reached for a cigarette and lit it. They didn't speak. Finally, the cigarette finished, he flipped it out of the window and started the engine.

She looked at him in surprise. 'Where are we going?'

'I'm taking you home,' he said sullenly.

'Why?'

'You know why.'

'Because I'm not in the mood to neck?'

'Not only that.'

'What else then?'

He glanced at her, his voice filled with resentment. 'I was coming home from the club after work last night and I saw you with Mr Thornton. You were driving.'

She smiled. 'Of course. He doesn't drive.'

'But he had his arm along the seat behind you. You were laughing. You never laugh with me anymore.'

'He was probably saying something funny,' she said.

'It wasn't only that. I saw the way you were looking at him. Real sexy like.'

'Oh, Bernie.' Suddenly she felt her face flushing. She hoped he would not see it in the dark. It was not until then that she realized how excited she'd been. She knew she had not been able to sleep until she had eased the feeling inside her, but she had not related it to Mr Thornton.

'Don't give me that "Oh, Bernie" crap,' he said, annoyed.

'You're jealous,' she said. 'You have no right to be jealous. Mr Thornton and I are good friends. He's helping me with my writing.'

'Oh, sure. A man like him's going to bother with a kid writer.'

'That's true,' she said heatedly. 'He thinks I'm pretty good. And he even talks to me about his work.'

'Does he tell you about all those wild parties in Hollywood?'

'He doesn't go to any wild parties,' she said. 'He just goes there to work.'

'Oh, yeah?'

She didn't answer.

'I might have figured it,' he said, bitterly. 'First you had the hots for the son, now the old man. Maybe he's the one you wanted all along. I remember that time you met him on the bus. You were wetting your pants even then.'

'I was not!'

'You were too,' he insisted. 'Too bad I didn't know then what I know now. Maybe people ain't so crazy after all. Everybody in town sees the way you go around teasing – not wearing a brassiere and all that. In a way I don't blame Walt for what he thought.'

Now she was angry. 'Is that why you see me?'

'If that's what you think, I won't see you.'

'That's okay with me,' she snapped.

'It's okay with me too,' he muttered. He stopped the car in front of her house.

She got out without a word and slammed the door. 'JeriLee!' he called after her. But she went into the house without looking back.

Her father looked up from the television set as she came in. 'Was that Bernie?' he asked.

'Yes.'

He saw the expression on her face. 'Is there anything wrong?'

'No. He's just stupid, that's all. I'm not going to see him anymore.'

He watched her march up the steps to her room, then turned back to the television set. But his mind wasn't really on the late show. He had a real problem to solve. The state bank examiners were due any day and somewhere in the maze of accounts there was almost three hundred thousand dollars missing, most of it from Walter Thornton's account.

CHAPTER NINETEEN

MR CARSON looked down at the sheet in front of him. 'Did you check all the transfer vouchers?'

'Yes, sir,' John said.

'What about bank cable advices?'

'They balance. We have all the receipts posted.'

'I don't understand it,' the bank president said.

'Neither do I,' John said. 'I've been worried sick ever since I discovered it.'

'When was that?'

'A few days ago.'

'Why didn't you come to me right away?'

'I thought I might have made a mistake,' John answered. 'So I went through the whole thing over again. But the answer was the same.'

Carson looked up at him. 'Don't say anything about this to anyone. Leave it with me for a few days. I want to think about it.'

'Yes, sir. But if the auditors should come in – '

Carson didn't give him a chance to finish. 'I know, I know,' he said testily. 'But I want to check the figures myself before we do anything about it.'

He waited until the door closed behind the cashier before he reached for the telephone and dialed. A guarded voice answered. 'Hello.'

'Mr Gennutri please. Carson calling.'

The voice became less cautious. 'This is Pete, Mr Carson. What can we do for you today?'

'I don't know,' Carson said. 'How do we stand?'

'You did good yesterday. That filly paid six ten. You got your marker down to eleven grand.'

'What about the other two?'

'They ran out.' The bookie's voice was sympathetic. 'They shouldn't have. I was sure you were going to hit me big.'

Carson was silent for a moment. 'I'm in trouble, Pete,' he said. 'I need money.'

'You're a good customer, Mr Carson. I could let you have ten grand.'

'I need more than that,' the banker said. 'Big money.'

'How much?'

'About three hundred thousand.'

The bookmaker whistled. 'That's too rich for me. You have to go to the big boys for that.'

'Can you get to them?'

'Maybe.' Caution returned to Gennutri's voice. 'What you got to give them for the money?'

'You mean collateral?'

'Yes. I guess that's what you bankers would call it.'

'Nothing much that's liquid. My house. The shares in the bank.'

'The shares in the bank,' Gennutri asked. 'What's that worth?'

'Five, maybe six hundred thousand,' the banker said. 'But it's non-negotiable.'

'You mean you can't sell it?'

'Not without the consent of the bank's board of trustees.'

'Would you have any trouble getting them to do that?'

'I would have to tell them why,' he said. 'And I can't do that.'

'It won't be easy then.'

'Would you try them for me? I'd appreciate it.'

'I will, Mr Carson,' the bookmaker said.

Carson's eyes fell on the newspaper lying next to the report on his desk. The page was turned to racing charts. 'Pete,' he said.

'Yes, Mr Carson?'

'Put a thousand across the board on Red River in the fifth at Belmont.'

'Gotcha.'

Carson put down the telephone cursing himself. It was stupid, and he knew it. But he couldn't help himself. The horse had a chance and the odds were long enough to make it a good bet. He stared down at the newspaper, a sinking feeling coming into the pit of his stomach. Somehow no matter how good they looked they never won when you needed them. He promised himself that if he straightened out this time he would never allow himself to get into the same trap again.

JeriLee came out of the warm pool. Walter put down his newspaper, picked up a large bath towel and draped it around her shoulders.

'Thanks.' She smiled.

He returned her smile. 'The October air has a way of getting to you.'

She looked up at him. 'In a way I'm sorry that winter is coming. There'll be nothing for us to do.'

'You can always come over and sit by the fire.'

'That would be nice.' She hesitated. 'But you'll be leaving soon. The play will be going into rehearsal in a few weeks.'

'Yes,' he said. 'That is, if we can get it cast.'

'I thought it was all set.'

'It is. Except for the girl.' He looked at her. 'Do you know of a seventeen-year-old actress who could play a child as if she were a woman?'

'I never thought about it. I would think there must be several.'

'Not really,' he said. 'The director should be here any moment to talk about it. We're going over some possibilities.'

'I'll dry and get out of your way then,' she said.

'No hurry,' he said quickly. 'You won't be in the way.'

'Sure?'

'I wouldn't say so if I weren't.'

'I'll get out of the wet bathing suit then,' she said.

He watched her walk into the cabana, then picked up his newspaper again. But he wasn't reading. He was thinking. The play was one thing. There he was in complete control. The characters did only what he let them. But life was different. Very different.

He heard the cabana door open and looked up. She was wearing faded blue jeans and a bulky knit sweater. She caught his glance and smiled. 'Would you like me to get you something to drink?'

'Yes, please,' he said. A tight hard knot suddenly gathered in the pit of his stomach. 'Scotch and water.'

'Okay.'

He watched her disappear into the house. The surge of feeling left him almost trembling. It was the first time he realized he had fallen in love with her.

'All right, Guy,' he said. 'If we don't find the girl we don't open in November. We'll go for next spring.'

'Can't do it,' the director said. He was a slim lanky man with large horn-rimmed glasses and an air of quiet confidence. 'We lose Beau Drake if we wait. He has a film commitment in May. And without him we'd have to begin all over again. We'll just have to take a chance and go with the girl we think is best.'

Walter shook his head. 'The play is chancy enough,' he said. 'If the girl lets us down it won't work.'

'I've never steered you wrong, Walter. There are ways to get around her.'

'I'm not rewriting,' Walter said stubbornly. 'If I wanted it to be something else I would have written it that way.'

Guy made a gesture of futility. 'It's your baby, Walter.' He glanced through the glass sliding doors at the pool. JeriLee was sitting there reading a newspaper. He turned back to Walter. 'Who's the girl? A friend of Junior's?'

Walter felt his face flushing. 'In a way.'

Guy was sensitive. 'That's a funny answer,' he said, probing. 'Sure she's not a friend of yours?'

'Come on, Guy. She's just a child.'

'How old is she?' He took a stab. 'Seventeen?'

Walter stared at him.

'Can she act?' Guy asked.

'You're crazy! She's a high school kid who wants to be a writer.'

'Has she any talent?'

'I think so. There's something extraordinary about her. If she keeps on the way she's going she's going to make it someday.'

'You have doubts?' Guy asked shrewdly.

'There's only one thing that could stop her.'

'And that is?'

'She's a girl and there's something very physical about her. She's really not aware of it but I have the feeling that a tigress is in there waiting to be unleashed.'

'You've just given me a perfect description of our girl,' Guy said. 'Now, if she could only act.'

Walter was silent.

'Ask her to come in here.'

As she came through the door, Guy played a hunch. Without waiting for an introduction, he spoke the opening lines of the play. 'Your father just called. He wants you to come home right away and said that he doesn't want me to see you anymore.'

His hunch was right. She had read the play. She answered him from the script. 'My father is insane. If he can't have me, he doesn't want anyone else to.'

'Anne! That's no way to talk about your own father.'

She looked at him with a demurely innocent smile. 'Don't act so shocked, Mr Jackson. Didn't you ever have any incestuous thoughts about your own daughter?'

Guy turned to Walter, who had been watching with fascination. 'What do you think?'

Walter was looking at JeriLee.

'She is the girl, Walter,' the director said.

JeriLee was bewildered. 'What's he talking about?'

Walter found his voice. 'He wants you to play the girl.'

'But I'm not an actress.'

Guy smiled at her. 'All it takes to be one is to be one.'

'It's not that easy,' she said. 'I've never really been on stage before except for a few school productions.'

Guy turned to Walter. 'It's up to you to convince her.'

Walter was silent and there was a strange expression on his face as he looked at her.

Guy walked to the door. 'I'm going back to the city. Give me a call when you decide what you're going to do.'

Walter didn't answer him.

JeriLee saw Walter staring at her. 'Are you angry with me?'

He shook his head.

'Then what is it?'

He found his voice. 'Suddenly I find out I'm like the father in my own play. I'm jealous of you.'

Carson looked at his watch. It was four o'clock. They should have the results of the fifth race by now. He dialed the bookmaker's number.

Gennutri answered the telephone with his customarily cautious voice. 'Hello.'

'Pete? What happened in the fifth?'

'Tough luck, Mr Carson. Your horse ran out of the money.'

Carson was silent for a moment. 'Did you get in touch with your friends?' he asked.

'I did.' Gennutri's voice was expressionless. 'They're not interested.'

'But surely they understand. I'm not just the usual horse-player. I'll pay them back.'

'Nothing personal in it, Mr Carson, but that's what they all say.'

He looked down at the newspaper still on the desk. There was a horse in the eighth race that could help out. 'Okay, Pete,' he said. 'Give me two thousand across the board on Maneater in the eighth.'

'Can't do it, Mr Carson.' Gennutri's voice was cool. 'You're into me for twelve grand right now and I can't give you any more markers until that's cleaned up.'

'But I've run more than that before,' he protested.

'I know,' the bookmaker said flatly. 'But things were different then. You weren't hurtin'.'

'A thousand then,' Carson said. 'You got to give me a chance to get even.'

'Sorry.' The bookmaker went off the line.

Carson stared at the dead phone in his hand for a moment, then slowly put it down. He sat there for almost an hour until he was sure everyone had gone home. Then he opened the small drawer in the bottom of his desk. He took out the revolver, put the muzzle in his mouth and blew the top of his head all over the wall under the picture of President Eisenhower.

CHAPTER TWENTY

WEARILY JOHN RANDALL glanced up at the big clock on the wall. Three o'clock. The bank guard was looking at him. He raised his hand, the guard nodded and turned to lock the door. At the same time the two tellers dropped the windows, closing their cages.

Frustrated, the crowd of people still in line in front of the tellers' windows surged toward him. He got to his feet. The news of Carson's suicide had hit Port Clare like a shock wave.

He glanced over his shoulder. The door of the president's office was closed. Behind it the state examiners were still going through the records. Several other large discrepancies had been found but the total had not yet been reached. Carson had been thorough. Transfers and approvals had been carefully forged. No one could understand how he had slipped up this time.

'When do we get our money?' an irate customer shouted at him from the crowd. 'Why are you closing the doors on us?'

'It's legal closing time,' he said patiently. 'And you will get your money. Whatever losses there have been are completely covered by insurance.'

'How do we know that?' another customer shouted. 'I remember they told us the same thing when the Bank of the United States failed back in thirty-two.'

'Things were different then,' John explained. 'Savings accounts are protected by the F.D.I.C. up to ten thousand dollars. The bank carries insurance against fraud and theft. Every penny will be replaced.'

'That's what you say,' the man replied. 'But you don't have the cash to give us back our deposits right now, do you?'

'No,' John said. 'But no bank has all the cash on hand to return to their depositors. Banks have the same problem as people. Cash comes in and goes out all the time. Like when you pay up your mortgage we have the money to lend to someone else or to give them a mortgage. Multiply that by hundreds and you understand how it works. It's really simple common sense.'

'I'm not stupid,' the man said. 'If I don't make the payment on the mortgage, the bank takes my house away. If the bank doesn't make our payment, what do we do?'

'The bank will make the payments.'

'What if you close?'

'We won't close,' John said stubbornly. 'We have assets enough to cover all our liabilities. All we need is time to convert them. And if you give us that time, I can promise that not one of you will suffer.'

'Mr Randall, why should we believe you after what happened?'

John looked the man squarely in the eyes. He spoke slowly and clearly so that they could all hear him. 'Because like you, Mr Sanders, I've worked for a living all my life. And I have every penny I've managed to save in the world in this bank. And I'm not worried about it.'

The man was silent for a moment, then turned to the others. 'I'm goin' along with Mr Randall. How 'bout you?'

There was a murmur among the crowd. Their hostility was dissolving. This was something they could understand. The word of one man.

'We'll go along too!' a man in back of the crowd shouted.

Sanders held out his hand to John. 'You'll keep your promise to us?'

John nodded. He didn't trust himself to speak. Several of the others grabbed at his hand and then he watched the crowd silently leave the bank as the guard opened the door for them.

As he returned to his desk, John saw that Arthur Daley and several of the other bank's board of trustees had come out of the president's office, where they had been closeted with the examiners, and were looking at him. Arthur nodded and they went back into the office.

Three days later John was elected president of the Port Clare National Bank.

John looked up from the breakfast table as JeriLee came into the room. 'You're early,' he said. 'Especially today.'

'What's so special about today? I'm always up early.'

'On Saturdays? When there's no school?'

She blushed. 'I wanted to get to the stores.'

He raised an eyebrow. 'You? I thought you hated shopping.'

'It's Mr Thornton's birthday tomorrow,' she said. 'I wanted to get him something special.'

'How old will he be?'

'Forty-eight.'

Surprise came into John's voice. 'I thought he was older.'

'Many people do. I guess it's because his first play was produced on Broadway when he was only twenty-three.'

'He's still older than I am,' John said. He was forty-three.

'Not much,' JeriLee said. 'The funny thing is that he doesn't seem old.' She looked at her father. 'You know what I mean.'

John nodded. He picked up his coffee cup. 'He was in the bank yesterday. We had a long talk.'

She took some coffee and sat down. 'What about?'

'Business mostly,' John said. 'He's been very nice about what happened. If he had wanted to, he could have made real trouble for us. If he had taken away his account, it could have started a run that would have closed the bank.'

'But he didn't.'

'No,' he answered. It was curious how things happened. He wondered if she knew that if it weren't for Walter Thornton he might never have been president of the bank.

It had happened the night the bank examiners had finished. The board of trustees had gone to see Mr Thornton. He had been the hardest hit of any individual. More than two hundred thousand dollars. They had asked him for time to replace the loss and to show his confidence in the bank by not taking the account elsewhere.

His agreement had been immediate. But conditional. Later Arthur Daley had told John the exact words Mr Thornton used. 'I will stay under one condition only. That is, if John Randall is made president of the bank.'

As Arthur had put it, the board was relieved. They had already come to that decision on their own so it was a simple matter for them to agree.

He watched her take some toast and butter it. 'We also spoke about you,' he said.

'Yes?' She waited until she swallowed. 'What did he say about me?'

'He said you really can write. And that you should take special care about what college you go to after graduating Central.'

'He told me that too.'

'Do you really want to become a writer?' John asked curiously. 'What happens if you get married and have a family?'

'Oh, Daddy!' She flushed. 'That's a long way off. I still haven't met a boy I would want to settle down with. And besides, writing is the one thing you do on your own. Many women writers are married and have families.'

'He says you should start making applications to college now. After all, you'll be graduating soon.'

'He promised to get me some information. Then I'll be able to make up my mind.'

'He mentioned that too. He said he would keep in touch with us.'

'In touch?'

John nodded. 'He's going to be gone for a long while. Hollywood, Europe, then back to Hollywood.'

She was silent for a moment. 'Did he say anything about a play on Broadway?'

'No,' her father replied. 'He never mentioned anything like that at all.'

She pressed the doorbell. Inside the house, chimes rang softly.

The door was opened by his secretary. 'Oh, JeriLee!' she exclaimed. 'I didn't expect you. We're in the midst of packing. I'll tell him you're here.'

The woman went into the library, closing the door behind her. After waiting a moment in the foyer, JeriLee walked through the living room and out onto the terrace. The pool was already covered for the winter and the cold November wind was tearing off the Sound. She shivered and pulled her jacket around her.

'JeriLee.' His voice came from the doorway.

She turned. 'It's really getting cold now,' she said.

'Yes,' he answered. 'Come back inside where it's warm.'

She followed him into the living room. 'I didn't expect to see you today,' he said.

'It's your birthday tomorrow,' she said, handing him the small gift-wrapped package. 'I wanted you to have this.'

He took it awkwardly.

'Open it,' she said. 'I hope you like it.'

Quickly he undid the wrapping. It was a small pocket memo and telephone book bound in black pinseal leather. And in a loop along the side was a small gold pencil. 'It's lovely,' he said. 'What made you think of it?'

'You're always looking for telephone numbers.'

He nodded.

'Happy birthday,' she said.

'Thank you.' He forced a smile. 'I'm getting old.'

'You'll never get old, Mr Thornton,' she said. 'The things you've written will keep you young forever.'

He felt a tightness inside him. 'Thank you. Really thank you. That's the nicest thing anyone ever said to me.'

She stood awkwardly for a moment, then she said, 'I guess I'll be going, Mr Thornton. I'm expected home for dinner.'

'JeriLee,' he said, without moving.

'Yes, Mr Thornton.'

His eyes were on her face. 'I'm going away tomorrow.'

'I know. My father told me.'

'I'll be gone a long time.'

'My father told me that too.'

After a moment he said, 'I've withdrawn the play. I don't think it's ready.'

She was silent.

He smiled. 'You're a writer,' he said. 'You'll find things like that happen sometimes.'

She nodded.

'You go off on the wrong track and suddenly you find that you don't know what you're talking about.'

'Or that you know too much. And you don't want to say it.'

His eyes fell. 'I'm sorry, JeriLee.'

Her voice suddenly broke. 'So am I, Mr Thornton,' she said and went out of the house.

He moved over to a window where he could watch her as she got into the car and drove away.

His secretary called from the library. 'Walter, do you want me to take your notes on the Chicago story?'

Unshed tears burned his eyes.

He didn't answer. JeriLee's car was at the corner and turning out of sight.

'Walter, do you – ?'

'I'll be right there,' he said.

CHAPTER TWENTY-ONE

IT HAD BEEN so long and yet not that long really. Seventeen years. What was that? Half her life to date. So much had happened since and still, if she pushed the right button in her memory bank, it all came back.

She glanced up at the clock on the wall over the hospital bed. It was four o'clock and the other woman had long since gone home. She was the only patient left.

The doctor came to the side of the bed and looked down at her through his glasses. He smiled. 'How do you feel?'

'Bored,' she said. 'When do I get out of here?'

'Right now. I'll sign the discharge.' He picked up the chart from the foot of the bed, made a note and then pressed the button for the nurse.

The big black lady came in. 'Yes, Doctor?'

'Miss Randall can go now,' he said. 'Help her with her things.'

'Yes, Doctor.' She turned to JeriLee. 'They's been a gen'mun waiting downstairs in reception for you since twelve o'clock.'

'Why didn't you tell me?'

'He said he'd wait. He didn't want to disturb you.' The nurse went to a small closet and took out JeriLee's clothes and put them on the chair next to the bed. 'You let me he'p you out of bed, honey.'

'I'm all right,' JeriLee answered. But when she was on her feet she felt strangely weak and reached for the hand the nurse held out to her. 'Thank you.'

The nurse smiled. 'You'll be okay in a few minutes, honey. Takes that long fo' you to git yo' legs back.'

She went to the bathroom and when she came out the doctor was still waiting for her. 'I want to see you in a week,' he said.

She nodded.

'And no sex until after I check you out,' he added.

She looked at him and smiled. That had been the furthest thing from her mind. 'Can I give head?' she asked.

He laughed. 'That's out of my area,' he said. 'Check with your dentist.'

'Okay, Doc.'

'Take it easy for a few days. Don't push things.'

'I will, Doc. Thank you.' He left and she began to dress. By the time she finished, the nurse was back with a wheelchair. JeriLee looked at it dubiously. 'Do I have to go in one of those things?'

'Regulations. Right to the door.'

'Let me put some lipstick on first,' JeriLee said. She looked in the mirror. A little color in her cheeks wouldn't hurt either. Hospital pallor didn't take long to set in.

At first she didn't recognize him. Dark mirror glasses, a false brown mustache and a wig covered his normally clean shaven face and curly black hair. She almost laughed aloud. He looked so ridiculous.

'How are you, JeriLee?' he piped, trying to disguise his deep voice.

'Just fine.'

'The car's right outside, Nurse,' he said.

The nurse nodded and rolled the chair to the car entrance and down the ramp. He had a rented Continental instead of using his own Corniche convertible. He opened the door and the nurse helped her into the front seat.

'Goodbye,' JeriLee said. 'Thank you.'

'You're welcome, honey. Good luck.'

He looked out a twenty-dollar bill and gave it to the nurse. 'Thank you,' he said.

The nurse looked at the twenty then at him, her shining dark face breaking into a big grin. 'Thank you, Mr Ballantine.'

He stood with his mouth open, then turned to JeriLee. 'How did she recognize me?'

JeriLee was giggling. 'You may be a star, George,' she said, 'but you still don't know a damn thing about makeup.'

He walked around the car and got in behind the wheel. 'I didn't want anyone to recognize me.'

'Don't worry about it. She's seen 'em all. Coming and going. She won't talk.'

'I can't afford any more talk,' he said, putting the car into motion. 'The studio's on my back enough as it is.'

'Don't worry.'

He looked at her. 'How do you feel?'

'Okay.'

'Just okay?'

'Okay.'

'Don't you feel better now that it's over?' he asked.

She looked at him. 'Do you?'

'Much. It was the right thing to do.'

She reached for a cigarette.

'Don't you think so?' he asked.

'If you think so,' she said.

He reached across and patted her hand. 'I'm right. You'll see. Tomorrow morning you'll wake up and you'll see that I was right.'

'Tomorrow morning I'm going to wake up so stoned that I won't even remember what happened today,' she said.

'What's the matter with you, JeriLee? What do you want from me?'

'Nothing,' she said. 'Absolutely nothing.' She shrank down into her seat.

What was wrong with men that always made them feel you wanted something from them they were not prepared to give? Especially when you asked nothing and wanted nothing. That they could not understand at all.

There had been only two men in her life who had not felt like that. Her father and Walter Thornton. All they wanted was to give to her. And maybe that was why she failed them. She did not know how to take.

'He's too old,' her mother said. 'He's older than your father. And what about his son? You'll have to see him.'

'No, I won't have to. He's moved to England with his mother,' she said. 'Besides it doesn't matter. I love him.'

Veronica looked at her. 'What do you know of love? You're still a child. You're not even eighteen yet.'

'What is love, Mother?' she asked. 'I like him, I admire him, I respect him, I want to go to bed with him.'

'JeriLee!'

'If that isn't love, then tell me what it is,' JeriLee said.

'It's not what you think it is,' Veronica said. 'Sex. You saw what almost happened with those boys.'

'Was that supposed to make me afraid of love?'

'That's not what I'm talking about,' her mother said. She

turned to John for help. 'Tell her, John. Make her understand.'

John shook his head. 'I can't,' he said. 'Love is what each individual person thinks it is. Love is what two people agree it is. And it is different for every person who loves.'

'But she's still a child,' Veronica said.

'Then you don't know your own daughter. JeriLee stopped being a child a long time ago.'

'He'll be fifty before she's eighteen,' Veronica said.

'If that turns out to be a problem it will be their problem. I'm sure they have both thought about it and they will have to solve it.'

'She still needs my signature on the marriage license,' Veronica said stubbornly. 'And I won't sign it.'

'Then it will be too bad. Because I will.'

Veronica grew angry. 'You can't. She's not your daughter!'

JeriLee could see the hurt on her father's face. But his voice was calm and quiet. 'Yes, she is,' he said. 'As much mine as her real father's. I love her and I adopted her. That's enough to satisfy the law.'

'Then you're willing to let everyone believe that what they've been saying all this time is true?'

'I don't care what people say, or think, or believe. What I care about is my daughter's happiness.'

'Even if you know she's making a mistake in the long run?'

'I don't know that and neither do you. But if she has made a mistake, I will still love her and try to help.'

Veronica turned to her daughter. 'For the last time, JeriLee. Please listen to me. There will be younger men, closer to your own age. You can grow up together, grow old together, have children together. Those are things you won't be able to do with him.'

'For God's sake, Mother.' JeriLee said, exasperated. 'He's not a cripple! I've already been to bed with him and he's a wonderful lover.'

'So that's it. Then the stories were true.'

The tears sprang to JeriLee's eyes. 'No. Only if you believe them.' She turned and ran from the house.

Wearily John looked at his wife. 'Veronica,' he said hopelessly, 'sometimes I wonder what I ever saw in you. You're such a goddamn fool!'

George pulled the Continental into the driveway of her house.

'Would you like to come in for a drink?' she asked.

He shook his head. 'I promised my agent I would meet him for a drink at the Polo lounge at five.'

'Okay.' She opened the door and got out. 'Thanks for coming to pick me up.'

'It's okay. I'm sorry. I didn't mean for it to become such a big deal.'

'It's not a big deal,' she said. 'Haven't you heard? It's easier than curing a cold.' She walked around to his side of the car. 'Sure you don't want to come in?' she asked, playing with his false mustache. 'We can't fuck but I can give you head. The doctor said so. And you always say I give the best head in town.'

'Well,' he said, 'maybe I can always be a half hour late. My agent won't mind.'

She laughed and pulled the false mustache from his lips and stuck it in the center of his forehead. 'Oh, George,' she said. 'Why do you have to be such a shit?'

Then she turned and, half laughing, half crying, walked up the driveway to her house. Locking the door behind her, she leaned back and let the tears run down her cheeks. What was there about her that always seemed to attract the shits?

It hadn't always been like that. Walter was not a shit. Not really. He was just weak. He needed even more reassurance than she did.

She walked through the house to her bedroom and fell on the bed with her clothes on. She stared up at the ceiling, her eyes dry once again. The telephone began to ring but she lay there making no move toward it. After three rings the answering service picked up.

She reached for the cigarette box at the side of the bed and took out a rolled joint. Slowly she lit it and inhaled deeply. The sweet calm went down into her lungs and spread through her body. She pressed a button and the tape deck went on, the music filling the room. She took two more tokes from the joint, then placed it in an ashtray, rolled over on her stomach and covered her face with her hands. Once again the picture of the little girl sitting at the top of the stairs and crying flashed before her eyes. Then it was gone. Abruptly she sat up in the bed. She was no longer that little girl. And she had not been for a long, long time.

Not since the day she and Walter were married and he had taken her down to New York and up, up, in the elevator to the apartment at the top of the building which looked out over the city.

Book Two
Big Town

CHAPTER ONE

IT WAS SPRINGTIME in New York. The young green of the new leaves on the trees in Central Park fluttered in the gentle wind and the children were playing in the first flush of May warmth. We walked past the benches filled with idlers. We neither spoke nor looked at each other, together yet not together, each thinking our own silent thoughts.

He didn't speak until we came out at the Avenue of the Americas exit at Fifty-ninth Street. We stood waiting for the light to change. As usual the traffic was backed up on both streets. 'You can take your time about moving,' he said. 'I'm making the ten o'clock flight to London tonight and I won't be back for a month.'

'It's okay. They told me the apartment would be ready.'

He took my arm as a truck making a turn came uncomfortably close, then as quickly let it go as we stepped out of the gutter. 'I just wanted you to know,' he said.

'Thanks, Walter, but I'm going home over the weekend. By Monday I'm sure everything will be in.'

The doorman who held open the door looked at us strangely. 'Mr Thornton,' he said. 'Mrs Thornton.'

'Joe,' I said. I was sure he knew about it. By now the whole world had to know. It had been in all the columns. The Thorntons were getting a divorce.

We were silent going up in the elevator to the penthouse. We stepped out into the corridor. 'I have my key,' Walter said.

His bags were already packed and in the foyer. He closed the door and stood silently for a moment. 'I think I could use a drink,' he said.

'I'll fix it for you,' I said, automatically starting for the bar in the living room.

'I can do it.'

'I don't mind. Matter of fact I can use one myself.'

I threw some ice in the two glasses and poured the scotch over it. We faced each other across the bar. 'Cheers,' he said.

'Cheers.'

He took a long swallow, I just took a sip. 'Six years,' he said. 'I can't believe it.'

I didn't speak.

'They went so fast. Where did they go?'

'I don't know.'

'Do you remember the first time I brought you here? It was snowing that night and the park was white in the darkness.'

'I was just a child then. A child in a woman's body.'

There was a bewildered expression in his eyes. 'When did you grow up, JeriLee?'

'It was happening a little bit every day, Walter.'

'I didn't see it.'

'I know,' I said gently. That was it. More than anything else. To him I would always be the child bride.

He finished his drink and put the empty glass on the bar. 'I'm going upstairs to try to get a nap. I never could sleep on those night flights.'

'Okay.'

'The car's picking me up at eight-thirty,' he said. 'Will you be here when I come down?'

'I'll be here.'

'I wouldn't want to go without saying goodbye.'

'I wouldn't want that either,' I said. Then the dam broke and my eyes filled with tears. 'Walter, I'm sorry.'

His hand touched mine for a brief moment. 'It's all right,' he said quickly. 'It's all right. I understand.'

'I loved you, Walter. You know that.'

'Yes.'

There was nothing else to say. He left the room and I heard his footsteps going up to the bedroom. A moment later the sound of the closing door echoed through the silent rooms. I dried my eyes with a Kleenex and went over to the window and looked down at the park.

The leaves were still green, the children were still playing, the sun was still shining. Spring was here. Damn! If that were true why was I shivering with the cold?

The apartment was empty after he left. I was on my way from the door to the kitchen to get myself something to eat when the telephone rang.

It was Guy. 'What are you doing?'

'Nothing. I was just going to fix myself some dinner.'

'Walter gone?'

'Yes.'

'You shouldn't be alone tonight,' he said. 'I'll take you out to dinner.'

'That's sweet of you.' I really meant it. Guy was a good friend to both of us. He'd directed me in my first play – Walter's play, the one he had been writing when we met. 'Can I get a rain check? I really don't feel up to it.'

'It'll do you good.'

'No, thanks.'

'Then let me bring up some sandwiches. I'll stop off at the Stage,' he said quickly.

I hesitated.

'Besides I have some ideas for the rewrite on your play,' he added. 'We can talk.'

'Okay.'

'That's better. I'll bring a bottle of wine and some grass. We'll have a nice quiet evening. Half hour okay?'

'Fine.' I put down the telephone and went up to the bedroom. I started for the closet to get a pair of jeans when the telephone rang again.

It was my mother. 'JeriLee?'

'Yes, Mother.'

'When did you get back?'

'This afternoon.'

'You could have called me,' she said in a peeved voice.

'I didn't have time, Mother. I went to the lawyer's office right from the airport. Walter and I still had some papers to sign.'

'Then the divorce is final,' she said disapprovingly. 'I didn't think Mexican divorces were legal in New York.'

'It's legal.'

'You should have called me. I'm your mother. I'm entitled to know what's happening.'

'You knew what was happening. I explained all that to you before I went to Juarez. Besides I'll be there all weekend and I'll tell you all the gory details.'

'You don't have to tell me anything if you don't want to,' she said stiffly.

I tried to keep from getting angry. I don't know what it is but she always had the ability to get me on the defensive. I looked around for a cigarette but couldn't find one. 'Damn,' I muttered.

'What did you say?'

'I can't find the damn cigarettes.'

'You don't have to swear,' she said. 'And you smoke too much.'

'Yes, Mother.' I finally found one and lit it.

'What time will you be out here?'

'Some time in the morning.'

'I'll have lunch for you. Don't eat too much for breakfast.'

'Yes, Mother.' I changed the subject. 'Is Daddy there?'

'Yes. Do you want to speak to him?'

'Please.'

His voice was warm and gentle on the telephone. 'How's my little girl?'

That did it. I could feel the tears start to my eyes again. 'Big and hurting,' I said.

All the sympathy in the world was in the one word. 'Rough?'

'Yes.'

'Hold your head up. You've got us.'

'I know.'

'It'll be all right. Take time. Everything takes time.'

I was under control again. 'We'll talk tomorrow. I can't wait to see you.'

'Me too.'

I had just enough time to take a quick shower and dress before Guy came.

He stood in the doorway with a silly smile on his face, a shopping bag in one hand and a bouquet of flowers in the other. He pushed the flowers into my hands and kissed me on the cheek. Even before he spoke I could tell from his breath that he was smashed. 'Happy, happy,' he said.

'You're crazy,' I said. 'What are the flowers for?'

'Celebrate,' he said. 'It's not every day that a man's best friends get divorced.'

'I don't think that's funny.'

'What do you want me to do? Cry?'

I didn't answer.

'I cried at your wedding,' he said. 'For all the good it did me. Now you're divorced and you're both happy. I guess that's worth a celebration.'

'You do everything backwards.'

'What the hell?' he said. 'It's just as good.' He walked into the living room and took a bottle of champagne out of the shopping bag. 'Get the glasses,' he said. 'Dom Perignon. Nothing but the best.'

Raising his glass, he said, 'Drink up to better times.'

I sipped. The bubbles tickled my nose.

'All of it.'

I emptied my glass and he refilled it. 'Again.'

'You're trying to get me drunk.'

'Right.' He nodded. 'And it won't hurt you one bit.'

It went down like champagne was supposed to. I began to feel warm. 'You're really crazy,' I said.

He looked at me out of those pale blue eyes and I suddenly realized that he wasn't as drunk as I thought. 'Feel better?'

'Yes.'

'Good. Then we'll eat. I'm starved.' He began emptying the bag on the bar. In a moment I was surrounded by the wonderful odors of hot corned beef and pastrami and garlic pickles. My mouth began to water.

'I'll set the table.'

'Why?' He picked up a sandwich and bit into it. He mumbled with his mouth full, 'You don't have to impress nobody.'

I stared at him. With Walter everything had to be in place. We never once had eaten in the kitchen.

He refilled my glass. 'Eat, drink and be merry.'

I picked up a sandwich and took a bite. Unexpectedly my eyes began to moisten.

He picked up on it right away. 'No. Please. No.'

There was a lump in my throat. I couldn't swallow. I couldn't speak.

'Don't cry,' he said. 'I love you.' Then he smiled and his face took on a mischievous look. 'That is, I love you as much as any queen can love a girl girl.'

CHAPTER TWO

I WAS A LITTLE BIT smashed, a little stoned and there was a pleasant buzz to my high. I sprawled back on the couch and looked down at Guy, who was stretched on the floor at my feet. 'Why don't you get up?' I asked.

He rolled over on his back and reached up to take the joint from my fingers. 'I don't know whether I can,' he said, taking a drag.

'Try. I'll help you.'

'What for? I'm happy here.'

'Okay. What were we talking about?'

'I don't remember.'

'The play. You had some ideas for the rewrite.'

'I can't talk about it now. I feel too good.'

I looked toward the windows. The night sky over Central Park was gray with the reflected light. 'Do you think the plane took off already?'

'What time is it?'

'Almost midnight.'

'It's gone,' he said.

I got to my feet and went over to the window. I held up my hand and waved at the sky. 'Goodbye, Walter, goodbye.' Then I began to cry. 'Have a nice flight.'

Guy struggled to his feet and weaved toward me. 'Hey, this is a celebration,' he said. 'Don't cry.'

'I can't help it. I'm alone.'

'You're not alone,' he said, putting an arm around my shoulders. 'I'm here.'

'Thank you. That's very nice.'

He led me back to the couch. 'Have another glass of champagne.'

I took a sip from the glass he put in my hand. Suddenly it didn't taste good anymore. I was coming down. I placed the glass on the cocktail table. It made a small wet ring on the polished surface. I stared at it. Usually I would wipe it quickly and place the glass on a coaster. Walter hated drink stains on his precious antiques. Now I didn't give a damn. 'I think I'll go to bed,' I said.

'It's early,' he protested.

'But I'm tired,' I said. 'It's been a long day. I was in court in Mexico at eight-thirty this morning. By eleven I was on the plane on my way back. I haven't had any rest in two days.'

'What did you do with your wedding ring?' he asked.

'I'm wearing it.' I held out my hand. The tiny gold band glimmered in the light.

He shook his head solemnly. 'That's bad. You have to get rid of it.'

'Why?'

'It's a symbol. You won't be free until you get rid of it.' He snapped his fingers. 'I've got it. In Reno there's a little bridge over a stream. When the women come out of the courthouse, they stand on the bridge and throw their rings in the water. That's what we have to do.'

'But we're not in Reno.'

'It doesn't matter. I know just the place. Get your coat.'

A few minutes later we were downstairs getting into a taxi. 'Central Park Lake,' he told the driver. 'The dock near the boathouse.'

'You crazy, mister?' the cabby asked. 'They don't rent out boats at night.'

'Drive, my good man,' Guy said with a lordly wave of his hand. He sank back into his seat as the cab started off with a jerk, made a U-turn and went into the park at the Avenue of the Americas entrance. He stuck his hand into his pocket and came up with another joint, which he promptly lit. He blew the smoke out contentedly.

Abruptly the taxi slowed down. The driver looked back at us. 'You better cut that out, mister,' he warned. 'You want to get us all busted?'

Guy smiled and held the cigarette toward the driver. 'Relax. Have a toke. Enjoy life.'

The driver reached back and took the joint. He took two good long hits, then passed it back. 'That's good grass, mister. You get it locally?'

'Brought it all the way from California last week. Can't get shit like that around here.' He passed me the joint. 'Here, baby.'

I sucked on it. It did make me feel good. Walter never really approved of my smoking grass except when we were alone. But it never made me any higher than he got on whiskey.

The taxi slowed down and came to a stop. 'We're here,' the cabbie announced.

'Hold the clock,' Guy said, opening the door. 'We'll only be a minute.'

'This place ain't safe at night,' the cabbie said.

Guy gave him the joint. 'Drag on that. We'll be right back.'

The cabbie took the joint with one hand and with the other picked up a tire iron from the floor. 'Okay,' he said. 'But God better help any spic or nigger that comes near.'

We went up the walk onto the dock, then stopped and leaned on the railing to look out over the water. It was absolutely still, not a ripple marred its surface.

'Take your ring off,' Guy said.

It wouldn't budge. My fingers were swollen. I looked at Guy helplessly. 'What do we do now?' I asked.

'Leave it to me.' He cupped his hands around his mouth and yelled at the taxi driver. 'Do you have a file there?'

In the night the sound of his voice was like an explosion.

The cabbie's voice echoed back. 'What the hell do you think I'm drivin'? A plumber's shop?'

Guy turned back to me. 'Cabs aren't what they used to be,' he said. He took my hand and led me off the dock and across the damp ground to the water's edge. 'Put your hand in it,' he said.

I knelt and stretched out my hand. I looked up at him. 'I can't reach it.'

'Give me your hand. I'll hold you.'

He gripped my hand firmly and I leaned forward. The water was cold against my fingers. 'Okay?'

'Okay.' After a few minutes my fingers began to numb. 'This water is freezing,' I said.

'Good. That should do it,' he said and let go of my hand.

It wasn't deep, but it was wet and cold and when I stood up the water came just below my knees. I took his hand and climbed out.

All the way back to the cab he apologized. I was so angry I couldn't speak.

The cabbie stared at us as Guy opened the door. 'You're not getting into my cab like that.'

'There's an extra ten dollars in it for you.'

'Got any more of that grass?'

'A couple of joints.'

'Ten bucks plus the grass,' the cabbie said quickly.

'Okay.'

We got into the taxi and he pulled away with a roar. 'We better get out of here,' he said with a glance in the rearview mirror. 'They pull you in for swimming in the lake.'

Guy had his jacket off and around my shoulders. I looked down at my hand. The ring was still there. Suddenly I began to laugh so hard that tears came to my eyes.

Guy didn't understand it. 'What's so funny? You're liable to wind up with pneumonia.'

I couldn't stop laughing. 'We were supposed to throw the ring in the water. Not me.'

I came down from the bedroom wrapped in a heavy terry cloth robe. He was sitting on the edge of the couch and got to his feet. 'You okay?'

'Fine.' I looked at the bar. 'Any sandwiches left? Swimming always makes me hungry.'

'Plenty. I made some coffee too.'

We were both sober now.

'I'm sorry,' he said.

'Don't be,' I answered. 'I enjoyed every minute of it. If you hadn't come over I probably would have spent the night being miserable and feeling sorry for myself.'

He smiled and picked up his own coffee cup. 'Good.' He looked at me thoughtfully.

'What are you thinking?'

'About you,' he said. 'About how things are going to change.'

I was silent.

'They are going to change. You know that, don't you?'

'I guess so, but I don't know exactly how.'

'For one thing,' he said, 'you're not Mrs Walter Thornton anymore. And that will make a difference. Doors won't open as easily.'

I nodded. 'I kind of figured that. I used to wonder whether people liked me for me or because I was Walter's wife.'

'Both,' he said. 'But being Walter's wife made it practical.'

'I'm still the same person,' I said. 'I have the same talents as I did when I was married to him.'

'True.'

'You're trying to tell me something,' I said. 'What is it?'

He didn't answer.

I had an intuitive flash. 'Fannon still likes my play. He is taking an option on it, isn't he?'

'He still likes it, but now he won't option until after the rewrite.'

I was silent for a moment. Earlier in the week Fannon had done everything except force the check into my hands. Now it was a different story. The divorce had been in the morning papers. 'Did he think Walter would rewrite the play for me?'

'Not exactly, but he probably thought that Walter would be there to help out if he was needed.'

I felt the resentment rising. 'Shit! Now he won't get the play even if he wants it.'

'You listen to me, because I'm your friend and I love you. I also happen to believe in you. So, lesson number one, Fannon happens to be the best producer in town for your play, and if he wants it you're going to have to give it to him.'

'He's a dirty old man. He makes me feel slimy the way he undresses me with his eyes every time we meet.'

'That's lesson number two. You're in a business that is controlled by dirty old men and fags. You'll have to get along with them.'

'Isn't there anything in between?' I asked.

'Bridgeport,' he said.

'I've been there.'

'Then you know what I mean. This is the Big Town. You make it here and you make it anywhere in the world.'

'I'm beginning to get scared,' I said. 'Somehow Walter made everything seem so easy.'

He reached out and took my hand. 'Don't be. You'll make it all right. You've got the talent. Now you've got to fight.'

'I don't know how,' I said. 'I've never had to before. I went right from my parents' home to Walter. And he never wanted to let me grow up.'

'That was always one of Walter's problems,' Guy said. 'He tried to rewrite life like he did his scripts. But things had a way of getting away from him and he never could understand why. Proof. You grew up in spite of it, didn't you?'

'Now I'm not so sure.'

'Well, I am,' he said, getting to his feet. 'It's after three. I'd better let you get some sleep.' I followed him to the door. 'You come to my office at ten o'clock Tuesday morning. We'll go over the play and then I'll buy you lunch.'

'Thank you, but you don't have to take me to lunch if you have something more important to do.'

'Lesson number three. When a director or a producer offers to take you to lunch you say, "Yes, sir." '

'Yes, sir.'

He laughed and kissed my cheek. I closed the door behind him, went back into the apartment and looked around the living room. Somehow it all seemed strange and foreign to me now. Suddenly I realized why.

I didn't live here anymore.

CHAPTER THREE

MY FATHER'S CAR was blocking the driveway so I pulled to a stop in front of the house. I had just cut the motor when my brother came out of the house and down the walk toward me. For a moment it was hard to believe that it was Bobby.

He was tall, over six feet and slim. Somehow the gray-blue Air Force uniform made him look older and taller than his twenty years. He came around the car and pulled open the door. 'Holy cow!' he said, sticking his head inside the car and looking at the wood-paneled dashboard of the Jaguar.

'You could say hello first.'

'A sister is a sister. But a new car is a joy forever,' he said, kissing me on the cheek.

'What are you doing in that unform? R.O.T.C. comes home with you now?' I asked as I got out of the car.

'Nope,' he said. 'I'm in. They accepted me for pilot training so I decided, Why wait? If I did, the war might be over before I graduated. I leave Monday for San Antonio.'

'What did Mother say?'

'You know.' He made a face. 'She hollered a lot.'

'She was right this time,' I said, opening the trunk.

He reached over and took out my small suitcase. 'Don't you start in,' he said, 'I got enough from Mother.'

I snapped the trunk lid shut and followed him up the walk. 'We have no business being in Vietnam,' I said. 'But as long as they can get kids like you to go, it will never end.'

'You're beginning to sound like all those other New York commies.'

'Shit, Bobby, I just don't like the idea of my kid brother having his head shot off in some stupid jungle.'

'I wouldn't worry about it,' he said. 'The President says it'll all be over by Christmas, and I'll be in school for two years so I'll probably miss it all anyway.'

He stopped on the front steps of the porch and turned to look back at the car. 'I didn't know you had a new car.'

'It's almost a year old.'

'Looks new.'

'Can't drive a car much in the city.'

'It's smooth,' he said. 'Expensive?'

'Five thousand.'

He whistled. 'Whose is it? Yours or Walter's?'

'Mine. I paid for it with my own money. Walter thinks anything other than a Cadillac isn't worth buying.'

'That means you get to keep it.'

'Of course.'

He looked at me. 'I'm sorry about the divorce. I liked Walter.'

I met his gaze. 'So did I. But we just weren't making it. The divorce was the best thing for both of us.'

He pulled open the door. 'You planning to go out tonight?'

I knew what he was getting at. 'You want to borrow the car?'

He nodded. 'I got a heavy date tonight. Sort of goodbye thing.'

I handed him the keys. 'Just be careful with it. It's a hot car.'

A grin crossed his face and for a moment I saw the little boy I had always known. 'Thanks, Sis. I'll handle it with kid gloves.'

Mother didn't really start in on me until after dinner, when she followed me out to the porch.

We were silent while I lit a cigarette. I saw the disapproving look in her eyes. 'Is your apartment ready?' she finally asked.

'Yes. I'm moving in on Monday.'

'I hope it's a safe building. I read stories in the paper every day about things happening.'

'It's safe.'

'Do you have a doorman?'

'No. Doorman buildings are too expensive. I can't afford it.'

'I'm surprised Walter allowed you to do that.'

'It's not his responsibility. We're divorced, remember?'

'I'm sure he would have given you more money if you had asked him for it,' she said.

Now I knew what she was getting at. 'Why can't you come right out and ask what's on your mind, Mother? Do you want to know how much alimony Walter is paying me?'

'You don't have to tell me. It's really none of my business.'

'I don't mind telling you,' I said. 'Nothing.'

'Nothing?' she echoed, disbelief in her voice. 'How could he do a thing like that? I think it's terrible.'

'I don't. I didn't want any.'

'But you told me about all the money he was paying to his ex-wife. Why shouldn't you get any?'

'I said I didn't want it, Mother.'

'But you were married for six years,' she protested. 'How are you going to live?'

'I can work, Mother. I've got a play that might be produced and I'm up for several parts in shows.'

'But if nothing happens what are you going to do for money then?'

'I have some money. Walter would never let me touch a penny of the money I earned. It's all in the bank.'

She was silent, waiting.

'Would you like to know how much I have?'

'You don't have to tell me. It's really none – '

'I know, Mother,' I said sarcastically. 'It's really none of your business but I'll tell you anyway. I should have about eleven thousand dollars.'

'Is that all? I thought you were getting seven hundred and fifty dollars a week while you were in the play. What did you do with all that money?'

'Taxes took a big part of it. Walter is in a top bracket and we filed a joint return. The car, clothes and furniture took the rest.'

'Maybe you ought to sell the car. I don't see why you need a car in the city at all. Especially an expensive car like that.'

'But I like it. I wouldn't have bought it if I didn't.'

'I wish you had spoken to your father and me before you did anything.'

I was silent.

'Walter was a good man. You shouldn't have left him like that.'

'I discovered I didn't love him anymore, Mother. It wouldn't have been fair to stay on with him, knowing that.'

'Are you in love with someone else?'

'No.'

'Then you shouldn't have left,' she said emphatically. 'You don't break up a good marriage on a whim.'

'It was not a whim,' I explained patiently. 'And if I had stayed on we would have wound up hating each other. This way we're still friends.'

'I'm afraid I'll never understand you, JeriLee. Do you know what you're looking for?'

'Yes, me.'

She was genuinely puzzled. 'What kind of an answer is that?'

I was tired and went up to bed early. But as soon as I lay down I was wide awake. I got out of bed and sat near the window with a cigarette. I wasn't even thinking. I remembered sitting in this same window staring at the same street ever since I had been a little girl.

The picture flashed through my mind. The little girl sat at the top of the stairs and cried. The little girl was me. But I was no longer a little girl, so why was I crying?

There was a soft knock. 'Are you still awake, honey?' my father whispered.

I opened the door. His face, framed by the hall light, was a little thinner and a little more lined than I remembered. 'Can't sleep?' he asked.

I shook my head.

'I can make you some hot milk.'

'I'll be okay.'

'I hope Mother didn't upset you. It's only that she worries about you.'

'I know. She didn't.'

'She has a lot on her mind. Bobby's signing up upset her more than she admits.'

'And now me. I guess it doesn't make things any easier.'

'We'll manage. All we want is for you both to be all right.' He hesitated a moment. 'You know that if there's anything you need, anything, all you have to do is call us.'

I leaned over and kissed his cheek.

He patted my hair gently. 'I don't like to see you hurting.'

'It's my fault,' I said. 'And I'll have to work it out myself. But it will get better now that I have the chance.'

He looked at me silently for a moment, then nodded. 'I'm sure it will,' he said. 'The last thing in the world you needed was another father.'

My surprise showed in my eyes. He didn't wait for me to speak. 'Walter's problem was the same as mine. Neither of us wanted to believe that you were growing up.' His smile suddenly warmed his face. 'I knew that the moment I saw you in his play. He would like nothing better than to keep you that girl forever. But the difference between life and the play is that life changes and plays don't. That girl in the play is still the same age today that she was five years ago. But you're not.'

I felt the tears running down my cheeks. He pulled my head against his chest. A thoughtful tone came into his voice. 'Don't feel bad, JeriLee. It could have been worse. Some people just never grow up at all.'

CHAPTER FOUR

I WATCHED MY FATHER walk down the hall into his room before I closed the door. I lit another cigarette and went back to the window.

The girl in the play never grew up at all. But I had been the girl in the play. Was I still the same girl? Was the growing up I thought I did an illusion? I still remembered that afternoon, the second week of rehearsals, when my growing up began.

I didn't want to do it. I kept saying I wasn't an actress. But Walter and Guy kept pressing and finally I gave in. At first I felt strange and awkward. An amateur among professionals. But I learned bit by bit. By the end of the first week they could hear me in the balcony. Everyone was so nice, so considerate, I began to feel more comfortable, more sure. Until that afternoon when it came at me from out of the blue.

Beau Drake had come from Hollywood to make his first appearance on the New York stage since he had left fifteen years before. He was a star and he knew it. He was a professional and never let anyone forget it, especially me. He knew and pulled all the tricks. Half the time I found myself playing the scene with my back to the audience, other times I would be hidden by his broad shoulders or upstaged and left hanging while the attention of the audience was directed to another portion of the stage.

In the beginning I didn't know enough to be bothered by it, but as I began to realize what he was doing, I started to get angry. I didn't want more of a role than the play gave me, but I felt I was entitled to what I did have. I began to fight back in the only way I could. By this time I recognized that he was a stickler for cue lines. The slightest variation in the reading would throw him off. And so I began to change the lines that Walter had written into my own language.

It was the second run-through of the afternoon and we were at the climax of the second act, the scene just before curtain, when he blew. 'God damn it!' he suddenly roared.

We froze. Dan Keith, who played my father, stared first at

him then at me. Jane Carter, in the wings waiting for her entrance, stood with her mouth agape while Beau marched angrily down to the center of the stage and leaned over the footlights.

'I'm not getting paid enough money to be Stanislavsky,' he shouted at Guy and Walter. 'If I wanted to run an acting school for stage-struck girls I could do better in Hollywood. If you can't get Mrs Thornton to say the lines that were written for her, you can find yourself another actor for my part. I'm walking!'

He turned and stalked off the stage. There wasn't a sound or a movement until we heard the door of his dressing room slam shut backstage. Then everybody began to speak at once.

'Quiet!' Guy's voice was firm as he came up on the stage followed by Walter. He looked at Dan and Jane. 'We'll break for a half hour.'

They nodded and left the stage silently. Guy and Walter looked at me without speaking. I remembered feeling just at that moment like a child defying her parents.

'You saw what he was doing,' I accused. 'It wasn't right. He was doing everything to make me look stupid.'

I had nothing more to say so I began to cry. 'Okay. I never said I was an actress. I'll go.'

Guy's voice was quiet. 'No. I'll decide that. I'm the director.'

'It's the best thing for the play,' I sobbed. 'He hates me. You won't have any trouble with another girl.'

'Beau is right,' Guy said. 'You were changing the lines on him. Why?'

'He had no right to do what he was doing.'

'You didn't answer my question.'

'You didn't answer mine,' I retorted.

'I don't have to. I wasn't tampering with the author's lines.'

'If you objected to it, why didn't you say something?'

'Because it wasn't time. What I want to know is why you did it.'

'It was the only way I could get him to let me play my part.'

Guy and Walter exchanged a communicative glance. 'That's not a good enough reason,' Guy said.

Suddenly I was no longer intimidated. 'Then how about this one? There was no way I could get myself to say those lines and still be the seventeen-year-old-girl you want me to be. Those lines are written for a thirty-year-old woman. I don't know any kids who talk like that.'

For a moment there was silence, then I caught a glimpse of Walter's set and guarded face. 'Oh, Walter, I'm sorry. I didn't mean it like it sounded. I – '

'It's all right,' he said stiffly. Abruptly he turned and walked off the stage.

I started after him but Guy held out a hand. 'Let him go.'

'What are you talking about? That's my husband walking out.'

'Not your husband. The playwright.'

'I hurt him. I'm going after him.'

'No, you're not. He's a pro, he'll get over it.'

'I don't understand.'

'Someone had to tell him. The lines weren't right. It was becoming more obvious every day. If the dialogue were right, Beau would not have had the chance to do what he did. He'd be too busy working on his own part.'

Over Guy's shoulder I saw Beau coming out of the wings. He seemed relaxed as he approached us. 'Everything okay?' he asked in a casual voice.

'Fine, now,' Guy answered as if nothing had happened.

Suddenly I understood and I felt the anger surging within me. 'You set me up for this,' I accused. 'Because none of you had the nerve to tell him the truth.'

'You were the only one he would take it from,' Guy said. 'Now he'll go back and rewrite until he gets those lines right.'

'You're a shit!' I snapped.

'I never said I was a saint.'

'The truth,' I said. 'Can't any of you tell the truth? Do you always have to manipulate others into doing your dirty work for you when the truth is so much simpler?'

'That's show business,' Guy said glibly.

'I don't like it,' I said.

'You better get used to it if you're going to stay in it.'

'I had no intention of doing that either.'

'If you plan to stay married to Walter, you'll get used to it whether you like it or not. Because he's going to be around for a long time. This is the only life he knows or wants.' He started for the wings without waiting for a reply. 'Rehearsal at two o'clock tomorrow,' he called back over his shoulder.

Beau and I were left alone on the stage. He smiled slowly. 'Just you and me, baby.'

'I don't think that's funny.'

'I'm sorry. I didn't mean for it to get so rough.'

When I didn't answer, a look of contrition came over his face. 'I couldn't help it. I guess I'm a better actor than I thought.'

That broke the ice. I began to smile. 'You're pretty good,' I said. 'But you're also a prick.'

He grinned. 'I've been called worse. But it's all for a good cause. Can I buy you a drink just to show there's no hard feelings?'

'I don't drink,' I said. 'But you can buy me a cup of coffee.'

It all worked the way they had planned it. By the time I got home that night Walter was working on the rewrite. He didn't come to bed at all and the next morning when I came down for breakfast there was a note on the table.

> Dearest,
> Have gone to Guy's for breakfast to go over the new lines. See you at rehearsal. Love,
>
> Walter.
>
> P.S. Please forgive me but I had to use your lines. They were better than anything I could dream up.
>
> W.

I felt the warm glow of approval, and later in rehearsal I noticed that the changes had already been incorporated. For the first time we were all together.

It wasn't until long afterward that I realized what that afternoon cost me. By that time Beau and I had already picked up our Tonys for best actor and supporting actress, even though the award for the best play had gone to another writer. It happened the week the play closed on Broadway after a year's run.

I had a suggestion to make to Walter about his new script and went into his study to give it to him. He listened to me impassively. When I finished he reached for the script I still held in my hand.

'You weren't supposed to read this,' he said.

'I didn't know that, Walter. I picked up the copy in the bedroom.'

'I forgot it.'

'I was only trying to help.'

'When I want help I'll ask for it.'

It was not until then that I really believed they had found the only way to get him to make the changes. He didn't care any more for the truth than the others in the business. All they were really interested in was their own egos.

'I'm sorry,' I said stiffly. 'It won't happen again.'

'I don't mean to sound harsh. But you can't know what it is until you do it yourself. You have some idea how difficult it is. You tried to write once yourself.'

'Then I'll find out,' I said. 'Now that the play is closed and I have the time to spare, I have an idea of my own that I want to try.'

'Good. If you have any problems you can talk to me about it.'

I didn't answer. But when I left the room my mind was already made up. He was the last person in the world I was going to go to for help.

That had been four years ago and the beginning of the end of our marriage. After that in a thousand subtle ways I became aware that he felt challenged. Now it was over. I hoped that he was no longer threatened.

I heard the telephone begin to ring downstairs and glanced at my watch. It was after two in the morning. I had been sitting at the window for over an hour. An impulse made me go downstairs to answer it. My parents were old-fashioned enough to believe that extension telephones were a needless extravagance.

The voice on the phone was harsh and strangely familiar. 'Veronica?'

'No. This is JeriLee.'

'JeriLee, I didn't know you were home. This is Chief Roberts. Do you own a blue Jaguar?'

My heart began to pound but I tried to keep my voice calm. 'Yes.'

'There's been an accident.'

'Oh, no!'

My parents had suddenly appeared behind me. My father reached and took the telephone from my hand. 'This is John Randall.'

He listened for a moment, then his face went white. 'We better get dressed,' he said as he put down the phone. 'There's been an accident and Bobby's in the hospital at Jefferson.'

CHAPTER FIVE

My brother never went to Vietnam. The car went off the road on the same curve that had killed my father fifteen years before. He lived only long enough to apologize to my mother.

'I'm sorry, Ma,' he whispered through the maze of tubes that ran in and out of his body. 'I guess I had too much to drink.' Then he turned his head away and went to sleep. And never woke up.

Mother seemed to turn to stone. For her it must have been like a nightmare revisited. No matter what we said or tried to do we received no response. The only question she addressed to Chief Roberts. 'Was he alone in the car?'

'Yes, Veronica. He dropped Anne off at her house fifteen minutes earlier. She said she asked him to stay and have a cup of coffee before he went home but he said he wanted to get JeriLee's car home so that she wouldn't worry about it.'

She nodded without speaking.

'Anne said they were planning to get married before he went off to training camp,' he said. 'Did you know she was pregnant?'

My mother stared at him.

'He hadn't said anything to us,' my father said.

'She said he was going to tell you this morning.'

'You spoke to her?' my father asked.

The chief nodded. 'The accident went out on the one o'clock news flash on the Jefferson radio station. She called here and I spoke to her. She's pretty broken up.'

'The poor kid,' I said. 'She's got to be scared to death.'

My mother turned on me angrily. 'Don't feel sorry for that slut! I warned Bobby that she would do anything to trap him.'

'I don't know the girl,' I said. 'But it can't be – '

'I do,' my mother cut in in an icy voice. 'I'm almost glad that he's beyond her reach.'

I felt my heart swell up and almost choke me. Suddenly I realized something I had never known before. I had never seen my mother cry. Never. Not even now. I couldn't stop the words. 'Don't you know how to cry, Mother?'

She looked at me for a moment, then turned to my father. Her tone was almost normal. It was as if I had said nothing. 'We'll have to make arrangements for the funeral, John . . . '

I couldn't stand it. I forced myself between them and looked deep into her eyes. The tears were running down my cheeks. 'Bobby's dead, Mother. Your only son is dead. Can't you spare him any tears?'

Mother's voice was cold and calm. 'You have no right to speak like that, JeriLee. It's your fault this happened. You shouldn't have given him the car.'

It was too much for me. In tears, I turned and walked down the short flight of stairs to the main floor, then out the front door.

The dawn was breaking in the east. The morning air was cold. I shivered but it wasn't from the cold. I finished a cigarette from my purse and was about to light it when a large calloused hand held a burning match for me. It was Chief Roberts.

'I'm sorry, JeriLee,' he said. There was genuine sympathy in his voice.

'I know.'

'I don't like to bother you at a time like this, but there are certain questions that have to be answered.'

'I understand. Go ahead.'

'The car registered and insured to you?'

'Yes.'

'You'll have to notify your insurance company. I ordered it towed to Clancy's garage on Main Street.'

I looked at him.

'It's totaled. There won't be anything they can do with it.'

I was silent.

'I can come by the house later and you can sign the accident report. You don't have to come down to the station.'

'Thank you.'

'Chief Roberts,' I called as he started to turn away.

'Yes?'

'That girl, Anne?'

He nodded.

'Tell her to call me. Maybe there's something I can do.'

'I'll do that, JeriLee,' he said. 'I've known her as long as I've known you. Since she was a baby. She's a right nice girl.'

'She has to be if my brother loved her.'

He nodded again, then looked up at the sky. 'It's going to be clear today.'

'Yes,' I said and watched the pudgy figure in the baby-blue uniform walk away from me.

He was right, I thought as I looked up. It would be a clear day. There wasn't a cloud in the sky.

The funeral was on Tuesday. Walter sent flowers from London and Guy came to hold my hand. When we came home afterward, Mother went right up to her room and closed the door. 'I guess I'll pack,' I said to my father. 'Guy offered to drive me back to the city.'

'I guess so,' he said. He looked tired. It had not been easy for him. He loved Bobby too.

'If you want me to stay, I will.'

'No. We can manage. It will be all right.'

'But will you be all right?' I asked pointedly.

He got the nuance. 'I'll be fine.' He hesitated a moment. 'Don't be angry with your mother. She's gone through a great deal.'

'I'm not angry. I just don't understand.'

'Then be charitable. Don't push her away. You're all she has left now.'

'I can't get through to her, Daddy,' I said. 'You know how many times I've tried. We don't think or feel alike about anything.'

'Keep trying,' he said. 'That's what love is about.'

I went over and put my arms around him. 'You never stop trying, do you, Daddy? You must love her very much.'

'I do. I see her faults. But they don't matter. I also see the good things about her. The strength and courage she had to go on with you two children after your own father died. Do you know she said she wouldn't marry me unless you approved? That she would never do anything that would make you unhappy?'

'I didn't know that.'

'Your aunt and uncle wanted to take you both off her hands so that she could be free to make a new life for herself. She wouldn't do it. She told them that you were her children, her responsibility, and that she was going to take care of you. The first thing she asked me about when I proposed was how I felt about the two of you.'

I kissed his cheek. He was lovely. And naïve. But then he loved her. He said so himself. So how could I expect him to see that all these wonderful things she said and did were not because she loved but because she thought they were the right things to do? I kissed his cheek again. 'I'll try to remember what you said, Daddy.'

The telephone rang. He picked it up, then held it out to me. 'For you.'

I took the phone from his hand. 'Give Guy a drink, will you, Daddy? I have a feeling he's dying of thirst.'

'I'm okay,' Guy said quickly.

Father took his arm and led him into the living room. 'I think I could use a whiskey myself,' he said.

'Hello,' I said into the phone.

The voice was soft and young and tired. 'Mrs Thornton?'

'Yes.'

'Anne Laren. Chief Roberts gave me your message. I wanted to call and thank you.'

'I meant it. If there is anything I can do . . . '

'No,' she said quickly. 'Nothing.' She hesitated a moment. 'Was everything all right? My flowers get there?'

'Yes. They were lovely.' I remembered. A blanket of yellow roses with just the small card and her name on it.

'I wanted to go, but the doctor wouldn't let me get out of bed.'

'Are you okay?'

'I am now,' she said. Again the moment's hesitation. 'I lost the baby, you know.'

'I'm sorry.'

'Maybe it's for the best,' she said. 'At least that's what everyone says.'

'I guess so,' I said.

She began to cry softly. 'But I wanted his baby. I really loved him.'

'I know.'

She stopped crying. I felt the control in her voice. 'I'm sorry. It's bad enough for you. I didn't want to make it any worse. I just wanted to thank you.'

'Anne,' I said, 'when you're feeling better, give me a call and come into the city. We'll have lunch. I'd love to meet you.'

'I'd like that,' she said. 'I will.'

My mother was standing at the foot of the stairs when I put down the telephone. 'Who were you talking to?' she asked.

'Anne.'

Her lips tightened slightly. 'Did you thank her for the flowers?'

'I thought you would do that.'

'If she loved him as much as she said she did, why didn't she come to the funeral?'

'Why didn't you ask her?'

Mother's eyes met mine. 'I called. But she wouldn't speak to me. I guess she was too ashamed of what she had done.'

'That wasn't the reason, Mother.'

'Then what was the reason?'

'She was probably too sick. She lost the baby.'

My mother's face suddenly went white and she seemed to stagger. I put out a hand to steady her. 'I'm sorry, JeriLee, I really am.'

I didn't speak but I could see the color slowly coming back into her face. A very strong lady, my mother. 'Now he's really gone,' she said.

We looked at each other for a long moment, then she took a tentative step toward me. I opened my arms. She came into them as if she were the child, and the tears finally came.

CHAPTER SIX

It was Wednesday, matinée day, and Sardi's was already crowded with ladies from the suburbs.

The bar was crowded too, but mostly with regulars. I nodded to several of them and the maitre d' came up to me. 'Mrs Thornton.' He bowed. 'So nice to see you again. Mr Fannon is expecting you.'

I followed him to Fannon's usual table. It was back against the wall separating the restaurant from the Little Bar – the most important location in the place. Everyone coming in or going out could see or be seen. I had heard he hadn't missed a week-day lunch there for fifteen years, except when he had been in the hospital, and then they had catered his meals.

He was sitting on the banquette. As I approached he tried to rise but his potbelly pressing against the table forced him to remain in a half crouch until I sat down next to him. He sank back into his seat with a sigh and kissed my cheek.

'You look beautiful, my dear,' he said in his hoarse voice.

'Thank you, Mr Fannon.'

'Adolph, my dear,' he said. 'Call me Adolph. After all, we're old friends.'

I nodded. We had known each other almost two years. That was a long run on Broadway, even for friendship. 'Thank you, Adolph.'

'A champagne cocktail for Mrs Thornton.' The waiter went away and he turned to me beaming. 'Nothing but the best for you.'

I liked champagne, but champagne cocktails made me nauseous. Nevertheless I smiled. 'Thank you, Adolph.'

'Taste it,' Fannon urged when the waiter returned with the cocktail.

I began to raise the glass toward my lips.

'Wait a minute, we must have a toast.' He picked up his own glass, which was supposed to look like vodka on the rocks but which everyone knew was nothing but water. Ulcers had taken away his liquor license. 'To your play,' he said.

I nodded and took a sip. The sickeningly sweet cocktail turned my stomach but I managed a smile. 'Very good,' I said.

A serious look came over his face. 'I have a very important announcement to make,' he said, putting his hand on my knee.

'Yes, Adolph,' I said, my eyes on his face.

'I've decided to do your play.' His hand was now halfway up my thigh. 'We'll go into rehearsal in August. I'd like to bring it to New York in October.'

Suddenly I forgot about his hand on my thigh. 'You mean it?'

'Yes. I loved the rewrite. I've already sent the script to Anne Bancroft.'

'You think she'll do it?'

'She should. She'll never find a better part. Besides she always wanted to do a play with Guy.'

'Is he going to direct?'

'Yes. I called him in California this morning and he's agreed.' His hand went the rest of the way up.

'Adolph, I never knew anyone who moved so fast,' I said pointedly.

He cleared his throat. 'When I like something, I like it. I don't believe in playing around.'

'Neither do I,' I said, looking into his eyes. 'But I'm soaking wet already and if you don't take your hand away, I'll come right here.'

He flushed and put his hand on the table, 'I'm sorry. In my enthusiasm I forgot myself.'

'It's okay. I just happen to be very excitable. And I've never known a man quite like you before.'

'No?' he asked in a questioning voice.

'You're something else. In a business full of wishy-washy people you have the strength of your convictions.'

'I make decisions,' he said, looking pleased. 'Like I told you, I know what I want.'

'That's what I admire about you.'

'We're going to be seeing a lot of each other. I'm not the kind of a producer who leaves it all up to the director. I get very involved with my plays.'

'I know. That's why I'm glad you're going to do it.'

'There's still work to be done on the script. We'll have to get started soon. I would like you to have my ideas before Guy gets back from the Coast.'

'You let me know when. I'll make myself available.'

'Good,' he said, obviously delighted with the way things were going. I had calculatedly told him everything he wanted to hear. His hand was on my knee again. 'My office is drawing up the contract. I thought a ten-thousand-dollar advance would be very fair. It's more than twice what I give anyone else for a first play.'

I believed him. Both Guy and my agent told me not to expect more than thirty-five hundred. 'That's very fair. Thank you, Adolph.'

'You deserve it,' he said, smiling. 'Besides from what I have heard you could use the money. I understand Walter didn't give you any alimony.'

'I didn't want any,' I said quickly.

'Most girls in this business don't feel like that.'

'That's their bag. I can work. I can take care of myself.'

His hand began to travel. 'That's what I respect about you.'

'I'm getting hungry,' I said, trying to divert him. 'I haven't had any breakfast.'

'Let's order then.'

But before he could signal the waiter, Earl Wilson of the New York *Post* came in and spotted us. His round face broke into a smile. 'Adolph, JeriLee, what are you two cooking up?'

'You've got a scoop, Earl. I'm putting on JeriLee's new play.'

'What kind of a part are you playing this time, JeriLee?'

'She's not acting in this one, Earl,' Fannon said. 'She wrote it.'

Earl whistled enthusiastically. 'That is a scoop.' He smiled at me. 'Did you have any help from your ex?'

'Walter had nothing to do with it,' Fannon said quickly. 'JeriLee was a writer before she was an actress. She only went into acting because Walter wanted her to do his play.'

'You got someone in mind for the lead?' the columnist asked.

'Anne Bancroft.'

Earl looked at me. 'How do you feel about it?'

'I'm thrilled,' I said and almost jumped out of my seat to prove it. Fannon's hand was on my cunt again.

The story was the lead item in the New York *Post* the next day.

> Adolph Fannon, noted Broadway producer, confided to us at Sardi's yesterday that he is planning to present

a new play on Broadway next season by Thornton's ex-wife. He also told us that Anne Bancroft is penciled in for the lead.

That was it. Walter Thornton's ex-wife. Although it had been two months since the divorce he never even mentioned my name.

I left the paper on the kitchen table and went into the living room just as the telephone began to ring.

It was Guy returning my call from California. 'Congratulations,' he said.

'I wanted to thank you. If it weren't for all the work you did on the play, Fannon would never have bought it.'

'I just made suggestions. You did the writing.'

'I'm glad you're going to direct it.'

'So am I.'

'He sent the script to Anne Bancroft.'

'He told you that?' Guy's voice was skeptical.

'Yes. He even told Earl Wilson, who ran it in today's column.'

Guy laughed. 'Don't you believe it. I'll give you ten to one she never got it.'

'Then why would he say something like that?'

'It's a flyer. He's smart. He figures she'll hear about it and be curious enough to ask her agent to get her a copy. That way she's asking him, he's not asking her.'

'Oh, Jesus.' I said.

'Did you get the contract yet?'

'My agent called this morning. He's got them. By the way, I'm getting a ten-thousand advance.'

'That's great. How are the payments scheduled?'

'I don't know. Why?'

'He never pays more than thirty-five hundred until the play opens on Broadway. What you'll probably get is a thousand on signing, a thousand when we go into rehearsal, fifteen hundred when we go on the road and the balance when and if we open in New York. Just don't spend it until you get it.'

'I don't know,' I said. 'He said a ten-thousand advance.'

'Everything you get before the show opens on Broadway is considered an advance,' he said. 'Check it with your agent.'

'I will,' I said. 'When are you coming back?'

'I should wrap up here in about a month.'

'Please hurry, Guy. I miss having you around.'

When Guy hung up I called my agent. The payment spread was exactly as Guy had explained it to me. Apparently I still had a lot to learn.

I sat down again at the kitchen table and took out my checkbook. Even with the thirty-two hundred I had gotten from the insurance company for my car I only had about a four-thousand-dollar balance. Furnishing the apartment had taken much more than I had figured.

I did some quick arithmetic. The apartment cost me about eleven hundred a month, including gas, electricity, telephone and a maid two days a week. Food, clothing and cabs came to another four hundred at least. With five months to go before we opened on Broadway, I'd be shaving it pretty close. And if the play didn't make it to Broadway, I'd be broke.

There was no getting away from it. I couldn't sit around and wait for the play to come through. I needed an acting job to get me through the summer. And I needed it right away.

CHAPTER SEVEN

I WAS ON TIME for my appointment at George Fox's office at ten o'clock the next morning and was ushered in almost immediately. George was senior vice president of Artists Alliance, Inc, and Walter was his personal client.

He was a short dapper man with gray hair and an easy smile. He came around the desk and kissed me on the cheek. 'Congratulations,' he said. 'Fannon's really high on your play.'

'Thank you,' I said, taking the seat in front of his desk. 'I am disappointed about the payments though. I had hoped that it would all be paid in advance.'

'They never do that,' he said quickly. 'Believe me, I personally went over your contract. You've got a very good deal for a first play. And more important, you have the hottest producer in town.'

'I know that. But I have money problems. I have to find some work if I want to make it until the play opens.'

'I can lend you some money,' he said quickly.

'There's no need for that. I can get by. What I need is some work.'

'Have you anything in mind?'

'Not really. I thought maybe I could pick up some work in summer stock.'

He looked doubtful. 'I shouldn't think so. All the shows are already packaged. They begin casting in January.'

'Some writing jobs then,' I said. I knew they were shooting next fall's TV programs.

'Pretty late for that too,' he said. 'That's usually wrapped up by January too.'

'Maybe there's an acting job in one of the pilots. After all, I have had stage experience. I saw in last week's *Variety* that they're short of new faces for TV.'

'They always say that but whenever possible they go with the tried and true. They like to play it safe. Besides all the action is out on the Coast and they would never pay your fare out even if they wanted you. In addition to everything else, they're cheap.'

'If there was a chance of my getting a few things. I'd pay my own way out.'

'I don't know. I'm really not up on the situation.' He thought for a moment. 'Let me put you together with a young man in our office who is into these things. I'm sure he'll find something for you.' He picked up the telephone. 'Ask Harry Gregg to come up here.'

A few minutes later Harry Gregg arrived. He was tall and thin with tousled hair and wore the black suit, white shirt, black tie and a reserved expression that was standard issue in the agency.

'Harry, let me introduce you to one of the agency's most important new talents as well as a close personal friend of mine, JeriLee Thornton . . . er, Randall. JeriLee, Harry Gregg, one of the agency's brightest and most up and coming young men.'

Harry smiled and we shook hands.

'I want you to do everything you can for her,' George continued. 'I'm making you personally responsible. We've already made a deal with Fannon to produce a play that she has written but I want you to explore other areas in which we might be of service.'

Before I knew it, I was out of George's office and sitting in Harry's tiny cubbyhole. 'Would you like some coffee?' he asked, pushing a pile of papers to one side of his desk.

I nodded.

'Two coffees,' he said into the phone. 'How do you take it?'

'Black. No sugar.'

A minute later his secretary came into the office with two plastic cups of coffee. It was very different than George's office. There the coffee was served from an elaborate silver set in genuine Wedgwood cups.

'Did George make the deal with Fannon for you?' Harry asked.

'No. I worked on it myself but mostly it was Guy Jackson. Without him it never would have happened.'

'I thought so.'

'What do you mean?'

'George is not a negotiator. He picks up packages.' He took a swallow of coffee. 'Is Guy directing?'

'Yes.'

'That's good. I like him,' he said. 'Are you friendly with your ex?' He saw the expression on my face. 'I don't mean to pry into your personal affairs, but it's important that I know how we stand.'

'Why?'

'Walter is one of the agency's most important clients. If he's down on you, the agency will bury you, no matter what bullshit they hand you.'

Suddenly I liked this young man. At least he was honest. 'We're friendly,' I said.

'Does George know that?'

'I don't know.'

'It would be helpful if he did. It would make my job easier. Right now, he probably doesn't know how things are between you.'

'Is that why I'm down here?'

'Don't quote me. But . . . yes.'

'I see.' I got to my feet. 'Is there any point in us talking then?'

'Sit down, sit down,' he said quickly. 'There's no point in going off half cocked. You've already got the play with us, you might as well go the rest of the way. We could get lucky.'

I returned to the seat and took a sip of coffee. I had always hated the taste of coffee in plastic cups.

'What are you looking for?' he asked.

'Work,' I said. 'Anything. Acting, writing.'

'Why?'

'I have to support myself.'

He was silent for a moment. I didn't know whether he believed me or not. 'Okay,' he said in a businesslike voice. 'We have to start somewhere. Do you have a portfolio?'

'Sort of.' I took a brown envelope out of my script case. 'Not very good though. They were all taken when I was in the play four or five years ago.'

He skimmed through the photographs. 'We're going to need new pictures. You looked like a kid then.'

'That was the part.'

'I'll need a complete layout. Face, character, cheesecake. Do you have a photographer?'

'No. But I know quite a few.'

'Do you think one of them would do it for you?'

'I don't know. I could ask.'

'If not, I know a very good one that would do exactly what we need for two hundred. And if you let him do a magazine layout on you, it could wind up costing you nothing and even making you a few dollars.'

'What kind of a layout?'

'You know. *Playboy.* You get fifteen hundred dollars.'

'I'd have to think about that,' I said. 'Wouldn't something like that screw up my career?'

'Your guess is as good as mine. Attitudes are changing. The studios aren't as uptight as they used to be.'

'Will he do the portfolio for the two hundred even if I don't go for the magazine deal?'

'Yes.'

'Then let's use him. I can afford that.'

'Okay. I'll set it up. Now, do you have a copy of the play that I can read?'

I took out a copy of the script and gave it to him.

'Is there a part in this for you?' he asked.

'The lead, but Fannon wants Anne Bancroft.'

'I'll read it,' he said. 'It will give me an idea of how you write.'

'I told George that I could go out to the Coast if you can line up a few guest spots on some of the pilot shows.'

At that moment the telephone rang. Listening, he said, 'Put him on,' then, 'Hello, Tony.'

He was silent for about two minutes. Finally he spoke. 'How old is this girl as you see her?'

The voice crackled on the other end. 'We may be in luck, Tony,' he said. 'I've just picked up a new client. Remember JeriLee Randall? Walter Thornton's ex-wife. She did a year on Broadway in his play and she's just the right age. Twenty-three, that's right. And she looks sensational. We got just one problem. I don't know whether she'll do a part like that. She's a very classy dame.'

He listened for a few more minutes, then interrupted. 'Send me the script, Tony. I'll talk to her and see what I can do.'

'No, Tony,' he said into the phone. 'I told you she's a very classy dame. She doesn't do cocktail interviews. That's not her style.' He paused for a moment, then looked over at me. 'What's she look like?' he echoed. 'She's sensational. Stacked like you would not believe, but very classy. Sort of a combination Ava Gardner and Grace Kelly. She's the kind who when she comes into your office you want to bend down and kiss her pussy out of sheer reverence. So send me the script and I'll get on it right away.'

He put down the telephone. 'I'm sorry I had to talk like that,' he apologized. 'But that's the only language that son of a bitch understands. He thinks he can fuck every actress who comes into his office.'

'Who is he?'

'Tony Styles. He's got a part open in a picture that starts shooting in New York next week and the girl he was counting on for the part got a job on the Coast.'

I had heard about him. I thought I might have met him once at a party in Hollywood with Walter. A vulgar little man with a dirty mouth. But he and his brother made pictures that made money. The Styles Brothers. 'What kind of a part is it?'

'Two weeks' work. A high class New York call girl who runs through the picture getting in and out of her clothes. He said she had some good lines but I'll know more when I see the script. He's desperate though and he might go as high at twenty-five hundred for the two weeks.'

'Can I read it after you get through?' I asked.

'Of course.' He looked at his watch. 'My God, it's lunchtime. Do you have a date?'

'I'm free.'

'Good. I'll buy you some lunch and we can talk some more.'

And lunch was different too. We had sandwiches in his office.

CHAPTER EIGHT

THEY WERE TWINS but you wouldn't believe it looking at them. Tony Styles was five four, pudgy and vulgar, while his brother John was six one, slim, esthetic-looking and quiet. Tony's own description was perhaps the best. 'John's the artist in the family. He's got everything. Good taste, good manners and class. Me, I'm the hustler. But we go good together. I shoot all the shit. John shoots the picture.'

I sat on the couch in his office with Harry next to me. Across the room Tony was seated behind the desk while John leaned against the wall. Beyond the standard greeting, John hadn't said a word, but his eyes were watchful.

'Did you like the script?' Tony asked.

'She loved it,' Harry said quickly.

John spoke for the first time. 'Really?'

I didn't like the tone in his voice. It was as if he doubted that anyone with good taste could like it. Unfortunately, he was right, I met his eyes. 'Not really,' I said.

Harry was silent at my side.

'What did you really think of it?' John asked.

I consoled myself with the thought that I wouldn't have gotten the job anyway. 'It's a piece of shit. Commercial shit probably. But shit anyway.'

Tony looked at his brother with a triumphant smile. 'See? I told you she'd like it.'

I laughed. He had to be completely crazy. I could see John's eyes smiling with me.

Tony turned back to me. 'Do you think you could do the part?'

I nodded, knowing that any girl with a good body would do just as well.

'We could add some dialogue. You know, give you some business. Make it interesting.'

'That would be nice.'

'Would you mind standing?'

I got to my feet.

'Would you take off your shoes, please?'

They weren't high heels but I slipped out of them. He turned to his brother. 'Not too tall, you think?'

John shook his head.

'Those tits real?' Tony asked. 'You're not wearing falsies?'

'I'm not wearing a brassiere, period,' I said.

Tony met my gaze without smiling. 'I had to ask, you know.'

'I know,' I said. My basic costume for the picture consisted of a brassiere and panties.

'Do you have a bikini with you?'

I nodded.

'You can change in there,' he said, pointing to a small door at the far side of the office.

It was a little private john. I changed quickly and went back into the office. I walked in front of the desk. He was watching me. I turned around slowly and stopped.

'Okay,' he said. 'One other thing. We shoot a few scenes separately for the foreign version. They ain't got the same hang-ups we Americans have. Would you object to a little nudity?'

I looked at him silently.

'Nothing vulgar,' he added quickly. 'Discreet. Good taste. But sexy. You know. Like Bardot or Lollobrigida. Quality.'

Harry was suddenly on his feet. 'That's out,' he said. He turned to me. 'Get dressed, JeriLee. We're leaving.'

I started back to the john. Through the closed door I could hear Tony protesting. By the time I came back into the room it had all calmed down. 'It's okay,' Harry said. 'You don't have to do the nude scenes.'

'I changed my mind,' I said. 'I don't want to do the picture at all.'

Harry stared at me, his mouth open.

I looked down at Tony. 'Nice meeting you both. Good luck with the picture.' I picked up my bag and walked out.

Harry caught up to me at the elevator. 'I don't get it,' he said, bewildered. 'I had you locked in for thirty-five hundred and you walk out.'

'I'm not a piece of meat,' I said. 'Let him go to the nearest butcher shop if that's what he's looking for.'

The doors opened and he followed me into the elevator. 'Okay. Now what do we do?'

'You tell me,' I said. 'You're the agent.'

'I'll try to think of something.'

By the time I got home there was a message on the answering service. Call John Styles. I hesitated for a moment, then dialed the number.

John Styles answered.

'This is JeriLee Randall,' I said. 'You asked me to call.'

His voice was quiet. 'I'm sorry if my brother upset you, Miss Randall. I'd like you to do the part. I wish you would reconsider.'

'What for? You know how I feel about the screenplay.'

'That's the script, Miss Randall. But films are a director's medium. The script can be changed. And I'm the director.'

My voice was skeptical. 'You mean that you'd rewrite for me?'

'No, Miss Randall,' the gentle voice replied. 'For myself.'

'But my part isn't important enough for that.'

'Right. But within the context of the film it can be valid. And I think that you're the one that can make it work.'

'Do I have time to think about it?'

'Not much. We'll have to have your answer by tomorrow morning. We go on the floor Monday.'

'I'll call you in the morning.'

'Thank you, Miss Randall.'

'Thank you, Mr Styles.' I put down the phone and called Harry on his direct line.

'John Styles just called me,' I said.

'I know. He called me first. I let him talk me into giving him your number.'

'Why'd you do that?'

'Two reasons. One, it's now five grand for the two week's work. Two. John says you'll be treated right and I believe him. He's got a good reputation.'

'Then what do we do now?'

'We take the job.'

'Right,' I said. And we did.

John Styles did something special with what began as a stereotyped role. Suddenly the hooker developed into a frightened desperate girl trying to survive in society with the only talents at her disposal. Still it was a small role and since I didn't have that much to do, I spent a good part of my time just hanging around the set.

John was good. In his own low-key manner he kept everything moving and under control. There were no flaps, no panic, no pressure. He just moved from shot to shot putting together his film. He came over to me after I had finished my last scene.

'You were very good, JeriLee. Thank you.'

'You made it possible,' I said. 'Thank you.'

He smiled. 'You were right for the part. I couldn't let my brother frighten you away.'

'I'm glad you didn't.'

'How about dinner tonight?' he asked. 'No shooting tomorrow.'

'Okay,' I said, surprised. He had given no sign of any special interest while we had been working.

'I can pick you up about eight o'clock.'

'Fine.'

'Twenty One, okay?' he said when I got into the cab.

'Lovely.' I hadn't been there for dinner since my divorce.

Chuck greeted us at the door as we came in. 'Mr Styles,' he said. Then he saw me and his eyes widened. 'Hi, Mrs Thornton.' He beckoned to a maitre d'. 'We have a table for Mr Styles in the main dining-room upstairs.'

'But I reserved in the bar,' John said.

Chuck flushed with embarrassment. 'It's a bit crowded in there,' he said quickly. 'You'll be more comfortable upstairs.'

'Okay, Chuck,' I said. 'Out with it.'

'Your ex is in there, Mrs Thornton. And the only table open is right opposite his.'

John looked at me.

'But I reserved in the bar,' John said.

The bar was crowded. We followed the waiter to our table. Walter was with George Fox. He didn't see us until after we sat down. When he did, he rose and came over to our table.

I held up my cheek for his kiss, then I introduced him to John. They shook hands with a display of show business cool but my legs were trembling.

Walter smiled. 'George told me how well you were doing. I'm pleased.'

'I've been lucky.'

'You've got talent. I always said that.' He looked at John. 'How's the picture coming?'

'Good. We've wrapped up here and move back to the Coast over the weekend.'

'Are you going out too, JeriLee?'

'No. I finished today.'

'Maybe we can have lunch one day next week then?'

'I'd like that.'

'I'll call you.' He smiled. 'Enjoy your dinner.'

I thought as I watched him walk back to his table that he looked a little tired. But then he was always a little tired. It seemed to be a condition of his existence.

'Why don't you?' John's voice interrupted my thoughts.

'Why don't I what?'

'Come out to the Coast with us.'

'That's ridiculous. What on earth for?'

'To get away. I think you need a change of scene.'

'Maybe I do. But I can't afford it. I have to stick around here and look for another job.'

'There's work out there too.'

'My agent thinks I have a better chance here. He doesn't want me to go out there except for a firm job.'

'Agents like to keep clients under their thumb.'

'I'd need a better reason than that.'

'Okay. How about this one? Because I want you to.'

I was silent, looking at him.

'No strings,' he said quickly. 'I'm not my brother.'

I shook my head. 'Not yet.' I took a sip of water. My mouth had suddenly gone dry. 'Maybe later. When I'm sure I can handle things.'

'Like what?'

'Myself.'

'I think you do very well.'

'I don't know yet.'

'Chuck is smarter than we are,' he said. 'It would have been better if we had gone upstairs.'

I felt the pressure of the tears behind my eyes but I managed a smile. 'You know something? You're absolutely right.'

Then we both laughed and it wasn't as bad after that.

CHAPTER NINE

IT WAS ABOUT one o'clock in the morning when the telephone rang. I had just dozed off, and I reached for the phone still in the fog of early sleep.

'Are you alone?' It was Walter.

I came out of the fog. 'Yes.'

'I had to call you.' He paused for a moment and I could hear the wheeze deep in his chest. He was still smoking too much. 'There were so many things I wanted to say to you when I saw you in the restaurant.'

I fished for a cigarette and lit it. The lighter made a loud rasping click.

'Are you sure you're alone?'

'I'm alone.'

'I thought I heard something.'

'It was my cigarette lighter.' I was getting annoyed. One of the most difficult things in our relationship had been his insatiable desire to know everything I had done and thought every minute of the day. 'I'm tired. You woke me. What was so important that you had to call me tonight?' I knew he had been in town almost a month.

'I just wanted to know one thing. Are you sleeping with John Styles?'

'No,' I answered without thinking. Then I got angry. 'Besides what difference would it make to you if I were? What I do is none of your business.'

'It would make a difference. I don't want to see you used.'

'Nobody's using me. Just because I had dinner with him doesn't mean that I'm sleeping with him.'

'That's not the talk around town. They said he paid you double the money they offered anyone else for that part.'

'Who is they?' I asked sarcastically. 'George Fox?'

He didn't answer.

'George is a prick. He's trying to make points with you. It could be that he can't get it through his head that maybe John thought I was worth twice as much as anyone else.'

'I know John Styles. That's not his reputation.'

'You've got him mixed up with his brother Tony.'

'No, I haven't,' he said. 'I've heard he's worse, in his own quiet way.'

'I'll believe that when I see it. He's been a perfect gentleman with me.' I ground out the cigarette. 'And if that's the only reason you woke me up, let me go back to sleep. I'm tired.'

'I'm sorry,' he said.

'Okay.'

'Can we still have lunch next week?'

'Yes, call me after the weekend.'

'Goodbye,' he said.

I hung up and rolled back on my pillow. There was no use trying to sleep now. I was wide awake. I got out of bed and went to the medicine cabinet in the bathroom. I was looking for a Librium or a Valium but there weren't any. Then I remembered.

The last time Guy had been here working on the play he had left me a joint. I went back into the living room and took it out of the drawer under the coffee table. It was a big one. Guy called it a bomber. Two tokes were guaranteed to put you away.

I carried it back into the bedroom and got into bed. I leaned back against the headboard, lit the joint and took the first hit deep into my lungs. I did it again, holding my breath for what seemed almost half an hour. I felt the warm easy feelings come over me. I took one more toke, then carefully pinched it out before I floated away on the tide. No sense wasting it. I already had a beautiful high.

I looked across the empty king-sized bed. Instinctively I put my hand out to where Walter would have been, then took my hand away quickly. Walter would never be there anymore.

Still I couldn't help remembering how it was when we were together and had a joint and got a little high. Sex was better than when we were straight. Walter didn't seem uptight and he lasted longer. Without it, he either came almost as soon as he entered me or he had problems getting hard. It got so that most of the time he either brought me off orally, manually or mechanically with the aid of a little vibrator. But even then it hadn't mattered. I had loved him and been perfectly happy. And if I got too uptight, I helped myself. It was something I could rely on, something I'd been into since I was fifteen.

Again I looked at the empty bed. There had to be something

the matter with me. Other girls were getting it. They had no trouble. But not me. I had even gotten a new birth control pill that had come out last year, thinking it would free me of inhibitions. But it didn't help.

I looked good, I knew that. Everybody told me that I was sexy, but nobody made a move, nobody touched. Something in me was putting them off. Even Beau Drake, who fucked everything that came his way, never laid a hand on me.

I remembered one afternoon when, over coffee between the matinée and evening performance, he'd gone into a vivid description of what he would do to me if we were alone. It was so vivid that when I got back to my dressing room my panties were soaking wet. I eased my tension while taking a shower but went through the whole evening performance in a state of sexual excitement.

By the time I got home that night I thought my cunt was on fire. The note from Walter on the night table said he was having a late dinner at Twenty One with George Fox and a producer.

I couldn't wait. I took off my clothes, stretched out naked on the bed and reached into the drawer of the night table for the little 'Green Hornet' – our name for the vibrator. I slipped my hand through the strap so that the motor rested on the back of my hand and plugged it in. The soft familiar sound filled the room and I put my hand between my legs.

I don't know how long I lay there riding the waves but suddenly I became aware that Walter had come into the room. I opened my eyes. He was standing looking down at me with a curious expression on his face.

'Walter . . . I – '

'Don't stop,' he said.

'I . . . want . . . ' I couldn't finish, as another orgasm flowed through me.

He knelt beside the bed, his face very close to me, but not touching me. 'What turned you on?' he asked.

'I don't know. Thinking of you. I . . . wanted – '

'What did you want? A big stiff prick?'

'No.'

He ignored my answer. 'A big stiff prick? One like Beau Drake's?'

At the mention of the name, I came again.

He didn't miss the reaction. 'So that's it,' he said softly.

'No, no. I want you. Give me your cock, Walter, please.'

He got to his feet slowly and stood looking down at me.

I pulled at his zipper and took him out. His penis was soft and fragile. I kissed it gently and took it in my mouth. But no matter what I did nothing happened.

After a moment he took my head between his hands. 'I'm sorry,' he said. 'I'm tired and I drank too much.'

I didn't speak.

'Sometimes I feel I'm too old for you,' he said. 'I wouldn't blame you if you took another man.'

'No, Walter, no!' I buried my face against his trousers. 'I only want you!' I began to cry.

Absently he stroked my hair. 'It's okay,' he said. 'I understand.'

But he really didn't. He only knew enough to manipulate my own sense of guilt. And in the end even I came to understand that.

Shit. I looked at the empty bed, then touched myself, feeling the tiny nerve endings. My buddy the Green Hornet called to me from the night table: Hey, baby! I'm always ready, whenever you are.

I spoke aloud. 'But you're not real. You're not alive.'

Don't quibble, baby. You can't have everything.

'Why not?' I asked. 'I want everything.'

That ain't human either, baby.

I shook my head. I had to be going around the bend, holding a conversation with a vibrator. Suddenly I was alone. The apartment was empty. Maryjane had left me.

I got out of bed, lit a cigarette and went to the living room. I looked out the window but there was nothing to see except the apartment houses across the street. It was not anything like Central Park South, where I had a view of the park and the city stretching out into the night.

I looked at the clock. Two in the morning. The trouble with being alone was there was no one to talk to. I wondered if the darkened windows of the city held other people like me. Alone with no one to talk to.

It was eleven o'clock on the Coast. Guy would still be awake. I put in a call. But his room didn't answer. He had not returned from dinner.

I sat there with the telephone in my hand and without thinking further dialed a number. By the second ring I had changed my mind and was about to hang up.

'I'm sorry,' I apologized. 'Did I wake you?'

'No,' John said. 'I was reading.'

'Your offer still open?'

'Yes.'

'You don't think I'm crazy, do you?'

'No.'

'I suddenly felt as if I had to get out of the city.'

'I'm glad,' he said quietly.

'When are we leaving?'

'The noon flight on Sunday,' he said. 'If you'll be downstairs I'll pick you up at ten-thirty.'

'Will you make a reservation for me at the Beverly Hills Hotel?'

'What for?' he said. 'You're staying with me.'

'I don't want to put you to any trouble.'

'It's no trouble at all. I've got a big house and a housekeeper that has nothing to do.'

When I put down the telephone my heart was pounding as if I had just walked up five flights of stairs. But when I went back into the bedroom and lay back on the pillows I slept like a baby.

CHAPTER TEN

THE HOUSE WAS on a hill in Malibu a few miles north of the more exclusive colony. A narrow staircase cut into the rocks led to the beach a hundred-odd feet below. The beach itself was a narrow cove between two rock formations, making it almost inaccessible to the wandering bather. A pool surrounded by flowers was built into the small garden which hung out over the ocean. Once in the pool, it felt as if one were swimming in the sky.

A studio car met us at the airport and drove us to the house. We were greeted at the door by his housekeeper, a small smiling broad-faced woman of Mexican Indian descent. She showed no surprise at my arrival. He said something to her in Spanish; she nodded and led me to my room.

A corner room with an ocean view on two sides, it was decorated in Mexican Mediterranean. The bed was Hollywood king sized and looked as if it were intended to sleep six people. She placed my suitcase on a small table against the wall and said something to me which I didn't understand.

As soon as she had left, John appeared in the doorway. 'Do you like it?'

'I love it. It's just beautiful.'

'It's simple,' he said, sounding pleased. 'But I did it all myself. It's just what I always wanted.'

'Have you had it long?'

'Two years. Since my separation. My wife and the children have the house in Bel Air.'

I looked at him.

'I had to tell you that. I wanted you to know how things are.'

I appreciated his honesty. 'Thank you.'

'The telephone, radio and remote TV control are on the side of the bed.' He started toward a small door at the side of the room. 'The bathroom is over here.'

I went through the door he opened for me. It was a large bathroom, double sink, sunken tub with built-in Jacuzzi, shower stall and bidet. I eyed the other door which was opposite the one we entered.

'That leads to the other guest room,' he said. 'But for all intents and purposes it's yours. I had it built this way because the kids share it when they stay over.'

'How many do you have?'

'Three. Two boys and a girl. The girl is fourteen, the twin boys are twelve. You're in her room.'

I nodded and followed him back into the bedroom. He turned to me. 'I suggest you take a nap before dinner. The time change is always tiring.'

'I don't feel tired,' I said.

'You will. It always hits me at dinnertime.' He walked to the door. 'We'll have dinner at eight o'clock if that's okay with you.'

'Perfect.'

He smiled. 'I'll see you then.'

When I opened my eyes the room was bathed in purple and violet light. I checked my watch. It was still set on New York time. Ten o'clock. I reset it and got out of bed. He had been right. The time change had caught up to me.

I went into the bathroom and turned on the water in the tub. I stared at the water, pale and sparkling green, spilling from the spout and put some lemon-scented Vitabath into the water. I stripped and got into the tub just as the automatic Jacuzzi went on.

I gave myself up to the currents. One of the jets seemed aimed right between my legs. It was lovely, even better than the Green Hornet.

Suddenly I was aware of the phone buzzing in the bathroom. I reached out of the tub and took it. 'Hello.'

'Are you awake?'

'Yes, I'm in the tub.'

'No rush. Dinner will be ready when you are.'

I laughed. 'I may decide to have dinner in the tub.'

'You like it?'

'The Jacuzzi is too much. I may decide to marry it.'

He laughed. 'Enjoy. See you in a little bit.'

I put back the phone but by then the water had turned cool so I got out. I took one of the giant-sized towels and rubbed myself briskly. Everything in California was large – the beds, the tubs, even the towels. I wondered if it signified anything. I gave up thinking about it, got into a pair of slacks and a shirt and went downstairs.

The table with a salad in a large wooden bowl in the center was already set next to the open patio door. Outside a charcoal fire was glowing in the barbecue.

I stopped in the center of the room, sniffing. 'What's that?'

'Baked potatoes in charcoal. I hope you like them.'

'Roast mickeys?' I said. 'I love them.'

He smiled and went to the bar. He turned on the Osterizer. 'I have two specialties,' he said. 'I make the best Margaritas and the best steaks in the world.' He pulled the cocktail glasses from the ice bucket and quickly rimmed them with salt, then stopped the machine and filled the glasses to the brim.

'Welcome to California,' he said as I took the glass from him.

The Margarita went down like liquid fire, sending a warm glow through me. 'Unbelievable,' I said. He couldn't know I had never drunk a Margarita before.

'I'll put the steaks on,' he said. 'By the time we finish two of these, they'll be ready.'

As if on cue, the housekeeper came into the room carrying two huge steaks on a wooden platter which she handed over to John. 'Buenas noches,' she said.

I smiled and nodded as she left.

'She usually has Sunday off,' he said. 'She only stayed to see that everything was right.'

I followed him out to the barbecue and watched him put the steaks on the grill. There was a hissing sound as the fat hit the coals.

'The steaks have been marinated in oil, vinegar and garlic,' he explained. 'Gives them a special flavor. Like it rare?'

I nodded.

'Good. So do I.'

By the time the steaks were ready I felt good, light-headed but good. I sighed with relief as I sat down at the table.

I watched him solemnly as he lit the candles and poured the wine. The wine glass was almost too heavy for me to lift. After the tequila the red wine was soft to the taste. 'Lovely,' I said, putting the wine glass down carefully.

'I think I overdid the Margaritas,' he said.

'No.'

'Are you all right?' he asked.

'I'm okay,' I said quickly. 'Just a little drunk.'

'You'll be all right after you eat something,' he said.

He was right about that. The steak, salad and baked potatoes were delicious and by the time we got to the coffee my head was clear.

'Do you smoke?' he asked after we'd finished our coffee.

I nodded.

'I have some great grass. Acapulco Gold. It goes great with cognac.' He looked at me. 'Feel up to it?'

'Lead on. You've already seen me drunk, you might as well see me stoned.'

I followed him to the couch. He opened a wooden cigarette box on the coffee table. 'I've got a few J's already rolled,' he said.

He lit the joint, then passed it to me while he went to get the brandy snifters and the bottle.

I took a big hit and let the smoke slowly out. I nodded. 'Mellow.'

'The best,' he said, taking it from me. He hit it again and gave me my brandy. I watched him chase the smoke down his throat with the cognac. 'Try it like that.'

I followed his example. It was dynamite. In a second I was up there. Suddenly it all seemed very funny. I began to laugh.

'Que pasa?' he said.

'I still don't believe it.'

'Believe what?'

'I'm here. You. Me.'

He took the J from my fingers. Hit, sip, back to me. 'It's not hard to believe,' he said.

'I've never gone anywhere with a man before except my husband,' I said. 'And here I've flown all the way across the country with you.'

'Are you having second thoughts?'

'No.'

'I don't want you to.'

'I don't have any.' I passed the joint back to him and giggled. 'I'm high as a kite already.'

He laughed. 'Feelin' good is how to say it.'

'I'm feelin' good.' I leaned against the back cushions. 'You sure know how to treat a girl.'

He didn't speak.

'I'm so relaxed,' I said. 'I feel all loose and lazy.'

'Whenever you're tired, you can go to bed. Don't worry about me.'

'You're a nice man, John Styles.'

'Thank you.'

'A perfect gentleman.'

He didn't speak.

Suddenly I was warm. I looked outside at the pool and got to my feet. 'Can I go for a swim?'

'Anything you want. There are bikinis in the small cabana. I think you'll find one that fits.'

I met his eyes. 'Do I have to?'

He shook his head silently.

I went outside, got out of my clothes at the side of the pool and dove in. The water was cool and refreshing. When I came up, he was still inside sitting on the couch. 'Come on in,' I called. 'It's great.'

He came out, the joint still in his mouth, undressed and slipped into the water.

'Isn't it great?' I asked. Without waiting for an answer I took the J from his lips and put it in my mouth. Then I went over on my back, sucking the smoke into my lungs. The sky above was diamond-studded velvet. 'Hey! This is really floating.'

Inside the house the telephone began to ring. I treaded water and looked at him. The phone rang again. He started to lift himself from the pool.

'You don't have to answer it,' I said.

'I've been expecting the call,' he said. 'It's my A.D. to give me the schedule for tomorrow.'

I watched him get out of the pool and run dripping to the telephone in the cabana. He was on the phone almost fifteen minutes. When he came back I had finished the joint. But it didn't seem to matter. My high was almost gone.

'The call is for six o'clock tomorrow morning,' he said.

I stared at him. 'You want to go to bed?'

'I'd better,' he said. 'Or else I'll be in a fog all day.'

I got out of the pool and into another one of those giant California towels, which he wrapped around me as carefully as if I were a baby. I picked up my clothes while he wrapped a towel around his waist, then followed him up the stairs.

I stopped at my door and turned to him. He leaned forward and kissed my cheek. 'Sleep well,' he said. 'I left the keys in the convertible for you. Anything else you want just ask Marcia.

I'll be leaving about five o'clock so I'll see you when I get home in the evening.'

I stood in the doorway, watching him walk down the hall to his room and close the door behind him.

I went back to the bathroom, dropped the towel, lit a cigarette and stared at myself in the mirror. There had to be something wrong with me. I didn't understand it. Cool was cool but his cool was too much. It had to be me.

'Damn!' I said angrily to myself in the mirror as I dragged on the cigarette and noticed that my hand was shaking.

I went back into the bedroom and took the Green Hornet from my suitcase, then looked around the bed for an outlet. I finally found it behind the giant headboard. There was no way I could get to it. That did it.

I threw the vibrator on the bed, walked out of my room and down the hall. I opened his door without knocking. He came out of the bathroom, the towel still around his waist, and stared at me.

In the mirror on the far wall I caught a glimpse of myself standing naked in his doorway. 'Is there anything wrong with me?' I demanded. I didn't wait for him to reply. 'Or am I supposed to believe that you flew me three thousand miles across the country in order not to fuck me in California?'

CHAPTER ELEVEN

INSIDE THERE WAS a small light glowing from the lamp in the far corner of the room. Outside there was the blackness of the night and the quiet pounding of the surf. I was on the side of the bed near the open window; he was toward the wall, half hidden in the shadow.

'What time is it?' I asked.

'Four o'clock.' The tip of his cigarette glowed in the dark. 'Time for me to get up.'

'I'm sorry.'

'What for?'

'I kept you awake. And you have to go to work.'

He was silent for a moment. 'I'll be okay. A shower and a red can work wonders.'

'Funny thing, I don't feel sleepy. I was so tired when we got off the plane. And now I'm not tired at all.'

He smiled. 'Youth.'

'Is that all it is?'

'I don't know.'

'Is it always like this?'

He looked at me but I couldn't see the expression in his eyes. 'What do you mean?'

'The first time. All night.'

'No.'

I reached and took the cigarette from him, then I laughed and gave it back.

'Why did you laugh?' he asked.

'Habit. I really didn't want the cigarette but I used to take Walter's away from him pretending that I did because he wasn't supposed to smoke.'

'Oh.'

'He had emphysema.'

He got out of bed without speaking.

'You're not angry with me because I spoke about Walter, are you?'

'No.'

I sat up in the bed. 'Are you sorry that I came out with you?'

'Are you sorry that you did?'

'No. But you didn't answer.'

'I'm not sorry.'

'Was I okay? I mean was it good for you?'

He smiled. 'You don't hear me complaining.'

'I mean it. I want it to be as good for you as it is for me.'

The smile grew broader. 'If it got any better I'd wind up in a hospital in less than a week.'

'I never knew it could be so good. I didn't want to stop.'

'I kind of thought it had been a long time for you. How long since your divorce?'

'Going on five months.'

'That can be a long time for a girl as sexual as you are. There's been no one else during that time?'

'No.' I didn't tell him there hadn't been much during my marriage either. Walter had his own routines. And I didn't know any better.

'I'd better get started,' he said, going toward the bathroom.

'I'll go downstairs and make coffee.'

'Know where the kitchen is?'

'I'll find it.'

I went back to my room, put on a robe and went downstairs. The housekeeper was gone. The kitchen was as neat as a pin and the coffeepot was ready to be plugged in. I opened the refrigerator and by the time he came down I had bacon and eggs and toast on the table.

'You didn't have to do that,' he said.

'I wanted to.'

He didn't eat very much but I ate like a truckdriver. I was famished.

'What are you going to do today?' he asked.

'I don't know. Sleep a little. Get some sun maybe.'

'Do you want to eat out or in?'

'Let's eat in and go to bed early.'

He smiled.

I felt myself blush. 'You'll have to get some rest. Living on reds isn't the best idea in the world.'

'Okay.' He got to his feet. 'I should be back about eight. I have to look at the rushes tonight.'

'I'll be here.' I started to get up.

'Stay there. I'll see you later.'

I watched him leave, then finished my coffee, stacked the dishes in the washer and went up to my room to bed. I crashed the moment my head touched the pillow.

The telephone beside the bed was buzzing, buzzing, buzzing. I rolled over, opened my eyes, then closed them against the burning sunlight. The telephone kept on buzzing. I looked at the flashing light and finally I picked it up. 'Yes.'

'Señorita, para usted.' The houskeeper's voice was pleasant.

'Thank you.' I stared at the phone for a moment, thinking it must be Mother who couldn't wait for me to call her. I pushed the button down.

It wasn't my mother. It was Harry Gregg. 'What are you doing out there?' he asked abruptly.

'Sleeping when you woke me up,' I said sarcastically. 'How'd you get my number?'

'For Christ's sake! It's three o'clock in the afternoon out there. What the hell were you doing all night?'

'Fucking, if it's any of your business!' I snapped. I was beginning to feel that everything they said about agents was true. Once they got you a job they felt they owned you. 'How'd you find out where I was?'

'Your service told me you were out of town but they didn't know where, so I called your mother. She told me.' His voice dropped to a conspiratorial whisper. 'I just got a call from Fox's office. He wanted to know where you were. Your ex is looking for you.'

'So?'

'I didn't tell him. Do you think your mother might?'

'No.' Not my mother. She wasn't about to admit that her little girl would go off across the country with a man. And even if she did, what difference did it make? Walter had no claims on me. 'Is that why you called?'

'No.' His voice returned to normal. 'I got you another job. Just as well you're in California.'

'I don't get it.'

'Got you a guest shot on *The Virginian.* They want to see you over at Universal this afternoon. Thirty-five hundred for the week.'

'How did that happen?'

'They saw some of the film you did in New York last week.'

'It's late,' I said. 'I'll have to do the whole works. Hair. Makeup. Everything. I won't make it. How about tomorrow?'

'They insist on today. They called me early this morning to get you on a plane. They said they'll wait at the studio until eight o'clock for you.'

I was silent.

'It's a good shot. Universal does a lot of film. If they like you, they'll keep you working.'

'Okay. Who do I have to see?'

He gave me the information and when he was finished his voice became conspiratorial again. 'What do I tell Fox? By morning he'll know you've been to Universal.'

'You think of an excuse. I don't give a damn what he tells Walter.'

'You better. George will make it rough for you if Walter gets angry.'

'Tell him the studio got to me before you did and that I was on my way out there.' I put down the phone and then got angry. I didn't like being intimidated. I decided to call him back. 'Is there anything wrong?' he asked as he came on the wire.

'Yes. I don't like being pushed. By Walter. George. You. Or anybody. And I don't owe any of them explanations.'

'Wait a minute! Don't get mad at me. I'm on your side.'

'Okay. Then tell them the truth. And if they don't like it, they can go fuck themselves!'

I felt better when I put down the telephone. I got dressed and was at the studio by six-thirty.

In the course of the next three hours about seven men came into the producer's office to talk to me. At the end of that time the only thing they didn't know was that I had a beauty mark high on my left buttock. Finally they all sat around the office in a semicircle looking at me.

The big man whose office it was finally spoke. 'I think she'll do. What do you think, fellers?'

There was a chorus of agreement.

'What kind of a part is it?' I asked finally.

'A very good part,' the big man said. 'Exciting, if you know what I mean. A real acting part.'

'Can I read it?'

'Of course you can. We'll give you a script first thing in the morning.'

'I'm supposed to start work in the morning.'

'That's right.'

'How am I supposed to learn my lines?'

'You'll have time. Your first setup isn't until the afternoon. You can read it while you're in Costume and Makeup.'

'Why can't I have it now?'

An uncomfortable look crossed his face. 'I don't think we have the final scripts back from the mimeo.'

'I can read one of the others. At least I'd get an idea of the character I'm supposed to play.'

'It's a good part,' he said defensively. 'Don't you take my word for it?'

'I take your word for it.'

'That's a good girl.' He got to his feet. 'Now you be here at seven tomorrow morning for Costume.'

'No.'

His chin dropped. 'What do you mean?'

'What I said. No. I think I'm entitled to read the part to see if it is something I can and want to do before I agree to it.'

'Of course you are, but we have an emergency here. We have to go on the floor tomorrow and it has to be settled tonight.'

'Then get me a script. I read quickly.'

His eyes hardened. 'You're pretty independent, aren't you, Miss Randall?'

'Not at all. I just feel I'm entitled to the same consideration that you demanded. You wouldn't agree to give me the part until I came out here and gave you all a chance to look me over. Well, I'm here because I understand that. As I see it, it's a matter of common courtesy.'

He stared at me for a moment, then smiled and turned to the man next to him. 'Okay, Dan, get her a script.'

'Okay, fellers, the meeting's over,' the big man said.

As they filed from the room I looked at the man behind the desk and said. 'I can go outside to read if you have work to do.'

'It's okay.'

I read it quickly. My instincts had been right. The part was for that of an Indian girl and I would be all wrong for it. It was one of those roles with a lot of scenes but very little dialogue. As a matter of fact I didn't know why they even needed the girl in the script at all. She served no real purpose and it would have been better if they had left her out.

'I don't think so,' I said, getting to my feet.

He stared up at me challengingly. 'It's not much of a part but you're on camera a lot.'

'I don't even have black hair or black eyes.'

'No problem,' he said. 'A wig and contact lenses will take care of that.'

'No, thank you.'

'Think of the exposure. Twenty million people will see you in one night.'

'I wouldn't be comfortable in the part.'

'It's a great opportunity. Don't pass it up. There's a lot of work out here. Do you know how many girls would give their ass to be standing where you are?'

'I have an idea. And I'm willing to bet that many of them would be more right for the part than I am.'

'But I want you. I backed myself into a corner to get you for this. I think you could give it something special.'

'Thank you. I genuinely appreciate that.'

'Look, it's late. Why don't we have a bite of dinner and talk it over?'

'I'm sorry, I have a date.'

'Then you won't do it?'

'No.'

I placed the script on the desk in front of him. 'Can I get a taxi?'

He looked at me as if he had already forgotten that I was there. 'Yes. Just ask my secretary. She'll call one for you.'

'Thank you. Good night.'

He nodded silently and I left the office.

I didn't get back to the beach until ten o'clock. By that time everything had gone wrong.

CHAPTER TWELVE

THE A.D. who had been on the picture with us in New York answered the door. 'Hello, JeriLee,' he said.

I looked at him. In New York it had been Miss Randall. 'Hello,' I said, trying but failing to remember his name. I went into the house and started down the steps to the main floor.

'Go easy on him,' he warned. 'The boss had a rough day.'

There was something about his voice that implied that we understood each other, that we were allies.

'Everything was a shambles. I don't think we got two minutes of film today. Then when he came home and you weren't here he hit the roof.'

'What for? I left a note saying where I went.'

'I don't know whether he got it,' he said.

'I'll explain to him.' I glanced at him. 'Coming down?'

'No. I was just on my way home.'

'Okay. Good night.'

John was seated on the couch with a drink in his hand. He looked up as I came into the room.

I bent over and kissed his cheek. 'Hello,' I said. 'I'm sorry I'm so late.'

'Where the hell were you?'

'Universal. I left a note.'

'I never got it,' he snapped. 'What the hell were you doing out there?'

'I explained it in the note. They called me for a job.'

'Here?'

I was becoming annoyed by his childishness. 'No. They sent a carrier pigeon.'

'Who else did you give my number to?'

'I didn't give your number to anybody. My agent figured it out for himself.'

'Then how come the whole damn world has it?' he demanded. 'In the two hours I've been home I've gotten half a dozen phone calls for you. Your mother, your ex-husband, your agent twice and Universal twice.'

'I didn't give it to anybody,' I retorted.

'Then how come everybody has it?'

'I don't know. I'm sorry. I didn't mean to be a bother.'

'Fuck it!' He got up and went to the bar and refilled his glass. 'This is all I needed.'

I watched him take another belt of the drink without speaking. I had never seen him like this.

'By now it will be all over town that you're out here with me.'

'What difference does it make? Nobody has any strings on us.'

'On you maybe. But you forget that I'm still married.'

'You said you were separated.'

'That's not divorced. I've always been careful not to give my wife a chance to nail me.'

'I'm sorry. I didn't mean to put you on a spot.'

'You weren't thinking. I told you what the score was.'

'Sure you did. After I got here. Why didn't you tell me in New York?' I answered without waiting for his reply. 'Because you knew damn well I wouldn't come.'

'I didn't expect the whole world to be calling you.'

I stared at him for a moment. 'I think you ought to call me a cab,' I said. 'It would be better for both of us if I checked into a hotel.'

Just then the telephone rang. John picked it up, then handed it to me. 'For you.'

It was Harry. 'What the hell did you do out there at Universal? They're boiling mad.'

'I did nothing,' I said. 'I just told them I never heard of a blue-eyed Indian.'

'They want you anyway. They're changing the part so that you're the adopted daughter of the chief, the only survivor of a wagon train who has been brought up as his own.'

'The part still stinks.'

'They got the hots for you. They also promised to give you some other jobs if you do this.'

'Sorry.'

'What the hell's got into you?' he shouted in exasperation. 'Just a few weeks ago you were begging for a job. You said you needed the money. Now that you've worked two weeks, you're suddenly nigger rich!'

'I'm not going to do it just to satisfy some producer's ego. They can find some other girl to run around in a torn Indian shirt with her boobs hanging out.'

'It's one o'clock in the morning here and I'm bushed,' he said. 'I'm going home to bed. You think about it and I'll call you in the morning.'

The moment I put down the telephone it rang again. 'Hello,' John barked. Then his voice changed abruptly. 'How's it goin', Chad?'

He listened, then glanced at me before he spoke. 'You're absolutely right, Chad, she's quite a girl. A good little actress too.'

I realized he was talking about me and listened to the rest of the conversation with a kind of stunned fascination. It was almost as if I were his property.

'I don't blame you one bit. She sounds perfect for the part.... Of course I'll talk to her, but you know these New York actresses. They have their own ideas. . . . Sure, she's right here. I'll put her on.' He held the phone out to me.

'Who is it?' I asked.

'Chad Taylor.'

'Who is he?'

'For Christ's sake, you spent the afternoon in his office at U.I.'

I took the telephone. 'Yes?'

'Did you talk to Harry Gregg, JeriLee?'

When I left his office I was still Miss Randall. Apparently we were now old friends. 'Yes, Mr Taylor.'

'Did he tell you how we solved your problem?'

I hadn't known it was my problem. 'Yes, Mr Taylor.'

'It's a hell of an idea. What do you think?'

'I still think the part stinks, Mr Taylor.'

'JeriLee, what makes you so difficult?'

'I'm not being difficult, Mr Taylor. I just know what I can and what I can't do.'

'If you'll keep an open mind about it,' he said almost pleadingly. 'I'll have a revised script for you to read in the morning.'

Suddenly I was tired. I had enough hassling for one day. 'Okay.'

'Can you come in around eleven o'clock? I'll send a car out for you.'

'Don't bother. I can get a cab.' I put down the telephone.

'You ought to do it,' John said.

'Why? Did you read it?'

'No, but the exposure would be good for you. The public will get to know your name. Maybe that way I can get my brother to increase the size of your billing.'

Another lesson. I was learning a lot today. Exposure is good because it helps the marketability of other products. Since there was nothing more for me to say, I turned to leave.

'Where are you going?' he asked.

'To pack.'

'Wait a minute. What's the rush?'

'I don't want to get nailed,' I said sarcastically.

He made a deprecatory gesture. 'I was just a little steamed. Debbie and I have an understanding. She doesn't expect me to lead a virginal life.'

'Oh, shit,' I said disgustedly.

'God, what a bitch day I had,' he said. 'Nothing went right.'

I didn't answer.

'I'll make us a couple of Margaritas and we'll take off our shoes and relax.' He went back to the bar. 'Maria's made arroz con pollo. You never tasted anything so good in your life.'

I still didn't speak.

He turned on the blender. Its soft hum buzzed through the room. 'You don't know what I went through.'

'It's not easy.'

He missed the sarcasm. 'We'll have dinner and go right to bed.'

'Will I have time for a bath first?'

'Of course, but that's a funny question. Why do you ask?'

'I feel dirty,' I said.

He didn't understand that either.

He came into my room about an hour after I had gone to bed.

'I've been waiting for you,' he said.

'You have another early call in the morning,' I said. 'I thought it would be better if you got some sleep.'

'I can't sleep, I'm too uptight.'

'I'm sorry.'

He came into the room and closed the door behind him. He sat down on the edge of the bed. 'What are you doing?' he asked.

'Nothing,' I said. 'Just lying here. Thinking.'

'About what?'

'Things. Nothing special.'

'You don't want to talk, do you?'

I reached for a cigarette and saw in his eyes the reflected light of the match. 'Do you?' I asked.

'You're angry with me.'

'No.'

'What is it then?'

'Things just aren't right. It's not going the way I thought it would.'

'You shouldn't have gone out. We were okay yesterday.'

It was exactly the kind of thing Walter would say. I didn't answer.

'Yes, I would have had a chance to absorb it. I wouldn't have been taken by surprise.'

'I didn't think I was doing anything wrong.'

'After all, you are my guest. I brought you out here.'

I was beginning to understand. It made some kind of sense. Not real sense. But crazy sense. It had something to do with property rights. Because he had paid the freight, I belonged to him. He was more like Walter than I had thought.

'Do you understand what I mean?'

'Yes.'

'Good,' he said in a satisfied voice. He got to his feet. 'Now, let's put it all behind us and go to bed.'

'I am in bed.'

An edge crept into his voice. 'I don't like to be used.'

'I'll leave you a check for the plane ticket before I go in the morning,' I said, thinking that I'd been more used than he.

'Don't bother,' he said in a cutting voice. 'I've given more money to a whore for a one-night stand.'

The door slammed behind him. I fought back the tears, too hurt to be angry. It wasn't fair. It just wasn't fair. Why did it have to be like this?

I didn't go to Universal in the morning. Instead I took the red eye back to New York that night.

CHAPTER THIRTEEN

HARRY SAW ME through the glass partitions that enclosed his office and rose to his feet. He shook his head. 'You did it. You really did it.'

'I thought it over,' I said. 'I didn't want the job no matter what they said.'

'You fucked yourself. In only two days you managed to do what would take most people a lifetime to accomplish.' A curious note of wonder entered his voice. 'You really fucked yourself.'

'All I did was turn down a job. I even called the studio and left word that I wasn't coming in.'

'Jesus,' he said. 'Universal's putting out the word that you're impossible to deal with and then I get a frantic call from Tony Styles that you screwed up his picture.'

'Tony Styles? I never even saw him!'

'He says you fucked up his brother's head and he had to close down the picture for two days so that John could stay in bed. He says he's going to cut your part down to nothing even if he has to shoot some of the scenes over with another girl.'

'I don't get it.'

'What happened between you two?'

'We just didn't agree, so I left.'

'Jesus,' he repeated. He picked up a sheet of paper. 'This memo got here just before you did. George wants to see me about you.'

'If George wants to talk to me all he has to do is say so.'

'You don't understand. You're not his direct responsibility anymore. You're mine. He tells me whatever he wants to do or say and I tell you.'

'What does that mean?'

'George doesn't like to make waves,' he said. 'George is Mr Nice Guy with everybody – Universal, Styles, your ex, even God himself.'

'So?'

'So we're in trouble. George must have picked up some of the flap and he doesn't want anybody mad at the agency.'

'Does that mean he's going to drop me?'

'I don't know,' he said. 'But if you have any friends he will listen to, now is the time to get to them.'

'But we have a contract.'

'Read the fine print. They can drop you any time they want.'

I was silent.

'Your ex. Would he put in a good word for you?'

'I don't want to go to him,' I said. 'It took me too long to get out from under.'

'Any other friends?'

I thought for a moment. 'Guy Jackson?'

He shook his head. 'George hates him. He signed with another agency after George broke his ass to get him.'

'Then there's nobody.'

Slowly he got to his feet. 'I might as well get it over with.'

'Do you want me to wait for you?'

'What the hell.' He shrugged. 'Might as well get it hot from the oven.'

By the time he got back half an hour later I had gone through the rest of my package of cigarettes and was beginning to work on his. He closed the door, went behind his desk and collapsed in his chair. 'Jesus,' he said. It seemed to be his favorite remark of the day.

'Okay,' I said. 'Let's have it.'

'They're dropping your acting contract but they're keeping you for writing even though I tried to get him to drop that one too.'

'I thought you were my friend,' I said sarcastically. 'Half a loaf is better than none.'

'You got a lot to learn. If they let you out of the writing contract, you would have a lever to get another agent. You have the play, which could bring him some income. But this way we keep all the money and you got no muscle.'

I stared at him. 'That's not fair.'

'I didn't say it was.'

'I'll go up and see him.'

'It won't do any good. You'll never get past his secretary. George has that down to a fine art.'

'Is there anything I can do?'

'Only one thing I can think of, but you won't like that either.'

'What's that?'

'Eat humble pie,' he said. 'Call Chad Taylor out at Universal.

Tell him it was that time of the month or something female like that and that you thought it over and decided you would do it. I happen to know they haven't cast that part yet.'

'You're sure?'

'Sure as I'm sitting here.'

'Is that your idea or is that what George told you to tell me?'

I could see the flush creep over his face. 'George's.'

'And if I don't do that, I'm finished here?'

He nodded silently.

I felt trapped. They were playing a game and all of them were on the same team. There was no way I could win. 'Okay,' I said finally. 'Get him on the phone for me.'

I was a better actress than I thought. I not only ate humble pie, I rubbed my face in it. And all the way to the Coast on the plane that evening I had a sick feeling in my stomach to prove it.

They had a car to pick me up at the airport and take me to the hotel. Even before I'd got my baggage the driver gave me a note from Taylor.

> Dear JeriLee,
>
> Keep dinner open. Will be by at eight thirty with the script. Dress for Chasen's. Regards.
>
> Chad

Short and to the point. There was no mistaking who was in charge. By now it didn't matter. I was so tired all I wanted to do was to get into bed and sleep.

The driver took me to an hotel-motel called the Regency on Hollywood Boulevard between Fairfax and Laurel Canyon. I had a small two-room suite on the second floor overlooking the pool.

'We put lots of New York people out here,' the driver explained. 'There's a short cut to the studio over Laurel Canyon.'

I thanked him as he placed my luggage on a small rack. As soon as he left I took off my clothes and closed the drapes to the sun. Then I turned down the big king-sized bed and called the operator to leave a wakeup call for seven-forty-five.

I was just drifting off when the telephone rang. It was Chad Taylor. 'Everything all right?'

'Perfect.'

'Good.' He sounded pleased. 'Dress up tonight. There'll be some important press people there.'

'Okay.'

'See you about eight-thirty.' He rang off.

I turned over and closed my eyes when the telephone rang again. I reached for it wearily. 'Hello.'

'JeriLee? This is John.' There was no sign of anger in his voice. It was as if nothing had happened.

'Yes.'

'I'm glad you came to your senses. I was beginning to worry about you.'

'I'm okay.'

'I thought we might have dinner. I remembered you liked the steaks on Sunday.'

'I have a date. Mr Taylor is bringing the script over this evening.'

'What are you doing afterwards?'

'Going to sleep. I'm wiped out.' Flying back and forth across the country wasn't my idea of fun.

'I have to see you, even if it's just for a minute.'

'We're going to Chasen's. He said there will be press there. I don't know what time I'll get back here.'

'We have to get some things straightened out.'

'It'll keep until tomorrow. If I don't get some rest, I'll die.'

'Okay,' he said finally. 'Meanwhile is there anything I can do for you?'

'No.' Then I changed my mind. 'Yes, there is one thing. Tell your brother to stop bad-mouthing me all over the country.'

I put down the phone but by that time I was too keyed up for sleep. I popped a Librium and waited for it to slow me down. Meanwhile I ran the tub and got into it. I felt the lassitude come back. Quickly I dried myself and jumped back into bed. This time I slept. But not for long. In less than an hour the telephone rang with my wakeup call.

In a fog, I popped a red and stood under an ice cold shower. Then I began the slow job of getting myself together.

The doorbell rang at exactly eight-thirty. I opened the door in a robe. 'Come in, Mr Taylor. I'll be just a few more minutes.'

'I brought the script with me.'

'Make yourself comfortable,' I said, heading back to the bedroom.

He followed me to the door. 'My flowers get here yet?'

'I haven't seen them.'

'They should have been here when you arrived. Damn secretary. Mind if I use your phone?'

'Help yourself.'

He disappeared back into the living room while I went into the bathroom. I put on two pair of false eyelashes, penciled in the liner quickly and checked the mirror. Not bad for a quick job.

He was standing in the doorway when I returned to the bedroom. 'She says she ordered them.'

'Don't worry. They'll get here. Thanks anyway.'

'Nobody does anything right these days. You gotta keep on their ass.' He didn't move from the doorway and something told me he was not about to. I opened the closet door and stood behind it while I slipped into my dress. It was the long black silk that clung to my body. When I came out from behind the door he gave a long low whistle.

'Not bad.'

'I feel a mess.'

'You don't look it.'

'Thanks.' I pulled the white angora stole from my bag and put it around my shoulders. 'I'm ready now.'

He looked at me critically.

'Anything wrong?' I asked.

'Do you have a fur?'

'I have, but I like the look of the white angora with the black silk.'

'Wear the fur. This is Chasen's.'

I stared at him for a minute, then took off the stole and put on the short chinchilla jacket.

'That's better,' he said. 'Class.'

I noticed the script on the table in front of the couch as we went to the door.

'Do you want to take it with us?' I asked. 'We can discuss it during dinner.'

He shook his head. 'Too many people there. We'll go over it when we get back.' He didn't give me a chance to answer. 'The car's right in front.'

'How do you like it?' he asked as he opened the door for me.

'Beautiful.'

He smiled. 'It's a classic. A 'fifty-five Bentley Continental convertible. They only made fifteen like this. There are only five that are still in use. This is one of them.'

'It's really something,' I said.

It was Tuesday night and Chasen's was jumping. But we had a large table near the door where everyone coming in or leaving could see us. I noticed there were only two places set.

'I sort of expected other people from what you said,' I said as I sat down.

'The restaurant is loaded,' he said. 'No place to talk shop. People will be stopping by. You'll see.'

He was right about that. He couldn't have displayed me any better if he had put me in Macy's window.

'Deviled ribs is the best thing on the menu. But since they always run out I ordered some in advance, along with a side dish of chili. How does that sound?'

'Good to me,' I said. By that time I would have eaten the tablecloth.

He signaled the waiter. First we had the cracked Dungeness crab with the mustard and tomato side sauces, then the ribs. Between the wines and the red I had popped my head was spinning. Somehow I managed to keep my conversation halfway intelligible, but it probably wouldn't have made any difference if I had gone totally dumb. He never stopped talking about his career and the fact that Universal would never have made it without him.

For dessert we each had three Irish coffees and by the time we got up to leave at one o'clock in the morning I could hardly manage to stand straight. As soon as we got back to the suite, he plopped himself down on the couch and picked up the script. 'Now we can go to work,' he said.

I couldn't believe my ears.

'We improved it,' he said. 'But that's not the important thing. I have other plans for you. Big plans. Do you understand?'

I could only shake my head. I didn't understand.

'The minute you walked into that office I knew you were the girl I had been looking for.' He paused to let the importance of his statement sink in. 'You know, I'm not staying on this show. I'm preparing a feature. A big picture. The deal's already closed.'

'Congratulations,' I managed to say.

He nodded. 'And you're the girl. The lead. Today's girl. Feisty. Tough. Sexy. Intelligent. That's why it was important that I got you for this show. I had to show them what I could do with you.'

I didn't speak. My head was beginning to buzz.

He opened the script. 'Now, let's go over this.'

The hammers were really beating my skull now. 'Chad,' I said. 'Mr Taylor.'

He looked up at me with a puzzled expression.

'It's not that I'm not grateful, I really am,' I said, speaking as clearly as I could. 'But if you don't let me get to bed, I'm going to pass out right here.'

His expression cleared and he rose with a rueful smile. 'Of course. I forgot the kind of day you've had.'

I followed him to the door. 'I'll see you in the morning,' he said.

I was beginning to feel dizzy.

'Don't worry about getting to the studio. I'll have a car and driver here for you at seven o'clock.'

I managed to nod.

He gave me a quick peck on the cheek. 'Good night,' he said, then drew back and looked at me. 'The next time we go to dinner don't wear a dress with so much decolletage. I had a hard-on all night and half the time I didn't know what the hell I was saying.'

I closed the door and felt the nausea rising. I just about made it to the bathroom. Then, still dressed, I threw myself across the bed and passed out.

CHAPTER FOURTEEN

I WAS NAKED and they were all staring at me as if I were a piece of meat. I tried to hide behind my hands but no matter which way I turned I couldn't escape their eyes. The white merciless spotlights tore at me from all sides.

Somehow, of all the men there, I didn't seem to mind the strangers as much as those that knew me. I didn't even seem to mind the way the men were all dressed in football uniforms, helmets, face guards, bright red sweatshirts with black numbers. And they were all wearing the same number – One. Perhaps the strangest thing about the uniform was that the heavy padded pants had no fronts and their huge cocks hung out almost to their knees.

Abruptly they all went into a huddle. I tried to hear what they were whispering but the words were lost. Then they broke from the huddle and went into a playing formation. The only man I recognized in the line was the center, Harry Gregg. Behind him I could see the faces of the backfield. George Fox as quarterback, halfbacks Chad and John and, not too far behind, Walter as fullback.

George straightened up and gestured violently toward me, then pointed at Harry. Responding to a compulsion I did not understand, I walked toward the line, got down on my knees and crawled between Harry's legs. Curling myself into a fetal ball, I hugged my knees close to my chest and pressed my face into my thighs.

I heard Harry grunt as he crouched even lower and forced his large hands between my arms until each one was firmly locked on my breasts. He nudged his knees against my buttocks and I raised myself slightly. He grunted again and I felt his long tool ram into me from behind. It was strange, but I felt nothing. Neither surprise, nor resentment, nor excitement. Then he exploded inside me and I felt his semen dripping down my legs as George shouted 'Hup!' in a strange hoarse voice.

Abruptly I was flung backward between his legs into George's hands. They felt rough and callused, not at all like the soft manicured hands I knew he had. Still locked in the fetal position, I felt his heavy hands pressed down on my breasts forcing me onto his cock. Then he was running, his cock moving in and out of me with his strides. A moment later I heard Walter's voice shouting 'Get rid of her! God dam it! Get rid of her!'

George's orgasm splashed into me, firing me into the air like a rocket. I felt myself spinning sideways, over and over, and the air was cold against my skin.

I was floating over them now and suddenly I felt free.

There was something about soaring high like a bird. Nothing could touch you except the wind. And the wind loved you. You were safe. Then I began to fall.

I looked down. Chad and John were running toward the center of the field.

I felt the fear knotting my stomach. I could hear myself screaming inside my head but no sound came out. I willed the wind to keep me up. But I kept falling, falling towards them until I could see their faces grim with the power behind their masks.

The scream finally tore from my throat. 'No! No! This is not a game. I am not a football!'

Then I woke up cold, sweating and shaking, with tears running down my cheeks. For a moment I lay staring into the darkness. Then, still trembling, I reached across and turned on the lamp.

The ghosts of my dreams fled before the light. I looked down at myself. My dress was totally crushed and the long skirt was ripped on one side where it had caught on the heel of my shoe while I was asleep.

I checked the time – almost five o'clock. Another two hours and the car would be here to take me to the studio. My mouth felt dry. I got out of bed and went into the bathroom.

The first thing I did was brush my teeth and rinse out my mouth. Then I looked at myself in the mirror.

My eyes were puffy and my face white and drawn. I stared at myself in disgust. It would take at least two hours to make myself presentable. I started the water running in the tub and I opened a jar of cream to begin removing my makeup.

I noticed my hands were still shaking and without thinking reached for a tranquilizer. Then I stopped. Between the pills and the drinking, I had really done a job on myself. There was no other explanation for that crazy nightmare.

I put the pill back in the bottle. There had to be a better way to keep going.

I spent two hours in Makeup and Hairdressing, where they toned down the blond in my hair and eyebrows and covered my body with a dark makeup that turned my skin to a dull copper. Then came the selection of my costume – a short loose-fitting chamois dress with a few touches of colored beads. They called it the Debra Paget. She had worn it last while playing the mother of Cochise in an old Jeff Chandler film. By ten o'clock I had been driven to the back lot where they were doing the filming.

Chad came over to the car as I got out. He kissed my cheek. 'You look sensational,' he said. 'Sleep okay?'

I nodded.

'Good,' he said. Chad then introduced me to the man who had ambled over to us. 'This is your director. Marty Ryan. JeriLee Randall.'

Ryan was wearing a faded blue shirt and cowboy jeans. His grip was firm. 'Glad to meet you, JeriLee,' he said with a Western twang.

'My pleasure,' I said.

'Ready for work?'

I nodded.

'Good,' he said. 'We're ready for your first setup.'

I felt a moment of panic. 'I just got the script last night,' I said quickly. 'I haven't had a chance to read it yet. I don't know my lines.'

'No problem,' he said. 'You don't have any dialogue in these scenes anyway. Come with me.'

I followed him down to the camera and sound truck, which was standing in front of the Indian camp set. A number of men in Indian costumes were seated around a wooden crate playing cards. Near the corral two wranglers were tending to the horses.

'Hey, Terry,' the director shouted, 'bring her horse over here.'

The smaller wrangler cut a large white horse out of the pack and started toward me. The director turned back to me. 'It's a simple shot,' he explained. 'You come from the tent over there, look around for a moment, then run to the horse, jump up and ride away.'

I stared at him, too dumbfounded to speak.

He mistook my silence for confusion. 'It sounds more complicated than it really is,' he explained gently.

I shook my head. 'Somebody made a big mistake.'

He was puzzled. 'What do you mean?'

'The script I read had no scenes of me on horseback.'

'We rewrote the script to give you more to do,' he said. 'We've given you a key part now. You're practically the chief of the tribe. You're in charge because your father has been wounded.'

'Sounds great,' I said. 'Except for one thing. I can't ride.'

'What did you say?'

'I can't ride,' I repeated.

He stared at me dumbly. Chad came up to us, sensing something was wrong.

'What's the matter?' he asked.

The director turned to him. 'She can't ride.'

Chad stared at me. 'You can't ride?'

I shook my head. 'I've never even been on a horse.'

'Holy shit!' Chad exploded. 'Why the hell didn't you say something?'

'You never asked me,' I said. 'Besides the script that I saw didn't have any riding scenes.'

'What do we do now?' the director asked him.

'We use a double,' Chad said.

'No chance,' the director said firmly. 'This is television. Every shot is in close. There's no way to fake it.'

Chad turned toward the wrangler. 'How much time do you think it would take to teach her?'

The little wrangler looked at me with slitted eyes, then shifted a wad of tobacco in his cheek and spat into the dirt. 'If she learns fast, about a week to do what's called for in the script.'

'We're fucked!' the director said in a disgusted voice and walked off.

'I knew it,' Chad said. 'I knew it. The minute you walked into my office, I smelled trouble.'

'Don't blame me,' I said angrily. 'I didn't want the damn part to begin with. But you couldn't take no for an answer.'

'How the hell was I supposed to know you couldn't ride?' he snapped.

'The only horses I ever saw were outside the Plaza Hotel in New York hitched to a carriage,' I said.

'I'm jinxed,' Chad said.

'What do you want me to do with Queenie here?' the little wrangler asked.

Chad gave him a look which left no doubt as to what he would like him to do. I turned to the wrangler. 'Is the horse gentle?' I asked.

'She's like a baby,' he said. 'Loves evvabody.'

'Help me up,' I said. 'Let me see how it feels.'

He squatted at the side of the horse, making a clasped cup of his two hands. 'Put your left foot in here,' he said. 'An' swang your right foot over.'

'Okay.' I followed directions and everything was going fine until the horse moved as I crossed my leg over her back. I kept right on going and wound up in a puddle of mud on the other side.

'Are you all right?' Chad asked in a frightened voice.

I raised myself up on one elbow. The mud was all over my face and dress. I stared up at them. 'Sorry, fellers,' I said. Then the absurdity of it all got to me and I began to laugh.

Thinking that I was becoming hysterical, they quickly helped me to my feet. 'Get a doctor!' Chad yelled. Then he turned to me. 'Don't worry, don't worry, everything will be all right.'

But I couldn't stop laughing and by that night I was off the picture.

CHAPTER FIFTEEN

CHAD DROVE ME BACK to the motel. On the way he stopped off at a package store and bought a bottle of scotch. Within an hour after we got to my room, he had put away half the bottle. It was almost eight o'clock when he finally got to his feet, weaving unsteadily. 'We better get something to eat.'

He was in no condition to drive. 'Maybe we ought to get something from room service,' I suggested.

'They don't have any. Do you think the studio's going to put you somewhere where you can run up room service charges?'

I didn't answer.

'We'll go out for something.'

'I don't want you driving,' I said.

'We can walk. There are a few places down the block on Sunset.'

'Okay,' I said.

We went to a restaurant on the north side of the street opposite Schwab's Drug Store. The place was dimly lit like most Californian restaurants and there was a piano player sitting in the bar area near the entrance. A few people sat around the piano nursing their drinks. We walked past them and a head waiter escorted us to a table.

'The prime ribs are extra good tonight,' he said.

Chad looked at me and I nodded. 'Make it two,' he said to the headwaiter. 'But first bring me a double scotch on the rocks.'

The ribs were as good as the man promised but Chad left his untouched while he drank his dinner.

'You're not eating,' I said.

'Don't be a woman,' he said.

I was silent. The waiter brought coffee and Chad took a sip. 'What are your plans now?' he asked.

'I'll probably go back to New York tomorrow.'

'Anything special doing back there?'

'I'll start climbing on my agent's back again.'

'I'm sorry about what happened,' he said.

'The luck of the draw,' I said.

'I want to thank you for trying to get on that horse,' he said. 'If you hadn't done that, I could have blown my job.'

I didn't understand but I kept silent.

'It gave us a perfect out. The doctor called it an accident. Insurance took over the delay in shooting. It didn't cost the studio one penny and this way everybody's happy.'

I still didn't speak.

He looked at me. 'Except me. I felt we could have done great things together.'

'Maybe we will someday,' I said.

'No.' He shook his head dolefully. 'It doesn't work like that. The pressure's too great. Each week there's another show. You got to go forward.'

'But what about the feature you were telling me about?' I asked. 'We can still take a shot at that.'

'Maybe, but that's why I wanted you in this show. The studio likes to go with people out of their own productions.'

'I'm sorry,' I said.

'Not your fault,' he said. 'You tried.'

The waiter came and refilled our cups.

'Have you ever been to Vegas?' Chad asked.

'No.'

'Why don't you stay then?' he asked. 'A gang of us are going down tomorrow night to catch Sinatra's opening. We'll have a few laughs and you can fly back from there.'

'I don't think so,' I said.

'There won't be any heat. You can have your own room.'

'No, thanks. I'm not up to it. I'm going home and spend the next few days in bed.'

He was silent for a moment. 'Anything serious between you and John?'

'No.'

'You didn't have to answer that,' he said quickly. 'It wasn't any of my business.'

'I already did,' I said.

'I don't want you to leave,' he said.

'Why?'

'If you go, I'll feel I've failed. And I don't like failing.'

I was beginning to get irritated. 'You mean you don't want me to leave until you lay me, is that it?'

'Not exactly. Well, maybe. I really don't know.'

'Why can't you say exactly what you mean?' I asked. 'Or is

that the way the men here play the game?'

'I'm not playing any game,' he said defensively.

'What's on your mind then?'

'Look,' he snapped, 'I don't see any reason why I should have to be cross-examined like this. I went out on a limb for you.'

'You're absolutely right,' I said. 'I apologize.'

He relaxed and smiled. 'Don't apologize,' he said. 'You were absolutely right. I do want to lay you.'

When I didn't answer, he signaled for the check. Back at the motel he followed me into the room and began to take off his jacket.

I stopped him. 'Are we friends?'

'Yes.'

'Would you understand it if I told you my head isn't ready for you yet? I've got too much shit goin' on in there that I have to get rid of before we can make it.'

He was silent for a moment. 'You're not putting me on?'

'It's straight. You're okay. I like you. I'm just not up there yet.'

He slipped his arm back into his sleeve. 'They'll think I'm crazy but I believe you.'

'Thanks, Chad.'

'Can I call you if I come to New York?' he asked.

'I'll feel bad if you don't,' I said.

I followed him to the door. 'I'll see you then,' he said, kissing me quickly.

The phone began to ring almost the moment I closed the door. It was John. 'I've been calling all night,' he said.

'I've just got back from dinner.'

'I know, but I've got to see you.'

'I've got to pack,' I said. 'I'm going back on the first plane in the morning.'

'I heard what happened out at the studio,' he said. 'But all I want is a few minutes. You can't go without giving me a chance to explain.'

I thought for a moment. 'How long will it take you to get here?' I asked.

'One minute,' he answered. 'I'm in the motel office downstairs.'

He was there as soon as I put down the phone. 'Come in,' I said.

He followed me into the room. I gestured at the half empty

bottle of scotch that Chad had left. 'Would you like a drink?'

'Yes, please.'

I took some ice cubes from the refrigerator and gave him a healthy drink. He looked drawn and tired. He took a good belt and some of the color seemed to come back into his face. I gestured at the couch and sat down in the chair opposite him.

'I don't know what got into me,' he said. 'I'm not usually like this.'

I didn't answer.

'I want to apologize,' he said.

'Don't. It's as much my fault as it is yours. I didn't know the rules of the game.'

'It wasn't a game,' he said. 'I care for you. I really do.'

There was nothing I could say.

He took another sip of his drink. 'I don't want you to go back tomorrow. I want you to come back to the beach with me so we can start over. This time it will be right. I promise.'

'It won't work,' I said gently. 'I know that now.'

His voice grew more earnest. 'It will. I know it will. Remember how beautiful it was that night? It will be like that again if you just give it a chance.'

Looking at him, I thought there was so much he didn't understand. All he could remember was the way he felt then. By some strange quirk he seemed to have erased everything that happened afterward.

But I could not. Everything that had happened between us came together in the way I viewed him now. And the way I felt about him had changed. But seeing him so abject, I knew that there was no way of telling him the truth without bringing him down further. So instead I lied.

'I have to go back,' I said. 'Fannon and Guy have some ideas they want me to work on right away. They're going to try to get the play on a month earlier than they'd planned.'

He took a deep breath. I could see some of the tension leave his face. This was the kind of rejection he could cope with. It was business, not personal. 'Was it beautiful for you too?' he asked.

I got to my feet. 'It was beautiful.'

He rose from the couch and reached for me.

I put a hand on his arm, stopping him. 'No.'

He looked at me questioningly.

'I'm exhausted,' I said. 'I wouldn't be any good tonight.' I remembered the nightmare. 'I've been going back and forth so much the last two days I feel like a football.'

He didn't speak.

'Do you understand that?' I asked. 'I'm not a machine. I'm human. And I have to get some rest.'

He nodded. 'I keep forgetting. Women don't adapt to the time changes as well as men.'

I stared at him. That made no sense at all. But all I wanted to do at this point was to go to bed, so I agreed.

'I'll let you get some rest then,' he said.

He kissed me. I felt nothing but he didn't seem to be aware of it. 'We'll be in touch,' he said.

'Yes.'

He smiled. 'I'm glad we were able to have this talk.'

'So am I.'

'Call me when you have time,' he said.

He kissed me again and I closed the door behind him. I walked back into the room and stared at the whiskey bottle. I picked it up and dropped it in the wastebasket. Then I went into the bedroom and undressed. I crawled naked between the sheets and closed my eyes. I remember the last thought I had before drifting off.

Oh, shit.

Men.

CHAPTER SIXTEEN

THE SNOW was still falling heavily as we came out of the darkened theater. Max, the fat little company manager, came hurrying toward us through the lobby.

'Mr Fannon took the limo back to the hotel. He had some important calls to make. He said that he'd send the car right back.' He was puffing with exertion. 'It won't be long,' he added.

I glanced at Guy. 'Feel like walking?' I asked.

'The snow will be up to our ass,' he said.

'What the hell. It's only three blocks. Besides I think it will do me some good.'

'Okay.' He looked at Max. 'Hold the car for the cast.'

'Yes, Mr Jackson.'

Heads down, we walked stolidly for two blocks before exchanging a word. A plow moved past us spraying snow to the sides of the street. We paused at the corner to let it go by.

The whole performance was running through my head. The echo of the actors' voices in an almost empty theater, the laughter that never came, the lines that fell flat, the critics' averted faces as they left. 'The play stinks,' I said.

'You're not being fair to yourself. Look what we had to open against. The worst fucking snowstorm in five years.'

'It wasn't snowing inside the theater,' I said. 'Nothing worked. And the cast kept blowing their cues. One after the other.'

'They were nervous,' he said. 'Tomorrow night they'll be better. That's why shows go on the road. To work out the kinks.'

We were almost at the hotel. 'We ran too long,' I said. 'I think if I took about five minutes out of each act it would help.'

'Ten minutes out of the first,' he said. 'That's where our big problem is. We don't hook them early enough.'

We pushed open the door and were hit by the blast of warm air from the lobby. 'Feel up to working tonight?' he asked as we went to the desk for our keys.

'That's what I'm here for.'

He grinned. 'Your room or mine?'

'Yours,' I said. 'I'll bring the typewriter.' Directors and stars got suites. Authors were the low end of the totem and got small singles. Unless they happened to be my ex-husband.

We walked to the elevator. 'I'll order some sandwiches and coffee,' he said.

'Give me a half hour to shower and change into dry clothing,' I said.

'Good enough,' he answered.

The first thing I saw when I entered my room was the giant basket of flowers on the dresser. I read the card.

> Love and success
> We're very proud of our little girl.
> Mother and Daddy.

I looked out the window at the falling curtain of snow, then back at the flowers and began to cry.

We had been working almost three hours when the knock came at the door.

'I'm sorry to bother you, Mr Jackson,' Max said apologetically, 'but Mr Fannon wants to see you up in his suite right away.'

'Tell him I'll be right there,' Guy said.

'What do you think he wants at this hour?' I asked.

'I don't know. Probably wants to tell me the play needs fixing and what to fix.' He slipped into a cardigan. 'Finish off that bit of the first act. I think we've helped it a lot. I'll be right back.'

It was a half hour before he returned. By that time I had finished the first act rewrite and was working on the second. I took one look at his face and knew it was bad news.

'He wants to close it down,' he said.

'He can't do that,' I said. 'We're entitled to more than one night.'

'He's the producer; he can do whatever the hell he wants. He controls the money.'

'Why?' I asked. 'We haven't even seen the reviews yet.'

'He's got them all,' he answered. 'He has spies at the newspapers. He's got slugs of every one just as they'll be in the papers tomorrow morning.'

'What did they say?' I asked.

'Slaughter. Every one of them. Bloody slaughter.'

'Did you tell him what we were doing?'

'I did,' he answered. 'He said we should have thought of that before we opened. I did manage to get one thing out of him though. I asked him not to make his final decision until after he talks to you. After all, it's your play.'

'He wants to see me now?' I asked.

He nodded.

'What am I supposed to tell him?'

'Explain to him again what we're doing. You got to convince him that the play has a chance. You know what we're doing is right. Don't let him cut us off at the pass. We got to get this play into New York.'

I got to my feet. 'What if he won't listen to me?'

For the first time in all the years I'd known him I saw the bitch come out. His lips drew back over his teeth in a contemptuous smile, and unconsciously his voice went a register higher. 'For Christ's sake, JeriLee! If he liked boys I'd suck his cock to get this play on Broadway. It's got to be worth that to you. You're a woman. Just this once try using your cunt instead of your head!'

All the way up to the Presidential Suite where Fannon was staying Guy's words kept running through my head. For me it wasn't only the money. If the play went on I would be alive at the agency. Without it I was dead.

He opened the door, wearing a red velvet robe that I thought existed only in old movies. 'Hello, my dear,' he said.

I bent slightly so that he did not have to stretch to kiss my cheek. 'Adolph,' I said.

'I have a cold bottle of champagne. I find it always helps to have a little lift when you're facing the facts of life.'

I followed him into the room without answering. The wine was in a bucket next to the window. Solemnly he filled two glasses and gave me one. 'Cheers,' he said.

We drank.

'Dom Perignon,' he said. 'Nothing but the best.'

I nodded.

'Guy told you about the reviews?'

'Yes, but I don't think it's fair to go on them. Comedy doesn't play in an empty house. That's why TV shows have laugh tracks. Too bad we can't do the same thing in the theater.'

He refilled the glasses. 'That's not being realistic. Believe me, my dear, I've had years of experience with these things. They never go right after a start like this.'

'But it will work, Mr Fannon,' I said. 'I know it will. Guy and I have been rewriting. We have got all the problems out of the first act and we can lick the others.'

'Cheers,' he said again and took another sip of champagne.

I wondered if he'd even heard me. 'You've got to give us the chance,' I said. Then in spite of myself I began to cry.

He led me to the couch, took some Kleenex from the desk and pressed it into my hand. 'There, there, my dear. You mustn't take it so hard. You must think of it as experience. After all, this is your first play. There will be others.'

I couldn't stop crying. 'It will work,' I said. 'I know it will work.'

He sat down on the couch beside me and drew my head to his chest. He stroked my hair gently. 'Listen to the words of a man almost old enough to be your father. I know how you feel. After all, I feel just as bad. I don't like to lose eighty thousand dollars. But it's better than going into New York and losing seventy thousand more. A man has to learn when to cut his losses. And, in a way, that's what you're doing. Nobody will remember the reviews you get in New Haven when it comes time to get your next play produced. But if you get bad reviews in New York they never forget it.'

'I don't care,' I cried. 'I know the play will work.'

He continued stroking my hair while the arm around my waist moved up toward my breasts.

I turned and let my breast fill his hand. 'Adolph,' I said, 'you don't know how much I've always admired your courage as a producer. You were the one man I felt would never quit on me.'

'I'm not quitting.' He cleared his throat. 'I'm just trying to be practical.'

This time I let him feel both breasts. A curious flush blotched his face.

Then abruptly he got to his feet. He picked up the champagne glasses and gave one to me. 'Drink it,' he ordered.

There was something in his voice I hadn't heard before. And I suddenly realized that this little monster was really a man. I drained my glass.

'I want to fuck you,' he said. 'And I know you're ready to fuck me. But, would you still be willing if I close the show?'

'No,' I said, looking into his eyes.

He stared at me for a moment, then emptied his glass. Suddenly he smiled and patted my cheek. 'I like you,' he said. 'At least you're honest.'

'Thank you,' I said. 'What about the show?'

'I'm closing it. But I promise you this. If you write another play, bring it to me. We'll take another crack at it.'

I rose to my feet. Suddenly I didn't feel cheap anymore. 'Thank you, Adolph,' I said. 'You're a real gentleman.'

He held the door open for me. I bent my cheek for his goodnight kiss, then went down to my room. There was no reason to see Guy.

The show closed in New Haven.

CHAPTER SEVENTEEN

'MODERN FURNITURE is a drug on the market,' the man said.

I didn't reply. Every used-furniture dealer who had come to look at the apartment made the same remark.

'The rugs belong to you?' he asked.

I nodded.

He looked down disapprovingly. 'White and beige. Bad colors. Hard to keep clean.' I had heard that before too.

The telephone rang. I answered, hoping that it was my new agent calling about an interview he was trying to arrange for me with an Italian producer.

It was the telephone company about their bill, which was already two months overdue. They were apologetic but said they would have to disconnect my service if a check was not in their office by the following morning. I told them it was in the mail and hung up. It wasn't but it didn't matter. By tomorrow I wouldn't live here anymore.

The furniture dealer was coming out of the bedroom. 'You moved some furniture out,' he said in an accusatory voice. 'I could tell from the marks on the rug. And I didn't see any silverware, dishes or pots and pans.'

'What you see is what's for sale,' I said. I wondered if he thought I was going to live in a suitcase. The things I needed were already in the small studio apartment I had rented on the West Side.

'I don't know,' he said doubtfully. 'It's tough merchandise to move.'

'It's practically new. Only about a year old. And I bought the best. It cost me over nine thousand dollars.'

'You should have come to us,' he said. 'We could have saved you a lot of money.'

'I didn't know about you then.'

'That's the trouble with people. They never learn until it's too late.' He gestured toward the couch. 'How much do you want for that?'

'Five thousand dollars.'

'You'll never get it.'

'Then make me an offer.'

'A thousand dollars.'

'Forget it,' I said, walking toward the door. 'Thanks for coming up.'

'Wait, you got a better offer?'

'Yes. Much better.'

'How much better? A hundred, two hundred?'

I didn't answer.

'If Hammersmith was here, he wouldn't give you more than twelve hundred,' he said.

He knew the competition. That was exactly the amount I had been offered.

'I'll take a chance,' he said. 'I'll give you thirteen hundred. That's my top offer.'

'No, thanks,' I said, looking at him steadily, holding open the door.

He appraised the room again quickly. 'How fast can I get the merchandise?'

'You can take it wih you right now as far as I'm concerned.'

'This afternoon?'

'If you like.'

'No mortgages, no time payments due? It's free and clear? You'll sign a paper?'

'Yes.'

He let out a reluctant sigh. 'My partner will think I'm crazy but I'll give you fifteen hundred. And that's absolutely my top offer.'

That was three hundred more than any offer I had received so far. And he was the fourth dealer I'd seen. 'Cash,' I said. 'Not a check.' A check wouldn't clear my bank in time to cover the rent and deposit check I had issued for the new apartment.

'Of course,' he said.

'Sold,' I said, closing the door.

'Can I use your phone?' he asked. 'I can have my truck here in an hour if you'll wait.'

'I'll wait,' I said.

I made it to the bank just before three o'clock. After making the deposit I came out into the mild May afternoon and decided that since I hadn't heard from my agent I would go to see him.

On the bus I did some calculating. I figured that after paying all my bills I would have about eight hundred dollars left.

Lou Bradley's noisy offices in the Brill Building were nothing like the elaborate offices of Artists Alliance.

And Lou wasn't exactly the kind of agent I would have preferred but I didn't have much choice. I had been to all the big ones – William Morris, A.F.A., C.M.A. – before coming to him. They were polite but not interested. It was as if I had suddenly become an untouchable. I tried to look at it realistically. After all, no one wanted to associate themselves with failure. And whether or not it was my fault, I had three good ones to my credit. Despite what John had told me, his brother had cut down on my part in the film, then there was the episode at Universal and, last but not least, the play.

It was the play that had hurt most, not only because it closed but because I began hearing all over town that Guy was dumping on me, saying that I had been uncooperative and had refused to make the changes he wanted. I tried to call him, convinced that I could make him stop, but I could never get him on the phone. Then after I had gotten back I received the notice from Artists Alliance canceling my contract.

I was bewildered. Harry Gregg had said nothing about it.

I picked up the phone and called him. His voice was guarded. 'Yes?'

'There has to be a mistake,' I said. 'I just got a notice that the office dropped my contract, and you never said anything about it.'

'That's not my job,' he said. 'That's upstairs.'

'But you knew about it?'

He hesitated. 'Yes.'

'Then why didn't you say something? I thought you were my friend.'

'I am. But I also have a job here. I don't mess in affairs that aren't my concern.'

'But we talked about plans, things you were going to do,' I said. 'And all the time you knew you weren't going to do any of them.'

'What did you expect me to say? "Don't bother me, baby, you've had it"?'

'You could have said something.'

'Okay. I'll say it now. Don't bother me, baby, you've had it.' The line went dead in my hands.

I was hurt and angry but I had no time for tears. I needed another agent and another job fast.

But I found neither quickly as I had hoped. The money from the last payment on the play had run out before I knew it. I guess my parents must have sensed something was wrong, because on my twenty-fifth birthday they sent me a check for twenty-five hundred dollars. Then I cried.

I had to wait half an hour for Lou to get off the phone. In that way he was no different than any other agent. They were all telephone freaks. Finally his secretary gave me the signal to go into his office.

He looked up at me, his eyes pale blue and watery in his thin face. 'Hi, baby,' he said quickly. 'I been thinkin' about you. I haven't been able to get the son of a bitch on the phone yet.' He yelled through the open door. 'Hey, Shirley, try DaCosta again for me.'

Then his voice dropped to a confidential whisper. 'I think he's with the boys.'

I was puzzled. 'Who?'

His voice went even lower. 'You know who I mean. The boys. Big Frank. Joe. Where do you think those guinea producers get their money from?'

'You mean the rackets?' I asked.

'Shh!' he said quickly. 'We don't use that word around here. The boys are all good guys. Friends. You know what I mean.' The phone buzzed.

'Hey, Vincenzo,' he said jovially, 'how's it going?'

He listened for a moment, then spoke again. 'That sounds real good. By the way, I got that girl I was talking to you about right here in my office and I was wondering if you could set an appointment to see her?'

He looked over at me and nodded into the phone. 'Would I steer you wrong? She's a real good looker, you know what I mean? Lots of experience. Broadway, films, Hollywood, everything.'

He covered the mouthpiece with his hand. 'He says he's all tied up the next two days, then he's going back to Italy. You free for dinner tonight?'

I hesitated.

'You don't have to worry about this guy. He's a perfect gentleman.'

I nodded. Even if I didn't get the job, dinner out was better than eating a hamburger alone.

'She says she's free,' he said into the phone, then covered the mouthpiece again. 'He wants to know if you got a friend?'

I shook my head.

'She says she hasn't. But don't worry. I'll send somebody up.' He nodded. 'Gotcha. Eight o'clock. Your suite at the Saint Regis.'

'You're lucky,' he said solemnly as he put down the phone. 'A guy like him don't usually go out of his way to see anybody. He's got his pick of all them Italian actresses. Loren, Lollobrigida, Mangano. Only trouble is their English ain't no good.'

'What kind of part is it?' I said.

'How the hell do I know? You don't ask foreign producers and directors for a script. They would think you were crazy or something. Half these guys make their pictures with no script at all. An' they win all the awards.'

'Maybe I'm not the type he's looking for,' I said.

'You're American, aren't you?'

I nodded.

'You're an actress?'

I nodded again.

'Then you're perfect for the part. Exactly what he asked me for. An American actress.' He got to his feet and, taking my arm, steered me to the door. 'Now you go home, take a hot bath and make yourself up real pretty. Wear a long sexy dress. These guys wear black tie for dinner every night.'

He held open the door to the outer hall. 'Don't forget. Eight o'clock at his suite in the Saint Regis. Don't be late. These guys are very prompt.'

'Okay,' I said. 'But you forgot one thing.'

'What's that?'

'To tell me his name.'

'Oh. DaCosta. Vincent DaCosta.'

DaCosta. The name was vaguely familiar but I couldn't recall where I had heard it before.

CHAPTER EIGHTEEN

As I walked down the carpeted corridor to the suite, the shouting grew louder. The noise was vulgar in the faded gentility of the Saint Regis halls. I stopped in front of the double doors and knocked at the wooden panels. The shouting continued. I could hear a woman's voice. But I couldn't understand what she was saying because she was speaking Italian. Thinking that they hadn't heard me, I knocked again.

The door was opened almost immediately by a tall good-looking dark-haired young man dressed in a conservative dark suit, white on white shirt and white tie. There was no sign that he was expecting anyone.

'Mr DaCosta?' I asked.

He nodded.

'JeriLee Randall,' I said. 'Mr Bradley asked me to be here at eight o'clock.'

His face cleared. 'Luigi sent you.' He smiled suddenly, revealing white even teeth. 'Come in.' There was no trace of accent in his English.

I followed him through the small entrance hall into the large living room. There were two men sitting on the couch, but they didn't glance in my direction. They were looking up at the woman in the flimsy short chemise who was shouting at the bald older man.

I stood in the doorway for a moment, not knowing whether or not to enter. Suddenly I recognized the woman. Carla Maria Perino. Just two years before, she had won the Academy Award for her performance in *Remnants of a War*. Then I recognized the bald man on the couch. It was her husband, Gino Paoluzzi, who had produced and directed the film.

Suddenly Paoluzzi's eyes glittered and he rose to his feet. He was a head shorter than she but there was a strange sense of power in him that made him seem larger than anyone in the room. His hand moved swiftly. There was the sharp sound of the slap across her face and the harsh guttural sound of his voice. 'Putana!'

Abruptly she was silent, then she dissolved in tears. He turned away from her and crossed the room toward me. The other man rose from the couch and followed him.

DaCosta came between us. 'This is Mr Paoluzzi, the famous director,' he said to me. 'He doesn't speak any English.' He looked at the director. 'Io presento JeriLee Randall.'

Paoluzzi smiled and I held out my hand. He gave a short half bow and kissed my hand in such a way that his lips seemed to brush his own hand, which covered mine.

Looking at me, DaCosta snapped his finger. 'I know you!' he said excitedly. 'Didn't you get a Tony award about five years ago?'

I nodded.

'I saw that play. You were fantastic.' He turned to Paoluzzi and began to speak rapidly in Italian. I could pick up only a few words. Broadway. Tony. Walter Thornton.

Paoluzzi nodded and looked at me with an expression of respect. He said something in Italian.

DaCosta translated. 'The Maestro says that he has heard of you. He is honored to meet you.'

'Thank you.'

DaCosta intrduced the other man, who was tall, gray-haired and paunchy. 'Piero Guercio.'

Again the strange hand kiss. 'How do you do,' he said in a strongly accented English.

'Signor Guercio is the Maestro's consigliere,' DaCosta said. He saw the puzzled expression on my face. 'Lawyer,' he added.

'Gino.' Her voice was a small plaintive cry.

It was almost as if they had forgotten that she was in the room. Her husband said something to her. She nodded her head and looked at me appraisingly.

Paoluzzi spoke again. This time I gathered he was telling her about me. After a moment she came toward us. 'Mia sposa,' he said to me.

We shook hands. I was surprised at the strength in her slim fingers. I turned to DaCosta. 'Tell her I'm a fan. I loved her performance in the film.'

DaCosta translated and she smiled. 'Grazie.' Then she left the room.

'She was upset because the maid burned a hole in her dress while she was ironing it,' DaCosta explained to me.

If that was all it took to bring on an outburst like that, I wouldn't have wanted to be around when something really went wrong.

'How about a drink?' he asked. 'We have everything.'

'A glass of white wine?'

'You got it.'

I took the glass from him and sat on the couch where he indicated. The men sat on chairs in a semicircle around me.

DaCosta translated for Paoluzzi. 'Are you working right now?'

'No, but I'm considering a few things.'

Paoluzzi nodded as if he understood. 'Do you prefer theater to films?' DaCosta asked, translating for Paoluzzi.

'I can't tell,' I said. 'I've never really had a film role that I felt was rewarding.'

Paoluzzi nodded, then spoke again. 'The Maestro says that Hollywood has destroyed the American film industry with their emphasis on television. At one time they led the world but now the leadership has passed to Europe. They are the only ones to make films that have any artistic or real values.'

I sipped my wine and we sat in awkward silence for a moment until there was a knock at the door.

DaCosta jumped up and hurried out into the foyer. He returned with a tall red-headed woman wearing a beaded green evening dress and a long black mink stole. The men got to their feet and kissed her hand as they were introduced. Then DaCosta looked at me. 'Marge Small, JeriLee Randall.'

There was an antagonistic look in the girl's eyes. 'Hi,' she said.

'Hi,' I replied.

'You're with the consigliere,' he said, pointing at Guercio.

She nodded casually. 'Okay.'

The attorney smiled at her. 'Would you like something to drink?'

'Yeah,' she said. 'You got some champagne?'

He nodded and she followed him to the bar, where he filled two glasses, one for her and one for himself. They stayed there, talking in low tones. I wondered what they were saying.

DaCosta interrupted my thoughts. 'The Maestro wants to know if you ever thought of working in Italy?'

'Nobody ever asked me,' I said.

'He says you would do very well there. You're the type they're looking for.'

'Tell him I'm available.'

Paoluzzi smiled, got to his feet, then vanished into the next room. DaCosta picked up the phone. 'Front door,' he said. 'Tell Mr Paoluzzi's chauffeur that we'll be down in ten minutes.'

'How long have you been with Lou?' he asked as he hung up the phone.

'A week now.'

He nodded, smiling. 'I don't know how the little bastard does it. He always comes up with a winner.'

'I'm a little confused,' I said. 'Mr Bradley told me you were a producer.'

He laughed. 'He never gets anything right. I'm a producer's rep. Paoluzzi's the producer.'

'I see,' I said, although I really didn't. 'What's the picture about?'

'Damned if I know. Every meeting we go to tells a different story. I'm willing to bet that none of them are what he's going to make. He's afraid that if he tells the real story someone'll steal the idea. It doesn't make my life any easier, I tell you.'

'Why?'

'I'm supposed to raise American financing for him and our money people don't work that way. They want to know what they're getting into.'

'You're Italian?' I asked.

'American. My parents were Italian.'

'You come from New York?'

'Brooklyn. My father and brothers are in business out there.'

Suddenly I remembered why his name was familiar. The DaCosta family. They certainly were in business out there. They owned the waterfront. One of the five families that divided up New York. Now I understand what Bradley meant.

He smiled, as if he had read my mind. 'I'm the black sheep of the family,' he said. 'I didn't want to go into the business. They all think I'm stupid for beating my brains out in show business.'

Suddenly I liked him. There was something disarmingly honest about him. 'I don't think you are,' I said.

The bedroom door opened and the Paoluzzis came out. I couldn't help but stare at her. None of the pictures I had seen of her had done her justice. Without a doubt she was the most beautiful woman I have ever seen.

I saw her swift appraising glance of Marge Small. In a moment she turned to me, and I knew the girl had been dismissed from her mind as if she never existed. 'I'm sorry I took so long,' she said in a soft pleasantly accented voice.

'It's all right,' I said.

DaCosta led the way to the car and opened the door. In the limousine he sat up front with the driver. The lawyer and Marge were on the jump seats and the Maestro sat between his wife and me. We went to Romeo Salta's, a restaurant only two blocks from the hotel.

At dinner there was no mistaking who the star was. We had the best table and Carla Maria the best seat. She got the same kind of treatment at El Morocco, where we went after dinner. Mysteriously, photographers appeared everywhere we went, and in a curious way it felt good even if it wasn't for me. It had been a long time since I had been around this kind of show business excitement.

'Dance?' DaCosta asked.

We went out onto the small crowded dance floor. The music was sedate. It was not until after one o'clock that they went into any rock. He held me closely as we moved slowly to the Sinatra record on the stereo system.

'Enjoying yourself?' he asked.

I nodded. 'It's fun.'

'Do you really have some jobs on the fire?'

'No.'

'I didn't think so.'

'What makes you say that?'

'You wouldn't be with Luigi if you did. He's generally a desperation area.' His eyes were serious as he looked down at me. 'You have talent, real talent. What went wrong?'

I hesitated. 'I don't know. Everything. It's like – one day it was all there and, the next day – nothing.'

'It's the breaks,' he said. 'It happens like that sometimes.'

I didn't answer.

'Carla Maria likes you,' he said.

I was pleased. 'I like her too. She's really a fantastic lady. You can tell her I said so.'

'The Maestro also likes you.'

'Good. He must be a great talent.'

He found an opening and steered me to a corner of the dance floor near the wall. 'He was wondering if you would be interested in doing a scene with Carla Maria.'

'I would,' I said quickly. Then I looked at his face and knew we weren't talking about the same thing. I felt myself turning red. I didn't know what to say.

'It's okay,' he said finally. 'You don't have to.'

'I'm surprised,' I said. 'I just didn't expect this.'

'They have their own ideas of fun,' he said. 'I'm just delivering the message.'

'Is that part of your job too?'

'That and a lot of other things.'

When we got back to the table Guercio and the other woman had gone. I caught the signal that passed between Paoluzzi and DaCosta, then the producer got to his feet and said something in Italian.

DaCosta looked at me. 'The Maestro apologizes but it's time to leave. He has appointments early in the morning.'

We all rose and almost caused a collision between captains and waiters rushing to move the table out of the way. Carla Maria and her husband led the way out of the club, DaCosta and I brought up the rear.

The limousine rolled up as we came out the door. 'The Maestro wants to know if we can drop you off on the way back to the hotel?' DaCosta said.

'No, thanks. I live over on the West Side. Tell him I'll grab a cab. And thank him for a lovely evening.'

DaCosta repeated it in Italian. Palouzzi smiled, bowed and kissed my hand again. Then he looked into my eyes and said something.

DaCosta translated the words. 'He says that he hopes he has the good fortune to work with you someday.'

'I do too,' I said.

I held out my hand to Carla Maria. She smiled. 'That is not the way we say good night in Italy.' She leaned forward, pressing her cheek against both of mine and making kissing sounds. 'Ciao,' she said.

'Ciao.'

They got into the limousine. DaCosta escorted me to my taxi and pressed a bill into my hand. 'Cab fare,' he said.

'No,' I said, trying to push it away.

'Take it. It's on the expense account.' He closed the door of the cab before I could protest again. 'Good night.'

'Good night,' I said as the taxi moved away from the curb.

'Where to, lady?' the driver asked.

I gave him the address.

'Was that Carla Maria Perino getting into that limo?' the cab driver asked.

'Yes.'

'Gee.' His voice was filled with a whispering wonder. 'She's really something else, ain't she, lady?'

'She really is,' I said, and I meant it. Then I remembered the bill I had in my hand. For a moment as I looked down at it I couldn't believe my eyes.

I had never seen a real five-hundred-dollar bill before.

CHAPTER NINETEEN

I CALLED HIM on the house phone at nine o'clock the next morning. He sounded sleepy.

'JeriLee Randall,' I said. 'I didn't mean to wake you.'

'It's okay,' he said.

'I just want you to know that I left the money you gave me in an envelope at the desk in your name,' I said. 'Thank you anyway.'

'Wait a minute!' He sounded wide awake now. 'Where are you calling from?'

'The lobby.'

'Don't go away. I'll be down in a minute. We can have a cup of coffee or some breakfast.'

'I don't want to be any trouble.'

'I want to see you.'

I put down the phone. In less than three minutes he came out of the elevator. He hadn't been asleep as I had thought. He was already shaved and dressed. He didn't speak until after we had gone into the restaurant and the waiter had brought us some coffee.

'You didn't have to do that,' he said.

'Neither did you.'

'You don't understand. It's all part of the business.'

'But it's not my business,' I said.

'You really are an old-fashioned girl, aren't you?'

'No. New-fashioned. I don't believe in taking money I haven't earned.'

'What are you going to do for a job?' he asked.

'Keep on looking,' I said.

'I'll talk to Luigi about you. I'll make sure he doesn't hustle you.'

'I'm not going back to him.' I hesitated. 'Is Paoluzzi really going to do a picture in which he needs an American actress?'

'Paoluzzi is only interested in doing pictures with his wife,' he said.

'Then there wasn't really a job?'

'No.'

'That's what I finally figured out. I guess I'm really stupid.'

'It's a stupid business. There are millions of girls and very few jobs. Even those with talent rarely make it.'

'I'll make it,' I said. 'I did it once.'

'Weren't you married to Walter Thornton?' he asked.

I knew what he was getting at. 'They gave me the Tony for acting, not because my husband wrote the play.'

'But everybody needs a friend,' he said. 'At least that gets you past the secretaries.'

'What are you getting at?'

'Paoluzzi kept me up half the night talking about you. He says you can get more work than you can handle in Italy – with the right kind of a sponsor.'

'Meaning himself?' I asked.

He nodded.

'No, thanks,' I said. I started to get up.

He put a hand on my arm to stop me. 'Don't be a fool. I could name a half dozen stars who made it that way including Carla Maria. And she was only seventeen when he found her in Naples a dozen years ago.'

'It's not my style. I came close to it once and it left me feeling like half a human being.'

'Independence isn't what it's cracked up to be,' he said. 'Most independent people I know are broke.'

'What about you? I notice you didn't go into the family business.'

He reddened slightly. 'That's different.'

'Why is it different?'

'Because I'm a man and you're a girl. I can take care of myself better than you can.'

'Maybe you can right now, but I'll learn. And when I do, there'll be no difference.'

'The world won't change. If you're smart you'll find some nice guy, get married and have a couple of kids.'

'Is that the only answer you have for me?'

'That. Or the other. And you already said you're not interested in the other.'

'You mean either I become a wife or a whore. There's no other way for me to make it?'

'Outside chance,' he said. 'One in a million.'

'My kind of odds,' I said. 'Thank you for the coffee.'

He took my hand. 'I like you. I'd like to see you again sometime.'

'I'd like to see you too. But on one condition.'

'What's that?'

'No business. No bullshit.'

He grinned. 'You're on. How do I get in touch with you?'

I gave him my number and we walked out to the lobby. 'I'll give you a call next week when I get these people out of town.'

'Okay,' I said. We shook hands and I went out into the street. The sun was shining, the day was warm. I didn't know why, but suddenly I was feeling up.

I didn't see him again for three months. And by then things were very different for both of us. My father died that summer and for the first time in my life I found out what it really meant to be alone.

There had been no work that summer, not even in summer stock. I made the rounds every day, read *Casting News* and answered every call. But without an agent I wasn't getting anywhere. Even for television commercials you needed an agent to get you inside the doors of the advertising agencies.

Every night I would return to my small apartment exhausted, but after only a few hours' sleep I would wake up and be unable to go back to sleep. I worked on my new play but it wasn't coming together. Everything I wrote seemed forced and artificial. Then, after a while, I didn't write at all. I would sit by my typewriter staring out the window at the night-darkened street, not even thinking.

Somehow my father sensed what was happening. And one day, without a word, I received a check for one hundred dollars. And from then on, the check came regularly every Monday. Without it I couldn't have managed.

I tried to talk to him about it one day. But he would say nothing except that it was something both he and Mother wanted to do because they loved me and had faith in me. When I went to thank Mother, she looked at me coolly. 'It's your father's idea,' she said. 'I think you should come back home and live with us. I don't hold with a young girl living alone in the city the way you do.'

After that I was even more determined to show her. I attacked my typewriter with new ferocity. But it didn't matter. Nothing good came of it.

I felt so totally alone. I had no friends – male or female. Show business camaraderie didn't seem to exist on the level on which I lived, at least not for me. And then suddenly one day I became brutally aware of something else – the fact that I was no longer young.

I had answered a cattle call for girls who were to play bits and extras in a beach scene for a film that would be shooting on Long Island. The audition was held in a large hall over the Roseland ballroom on Broadway and we all had to appear in bathing suits and bikinis. I was almost last in a line of about thirty girls. I stood waiting to walk past the casting director and the producer, hoping that all the jobs would be filled before I got my turn.

My figure had always been good. I knew that. And I made sure that I kept it that way by spending a half hour every morning doing exercises. I heard my name being called and walked out across the small stage.

In the center of the stage I paused, turned around slowly as we had been instructed, and then walked away from them, swinging my hips suggestively. I had almost reached the end of the stage when I heard the producer whisper, 'No.'

'But she's got a great figure and a sensational ass,' the casting director rasped.

The producer was trying to whisper, but I could hear him. There was a tone of finality in his voice. 'Too old. She has to be at least twenty-five.'

I went around behind the stage to get my clothes. The other girls chattered as they dressed, but none of them seemed to have anything to say to me. The producer's words were beginning to sink in. Too old. They were all younger than I – seventeen, eighteen – bright and fresh and untarnished.

Suddenly I wondered what I was doing trying to live in a world I had outgrown.

Broadway was sweltering in the July heat, but I decided to walk back uptown to my apartment.

By the time I got to my street I was perspiring and exhausted. I decided to go into the liquor store, where I bought a cold bottle of white California wine. Then I went up to my apartment and began to drink. Within an hour I was smashed. The wine worked better on an empty stomach and I had not eaten that morning because I did not want my stomach to bulge when I got into my bikini.

I sat at the window, staring out at the hot streets. Shit. What was the matter with me?

The telephone began to ring, but since I was expecting no calls I decided not to answer. But when it continued to ring I finally picked up.

It was my mother. From the steely control in her voice I knew it was something bad. 'JeriLee? Where have you been all day? I've been trying to get you.'

I was angry, yet somehow frightened. 'For Christ's sake, Mother! I was out looking for a job. What do you think I've been doing?'

The steel was still there. 'Your father had a heart attack this morning. He died before they could get him to the hospital.'

The pain seemed tightened around my heart. Then I found my voice. 'I'll be home right away, Mother.'

CHAPTER TWENTY

IT SEEMED as if the whole town turned out for his funeral. Many stores closed during the morning and the crowd at the church spilled out into the street. The words of the minister were carried to them by loudspeaker.

'John Randall was a good man. He gave freely of his life and time for the welfare of his neighbors. Many of us here today have been enriched by his aid and kind advice. We shall miss him. And we shall always remember him.'

Then the flower-laden coffin was carried out to the hearse and borne to the cemetery, where he was laid to rest. Later after the neighbors had all gone home, Mother and I were alone.

'Let me make you a cup of tea,' I said.

She nodded. 'He hadn't been feeling well that morning before he went to work,' she said, sipping her tea. 'I wanted him to stay home and rest. But he said he had too much to do. His secretary said he was dictating a letter when he suddenly slumped over his desk. She called for help right away. But there was nothing anyone could do.'

'Try not to think about it now,' I said.

Her eyes met mine. 'Sometimes I think I did not give him enough. He might have wanted a son of his own. But he never said anything. He knew how busy I was with the two of you.'

'He loved you,' I said. 'He was happy.'

'I hope so,' she said. 'I would not like to feel that I cheated him of anything he wanted.'

'All he ever wanted was you, Mother,' I said.

We were silent for a long time.

'You know many things will have to be changed now,' she said finally. 'Without Father's income, we'll have to cut back.'

I didn't speak.

'I was thinking it might be a good idea if you came back home to live.'

'What would I do, Mother?' I asked. 'There's no work for me here.'

'I won't be able to continue sending you the hundred dollars a week.'

'I can understand that Mother. I'll manage.'

'How?' she asked directly.

'I'll get something soon,' I said. 'And I'm almost finished with my new play. Fannon promised me that he would put it on.'

'What if it fails like the other one?' she asked.

'Then I'll try again,' I said.

She rose from her chair. 'I think I'll go up and lie down,' she said. She started from the room, then turned back. 'You know there's always a room for you here if things don't work out.'

'Yes, Mother. Thank you.'

I watched her slowly climb the stairs to her room. She was still a good-looking woman. Her back was straight and she held her head high. Suddenly I had a feeling of admiration for her. I wished I could be like that. She always seemed to know exactly what she had to do.

My apartment was hot and musty. I threw open the windows. Even with the noise of the traffic it was better than the dank dead smell of the closed-up rooms.

I picked up the mail that had accumulated in the week I'd been away. It was mostly bills.

Idly I opened the latest copy of *Casting News*. I went through the casting calls and open auditions. There was really nothing for me. Then an ad caught my eye.

> WANTED! ACTRESSES, MODELS, SHOW-GIRLS! WORK IN YOUR SPARE TIME. MEET IMPORTANT PEOPLE. If you are between assignments, over twenty-one, not less than 5′ 5″, good figure and conversationalist, and can give us at least four nights out of the week, we have a job that might interest you.
>
> STARTING SALARY $165 per week, including all Social Security and Unemployment Insurance Benefits plus Costume and Tips. Increases after three months. Based on a forty-hour work week.
>
> IF INTERESTED APPLY:
> TORCHLIGHT CLUB, EAST 54th STREET OFF PARK AVENUE, MONDAY THROUGH

FRIDAY THIS WEEK BETWEEN 2 p.m. and 5 p.m.

*IMPORTANT – NO HUSTLERS! ALL EMPLOYEES WILL REQUIRE N.Y.P.D. AND N.Y.S.A.B. LICENSES AND APPROVALS.

I reread the ad slowly, thinking that it must be a new club. The only two I knew of were the Playboy and the Gaslight. In my financial condition, a hundred and sixty-five dollars a week sounded good, and they had to be legitimate. They did require police department and state liquor board licenses. The hours seemed right for me too. It would leave me time to write and follow up any other job that might turn up.

I checked my watch. It was almost noon. And it was already Thursday. The ad had been in all week. If I wanted to get a crack at it I had to move quickly. Having made up my mind, I went into the bathroom, dumped a whole bottle of bath salts into the tub and turned on the water. While the tub was running I lined up all my makeup including the false eyelashes on the shelf over the sink. I was determined to look my best.

It was a wide gray stone building with black-painted double doors. On either side of the door were heavy brass coach lamps that matched the brass plate on the door. The letters etched into the brass and read simply, 'Torchlight'.

I tried the door but found it locked. I checked my watch. It was after two o'clock. Then I saw the small buzzer almost concealed under the brass plate.

When I pressed it the door opened automatically and I stepped inside. There was a smell of new paint and in some of the rooms off the entrance hall I could see workmen hammering and tacking draperies on the walls and over the windows.

One of the workmen saw me. 'Upstairs,' he said, pointing. 'The front room.'

The girl sitting behind the desk looked at me with a bored expression.

'I came in answer to the ad,' I said.

Her expression didn't change. 'All the jobs are filled.'

'The ad said interviews all week.'

'I can't help that. We had over four hundred girls here in the first two days.' She reached for a piece of paper. 'The place was a madhouse. You can leave your name and number if you like. We'll get in touch with you if there's an opening.'

The telephone on her desk buzzed. 'Yes, Mr DaCosta. Right away, Mr DaCosta,' she said. After putting down the phone, she looked up at me. 'Do you want to leave your name or not?' she asked impatiently.

I played my hunch. 'Tell Mr DaCosta that JeriLee Randall is here.'

The expression on her face changed suddenly. 'Why didn't you say so? I've heard him mention your name,' she said, picking up the phone again. 'Mr DaCosta, JeriLee Randall is here to see you.' She listened for a moment, then looked at me. 'Next floor up, first door on the right.'

He was standing in the open doorway waiting for me, a smile on his face. 'How did you know I was here?'

'I didn't,' I said. 'But I heard the girl downstairs say the name DaCosta and I took the chance it was you.'

'I've thought of calling you many times,' he said. 'But something always came up.'

'It's okay,' I said.

'How's it been going?'

'Not good. I came in answer to the ad. But the girl says that all the jobs are filled.'

His face grew suddenly serious. 'Do you have any idea of what the job is?'

'Only what I saw in the ad.'

He walked around behind his desk. 'It's a kind of super-expensive Playboy Club with extras – sauna, swimming pool, massage – as well as a cocktail lounge and restaurant. There'll also be a discotheque in the basement.'

'Sounds like quite an operation.'

'It is,' he said. 'We have eight hundred people who have already laid down six hundred dollars apiece for membership. We've been looking for some very high class girls to act as hostesses. They have to be very special type girls because they will set the tone of the place. Just as the Bunnies do over at Playboy.'

'How will your hostesses be different?' I asked.

'First, they won't have to wear those silly costumes. Each hostess will wear a gown especially designed for the room in which she works. Second, they have to be able to talk, to be friendly without being pushy. They must make the members feel comfortable, almost as if they were in their own home.'

'Sounds like a good idea,' I said.

'It is,' he said. He looked at me. 'Would you like to see some of the gowns?'

I nodded.

He went to a closet in the corner of the room and took out two gowns. One was Grecian, soft and flowing and very decollete. The other was a granny dress of flowered chiffon with a square deep-cut peasant neckline. He held them in front of the window. They were almost transparent. 'The girls wear these,' he said. 'And nothing else.'

I was silent.

'No bras, no panties, nothing but high-heel shoes.' He put the gowns back in the closet and returned to his desk. 'What do you think?'

'I didn't think I was applying for a job in a kindergarten,' I said.

There must have been something in the expression on my face that made him come suddenly toward me. He put his hands on my arms and looked down into my eyes. 'What happened?' he asked.

'My father died,' I said. Then the tears came and I buried my face against his jacket. 'And for the first time in my life I'm frightened.'

CHAPTER TWENTY-ONE

I LOOKED UP at the wall clock. It was after eleven. The ten o'clock changeover should have been completed by now. It was time to begin the check. I stopped and looked in the full-length mirror on the door of my small office.

The sheer floor-length granny clung smoothly. I was satisfied. The first few days I had felt very self-conscious about wearing it, but I'd since learned that no one seemed to pay any attention, so I'd stopped thinking about it.

I took the elevator down seven floors to the disco in the basement. It was my job to see that all the stations were covered and make sure that there was always someone to replace the absentees, as well as to arrange work schedules. The club had been Vincent's idea and it had succeeded even beyond his expectations. Now, six months after the opening, membership applications were backed up for two years. It wasn't what Vincent really wanted to do but his family had been on his back after allowing him two years to chase film deals that always seemed to evaporate into thin air. And when the Paoluzzi business fell apart his father had drawn the line. Vincent was offered two choices. Either he got into what they considered a proper business or he had to come in with them. Vincent chose the lesser of the two evils. It cost his family more than two million dollars to open the club but they didn't seem to mind. The money was insignificant. The important thing was that their son was making something of himself.

The loud music echoed in the partially filled disco. It was still a little early for any action there.

Dino, the stocky little maitre d' came over to me. 'Everything's cool,' he said. 'Come down later. We're trying out a new D.J. He's supposed to be terrific.'

'I'll try to make it.' He gave me the checklist of the girls that were working and I went up to the cocktail lounge on the ground floor. Angelo was at the desk in the corner. 'It's good tonight,' he said.

I collected his list and went up another flight to the restaurant.

The dining-room was just beginning to thin out. Carmine hurried over to me. 'I'll need a couple of extra girls Saturday night,' he said. 'I'm just about making it now.'

'I'll take it up with Vincent.'

'Do it for me, baby. We got to keep up the standards. We can't afford to fuck up.'

All the floors above the third were reserved for members only. I decided to look into the health club. There were a few men lolling about in the raised swimming pool and some girls sitting around the edge looking bored. They paid absolutely no attention to the fact that the men were nude.

Tony came out of his little office. 'Quiet,' he said. 'There's nobody in the steam or sauna.'

The gym and massage parlor floor above was just as empty. Only one of the little booths had the curtain drawn. 'It's dead tonight,' Rocco, the trainer said. 'Nobody's got a hard-on. They're all staying home with their wives.'

I laughed.

His face was serious. 'It's not funny. The girls are beginning to practice on each other. I caught Joan giving Sandy a massage.'

'You can't let that happen,' I said with a straight face. 'You'll have to make some sacrifices and let them practice on you.'

He stared at me in disbelief. 'My wife'll kill me!'

I laughed and went upstairs. There was absolutely nothing happening on the sixth floor, which had private rooms for guests who wished to stay the night. Gianni and his two girls were playing gin. I waved and went up to the office.

I put the checklists in a time box for the bookkeepers, lit a cigarette and went to Vincent's office. He hadn't come in yet. That was strange. When I had left his apartment just before eight o'clock he had said he would be in by ten. Since there was nothing else for me to do at the moment, I thought I might go down to the disco and check out the new D.J. A hip D.J. made all the difference. The right music for the right crowd kept the room jumping.

But I made no move to go. I really wasn't in the mood. I didn't feel like talking to anyone. It wasn't easy having to smile at people all the time, pretending to be interested in what they were saying.

I ground out my cigarette. What I really wanted to do was get stoned. But I couldn't do that either. The rules were very strict.

No grass, no coke, no drugs on the premises. 'We take absolutely no chances,' Vincent said. 'Everybody'll be looking to bust us if we make it. We make sure we don't give them a handle.'

But at his apartment it was different. He had everything from grass and angel dust to poppers, which he loved to use while we were balling. But there was never anything on him. I used to wonder sometimes how the stuff got there but I didn't ask. There were some things I just didn't talk to him about and that included his family.

I remembered the only time I had seen his father and his two older brothers. They had come in one night shortly after we opened. There were two other men with them. Vincent took them right up to the office. About a half hour later they came down and Vincent gave them a tour of the club.

I happened to be at the entrance as they were on their way out. Vincent saw me but made no move to introduce us. His father was a thin gentle-looking little man with iron-gray hair and black impenetrable eyes. Vincent bent over him and kissed him on each cheek.

The old man smiled, gently touched Vincent's face and nodded. 'It is good, my son,' he said. 'We are proud of you.' Then he turned and left, followed by the others.

Vincent glanced at me and, without a word, took the elevator up to his office. A few minutes later I followed him.

There was a bottle of scotch on his desk and he was refilling his glass as I came in. I had never seen him take a drink at work before. 'It's okay,' he said quickly. 'It's okay.'

But I noticed that his hand was shaking as he carried the glass to his lips. He took a swallow of the drink. 'I want to fuck you,' he said.

There was a strange expression in his eyes. Somehow I knew he was afraid of what my answer would be. 'Okay,' I said.

'Right away.'

'Shall I lock the door?'

'Not here. At my place. Change your clothes.'

Minutes later we were on our way. We didn't say a word until we walked into his apartment, which was only a few blocks from the club on Sutton Place, overlooking the river.

He turned on the light and crossed to a built-in bar. 'Do you smoke?' he asked.

I nodded.

He lit a joint for me and another for himself. It was sweet

stuff. Very easy. Usually it took only two tokes for me to get stoned but this time it didn't seem to be working.

'Come on,' he said.

I followed him into the bedroom. He turned toward me, taking off his jacket. 'Strip.'

I put the joint in an ashtray and began to undress. I bent down to unfasten my shoe straps, and when I straightened up he was naked. He stared at me for a moment, then opened a drawer in the night table beside the bed. He brought out a yellow box, a small white vial of powder and a tiny gold spoon. He came toward me with the vial and spoon.

He took the cap off the vial and spooned out some white powder. Then he held it to his nostril and snorted. Afterward he took a deep breath and repeated the process under his other nostril. His eyes began to lighten. 'Bang,' he said, holding out a spoonful of powder to me.

'What is it?' I asked.

'Coke,' he said. 'Take it. It won't hurt you.'

He held the spoon to my nose. I snorted. The powder made me sneeze. He laughed and held the spoon under the other nostril. I snorted again. This time it only stung a little.

'How is it?' he asked.

'I don't feel anything.'

'You will.' He laughed. 'Takes a few minutes.'

He was right. Already my nostrils were numbing and there was a dryness in my mouth. Suddenly I was up there. He had been watching me. 'Good?'

'Way out.'

He put down the vial and pulled me toward him. His mouth was rough and bruising and I could feel his hands gripping hard into my arms. We stumbled and almost fell across the bed. I felt his teeth biting into my breasts, hurting my nipples. I moaned in pain and he raised his head.

His eyes stared into mine. 'I'm crazy about you. Do you know that?' he said, almost angrily.

I shook my head. My pain seemed like nothing compared with his. His world of pain was far beyond me.

He reached across to the little yellow box and pulled out an amyl nitrate capsule. Holding it in his hand, he pushed my legs back in a jackknife position against my chest and rose to his knees, poised over me. His entire body seemed like a tense steel spring.

There was a strange faraway glaze over his eyes. Then, before I had the chance to be frightened, he fell forward across me. I could feel the length of him pushing into me and at the same time he broke the popper.

My head seemed to explode with the rush of blood and heat to my brain and at the same moment his orgasm began. He raised himself away from me suddenly, digging his arms into the mattress on either side of me. His eyes were closed and his face contorted.

'No! Oh, Christ! No!' he almost screamed, trying to control his spasms. 'No, no, no!'

I pulled him down to me. 'Don't fight it, don't hold it back. Let it come.'

He shivered for a moment more, then it was over. He lay very still, his chest heaving against me. Then abruptly he began to cry. Hard, wracking sobs.

I held his head to my breasts and stroked his hair. 'It's all right,' I said. 'It's all right.'

He raised his head to look at me. His eyes were wet with tears. 'You don't understand,' he said. 'Damn them!'

I waited for him to go on.

'They finally got what they wanted,' he said. 'They wanted me in the family business, and like it or not I'm in it.'

'Don't talk about it,' I said. 'It will be all right.'

'No. The club was supposed to be mine. They loaned me the money for it. But now they don't want the money back. We're all partners. After all, aren't we family?' he asked bitterly.

'Is that why they were at the club tonight?'

He nodded. 'I would have been better off if it had bombed. At least that way they would have forgotten the whole thing. It would have been just another of Vincenzo's crazy ideas.'

'I didn't know they were like that. From everything I've heard, Italian families always kept their word to each other. No matter what happened.'

'Except when it comes to money and power. Cosa nostra is just a word for the newspapers. My father got rid of his brother in order to become the head of the family, and when he's gone my brothers will kill each other to take his place.'

I was silent for a moment. 'What happens now?'

'Nothing,' he said. 'I run it just the same as before. Only now we cut the profits four ways.'

'What happens to the money they loaned you? The two

million dollars. Do you have to pay it back?'

'Of course not. It's the family business now. The business will pay it back out of their share.'

'Then you're ahead,' I said, looking at him. 'My father was a banker and I remember he once told me that any loan you did not have to repay personally was a clear profit. You just made yourself a half million dollars clear.'

Finally he began to smile. 'You're a strange girl,' he said. He swung his legs off the bed. 'Care for a drink?'

'No, but if you have another stick I'd like it.'

He came back into the bedroom with a cigarette box full. I lit one and leaned back on the pillow inhaling gently. This time it worked. I began to feel very mellow.

He was standing at the side of the bed looking down at me. I passed him the joint. He took a few tokes then I reached up for him.

'Come here,' I said. 'You owe me one.'

He came down into my arms and this time we made love. The next day I moved everything except my typewriter and papers into his apartment. I didn't give up the apartment, because I always wanted a place to go to where I could work.

CHAPTER TWENTY-TWO

BY THE TIME I went back down to the disco it was jammed. There was just about enough room on the floor to move up and down in time with the beat. The rest of the room was filled with people huddled around tiny tables without an inch of space between them.

Dino came over to me, a wide grin on his round face. 'The new boy's good,' he said. 'He keeps them movin'.'

I looked across the dark room to where the D.J. was working at two turntables which were raised on a platform slightly above the floor. He was a tall slim black boy, dressed in an outlandish costume – safari wide-brimmed hat, hand-made chamois shirt and wide bell-bottomed chinos. He held an earphone to his ear while he placed a new record on the second turntable and marked the disk. When he finished he put the headset down, looked at me and smiled.

There was something vaguely familiar about his smile. I nodded and made my way through the crush of people to the turntable. When I stopped in front of the stand, he smiled again. 'Hello, JeriLee,' he said shyly.

I couldn't keep the surprise from my voice. 'Fred! Fred Lafayette!'

He grinned. 'You remembered.'

I held out my hand. 'I can't believe it,' I said.

'Yep. Here we are. Right back where we started. Me up on the stand, you down there on the floor workin'.'

'But your singing,' I said. 'What happened?'

'You know, girl. Mellow singers like Nat King Cole just ain't cuttin' it today. The world is rock happy.' He let go of my hand. 'How long has it been? Ten years?'

'Just about.'

'I used to read about you in the papers,' he said. 'Then I sort of lost touch. You divorced that man, didn't you?'

I nodded.

'You look real good,' he said. 'You grew up pretty.'

'I feel old.'

'That's no way to talk. You're still a kid.'

'I wish it were true,' I said. 'My father died.'

'I'm sorry to hear that. He was a nice man.'

'Yes.'

'I saw you when I came into work an' thought I recognized you.'

'Why didn't you talk to me?' I asked.

'When I checked to see if I was right I was told to keep off. That you were the boss's lady.' His eyes searched mine.

'That's true. But you should have said something anyway. After all, we're old friends.'

Before he could answer, Dino was at my side. 'Vincenzo just came in. He wants to see you right away.'

'Okay,' I said. I looked up at Fred. 'I hope you like it here. Maybe we could get together for a cup of coffee sometime.'

'Sure,' he said. He picked up the earphone and began placing another disk. 'You let me know when.'

I pushed my way back to the door and went up to the office. Vincent was on something. The expression in his eyes was too bright. His voice was angry. 'What the hell were you doing holding hands with that nigger?'

'We were shaking, not holding hands,' I said. 'He's an old friend. He saved my life once.'

'I don't give a shit what he did. I'm going to fire the cocksucker!'

'You do,' I said, 'and you fire me too.' Fred had been more right than he knew when he said we were back where we started. It looked as if I were going to cost him another job.

Vincent suddenly calmed down. 'He really saved your life?'

'Yes,' I said. 'A couple of kids were beating me and trying to rape me. He got me away from them just in time.'

Vincent was silent for a moment. 'How old were you?'

'Sixteen.'

'I guess it's all right then,' he said. 'You really are old friends.'

I didn't answer.

'Change your clothes,' he said. 'We're gettin' out of here.'

'Where are we going?'

'Over to El Mo. I'm onto something. We're goin' to meet some people there.'

'About what?'

'About a movie,' he snapped. 'How long do you think I can stand a stinking joint like this before going crazy?'

'Does your family know about it?'

'No. And I don't give a damn! Now change your goddamn dress and stop asking so many damn questions.'

We walked into El Morocco and it was like a rerun of the first time we had met. The Paoluzzis were at the best table. Only one thing was different. Instead of the Italian lawyer there was a hard compact medium-sized man in a dark suit who was introduced only as Frank.

Paoluzzi kissed my hand in that strange way he had and Carla Maria pressed her cheek to mine.

'Everything settled?' Vincent asked as we sat down.

Frank nodded. 'You'll have my check for a million dollars in the morning.'

Vincent suddenly smiled. 'This calls for a drink. Another bottle of champagne,' he said to the headwaiter.

Frank got to his feet. 'It's already past my bedtime. I'd better get going.' He shook hands formally with the producer and Carla Maria, then said something in Italian to which they responded with smiles and nods. 'Good night, young lady,' he said to me. 'Nice meeting you.'

'Nice meeting you,' I replied.

'Good night, Vincent. Don't forget to give my regards to your father.'

Vincent got to his feet. 'I won't, Uncle Frank. Good night.'

I watched him walk toward the door. There was something about the man that radiated power. Even the headwaiters seemed to bow more deferentially than usual. He went up the few steps to the entrance to the street and I saw two men come from the little bar and join him. They walked out together.

'To the film,' Vincent said, raising his glass of champagne.

'And you're going to be in it,' Vincent said to me. 'The second lead next to Carla Maria.'

'You've got to be joking.'

'I'm not. It's part of the deal.'

'How did you manage to do it?'

He laughed. 'Simple. I couldn't get the money anywhere else so I put it up myself.'

'Where did you get it?' Then it dawned on me. 'Is that the money your Uncle Frank was talking about?'

'I put up my share of the club as security.'

'Does your father know?'

'What difference does it make? I have the right to do what I like with my share.'

I was silent.

He refilled my glass. 'Stop thinking about it and drink up. You're going to be a star, baby.'

It was a little after three o'clock when we came out of El Morocco. Vincent pushed me toward the limousine. 'You go to the hotel with them,' he said. 'I'll run over to the club, make sure that everything is okay and then join you.'

'I'm tired,' I said. 'I'd just as soon go home to sleep if it's all right with you.'

He was smiling but I could tell from his eyes that he was angry. 'It's not all right with me. You go with them. I have some things to settle with Dino and they have to be settled tonight.'

I knew better than to argue with him when he was in that mood. I got into the car. He waved his hand and started walking up the street as the limo moved down to First Avenue.

Carla Maria smiled at me. 'I am glad you are to be with us at last.'

'I am too,' I said. 'It's like a dream come true. Making a picture with the two of you.'

She reached across her husband and patted my hand. 'You Americans are so funny.' She laughed. 'I mean tonight.' She read the expression on my face. 'Didn't Vincent tell you that we were going to spend the night together?'

I shook my head. 'He said that he would meet us later.'

She said something to her husband in Italian, then spoke to me. 'We will call Vincent from the hotel and straighten this out.'

'No.' I reached across to the front seat and tapped the driver on the shoulder. 'Could you stop the car here, please?'

The driver pulled to the curb. Neither of them said a word as I got out. I flagged a cab and went to the apartment.

I had just finished undressing when Vincent came storming in. He stood in the bedroom doorway shouting at me. 'You goddamn stupid bitch! After all I went through just to get them to agree to let you have the part.'

'You should have told me what you had in mind,' I said.

'Well now you know, so get yourself dressed and haul your ass over there!'

'No. I told you once before it wasn't my game.'

'You like going around town begging for jobs and starving better?'

I didn't answer.

'Remember what it was like the day you came into the club? You were on your ass when I took you off the streets. Now you think you can shit on me!'

'I'm not dumping on you.'

'Yes you are!' he yelled. 'We can blow the whole deal just because you won't go along with it.'

'No you won't,' I said. 'The million dollars you're getting for him is the important thing. Not me.'

'You're part of the deal too!' he shouted.

'You had no right to do that without asking me.'

'I had no right to commit the money either,' he yelled. 'But I did it. Now don't you fuck it up or I'll wind up in a sewer someplace.'

I stared at him.

He suddenly slumped into a chair and covered his face with his hands. After a moment he looked up at me. There were tears in his eyes. 'The only thing my family respects is success. If the picture goes over, everything will be all right.'

I didn't speak.

'Please,' he begged. 'Just this once. Afterwards you can do anything you want. It's the only chance I have to get out from under them.'

I didn't move.

'They'll bury me if this deal doesn't go through. My father and Uncle Frank haven't spoken in years. I don't dare give him a chance to get that share of the club.'

'You already have,' I pointed out.

'Not if the picture is made. Uncle Frank promised to keep it quiet if he gets paid back.' He put his hands over his face again and began to cry.

I stood looking at him for a long minute, then I slowly began to get dressed. As I walked past him to the door he stopped me.

He went to the night table, took out a few joints, the vial of coke and a box of poppers. He put them all in my handbag. 'This might help,' he said.

I didn't speak.

He bent and kissed my cold lips. 'Thanks. I love you,' he said.

I turned and went out the door. Even then I knew I would never come back.

Ten minutes later I was at their hotel suite. Carla Maria opened the door with a smile. 'I am so glad you have coming,' she said.

I laughed suddenly. It wasn't only her English. The whole thing just was beginning to feel ridiculous. I immediately lit a stick, then I took a double hit of coke and chased it down with two glasses of champagne.

By the time we made it to the bedroom I was as high as a kite and nothing seemed to matter. Much to my surprise I even began to enjoy it. I never dreamed that a woman's touch could be so delicate and so exciting. And the tricks Carla Maria could do with her tongue made the Green Hornet seem like a child's toy. It was as if a whole new world were opening up for me.

And when I woke up in the morning beside her and saw how beautiful she really was, I knew I had loved every moment of it.

CHAPTER TWENTY-THREE

I WAITED UNTIL after noon, when I thought he would be at the club for the morning accounting, before going back to the apartment for my clothes. I let myself in and went through to the bedroom. I had guessed wrong. He was in bed, still asleep.

I started to back out of the room quietly but he awakened and sat up in bed rubbing his eyes. 'Good morning,' he said, smiling.

I didn't answer.

'Come on now,' he said. 'It wasn't so bad, was it?'

'No.'

He was wide awake now. 'Did she eat your pussy?'

'Yes.'

'Did you eat hers?'

'Yes.'

I could sense he was getting excited. 'What did Gino do all the time you were together?'

'Once he came into the room and watched us.'

'Did he fuck her?'

'I don't know.'

'Did he fuck you?'

'I don't know,' I repeated. 'I remember he fucked one of us but I don't remember which one.'

'What did he do afterward?'

'He went back to his own room to sleep.'

'And what did you do?'

'We snorted the rest of the coke, popped a few more ammies and kept on balling.'

'Jesus!' he exclaimed. He got out of bed. I was right. He was excited. 'I wish I had been there. It must have been something to watch.'

I didn't speak.

'Let's ball.'

'No.' I let a moment pass. 'I'm all fucked out.'

'There's always room for one more.'

'No.' I went to the closet and took down my suitcases.

'What are you doing?' he asked.

'Packing.'

'What for?' He seemed genuinely puzzled.

'Because I'm moving out. Why the hell do you think I would be packing?'

'For Christ's sake, you don't have to be so pissed off about it. You said you had a good time, didn't you?'

'That has nothing to do with it,' I said. 'I don't like lies, and you lied to me.'

'Shit, baby,' he said. 'That was an important deal. You might have blown it for us.'

'You mean I might have blown it for you. There never was anything in it for me.'

He stared at me without speaking.

'All that crap you gave me about being in the picture was just that. Crap. Carla Maria told me this morning that she didn't know what you were talking about last night. There isn't any part in the picture for me. Why couldn't you have told me the truth?'

'I wasn't lying about my family. My father would – ' He stopped when he saw the expression on my face.

'You were lying about that too,' I said. 'Carla Maria told me that Frank and your father are partners in the deal, that each is putting up half the money.'

'Aw Christ, honey,' he said, coming toward me. 'It's over. Everything worked out. You know I love you.'

'You're right. It is over. You can stop lying now.' I began to take my clothes out of the closet and put them in the suitcases. 'Just let me pack.'

'Where are you going?' he asked.

'To my apartment.'

'Jesus, you're not going back to that dump?'

'Would it make more sense if I told you that I was going to Italy with Carla Maria?'

'I wouldn't believe you,' he said.

I opened my bag and handed him the airline ticket. 'Would that convince you?'

'Well I'll be a son of a bitch.'

'You're beginning to tell the truth,' I said, taking back the ticket.

He shook his head. 'To think you turned out to be a goddamn dike.'

I laughed. 'Little boys shouldn't play with fire. They might burn their fingers. But don't worry about it. I already told her I wasn't going. I don't intend to be a whore for either one of you.'

Relief crossed his face. 'You've had a rough time,' he said. 'Why don't you just hop into bed and get some rest. You can even have the night off.'

'I'll do that. Just as soon as I get to my place. And don't worry about giving me the night off. I've just quit.'

'Don't be stupid,' he said. 'We can still be friends.'

'Maybe you can. But I can't.'

'What are you going to live on?' he asked after a few minutes.

'I've saved some money,' I said. 'And I have a play to finish. I haven't had much time to work on it lately.'

'You haven't got that much money,' he said.

'When it runs out I'll find another job,' I said. 'But I'm not going to stop writing. Not ever again.'

Two nights later my doorbell rang. I got up from the typewriter and answered the door.

'Hi,' Fred said. 'I just happened to be in the neighborhood so I thought I'd take a chance and see if you were in.'

'How did you get my address?'

'From the girl in the office.'

'Aren't you supposed to be at work?'

He smiled. 'I got fired. I was just hoping that I wasn't the reason you got fired too.'

'I wasn't fired. I quit.' Then realizing that he was still standing in the hall, I said, 'Come on in.'

I saw his eyes moving around the room.

'Excuse the mess,' I said quickly. 'But I've been working.'

'I didn't mean to disturb you.'

'No, it's okay. I'm glad you came. I needed a break and I have some cold white wine in the fridge.' I offered to take his jacket but he made no move to take it off.

'I thought if you hadn't eaten we could go out and get some chink's.'

I grinned. 'You just talked me into it. Give me one minute to get into some other clothes.'

'Don't pick out anything too fancy,' he said. 'I got a rich man's taste but a poor man's pocket.'

'Jeans okay?'

'Fine,' he said.

I slipped into the jeans and a clean shirt behind the closet door. 'How's that?' I asked.

'Perfect.'

'Now if you give me another minute to brush my hair and put on my face.' Ten minutes later I came out of the bathroom, and found him still standing where I had left him.

'You could have sat down,' I said.

'I didn't think of it. I was happy where I was.'

The cold night air felt good. I had been inside all day. 'Do you know a good Chinese restaurant around here?' he asked.

'There's one over on Seventy-second near Broadway. We can walk.'

We chatted all the way through our meal of egg rolls, spare-ribs, won ton soup and lobster Cantonese with fried rice. Back at my house he stopped at the outside door.

'I still have the wine in the fridge,' I said.

'I don't want to put you out none.'

'Come on,' I said.

It was two o'clock in the morning when Fred got to his feet. 'I'd better let you get some sleep,' he said. 'I feel guilty enough about keepin' you from working.'

'It was fine,' I said, opening the door for him.

'Thank you.' I stood on my toes to kiss him good night.

His lips touched mine gently, and suddenly something happened. A warmth rose between us and I moved into his arms. I pulled him back into the apartment and kicked the door shut.

Later, much later, when we lay quietly in each other's arms, his soft voice whispered in my ear. 'You know, JeriLee, I've always loved you. Even way back then.'

'You don't have to say that if you don't mean it, Fred. I'm happy enough just being with you.'

'But I do mean it, JeriLee.'

'I don't want you to lie to me. I'm tired of people saying things they don't mean.'

'I'm not lying to you, JeriLee,' he said patiently. 'I loved you then. I love you now. And, in a way, I guess I always will.'

Because I could feel the truth in him I began to cry. Two days later he moved into the apartment with me.

Book Three
Any Old Town

CHAPTER ONE

THE DREAM was there. It was always there. The little girl at the top of the stairs. But in the split second between sleeping and waking it was gone. JeriLee heard the soft gentle humming of a song through the closed bedroom door and rolled over sluggishly. A sharp pain much like the headache after a hangover knifed through her temples.

It was, as the doctor had told her to expect, the after effect of the anesthetic.

After a moment the pain subsided and she got out of bed. She made her way to the bathroom, quickly swallowed two Bufferin and sat on the toilet. She felt congested and swollen, as if she needed to have a bowel movement. But after a moment when nothing happened she gave up and simply decided to change the tampon.

She looked at it curiously before discarding it. It wasn't as bloody as she thought it might be, no more so than an ordinary period. So far the doctor had been right.

Angela's voice was soft through the closed bathroom door. 'JeriLee. Are you all right in there?'

'I'm fine.'

'The coffee is made,' Angela said. 'I'll have breakfast ready by the time you come out.'

'Thank you. But I'll be a few minutes. I want to shower first.'

'It's okay. Take your time.'

JeriLee realized as she stepped into the stall shower that it had been more than a month since Angela had been to see her, and she wondered why she had chosen to come today of all days.

Coffee and orange juice were waiting on the night table when JeriLee emerged from the bathroom. The sheets felt cool and crisp against her skin and she realized that Angela must have changed them while she was showering. She propped the pillows behind her, drained the glass of orange juice and had just finished pouring her first cup of coffee when Angela came back carrying a tray laden with scrambled eggs, bacon and toast.

'I didn't think I'd be hungry,' JeriLee said.

Angela's gentle eyes smiled. 'Eat then. If you want more I can make it.'

Angela sat on the chair next to the bed and poured herself a cup of coffee. 'Aren't you eating?' JeriLee asked.

Angela shook her head. 'I just want some coffee.'

'What made you come today?' she asked after a moment.

Angela's eyes were steady. 'I thought you could use some help?'

'You knew?'

Angela nodded. 'Everyone knows. George can't keep his mouth shut and your agent wasn't much better.'

There were no secrets anywhere, she thought, taking another bite of egg. 'You're not working today?'

'No. We've taped all our shows for the week. I'm not due back in the studio until Monday.'

Angela was the ingenue on a daily television show, *The Stars Never Fall*. Every afternoon at two o'clock housewives all over the country turned on their sets to watch it. It was probably the most successful soap in history. In the five years Angela had been on the show it had always been number one in its time slot.

JeriLee wiped up the plate with a piece of toast. 'That was good,' she said.

'Food always helps,' Angela said.

JeriLee smiled. 'My mother always said that.'

Angela picked up the tray and started for the door. 'If there is anything else you want,' she said, 'I'll be here.'

'Angela,' JeriLee called.

The girl looked back.

'Thank you, Angela,' JeriLee said.

Angela's eyes filled with tears and she turned, closing the door behind her with her foot.

JeriLee stared at the closed door. Angela cared about her. She had always known that. She cared about Angela too. But there was a difference. The difference was that she loved Angela but Angela was in love with her.

Angela – tall, slim, beautiful – so cool on the outside but so frightened and fucked up on the inside. Why had it happened? It should have been so easy for her. But nothing ever brought her any real satisfaction. Her search for love was endless and unrequited.

Still it had to have begun somewhere for Angela, just as it had to have begun somewhere for her. But it was difficult to tell exactly where. We are the sum total of our experiences to any given point. And the point was always changing.

For JeriLee it had started somewhere between Port Clare, New York and Los Angeles and all the way stops and towns in between – Pittsburgh, Gary, Chicago, Des Moines, Phoenix, Las Vegas. She'd been to all of them. And she'd had them all – all the way to the madhouse.

Strange that that should come back to her now. A cold shiver of fear ran through her. Did it mean she was sliding back, back into the world of fear where everyone was a stranger?

No! she thought. She was not going back. It would never be like that again. Never would she let herself be used, not by anyone, not for any reason, even love.

She would give only what she could give. Too many times she had tried to be what others wanted her to be. And it hadn't worked. She could not be all things to all people. She could not even be all things to one person. And it was not until she recognized that in herself and saw the limitations of her own capacities that she began to be able to accept herself and give up some of the guilt.

She knew she couldn't run the mile in four minutes, or soar like a gull in the morning wind. And there were mornings when the day seemed to stretch into disaster. But there would always be those times, those days, and if she recognized them not as signs of failure and weakness, but as part of her basic humanness and right to be imperfect, she would never have to be afraid again.

That was the one thing she had learned and it had helped. At least now she could stand alone without the need to clutch and cling for support. Still it would be good if there were someone. It was not fun to be alone.

She lit a cigarette and leaned back against the pillows. That was the heart of it. Aloneness. All of it, all of them, the men, the women. When it was over and they were gone you came back to being alone. Still she knew that just outside the window there was a world filled with people.

What was it Angela had said to her one morning while they were lying on the bed together, the Sunday papers spread between them. 'You never seem to want anything, JeriLee. You never ask anyone to do anything for you, not even to get you a cup of coffee. Just once I would like you to ask me to do something. At least that way I would feel needed.'

'Is that what you want – to be needed?'

Angela nodded. 'How else can I tell that I mean something to you?'

'Isn't it enough that we're together, that we've been balling all night? Doesn't that mean anything?'

'That's sex. I know I'm not the only one you sleep with and there's nothing you can do with me that you don't do with others. But I want more. I want to be important to you.'

'Would you feel better if I couldn't function without you?' JeriLee asked.

Angela didn't answer.

Suddenly she was angry, more with herself than with Angela. 'I haven't lied to you, have I?' she demanded. 'I told you exactly where it would be with us, didn't I?'

Angela nodded, misery in her eyes. 'Yes,' she answered in a small voice.

'Then what more do you want from me?'

'I want you to love me.'

'I can't love you the way you want me to. I can only love you the way I do.'

'Don't be angry with me, JeriLee.'

She walked over to the window and looked out into the bright California sunshine. Down below them the traffic on the Strip was beginning to come alive. 'There's a whole world out there, Angela,' she said. 'And somewhere there is someone who will love you the way you want to be loved. All you have to do is give that world a chance.'

Angela came to the window and stood beside her. 'Is there someone out there for you too, JeriLee?' she asked.

A sudden sorrow flooded JeriLee, a knowledge of her own and Angela's pain. It was as if they were sisters, even more than sisters. Suddenly they moved toward each other and their tears mingled.

'I hope so,' JeriLee said softly. 'I should hate to think there weren't.'

Then they had gone back to bed and made love and in the sweet agony of their sex they had discovered their sameness and their separateness. But by the time Sunday had gone they knew that the affair was over, even though a residue of their love would remain with them.

The next morning when Angela had gone to work she had

taken her small suitcase but she had not returned JeriLee's key. Suddenly she realized how Angela had come into her apartment this morning. But right now she was tired. The pain throbbed in her pelvis, a reminder of yesterday.

The telephone rang and she picked it up. 'How are you feeling?' the doctor asked.

'Okay,' she answered. 'The pain just started up again but I'm not bleeding as much as I thought.'

His voice was matter-of-fact. 'You'll bleed a little but don't be frightened, and keep taking some aspirin to kill the pain. Stay in bed if you can. If you need someone to take care of you I can send over a practical nurse.'

'That's okay. A friend of mine is here.'

'Good. I'll look in on you this afternoon on my way back from the hospital.'

'Thank you.'

A moment later the door opened. 'Everything all right?' Angela asked.

'Yes. It was the doctor. He's coming by this afternoon.'

'Is there anything I can do?'

'Nothing, thanks. He just told me to stay in bed and rest.' She leaned back against the pillows. 'I think I'll try to sleep.'

JeriLee stared at the closed door. Which, she wondered, was the stronger – needing, or the need to be needed? She didn't know the answer. Probably never would.

Suddenly she remembered what Fred had said many years ago: 'We're good for each other, baby, because we need each other.' She had agreed with him then. But neither of them had really known what their needs were. And in the end it turned out that she had been feeding on herself.

CHAPTER TWO

THE CHATTER of the typewriter keys stopped. She sat at the small table staring at the words on the page, their sound still echoing in her mind.

'I love you. I don't love you. How the hell do I know how I feel?'

She rose from the chair and went to the window. The city street was dark and deserted except for a garbage truck that was collecting refuse from the restaurant across the street. The radio clock told her it was two-thirty in the morning. She went back to the table, took a deep drag on the cigarette and ground it out in the ashtray already littered with broken butts. Without sitting down, she hit the keys, forming the final word: CURTAIN.

Almost angrily, she tore the page from the typewriter and put it in the box on top of the rest of the neatly typed pages. It was finished.

The momentary anger passed and now she felt drained and empty. Tomorrow, with the realities she had put off day after day while clinging to her writing, loomed in front of her. Tomorrow she would have to think about money, about paying bills. Tomorrow she would have to go beyond her own walls, back into the world of people, back into the marketplace which sat in judgment upon her work.

She felt the nervousness rise within her, and she started to tremble. What are you afraid of, JeriLee? she asked herself. You've done nothing wrong. You've been working. You had a reason not to leave the cocoon.

But her hands were shaking to the point that she couldn't hold them still. She went into the bathroom and took the vial of Valium from the medicine cabinet, then popped a ten-mg blue, which she flushed down with a swallow of water.

She looked up at the clock. Two-thirty-five. It would be an hour and a half before Fred got home. He had a weekend gig at a bar on West Forty-ninth Street and wouldn't be out until after three o'clock. The tightness began to disappear from the pit of her stomach. She was beginning to feel better now. Her confidence was returning.

It was done. The play was finished. Tomorrow she could get on with her life. There was nothing to be afraid of, except what was in her head.

The first thing she had to do was get the play to Fannon. He had promised that he would do it. The next thing she had to do was to go to a beauty parlor. No, first she would go to the beauty parlor, then she would take the play to Fannon. She wanted to look her best when she walked into his office.

She began to separate the originals and the carbons. In a few minutes she had them all neatly together, each copy in its own ring binder. It wasn't a bad job. The typing service couldn't have done better – and they charged more than a hundred dollars for five copies. Quickly she stacked them on the shelf, put the cover over the typewriter and wheeled it into the closet. The room looked strangely empty. It was the first time in almost six months that the typewriter wasn't the main feature.

A feeling of elation came over her. This was an important moment. A time to celebrate. This was a night for champagne and caviar. She opened the cupboard – Gallo chablis and Planter's peanuts. That wasn't so bad either.

She put the bottle of wine into the freezing compartment, placed a tablecloth and two candles on the small table and emptied the can of peanuts into a glass bowl. Quickly she straightened the rest of the room, even emptying the wastebasket of all the rejected pages. Now there was no messy trace of work. She lit the candles and turned off the lights, then stepped back to observe the effect. The warm yellow glow flickered through the room.

Satisfied, she went into the bathroom and stripped off her shirt and jeans. She still had time to shower and do something with her hair before Fred came home. After all, it was a special night and she wanted to look special.

Despite the efforts of the conditioners, the air was still heavy with the smell of cigarettes, beer and sweat. Fred looked at his watch. A quarter to three. Only fifteen minutes to go. He looked down at the white keyboard of the piano. There was a nothing feeling to playing and singing. Nobody listened, and if they did they couldn't hear over the noise.

From his perch near the back of the room he looked down the bar. The bar girls were hustling. It was a good night. Maybe fifty per cent of the men were in uniform. Now he knew why the owners fought so hard to keep off the armed services' banned list. Without servicemen there was no business.

'Fred.' He turned and saw Licia standing behind him. She was a big honey-colored girl with a lustrous Nancy Wilson wig. The unofficial chief bar girl, she had a quiet air about her that belied her inner toughness. And for whatever reason, nobody fooled with her, neither the girls nor the customers. She talked with them, had drinks with them, but when the bar closed she left alone.

'Got a request for the piano player?' he asked, hitting an opening chord.

'Yeah. The man wants you to stay on till four o'clock.'

'Shit,' he said, continuing with the song. 'I'm beat. I been up here for five solid hours.'

'You get double for the extra hour,' she said.

That was ten dollars. He was getting twenty-five dollars for the five hours of regular work. 'How come the man's suddenly so big?'

'Look at that crowd,' Licia said. 'He knows they see you get down from that piano they figure the night's over and begin to leave.'

Fred wondered if JeriLee was waiting up for him. Chances were that she had already gone to bed. 'Okay,' he said. The extra ten dollars looked good. It was his first gig in more than three weeks.

JeriLee looked up at the clock. It was half past three. He should have been home by now. She began to feel the tightness gather inside her again.

It was stupid. She would have to get a better grip on herself. There was nothing to be nervous about. She'd finished the play.

A joint would help. She went into the bedroom and took the small cellophane bag full of grass from the table next to the bed. They liked having a joint before sex. A few tokes made everything easy.

Sitting on the couch concentrating intently on rolling the joint gave her something to do. She licked the paper carefully and looked at her handiwork. The joint was smooth and neat, the ends tightly rolled. She struck a match and lit up.

She took the first toke deep into her lungs and held it there.

There was something reassuring about its smarting sweetness. She took another hit and could feel the tension ease. This was better. She looked up at the clock again. Three-forty-five. It wasn't so bad.

Suddenly she felt dry and thirsty. Grass always did that to her. She took the wine from the refrigerator and poured a glass. She was beginning to feel a little high. Fred would be surprised when he came in and saw her like this.

Usually she was either sleeping fitfully or hunched tensed over the typewriter. It couldn't have been that good for him but only once had he complained. 'Baby, looks like you forgot how to have fun. You can't always live uptight like this.'

It had been a bad day. 'What the hell do you know?' she had shouted. 'You get a gig, you don't get a gig, you don't get a gig, you don't have to dig something out of yourself when you don't even know whether it's worth anything or not, whether it's good or bad, right or wrong. You go to work if you have a job. If you don't you sit around here drinking beer and smoking grass and staring at me night and day. Fuck it. Nothing bothers you.'

He stared at her for a moment, then went into the bathroom, closing the door behind him. A little while later she heard the sound of the shower. By the time he came out, her temper had gone and she felt contrite.

'I'm sorry,' she had said. 'I didn't mean to yell like that.'

He nodded and without speaking went into the bedroom and came out with a joint already rolled. He lit it and passed it to her. 'You'll be okay,' he said. 'Once you've finished the play.'

Well now it was finished and she was feeling good. She took another toke and chased it down with some wine. Feeling good and freed for the first time in a long while. She felt the warmth growing inside her and touched herself with a sense of excitement. She was wet. This hadn't happened for a long time. God, she was horny. She couldn't wait for him to come home. He didn't know it but he was about to get the most mind-blowing sex he had ever had.

CHAPTER THREE

At four o'clock the bar closed. In less than ten minutes all the customers and most of the bar girls had gone. The bartenders wasted no motions. Any customer that showed signs of lingering over his drink suddenly found it missing from the bar in front of him.

Fred wearily gathered up his sheet music and placed it in his leather folder, then made his way to the front cash register to collect his pay. The bartender had his back toward him, counting out the cash. Fred stood patiently, waiting until he was finished. He knew better than to interrupt him.

Licia suddenly appeared at his shoulder. 'The man wants to buy you a drink,' she said.

'Okay, bourbon and water,' Fred said gratefully.

'Jack Daniel's and water,' she called out. 'The bar whiskey is piss,' she said. 'It's cut by fifty per cent.'

'Thanks.'

The bartender put the drink in front of him and went back to the register. 'Right on,' he said, taking a sip.

'The man likes you,' she said. 'He says you know your music.'

'Thank him for me,' Fred said. It had been a long time since anyone had said something nice to him about his music.

'What are your plans?' she asked suddenly.

'What do you mean?'

'Work,' she said.

'Find another gig.'

'You don't have a job during the day?'

'No, there's only my music. I don't know anything else.'

'How do you keep busy?'

'Lookin' for gigs,' he said. 'And there's some songs I been workin' on.'

'You write songs?'

He nodded. 'Only trouble is I can't get anyone to listen to them. The publishing companies are all locked up with big names an' the only thing they're interested in is rock. Shove a guitar on some kid dressed in hippie clothes an' a beard an' they fall all over themselves to sign him.'

'Maybe the man can help you,' she said. 'He's got connections with a few music companies.'

'I'd appreciate it,' he said.

'Let me go talk to him,' she said.

He watched her walk to the back and disappear into the office between the men's and the ladies' toilets. He was sure that nothing would come of it but he was grateful that she'd shown an interest. In all the time he had been with JeriLee, the subject of his writing had never come up. She was too into her own work. There was no room in her head for anything else.

When Licia came back, she said. 'He told me to tell you he has a piano up at his place. If you want to come up there, he'll listen to your songs.'

'Now?' he asked. 'It's four o'clock.'

'The man is night people,' she said. 'This is the middle of the afternoon for him. He don' get out of bed until seven o'clock.'

Fred thought for a moment. JeriLee was certainly asleep by now. He didn't really expect anything, but any chance was better than no chance at all. 'Okay,' he said.

'Give Fred thirty-five dollars,' she said.

The bartender quickly counted out the money and Fred put it in his pocket. 'Thanks,' he said.

'Come on then,' she said. 'I got my car parked up at the Radio City garage. The man tol' me to bring you up to his place.'

The car was a silver Cadillac convertible with black leather and a black top. He sank back into the seat beside her and took a deep breath. Two things always turned him on. The smell of a new car or a new pussy. Somehow they always came together in his head, and this car smelled new.

She hit the tape deck as they moved onto Forty-ninth Street. It was Nat King Cole singing 'Too Young' – one of his biggest hits 'There'll never be another like the King,' he said.

'The King is dead,' she said quietly.

She cut expertly into the Avenue of the Americas going uptown. She had the lights timed perfectly. They were in the park before he knew it.

'Nice car,' he said.

'I like it,' she said tonelessly.

They left the Park at Seventy-second and Fifth and went across town to York Avenue. She turned in at one of the new buildings on the corner of York and went down the ramp into the garage. She pulled to a stop and got out without waiting for an attendant. 'The elevator's over here,' she said.

The elevator operator seemed to know her. He touched his hand to his forehead. 'Good morning,' he said.

'Good morning,' she answered.

He knew where they were going. The car stopped at the seventeenth floor without her saying a word. Fred followed her down the carpeted corridor. She had to be pretty thick with the man. They hadn't even called up to announce her the way they usually did in this kind of building. He watched her come to a stop in front of one of the doors and take a key out of her purse. He nodded to himself. Yeah. She was thick with the man. Real thick. She even had her own key.

The lights in the apartment were already on and he followed her through a large entrance hall into an even larger living room. Windows surrounded the room, allowing a view of the East River, the Triborough Bridge uptown and the Queenboro Bridge at Fifty-ninth Street. A white baby grand piano stood in an alcove near the corner windows. He stood in silent admiration. The only time he had ever seen anything like this was in the movies.

'Quite a place the man has here,' he said.

She glanced at him without comment. 'Jack Daniel's and water?' she asked.

He nodded.

She fixed his drink and waited while he tasted it. 'Okay?' she asked.

'Fine.' He nodded, then turned in response to the sound of footsteps.

A white girl with long brown hair and blue eyes came into the room wearing a white dressing gown. 'I was asleep,' she said to Licia, 'but I heard voices.'

'Sorry we woke you, honey. But Fred here came to play for us.' She turned to him. 'Fred, this is Sam. Short for Samantha. Sam, this is Fred – ' She looked at him questioningly.

'Lafayette,' he said quickly.

'Fred Lafayette,' Licia repeated.

The girl held out her hand. 'Nice to meet you.'

'Nice to meet you,' he said. Her touch was cool. He turned back to Licia. 'The man here yet? I can start any time he's ready.'

Licia looked at him steadily. 'You can start now.'

He stared at her. Suddenly it all made sense. He had worked the bar at least four times and had never seen the man.

'You?' There was a note of wonder in his voice.

She nodded.

He put his drink down on a small coffee table. 'I think I better go,' he said. 'I don't like being put on.'

Licia's voice was steady. 'Nobody's putting you on. You said you can't get anybody to listen to your music. Well, I can, if I think it's worth a shot.'

He met her eyes. 'You do this often?'

'First time.'

'Why me?'

'I studied music in college,' she said. 'But I have no talent. I can fake it but that's not the real thing. And I know the real thing when I hear it. I heard some of the things you did in the bar. You have a style all your own. You made those songs sound like you wrote them.'

He was silent for a moment. 'You manage the Green Bar?'

'I own it,' she said simply. 'An' just in case you have any wrong ideas about my being interested in your fat black dick, get them out of your head. I'm happy the way I am. I just happen to dig your music, an' if you got what I think you have we can all make a buck out of it.'

He looked first at her, then at the girl, and realized he had been very slow on the uptake tonight. 'What do you like?' he asked. 'Fast, slow, ballad, pop, country or blues?'

'You just play what comes into your head,' she said. 'I'll listen.'

'I'm going back to bed,' the girl said suddenly.

Licia's voice was easy. 'Okay, honey.'

The girl left the room without saying good night. 'I can come back tomorrow if you like,' Fred said.

'No reason to. I brought you up here to play. You play.'

Licia followed him to the piano. He smiled, responding to his charged-up feelings. It had been such a long time since all he had to do was play the music that was in his own head.

He hadn't gone more than eight bars into his first song when Licia knew that her hunch had been right. It was magic. Sheer magic.

CHAPTER FOUR

JERILEE HAD FALLEN asleep on the couch but the sound of his key in the lock woke her up. She sat up quickly. The room, now flooded with sunlight, reeled for a moment and she had a buzzing sensation behind her temples.

She looked at the empty wine bottle standing between the two burned-out candles. She couldn't believe she had drunk the whole bottle of wine herself.

Fred stood in the open doorway, surprised to see her on the couch. 'I didn't think you'd be awake,' he said.

'I tried waiting up for you but I fell asleep. What time is it?'

'Almost nine o'clock,' he answered. He saw the wine bottle and the candles. 'You've been celebratin'. What's the occasion?'

'I finished the play.'

He was silent for a moment digesting the news, then he smiled suddenly. 'Congratulations, honey. That's worth a celebration.'

'You didn't tell me you'd be out all night.' She didn't mean it to sound reproachful but it did.

'I didn't know. It was unexpected.'

'You could have called me.'

'I thought you might be asleep.' He bent over the couch to kiss her. 'I got some good news too.'

She caught the scent of Jack Daniel's on his breath. 'You've been drinking.'

'A little,' he admitted.

'What's the good news?'

'I auditioned for the lady that owns the Green Bar. She's goin' to help me find a publisher and record company for my songs.'

'What songs?'

'I got a few numbers I been doodlin' with for years,' he said.

'You never said anything to me.'

'You never asked me. Besides you always had so much on your mind. And nothin' was happening anyway. At least not until tonight.'

She felt a twinge of jealousy. 'A lady owns the Green Bar?'

He nodded.

'You stayed down there and played for her?'

'No. She took me up to her place. She had a baby grand up there.'

'Oh.' She got to her feet. There was a sour taste in her mouth. Suddenly she was depressed. The excitement of finishing the play had disappeared. 'I'm going to brush my teeth and go to bed.'

He followed her to the bathroom door. 'Ain't nothin' like you're thinkin',' he said.

She looked at him in the bathroom mirror. 'How do you know what I'm thinking?'

'It was all straight.'

'Sure,' she said sarcastically. 'You spent six hours after work in her apartment just playing the piano.'

'That's right.'

She squeezed the toothpaste carefully from the tube. 'You don't have to lie to me. You don't owe me any explanations.'

'I'm not lying.'

'I don't want to talk about it,' she said and began brushing her teeth.

'What do you do now?' he asked when she returned to the bedroom.

'Take a copy of the play over to Fannon.' She got into bed, reached for the alarm clock and set it for noon. 'But first I want to get over to the beauty parlor and get my hair washed and cut.'

'It looks okay to me.'

'It's not. It's been months since I had it cut.' She leaned back against the pillows. 'I have to get some sleep.'

He left the room, closing the door behind him. The heavily draped room was suddenly dark and she lay in the bed staring at the wall. She didn't like the way she was acting but she couldn't seem to help it. He had no idea how uptight she was, how important her writing was to her. He had never seemed curious enough to want to read what she had written, and she had the feeling that as far as he was concerned her work had nothing at all to do with him. The only communication they had between them was sex.

The alarm aroused her from a deep sleep. The sound jangled her nerves and she groped with shaking hands to turn it off. After putting on the bedside lamp, she lit a cigarette and took a few drags. She was feeling somewhat calmer when the telephone rang.

It was a woman's voice. 'May I speak to Fred, please?'

'Just a moment.'

Fred was asleep on the couch. She touched his shoulder. 'Phone call for you,' she said.

'Who is it?'

'I didn't ask.'

He picked up the telephone beside the couch as she went back into the bedroom. She closed the door behind her and hung up the extension. In the bathroom she stared at herself in the mirror and didn't like what she saw. Her face had an indoor pallor and there were tension lines around her mouth and eyes that she had never noticed before.

She thought about the sound of the voice of the woman on the telephone. Whoever she was, there was no doubt that the lady was in control. She wondered what the woman looked like, how old she was, then suppressed an impulse to eavesdrop on the extension.

What was the matter with her? These were not her kind of thoughts, that was not the kind of thing she would do. There were no strings between her and Fred; he didn't own her, she didn't own him. They were together only because they wanted to be. Any time either one wanted to leave, they were free to do so. But for six months they had been cooped up with each other, and that kind of togetherness sometimes played funny numbers in your head.

She wished now that she hadn't answered the telephone. But then Fred wouldn't have answered it either. He never did – because of her mother.

Her mother had gotten very angry when she discovered they were living together. She hadn't approved of JeriLee's way of life before but living with a black man was going too far. And she made no bones about telling them exactly how she felt. There was no doubt in her mind that Fred had completely destroyed JeriLee's life.

At one point she threatened to have JeriLee committed until JeriLee pointed out that she no longer had the power. Since then communications between them had completely broken down. It had been four months since JeriLee had seen her and weeks since they had spoken on the telephone.

Maybe what she needed was a shrink. But even if she had one, there was no way she could pay him.

She scanned the shelves of the medicine chest. Pills weren't as expensive as a psychiatrist. She took down the vial of Quaalude 500 mg. Just what she needed. Librium relaxed her muscles, Valium helped her sleep, but Quaalude did a double trick. It both calmed her and made her feel good at the same time. She popped the pill and stepped under the shower, turning the cold water on full blast.

Wrapped in a bath towel, she sat on the edge of the bed and dialed Fannon's office.

'Adolph Fannon Productions,' a woman answered.

'Mr Fannon, please. JeriLee Randall calling.'

'Just a moment, please.' Suddenly she felt her heart begin to hammer inside her chest. It had been more than a year. She wondered if he would remember her or his promise.

There was a click, then his voice. 'JeriLee. So good to hear from you.'

She made her voice light and casual. 'It's good to talk with you, Adolph.'

'It's been too long,' he said warmly, then he became more businesslike. 'You finished the play?'

'Yes,' she said, relieved that he had remembered.

'When do I get to see it?'

'I can bring it by whenever you want.'

'That isn't the way old friends do business. You come to dinner with me. We'll talk about it first. Then I'll take it home and read it.'

She smiled to herself. She knew that the play would be read by his entire staff before he looked at it, but even so it was nicer than just dropping it off at the office. 'I'd like that,' she said. 'When do you want to have dinner?'

'How about tonight?' he said. 'Are you free?'

'I can be.'

'Good. Sardi's at eight-thirty. The theater rush should be over by then and we'll be able to talk.'

'Eight-thirty,' she repeated. 'I'll be there.'

It wasn't until she put down the telephone that she realized how nervous she had been. Her hands were shaking again. She would need another Quaalude before going to dinner. It was very important that she hold herself together.

CHAPTER FIVE

WHEN SHE LET HERSELF in after dinner the apartment was empty. It was almost eleven o'clock. The note on the table was brief and to the point. 'Have gone to a meeting. Should be back around midnight.'

JeriLee felt a twinge of annoyance. She had not left for dinner until eight and Fred had said nothing to her about a meeting. She crumpled the note and threw it into the wastepaper basket. Restlessly she went into the bedroom and changed into shirt and jeans. Now that the play was finished, the apartment suddenly seemed confining.

She roamed aimlessly through the living room, then went to the kitchen and poured herself a glass of white wine. She had to start thinking about getting a job.

'I'll have to go back to work, I guess,' she had told Fannon when he asked about her plans. 'Do you have anything for me in any of your shows?'

'I don't think so. It's been a bad season. I don't have any shows on the road this summer.'

'I'll have to look around then,' she said.

'Who's your agent now?'

'I don't have any,' she said quickly. 'I sort of let everything drop while I was working on the play.'

He had looked at her without speaking. She knew that he knew what had happened. 'Now that I finished the play I thought I might go over to William Morris.'

'You can tell them that I'm interested in the play if that would be of help,' he said.

She looked at him gratefully. 'Thank you, Adolph,' she said sincerely.

'Anything I can do,' he said, moving his hand along her thigh, 'just call.'

'I will,' she said.

He put her into a taxi in front of the restaurant. When the cab turned the corner on Broadway she told the driver to drop her at Forty-second Street. She took the subway uptown from there.

Taxis were too expensive these days.

Strange how things had changed. For a long time cabs had been her only way of getting around town. But that seemed like a long time ago. Sardi's too was different now.

A little more than a year ago when she walked into the restaurant it seemed as if everyone knew her.

This time the maitre d' had looked at her with a blank expression even after she had asked for Fannon's table. She wondered if she had changed that much.

'Mrs Thornton, of course,' he answered with a professional smile when Fannon asked if he remembered Miss Randall. 'I thought it was you. But you've changed your hair style. I wasn't sure. Welcome back.'

Welcome back? Where was she supposed to have been, the Arctic Circle? 'Nice to be back,' she said, hating the words as she spoke them.

It was the same with other people who stopped by the table to talk to Fannon. In each case she had to be introduced and she could tell by their expressions that her name rang no bells. Broadway didn't have a long memory, that was for sure.

She had almost finished the wine when the telephone rang.

Fred's voice sounded happy in her ear. 'How'd the dinner go?' he asked.

'Fine,' she said. She could tell that he had been drinking.

'He goin' to do the play?' he asked.

'I don't know yet,' she said. 'He's got to read it first.'

'We're havin' a celebration up here,' he said. 'I just signed a management contract with Licia and she broke out a bottle of real champagne. Hop in a cab and come on up.'

'Maybe I'd better not,' she said hesitantly. 'It's late.'

'Come on, honey,' he said. 'There's just Licia, her lawyer an' me.' She heard another voice in the background. 'Change of plan, honey.' He laughed. 'You wait there, we comin' to get you. Goin' to do a little finger popping tonight.'

Then he clicked off. Maybe it was just as well, she thought. Without work the apartment was depressing.

Arthur's was jammed. The music reverberated from the speakers over their heads and they had to shout in order to be heard. There had been a long line at the door when they had pulled up but, without hesitating, Licia had gotten out of the car and left it for the doorman to park. Then, as if by magic, the door was opened and a good table found for them. She seemed to know everyone in the discotheque.

It wasn't until they got out of the car that JeriLee realized how tall Licia was – at least five ten, she guessed. There was something statuesque about her, a composed strength that revealed itself in the way she moved and walked. By comparison, the girl Sam with her selfish petulant look seemed soft. Marc, the lawyer, was a young man with a shrewd Jewish face which created immediate feelings of distrust.

As soon as they had reached their table and the waitress had taken their order, the lawyer and Sam got up to dance. In a moment they were lost in the press of people on the dance floor.

Fred, sitting between Licia and JeriLee, smiled. 'You two are goin' to like each other,' he said. 'You're both very independent ladies.'

Meeting Licia's eyes, JeriLee had the feeling that she and Licia already knew each other. There was a kind of recognition that went beyond the spoken word. She felt herself flushing.

Licia smiled. Her voice was casual. 'I know we will.'

'Yes.' JeriLee nodded.

When the waitress came with their drinks, Licia picked up her glass of orange juice. 'To the music man,' she said.

Fred laughed as they clinked glasses. 'I hope neither of you will be disappointed,' he said.

'I don't think we will,' Licia said, looking at JeriLee.

JeriLee felt herself flushing again. 'We won't be,' she added.

'Why don't you two dance?' Licia suggested. 'Don't worry about me. I'm okay here.'

Fred looked at JeriLee. 'How about it, honey?'

She nodded and got to her feet. The floor was crowded with bodies and after a moment JeriLee gave herself up to the pulsing beat. She loved to dance, especially to rock. There was something exhibitionistic about it that appealed to her. It was a form of dancing that seemed to have been made for her alone.

Fred leaned toward her. 'What do you think of Licia?'

'She's a very special lady.'

Fred nodded, his body moving with the beat. 'Smart too. She's got interests in a lot of things besides the Green Bar. Record stores, music companies and some clubs in other cities.'

'Sounds good,' she said.

'Real good,' he said. 'At least we don't have to scratch for dough no more. She's guaranteeing me a hundred and fifty bucks a week for the next year at least.'

'And what does she get for it?'

'We'll be fifty-fifty partners. We're putting all my songs into a publishing company and everything else, including records and club dates, will spring from that.'

'What does she put in besides the money?' JeriLee asked.

'Her contacts. She knows everybody in the business, and with the things she's into she's got a lot of muscle. People are goin' to try to please her.'

'Sounds good.'

'It is good.'

She met his eyes without answering.

'There ain't nothing between us but business. Sam's her girl friend.'

Suddenly it was beginning to fall into place. JeriLee had known there was a quality about Licia that reminded her of someone else. Now she knew who it was. It wasn't a physical resemblance, it had more to do with the way Licia looked at her when they met. Carla Maria had given off the same subtle vibrations. Perhaps it was that experience that had given her a new kind of awareness. Through a break in the crowd she saw Licia glance at her meaningfully and she felt her face flush.

Licia knew just as Carla Maria must have known. Could it be that she was telegraphing a message without realizing it? Was it possible that there was a latent lesbian crawling around inside her skin waiting to get out?

She had been so into her own thoughts that she hadn't heard Fred. She brought herself into focus on him. 'What?' she asked. 'So much noise I couldn't hear.'

'She wants me to get some new threads. She's advancing the bread. She wants me to have a superhip Sam Cooke kind of look.'

She nodded without speaking.

'We're goin' to get a few tapes together, then Marc and me are goin' out to Detroit to see some of the biggies at Motown. She thinks we can swing there.'

For the first time she realized how young he was – not in age, he was older than she – but in naïveté. His dreams were dreams she had had many years ago.

Suddenly she felt old and depressed and in need of a drink.

She touched Fred's shoulder and they left the floor.

As they reached the table, Sam returned alone. 'Marc left me on the floor.' She pouted. 'There was someone he wanted to talk to and I still feel like dancing.'

'That's Marc, always hustling.' Licia smiled. 'Why don't you dance with her, Fred?'

'Sure thing.'

JeriLee slid into her seat, carefully reserving Fred's seat between her and Licia.

'Fine bunch of freaks here tonight,' Licia said.

JeriLee nodded.

'Half of them are stoned. The other half are showoff smart-ass freaks who are here because this is the in place to be.'

'Which club are you in?'

'Neither. One, I really like watchin'. Two, I'm working.'

'You have a piece of this place?'

'I have an idea for opening a place like it when the time is right.'

'When will that be?'

'A year or two. When this place is gone. There's only room for one of these places at a time.'

JeriLee didn't answer.

'Fred tell you about our plans?'

'Yes.'

'What do you think?'

'I'm happy for him. He deserves a break.'

'You're not in love with him, are you?'

'No.'

'He's in love with you. He wants to marry you.'

'Did he say that?'

Licia nodded.

'Shit.' JeriLee picked up her drink. He was not supposed to go that far.

'Sister,' Licia asked, as if she had tuned in to her head, 'what is a woman like you doin' messing around with a boy like that?'

'It's better than being alone. And besides there are no real men around.'

Licia reached across the table and pressed JeriLee's hand.

In the same tone of voice and without moving her hand away JeriLee said, 'Sister, why is a woman like you messing around with a girl like that?'

Licia's eyes widened in surprise, then she laughed as she withdrew her hand. 'It's better than being alone. And besides there are no real women around.'

Suddenly there was an easiness between them. JeriLee laughed. 'I like you,' she said. 'At least you're honest.'

'I like you too.'

'But there's one thing I don't understand. Why are you doing all this for him?'

'Partly the money, but that's not all of it,' Licia hesitated.

'What's the rest of it?'

'You wouldn't understand.'

'Try me.'

Licia's voice was soft but with an undertone of toughness. 'This is a man's world and I've gone about as far as a woman can go alone and still be tolerated. Men don't like women who want to go all the way by themselves.'

'I still don't see what Fred has got to do with it.'

'I'm going to make him a success because we both need it for our own reasons. With him in front, ain't nobody goin' to stop me. I'll go all the way.'

'I still don't see it. What do you mean with him in front of you?'

Licia reached for JeriLee's hand again. 'I'm sorry. I didn't mean to be obscure,' she said quietly. 'You see, I'm going to marry him.'

CHAPTER SIX

JERILEE FOLDED the last shirt and placed it carefully in the suitcase. The new and expensive luggage, a gift from Licia, looked out of place on the bed. 'That should do it,' she said.

'Yeah.'

'Finish dressing. Marc should be here any minute now.'

'Okay.' He buttoned the collar of his shirt and went over to the mirror to put on his tie. When he had finished he slipped into his jacket and turned to her with a smile on his face. 'How do I look?'

'Great.'

He came over and kissed her. 'It's only the beginning. When I come back Licia wants us to get a better apartment. One where we can have a piano.'

She snapped the last bag closed without speaking.

'Hey, don't be down,' he said. 'I won't be gone that long. Detroit, Nashville, Los Angeles. Just a week in each place.'

He didn't understand.

'While I'm gone you start lookin' for another place. That way by the time I get back – '

'No,' she interrupted him.

A puzzled expression came over his face. 'What is it, honey?'

'I'm not moving.'

'Come on. It's time we got out of this dump.'

'I'm not moving,' she repeated.

'We can afford it, honey.'

'You can afford it.'

'What difference does it make? We never fussed about the bills here.' He put his arm around her. 'Besides, baby, it's time we got married.'

She buried her face against his shoulder. 'No,' she said, her voice muffled against his jacket.

He held her away from him. There was genuine bewilderment in his voice. 'Why not?'

She blinked back her tears. 'Because it wouldn't be right.'

'Is it because I'm black?'

'You know better than that.'

'I don't know. There are girls who'll make it with black guys but won't marry them.' There was a subtle edge in his voice.

'You know that's not it.'

'What is it then? I know it was okay with you for me to move in here. We were good for each other.'

'That's right. Then. But that was not forever. Now it's different.'

'The only difference is that now I'll be bringin' home the bread. And I can take care of you proper.'

She chose her words carefully. She cared too much for him to want to hurt him. 'I'm glad you're making it. You deserve everything you get. But don't you see, I've got to make it too. I've got to do my own thing.'

'I won't be stopping you. I jus' want to make it easier for you. Take the nickel and dime heat off.'

Her eyes were dry now, her voice steady. 'If that was what I wanted I would never have divorced Walter.'

'I don't understand you.'

'Sometimes I don't understand myself. I only know that I want to be free.'

'If you loved me you wouldn't feel like that.'

'Maybe that's it. I love you but not in the same way you care about me. It's like we're very close and we're friends and everything is good between us – the vibes, the sex, everything. It's great as far as it goes but it's not enough for me. Something is still missing. Maybe it's inside me, something I may never find, but until I do I won't be ready to give myself up to a relationship. And I won't be able to do that until I feel free and whole.'

'If we get married, we can start a family,' he said. 'That'll get you together.'

She laughed. That was the ultimate male answer. A baby made everything right. Maybe it did. For them. But that was not what she wanted. 'That's not exactly what I meant by freedom. I don't know if I ever want a family.'

'It ain't natural. Every woman wants a baby.'

'I don't. Maybe I will someday. But not now.'

The buzzer sounded from downstairs. He went over to the window. 'Marc is double parked,' he said.

'You'd better get going.'

'I'm not takin' no for an answer.'

'Don't fight it. You have your own life and your own career.

Leave me to mine.'

The buzzer sounded again.

'You mean you don't want me to come back?'

Her eyes fell, then she raised her head and nodded. 'I think it would be the best thing for both of us.'

When the buzzer sounded again, insistently, he erupted with anger and frustration. 'I'm coming! God damn it! I'm coming.'

He stood in the doorway. Anguish altered his voice. 'JeriLee.'

She reached up and kissed his cheek. 'Good luck, Fred. Sing pretty for the people.'

He put down the bags and took a step toward her. She drew back. His voice grew thick with pain. 'Fuck you, JeriLee,' he said. 'An' fuck your bullshit honesty or whatever you call it. It's just your excuse for the fact that you don't give a shit for nobody but yourself!' Then he was gone, leaving the door open behind him.

Abruptly she covered her face with her hands.

He was right about what he said. She knew enough to recognize the truth when she heard it. Her own mother had said the same thing.

There had to be something wrong with her. Why else couldn't she be satisfied with the same things as other people? Why did she always want more, why did she always feel incomplete?

When the doorbell rang she swore to herself and checked her watch. She had just an hour before she was due at Fannon's office. 'Who is it?' she called.

'Mr Hardy, the super.'

Shit, that was all she needed. She put an expectant expression on her face and opened the door. 'Mr Hardy.' She smiled. 'I was just about to call you. Come in.'

'I came about the rent,' he said in his peculiar thin voice.

'That's what I was going to call you about,' she said quickly.

'You got it?'

'That's what I wanted to explain,' she said. 'You see – '

'It's the twentieth of the month already,' he interrupted. 'The office is on my back.'

'I know, but I'm waiting for a check. I was going out just this minute to see the man who's going to produce my play. Adolph Fannon, the famous producer. You've heard of him, I'm sure.'

'No. The office wants me to give you an eviction notice.'

'Come on, Mr Hardy. What are they worried about? They have a month's security.'

'They'll apply it to this month's rent if you leave.'

'I've always paid. You know that.'

'I know it, Miss Randall, but I don't make the rules. The office says the rent ain't paid by the twentieth, serve the notice. That way you're out by the end of the month and nobody's the loser.'

'I'll pay you by Friday.'

'That's three days from now. They'll have my ass.'

'I'll make it up to you. Be a nice guy, Mr Hardy.'

He looked around the apartment. 'I ain't seen your boy friend around the last few weeks. He split?'

'No,' she said. 'But he's gone.'

'I'm glad, Miss Randall. I never told the office that you had someone here with you. You know your lease calls for only one person, and besides they find out you got a Negro in here they'd a gone through the roof. They don't have no spics or Negroes living in this building. They don't want the place run down.'

She had taken all she could. 'Mr Hardy,' she said in a cold voice, 'why don't you just go back and tell your office to go fuck themselves!'

He stared at her with an expression of shock. 'Miss Randall, what kind of language is that for a nice girl like you to use?'

'Mr Hardy, the office may own the building but they don't own the tenants. Nobody has the right to tell me how or who to live with. The only thing they have a right to is the rent, which I said I'll pay you on Friday.'

'Okay if that's how you feel about it,' he said, taking an official-looking piece of paper from his back pocket and pressing it into her hand.

She looked down at the words printed boldly across the folded page: EVICTION NOTICE. 'Why give me this?' she asked. 'I said I would pay you on Friday.'

He went to the door. 'You can always give it back to me with the rent,' he said. 'That's just in case you don't.'

CHAPTER SEVEN

THE MOMENT she saw Fannon she knew it wasn't going to be good.

'I wanted to get back to you sooner,' he said after kissing her on the cheek. 'But things have been hectic.'

'That's all right. I understand.'

'Cigarette?'

'No, thanks.'

'You look tired.'

'I haven't been sleeping too well. The nights have been hot and the air conditioner broke down.'

'You should get out of the city. What you need is some country air.'

She looked at him without answering. There was no point in telling him that she didn't have the money.

He picked up the copy of her play and stared at the cover. 'I like you,' he said abruptly.

She tried to keep her voice light. 'But you don't like my play?'

His eyes seemed to bore into her. 'Do you like your pills sugar coated?'

'I'll take it straight.'

'I don't like your play.' He cleared his throat. 'I wanted to, believe me. I think you can write. But this doesn't work. It's an emotional exercise, a series of scenes that don't go together, a story that doesn't work. But I haven't given up on you. I think someday you're going to write a play that will turn this town on its end.'

'But not this time,' she said tightly.

'Not this time.'

'Not even if I rewrote it?'

'It still won't work. There's no real story, no focus. It's all open and spread out, like a kaleidoscope. Every time you turn it you lose the picture. By the time I finished reading it I was too confused to understand what I had read.'

'Then what do you suggest?'

'I'd put this on the side. Maybe in time it will straighten itself out in your head. Then you can go back to it. Right now it won't work. I think you ought to start on something else.'

She didn't answer. It was easy enough to tell someone to do something else as long as you didn't have to do it.

'Don't get discouraged,' he said. 'Every successful playwright has had plays that don't work. The important thing is that you keep writing.'

'I know,' she said, meaning it.

'I'm sorry,' he said, getting to his feet.

She looked up at him, realizing the meeting was over. She managed to keep her voice steady. 'Thank you anyway.'

He came around the desk, gave her the script and kissed her cheek again. 'Don't be a stranger,' he said. 'Keep in touch.'

'I will.'

'Call me next week, we'll have lunch.'

'Yes.' She hurried through his secretary's office, fighting back the tears. She didn't want anyone to see her. All the way down in the elevator she was fighting back the tears.

When she reached the street, she saw a trash basket at the curb. In a fit of rage and self-pity she flung the script into the wire basket.

She had gone almost a block before turning and running back to retrieve the script from the bottom of the basket.

Maybe she had unconsciously thought that it should have been discarded, even while she was working on it. But there was no way she could have stopped herself. She was too much into it. She had to write it out.

Now it was over and she would have to begin again. But where? And how? There were other things she had to take care of first, like the rent and the bills. She would have to get some money to carry her over until she could find a job. Then maybe everything would fall into place.

'Hello,' her mother answered.

'Mother, I need help.' There was no point in wasting time on the preliminaries. The moment her mother heard her voice she would know the reason for the call.

'What is it this time?'

JeriLee kept her voice calm. 'I need two hundred and fifty dollars to get me past this month's bills. I'll pay you back as soon as I get a job.'

'Why don't you ask your friend? I'm sure he can give you something.'

'He's gone, Mother,' she said, controlling her voice. 'We broke up almost a month ago.'

Her mother was silent for a moment. 'It's about time you came to your senses,' she said finally.

JeriLee didn't reply.

'What about your play?' her mother asked. 'Did you finish it?'

'Yes,' JeriLee answered. 'It's not good. I took it to Fannon. He won't do it.'

'There are other producers.'

'It's not good, Mother,' she repeated patiently. 'I reread it. Fannon was right.'

'I don't understand it. Couldn't you have seen that while you were working on it?'

'No,' JeriLee answered.

'I don't know, JeriLee,' she said, sounding discouraged. 'Why can't you be like other girls? Get a job, get married, have a family.'

'I'm sorry, Mother. I wish I could be. It would be a lot easier all around. But I'm not.'

'I can let you have a hundred dollars,' her mother said finally. 'The market went down and there isn't much money coming in.'

'It won't be enough. The rent alone is a hundred and seventy-five.'

'That's all I can spare this month. If things pick up, maybe I can give you a little more next month.'

'At least give me the money for the rent. They gave me an eviction notice today.' JeriLee was angry with herself for pleading but she felt she had no choice.

'You can always come home to live.'

'What would I do? There's no work for me.'

'You're not working anyway.'

JeriLee lost her patience. 'Mother, either you're going to give me the money or you're not. There's no point in our going around in a circle.'

'I'll put a check in the mail for a hundred dollars,' her mother said coolly.

'Don't bother!' JeriLee said, slamming down the phone. It happened every time they spoke to each other. There seemed to be no way they could communicate.

She went back to the couch and started flipping through the

pages of *Casting News.* Nothing. The business was dead and the few things that were going were all locked up by the agents.

On the last page was another ad for the Torchlight Club. It was in the paper all the time now. The turnover in girls was obviously tremendous. On an impulse she picked up the telephone and dialed the club.

'Torchlight Club,' a woman's voice said.

'Mr DaCosta please.'

'Who is calling?'

'JeriLee Randall.'

'Just a moment, please.' There had been no sign of recognition in the woman's voice.

There was a click, then he came on. 'Hello,' he said cautiously.

'Vincent, this is JeriLee.'

'How are you, baby?'

'Okay,' she said. 'You?'

'Never been better,' he said. 'How come the call?'

'I need a job.'

He was silent for a moment. 'You still got that nigger living with you?'

The question took her by surprise. She had not known that he knew about Fred. 'No.'

'It's about time you came to your senses,' he said. 'A guy like that is nothing but bad news.'

She didn't answer.

'What about the play you were writing?'

'It didn't work. I'm junking it.'

'Too bad,' he said, but there was no sound of sympathy in his voice. 'What kind of a job are you looking for?'

'Anything,' she said. 'I'm busted.'

'Your old job is filled. We got a guy doin' it.'

'I said anything,' she replied. 'I know the whole setup. I can fit in anywhere.'

'Okay. Come on over an' we'll talk about it.'

'What time?'

'Just a minute, let me check my book. I'm locked in tight all afternoon,' he said. 'How about seven o'clock at the apartment? We can have a drink and talk there without anybody bugging us.'

'Okay,' she said. 'I'll be there.'

She got up and went into the bathroom. There was one

Valium left in the bottle. She swallowed it and looked at herself in the mirror.

Her eyes looked strained and red but a few drops of Visine would clear them up. Maybe things weren't so bad after all. If she did get a job she was sure that Vincent wouldn't mind giving her an advance on her salary.

CHAPTER EIGHT

A WOMAN LET HER into the apartment. 'Vincent's in the shower,' she said without introducing herself. 'He'll be out in a minute.'

'That's okay,' she said.

'Would you care for a drink?'

'Thanks. Vodka and tonic.'

The woman nodded and went behind the bar. JeriLee watched her. She was very pretty in a showgirl way – heavy eye makeup, lots of false eyelashes and carefully styled shiny black hair that fell to her shoulders. 'Okay?' she asked as JeriLee tasted her drink.

'It's fine.' JeriLee smiled.

The woman went back to the bar and picked up her own drink. 'Cheers,' she said, raising her glass to her lips.

'Cheers,' JeriLee replied.

'Sit down,' the woman said, gesturing to the couch. She climbed up on the bar stool and swung around facing JeriLee.

The telephone began to ring. Automatically the woman made a gesture toward it, then checked herself. It rang again, the sound cutting off in the middle. 'He doesn't like anyone to answer his private phone for him,' the woman explained.

JeriLee nodded.

'He's crazy. You know that, don't you? His whole family is crazy.'

JeriLee didn't answer.

'His brothers are worse.'

'I don't know them,' JeriLee said.

'Consider yourself lucky then.' She took a bottle of scotch from the bar and refilled her glass. 'Jesus, what a family.'

They fell silent, the woman staring morosely into her glass. Through the closed door there was the faint sound of Vincent's voice on the telephone. Then abruptly the bedroom door opened.

He was wearing the white terry cloth bathrobe that she remembered. 'You're here,' he said.

'Yes.'

'I thought I told you to tell me when she got here,' he said to the woman in a harsh voice.

'You were in the shower,' she said. 'Then you got on the phone.'

'Stupid cunt,' he said. 'Fix me a drink.'

Silently the woman got down from the stool and poured some scotch over the rocks. He took the drink and walked over to JeriLee. 'You don't look so good,' he said abruptly.

'I'm tired.'

'The nigger fuck you out?'

She didn't answer.

'Everybody knows about them,' he said. 'All their brains are in their cocks.'

She put down her drink and rose from the couch. 'I don't have to listen to that,' she said.

His hand gripped her arm tightly. 'You want a job, you listen whether you like it or not.'

It was not until then that she saw the glittering brightness in his eyes and knew he was coked to the ears. He had probably taken a few snorts before he came out. 'What about the job?' she asked.

He let go of her arm. 'I told you you'd come crawling back.'

She didn't answer.

'What makes you think I'd give you a job?' he asked. 'What can you do better than anybody else?'

She kept her silence.

'Maybe the nigger taught you some new tricks.' Abruptly he pulled at his belt and the robe fell open. 'Show me,' he said. 'Get it hard. I got room for a good cocksucker up in the massage parlor.'

'I think I'd better go,' she said.

'What's the matter? Isn't it big enough for you anymore?' He laughed harshly. 'Everybody knows they're hung like horses.'

She turned and started for the door. He caught her arm. 'Maybe I was all wrong. Maybe you'd rather make it with her than with me?' He called over his shoulder to the woman. 'Come here.'

'Jesus, Vincent,' the woman said in a disgusted tone of voice.

'Come here, bitch!' he said angrily.

Slowly the woman got down from the stool and came over to him. He turned back to JeriLee. 'Would you like to go down on her?' he asked.

'I told you he was crazy,' the woman said.

Vincent stared at the woman wildly and for a moment JeriLee thought he was about to strike her. Then abruptly he dropped JeriLee's arm and walked back to the bar, where he refilled his drink. 'Go on, get out of here. Both of you,' he said. 'You cunts are all alike.'

Silently JeriLee opened the door and the woman followed her out into the hall.

'He's got to be higher than the Empire State Building,' the woman said as they waited for the elevator. 'He's been snortin' coke ever since he got home.'

When they came out of the building, the woman signaled for a cab. 'Can I give you a lift?' she asked.

'No, thanks. I think I'll walk.'

The woman fished in her purse, then held her hand out to JeriLee. 'Here's my phone number,' she said. 'Give me a call sometime.'

Automatically JeriLee's hand closed over the folded paper. The cab door closed and the taxi took off. JeriLee looked down at her hand. The folded twenty-dollar bill lay flat in her palm.

'Oh, no!' She took a step after the cab. But it had already turned the corner. She stood there for a moment, blinking back the tears that suddenly came to her eyes.

'Taxi, miss?' the doorman asked.

'No, thank you.' The evening breeze was beginning to come in off the river as she boarded a crosstown bus on Fifty-seventh Street.

The driver looked down at her hand as she held the bill toward him. A tone of disgust came into his voice. 'For Christ's sake, lady,' he said. 'Can't you rich East Side broads get it through your heads that there are poor people in this world?'

'I'm sorry,' she said, searching in her bag and finding a quarter. She looked out the bus window and blinked her eyes. It really would be funny if it weren't so sad.

The only kindness she had known during the whole depressing day had come from a stranger, a woman whose name she had never thought to ask. But then they were both female in an alien world. Only a woman who had been there herself could sympathize with one who was there now. She was sorry she hadn't taken the cab with her. It would have been good to have someone to talk to.

Suddenly she thought of Licia. There was something about

her that was solid and strong. Fred had said that she was into a lot of businesses. Maybe she would be able to help her find a job. She made up her mind to call her when she got back home.

The downstairs buzzer sounded. She took a last quick look around the apartment as she went to press the button that unlocked the outside door. It looked as good as it ever could. She opened the door and waited.

The sound of footsteps came from the landing below. 'Up here,' she called. 'One more flight.'

Licia's head appeared as she came up the stairs.

'I forgot to tell you there was no elevator,' JeriLee said.

Licia grinned. 'That's all right,' she said easily. 'I never knew there was such a thing as elevators until I was fourteen years old.'

JeriLee closed the door behind her. 'I didn't mean to interfere with your work.'

'You're not,' Licia replied. 'I usually take Tuesday nights off.'

'Would you like a drink?' JeriLee asked.

'Do you have any fruit juice?'

JeriLee shook her head. 'Some white wine?'

Licia hesitated. 'Okay.'

JeriLee quickly filled two glasses and gave her one. Licia sat down on the small couch and put the glass on the cocktail table. JeriLee sat opposite her, suddenly feeling awkward and embarrassed. She took a quick drink of the wine. 'I shouldn't have called you,' she said. 'I'm sorry.'

The black girl looked at her steadily. 'But you did.'

JeriLee's eyes fell. 'Yes. The roof was caving in. I felt I had to talk to somebody. The only one I could think of calling was you.'

'What happened to the play. Fred told me that Fannon was going to do it.'

'It wasn't any good. I didn't know it then but I know it now. I screwed it up.'

Licia's voice was easy. 'Those things happen. I put some money into a few shows. Nothing happened.'

'Now I've got to get a job. I can't fool around anymore.'

'Fred told me that you wouldn't take any money from him.'

JeriLee nodded.

'Why?'

'Fred has his own plans. I had mine. They didn't go together. It wouldn't be right to take his money.'

Licia was silent for a moment. 'What kind of a job are you looking for?'

'I don't know,' JeriLee said. 'I'm an out-of-work actress and an unsuccessful writer. The only thing I know is that I want to make enough money so that I can continue writing.'

'How much would that take?' Licia asked.

JeriLee laughed, embarrassed. 'A lot more than I'm probably worth on the job market. At least a hundred and fifty, two hundred a week.'

'That's a lot of bread,' Licia said.

'I know,' JeriLee said. 'But this place costs me over two hundred a month with the utilities.'

'What you need is some man to keep you,' Licia said.

'Is that how you did it?'

'Yes,' Licia said evenly. 'I have an eight-year-old son. When he was born his father gave me twenty-five grand to get lost. He didn't want his nice white world to get fucked up.'

'I'm sorry,' JeriLee said quickly. 'I had no right to say something like that.'

'It all worked out,' Licia said quietly. 'My boy lives in the country with my mother. And the friends I made when I was with his father helped me get started in business.'

JeriLee emptied her glass and refilled it. 'You don't drink?' she asked, noticing that Licia's wine was untouched.

'Never liked it,' Licia said.

'What's happening with Fred?' she asked.

'He's working,' Licia said. 'He's in L.A. right now. He's getting an album together for one of the record companies. When that comes out, they're goin' to send him around the country on a tour. They think he's got a real good chance.'

'I'm glad for him,' JeriLee said. 'He's a good person.'

'You haven't changed your mind about him?' Licia asked. 'He still wants to marry you.'

'No.' JeriLee shook her head. 'It wouldn't work. We make it in bed and we make it as friends. But that's as far as it goes. If we did get married we'd only wind up tearing each other apart. There's only room for one career in Fred's life.'

'You wouldn't consider giving up yours?'

'I would have remained married to my first husband if I felt that way.'

Licia was silent for a moment. 'Have you had dinner yet?'

'No.'

Licia smiled. 'What do you say we get something to eat? Somehow problems never seem as heavy on a full stomach.'

CHAPTER NINE

THE SAWMILL RIVER PARKWAY was deserted. Disregarding the posted limit, Licia calmly moved the big car up to seventy miles an hour. JeriLee looked at the clock on the dashboard. It was almost nine-thirty. 'Are you sure it will be all right with your mother, bringing someone up to dinner at this hour of the night?'

'My mother's used to it. We're all night people in my family.' She began to slow down. 'Besides we're almost there. We get off at the next exit.'

'You like driving?' JeriLee asked.

Licia nodded. 'Especially this car.' She laughed. 'It used to be a pimp's hog. Man, when he got it he was on top of the world an' he shit down on everybody. Then he got heavy into horse an' completely lost control. His girls georgied on him an' he had to sell it to feed the habit. I got it for practically nothing because he still had some payments on it. But he was one guy I didn't mind shaftin'. He had to be the world's number one prick.'

They turned off the main road onto a narrow road that wound its way through the trees to the top of a small hill where a few houses were clustered. 'We're here,' she announced, pulling into the first driveway on the left.

The front door opened as they got out of the car and a boy came running down the steps and across the lawn. 'Mommy! Mommy!'

Licia bent forward and he leapt into her arms. He put his arms around her neck. 'You came just at the right time,' he said. 'There's nothing but commercials on.'

Licia laughed and kissed him. 'I swear you're goin' to wind up with square eyeballs from watchin' the tube like that. JeriLee, this is my son, Bonny,' she said, putting him down. 'Bonny, JeriLee.'

The boy came to her, his hand outstretched. 'Hello,' he said. 'Do you like television?'

JeriLee laughed. 'Yes.'

'Good,' Bonny said. 'We can watch it together. There's a good show just starting.'

'You're going to bed, young man.' The woman's voice came from the open doorway. 'You've got school tomorrow.'

Bonny turned back to Licia. 'Mommy?'

Licia took his hand and they started toward the house. 'You heard Grandma.'

'But you just got here,' he said. 'I won't even be with you.'

She laughed. 'You wouldn't be with me anyway. You'd be with the TV.'

Licia's mother was a tall woman and if it weren't for the fact that her hair was flecked with gray she might have passed for an older sister. Her smile was warm and her hand firm as JeriLee took it. 'Nice to meet you,' she said.

The house was warmly decorated. Bonny went right to the color television set. 'Just ten more minutes,' he said.

'Okay,' Licia's mother answered. 'Then you go right upstairs.'

They went to the kitchen. A table had been set up on the screened-in back porch. A charcoal-fired barbecue was glowing in a corner. 'I got steaks and salad,' Licia's mother said. 'I wasn't expecting company.'

'That's fine with me,' JeriLee said.

'I make great fried chicken, barbecued ribs and greens, but Licia won't eat soul food. She says it's too greasy an' she's always on a diet.'

'Mother.' Licia laughed.

'Okay,' her mother said. 'You see if'n you kin get your son to bed. I'll put the steaks on.'

'How do you like yours cooked?' she asked JeriLee.

'Rare.'

'Like Licia.' The older woman sniffed. 'I like mine cooked through. I don't hold with eating raw meat.'

JeriLee smiled. 'Is there anything I can do to help?'

'No. I'm used to managin'. But maybe you like a cold drink? We got all kinds of fruit juices. We don't hold with liquor and no soda pop in this house.'

'Anything you have will be fine, Mrs Wallace.'

'Licia likes orange juice, but my favorite is Hawaiian Punch.'

'I'll have some of that.'

Mrs Wallace smiled. 'I'll put ice cubes in it. Don't taste as sweet that way.'

The meat was sizzling when Licia returned. 'Those steaks smell good,' she said.

'I had the butcher at the A and P cut them special for me,'

her mother said. 'He didn't charge me extra either.'

'My mother's got everybody in the A and P under her thumb,' Licia told JeriLee.

Licia walked over to the grill. 'The meat looks about ready to me.'

Mrs Wallace got out of her chair. 'Now you come right back here an' set down,' she commanded. 'I'm the one who does the cookin' in this house.'

'Yes, Mother,' Licia said meekly. She looked over at JeriLee and smiled.

JeriLee returned her smile without speaking.

It was after eleven o'clock by the time they finished. During the meal, Licia's mother didn't stop talking. It was apparent that a week's worth of problems and conversation had been stored up inside for this one night. Licia listened patiently – Bonny's school, shopping, the plumber. All the normal trivia came pouring out. And in the telling there was a feeling of pride. She had coped. Licia's approval was obviously very important to her mother. And the woman glowed when Licia gave it to her.

Licia's voice came from behind her. 'Not much like the city.'

Her mother was surprised. 'You're not stayin'? I got your room all fixed up for you.'

'Maybe JeriLee's got some things to do in the morning, Mother,' Licia said.

'Do you?' she asked bluntly.

'I don't want to put you out,' JeriLee said.

'It's no trouble,' Mrs Wallace said quickly. 'There are twin beds in Licia's room.'

Licia smiled. 'My mother's used to gettin' her own way.'

JeriLee nodded, got to her feet and picked up her plate. 'Let me help you with the dishes,' she said.

'You don't have to do nothin', girl,' Mrs Wallace said. 'We got an automatic KitchenAid dishwasher in this house.'

There were three bedrooms on the upper floor. Licia had the master bedroom. It was in one corner of the house, separated from the other rooms by a large bathroom. Licia paused in the upper hallway and kissed her mother. 'Good night, Mother.'

'Good night, Mrs Wallace. Thank you,' JeriLee said.

The older woman nodded and went down the hall to her room. JeriLee followed Licia. A small lamp was glowing between the beds. Licia crossed to the bathroom. 'I'll put out a new toothbrush for you. I have extra nightgowns in the closet. I'll get one for you.'

'Thanks.' JeriLee walked to the open window and breathed deeply of the night air. It smelled fresh and green.

Licia's voice came from behind her. 'Not much like the city.'

'I'd almost forgotten what fresh air really smells like.'

Licia took out a neatly pressed nightgown. She held it up. 'This okay?'

'Fine.'

'You can use the bathroom first,' Licia said, holding the nightgown toward her.

She took the gown and went into the bathroom, closing the door behind her. Quickly she undressed and folded her things neatly over the hanger. She took the toothbrush from its package and brushed her teeth, then washed her face. She had been feeling all right up to now but suddenly she was nervous. She rummaged through her purse. If she remembered correctly, there was a ten-mg Valium in her pill box. When she found it she swallowed it quickly. She felt reassured. Valium always put her to sleep.

Licia smiled as she came through the doorway. 'That gown's a little big on you.'

JeriLee looked down. The hem was dragging on the floor. 'I guess it is,' she said.

Licia gestured to the bed nearest the door. 'This one's yours.'

JeriLee nodded. She went to the bed and sat down. Automatically she reached for a cigarette and lit it.

Licia seemed to sense her nervousness. 'Are you okay?'

'I'll be all right. It's just been a bad day, that's all.'

'You don't have to worry,' Licia said in a low voice. 'I didn't bring you up here to hit on you. I never figured we'd be staying.'

'It's okay. I'm glad you did. It's the only good thing that's happened to me all day.'

'Good,' Licia said, going to the closet. Quickly she pulled her blouse off over her head and stepped out of her skirt. She reached behind her to unfasten the brassiere.

JeriLee ground out her cigarette. When she looked up, Licia had slipped into a beige-colored peignoir that was almost the same color as her skin. JeriLee slid down into the sheets.

Licia sat down on the other bed. 'What do you think of my little family?' she asked.

'There's a lot of love here.'

Licia smiled. 'That's why I keep them here. Ain't no way you can get that feeling in the city.'

'You're doing the right thing.'

'Bonny's growin' fast though,' Licia said. 'A boy like that needs a father.'

JeriLee didn't speak.

'You think he'd put Fred off?' Licia asked.

'Fred loves kids,' JeriLee answered.

'What about me?' Licia asked. 'He ever say anything about me?'

'Only that he liked you. He respects you.'

'But he knows about me. He's seen me with Sam.' Licia was silent for a moment. 'It ain't that I don't like men. I just went off them. With them everything's a battle. They don't make love, they make war.'

'Fred's not like that. He's a very gentle man.'

Licia rose to her feet. 'I don't know,' she said hesitantly. 'I got to think some more about it. I don't want to make any mistakes.'

'You won't,' JeriLee said. 'You'll do the right thing.'

'You really think so?'

'I think so.'

Licia smiled suddenly. 'Enough of my problems. You go to sleep.' She turned off the light. 'Good night.'

'Good night.' JeriLee watched her go into the bathroom and close the door behind her. Then she looked up into the dark. After a few moments she heard the sound of the water running and closed her eyes. She didn't hear Licia come out of the bathroom. She didn't feel Licia's kiss, light on her cheek, or hear her soft murmur. 'Poor little baby.' She was fast asleep.

CHAPTER TEN

THE FUCKING California sunshine, she thought as she opened her eyes. Christ. What I wouldn't give for just one rainy day.

Then she was wide awake and thinking about Licia. For a moment she could almost smell the warm sweetness of her and the smooth sensation of the honey-colored skin against her fingers. Then she heard the voices through the closed bedroom door and the thought was gone.

She sat up in the bed and listened. The voices, a man's and a woman's, were muted. Then the man's voice grew more insistent. A moment later the door opened softly.

Angela peeked into the room. 'Are you awake?'

'Yes.'

'You were asleep when I looked in just a moment ago. I didn't want to wake you.'

'That's okay. Who's out there?'

'George.'

'Shit!' JeriLee said. 'What does he want?'

'I don't know. He just said it was important that he see you. I'll tell him to go away, that you're not feeling well enough.'

'No.' JeriLee swung her feet off the bed. George was too self-centered just to pay a courtesy call. It had to be something else. 'I'll see him. Just ask him to wait a minute while I go to the bathroom.'

'Okay. You let me know when you're ready. I'll send him in.'

'No. I'll come out there.'

'Don't you think you should stay in bed?' Angela asked disapprovingly.

'What for? I'm not sick. All I had was a lousy little abortion.'

The door closed behind Angela, and JeriLee went into the bathroom. She sat down on the john and changed the tampon. She was bleeding more than she had in the morning and she was still sore. She took two aspirin and a Percodan for the pain. Then she washed her face with cold water. She began to feel better. She touched up her lips, used some rouge on her cheeks and brushed her hair quickly.

George got to his feet as she came into the room. 'Hey,' he said, 'you don't look sick at all.'

'Makeup.' She smiled. She sat in the easy chair opposite him. 'What's up?'

'I wanted to talk to you,' he said. 'I wanted to tell you how sorry I was about what happened.'

She looked at him without speaking.

'We shouldn't have rushed it,' he continued. 'We should have kept the baby.'

She couldn't keep the surprise from her voice. 'You've got to be kidding!'

'I'm not,' he said earnestly. 'I mean it.'

'But what about your wife?'

'It would have been okay with her,' he said, his blue eyes clear and untroubled. 'We talked about it last night. We could have adopted the baby and there would be no problems.'

'Oh, Jesus!'

'Rosemary would love to have a baby. She loves kids,' he said.

'Then why don't you have one?' she asked.

'It's that damn series she's in,' he said. 'She's got a three-year contract firm. And that's big money, especially with the residuals. She'd blow it all if she got pregnant.'

'And how was I supposed to support myself all the time I was walking around with a big belly?' she asked sarcastically.

The sarcasm went over his head. 'We talked about that too. You could have lived with us. That way we all would have had a part in it.'

'I don't believe it,' she said, shaking her head.

'It would have worked,' he said. 'We were at a party last night at my shrink's. Everybody agreed it was a good idea.'

'Everybody?'

He nodded. 'Everybody. You know my shrink. He's got the most important patients in town. And once a month we meet at his house for a sort of consciousness-raising session. That's how the whole thing came up.'

JeriLee knew his psychiatrist. If you didn't need him when you went to him, you would by the time you finished your first visit. That is, if you were a big enough name and could afford the hundred dollars an hour.

'That really does it,' she said in a disgusted voice. 'It took me two years to get this town to take me seriously and in one evening you hung the cunt label back on me.'

'It wasn't anything like that, JeriLee,' he said sincerely. 'We're all very honest and open with each other. They all respect you.'

'Sure,' she said.

'Really. Take Tom Castel, for example. He's producing your picture over at the studio.'

'What about him?' she asked wanting him to confirm what her agent had told her.

'He said that he's talking to your agent about you writing the script based on your book. He says that he's convinced that you're the only one to do it. Especially after Warren's scripts turned out such a disaster.'

'Then what is he waiting for?' she asked. 'Why doesn't he sign me?'

'He says the studio won't let him go without a star.'

'Shit,' she said disgustedly. 'Nothing ever changes. Which comes first, the chicken or the egg?'

'He said the studio wants me for it. They'll give him the go-ahead if I commit.'

She couldn't contain herself. 'For Christ's sake, what's stopping you then?'

'That's why I had to see you,' he explained patiently. 'I read the book. I don't know whether I'm right for the part. It calls for an older leading man.'

'Don't worry, you can do it,' she said firmly.

'But the age,' he protested.

'Remember Jimmy Dean in *Giant*? He played a forty-year-old man when he was still in his early twenties. And you're as good an actor as he ever was. You've got the same quality and excitement.'

She could see the actor's ego take over. 'Do you really think so?' he asked. 'Jimmy Dean?'

She nodded. 'What do you think turned me on to you in the first place?'

'I'll be damned,' he said in a wondering voice. 'I never thought of that.'

But she could see that he was pleased. 'If you do it I could write the ass off it,' she added. 'Together we could make sure that everything was perfect.'

He nodded thoughtfully. 'It's really a hell of a part.'

'Once in a lifetime,' she said. 'An actor's dream. It will put you right up there with McQueen and Redford.' She laughed. 'George Ballantine. Superstar.'

He laughed, then his face grew serious. 'But what about the director?' he asked. 'Jimmy Dean and Kazan and George Stevens. We'll need a top man. Coppola, Schlesinger, someone like that.'

'You name him, we'll get him.'

'I'll have to think about it,' he said. 'I'll talk it over with my agent.'

'You tell him what I said. The important thing is that we can work together.'

'Sure.' But he was already thinking of something else. 'Do you think Rosemary could play the girl?'

'I thought you said she was firm in the series?'

'She could get out for a feature,' he said. 'Besides it would look better if we were all together on the project. Especially after what happened.'

'Why not?' She nodded. 'It would be great box-office chemistry.'

'I've got an idea,' he said. 'Why don't you come over to the house for dinner tomorrow night? I'll have my agent over and we can all talk it out.'

That was the last thing in the world she felt like doing. 'Why don't you explore it first?' she suggested. 'Maybe we can get together on the weekend when I get my strength back.'

'Fine,' he said, getting to his feet. A rueful expression crossed his face. 'Shit,' he said, putting his hands in his pockets.

'What's the matter?'

'I don't know what there is about you, JeriLee,' he said with an embarrassed laugh, 'but every time I'm around you I get a hard-on.'

'You do say the nicest things.' She laughed. She got to her feet and kissed him lightly on the cheek. 'But you'll also have to save that until I get my strength back.'

'He's gone?' Angela asked, coming out of the kitchen.

JeriLee nodded.

'I don't like him,' Angela said flatly. 'It was his fault you went through all this and he didn't give a damn how you were feeling. He would have gone right into your bedroom if I didn't stop him. The selfish chauvinistic son of a bitch.'

JeriLee looked up at her and laughed. 'And besides that, he's an actor, which makes it even worse.'

'I don't see what's so funny,' Angela said. 'I wouldn't talk to a man who put me through a thing like that.'

JeriLee shook her head. 'It wasn't all his fault,' she said. 'It still takes two, you know. And if I hadn't been in such a hurry I would have stopped to put in my diaphragm.'

The doctor straightened up. 'You're doin' okay,' he said. 'You can start getting out tomorrow if you don't overdo it. If you get tired I want you to come home and go to bed.'

'Okay, Sam.'

'Come into the office after the weekend,' he said, 'and we'll give you a final check.'

'I'm beginning to feel like a used car.'

He laughed. 'Don't worry about it. You should have another fifty thousand miles left in you. Besides I have an idea for a new part that should make the motor run without any more problems like the one you just had.'

'What's that?'

'I just received the clinical reports on a new I.U.D. they've been testing. It's a small copper coil and I think you'll be able to tolerate it.'

'Order one. I'll try anything.'

'I already did,' he said. 'Goodbye.'

'Goodbye, Sam,' she called after the doctor, then picked up the ringing phone. 'Hello.'

It was her agent. 'Who was that?'

'My doctor,' she said wearily. Agents were all alike. They had to know everything.

'What did he say?'

'I'll live. I can start going out tomorrow.'

'Good,' he said. 'We have to have a meeting.' His voice lowered to a confidential whisper. 'I've got some very big news but I don't want to talk about it on the phone.'

That was another quality of agents. Everything had to be top secret. None of them would trust the telephone even if they were reading the headline from the daily newspaper. 'Is it about George doing my picture?'

The surprise showed in his voice. 'I thought you were in bed. How did you find out about it?'

She laughed. 'For Christ's sake, Mike, you know about George and me.'

'No, I don't,' he said. 'What about George and you?'

'That was George's baby that I aborted.'

'The son of a bitch!' he erupted. Then there was a moment's silence and his voice lightened. 'But that should make things easier for us. He has to listen to you. You can make him take the part.'

'I can't make him do anything,' JeriLee said. 'All I can do is try to talk him into it.'

'He owes you something,' Mike said.

'Nothing,' she said flatly. 'That's not the way I live. I'm a big girl. I didn't do anything I didn't want to do.'

'Can you come into the office in the morning?' he asked. 'I've got to make you understand how important this is.'

'Eleven o'clock okay?'

'Fine,' he said. 'I'm glad you're feeling better.'

'So am I,' she said. The phone clicked off and she put it down. He was a good agent but he lived in an ancient world.

Angela was on the couch reading the trades. She looked up. 'What did the doctor say?'

'I'm better. I can go out tomorrow.'

'That's good,' Angela said. 'Have you thought about dinner?'

JeriLee shook her head.

'Steaks or chicken?' Angela said. 'I took both out of the freezer.'

'Steak,' JeriLee said promptly. 'I need the strength.'

Angela got to her feet. 'I'll get started then,' she said. 'I'll fix salad and french fries.'

'We'll have a bottle of red wine with dinner,' JeriLee said. 'The good wine. The Chambertin you gave me. I was saving it for a night like this.'

Angela smiled. 'You didn't forget?'

'I didn't forget,' JeriLee said.

'Candles on the table?' Angela asked.

'The works,' JeriLee said. 'I'll roll a couple of joints. We'll have one before dinner and one before we go to bed.'

Angela smiled. There was a happy sound in her voice. 'It will be just like old times.'

JeriLee watched her go into the kitchen. There was something very touching about her. Like old times.

Only the very young could think like that. Or the very old. There was no such thing as old times. Only good times and bad times. And sometimes the good came with the bad and the other times the bad came with the good. It all depended on where you were in your head.

Like the time JeriLee Randall became Jane Randolph. Or the time Jane Randolph went back to being JeriLee Randall. She didn't know which. And that wasn't even old times.

It hadn't been that long ago.

CHAPTER ELEVEN

THE AMBER SPOT set in the ceiling over the tiny platform on which she was dancing blurred everything in front of her and the loud acid rock drowned out all other sounds in the crowded club. Her face and body were covered with a fine patina and the perspiration ran in rivulets between her naked breasts. She gulped for air between smiling parted lips. She was beginning to feel exhausted. Her back and arms were aching, even her breasts were sore from the gyrations of the dance. Suddenly the music stopped in the midst of a wild movement, taking her by surprise. She stood for a moment, then raised both arms over her head in the standard gogo dancer's bow, giving the customers one last free look as the spot died.

As she looked challengingly at the men staring at her from the crowded bar, their eyes fell from her gaze. There was no applause, only the beginning of the swell of conversation. She dropped her arms, came down from the platform and went through the small curtain behind it.

Through the sound system she could hear the voice of the club manager. 'Ladeez an' gentlemun, it is with great pride that World à Gogo presents the star of their show, direct from San Francisco, the girl you have all read about, the girl you all want to see, the original, the one and only, the Blond Bomber, Miss Wild Billy Kichkok and her twin forty-eights!'

Billy was waiting behind the curtain, her giant breasts thrusting forward against the thin silk kimono. She was holding a small vial in one hand and a short hard straw in the other. 'How's the crowd out there tonight, Jane?' she asked.

'Okay, Billy,' JeriLee answered, reaching for her terry cloth robe. 'But it's you they came to see. All I could do was try and warm them up for you.'

'Fuckers, all of them,' Billy said without rancor. She put the straw in the vial and held it to her nostril. She snorted once in each nostril. Then she held the vial toward JeriLee. 'Want a hit, Jane?'

JeriLee shook her head. 'No, thanks. It'll keep me up the rest of the night and I want to get some sleep.'

Billy put the vial of coke and the straw in the pocket of her kimono. 'The gogo dancer's maiden aunt,' she said.

JeriLee nodded. Coke, bennies and ammies. Without them the girls couldn't make it through their nightly four to six half-hour turns, seven nights a week. Billy slipped out of her kimono and turned to her. 'I look all right?'

JeriLee nodded. 'Fantastic. I still don't believe it.'

Billy smiled. Her eyes were beginning to shine as the coke hit. 'You better believe it,' she said, touching her breasts proudly. 'Carol says that hers are bigger than mine but I know better. We went to the same doctor and he told me she stopped at forty-six C and mine are a real forty-eight D.'

JeriLee knew she was talking about Carol Doda, San Francisco's first topless dancer. Billy hated her because Carol got all the publicity. 'Good luck, Billy,' she said. 'Go out there and kill them.'

Billy laughed. 'I know how,' she said. 'If they don't applaud, I'll just drop these on their heads.'

Billy disappeared through the curtain and the music stopped. JeriLee knew that the club had gone black while Billy took up her position. A moment later there was a roaring from the crowd as the amber spot went on. Then the music crashed and the applause and the whistles began.

JeriLee smiled to herself as she started back to the dressing room. Tits were what they had come to see. Now they were happy.

There was no one in the dressing room she shared with two other girls. She closed the door behind her and went directly to the small refrigerator. The pitcher of iced tea was half empty. Quickly she opened a tray of ice cubes and emptied it into the pitcher. Then she poured the tea into a tall glass, spiked it heavily with vodka and took a deep swallow.

She felt the cold liquid running down her throat and gave a light, gentle sigh of relief. Vodka and iced tea helped. It gave her a lift while replacing the fluids she sweated out during her turn.

Slowly she took off the short blond wig she wore and shook her own long brown hair down around her shoulders. Gogo dancers didn't wear their hair long. The customers didn't like it. Sometimes long hair covered the breasts. She opened a jar of

Abolene and began to remove the heavy layer of makeup from her face.

The door opened and the manager came in. She looked at him in the mirror. He took out a handkerchief and mopped his face. 'It's murder out there,' he said. 'There isn't enough space to breathe.'

'Don't bitch,' she said. 'Last week you were complaining you could shoot pigeons in there.'

'I'm not complaining.' He put his hand inside his jacket, took out an envelope and tossed it on the makeup table. 'That's for last week,' he said. 'Better count it.'

She opened the pay envelope. 'Two hundred forty dollars,' she said. 'It's all there.' She glanced down at the payroll slip. The gross was three hundred and sixty-five dollars but with deductions, commissions and expenses all that was left was two forty.

'You could have doubled that in cash if you'd have listened to me.'

'It's not my game, Danny.'

'You're a strange one, Jane. What is your game anyway?'

'I told you, Danny. I'm a writer.'

'Yeah. I know what you told me,' he said without belief. 'Where you goin' next?'

'I open in Gary on Tuesday.'

'Topless World?'

'Yes.'

'Good spot,' he said. 'I know the place. Lots of action down there. The manager's name is Mel. Give him my best.'

'I'll do that, Danny,' she said. 'Thanks for everything.'

There was a sound of applause from the room as he opened the door.

'Wild Billy really turns them on,' she said.

He smiled. 'She puts on a show. Too bad there aren't more like her. Ten girls like her and I can retire in a year.'

She laughed. 'Don't be greedy, Dan. You're doin' all right.'

'Ever think of having yours done up like that?'

'I'm happy the way I am.'

'She pulls a grand a week, for just one turn a night.'

'Good luck to her,' JeriLee said. She took another sip of her iced tea. 'I couldn't walk around with a pair like that. I'd keep falling on my face.'

He laughed. 'Goodbye, Jane. Good luck.'

'Bye, Danny.'

She turned back to the mirror and finished removing the makeup from her face and throat, then went over to the sink and washed with cold water. After lighting a cigarette she finished her iced tea. She was beginning to feel better. Maybe she could get a little work done when she got back to the motel. Tomorrow was Sunday and she could sleep late. She wasn't making the connecting flight to Chicago until Monday morning.

She saw the car – shining silver and black top – when the taxi dropped her off in front of her motel.

The night clerk looked up from the switchboard in the office. 'Your friend came in a couple of hours ago. I gave her the key to your room.'

JeriLee nodded.

'Are you leaving tomorrow, Miss Randolph?'

'No. Monday.'

'Okay. Just checking.'

She went outside and down the walkway to her room. A faint light filtered through the drapes. She tried the door. It wasn't locked.

Licia was sitting on the bed, the pillows propped behind her, reading. She put down the newspaper and smiled as JeriLee came in. 'Pittsburgh ain't New York,' she said. 'The late show goes off at two a.m.'

JeriLee smiled and glanced over at the table. The portable electric typewriter Licia had given her was exactly as she had left it, the page still in the roller. 'You're right about that,' she said. 'It's not New York.'

She put down the small suitcase she had brought back from the club. 'Care for a drink?' she asked, opening the door of the refrigerator.

'Orange juice, if you have it,' Licia said.

'We have it.' She placed the bottle of Tropicana on the small table. From the shelf above she took down a jar of iced tea mix and a bottle of vodka. 'I'll get some ice,' she said and went out in the corridor to the machine. When she got back to the room, Licia was rolling a couple of joints. JeriLee fixed the drinks – iced tea and vodka for herself, orange juice on the rocks for Licia. 'Cheers,' she said, slumping into the easy chair.

Licia passed her a joint. 'I figured you can use one of these.'

'You were right.'

'How's it coming?' Licia asked, nodding toward the typewriter.

'It's not,' she said flatly. 'I can't seem to get on.'

'What you need is a vacation,' Licia said. 'You've been on the road for four months. You can't work both ends of the clock.'

'That's not it,' she said. 'It seems that I've suddenly forgotten how to put words together. Like I can't get down on paper what I mean.'

'You're tired. You got to stop pushing yourself, honey, or you'll push yourself into a breakdown.'

'I'm okay.'

Licia looked at the glass in JeriLee's hand. 'How many of those do you put away in a day?'

'Not that much,' JeriLee said, knowing it wasn't true. It seemed that almost every time she went for a drink lately the vodka bottle was empty. 'It's cheaper than coke and bennies and it works almost as well.'

'Alcohol does things to your gizzards,' Licia said. 'At least when the other stuff is out of your system it's out.'

'I don't know about that,' JeriLee answered defensively. 'Too many reds can scramble your brains.'

'I'm not talkin' about speed,' Licia said.

JeriLee fell silent.

'Look, honey,' Licia said quickly. 'I'm not preachin' at you. I just worry about you.'

'I'm okay,' JeriLee answered quickly, then changed the subject. 'I didn't expect to see you this weekend. Where's Fred?'

'He got held over at the Fairmont in San Francisco,' Licia answered. 'He comes into the Waldorf next week.'

'I thought it was this week,' JeriLee said. The grass and the vodka were reaching her head. She giggled. 'How does he take to being married?'

'He's not complaining.' Then Licia laughed too. 'Not that he's had much of a chance. In the four months we've been married, I don't think we've had more than ten days together. He's really getting it together.'

'I'm glad,' JeriLee said. 'He's beginning to get more airplay. I hear him all the time.'

'F.M. mostly,' Licia said. 'They dig middle of the road. We're pushing A.M. radio though. That's the one that pays off.'

'You'll get it,' JeriLee said confidently. She took another drag of the joint, leaned her head back against the cushion on the chair and closed her eyes.

'Tired, honey?'

JeriLee opened her eyes. Licia had come around behind her chair and was bending over her. She nodded without speaking.

Gently Licia began to stroke her forehead with her fingers, then moved slowly down to her neck to massage the taut muscles. 'How does that feel?' Licia asked.

JeriLee closed her eyes. 'Good.'

'How would you like me to fix you a nice warm bath?' Licia asked. 'I brought some new bath oil with me.'

'Sounds lovely,' JeriLee said, her eyes still closed. She heard Licia begin to run the water in the tub. A few moments later she felt rather than heard her return. She opened her eyes.

Licia was kneeling at her feet, unfastening her shoes. She massaged her feet. 'Poor tired little feet,' she murmured. She looked up at JeriLee. 'You're beautiful, do you know that?'

'You're beautiful yourself,' JeriLee said, looking at her steadily.

Licia ran her tongue across her lips. 'I can smell your perfume from here.'

'Is it strong?' JeriLee asked quickly. 'I didn't have time to shower after the turn.'

'It's fantastic.' Licia smiled. 'It's a real turn-on. I'm wet already.'

JeriLee stared into her eyes. 'So am I,' she said.

CHAPTER TWELVE

EXCEPT FOR THE faint rays of sunlight coming through the cracks in the drapes, the room was dark when JeriLee opened her eyes. She rolled over on her side and looked at Licia, half buried in the pillow, one arm over her eyes.

In the semi-darkness the black girl's nudeness was like a statue carved out of the night, the full breasts and long jutting nipples like antennas on top of twin peaks falling down into the valley of her flat hard belly, then rising abruptly to the abundantly fur-covered mountain of her pubis. She fought the sudden impulse to touch her, to feel again the hot wetness of her, to taste the mildly salty flavor of her skin. But Licia was fast asleep and she didn't want to waken her. Silently she crept from the bed and went into the bathroom.

Licia was sitting up in bed when she returned. 'What time is it?' she asked.

'Almost one o'clock.'

Surprise echoed in Licia's voice. 'I don't believe it!'

JeriLee laughed. 'We didn't get to sleep until seven this morning.'

'I never had sex like that,' she said. 'I never wanted to stop. I just kept on coming and coming and coming.'

'The same thing was happening to me,' JeriLee said.

'I've never tasted cunt like yours,' Licia said. 'It's like you're flowin' pure honey. I even lick my fingers after we ball.'

'You better stop talkin' like that.' JeriLee laughed. 'You're turning me on again.'

'Keep the good thoughts,' Licia said, starting for the bathroom. 'I'll be right back.'

Just then the telephone began to ring. 'You expectin' any calls?' Licia asked.

'No.' The telephone kept on ringing. JeriLee picked it up. 'Hello.'

She held the phone toward Licia. 'It's for you. Fred's calling from New York.'

'Hello. This is Mrs Lafayette.' She paused, covering the

mouthpiece with her hand. 'The operator's getting him,' she said in a worried voice. 'I hope nothing's wrong.'

There was a crackling in the phone. 'Fred, darling, is everything all right? I thought you were staying on in San Francisco.' She listened a moment, then her voice lightened. 'That's fantastic! Of course I'll be there. If I leave now I can be in New York by nine o'clock, it's turnpike all the way. No, it's perfectly all right. I had some business with the club down here and since I didn't expect you back until next week, I thought I'd stay over and kill some time with JeriLee and see how she was doin' ... Yes, she's fine. Going on to Gary tomorrow ... Sure I will. 'Bye, honey. Love you.'

JeriLee looked at her without speaking.

'It's okay,' Licia said quickly. 'He's cool.'

'You sure?'

Licia nodded. 'He's too up to think of anything. Lou Rawls came down with laryngitis and they called Fred to replace him on the Pearl Bailey special that they're taping tonight. It's the break we've been waiting for.'

JeriLee was silent.

'I'll grab a shower and get started,' Licia said. 'I don't want to get caught in the weekend traffic going into the city.'

'I'll order some breakfast meanwhile.'

'Just orange juice and coffee for me, honey.' She saw the expression on JeriLee's face. 'Don't be upset,' she said quickly. 'I tol' you everything was cool.'

'I'm okay.'

Licia laughed. 'There's nothin' to worry about. Fred's just like every other man. They can't imagine anything in the world's better than their cocks.'

Through the window JeriLee watched the silver car turn out of the motel driveway onto the approach road leading up to the turnpike ramp. She let the curtain fall and absently began to straighten up the room. The odor of grass and last night's sex hung over the unmade bed. She pressed the vent button on the air conditioner and the whine of the compressor filled the room with a low hum.

Then she went and stared down at the page in the typewriter. Suddenly she was depressed. Angrily she pulled the sheet from the machine, crumpled it, and threw it on the floor. 'Fuck it!' she said aloud.

She opened the refrigerator door. There were still some ice

cubes left in the bucket. She threw them into a glass and made herself a vodka and tea. Sipping the drink, she crossed the room to the bed and lit one of the joints that Licia had left on top of the night table. The grass picked up on last night's high and almost immediately she was up there.

She threw off her terry cloth robe and lay back on the bed. She dragged on the joint slowly and with her free hand began to manipulate herself gently. A slow easy lassitude crept over her. She closed her eyes.

Licia's head was between her legs, Licia's tongue was licking at her clitoris, Licia's mouth was sucking the juices from her.

Suddenly she felt herself pop, almost like a balloon deflating. She opened her eyes. The empty room was a prison and the walls were closing in on her.

Quickly she reached for her drink and drained the glass. Then she pulled open the drawer of the night table and took out the vibrator.

This was a modern Green Hornet. It had been made in Japan. Executive size, they called it – no cords, battery-powered with two speeds.

She turned the vibrator on low. Closing her eyes she pressed it gently around her pubis, stroking lightly over her clitoris. She squeezed her eyes closed and inserted the phallus-shaped vibrator.

Now she could see Licia stopping the car and running into the apartment. Fred was sitting at the piano and when he stood up he was naked, his cock hard as rock. Then Licia was naked too and kneeling in front of him, peeling back the thin black skin exposing the glistening glans. He disappeared into her gobbling mouth but then suddenly he pushed her backward onto the white carpet and her legs were going up in the air to encircle him. Her cunt gaped open and he began to bore into her.

'No!' JeriLee screamed aloud. 'That's mine!' Torn from her fantasy, she opened her eyes and stared down at the vibrator tingling in her hands. It was nothing.

Switching it off, she threw it down on the bed and rolled over on her side, fighting back the tears.

JeriLee didn't know why she was so upset. Licia had said she would get jobs for her and she had kept her word. She was supporting herself and writing and should have been happy, but she wasn't.

'I'm not jealous,' she said over and over to herself. 'I'm not jealous.' But every time she blinked her eyes she saw Licia and Fred balling on the soft white rug.

She looked down at her hands. They were shaking again. She went into the bathroom and popped a Quaalude.

In the mirror she saw the black hollow circles under her eyes. She looked awful. She splashed some cold water on her face.

If she was jealous, was it of Fred because Licia was fucking him? Or of Licia because Fred was fucking her? She just didn't know.

It had been nine months since her affair with Licia had begun, and almost a year since she had been with a man. Until now she had not thought about it.

It was almost midnight when she came into the club. The music was blasting and a girl was writhing in the amber spot on the platform behind the bar. She went through the dark club to the manager's office in the back.

Danny looked up from his desk as she came in. 'I didn't expect to see you again,' he said with surprise.

'I had nothing to do,' she said. 'I was bored.'

He gave her a shrewd glance. 'I thought your friend came down to see you.'

He knew, but how. How did they all know everything about everybody. 'She had to go home to her husband,' she said.

'What are you looking for?' he asked.

'A cock,' she said flatly. 'The biggest hardest cock in town.'

'I don't know,' he said after a moment. 'Wild Billy has an eye for you.'

'I had that last night,' she said. 'Tonight I want cock.'

'There's a half a dozen guys out there, any one of them would spring for fifty or a hundred. I get half.'

'You can keep all the money,' she said.

'Okay. Want to come outside and take your pick?'

She laughed and for the first time he saw the contracted pupils in her eyes and knew that she was coked out of the world. 'Don't bother,' she said. 'Just collect your money. I'll take all of them.'

CHAPTER THIRTEEN

AT THE BACK of the club there was an old rickety wooden porch that looked out on the ocean. Off to the right JeriLee could see the Santa Monica Pier and overhead the landing lights of the jet planes as they turned over the water and headed for the airport. The night air was turning cool and she pulled the terry cloth robe more tightly around her. She listened abstractedly to the muffled sound of music coming from the club.

Just one more turn and she was finished for the night. The club owners hated it but she was grateful for the California two o'clock law. In some states she worked until four in the morning, in others until daylight. She wondered vaguely if Mike would pick her up. You never knew about him. He lived in a world all his own.

She had met him the day she arrived in California almost a month ago. It was a Sunday and he'd been working in the real estate office she went to when she decided that she wanted to rent an apartment instead of staying at a motel. Besides being cheaper, she had thought it would be easier to write there than in a motel. It would be quieter and she had eight weeks of bookings in the Los Angeles area.

Tall, tanned and with his hair bleached almost white from the sun, he didn't look at all like a real estate agent. In jeans and bare feet he looked out of place seated behind the desk.

'What do you do?' he asked, beginning to fill in the information form.

'I'm a writer,' she answered.

'A writer?'

'Anything wrong with it?'

'With your body and your legs, I figured you for an actress or a dancer.'

'I do that too.'

'I got a three-month sublease I think would be perfect for you.'

'I only need it for two months.'

'I think I could talk the owner into it,' he said.

He closed the office and took her out to his car. It was a customized VW with giant balloon tires. The top was completely cut away, with a roll bar running from side to side over the middle of the car. 'This is a great place,' he said as he moved the car out of the parking lot. 'Quiet. Two minutes from the beach. Great bathroom. Even has a bidet.'

'A bidet,' she repeated. 'Sounds expensive.'

'You'll love it,' he said confidently. 'Only three hundred a month. A French lady fixed it up.'

'Sounds too good to be true. Why did she leave it?'

'Her romance broke up. She went back to France.'

The bedroom was small, as was the living room, and the kitchen was little more than a closet. But he was right about the bathroom. By far the biggest room in the apartment, it had a shower stall, sunken tub, two sinks and a bidet.

'What do you think?' he asked.

'It's small,' she said.

'Great for a writer. You alone?'

'Yes.'

'You don't need anything bigger then.'

'But I only want it for two months.'

'No problem. Give me a check for two months plus seventy-five dollars cleaning charges and you can move in this afternoon.'

'Okay,' she said, taking her checkbook from her purse. 'Who do I make the check out to?'

'Me,' he said. 'It's my place.' He put his hand in his pocket and took out a small linen tobacco pouch tied with string. With his other hand he pulled out a pack of Zig Zag cigarette papers. 'Do you smoke?' he asked.

She nodded silently, watching him roll the joint expertly with one hand. From his back pocket he took out a wooden match and struck it along the side of his jeans. He lit the joint carefully and held it out to her.

'Two tokes of this and you're away,' he said. 'Got it straight from Mexico.'

She took a deep hit. He was right.

'Sit down,' he said. 'It'll only take me ten minutes to get my shit together and put it in the car. Then we'll go and pick up your stuff.'

'What about the office? Don't you have to go back?'

'I only work there Sundays because the owner likes to go

fishing. Besides I did all the business I have to do today.'

'Where do you work the rest of the week?'

'I don't. Gave it up when I got out of the army. Ruins your sex life and gives you ulcers.'

'What do you live on then?' she asked.

'This apartment. It's enough to keep me.'

'Where do you stay when you're not here?'

'I have friends,' he said. 'Never have trouble crashing someplace. It's amazing how many people are just looking for company and someone to talk to.'

She took the cigarette from him while he went into the bedroom to get his things. She took another drag. He was probably right. Dropping out was a way to go. And he didn't look as if he was suffering from it.

He was back in a few minutes with an olive-green duffle bag only half full. 'Ready?' he asked.

'Good grass always makes me thirsty,' she said.

'I'd offer you a glass of wine, but there isn't any.'

She didn't speak.

'There's a liquor store down the block,' he added. 'I can run down there and get a bottle.'

'That's a good idea.'

'But I haven't any cash,' he said without embarrassment.

She opened her purse and took out two dollars. 'That enough?'

He grinned. 'This is California. I'll get two bottles.'

They smoked, drank and balled through the afternoon, and when night came they went to her motel and got her things so that she could move in. But he didn't move out.

She awakened early the next morning with the sunlight streaming into the room. The bed beside her was empty. She hadn't heard him leave.

In the small kitchen she found a small kettle which she filled with water and put on the stove to heat. She opened the closet door but couldn't find anything but two lonely tea bags. She took one down and placed it in a cup. It would have to do.

She went back into the bedroom and began to unpack. She was setting up the portable typewriter on a table near the window when he returned.

He came into the room, a bag of groceries in his arms. 'You're up,' he said, surprise in his voice.

'Yes.'

'I thought you could use some groceries,' he said, crossing the room to the small kitchen and placing the large bag on the table.

'Did you get some coffee?' she asked. 'I couldn't find any.'

He began to empty the bag. Eggs, butter, bacon, bread, orange juice, milk. Finally he held up a jar. 'Instant okay?'

'That's fine.'

'I don't drink it myself. Caffeine is bad for you.'

'I can't get moving in the morning without it,' she said.

'Why don't you finish whatever you're doing?' he suggested. 'I'll make breakfast.'

She stood there hesitantly.

'I'm a good cook,' he said quickly.

She smiled. 'Okay.'

'Hungry?'

'Starved.'

The water in the kettle began to boil. Quickly he made a cup of coffee and handed it to her. 'That should help,' he said. 'I'll have breakfast in a jiffy.'

By the time she had finished setting up her work table with all her papers he called her.

She looked down at the table approvingly. He had set it very attractively with green placemats and white plates.

He gestured to the seat near the window. 'You sit over there.' He placed three eggs and six slices of bacon on each of their plates. Then he opened the oven door and took out the warm toast. 'Okay?' he asked, sitting down.

'Beautiful,' she said, picking up her orange juice.

'Coffee now?'

She nodded.

'By the way, how'd you pay for this?' she asked. 'I thought you didn't have any money.'

'I didn't, but the market always gives me credit when I have a boarder.'

She was silent for a moment. 'Do you do this often?'

'It all depends on who rents the place,' he said. 'I don't rent to gays.'

'Only girls?'

He grinned. 'Preferably. Once or twice I let it to couples. But they usually don't stay too long. It's really too small for them.'

She finished her food and drained her cup. Quickly he was on his feet, bringing her more coffee. She looked up at him and smiled. 'You do give good service.'

He returned her smile. 'I try. And when I find a good tenant I try even harder.'

'What other services do you provide?'

'Everything – laundry, housecleaning, chauffeuring. You don't have to rent a car with me around. I'm always available.'

'What do you do when your tenant's friends come over?'

'I'm very discreet,' he said. 'I disappear.'

'I work at home during the days.'

'That's fine with me.'

'I work outside nights.'

'Are you trying to tell me you're a hooker?'

'No.' She laughed.

'I don't understand you then.'

'I begin work over at the Rosebud on Airport Boulevard tonight. I have eight weeks of bookings around L.A.'

There was an expression of shock in his voice. 'But that's a topless joint!'

She laughed again. 'I told you I was a dancer.'

'But, the typewriter.' He sounded confused.

'I told you I was a writer too,' she said.

'What else do you do?'

'I used to act,' she said. 'As a matter of fact, I thought I might check into what's going on while I'm out here.'

'Business stinks,' he said. 'I have friends who are in it. The only work around is in pornos.'

'You never can tell,' she said. 'And since I'm out here, it won't cost anything.'

'I have a friend who's an agent,' he said. 'Maybe he can help you. Would you like to meet him?'

'I can talk to him,' she said.

'I'll fix it up.'

She sipped at her coffee. 'I'll have to rent a car. Do you know a place where I can get one for a decent price?'

'I told you chauffeuring was part of the service,' he said. 'All you pay for is the gas.'

She looked up at him without speaking.

He smiled suddenly. 'Okay. I got the message.'

'It's nothing personal,' she said. 'I'm just used to being alone.'

'I dig that,' he said. 'But look at it this way. Why go through the hassle of having to do everything yourself? From what I hear, you're going to be a very busy lady. Working day and night besides all the other shit you want to get into. Why don't you give the service a try for a week? If it don't work out, you can drop it. There'll be no hard feelings.'

She thought for a moment. In a peculiar way it made sense. 'Okay,' she said finally. 'How much extra does it cost?'

A hurt tone came into his voice. 'I told you there was no charge. The only thing you pick up is the expenses and the most expensive thing about me is orange juice. I drink three quarts a day.'

She laughed. 'I guess I can afford that.' She got to her feet. 'I'll finish straightening up my things and then I'm going back to sleep. I like to be in good shape for the first night on a new job.'

'What would you like for lunch?'

'No lunch.'

'Dinner then?'

'It'll have to be early,' she said. 'Six o'clock. I have to be on the job at eight.'

'Okay. What do you want to eat?'

'Make it steak, tender and rare.'

She went into the bedroom and closed the door behind her. She drew the drapes, darkening the room, then popped a Valium 10 and stretched out on the bed.

She felt the tranquilizer taking hold. Maybe it would work. She was always so wound up running around that she almost never had time to really rest. Walter had once said there was nothing like having a houseboy to take care of one. He could very well be right.

She felt herself sinking into sleep. Then another thought ran through her mind. Licia. She had promised to call her as soon as she found a place. She tried to rouse herself but the pill had taken too strong a hold. She gave herself up to the quiet. There would be time to call Licia between turns at the club.

CHAPTER FOURTEEN

THE FOG was beginning to obscure the lights of the Santa Monica Pier. In another few minutes they would be completely gone. The door opened behind her.

'Five minutes, Jane,' the manager said.

She threw her cigarette over the railing and went into the club. 'Mike show up yet?' she asked the manager, who followed her into the dressing room.

'I haven't seen him.'

He watched while she checked her makeup. Quickly she brushed a little rouge around her nipples and plucked them to make them more prominent. 'A little coke'll really get them up there,' he said.

She grinned at him in the mirror. 'It's too expensive to waste like that. You don't pay me enough.'

He laughed. 'I got a little stash. I'd be willing to put it on for you for free.'

She laughed with him. 'I'll bet.' She turned toward him. 'How do I look?'

He nodded without speaking.

'Anything wrong?' she asked.

He shook his head.

'What is it then?'

'I just got word from the owners. We're going bottomless next week.'

'Total?' she asked.

'No. The girls will still wear pubic pasties.'

'Hell,' she said in a disgusted voice. 'When do we start giving them fuck shows?'

'Don't be like that, Jane,' he said. 'You know our business has gone to hell. Almost all the clubs around have gone bottomless. We held out as long as we could.'

'Good luck,' she said. 'I'm moving on to Zingara's in the valley next week.'

'Same management, same policy,' he said.

'I got a firm booking.'

He was silent for a moment. 'Not if you don't show your ass.'

'They can talk to the booking agent about that.'

'They already did,' he said. 'He agreed to an extra forty bucks a week.'

She was silent.

'Don't be a fool, Jane,' he said. 'Forty bucks is forty bucks. The management likes you and so do the customers. What's a little skin more or less between friends? Don't ruin a good thing.'

Suddenly she could feel the weariness seeping through her. 'I need a pop,' she said. She took her handbag from the locked drawer of the dressing table, rummaged through it and came out with a yellow net-covered ampule. Holding it under her nose, she crushed it between her thumb and forefinger.

She sniffed deeply, and felt the rush of heat from the amyl nitrite flood her brain. She took another deep sniff, then dropped the broken ampule into the wastebasket. The first wave of heat had gone, leaving her up and somehow stronger. 'I do a hell of an act with an executive-size vibrator,' she said.

He smiled. 'We can't go that far but I'll be glad to give you a private audition.'

She laughed. 'I'll bet.' Then she turned serious. 'I don't suppose I have any choice, do I?'

'Not if you want to work for us.'

She thought for a moment. The management that controlled this club also controlled the other clubs she had been booked into. For her that represented eight weeks' work. By the time she found replacement bookings the two months would be gone, along with the money she had managed to put together during the last six months. In addition she wouldn't have the chance to follow up on the contacts she was trying to make while she was on the Coast. The gent Mike had introduced her to thought he might get something for her. Finally she nodded. 'Okay.'

He smiled. 'Smart girl. I'll let the boys know. I wouldn't be surprised if they don't hold you over on the whole circuit.'

She watched him leave the dressing room then turned back to the mirror. She still looked good. No way could they take her for twenty-eight, but then there was no way they could take her for twenty-three either. The body was still firm, but the lines were beginning to show in her face. Still, the one place she really felt age was inside her head.

The music pounded at her from the four speakers. She was dancing on the tiny platform behind the bar – the lead spot. There was another girl on the platform in the back of the room but the real action was at the bar.

As she moved she let her eyes wander down the bar. Mike was pushing his way in and there was a man following him. Although she couldn't remember his name, she recognized him as a producer she had met at the agent's office. He made motorcycle pictures – cheap action quickies, as the trade called them. She wondered why he was with Mike.

Mike held up his usual glass of orange juice in a gesture of recognition. She nodded and smiled. The timing mechanism in her head told her that she had about five minutes left of her turn. Time enough to give the producer something to stare at. She let herself get into the music and go.

She was sipping an iced tea and vodka when they came into the dressing room.

'This is Mr Ansbach,' Mike said.

Ansbach held out his hand. 'We met at the Gross office.'

'I remember,' she said, shaking his hand.

'You really can dance.'

'Thank you.'

'I mean it. Really dance. Not just shake your tits and ass.'

'Thank you,' she repeated.

'Mr Ansbach stopped at the apartment,' Mike explained. 'He said he had to see you right away. I thought you wouldn't mind if I brought him over.'

'I don't mind.'

'I'm glad now I did come,' Ansbach said. 'I was interested in one of your story ideas. Gross gave me several of them to read.'

'Which one?' she asked.

'The one about the dancer in a sleazy club in Gary who gets ripped off by a gang of bike riders.'

She nodded. 'Those things happen. And I know the girl it happened to. It was pretty hairy. She wound up in a hospital for six weeks.'

'I know they do, but for the movie we have to give it an upbeat ending.'

She didn't answer.

'Now that I've seen you dance, I got another idea. Maybe you can do the part. Mike told me you were an actress too. If you can act half as good as you write and dance, we're home free.'

'I'm locked in on the circuit for another eight weeks.'

'That's okay,' Ansbach said quickly. 'We'll need that much time to get the script ready.'

'I'll need more time than that to write it. It was just a story idea.'

'You don't have to write it. I have writers who know how I work and can get it together in no time.'

'Did you talk to Gross about it?'

He nodded. 'He tried to call you but there was no answer, so I got your address from him and decided to give you a try myself.'

'How much are we talking about?' she asked.

'Not much. We haven't got big money. Ten-day shooting schedules. Non-union crews. All location, no sets.'

'I understand that.'

'Two hundred fifty dollars and screen credit for the original story. If we decide you're right for the part, and I don't see why you're not, three seventy-five a week, two-week guarantee.'

She was silent.

'It's not much money,' he said quickly. 'But it's a beginning. You got to start somewhere, Miss Randolph.'

'Can I talk to Gross about it?'

'Of course. But try to get back to me tomorrow. I'm committed to start a picture by the end of next month and if it's not yours I'll have to set another.'

'I'll get back to you,' she said.

He held out his hand. 'Very nice meeting you, Miss Randolph. You're a very talented young lady. I hope we can work together.'

'Thank you, Mr Ansbach.'

She watched the door close behind him, then turned to Mike. 'What do you think?'

'Could be.'

'You don't sound up about him.'

'He's a weasel. Just get your money up front whatever you do.'

'I'll rely on Gross to take care of that.' She turned back to the mirror and began to cream her face. 'I won't be long,' she said.

He looked at her reflection in the mirror. 'The word on the beach is that the club is going total next week.'

'News travels fast.'

'Going along with them?'

'Do I have a choice?'

He was silent for a moment. 'You're a strange lady. I really don't understand you. What's so important about making all that bread?'

'Try living without it.'

'I don't need that much.'

'You're not a woman. You can turn it on any time you want. It's not that easy for me. I've been without and I know what it's like.'

'Still goin' to do it if you get the picture?'

She nodded.

He got to his feet. 'I'm goin' to try and talk the bartender into giving me another orange juice.'

'Okay.' She thought as she removed the rest of the cream from her face that he was acting strange, not at all like himself.

But she didn't know why until he stopped the car in front of the apartment. When he made no move to get out she turned to look at him. 'Aren't you coming in?'

'I'm crashing somewhere else tonight.'

'Anything wrong?'

'You have a friend visiting you.'

He put the Volks into gear and drove off before she could ask another question. She turned and walked up to the house.

Licia was waiting for her in the living room.

CHAPTER FIFTEEN

LICIA'S VOICE was gentle and concerned. 'You okay, baby?'

JeriLee closed the door and met Licia's eyes. 'I'm okay.'

Licia kissed her cheek, her lips soft against JeriLee's face. 'I was worried about you. You been out here over two weeks and I didn't hear nothin'.'

'I was working.' JeriLee went into the kitchen, with Licia following. She took out a container of orange juice. 'Want a drink?'

Licia gestured at the four containers of orange juice. ''Bout time you got smart. That stuff's better than what you been drinking.'

JeriLee filled a glass. 'It's not mine. It's Mike's. He's a juice freak like you.'

JeriLee took out the pitcher of iced tea and made herself a drink. 'That stud livin' here with you?' Licia asked.

'Yes,' she answered flatly.

'Serious stuff?'

'No.'

'Then what's he doin' here?'

'He's the landlord.' JeriLee walked back into the living room, kicked off her shoes, and sank into the couch. 'He makes it easy. He drives, cooks, cleans.'

Licia sat in the chair opposite her. 'Fucks too?'

JeriLee didn't answer.

Licia reached for a cigarette, then stopped and looked at JeriLee. 'Got a joint?'

As she began to roll the joint, she noticed that her hands were shaking. There was no reason for her to be jumpy. Licia hadn't changed, she hadn't changed, they were still the same people they had been when they were last together. The grass would help. It would take the edge off. She rolled a bomber big enough to put them both way up there. Carefully she licked the paper, sealed the cigarette and went back into the living room.

Licia had her suitcase open on the couch. She held out a red velvet Cartier box to JeriLee. 'I brought you a present,' she said. 'Open it.'

Inside, JeriLee found a long rope of oval jade beads.

'Do you like it?' Licia asked anxiously.

'It's beautiful. But you shouldn't have done it.'

Licia smiled. 'Let me put it on you.'

She took the necklace and placed it over JeriLee's head. After a moment she nodded. 'Look at yourself in the mirror.'

She followed JeriLee into the bedroom. The jade was warm against her skin. JeriLee met Licia's gaze in the mirror. 'Why, Licia?'

Licia moved closer, placing her cheek against JeriLee's. Her lips brushed against her hair. 'Because I love you and missed you.'

JeriLee was silent.

Gently Licia turned her around and kissed her on the mouth. 'I missed you so much, baby,' she murmured. 'You can't know how much I wanted to hold you and kiss you and make love to you.'

Suddenly JeriLee felt the tears coming to her eyes and in a moment she was sobbing almost hysterically. Tenderly Licia drew her head down to her breast. 'There, baby, there,' she said soothingly. 'I understand.'

She led JeriLee back into the living room and picked up the joint. She lit it, took a deep toke, then handed it to JeriLee. 'Take a good hit,' she said. 'You'll feel better.'

JeriLee took the smoke deep into her lungs. The grass was good. Mike was right. He got nothing but the best. She took another hit and felt the sudden easing of the tensions. She dabbed at her eyes with a Kleenex. 'I don't get it,' she said in a puzzled voice. 'I go up and down like a yoyo.'

Licia took the joint from her and sucked on it. Her eyes watched JeriLee thoughtfully. 'You've been workin' hard, honey. You can't burn it at both ends without paying for it.'

'I have to, Licia, if I don't want to stay in this business until I shake my tits down to my knees.'

'You're a long way from that,' Licia said.

'It doesn't feel like that at three in the morning after you've done six turns.'

'It's not a bad rap, and the money is good,' Licia said, passing the joint back to JeriLee. 'Who was that little man here with the stud when I came in?'

'He's a producer. He's interested in buying one of my stories for a film. I might even play in it.'

'Is he legit?'

'My agent says so.'

Licia was surprised. 'You have an agent? You have been busy. How did you get to him?'

'Through Mike. He knows everybody.'

'What does Mike do?'

'Nothing.' She smiled. 'He lives off this apartment.'

There was a faint note of resentment in Licia's voice. 'He's a pimp.'

'That's not fair. You don't even know him.'

'Maybe, but where I come from, a man don't work, he's a pimp.'

JeriLee was silent.

Licia took the joint from JeriLee and put it in an ashtray. 'I'm not hitting on you, honey,' she said, drawing JeriLee to her. 'I'm not holding Mike against you. I know what girls need. Even I can dig a good hard cock once in a while. But I never forget what they really want. There ain't a man in the world who won't put you down if he has the chance.'

JeriLee was suddenly weary. She felt the energy drain from her. 'Mike isn't like that,' she said.

'We won't talk no more about it,' Licia said soothingly. 'You're wiped out. You go to bed and get a good night's rest. We got the next few days to catch up on our talk.'

'How long can you stay?'

'I got a week. Fred's working in Seattle. I said I'd meet him in Frisco.'

JeriLee didn't speak.

'I thought it would be nice if you could get some time off. Maybe we could go somewhere and catch up on our rest. I've been going at it pretty hard too.'

JeriLee shook her head doubtfully. 'I don't know.'

'We'll see. Now you go off to bed before you fall on your face.'

'What about you?'

'I'll finish unpacking first. I won't be too long.'

Licia watching the door close, was annoyed with herself. She should have known better than to let JeriLee get this far away from her. Especially here where the things JeriLee really wanted were at the tips of her fingers.

She looked around the small apartment. After a moment she had made up her mind. Tomorrow she would look for a more comfortable apartment for JeriLee. Something with enough room for both of them.

The sooner she got JeriLee out of here the better. She could no longer leave JeriLee on her own as much as she had. No matter how much it screwed up her own life, she would have to find a way to bring her back to New York.

CHAPTER SIXTEEN

LICIA AND JERILEE came out of the dust-covered aluminum camper into the bright sunlight. JeriLee's face was covered with carefully applied smeared dirt and blood.

The A.D. peered at JeriLee's face anxiously and called to the makeup man. 'I think we can use a little more gore. And rough up the bike suit a bit.'

'Where are they shooting now?' JeriLee asked.

'They're on the road. They should be here in about fifteen minutes. They better,' he muttered, scanning the sky. 'Or we're going to lose the light.'

JeriLee followed the makeup man to a small table set under a tree. A wooden crate served as a seat. The makeup man went to work on her face and then with a small razor blade made several cuts and nicks in her bike suit.

Just as he finished with JeriLee they heard the roar of motors. A moment later the big black Harley Davidson screeched up the ramp past the camera. Behind through a cloud of dust came the pursuing souped-up beach buggy. As it sped past the camera they heard the shrill whistle of the A.D. and the director's shouted 'Cut!'

The motors stopped and the crew immediately began resetting the cameras. The sun was beginning to slide slowly down the sky toward the ocean and they worked feverishly to gain time against the dying light.

The stunt driver on the bike flipped up his visor. He took a can of beer from the outstretched hand of one of the crew and walked to the edge of the platform that hung out over the ocean.

'Is he really going over it?' Licia asked JeriLee.

JeriLee nodded.

'That's a seventy-foot fall.'

'That's his business.'

'It's not my kind of business,' Licia said.

The director came up with the driver of the dune buggy, who was wearing a long blond wig and black vinyl bike suit exactly like JeriLee's.

'You know what you have to do?' the director asked the stunt man.

'Yeah, the minute Tom goes over the cliff I get out of the car and JeriLee gets in.'

'It has to be fast,' the director said. 'We've only got one camera to work with. It will pan out after Tom, then back to the car. The other camera will pick up his fall. You got maybe thirty seconds, no more.'

The stunt man nodded. 'Okay.'

The director turned to JeriLee. 'Once you're in the car wait for my signal before getting out. Then you walk to the edge and look down. Take a long beat then turn and walk slowly along the cliff toward the cops who will be approaching you. I'm going to try to catch you in silhouette against the setting sun.'

JeriLee nodded.

'We'll be ready in five minutes,' the director said. 'They're getting the shot of the patrol car coming on the ramp now.'

'How are you holding up, honey?' Licia asked.

'Okay.'

'You look tired. It's been a long day.' She took a pill from her bag. 'Better take this. It'll keep you going.'

'It'll also keep me up half the night.'

'Don't worry about it,' Licia said. 'We'll get you to sleep. This is the last scene in the movie and I don't want you to look wasted.'

JeriLee took the red and swallowed it with a swig of water from the canteen. She felt the instant burst of energy. Her eyes began to shine.

'Feel better, honey?' Licia asked.

'Much better.' JeriLee laughed thin and high. 'I can go another ten hours.'

It was dark when she awoke. There was the faint hum of voices through the closed door to the living room. Her mouth was dry and her tongue felt swollen. She got out of bed and went into the bathroom. Thirstily she drank a glass of water, then brushed her teeth vigorously to get the brackish taste from her mouth. She put on the terry cloth robe hanging on the door and went out into the living room.

The voices were coming from the television set. Licia looked up from her chair.

'What time is it?' JeriLee asked.

'Eleven o'clock.'

'I told you to wake me at eight. I was due at the club at nine.'

'It's okay. When I saw how deep you were sleepin', I called the club and told them you were sick.'

'It's not okay. They know I was making the picture. They'll figure I didn't want to show up.'

'Then screw 'em. You can get plenty of jobs where you can show your ass.'

'You know better than that. This is a good club. Most of the places are hustlers' joints.'

'Calm down, honey,' Licia said soothingly. 'Let me make you a cup of tea. You can't keep this up or you're goin' to collapse.'

'I got to. I have to keep working.'

'Do you? You've been at it steady for about eight months now. You gotta have some money in the bank.'

JeriLee's eyes fell. 'It costs money to live.'

'I know it does, honey, but you only got into this to get enough money to write. You must have enough now to keep you while you get back to work on that play you want to do.'

JeriLee was silent.

'Face it, baby,' Licia said. 'Writin' motorcycle pictures ain't whut you started out to do. An' you didn't even write that. They just took your idea and turned it around to suit themselves. You didn't write no sex and sadism story but that's what they made out of it.'

JeriLee still didn't answer.

'You don't belong out here,' Licia said. 'You'll only wind up trapped in all this shit an' never write the kind of thing you really want to do.'

'At least I got paid for what I wrote,' JeriLee said defensively. 'And they talk to me. That's more than I get back East. Maybe this is the beginning of something.'

'It's the beginning all right,' Licia said. 'The beginning of the end. Nobody ever makes it out of these pictures. There's only one way to go after this – down, into straight pornos.'

'What makes you such an expert all of a sudden?'

'I didn't just sit here while you were out shootin' this movie. I did a lot of checking on my own. What you made is a double- or triple-bill drive-in movie that nobody watches anyway. The only reason they go to the drive-ins is for hamburgers, hot dogs and screwing.'

'Gross says that he can get me a few more pictures after this. He says Ansbach is happy with the film.'

'But they'll be the same kind of pictures.'

'I don't know.'

'You'll see. It'll be like the clubs. Each time you'll have to take off a little more. Next thing, fuck shows.'

JeriLee was silent. She knew that a lot of what Licia said made sense.

'I'm not pushin' you, honey,' Licia said earnestly, taking her hand. 'But someday JeriLee Randall will want to come back and by that time it may be too late. Jane Randolph will have taken over for good.'

'I need a drink,' JeriLee said.

'Don't drink. Take a Librium.'

'I took two before I went to sleep.'

'Take another. A drink will only charge you up. What you need is more sleep.' She rose from the couch. 'I'll get it for you.'

JeriLee took the pill with a swallow of water, then Licia pushed her gently back onto the couch. 'Now you just sit there and relax while I fix a nice bath for you. After that you go back to bed and I don't want to hear a sound out of you until morning.'

JeriLee took Licia's hand and squeezed it. 'I don't know how I'd have gotten through the last few weeks without you,' she said gratefully.

'I love you, honey. I want to take care of you.'

The tranquilizer wasn't working. Restlessly JeriLee sat up in bed and turned on the light.

The bedroom door opened. 'You okay?' Licia asked.

'I can't sleep.'

Licia sat down on the edge of the bed. 'You need a vacation. A change of scenery.'

JeriLee started to laugh.

'What you laughin' at, honey?'

'Look who's talking? When's the last time you ever took a vacation? Even out here, you're always on the telephone running your business.'

'There's a difference. I'm doin' what I want to do. You're shootin' off in so many different directions, you don't know what you want anymore.'

'I know what I want. I want to write.'

'Then do it.' Licia paused for a moment. 'If it's money that's holdin' you up, forget it. I got enough money to let you do what you want.'

'I don't want your money. You've done more than enough already.'

'You're being childish.'

'I'm not,' JeriLee answered stubbornly. 'It's important that I take care of myself.'

'You wouldn't feel like that if I were a man, would you?'

Licia's sudden coolness took JeriLee by surprise. 'What makes you say that?'

'It's the truth, isn't it? It's okay for a man to support you but you can't accept it from another woman.'

'That's not true.'

'Would you give the same answer to that stud if he offered?' Licia asked. 'I'll bet you wouldn't. You'd fall down on your knees and suck his cock in gratitude.'

'Don't say that, Licia. You know better. If that was what I wanted I could have had it a long time ago. It doesn't make any difference whether it's a woman or a man. I still have to make it on my own.'

Licia laughed harshly. 'You talk a lot about the truth but you don't face it, honey. Why did you call me when you had no place else to go? Because you knew in your secret little heart that I wanted to ball you. And that was okay if we kept it on an airy fairy level but now we're down to the gut and you don't like that. Why don't you come out of the closet, baby, and admit what you are? You're no different than me. You want cunt just as much as I do.'

JeriLee's eyes were wide and staring. With trembling hands she reached for a cigarette. Licia took it from her and put it in the ashtray.

'You'll wind up setting fire to the bed,' she said. As she removed her robe, her honey-colored skin shone in the glow of the lamp. Gently she drew JeriLee's face to her breasts. Her voice was husky as she spoke. 'Here, baby,' she said softly. 'Mother knows what you want. Mother knows what you need. Let Mother take care of you.'

JeriLee closed her eyes and inhaled Licia's warm musky smell. She wanted to sink into the safety of Licia's arms, but she suddenly knew that she could not.

What Licia offered was no different than what men had offered. Sex was still the currency of payment. The fact that she was a woman didn't make it a fair trade item. Freedom was the right to be yourself. It was not something that could be bought and paid for. It was earned by being honest with yourself, whether or not you liked what you saw.

She pulled away from Licia and looked into her eyes. 'You were right,' she said. 'I was not being honest. Not with myself and not with you. I'm sorry.'

Licia didn't speak.

'I'm grateful for what you've done,' JeriLee said. 'I want to be your friend. And I want to make love to you and have you make love to me because I enjoy it. Maybe more than any other kind I know. But I'm not in love with you any more than I am with anyone else. Maybe I'm not capable of love in the same way other people are. All I know is that I don't want to own anybody and I don't want anybody to own me. I have to be free.'

Licia's voice was dull with pain. 'Even if it means being alone?'

JeriLee looked at her for a long moment, then nodded slowly.

Licia's eyes filled with tears. And this time it was JeriLee who drew the woman's head to her breast and comforted her.

CHAPTER SEVENTEEN

MARC GROSS ASSOCIATES consisted of one harried secretary and an answering service. Gross himself was a young man who had worked for several of the big agencies before striking out on his own. He drove a Lincoln Continental on which payments were always two months behind and was given to continually dropping names and talking about the big deals that were always pending. Despite it all, he was a likeable young man and did the best he could for the clients who happened to drift through his door. The real problem was that the most promising talent was always grabbed up by the more established agencies while he had to make do with the hopefuls.

As JeriLee came into the office he got to his feet, a genuine smile on his face. She was one of his few working clients. 'No calls while I'm talking with Miss Randolph,' he told his secretary.

'We've got a lot of work to do,' he said importantly.

JeriLee nodded without speaking.

'Ansbach tells me that the film on you is sensational. I got him to promise me some clips so that we can have something to show around before the picture comes out. The idea is to lock up a few more jobs and build some continuity for you as a performer.' He stopped suddenly and stared at her. 'Was that a blond wig you wore in the picture?'

She nodded.

'I saw some stills. You should wear it all the time. Helps build the image.'

'It was all right for the part. But it's not me,' she said.

'Doesn't matter. That's what the producers want. Gives you a raunchy look.'

'A hard look you mean.'

'A matter of opinion. I call it the "I.F." look.'

'What's that?'

'Instant Fuck. Jumps right out of the pictures.'

'I'm a little too old to go the sexy blonde route.'

'Not true. You're just the right age. These days men are looking for a little more than the dumb blonde. They want a more experienced look, a woman who seems to know what they want and can give it to them. I'm setting up some interviews for you right now and I want you to wear the wig when you go to them.'

'Okay.'

'When are you going back to work in the club?'

'I start tonight.'

'Good. We got to promote that. Okay if I bring some producers over?'

She looked at him doubtfully. 'Don't you think that will frighten some of them away. I can't see the studios being crazy about that association.'

'Fuck the studios. That's not where the action is. It's the independents who are setting all the trends. The studios do nothing but try to catch up.'

'I can't see building a career on motorcycle pictures.'

'What's wrong with them? Jack Nicholson didn't do so bad. He made about four of them before *Easy Rider* and look where he is now. One of the biggies.'

She was silent.

'I know the money isn't much, but there's a lot of work in that field.'

'I don't know.'

'Ansbach wants to use you again,' he said. 'And it's not a bike picture this time.'

'What is it?'

'A story of a women's prison camp. There are a couple of good parts in it but you've got the lead if you want it.'

'Do you have the script?'

'You know how he works. The script won't be ready until he starts shooting. But here's a copy of the treatment,' he said, holding out some pages. 'While you're reading, I'll make a couple of calls.'

'You want me to read it now?'

'It's the only copy I have, and I need it. He wants me to find some other girls for him. It won't take long. It's only about twelve pages.'

She had finished reading before he was through his second telephone call. 'What do you think?' he asked.

'I don't think it's for me.'

'It's the big part.'

'It's out-and-out S. and M.'

'It's what the audiences are buying.'

'I don't like it. There's not even a pretense of a story line. Just one scene after another of girls going down on girls and girls beating up on girls.'

'That's what those prisons are like. Besides it's just a treatment. The script will be better.'

'I can't see how a film like that can do me any good. I wind up seeming to be the dike of all time.'

'You're an actress. It shouldn't be too difficult for you to get into it.'

She detected the subtle change in his voice. 'What do you mean?'

'Come on, Jane,' he said, putting on the charm. 'We're both adults. I know what you're into. I'm not exactly blind, you know.'

She didn't answer.

'I've met your friend from back East.'

She felt herself flush. 'What I do is my business,' she said shortly. 'I think it's a lousy idea and I don't want any part of it.'

'Wait a minute,' he said placatingly. 'Okay, okay. Ansbach and I thought you might go for it. There will be other things.'

'What about the story ideas I gave you?' she asked.

'I'm circulating them. I'll keep you informed.'

'Good. You can reach me at the apartment during the day. I'll be at the club at night.'

'You'll hear from me soon. I'm setting up appointments for you over at Warner and Paramount.' He followed her to the door. 'What about that screenplay you told me you were working on?'

'I'll show it to you as soon as I finish.'

'Don't forget. I got a hunch we can really break through with that one.' He kissed her cheek. 'We'll keep in touch.'

'I didn't expect you back so soon,' Licia said as JeriLee came into the apartment.

JeriLee looked at the closed suitcases standing by the door. 'You weren't going to leave without saying goodbye?'

'I don't like goodbyes any more than you do.'

JeriLee was silent for a moment. 'Where are you heading from here?'

'Chicago,' Licia said. 'I spoke to Fred. I told him everything was straightened out here. He was very nice about it. He didn't complain that I was spending too much time with you.'

The doorbell rang and JeriLee opened the door.

The man touched his cap. 'You called for a taxi, ma'am?'

She gestured toward the suitcases. When the taxi driver left, she and Licia stood looking at each other.

Licia broke the silence. 'I guess I better be goin'.'

JeriLee felt the pressure of the tears against her eyes, 'I don't want you to leave like this. I don't want you to be angry with me.'

Licia's voice was even. 'I'm not angry, honey. It's just that last night you let me know exactly where I stand. Nowhere.'

'But we can still be friends.'

Licia let a deep breath escape her lips. 'Sure, honey. But the kind of friends I want to be and the kind of friends you want us to be are two different things.' She forced a smile. 'I better get movin'. Planes don't wait.'

They moved toward each other and their lips met gently. ''Bye, baby,' Licia whispered.

They heard a sound behind them and turned to see Mike standing in the doorway. 'You leaving?' he asked.

Licia nodded and walked past him, then looked back at Mike. 'Now you look after my little girl real good. Hear?'

Mike nodded.

'Anything wrong?' Mike asked as the door closed behind Licia.

JeriLee shook her head, tears blurring her eyes. 'What brought you over just now?' she asked.

'Licia called me. She said you wanted to see me.'

Licia would do something like that. 'I can use a drink,' she said.

'Vodka and iced tea coming up,' he said quickly. He returned a moment later with the drink in his hand. He gave it to her, smiling. 'Want the service put back on?' he asked.

She nodded slowly.

'Great! I can get my shit together and be back here within an hour. Should I pick up some steaks for tonight?'

She nodded again.

'Hey, it's goin' to be fantastic. Now that I now where your

head's at, it will be even better. I got a couple of cute friends you really will dig.'

He was gone before she could answer. She started to roll a joint. Being a little bit stoned would ease the pain of feeling that she just couldn't seem to communicate with anyone.

CHAPTER EIGHTEEN

JERILEE GLANCED at her watch, then across the elegantly furnished room at Mike. It was after seven and she was due at the club at eight. Mike was standing at the bar talking to their host. She put down her vodka and tonic and went toward them. As she approached they fell silent.

'I'm sorry to interrupt, Mr Jasmin,' she apologized, 'but I have to leave for work.'

The tall gray-haired man with the deeply suntanned face smiled. 'It's quite all right. Now that we've met, you must have Mike bring you here more often.'

'Thank you.' She smiled and turned to Mike. 'If you want to stay I can call a cab.'

'No,' he said quickly. 'I was getting ready to leave myself. I'll drop you at the club.'

'I'll have Rick's bags put in your car then,' Mr Jasmin said.

After speaking briefly to one of the barmen, Jasmin returned to them. 'I'll walk you to your car,' he said.

Jasmin pointed to the pool as they stepped out on the terrace. 'We have a Sunday brunch around the pool every week,' he said. 'Lots of bright fun people. Come by if you feel like it.'

'Thank you,' JeriLee said, thinking that if they were anything like the people she had just seen they wouldn't be much fun. All the men seemed like reserved business types and the few women who were there had nothing at all to say to one another.

Surrounded by Cadillacs, Mercedeses and Continentals, Mike's VW stood out like a sore thumb. As they got to the car, two men came out of a back door, each carrying a large black valise.

'Put them in the back seat,' Mike told them.

'Thanks for the drinks, Mr Jasmin,' Mike said.

'My thanks too, Mr Jasmin,' JeriLee added.

Jasmin smiled at her. 'You're welcome. And please try to come Sunday.' He was still smiling but there was a hard edge in his voice as he said to Mike, 'Rick says to take good care of his things now.'

'I will, Mr Jasmin,' Mike said quickly. 'You tell him he's got nothing to worry about.'

As they pulled out of the driveway, JeriLee looked across at Mike. 'That was a strange cocktail party. Nobody seemed to want to talk to anybody else.'

'You know businessmen. Heavy types.'

'What does Jasmin do?'

'He's a financial man of some kind,' Mike answered. 'Usually his parties are a little better but today's was a real downer. I'm sorry I dragged you to it.'

'It's okay. I'd been at that typewriter long enough. It was good to get away.' She glanced at the black valises in the rear seat. 'What are you doing with those bags?'

'A friend of mine is going out of town for a while and I promised to keep them until he gets back. He left them at Jasmin's for me to pick up.'

'Was he there? I don't remember meeting him.'

'He was gone before we arrived.'

'Why didn't Jasmin keep the bags? He certainly has more room than you have.'

'You don't ask a man like Jasmin to do things like that. Besides, it won't be any problem. I'll just stick them up in my closet until he comes back. They won't be in your way.'

They were silent until he pulled the car into the parking lot in front of the club. 'Maybe we'll go out there for Sunday brunch like Mr Jasmin said. I think he likes you. He's not the kind of man who invites everybody.'

'We'll see,' she said noncomittally.

'It'll do you good to get out a little more. You've been inside for more than two weeks now.'

'I want to get this screenplay finished first.' She looked at him. 'Picking me up after work?'

'I'll be here.' He glanced back over his shoulder as a car pulled into the parking lot driveway behind him. 'I better get moving,' he said nervously. 'I'm blocking traffic.'

JeriLee watched him pull out of the driveway. There was something strange about him. She couldn't quite put her finger on it but she sensed a tension in him from the moment they had arrived at the Jasmin house.

The manager came rushing up to her. 'You'll have to go on first,' he said. 'Anne just called in sick.'

She smiled. 'No sweat, Jack. I'll be ready in ten minutes.'

Mike opened the door for her and she went past him into the apartment. 'Care for a drink?' he asked.

She shook her head wearily. 'I'm really bent. I had to take nine turns tonight. One of the girls didn't show up.'

'That's too much.'

'I ache all over. I think I'll take a Nembutal and really crash.'

'You do that. A good night's sleep is the best thing for you. I think I'll smoke a joint and read the papers before I come to bed.'

'Okay,' she said. The hot shower eased some of the aching in her muscles. After drying off, she pulled her terry cloth robe around her, popped two sleeping pills and went back into the living room.

Mike was sitting at a chair in front of the window. The faint sweet smell of weed hung in the air.

'I'll have a drag,' she said, taking the joint from him. She took a toke, then passed it back .'I thought you were going to read the paper,' she said.

'I got bored,' he said. 'The same old shit all the time.'

'Are you sure you're all right?' she asked.

'Me? Sure. Fine. Never better.'

She nodded as if accepting his reassurance. Whatever was wrong wasn't her business, especially if he didn't want to talk about it. 'Good night,' she said.

'Good night.'

She went into the bedroom and closed the door. She was asleep almost before she could turn off the light.

The sound of voices reached into the dark and pulled her awake. She moved sluggishly, trying to clear her head. The voices were louder now. Suddenly the bedroom door was flung open.

A man reached in and turned on the lights. His voice was harsh. 'Okay, sister, out of bed.'

For a moment it seemed like a dream. She was still groggy from the sleeping pills. 'What do you want? Who are you?' She reached for the phone. 'You better get out of here before I call the police.'

'We are the police, lady. We want to talk to you.'

She pulled the covers up around her chest. 'What about?'

'The two valises your boy friend picked up this afternoon. Where are they?'

Mike suddenly appeared in the doorway behind the policeman. 'You don't have to talk to him,' he shouted. 'Tell him you want to talk to your lawyer!'

A uniformed policeman came up behind Mike and pulled him away from the door. 'Keep your fuckin' hands off me!' Mike yelled.

JeriLee stared at the plainclothesman. 'What's all this about?'

'Your boy friend's movin' dope. This time we got him. We saw those bags come in here. We didn't see them come out.'

'This time?' she asked, bewildered.

'Third time and out. We picked him up twice before but couldn't make it stick. This time we'll tear the place apart if we have to.'

'You can't do that without a warrant!' Mike shouted.

The plainclothesman took a paper out of his pocket. 'We've got it. We would have been in here sooner but the judge didn't sign it until a half hour ago.' He turned back to JeriLee. 'Better get something on and get out of here.' He walked back into the living room, leaving the door open.

JeriLee put on her terry cloth robe and went into the living room. Surrounded by three plainclothesmen and two uniformed policemen, Mike was sitting sulkily on the couch.

The man who had spoken to her in the bedroom gestured to the men behind him. 'I'm Detective Collins, county police. Detective Millstein and Special Agent Cochran of the F.B.I. Now about those two valises?'

'You don't have to talk to him,' Mike snapped. 'You got to inform her of her rights.'

'You're a lousy lawyer, Mike,' Detective Collins said without a smile. 'That's only if you arrest someone. I haven't arrested her. Yet.'

JeriLee felt the panic rising. 'What are you arresting me for? I haven't done anything.'

'I didn't say you had, sister,' Collins said.

'Don't listen to him, Jane,' Mike said. 'He's trying to trick you.'

For the first time the F.B.I agent spoke. 'Why don't you make it easy on yourself, Mike, and tell us where the valises are? It would be a shame to mess up this nice apartment.'

Mike didn't answer.

'Might as well, Mike. You're nailed this time. We picked Rick up at the airport with two of the suitcases on him. We also picked up Jasmin early this evening and we saw you bring the suitcases here.'

Mike stared silently at the floor.

The agent turned to JeriLee. 'How about it, miss? Do you know where the suitcases are?'

'No.' She stared at Mike, who wouldn't look at her. She was beginning to get angry. How stupid she had been to believe his bullshit about not working, about how living off the apartment was enough for him. Sure it was. If he pushed a little shit on the side. She looked at the agent. 'But I think I know where they might be. There's a locked closet in the hall going into the bathroom where he keeps his personal things.'

'Do you have a key?'

'No. He has.'

The agent held out his hand to Mike. Sullenly Mike took a key from his pocket and gave it to him. The agent gave the key to the other detective. 'Let's go.'

Detective Collins took JeriLee by the arm and one of the uniformed policemen gestured to Mike. Mike got to his feet and they went through the bedroom to the narrow hallway.

The two suitcases were just inside the closet door. The detectives pulled them out and placed them flat on the bed. Collins tried to open one, then straightened up. 'It's a combination lock. Got the number, Mike?'

'No,' Mike answered. 'Why should I? I'm just minding them for a friend. I don't even know what's inside them.'

Collins laughed. 'I'll bet.' He took a small instrument from his pocket and played with the locks for a moment. He pressed the release buttons and the valises snapped open.

JeriLee stared at the neatly wrapped bricklike squares. There were twenty of them in each valise. Collins took one out, tore a corner of the paper and smelled it. He nodded, holding it out to the federal agent. 'The information was right. We can take them in and book them now.'

Collins turned to Mike and took a small white printed card from his inside coat pocket. 'This is official, Mike. I am required by law to inform you of your rights. Anything you say may be used against you in the court of law. You have the right to remain silent or to consult an attorney before speaking to the police and to have an attorney present during any questioning now or in the future.' His voice seemed to drone on interminably and at the end of his speech he turned to JeriLee. 'I'm taking you in too, sister.'

'What the hell are you arresting her for?' Mike demanded. 'You heard her. She don't know anything.'

'That's up to the judge,' Collins said. 'I got my job to do. You're under arrest. I am required by law to inform you of your rights,' he said to JeriLee, again reading from the card.

'You're making a mistake,' JeriLee said. 'I had nothing to do with this. I'm just renting the apartment from him.'

'Funny kind of renting,' Collins sneered. 'You been living here with him for almost two months now. I wish I could find a tenant like that.'

'But it's true,' JeriLee insisted. She felt the tears rising and fought to keep them down.

'You can explain that to the judge,' Collins said. 'You got five minutes to get dressed or I take you in like that.' He turned to the uniformed policeman. 'Take him out to the car, then one of you come back and help Millstein carry out the evidence.'

As the patrolmen left the room, he looked at JeriLee. 'You're not dressing, sister,' he said.

'What do you expect me to do with all of you standing here?'

Collins laughed. 'I'll put on a record. You can give us a show at the same time. Or isn't the crowd big enough for you?'

She glared at him without speaking.

'I caught your act a few times.' He grinned. 'You shake it real good. We wouldn't object to a little private show.'

Detective Millstein spoke for the first time. 'You can dress in the bathroom, miss,' he said. 'We'll wait out here.'

JeriLee nodded gratefully, still fighting back the tears. She took jeans and a shirt from the closet and some underthings from a drawer and went into the bathroom and closed the door. She splashed cold water on her face but she was still feeling drugged from the Nembutals. She had to wake herself up.

She searched frantically through the medicine cabinet for the Dexamyl. There were two left in the bottle. They would do it.

Quickly she finished dressing and ran a comb through her hair. When she came out of the bathroom Detective Millstein was the only one waiting for her.

'Where are the others?' she asked.

'On the way in,' he said. 'Ready?'

'I'll get my bag.' She took it from the top of the dresser. 'Look, you seem like a regular guy. Do I have to go in?'

He nodded.

'What are they going to do with me?'

'They'll probably let you go,' he said. 'But you'll have to come in anyway. Your boy friend was involved with a pretty big mob. And there was forty keys of grass in those bags.'

'Shit, all I did was rent an apartment. And who ever heard of asking a landlord for references?'

He laughed. 'I'm sorry, miss.'

They went outside. On the way down the steps, he stopped her. 'Don't you think you ought to lock your door, miss? You wouldn't want to get back here and find that you've been burglarized.'

CHAPTER NINETEEN

DAWN WAS BEGINNING to break as they pulled up the ramp in front of the police station. 'Shit!' Millstein cursed when he saw the crowd of reporters and the TV camera truck parked in front of the building. 'That asshole Collins couldn't wait to get his picture in the papers.'

He kept the car going past the station and down the off ramp. He circled around the block. 'How do you feel about publicity?' he asked.

'I don't like this kind.'

'I'll try to get you in the back way. Maybe they haven't covered it.' He turned the car up the street. 'You got dark glasses in that bag?'

'Yes.'

'Put them on. At least it will keep them from getting a clear shot of your face.'

She opened her bag. She put on the glasses. 'How does that look?'

He glanced at her. 'Okay. There's a newspaper on the back seat. Take it. You can hold it over your face when we go in.'

'You're a good man, Charlie Brown,' she said.

'Millstein,' he said, unsmiling. He turned the car into the parking lot in the rear of the station. There were not as many reporters as out front but they were all around the car even before he came to a stop. 'You don't get out of the car until I come around to your side and let you out,' he said.

The flashbulbs began exploding as they tried to shoot pictures through the closed windows. She held the paper up around her face until she heard the door click and the sound of his voice. 'Come on now, miss.'

He walked her rapidly to the door and she kept her face pressed into the paper. She could hear the reporters shouting.

'Come on, Jane, give us a good picture.'

'The publicity will sell out your next show.'

'Show 'em you got something else besides tits and ass!'

She heard Millstein's voice. 'Watch it. There's a step up here.'

She stumbled and almost fell but he held her up and a moment later they were through the door. 'You okay?' he asked.

She nodded.

'We'll have to walk up two flights,' he said. 'The elevator isn't running at this hour.'

'Okay, and thanks,' she said as they started up the stairs.

He smiled almost shyly. 'It's okay.' He stopped on the second landing. 'You'll have to be booked, you know. There'll be reporters in there but no photographers. You don't have to talk to them. I'll try to get you through as quickly as I can.'

They entered the large room through the back door. They were almost at the sergeant's bench before the reporters saw them. They surged toward her hurling questions. They had been well briefed. They all knew her name and where she worked. She kept her head down, not looking at any of them.

Millstein was as good as his word. He whispered across the desk to the sergeant, who nodded and gestured to a side door. Millstein led her through the door into a small room. 'The sarge is a friend of mine,' he explained. 'He'll bring the booking sheet in here away from the mob.'

'What did you say to him?' she asked.

He grinned. 'I asked him if he really wanted to help Collins make lieutenant.'

She began to laugh and suddenly the laughter caught in her throat. The pills she had taken were making her crazy. There was nothing for her to laugh at. Those windows she was looking at had bars on them. This was not a movie or a play. This was for real.

She opened her bag and began searching for her cigarettes. She was sure there had been a pack in there. Finally she looked up at Millstein. Her voice was shaking. 'Do you have a cigarette?'

Silently he fished a pack from his pocket and held it toward her. 'Ever been through this before?' he asked quietly.

She shook her head. 'No,' she said, taking a drag of the cigarette. 'It's scary. Really scary.'

He didn't speak.

'What happens now?'

'After the sergeant finishes the booking report, you turn over your valuables to the property clerk. Then we take your fingerprints and photograph. After that we take you up to the women's holding section, where a matron will search you and assign you a cell until court opens in the morning.'

'I have to stay here until then?'

He nodded.

'In the movies you see people getting out on bail or something.'

'Yes, but it takes a judge to order it.'

The sergeant came into the small room carrying a large gray-green ledger. 'Name, age, address?' he asked quickly, after seating himself at the table.

She hesitated, and looked at Millstein, who nodded. 'Jane Randolph, 11119 Montecito Way, Santa Monica, twenty-eight.'

'Okay. Collins already filled in the charge sheet,' he said to Millstein.

'What did he say?'

The sergeant read from the ledger. 'Transportation and possession of eighty kilos of marijuana with intent to sell.'

'That's not true,' JeriLee protested. 'I had nothing to do with it.'

Ignoring her outburst, the sergeant rose to his feet. 'Do you want to take her over to property or shall I call a matron?'

'I'll take her over,' Millstein said. 'We go through that door,' he said, gesturing to the other side of the room.

JeriLee followed him through the door and into a corridor. They stopped in front of an open counter window in the wall opposite the door. Millstein pressed a small bell to call the clerk.

'It's not fair,' she said. 'Collins paid no attention to what I said.'

A shirt-sleeved policeman appeared behind the counter. 'Empty your bag on the counter and take off your rings, watches and any other jewelry,' he said in a mechanical voice. 'Name and number?' he asked.

'Jane Randolph,' she answered. 'What number?'

He didn't look up from the paper. 'Every prisoner has a booking number.'

'I've got it.' Millstein gave him a slip of paper. 'It's just routine,' he said soothingly.

She opened her bag and emptied it on the counter. She slipped her watch from her wrist and put it down. The clerk began listing the items in her bag. She dragged on the cigarette and Millstein noticed the trembling of her fingers. 'Take it easy,' he said. 'I'll stay with you and try to make it as easy as I can.'

She nodded but he saw the animal-like glaze of fear in her

eyes. As if in a daze, she signed the inventory, went through the fingerprints, mug shots and body search. It wasn't until they followed the matron down the corridor to a holding cell that he saw her stiffen. The matron opened the steel-barred door.

JeriLee turned to Millstein. There was an edge of hysteria in her voice. 'Do I have to go in there?'

He looked at her for a moment. There was something about her that touched him, maybe because he was convinced that she had been telling the truth. They had been on the case for two months and this was the first time there was any suggestion that she might be involved. But Collins didn't give a damn. He was bucking for lieutenant and the district attorney was behind him all the way. Both of them were looking for a big score and didn't care who they hurt. He glanced at his watch. It was almost half past seven. The court would be open in an hour and a half.

'It's okay,' he said to the matron. 'I'll take her over to the conference room and stay with her.'

The matron was a cynical woman who believed that cops were no different than other men, especially when it came to attractive women. 'Okay, Officer,' she said in a flat voice. 'It's your sleep.'

JeriLee's knees went weak as they turned away from the cell.

The conference room was small, with a few chairs and tables and a long couch against one wall. The detective led her to the couch, sat down opposite her and held out a cigarette.

'I couldn't have gone in there. I don't know what I would have done,' she said, accepting his light.

His voice was not unsympathetic, just matter-of-fact. 'You'll have to go there sooner or later.'

'Maybe the judge will let me out.'

He was silent for a moment. She really didn't know what she was facing. The procedures were designed for delay, not speed. 'Do you have a lawyer?' he asked.

She shook her head.

'Do you know one?'

Again she shook her head.

'Then the judge will assign your case to the public defender.'

'Is that good?'

'It's better than nothing.' He hesitated. 'If you have any money, you'd be better off getting your own attorney. The D.A. will make mincemeat out of the public defender in this case. He's after a big score and he won't make any deals. What you need is a lawyer with clout. Someone the D.A. and the court will listen to.'

'I don't know anyone like that.'

He was silent for a moment. 'I do. But he's expensive.'

'How expensive?'

'I don't know.'

'I have some money. Do you think he will talk to me?'

'He might.'

'Would you call him for me?'

'I'm not allowed to do that. But I can give you his telephone number. You can reach him at home now. You're allowed one phone call.'

The matron came into the cell with her lunch tray.

JeriLee looked up at her from her cot on which she was sitting. 'What time is it?'

'Twelve o'clock,' the matron answered, placing the tray on the small table against the wall.

JeriLee looked at the sickly sandwiches. 'I'm not hungry,' she said.

'Might as well eat. Court won't open again until two o'clock. You won't hear anything before then.' She left the cell, closing the steel-barred door behind her.

It had been more than two hours since the lawyer had left her. A tall man quietly dressed in a dark suit with silver-gray hair and a florid complexion, he had listened, without comment to her story. When she had finished he asked her one question. 'Are you telling me the truth?'

She nodded.

'It's important. I don't want the D.A. springing any surprises on me.'

'It's the truth, I swear it.'

He looked at her for a moment. 'Five thousand dollars,' he said.

'What?'

'Five thousand dollars. That's my fee.'

'I haven't got that much.'

He rose from his chair. 'I'm sorry,' he said.

'That's a lot of money,' she protested, looking up at him.

'You're in a lot of trouble,' he said, returning her gaze. 'You're right in the middle of the biggest California drug bust of the year. It's not going to be easy to make the D.A. and the judge listen.'

She was silent for a moment. 'I have about thirty-five hundred in the bank,' she said. 'I can pay off the rest when I go back to to work.'

He sat down again. 'We have to get you off now. The charges must be dismissed. If they bind you over for trial and you have to go before a jury, you're dead.'

'I don't understand. I'll tell them the truth. Exactly what I told you.'

'It won't matter. You have to understand the rednecks they have on jury panels out here. The minute they hear the kind of work you do, they'll decide you're guilty. The way they think, only an immoral woman will dance naked in public.'

'What's the difference between the men who come into the club and watch me and the jury?'

'The same man who came into the club would go against you in the jury box.'

'Then what are we going to do?'

'Let me think,' he said. 'Do you have your checkbook with you?'

'It's down in the police property room.'

When he left a few minutes later he had her check for thirty-five hundred dollars as well as a signed note for fifteen hundred dollars. 'Try to relax,' he said. 'You'll be hearing from me soon.'

It was the middle of the afternoon by the time he reappeared.

'What happened, Mr Coldwell?' JeriLee asked after the conference room door had been locked behind them.

'I got it all worked out with the D.A.,' he said. 'He agreed to separate your case from the others and to dismiss charges if you will agree to act as a material witness for the prosecution.'

'What does it mean?'

'It means you're free. All you have to do is appear at the trial and tell your story exactly as you told it to me.'

'I can walk out of here right now?'

'In a few minutes. First you have to appear before the judge who will issue the necessary order.'

'What are we waiting for then?'

'Okay,' he said. 'Just remember one thing. Whatever the judge asks you to do, you agree, all right?'

She nodded.

He knocked at the door. 'Can Miss Randolph wait here for a

moment while I go down to the D.A.'s office and let him know we're ready to appear in court?' he asked the matron.

She looked at JeriLee doubtfully.

'It won't be more than a minute, I promise you,' he said quickly. 'They're dropping the charges against her and I think she's spent enough time in the cell.'

'Okay. But don't be long. It's against regulations.'

'I appreciate it.' The attorney glanced at JeriLee. 'Be right back.'

JeriLee smiled. For the first time in twelve hours she didn't have a feeling of dread hanging over her.

CHAPTER TWENTY

COLDWELL HAD TAKEN JeriLee out through the back entrance and put her in a cab. 'The reporters will have your home address within a day or two,' he said. 'If you don't want to be bothered by them, my advice is to get out of there as soon as you can.'

'I can't stay there anyway,' she said. 'Mike is my landlord. What's going to happen to him now?'

'The judge set one hundred thousand dollars bail for each of them. My guess is that they'll all be out before nightfall.'

'Mike hasn't got that kind of money.'

'He's concerned with some big people. They take care of their own.'

She was silent. It was still hard for her to believe.

'You keep in touch with me,' Coldwell said. 'When you move let me know where I can reach you.'

'Okay,' she said.

It was after five when she got to the apartment. As she came up the steps, she noticed that the door was open. That was surprising. She remembered distinctly having locked it when Millstein had reminded her. Slowly she went inside.

The living room was a shambles. Her portable typewriter had been smashed. There were crumpled sheets of paper scattered around the room, and in the fireplace was a pile of ashes.

She picked up a sheet of paper from the floor. It was blank. A wave of fear came over her. She rushed to the fireplace and pulled out some paper that hadn't been entirely consumed by the fire.

She had been right. All the work she had done in the last few weeks, the screenplay she had almost finished, had been destroyed – burned in the fireplace.

Dully she rose to her feet and went into the bedroom. That room too had been overturned, the contents of the drawers and closets lay around the room in shreds. But that almost didn't matter. What did matter was the words that had been lost. The words that might never be replaced.

The tears were running down her cheeks as she went to the

bathroom. All the pills from the medicine cabinet had been strewn in the sink and tub and water run over them so that their effectiveness was destroyed. At that moment the telephone began to ring.

She picked it up in the bedroom. 'Yes,' she answered in a cracked voice.

'Jane Randolph?'

'Yes.'

'This is a friend calling to give you a little friendly advice. Get out of town. Go as far away as you can. Or the next thing you'll find broken in your apartment is you.'

'But – ' She was holding a dead phone. Whoever it was had already gone off the line. She replaced the receiver and slowly began trying to straighten up the room.

It was close to eight when she came into the club and she was almost at the dressing room door when the manager caught up to her.

'Wait a minute,' he said. 'Come down to my office.'

She followed him down to the cubbyhole that served as the office. He closed the door carefully behind him and his voice dropped to a whisper. 'I didn't expect you tonight. When did you get out?'

'This afternoon.'

'I got another girl,' he said.

'That's okay. I could use a night's rest. I'll be in tomorrow.'

'No.'

'What do you mean, Charlie?'

'I got word from outside. I have to let you go.'

'You gotta be joking.'

'No, they were very specific. You're out.'

'They have to be crazy. All that shit in the papers will do nothing but bring in business.'

'Don't you think I know it?' he wailed. 'But they control the place. If I don't do as they say, zap! I'm finished. No license.'

'Okay,' she said. 'There are other places I can work. They won't pass up the business.'

'Janey,' he said earnestly, 'I'm a lot older than you and I'm going to talk to you like a father, like an uncle. You're a nice girl but you got mixed up with some very bad people. There ain't no place in this town that's going to give you a job. My advice is to go away from here. A long way.'

'They got to you too,' she said coldly.

'There's nothing I can do. I got my own family to support. But you, you better do as I say. You hang around here and something will happen to you. I know these guys and I know what they already did to some girls who didn't listen to them. It ain't very pretty.'

'I was alone at the apartment,' she said. 'They didn't come near me.'

'You're still today's news,' he said earnestly. 'Believe me, they'll wait. Then one day when the papers have forgotten all about you they'll pay you a visit.'

'I don't believe it.'

'Believe it,' he said sincerely. 'If you were my own daughter, I couldn't give you better advice.' He opened a small desk drawer and took out an envelope. 'I owe you a day's pay,' he said. 'But you did some extra turns so I'm giving you a hundred even. Okay?'

She took the envelope without speaking.

'You take that money,' he said, 'and buy yourself a plane ticket to someplace else.'

'Sure,' she said. This hundred plus the thirty in her bag and the twenty she had in the bank after paying off the lawyer was all she had in the world. She opened the door. 'Thanks, Charlie.'

'Good luck, Janey.' What a business, he thought. If the girls weren't in one kind of trouble, it was another.

'You fucked up, Jane.' Marc Gross's voice was harsh and complaining as if what had happened to her was a reflection on him and his business. 'I had it all set for interviews at Warner, Twentieth and Paramount, but as soon as they saw the morning papers they canceled.'

'Today's papers reported that the charges against me were dropped.'

'It doesn't matter. They don't like the publicity.'

'What about the story ideas you sent out?'

'They're starting to come back. And not even by mail. They're so anxious to get rid of them they're shooting them back by special messenger.'

'What about Ansbach's prison picture. Can I still do that?'

'It's already cast. You didn't think he was going to wait for you forever?'

It had only been a few weeks, but she didn't argue. 'Okay,' she said, looking directly at him. 'Did they get to you too?'

His face flushed. 'I don't know what you're talking about.'

'I think you do,' she said evenly. 'Didn't someone call and tell you that it might be a good idea if you had nothing to do with me?'

'I get crank calls all the time. I don't pay any attention to them.'

She was silent for a moment watching him. 'I'll have my screenplay back from the typist tomorrow,' she lied. 'I'll send it in to you.'

He hesitated, then cleared his throat. 'I've been thinking about the screenplay. I'm afraid it's really not the kind of thing I can sell.'

'Why don't you just read it first, then decide?'

'I'd only be wasting your time.'

She smiled humorously. 'You're a lousy liar, Marc. But even worse, you're a lying coward.' She got to her feet. 'I'll let you know where you can send my stories when you get them all back.'

JeriLee stood on the sidewalk for a moment undecided about what do do. Then she saw the coffee shop on the corner. It was past the lunch hour rush and she found an empty booth and slipped into it. 'Just coffee,' she said when the waitress came up to her.

She was engrossed in her thoughts and for a moment didn't notice the man who took the seat opposite her. When she did look up, there was surprise in her voice. 'Detective Millstein!'

He smiled shyly. 'Coffee,' he said to the waitress.

'Are you following me?'

'Not officially,' he said.

'What do you mean?'

'I had some time off, so I thought I'd see how you were doing.' He didn't tell her that he had picked up word that she might be in big trouble.

'I'm not doing so well,' she admitted. 'My job is gone and just now I found out that my agent doesn't want to represent me anymore. And yesterday when I got home I found my apartment a wreck – my clothes torn and my manuscripts burned. Besides that I got a telephone call telling me to leave town.'

'Did you recognize the man's voice?'

'Never heard him before.'

'Why didn't you call the police?'

'Would it have done any good?'

He was silent for a moment, then shook his head. 'What are you planning to do now?'

'I don't know,' she said. 'I've got exactly a hundred and thirty-six dollars between me and the poorhouse. I'm trying to make up my mind whether to stick around here and invest it in a month's rent in some cheap place and keep trying to get some work. Or, take eighty-seven dollars and buy a plane ticket back to New York.'

'Can you get a job back there?' he asked.

She shrugged. 'I don't know. But at least nobody there wants to keep me from working. What do you think I should do?'

'Officially, I have to tell you to stay here. You gave your word to the court that you would appear as a material witness.'

'You're not following me officially, so you can tell me what you think unofficially.'

'I'll deny it if you ever quote me.'

'I won't quote you.'

He took a deep breath. 'I'd buy that ticket.'

'Do you think these men will really do what they say?'

'I don't know. But they're a very rough crowd and they might. I wouldn't like to take the chance. There's no real way we could protect you short of keeping you in jail.'

'If only I could get a few more bucks together, I'd feel better. I hate to go back broke.'

'I could lend you a few dollars. Fifty, maybe even a hundred. I wish it could be more but a cop doesn't make that much.'

'No, thanks,' she replied. 'You've done enough already. Shit,' she went on after a moment of silence, 'just when I thought I was getting it all together.'

'I'm sorry.'

'It's not your fault. If you're off duty, would it be against the rules for you to help a friend pack and then maybe take her to the airport?'

'No.'

'Would you?'

'Yes.'

Millstein watched the skycap tag her suitcases and put them on the rack. 'Gate twenty-three, ma'am,' the skycap said, taking the dollar tip. 'They're boardin' now.'

She held out her hand. 'Thanks. You're a nice man, Detective Millstein.'

'Good luck. I just hope things work out for you.'

'That makes two of us.'

'If you come back this way, give me a call.'

She didn't answer.

'You know you're still young. Why don't you find a nice young man and get married?'

'And settle down and have some kids?'

'There's nothing wrong with it,' he said defensively.

'I guess not. But it's not for me.'

'What's better, the way you're living? From hand to mouth, like an animal.'

'You're a strange man for a policeman, Detective Millstein.'

'I can't help it. I'm a Jewish father. I have a daughter almost your age and I keep thinking the same thing could happen to her.'

A sudden smile brightened her face and she kissed his cheek. 'Don't worry. It won't happen to her, because she has you for a father.'

He put his hands on her arms. 'Let me give you some money.'

'I can manage. I have friends. It will be okay.'

'Sure?'

'Sure.' With tears in her eyes she started into the terminal. When she reached the door she turned and waved.

He waved back and waited until she disappeared in the crowds. He sat behind the wheel of his car for a long time before starting the engine. He was sad in a way that he really didn't understand.

What caused girls like this to waste their lives? He wondered what would happen to her now. Chances were that he would never know. She would drop from sight and he would never hear of her again. Another loser in a world full of losers.

But he was wrong. He did hear from her again. It was a year later and he had almost forgotten her name. The letter came from Creedmore State Hospital and was written in pencil in a neat almost schoolgirlish hand.

Dear Detective Millstein,
You may not remember me. I am Jane Randolph, the girl you took to the airport last year. You were very nice and I never forgot it. You told me to give you a call, remember? I never got back to California because I had a nervous breakdown. I have been in the hospital for almost six months now and I am much better and feel perfectly able to take care of myself. The doctors are considering letting me leave here and it would be very helpful if you would be kind enough to write them a letter about me, telling them that you think I am okay and will not be a problem any more. Even if you don't write a letter, I will understand and still be grateful for your kindness to me the last time we met.

Your friend,
Jane Randolph.

Millstein thought of his wife who had died fifteen years ago, leaving him with a five-year-old daughter, and of his daughter, who was now in her third year at U.S.C. Somehow the girl Jane Randolph had reminded him of her, and perhaps that was why she had touched him so deeply.

He started to write the letter she had requested, then stopped. What was there for him to say? He didn't even know her. He crumpled the sheet and threw it into the wastepaper basket. After a long moment of debate with himself he reached for the telephone.

'Lieutenant Collins,' the harsh voice answered.

'Dan, is it okay if I take a week of my vacation now? A friend of mine is sick in a hospital in New York . . . '

CHAPTER TWENTY-ONE

THE RECEPTIONIST'S voice was impersonal. 'Patient visiting hours are five to seven p.m. daily.'

'I'm sorry,' he said. 'I just arrived from California last night. I didn't realize.'

'Who was it you wanted to see?'

'Jane Randolph.'

'Jane Randolph,' she repeated. She glanced down at a paper in front of her. 'If you'll take a seat over there. I'll get in touch with her doctor and see what we can do.'

'Thank you,' he said, taking a seat near the window from which he could see the snow-covered trees. He couldn't remember the last time he had seen snow.

He was still amazed that he was really here. He remembered what his daughter had said when he told her why he was going East. She had stared at him for a moment, then flung her arms around his neck, the tears coming to her eyes. 'You're beautiful, Daddy. Just beautiful.'

'I'm probably just an old fool. The girl must have sent letters like that to everyone she knows.'

'It doesn't matter, Daddy.' Susan had said. 'She's crying for help and you're answering. That's what matters.'

'Something in her letter got to me. I remember how frightened she was the day I met her.'

'Was she pretty?'

'In a way, I guess. Maybe underneath all that makeup she had on.'

'Were you attracted to her, Daddy?'

'What do you mean?'

'You know what I mean, Daddy.'

'Why does it always have to be something like that?' he said indignantly. 'Stop acting like a romantic child.'

She laughed aloud and kissed his cheek again. 'I'm not the romantic in the family, Daddy. You are.'

He stared at the frosting of snow outside the window. Maybe she was right after all. He was here, wasn't he?

A white-uniformed nurse stopped in front of him. 'Are you the visitor for Jane Randolph?'

He nodded, getting to his feet.

'Would you follow me, please. Dr Sloan would like to see you.'

A young redbearded man in a white coat rose from behind the desk and gripped his hand firmly. 'I'm Dr Sloan, Jane's doctor.'

'Al Millstein.'

The doctor toyed with an unlit pipe. 'Reception mentioned that you came in from California.'

Millstein nodded. 'I hope I can see her. I'm sorry I didn't know about the visiting hours.'

'That's okay. Matter of fact I'm glad you came when you did. I might have missed you otherwise. Are you related to Jane?'

'No. Just a friend.'

'Oh. Have you known her a long while?'

'Not really. Just a few days.'

'I don't understand. You knew each other only a few days and yet in all the time she's been here you're the only person she has written to or tried to get in touch with.'

'You knew about the letter?'

'We encouraged her to write. We thought we could get a line to her family that way.'

'You mean that no one's come to visit, no friends, no family?'

'That's right. As far as we know she's completely alone in the world. Until she wrote you, we had no contact with anyone that she knew.'

'Jesus.'

'Since you're here I must assume you want to help her. The first thing I have to know is exactly what your relationship with her was.'

'I'm afraid I'm going to shock you, Doctor.'

'You don't understand, Mr Millstein. In my profession one learns never to be shocked at anything. I already assumed that you had been lovers.'

Millstein laughed aloud. 'I'm sorry but you're wrong, Doctor. I only saw her twice and that was never part of it.' He saw the puzzled expression on the doctor's face and continued. 'I'm a detective with the Santa Monica police and the only contact I've had with her was as her arresting officer.'

'If that is all, why did you come?'

'I felt sorry for her. When I met her there was a very good chance they would send her to jail for something she didn't do. I couldn't stand by and let that happen. When I got her letter, I felt the same way. Something was happening to her that was beyond her control. I had to see what I could do to help.'

The doctor was silent as he filled and lit his pipe.

'She said in her letter that you were considering letting her out,' Millstein said.

'We have been. She's really done very well since she's been in here. But there were a few things still puzzling us. That's why we've been hesitating.'

'What things?'

'Before we get to that, you should know why she is in here.'

Millstein nodded silently.

'She was committed here from the East Elmwood General Hospital last September to undergo detoxification. She had a severe problem of chemical drug abuse.'

'How bad was it?'

'She was suffering from paranoia and hallucinations resulting from the combined use of various drugs such as L.S.D. and amphetamines in addition to tranquilizers, barbiturates and marijuana. Before being sent here she had a record of three arrests, two for prostitution and soliciting, one for physically attacking a man she claimed had been following and annoying her, which was, of course, not true, but a typical symptom of drug-induced psychosis. In addition she had twice attempted suicide. The first time she tried to throw herself in front of a subway car but was saved by the alertness of a subway patrolman. The second time she took an overdose of barbiturates, which was pumped from her stomach by a fire department rescue squad. It was the last arrest which led to her being sent here. The man she had attacked dropped the criminal charges against her but she was still hallucinating and she was committed to Creedmore by the examining panel at East Elmwood.'

Millstein was silent.

'Were there any signs of this problem when you knew her, Mr Millstein?' the doctor asked.

'I don't know, but then I'm not a doctor. What I did notice was that she was highly nervous and at one point very much afraid.'

'Do you know if she was on drugs then?'

'Not really. But in California we assume that all the young

people are on something. If it's not grass it's pills. If they don't overdo it we try to look the other way. Otherwise we wouldn't have jails big enough to hold them all.'

'Well, anyway, I think we have the drug problem cured, at least temporarily. We cannot know what will happen when she gets outside again.'

'You're going to release her then?'

'We'll have to. She comes up for re-evaluation by the panel in another two weeks. She'll clear it without any problems I'm sure.'

'But you're still not satisfied, are you?'

'Frankly speaking, no. I feel that we haven't gotten to the real problem, whatever it was that pushed her to this. That's why I wanted to get in touch with her friends or family. I'd feel better if I knew she had someplace to go and people who cared about her. I would want her to go into therapy.'

'And if she doesn't?'

'She could slide back. The pressures would be the same as before.'

Millstein reflected on what a fool he had been to think there was anything he could do. He should have sent the letter and forgotten about it. He wasn't God. He couldn't stop anyone from going to hell in their own way.

'Did she ever mention the name JeriLee to you?' the doctor asked.

'No, who was she?'

'She was Jane's sister. Sort of an idol, I guess. The bright child in the family, the one that got all the attention. Jane loved and hated at the same time – true sibling rivalry. Part of Jane's problem was that she wanted to be JeriLee and couldn't. By the time she realized that was what she wanted, she had gone too far in another direction and couldn't get back.'

'Did you try to locate the sister?'

'The only way we could do that was through Jane and she said JeriLee was dead.' He looked at the detective. 'We don't have the facilities for personal investigation out here.'

'You mean you don't believe her story?'

'I neither believe nor disbelieve it. I just don't know.'

'I see.' Millstein nodded slowly. 'May I see her now?'

'Of course.' He pressed a button on the desk. 'Thank you for coming in and talking to me.'

'Thank you, Doctor. I just hope I have been of some help.'

'In my business, everything helps,' the doctor said as the nurse came into the room. 'Would you please take Mr Millstein to the visitors' room and bring Jane to see him.

'One more thing, Mr Millstein. Try not to express surprise when you see Jane. Remember that she's just gone through chemical and electrical shock therapy, which tends to slow down reactions and create some temporary amnesia. The treatments have been halted now but the effects will not wear off for a few more days.'

'I'll keep it in mind, Doctor.'

The visitors' room was small but comfortable with gaily printed curtains at the windows.

She came into the room hesitantly, half hiding behind the nurse. 'Jane, here is that nice Mr Millstein come to see you,' the nurse said in a professionally jovial tone.

'Hello, Jane,' he said, forcing a smile. She was thin, much thinner than he had remembered. Her hair was long but brushed neatly and her eyes very large in her pinched face. 'It's nice to see you again.'

For a moment she looked at him without recognition. Then a light seemed to dawn in her eyes and she smiled hesitantly. 'Detective Millstein.'

'Yes.'

'My friend, Detective Millstein. My friend.' She took a step toward him, the tears coming to her eyes. 'My friend, Detective Millstein.'

'Yes, Jane. How are you?'

She took his hand and pressed it to her face. 'You've come to take me out of this place? The way you did the last time?'

He felt the lump in his throat. 'I hope so, Jane. But these things take time, you know.'

'I'm better now. You can see that, can't you? I won't do any of those foolish things anymore. I'm all cured.'

'I know that, Jane,' he said soothingly. 'You'll be out soon.'

She rested her head against his chest. 'I hope so. I don't like it here. They hurt you sometimes.'

He stroked her head slowly. 'It was for your own good. You've been a very sick girl.'

'I know I was sick. But you don't cure sick people by hurting them more.'

'It's over now,' he said reassuringly. 'Dr Sloan told me the treatments are all finished.'

'You got my letter?'

'That's why I'm here.'

'You're the only friend I have. There was no one else to write to.'

'What about JeriLee?'

A frightened look came into her eyes. 'You know about her?' she whispered.

'Yes. Dr Sloan told me about her. Why didn't you write her?'

'Didn't he tell you that she was dead?'

'Is she?'

She nodded.

'Was she nice?'

She looked up at him, her eyes shining. 'She was beautiful. Everybody loved her. Everybody wanted to take care of her. And she was so bright she could do anything she wanted. When she was around, you couldn't see anyone else. At one time we were very close, then we drifted apart and when I went looking for her it was too late. She was gone.'

'How did it happen?'

'What?'

'How did she die?'

'She committed suicide,' she whispered.

'How?'

There was a tortured look on the face. 'She took pills, fell in front of a train or jumped off a bridge,' she cried in a pain-filled voice. 'What does it matter how she died? It only matters that she's gone and I can't get her back.'

He put his arms around her shoulders as she sobbed convulsively against his chest. He could feel the thin sharp bones through the cotton dress.

'I don't want to talk about her anymore.'

'All right. We won't talk about her anymore.'

'I have to get out of here,' she said. 'If I don't I will really go crazy. You don't know what it's like in here. They don't let you do anything. It's as if we're less than animals.'

'You'll be out soon.'

'I want to go back to work. When I get out I know an agent that will get me a job dancing again.'

He remembered the typewriter in her apartment and the

scripts she told him the agent was returning to her. 'How about your writing?' he asked.

'Writing?' she asked, a puzzled look in her eyes. 'You must be mixed up. I wasn't the writer. JeriLee was.'

CHAPTER TWENTY-TWO

POLICEMEN OFTEN spend their time walking backwards through other people's lives, retracing the steps from the grave to the cradle. It was a habit Millstein had fallen into over the years.

After his talk with Jane he had gone back to Sloan's office. 'I didn't expect to see you, Mr Millstein,' the doctor said in surprise.

'You said something about not being able to carry out a complete investigation of your patients, Dr Sloan, and that you sometimes thought it would be very helpful.'

'Yes, I said that.'

'You thought that if you knew more about Jane perhaps you could do more to help her?'

'I think so.'

'I've got a week off. Would you object to my help?'

'I would be most grateful, Mr Millstein. Almost anything you can find out will be more than we know. Do you have any ideas?'

'I have some, Doctor. But I'd prefer to wait and get something firm before I go shooting my mouth off.'

'Okay. What can I do?'

'You could let me read that commitment paper on her.'

'You've got it.'

Millstein read it quickly. There wasn't much information. He looked at the doctor. 'Where would I get the details behind this?'

'You'd have to go back to the source. In this case East Elmwood General. Back of them are the courts and the police, but you'd have to get that information from East Elmwood's files.'

After leaving the hospital, he had gone back to his hotel and stretched out on the bed. The time change had finally caught up to him. When he awoke it was almost dinnertime. He looked at his watch. It would be after four o'clock in California. His daughter would be home from school by now.

Her voice was bright as she answered the phone. 'Did you see her, Daddy?' she asked.

'Yes.'

'How was she?'

He put it all in one word. 'Sad.'

There was silence at her end.

'I don't know if I can make myself clear, Susan, but it's as if she split herself in two parts and one part of her is dead.'

'Poor thing. Is there anything you can do? Was she glad to see you?'

'I don't know if I can do anything. And, yes, I think she was glad to see me. Do you know what she told me, Susan? She said that I was the only friend she had. Imagine that. And we scarcely knew each other.'

'I can't imagine anyone being so alone. I hope you can do something for her, Daddy. You will try, won't you?'

'Yes.'

'I'm very proud of you, Daddy,' she said.

The hospital was set apart from the rest of the buildings around it. Across the street was a small park, on the corner opposite a large diner with a sign advertising breakfast for sixty-five cents. He paused on the cement steps listening to the voices of the people making their way in and out of the hospital. Most of them were speaking Spanish. Not with the soft accent of the Mexican that he was used to, but still the language of the poor.

A few minutes later he was seated in front of Superintendent Poole's desk in a small office on the ninth floor. To get there he had to pass through the steel-barred gate that separated the women's psychiatric detention center from the rest of the floor.

Mrs Poole was a good-looking middle-aged black woman, with a warm smile and sympathetic expressive eyes. She looked down at the copy of Jane's commitment report that he had been given by Dr Sloan. 'Jane Randolph?' she said in a puzzled voice. 'We have so many girls in here, Officer.'

He nodded.

She picked up the telephone. A moment later a young uniformed policewoman brought in a file. 'I think this is what you may be looking for,' Mrs Poole said.

The name was typed on the corner of the file. Jane Randolph.

It was followed by a number and a date. The date was five months old.

'May I make some notes, Mrs Poole?'

'Of course. If you don't understand some of the abbreviations I'll be glad to explain them.'

He spread the file on the desk and took out his small notebook. Most of it was simple enough. Arrest record, charge, arresting officer, disposition. He copied the important data. It wasn't until he reached the final page that the hieroglyphics baffled him. 'Mrs Poole?' he asked, handing her the page.

'This is our report on her condition and treatment here. Briefly it says that she was admitted in a highly agitated and violent state apparently caused by drug abuse which had induced hallucinations. A bad trip, in plain language. She was kept under chemical and physical restraints for the two days she was here because of the recurrence of the hallucinations and the damage she might do herself and others. At the end of the second day, we were notified that the criminal charges against her had been dropped, and since we no longer had jurisdiction over her our doctors applied to the court for a commitment order. The following morning she was transferred to Creedmore for further treatment.'

'I see. Is there anything further you can tell me about her?'

'I'm sorry, Officer. Unfortunately she is only one of many that pass through here and she wasn't with us long enough for us to make any kind of appraisal.'

'Thank you for your help, Mrs Poole.'

She held out her hand. 'I'm sorry I couldn't give you more information, Detective.'

He studied his notes in the taxi on the way back to the city. Maybe he would come up with something more at Midtown Precinct North. The police there should at least remember her. Every one of her arrests had been made in that precinct.

'You come back at eleven tonight and see Sergeant Riordan who's head of our pussy posse,' the desk sergeant told him. 'He'll fill you in on her. He knows every cunt in the Broadway area.'

When he returned a little after eleven that night he found Sergeant Riordan, a tall man in his late thirties, sitting in the corridor in front of the women's holding cells morosely nursing a cardboard container of coffee.

'What brings you here?' he asked after Millstein had told him he was looking for information on Jane Randolph. 'She kill somebody out there?'

'What makes you say that? Do you remember her?'

'Fuckin' right I remember her. Every time she came in here she practically started a riot. She was always on something. Spaced out of her mind. It got so I told my boys that if they came across her to look the other way. We got enough troubles in here without cuckoos like that around.'

'Did she ever talk about herself or her family?'

'Who could talk to her? I told you she was nuts. Nothing she said made sense. There was always somebody after her. Somebody who wanted to kill her. The last time we had her in here she had beat up on some poor tourist and wrecked his camera. She was yelling that he was a gun from Los Angeles out to knock her off. The poor bastard was from Peoria and was scared out of his fuckin' mind. I think he grabbed the next bus home. He never showed up to file charges.'

'What about the other times? Did she say anything then?'

'The first time we picked her up she was brought in by one of my boys dressed like a tourist. She saw him on East Fifty-fourth between Madison and Fifth. She asked him if he'd like a massage up in his hotel room for twenty bucks. He kept on walkin'. There's no law against getting a massage. She followed him. This time she said that for an extra tenner she'd blow his ears off. She told him she really didn't give great massages but she was the best cocksucker in the world. He thought that was funny and wasn't even going to pick her up because she didn't look like no pro to him. Just a kid down on her luck. He kidded her. How about skipping the massage and just going for the blow job for ten bucks, he said and began to walk away. She came after him. Cheap motherfucker, she says, and belts him in the chops. So there's nothing else he can do but bring her in.

'We fill out her sheet and take her over to the tank where we keep all the whores until we can ship them downtown. She takes one look and goes berserk. You ain't going to put me in there like a monkey in a cage, she yells as we shove her through the door. A minute later the whole tank is in an uproar. We finally manage to get her out from underneath a pile of six of the toughest mothers you ever saw, then we get her into restraint and throw her into solitary. We were glad when we could send her downtown in the midnight van.'

'What happened to her that time?'

'I don't know. I heard she got bailed out but I don't know. Once they get downtown we lose track of them.'

'By downtown, you mean night court?'

'Yes.'

'What about the next time you had her in?'

'That was a funny one. We picked her up in a massage parlor called The Way Out with three other girls and seven guys.'

'I thought you didn't bust massage parlors.'

'We don't, but this was different. They was making a porno movie and it got hot in there from the lights so they left the windows open and one of the neighbors called it in.'

'How was she then?'

'On a speed trip. Made no sense at all. Just kept yelling at all the cops to come and lay her while she kept playing with herself with a big vibrator.'

'What happened to her that time?'

'Some smart shyster got them all off on a technicality about an improper search warrant.' Riordan shook his head. 'I been on this job for six years now and it ain't worth a shit. You get no appreciation and the only thing everybody wants to know is how much ass am I getting.'

'I was wondering about that. How much are you getting?'

Riordan laughed suddenly. 'You small-town cops are all alike. I get enough to keep the skin back. And even with that it's still a lousy job.'

'Better than pounding a beat,' Millstein said, holding out his hand. 'Thanks, Sergeant.'

'Any time. Where you going next? Night court?'

Millstein nodded.

Riordan wrote a name on a piece of paper. 'My brother-in-law is the court clerk down there. Jimmy Loughran. Tell him you spoke to me. He'll give you anything you want.'

CHAPTER TWENTY-THREE

'TO YOUR RIGHT. Apartment seventeen-B,' the elevator operator said.

He walked to the end of the green-carpeted hallway and pressed the buzzer. From inside he heard the soft sound of muted chimes.

The door was opened by a slim blonde girl.

'Mrs Lafayette, please. I'm Mr Millstein.'

'She's expecting you. Come in.'

He followed the girl into the elegant all-white apartment.

'Can I get you a drink?'

'No, thank you.'

'I'll tell Mrs Lafayette that you're here.' He had seen apartments like this only in movies. The wide terrace outside the windows, spotted with plants and dwarf trees, was like a miniature garden in the sky. There were two photographs in silver frames on the white baby grand. One was a head shot of a good-looking young black man, his lips parted in a warm smile. There was something familiar about him and although the detective couldn't place him he knew that he had seen the man before. The other photograph was of a boy, about ten years old, standing with a gray-haired woman in front of a small white wooden house.

He didn't hear the footsteps in the soft white rug. 'Mr Millstein.'

He kept the surprise from his face when, turning around, he saw that she was black. She was tall and he immediately sensed the strength in her. Suddenly the name rang a bell. He knew now who the young man in the photograph was.

'Mrs Lafayette.' He gestured to the photograph. 'Your husband?'

'Yes. That's my son and my mother in the other photo.'

'My daughter has some of your husband's albums. Even I like the way he sings. He doesn't drive me up the wall the way some of them do.'

'Fred sings pretty but that isn't why you wanted to see me, is it? You said you had some news about Jane Randolph for me.'

This was a woman who came right to the point. 'You're a friend of Jane's?' she asked.

He nodded, then seeing the expression on her face, he said, 'You doubt it?'

'It's hard for me to believe that a policeman would be her friend. Especially one who comes all the way from California trying to get a line on her.'

He took her letter from his pocket and gave it to her without speaking.

She read it quickly, then looked up. 'What happened?'

'That's what I'm trying to find out.' Briefly he told her what he knew, including how he had gotten her name from the clerk at night court as the person who put up bail the first time she had been arrested.

There was a strange softness in the black woman's eyes. 'What happens to her now?'

'I don't know. The doctor told me that she comes up for re-evaluation in two weeks. They are considering letting her out but he's concerned about how she will handle herself after she gets out.'

'Shit, poor JeriLee.'

'JeriLee?'

'That's her real name. Didn't you know that?'

'The only JeriLee she mentioned she said was her sister.'

'She never had a sister. Her name is JeriLee Randall. I was the one who gave her the name Jane Randolph when she began dancing. She didn't want people in the business to know what she was doing. She was afraid if the word got out that she was dancing topless they'd never take her seriously as a writer or an actress after that.'

'Was she any good?'

'I'm no judge,' she said. 'But I know she once won a Tony as an actress on Broadway and another time she had a play produced, although it never got to Broadway. So she had to have something. She was always writing. That's why she worked as a dancer. It gave her the days to write.'

'Did she ever talk about a family?'

'She has a mother. But they're on the outs. Her mother never believed in the same things she did.'

'Do you have her mother's address?'

'Some small town on the island. My husband knows it. I can get it from him.'

'That would help.'

'I'll have it for you tonight then. My husband's on his way to Miami for an engagement.'

'Did you ever see Jane after that time you put up bail for her?'

'I took her to lunch the same day. I offered to help her but she turned me down. She said when she had the money she would repay the bail I had laid out. I told her I thought she was being a fool doing what she was and that I would give her the money to let her write and there wouldn't be any strings attached. But she turned me down flat out.'

'Why do you think she did that?'

'Because we were lovers once. And maybe she didn't believe me when I said "No strings".'

'Was she a lesbian?'

'No. I am. She's not. It would have been easier for all of us if she had been. She's bi. It took me a long time to understand that her reaction to our sex was purely physical. It never was like that for me at all. I really loved her.'

'Would you still be willing to help her if she wanted it?'

'Yes, but she won't take it.'

'What makes you so sure?'

'Because I know her. She has this crazy idea about freedom and independence. She won't take from anyone – man or woman. She left a rich husband for the same reason. She wants to do it all herself, and to be recognized for it.'

He was silent.

'Listen, she knew where I was, a phone call would have brought me any time, but look at the trip she took rather than pick up that phone.'

'She called you once before. Maybe she will again.'

'Twice before,' she said, a distant look in her large dark eyes. 'There won't be a third time.'

For the first time since coming East he felt better. Maybe it was being on the road in a rented car. The Long Island Expressway might have been freeway in California except for the white fields of snow stretching out on either side. He turned off at the Port Clare exit sign.

Fifteen minutes after coming off the expressway he pulled up in front of the house.

It was comfortable-looking and the neighborhood was a good one – well-established middle class. The one thing that distinguished the Randall house from others around it was that the shades were drawn and the driveway and front walk were covered with snow. It looked empty.

He got out of the car and made his way through the snow to the front door. He pressed the bell and heard the echoing sound in the house but there was no answer. He turned around at the sound of a car in the street behind him.

A police car had pulled up behind his. A young patrolman stuck his head out the car window. 'What are you doing up there, mister?'

'I'm looking for Mrs Randall.'

'She's not at home.'

Millstein began to pick his way through the snow back to the sidewalk. 'I can see that. Do you have any idea of where I could reach her?'

'Nope.'

'You were here within two minutes of the time I was. You must have a pretty good system out here.'

'This is a small town. One of the neighbors reported you the minute you stopped your car.'

'Maybe you can help me.' Millstein took his wallet out of his pocket and showed the patrolman his badge.

'Yes, sir,' the policeman said respectfully.

'It's very important that I locate Mrs Randall.'

'I'm afraid you're out of luck, sir. She got married again about two months ago and she and her new husband went off on one of them long world cruises. They won't be back until the summer.'

'Oh.'

'Is there anything else I can do, sir?'

'No, thanks, Officer.'

The detective closed his small black notebook and put it back in his pocket. 'That's it, Dr Sloan. You got it all.'

'I never bought her story about her sister.'

'Neither did I.'

'She wasn't trying to kill herself. What she really wanted to do was kill her dreams. Somehow she began to feel that whatever talent she had made it impossible for her to live in the same world as other people. Society tried to force her into its mold and she couldn't make it. The only thing left for her to do was to kill JeriLee. Then she would be all right.'

'You've passed me, Doc,' Millstein said. 'What happens to her now?'

'She'll get out,' he said somberly. 'We have no real reason to hold her anymore, she's no danger to anyone. She's off drugs, which was why she was sent here. We've done all we can. We're not equipped to give her what she needs now.'

'What if she falls back?'

'Then she'll be back here.'

'But she could kill herself this time.'

'It's possible. But like I said, there's nothing we can do about it. It's too bad that there isn't anyone who cares enough to keep an eye on her. She needs friends more than anything else. But she's cut herself off from everyone.' He was silent for a moment looking at the detective. 'Except you.'

Millstein felt himself flush. 'What do you expect me to do about it?' he demanded almost belligerently. 'I scarcely know the girl.'

'That was last week. This week you probably know more about her than she does herself.'

'I still don't know what I can do,' the detective said stubbornly.

'You might make the difference between life and death for her.'

Millstein was silent.

'It won't take much. Just give her a secure base where she can find herself again.'

'That's crazy.'

'Not so crazy. There has to be something between the two of you. She wrote you. And you came. You didn't have to. You could have sent a letter or done nothing at all. Right now you're probably the one person in the world she completely trusts.'

'Doctor, I'm beginning to think one of us should be committed.' He paused for a moment, shaking his head. 'Or maybe both.'

CHAPTER TWENTY-FOUR

MILLSTEIN CAME into the house after his four o'clock tour of duty. He paused in the small hallway listening for the familiar sound of the clicking typewriter. Hearing nothing, he went into the living room, where his daughter was reading a book. 'Where's JeriLee?' he asked.

'At the shrink's.'

He looked puzzled. 'I thought it was Tuesdays and Fridays.'

'This is something special.'

'Something wrong?'

'No, Daddy. Something good. She heard from the attorney in New York that the shrink suggested she send her novel to. He has a publisher interested in the book and they want to send her fare to come in and talk to them about it.'

'Hmph,' her father growled. 'I know about those New York shysters. I better run a check on him. What's his name?'

Susan laughed. 'Paul Gitlin. And stop being so overprotective, Daddy. She told me he only represents biggies, like Irving Wallace and Gay Talese.'

'I'm not being overprotective. It's only six months since she's been out of the hospital.'

'And look what she's done in that six months. A month after she was here she got a job nights as an operator at the answering service so that she could write and see her shrink during the day. She's written two original screen stories, one of which Universal bought, and now she's almost completely finished with a novel. You got to give her some credit, Daddy.'

'I'm not taking anything away from her. I just don't want her to run herself down.'

'She's fine, Daddy. She's not the same woman you brought home. She's beautiful, Daddy. Inside and out.'

'You really like her?'

Susan nodded.

'I'm glad. I was worried about how you would feel.'

'I have to admit I was jealous at first. But then I saw how much she needed us. Like a child needing approval. Then before my eyes I watched her grow. I watched the woman emerge. It blew my mind. It was like one of those stop motion films where the rose buds and opens all in a few seconds. She's a very special lady, Daddy. And you're a very special man to have seen that in her.'

'I could use a drink.'

'I'll fix it for you.' In a moment she was back with a whiskey on the rocks.

'That helps.'

'Rough day?'

'The usual. Just long.'

She watched him sink into his favorite chair. 'You know she's going to leave soon, don't you, Daddy?' she asked softly.

He nodded without speaking.

'You did what you said you'd do. You gave her back herself. She's strong now. She's learned to walk. Now she wants to fly. You can support a child walking, but flying is something they must do on their own. You'll have to get used to the idea, Daddy. Someday it will be my turn.'

'I know that,' he said, his voice husky.

'You love her, don't you, Daddy?'

'I guess so.'

'Strange, I felt that the moment you told me you were flying East to see her. You know she loves you too, Daddy. But not the same way.'

'I know.'

'I'm sorry, Daddy.' There were tears in the corners of her eyes. 'I don't know if it will help but there's something I think you should understand. JeriLee isn't like the rest of us. She's very special and apart. She'll never be able to love the same way we do. She has her eye on another star. But for her it's something inside herself, while the rest of us may look for it in another person.'

She was kneeling on the floor in front of his chair and he pressed his lips to her forehead. 'What makes you so smart, Daughter?' he whispered.

'I'm not so smart, Daddy. Maybe it's just because I'm a woman.'

Sunlight filtered to a soft glow by bamboo drapes warmed the yellows, oranges and browns of the office. The two women sat in comfortable easy chairs near the window, a triangular table between them. The doctor's chair had a small writing arm not unlike the old schoolroom chairs.

'Excited?' Dr Martinez asked.

'Yes. Very. But I'm also afraid.'

The doctor was silent.

'I didn't do so well the last time I went back East,' JeriLee said.

'Circumstances were different then.'

'Yes I suppose so. But what about me? Was I different too?'

'Yes and no. What you have to remember is that you were living under different pressures then. Those pressures are no longer valid. In that respect, you are different.'

'But I'm still me.'

'You are more you now than you were then. And that's good. As you learn to accept yourself, you grow stronger.'

'I called my mother. She wants me to come and stay with her while I'm working on the book. She wants me to see her new husband. I've never met him.'

'How do you feel about that?'

'You know how I feel about my mother. She's okay in small doses. But after a while we go at each other like cats and dogs.'

'And you think it will be like that this time?'

'I don't know. She's usually okay if I'm not laying any problems on her.'

'It could be that you're both more mature now. Maybe she's learned just as you have.'

'Then you think I should stay with her?'

'I think you should think about it. It could be a very important part of your coming to terms with yourself.'

'I'll think about it.'

'How long do you think you'll be there finishing the book?'

'At least three months. Maybe more. That's another thing that's been troubling me. I won't have you to talk to.'

'I can refer you to a couple of good doctors there.'

'Men?'

'Does it make a difference?'

'I know it shouldn't. But it does. Both doctors I went to before I came to you seemed to treat me as if I were a child to be cajoled into being reasonable and behaving myself. I could be wrong but I think sex had a lot to do with it.'

'I'm not clear what you mean.'

'If I were a housewife with the kind of problems they're used to hearing they could probably deal with me. But I'm not. When I tell them I don't want to marry or have children, that what I really want is to be able to take care of myself without having to depend on anyone, they just don't understand. I don't want to settle for a second-place existence. I want to make my own choices.'

'There's nothing wrong with that. Theoretically we all have that right.'

'Theoretically. But you know better, and so do I. One of the doctors told me jokingly that some good sex would straighten me out. Only I had the feeling that he wasn't joking. If I'd given him any encouragement I think he would have volunteered his services. The other kept trying to convince me that what he called the old-fashioned virtues were best – marriage, home and family. According to him that is the true purpose of women.'

'You'll find many women who go along with that.'

'Okay. But that's their bag. They made their choice. I want to make mine. I don't suppose I've said anything you haven't heard before.'

'I've heard similar things.'

'I even have it in business. I almost sold my second screen original until I met the producer. Somehow things got mixed up in his head and he thought the purchase price included me. When I told him a fuck wasn't included in the sale of a story he said he liked and wanted, he dropped the whole thing. That never would have happened if a man had written it.'

'I know of one woman you would like,' she said. 'It would all depend on how busy she is. She's an active feminist and I think she would like you too.'

'I'd like to see her if I can.'

'When you have a departure date let me know and I'll try to arrange it.'

'Thank you. There's one other thing I want to talk to you about.'

'Yes?'

'It's Al. Detective Millstein. I owe him a lot. Much more than money. I don't know how to tell him that I'll be leaving.'

'Don't you think he knows?'

'I think he knew I'd be going sometime. I just think he never thought it would be this soon. I don't want to hurt him.'

'He's in love with you?'

'Yes, but he's never said anything. Never made a move toward me.'

'How do you feel about him?'

'Grateful. Loving. As if he were my father or my brother.'

'Does he know how you feel?'

'We never really talked about it.'

'Then tell him. I'm sure he'd prefer to hear your true feelings rather than any polite evasions. At least this way he will know that you really do care about him.'

Millstein heard the sound of her car in the driveway, then her footsteps stop outside the front door as she searched for her key. He looked up as the door opened.

Her sun-tinted hair fell to her shoulders. She smiled and her face was flushed beneath the tan. 'You're home early,' she said.

'I had the eight to four today.' He could feel the excitement in her. It was difficult for him to believe that she was the same pale frightened girl that he brought from New York. 'I heard the good news.'

'Isn't it wonderful?'

'I'm very happy for you.'

'I can't believe it. It's like a dream come true.'

'Believe it. You worked very hard for it. You deserve it.'

'You made it possible, Al. Nothing would have happened if it weren't for you.'

'It would have happened. It just might have taken a little longer.'

'No. I was heading for the sewer and you know it.'

'You'll never get me to believe that. If I had ever thought that, I wouldn't have brought you with me. There's something special about you. I saw that the first time we met.'

'I'll never understand how you could see anything through all that shit I had pulled over me.'

'When do you plan to go?'

'I don't know. They said they would let me know next week when they want me to come in. I may stay at my mother's.'

He didn't speak.

'I spoke to the shrink about it. She thinks it might be good for me if I could handle it.'

'And when the book is finished, what do you plan to do then?'

'I don't know.'

'Would you come back out here?'

'Probably. I like living in California. Besides this is where it's at for me. Screenplays, television, work.'

His voice was suddenly husky. 'You always have a home here with us, if you should want it.'

She sank to her knees in front of him and put her hands over his. 'You've done enough, Al. I can't lay any more on you.'

'You're not laying anything on us. We love you.'

'And I love you both. You're like family to me. Even more than family. Maybe the only other person I knew that would have done what you did was my father. You have the same gentleness that he did. Mixed up as I was at the time, I knew that. Maybe that was why I wrote you.'

He understood what she was telling him. And though there was a feeling of deep disappointment, there was also the great satisfaction of knowing that she cared enough to let him know how she felt. He leaned forward and kissed her cheek. 'We'll miss you,' he said.

Her arm went around his neck and she held her cheek against his. 'I won't give you the chance. We'll always be very close.'

He was very still for a moment, then he drew back. He smiled. 'Hey! Are you going to give me a chance to read that book they're all making such a fuss about?'

She laughed. 'Of course. I thought you'd never ask.' A moment later she laid the boxed manuscript on his lap. 'Promise you won't read it until you go to bed. I couldn't stand watching you read it.'

'Okay,' he said. But he didn't really know why she wanted him to wait until after he picked up the manuscript: '*Nice Girls Go to Hell*, a novel by JeriLee Randall.'

Beneath that was a short paragraph.

'This book is dedicated to Al Millstein – with gratitude and affection for being the Loveliest Man I know.'

His eyes blurred with tears and it was several minutes before he turned to page one.

I was born with two strikes on me and no balls.

HAROLD ROBBINS

I was a girl child. Destined to be delivered direct from my mother's womb into the bondage of my sex. I didn't like it even then. I proceeded to piss all over the doctor who was slapping my ass.

CHAPTER TWENTY-FIVE

ANGELA OPENED the bathroom door while she was in the shower. 'Your agent's on the phone,' she shouted. 'He says he has to talk to you right away. It's very important.'

'I'll be right out.' JeriLee stepped out of the shower and wrapped a large bath sheet around her.

'What is it?' she said into the phone.

'Can you get over to the studio right away? Tom Castel wants to see you.'

'What about our appointment? I'm supposed to be at your office in an hour.'

'I can wait. I think this is our big chance. I've got him holding on the other line to let him know when you'll be there.'

'An hour okay?'

'Make it three quarters of an hour. It looks more sincere.'

'Okay.' She laughed. An agent was an agent. He even negotiated the time with you.

The doctor had been right. He had said she would feel better by today and she did. Outside of a mildly heavy feeling in her groin there was no pain at all.

Back in the bathroom she finished drying herself, then pulled the shower cap from her head and shook out her hair. It would need only thirty seconds with the blow dryer. She would use very little makeup today, just a touch of mascara and some light lipstick. They all knew what she had gone through.

Angela came into the bedroom while she was dressing. 'What did he want?'

'I'm due at Castel's office in twenty minutes.'

'Want me to drive you?'

'I think I can manage.'

'Are you sure? I'm clear today. I've nothing else to do.'

'Okay.' She nodded.

'How you feeling, baby?' Tom Castel asked, kissing her cheek.

'Fine.'

'Tough shit about what happened. George should never have put you in a spot like that.'

'It was my own fault.' she said, moving toward the chair in front of his desk.

'No, over there,' he said solicitously, taking her by the arm and leading her to the couch against the wall. 'You'll be more comfortable. Coffee?'

She nodded and he pressed a button on the side of his chair. A moment later his secretary came in with two cups.

'The old man said to come right over. That it was important.'

'How badly do you want your picture made?'

She couldn't resist. 'I don't want it made badly. I want it made well.'

'Don't get flip with words, JeriLee. I know you're a writer. You want the picture made or don't you?'

'I want the picture made.'

'Okay then,' he said seriously. 'I'll tell you how to get it done. I got the studio to agree to give me a go on the picture if George does it. You get George to do it.'

'Why me? You're the producer. Isn't that your job? And besides, isn't he under contract to the studio?'

'That's right. But he's got the right of approval over what pictures he will do, and I can't seem to pin him down. He should listen to you. After all, he did knock you up and you took care of it without making a fuss. I figure he owes you one.'

'What if he won't do it?'

'You blow fifty grand and five points.'

'What do you lose?'

'Nothing. I got a contract. If I don't do this picture, I do another. But I'd like to get this one made. I think there's a buck in it for all of us. Besides I want to work with you. I think we could come up with a real winner between us. I loved the book.'

'Thanks.'

'You don't know me. I'm dynamite when I get going. Work day and night. I got a place out at the beach where nobody can get to us.'

She nodded. She had heard about his place at the beach from friends. The only one that believed he went out there to work was his wife. 'Okay,' she said. 'I'll see what I can do.'

'Great. I arranged to meet George for lunch at the commissary. I told him you'd be joining us.' He smiled. 'I know you can sell him, baby. Just give him another whiff of that gorgeous pussy.'

'Christ, Tom,' she said disgustedly. 'It's going to take more than that to get him.'

'You don't know your own power, baby. He says that you've got the super body of all time and that he can't keep from getting a hard-on whenever he's near you.'

'When did he say that?'

'Just this weekend. We had a C.R. session out at the shrink's. It just – '

'Happened to come up,' she finished, interrupting him. 'I know I heard all about it.'

'I must say he made out a hell of a case for you. Are you really as good as he says you are?'

'Oh, sure,' she said, getting to her feet. 'I'm a real ball breaker.' She walked toward the door. 'Where's the john? I think I have to throw up.'

'First door on your left,' he said quickly. 'I'm sorry, I forgot you still weren't feeling well.'

'Don't worry about it. That's one of the problems of being a woman. Some things just turn your stomach.'

'It's really a very simple deal,' she explained to her agent. 'Castel gives me the job if I get George to do the picture. On top of that he already told me that we'd be working together out at his place on the beach and he made sure to tell me that he works day and night.

'George says that he loves the whole idea. That he believes in me as a writer and admires Castel as a top producer, for him the key is the director and he happens to know that Dean Clarke is available because Dean's wife coldcocked the picture he was going to do at Warner's.'

'Dean Clarke would be a good director for the project. And I say so even if he's not my own client.'

'But you know Dean's problem. If he doesn't get his wife's approval he won't do it. And that's another problem for me. She wants the same thing from me that George and Castel want. I've been ducking her ever since we met at a N.O.W. meeting.'

'Pictures have been made even with worse problems.'

'I've heard of fucking one guy to get a job in this business. But did you ever hear of anyone who had to fuck everybody on the damn picture? Before it's over they'll have me matched up with everyone except the hairdresser and that will only be because he's gay.'

'Now don't get excited. Let's talk this out.'

'Okay.'

'If I could get Castel to go for seventy-five thousand and seven and a half points, would you do it?'

'You're not listening. I wasn't talking about the money. I just don't think I should have to screw for the deal, that's all.'

'I agree with you. But since you're doing it anyway, I don't see what's such a big tsimiss you're making.'

'I didn't have to screw anybody to get them to buy the book, why should I do it to get them to make the picture?'

'They didn't make the picture yet, did they?' the old man asked shrewdly. She started to speak but he held up his hand. 'Listen to me, then you can talk. It's almost three years since they bought your book. They did two scripts on it. They were no good and there was no picture. Don't tell me that your book sold forty thousand in hard cover, a hundred thousand in book club and a million in paperback, or that you did fifty radio and TV shows and that *Time* magazine had you on its cover as Women's Lib writer of the year. I know it, you know it and the studio knows it. What the studio also knows is that it all happened three years ago. Since then there have been other books. And, believe me, they would much rather make a fresh start on something new than throw more money into something they have already failed with twice. You talk about what you have to do to get this picture made? Let me tell you what I had to do. For the last year while you were giving away your fucks for free, I was wining, dining and sucking up to every executive at the studio that I thought could push your picture into production.

'Well, I finally got it back on the active list. I got them to turn it over to Castel, one of their top producers, because I know he's a hustler, that he would find a way to get them to make the movie. Well, he found it and now you're complaining.

'I'm an old man. I don't have to work so hard. Soon I will turn the office over to my younger associates. You don't want to make the picture? It's okay by me. It's your book, it's your life, it's your money. I'm a rich man. I don't need it. All I get is a lousy ten per cent anyway.' He shook his head sadly. 'So go home. We'll still be friends. You'll write other stories, other books. I'll make other deals. But it's really too bad. It might have been a very important movie.' He held up his hand. 'Now you can talk.'

She started laughing hysterically.

'You think what I said was funny?'

'No. It's just that suddenly everything has become so unreal.'

'Then let me bring you back to reality.' His voice cut like a cold knife. 'In this business there is only one truth. It always has been and it always will be – make the movie. Just that. Nothing more, nothing less. Make the movie.

'I don't give a damn what you do, who you sleep with. I don't care if you want to remake the world. You can do anything you want but first you will have to deal with the truth. Make the movie. It's the only thing you can do that will validate you. If you don't do it, you're just another broad who couldn't cut it in this town.'

'And you don't care who I have to fuck to get it done.'

'I don't give a damn if you have to climb up on the cross and fuck Jesus Christ. You get that movie made.'

'I don't really care that much anymore,' she said in a tired voice.

'I don't believe that. If you hadn't cared you wouldn't have come out here three years ago. You would have stayed back East and written another novel.'

'That's what I should have done. I know that now.'

'It's not too late. The planes still fly both ways.'

He saw the tears come to her eyes but before he could say anything to her she rose from her chair and walked out of the office. He picked up the telephone and a moment later had Tom Castel on the line.

'I just finished talking to her, Tom,' he said in a confidential tone. 'Believe me, there's no way you can get her to go for less than a hundred grand. I'll get her to buy the seven and a half points but you'll have to come up with the cash. Right now she's fed up with this town. I have all I can do to keep her from getting on the next plane back East. All she really wants to do is write her next novel.'

JeriLee took a Kleenex from the container on the dashboard and dabbed at her eyes. 'We can go home now,' she said.

Silently Angela put the car into gear and they rolled out of the parking lot. JeriLee lit a cigarette and looked out of the car window. 'Shit,' she said.

'What's wrong?'

'I just discovered something about myself and I don't like it,' she said. 'People don't only get fucked by systems, they also get fucked by their dreams.'

'You lost me.'

'We're all whores,' JeriLee said. 'Only the currencies are different. By the time we get home the old man will be on the phone telling me he got a hundred grand to do the picture. And I'll say okay.'

'That's a lot of money.'

'It's not the money. That's where the old man is smart. He knows it. And uses it. He knows that I want that picture made more than I want life itself. I didn't fool him for a minute.'

'I don't see anything so bad about it.'

Suddenly JeriLee laughed. 'That's what's so beautiful about you. You're the last of the innocents.'

'It's been a rough day,' Angela said. 'Let's get stoned when we get home.'

JeriLee leaned across the seat and kissed Angela's cheek. 'That's the first sensible idea I've heard all day.'

Epilogue
Tinsel Town

ON STAGE the singer was drawing out the last anguished note of the song. In the small crowded control room high in the back of the large auditorium there was a hum of quiet frenzy. This was not just an ordinary television program. This was the live telecast of motion pictures' finest hour, the Academy Awards.

The applause came up as the singer finished. He bowed graciously to the audience, his fixed smile masking his anger. The orchestra had mangled his arrangement and drowned out his best notes.

A voice echoed through the speakers in the control room. 'Two minutes. Commercials and station break.'

'What song was that?' the director asked.

'Second,' someone answered. 'No, third.'

'It stinks,' he said. 'What's on next?'

'Best screenplay award. We're picking up the nominees now.'

The director looked up at the screens. The five center screens each showed a different person, four men and a woman. The men in their elaborate dinner jackets appeared nervous. The woman seemed almost oblivious to everything going on around her. Her eyes were half closed, her lips slightly parted, and her head nodded gently as if she were listening to some inner music. 'The girl is stoned,' he said.

'But she's beautiful,' a voice answered.

The countdown from the commercial began. The moment it was over a light flashed over the screen that was picking up the master of ceremonies returning to the podium. The director punched in a closeup of the emcee, then cut to a medium shot of two stars, a young man and woman, approaching the podium to the applause of the audience. The applause faded away as they began to read the list of the nominees.

As their names were being called out, the men were trying without success to appear nonchalant, the woman still seemed to be in another world.

With the usual pomp, the envelope was called for and ceremoniously opened. 'The award for the best screenplay goes to –'

The young actor paused for the dramatic moment. He looked at his companion.

She picked up the announcement, her voice suddenly shrill with excitement. 'Ms JeriLee Randall for *Nice Girls Go to Hell*!'

The director punched in on the woman. At first she didn't seem to have heard. Her eyes opened and her lips parted in a smile. She began to rise from her seat. Another camera picked her up as she made her way down the aisle to the stage. It wasn't until she had climbed the few steps and turned to face the audience that they had a clear full shot of her.

'Jesus Christ!' A voice broke the sudden hush in the control room. 'She's got nothin' but tits and pussy under that dress.'

'Want to go to closeup?' the A.D. asked.

'No way,' the director answered. 'Give the yokels a treat.'

Up on the stage the woman clutched the Oscar to her and moved toward the microphone. She blinked her eyes for a moment as if to hold back her tears but when she opened them they were clear and shining.

'Ladies and gentlemen of the Academy . . . ' Her voice was quiet but distinct. 'If I were to tell you that I'm not thrilled and happy at this moment I would be very wrong. This is something that happens only in a writer's wildest dreams.'

She paused for a moment until the applause died away. 'Still, there is within me a lingering doubt and a feeling of sadness. Did I earn this award as writer, or as a woman? I know there would be no doubts in the minds of any of the four gentlemen who were nominated had they won. But then all they had to do was write their screenplays. They didn't have to ball everybody on the picture except the prop man in order to get it made.'

A roar came up from the audience and panic hit the control room. 'Go to tape,' the director ordered. 'Delay five seconds.' He half rose from behind the control console and peered through the small window down into the theater. 'Get me some audience reaction shots,' he yelled. 'All hell's breaking loose down there!'

The images leaped onto the small screen. There were women rising to their feet applauding, shouting encouragement. 'Right on, JeriLee! Tell it like it is, JeriLee!' The camera zoomed in close on a shot of a dinner-jacketed man trying to pull the woman he was with back into her seat. The director cut back to JeriLee as her voice came on again.

'I do not intend to ignore the custom of thanking all the people who made it possible for me to win this award. So my first thanks go to my agent, who told me the only thing that mattered was getting the picture made. He might be relieved to know that I did not have to climb up on the cross. All I had to do was climb on the producer's cock, lick the star's ass, and eat the pussy off the director's wife. My thanks to all of them. Maybe they did make it possible.'

'Holy shit!' the director whispered. The noise from the audience was beginning to drown out JeriLee's words. 'Cut the audience mikes,' he ordered.

Her voice came over the crowd. ' . . . Last, but not least, I want to express my appreciation to my fellow members of the Academy for electing me their Token Woman Writer, in honor of which I want to unveil a painting I had done especially for them.'

She smiled gently as her hand reached behind her neck. Suddenly her dress fell from her body. She stood motionless on the stage, a huge inverted golden Oscar painted on her nude body. The gold paint covered her breasts and stomach, the flat head of the figure disappeared into her pubic hair.

Pandemonium broke out in the auditorium. The audience came to its feet, staring, cheering and booing as men rushed from the wings to surround JeriLee. Someone threw a coat around her. Contemptuously, she threw it off and marched from the stage in naked dignity.

There was a dazed happy expression on the director's face as the screen went to black for the commercials. 'The Academy Awards will never be the same after this.'

'Do you think we got on the air?' someone asked.

'I hope so,' he answered. 'It would be a shame if truth didn't get as much of a chance to be heard as bullshit.'

The car moved up the hill and came to a stop in front of the house. JeriLee leaned across the seat and kissed the man's cheek. 'My friend, Detective Millstein. Detective Millstein, my friend. You have a talent for turning up when you're most needed.'

He smiled. 'I wasn't far from the theater, I was watching the show in a bar when you came on.'

'I'm glad.' She got out of the car. 'I'm wiped out. I'll go right to bed.'

'Will you be okay?'

'Don't worry, I'm fine. You can go back to work.'

'All right.'

'Give Susan and the baby a kiss for me.'

He nodded and watched her go into the house before he turned the car around and went back down the hill.

The telephone was ringing when she came in the door. It was her mother. 'You really did it this time, JeriLee,' she said. 'I'll never be able to hold my head up in this town again.'

'Oh, Mother.' The line went dead in her hand. Her mother had hung up. Just as JeriLee put down the phone it rang again.

This time it was her agent. 'That was a brilliant publicity stunt,' he chortled. 'Never in all my years in the business have I ever seen a star made in one night.'

'It wasn't a publicity stunt.'

'What difference does it make?' the old man asked. 'You come into the office tomorrow. I got at least five firm offers on which you can write your own ticket.'

'Oh, shit,' she said and hung up the phone. It began to ring again but this time she didn't answer. Instead she lifted it up, pressed down the cradle to disconnect the call and left the receiver off the hook.

She went into the bedroom, found a joint, lit it and went back to the front door. She went outside. The night was warm and clear. She sat down on the porch steps and looked out over the city. Her eyes suddenly began to mist.

She sat at the top of the stairs and cried. And far down the hill, below her, the multicolored lights of Los Angeles shimmered through her tears.

DREAMS DIE FIRST

This book is for
Grace
because Grace is for me

BOOK ONE

The Down Side

Chapter One

It was five o'clock in the afternoon when I woke up. The room stank of [illegible] and cheap [illegible] wine. I rolled out of [illegible] the together. [illegible] was naked and [illegible] there. even when I didn't [illegible].

I [illegible] the [illegible] and opened the [illegible] in Southern California. [illegible] wind blasted the [illegible] cold shower [illegible] and [illegible] the [illegible] down.

Some of the rain hit the boy, but it didn't waken him. He merely rolled over on his side and curled into a ball, his knees tucked up against his chest. I circled around him to get to the bathroom. I still had half an hour to get over to unemployment and collect my check. If I rushed, I could make it.

Ten minutes later I was on my way out the [illegible]. The Colonel's [illegible] '68 Jaguar [illegible] traffic [illegible] the [illegible] and waiting for me. He raised his hand, and I walked across the rain-swept sidewalk and got into the car.

"I [illegible] not [illegible] yet," I said before he could speak. "I was on my way to unemployment."

His [illegible] face creased in an easy smile. "[illegible] Okay, Garrett. I figured that. I'll drive you." He moved into the traffic, [illegible]

"[illegible] you [illegible] after the small fry."

He was still smiling. "Lonergan believes that if you look after the pennies, the dollars will take care of themselves."

I had no answer for that. I'd been into Lonergan for so long I'd almost forgotten what it all meant. Three, maybe four months ago, when I ran short after my first unemployment check. I'd never been caught up after that. It was like trying to

Chapter One

It was five o'clock in the afternoon when I woke up. The room stank of stale cigarettes and cheap sour red wine. I rolled out of bed and almost fell as I stumbled over the boy sleeping on the floor beside my bed. I stared down at him in surprise. He was naked and I couldn't remember how or when he got there. Even worse, I didn't recognise him.

He didn't move as I walked across the room, rolled up the shade and opened the window. The song says it never rains in Southern California. Don't you believe it. The way the wind blasted the water over me, it was like stepping under a cold shower. I swore and pushed the window down.

Some of the rain hit the boy, but it didn't waken him. He merely rolled over on his side and curled into a ball, his knees tucked up against his chest. I circled around him to go into the bathroom. I still had half an hour to get over to unemployment and collect my check. If I rushed, I could make it.

Ten minutes later I was on my way out the front-door. The Collector, whose new red '68 Jaguar blocked the rush-hour traffic coming from the freeway onto Highland, was sitting and waiting for me. He raised his hand and I rushed across the rain-swept sidewalk and got into the car.

"I haven't got my money yet," I said before he could speak. "I was just on my way to unemployment."

His shiny black face creased in an easy smile. "That's okay, Gareth, I figured that. I'll drive you." He moved into the traffic, disdainful of the blasting horns behind him.

"Business must be bad if Lonergan is sending you after the small fry."

He was still smiling. "Lonergan believes that if you look after the pennies the dollars will take care of themselves."

I had no answer for that. I'd been into Lonergan for so long I'd almost forgotten when it all began. Three, maybe four months ago, when I ran short after my first unemployment check. I'd never been caught up after that. It was like taking an instant ten-dollar cut. Every week I gave him my unemployment check for sixty dollars and he gave me back fifty in cash. If I could have made it one week without the fifty, I would have been even. But no way. Without it, it was wipeout time.

The Collector turned into the parking lot and pulled up in front of the entrance. "I'll be right here," he said. "Go get it."

I jumped out of the car and dashed for the door. I made it just as the guard came to lock up. Verita, the Mexican girl, was at my regular window. "For Chris' sake, Gary," she complained. "Why you come so late?"

"Why do you think? I was out looking for a job."

"Oh, yeah?" She pulled the forms out of the drawer and pushed them toward me. "It was raining and you stayed in bed for wan more fuck waiting for it to stop."

"Only when you're with me, baby," I said, signing the form. "Ain't no other lady can keep me coming back like that."

She smiled as she gave me the check. "I bet you say that to all the girls."

I folded the check and stuck it in my pocket. "Not true. You ask them."

"I make dinner home tonight," she said. "Good enchiladas. Tacos with real beef. Red wine. You come?"

"I can't, Verita. Honest. I got a meeting with a guy about a job."

She made a face. "Whenever a man say, 'Honest' to me, I know he lying."

"Maybe next week," I said, starting for the door.

"There won't be no next week," she called after me.

But I was already at the door and it wasn't until I was back in the car that I found out what she meant.

The Collector had the pen ready for me. I took it, signed the check and handed it over to him. He looked at my signature and shoved the check in his pocket. "Good." He nodded; then his voice went flat. "Now get out."

I stared in surprise. "But you didn't give me my fifty."

"No more," he said. "Your credit just ran out."

"What're you talking about? We got this standing arrangement."

"Only as long as you get your checks. You don't stay on top

of things the way Lonergan does. He knows this is your last check and that you're not eligible now for another three months."

"Shit. What do I do now? I'm busted."

"You could go back to work," he said. "Instead of trying to pick up clap from small boys."

There was nothing for me to say. It seemed Lonergan knew it all.

The Collector reached across me and pushed open the door. I started to get out and the Collector put a hand on my arm. "Lonergan tol' me to tell you if you really want to go back to work to come an' see him tonight about twelve-thirty at his office in back of the Dome."

Then he pulled the door shut and drove off, leaving me standing with the rain pouring down my face. I fished through my pockets and came up with a mangled package of cigarettes. There were maybe three left. I went back against the building, out of the wind, and lit one.

When I looked up, I saw Verita driving out of the lot in her old Valiant. I waved. She stopped and I ran over and got in.

"My appointment isn't until twelve-thirty if your offer is still good," I said.

She had a small studio apartment just off Olivera Street. If you angled yourself at the window, you could look out and see the bright lights down the street which was always busy. The Chicanos didn't seem to mind the rain. After dinner was walk-around time. That was when they went – and stayed – out, dragging their kids with them until everything closed up at two in the morning. Then the poor ones took the kids home and those that could afford it made for the after-hours places. Mexicans don't like to sleep at night.

"Here's Johnny!" Ed McMahon's voice came from the television set at the foot of the bed behind me. I raised my head.

Her hands pushed me down between her legs again. "Don't stop, Gareth. That's so good."

I looked up at her. Her face held the grim concentration that came over it as she reached for an orgasm. I put three fingers into her and rolled her button gently between my teeth. I felt her body arch and spasm as she hit it. Her breath rushed out with an explosive gasp. I could feel the still-trembling buttocks in my hand. I waited a moment until she stopped and opened her eyes.

She shook her head slowly. "You do it so good, Gary. Nobody do it like you."

I was silent.

Her fingers came down and tangled with my hair, brushing it back from my eyes. "I love to see your blond head down there between my legs. My hair is so dark and yours is so white."

I rolled over and began to get out of bed.

She stopped me. "Do you have to go? It's still raining. You can stay with me tonight."

"I wasn't lying. I have an appointment about a job."

"Who gives job interviews at twelve-thirty at night?" she asked sceptically.

I reached for my jeans. "Lonergan."

"Oh." She rolled out of bed and made for the bathroom. "I go wash my pussy. I be right back. I drive you over."

We were silent in the car until she pulled to a stop in front of Lonergan's place behind the Cinerama Dome. "You want me to wait for you?"

"No. I don't know how long I'll be."

She hesitated a moment. "He's not a good man, Gary. Be careful."

I looked at her questioningly.

"He waits for people who have no money. Then he sucks them in. I know boys and girls who are working the streets for him. Sometimes he has the Collector wait for them outside the office on the day they get their last check. Like he waited for you."

I was surprised. I didn't think she had seen him. "I don't intend to walk the streets for anybody."

Her eyes were shining. "You have money?"

"I'll manage."

She opened her purse and took out a ten-dollar bill. She pressed it into my hand. "Take it," she said earnestly. "Nobody should see Lonergan without money in his pocket."

I hesitated.

"It's a loan," she said quickly. "You pay me back when you get a job."

I looked down at the ten, then nodded and put it in my pocket. "Thanks." I leaned across the seat and kissed her.

The rain had eased off. I waited until she put the car in gear and drove away before making my way into the Silver Stud bar.

The bar was almost empty except for a few hustlers nursing their drinks. They looked me over quickly and just as quickly wrote me off. It was still too early for the rich queens to come down from the hils. I walked down past the bar. Lonergan's office was upstairs off a staircase at the back of the room.

The Collector was sitting at a table in the dark near the staircase. He held up a hand to stop me. "Lonergan's running late. He ain't here yet."

I nodded.

He pointed to a chair. "Sit down an' have a drink."

I looked at him with raised eyebrows.

His face broke into a smile. His teeth were sparkling white in the dark. "I'm buying. What's your pleasure?"

"Scotch rocks." I slipped into the chair.

The waiter put the drink in front of me. I took a mouthful and savoured the taste. It felt crisp and clean.

"You look beat, man," the Collector said. "Like you been eatin' a little too much Mexican chilli tonight."

"How come you know so much about what I do? I must be real important."

The Collector laughed. "You not important. Lonergan is. An' he likes to be informed about people he plans to do business with."

Chapter Two

Lonergan came in about one o'clock. He walked right past the table at which we were sitting without even a glance in our direction and went up the stairs, followed by his bodyguard. I started to get out of my chair.

The Collector waved me back. "When he wants to see you, he'll send for you."

"He went by so fast he never even saw me."

"He saw you. He sees everything." He signalled for another drink.

I raised my glass and looked down the bar. It was beginning to get busy. The Beverly Hills and Bel Air queens were coming in after their society dinner dates. They had the air of those who, having done their duty, were now seeking a little fun. One of them who saw me looking must have thought I was casing him. He took a few steps toward me, then saw the Collector and went back to the bar.

The Collector gave a short laugh. "You pretty. With that white blond hair you can make a good buck playin' cowboy."

"Is that the kind of job Lonergan wants to talk to me about?" I asked.

"How the fuck do I know, man? He don' take me into his confidence."

Half an hour later the bodyguard signalled me from the foot of the stairs. I left my drink on the table and followed him up the steps. He opened the door of the office, closed it behind me and remained out in the hall.

The soundproofing and the faint hum of the air-conditioning unit cut out all noise from the bar. The room was starkly furnished and dominated by a large desk. A shaded round fluorescent lamp illuminated the papers on the desk blotter.

Lonergan was behind the desk, his face half hidden in the shadows. He looked up. "Hello, Gareth." His voice was as noncommittal as his tie, white shirt and Brooks Brothers three-button jacket.

"Hello, Uncle John." I made no move to the chair in front of the desk.

"Sit down," he said.

Silently I sat down in the stiff-backed chair.

"Your mother hasn't heard from you in more than two months."

I didn't answer.

There was no reproval in his voice. "She's worried about you."

"I thought you kept her informed."

"I don't," he said flatly. "You know my rules. I never involve myself in family affairs. She's my sister, you're her son. If you have problems in communication, you solve them."

"Then why bring it up?"

"She asked me to."

I started to get up. He raised his hand. "We're not finished. I said I had a proposition for you."

"The Collector said it was a job."

He shook his head. "People are stupid. They never get messages straight."

"Okay," I said.

His eyes glinted behind the small old-fashioned gold-rimmed glasses. "You're getting kind of on in years for the rôle you're playing. Somehow thirty-year-old hippies seem out of date."

I didn't answer.

"Kerouac, Ginsberg, Leary. They're all rapidly disappearing into yesterday. Even the kids aren't listening anymore."

I fished the last cigarette from my pocket and lit it. I didn't know what he was getting at.

"Where have all your heroes gone?"

"I never had any heroes. Except you, maybe. And that went out the window when my father jumped."

His voice was empty. "Your father was a weak man."

"My father couldn't face the thought of going to jail for you. He chose the quick way."

"He could have done four to six on one hand. When he got out, he would have been in clover."

"If it was so easy, why didn't you do it?"

A shadowed smile crossed his lips. "Because I have a business to run. Your father knew that when we made our deal."

I dragged on the cigarette without speaking.

He picked up a sheet of paper from his desk. "Do you know even the FBI gave up on you? They didn't think you were worth keeping an eye on."

I smiled. "That's not very flattering, is it?"

"Would you like to know why?" He didn't wait for me to answer. "You were too intellectual. They said you'd never make a good revolutionary. You always saw both sides of a problem and found reasons for each of them."

"Is that why they went to the trouble of fucking up the jobs I got?"

"That was before they had you figured. Now they don't give a damn."

"That doesn't help me now. The damage is done. Every prospective employer has it in his records."

"That's why I sent for you." He paused for a moment. "Maybe it's time you went into business for yourself."

"Doing what? You going to buy me a taxi, Uncle John?"

"How about a weekly newspaper of your own?"

My mouth hung open. "You're putting me on."

"No." His voice was flat.

"There's got to be a hooker in this somewhere."

"Just one. I own the advertising. You can do what you like with the rest of the paper. Use it to say whatever you want to say. I don't give a damn."

"Advertising is where the money is. Where do I get mine?"

"Circulation. You keep the net receipts and I'll throw in ten per cent of the advertising revenue to help with the costs."

"Who will own the paper?"

"You will."

"Where does the money to start it come from?"

"It's already started," he answered. "You may have seen copies of it around. The *Hollywood Express.*"

I ground out the cigarette. For a moment I had felt elation. But now it was gone. The *Hollywood Express* was a throwaway sheet. Every once in a while I would find a copy stuffed in my mailbox.

He knew what I was thinking. "What did you expect? The *LA Times?*"

"The *Express* is not a newspaper."

"That's a point of view," he said. "To me eight pages of newsprint is a newspaper."

I fished for another cigarette but came up empty. He pushed a box across the desk. I took one and lit it.

"Your unemployment's run out. There's not a paper or magazine that would touch you and you know it. You're not a good enough writer to make it freelance in the magazines or slicks, and your novel has been turned down by every publisher including the vanity press houses."

"Why me, Uncle John?" I asked. "You got to have better than me on your list."

His eyes met mine. "Put it down to vanity." He permitted himself a faint smile. "You got something going inside you. Maybe it's the way you look at yourself. Or society. You're sceptical about everything. And still you believe in people. It doesn't make sense. Not to me anyhow." Abruptly he changed the subject. "How long has it been since you got out of the army?"

"Five years. They kept me in for a year after I got back from Vietnam. I guess they didn't like the idea of a Green Beret getting out and spouting off against the war."

"You could get a GI loan to take over the paper," he said.

"You really are serious about it, aren't you?" The amazement showed in my voice.

"I always am about business," he said flatly.

"And what's in it for you?"

He took off his glasses, polished them, then put them back on his nose. His eyes were hard and bright. "Four pages of classified ads at a thousand dollars a page. That's four thousand a week."

"Impossible. That rag couldn't sell ten lines a month."

"That's my problem. For your ten per cent of the ads all you have to do is write them."

"You mean make them up? Just like that?"

He nodded.

"Who pays for them?"

He shrugged his shoulders. "The money comes in in cash. A dollar a line, four to ten dollars an ad. We just process it through the advertising agency and you skim off your ten per cent."

Now it all began to fall into place. My uncle had to do a big cash business. This was as good a way to wash the money as any I had ever heard. The going rate on the street for turning black money into white was forty to fifty. He had it figured for only ten per cent. "I'll have to think about it," I said.

"You do that. Tomorrow morning Bill will pick you up at your place and take you over to the paper so that you can look over the setup."

"Bill?"

"The Collector."

"Oh." Until now I had never known he had a name. I got to my feet.

"You meet me here tomorrow night at the same time and give me your answer."

"Okay." I started for the door.

"By the way . . . that boy up at your place. Better get yourself a shot of penicillin. He's got a bad clap." He took a twenty from his pocket and threw it on the desk. "In case you haven't got the money, there's enough there for you and the Mexican girl you had dinner with."

I looked down at the money then up at him. "I have enough," I said and closed the door behind me. I went down the stairs and through the bar to the street.

Now I was sorry I hadn't had Verita wait for me. Slowly I started walking back downtown. It would take at least an hour for me to make it back to her place. But I owed her that.

I couldn't remember anything about last night. I shook my head angrily.

I used to have times like that when I had first come back from Vietnam. Times when I would lose a day or night. After a while the blackouts stopped. Now I wondered if they were coming back.

Chapter Three

A muggy, steamy smell rose from the streets as the heat baked the rain off the concrete. The streets were narrower as you came down into East LA. The old houses leaned together as if to hold one another up. Now that the lights were out, the streets were almost totally dark. Even so, I was aware of life and movement within the shadows. It was something I sensed, yet did not see. Suddenly I found myself walking out in the middle of the street, my eyes searching the darkness. It was almost as if I had returned to Vietnam.

I felt as if I were going crazy. This is Los Angeles, I told myself. I'm walking down a street in the city, not up a jungle path.

I didn't see it. I didn't hear it. But I knew it was there and spun to one side. In the dark the loaded sock whistled by my head.

When I straightened up, he was standing there, a silly grin on his cream-coloured face. The sock hung limply from one hand; the other hand held the inevitable bottle of orange juice. 'I'm goin' tuh hit you, Whitey,' he said.

His eyes were out of focus and he was weaving slightly to some music that only he could hear. 'I'm goin' tuh hit you, Whitey," he repeated, still smiling that inane smile.

I stared at him, trying to penetrate his heroin fog. "You do and I'll kill you," I said quietly.

Somewhere in his head the music had come to a stop. He no longer weaved; his eyes struggled into focus. He sounded puzzled. "Why would you do a thing like that? I didn't do nothin' to you."

Just then a car turned the corner and in the approaching headlights I could see him clearly for the first time. He was just a kid. Seventeen. Maybe eighteen. A straggly moustache and beard tried vainly to cover the pimples that were still on his face. Slowly we separated, moving backward toward opposite sides of the street as the car passed between us.

By the time the car went by he had disappeared back into the shadows from which he had come. I searched the street but saw nothing. Still, I didn't move until the radar in my head told me he was really gone. Then I went back into the middle of the street and kept on walking.

You're getting old and stupid, Gareth, I told myself. You have no right feeling sorry for a junkie. That loaded sock could have broken your skull. But I did feel sorry for him. If you'd never known the sweet surcease from pain the needle could give you, you might feel differently. But if you knew, all you could feel was sorrow at the waste. And I saw more men in Vietnam wasted by the needle than by bullets.

It was three-thirty by the time I leaned on her doorbell. After a moment her voice came tinny and frightened through the brass speaker. "Who is it?"

"Gareth. Can I come up?"

"Are you all right?"

"I'm fine. I have to talk to you."

The buzzer sounded and I pushed the door open and went up the stairs. She was in her doorway waiting for me. I followed her into the apartment and she locked the door behind us.

"I'm sorry if I woke you."

"It's okay. I couldn't sleep anyway."

I heard the sound of the television set coming from the bedroom. I reached into my pocket, took out the ten-dollar bill and held it out to her. "I didn't need it," I said.

"You didn't have to come back for that."

"Take it. I'll feel better."

She took it. "Would you like a cup of coffee?" she asked.

"That would be fine."

I followed her across the room and sat at the table while she made a cup of instant and put it in front of me. She took one for herself and sat down opposite me. Her eyes were questioning.

I took a sip of the coffee. It was hot and strong. I met her eyes. "I may have picked up a dose and given it to you," I said.

She was silent for a moment, but when she spoke, her voice was uncomplaining. "Why did you not say something before?"

"I didn't know."

"How did you find out?"

"Lonergan. He told me I'd better get a shot of penicillin. You too."

She sipped at her coffee.

"Do you have a cigarette?" I asked.

She nodded, took a pack from the drawer and pushed it toward me. "I'm sorry," I said. "I'll go now if you want."

"No," she said. "I'm not angry. Most men I know would have said nothing. I'll go to the doctor tomorrow."

"I'll give you the money for the shot as soon as I can."

"It will cost nothing. My doctor works at the clinic." She was silent again for a moment. "Is that all Lonergan wanted to see you about? He has no job for you?"

"No job. He wants me to buy a newspaper."

"A newspaper? Buy one? He must be crazy."

"He is, but that's not the point."

"What does he expect you to use for money?"

"My GI loan. He said he could get one for me."

"And what does he get out of it?" she asked suspiciously.

"The advertising. That goes through his company."

"I don't know what kind of newspaper you can buy like that."

"*The Hollywood Express.*"

"That one," she said in a strange voice.

"You know something about it?" I asked. "Tell me."

"It's not good," she said, shaking her head. "Nothing but trouble."

"How?"

"In the office we have a list. Tax-delinquent employers and companies that do not pay the withholding taxes. The *Express* owes about thirty thousand with interest. If you buy it, you could become liable for it."

"Do you think Lonergan knows that?"

"He knows everything else," she said flatly.

I nodded. It was much too obvious for him to miss. I wondered what he had in mind. It made no sense for him to stick me into that kind of jam.

"Did you say you would do it?"

"I told him I would think about it. I'm supposed to look it over tomorrow morning."

She reached for a cigarette. "I would like to go with you."

"Why? What could you do?"

"Nothing maybe. But I am a CPA. And at least I will understand the books."

"Certified public accountant – state licence and all?"

She nodded.

"Then what are you doing at unemployment?" As soon as I asked the question, I felt stupid. There could be few, if any, jobs for Chicano accountants. "I would be grateful if you would come."

She smiled. "Okay. What time?"

"The Collector's going to pick me up in the morning. I'll go on home now and let you get some sleep."

"It's after four. You stay here. I'll drive you over in the morning."

"But what about your office?"

"It's Saturday." She reached for the coffee cups and put them in the sink. "The office is closed."

The Collector's red Jag was already in front of my house when we pulled up at ten o'clock in the morning. I walked over to his car and stuck my head in the window. "Don't you ever sleep?" I asked.

He grinned. "Not on Lonergan's time." He glanced in the rear-view mirror at Verita's car. "How'd the chick take the bad news?"

"She's not mad."

"I figured that when I saw her drive you over to the clinic at Cedars. You got your shots?"

I nodded. "I don't get it. Lonergan has to have more important things for you to do than to follow me around."

"I just do what I'm told." He pulled out a cigarette and stuck it in his mouth. "Ready to go?"

"I just want to go upstairs and change. Then we'll be right with you."

"We?"

I nodded my head toward Verita, who was walking toward us. "She's coming along."

"What for? Lonergan said nothing about her."

"She's my accountant. Even Lonergan knows that nobody buys a business unless their accountants go over the books."

For the first time he wasn't as sure of himself. "I don't know."

I pointed to the telephone under his dash. "Call him and check it out. I'm going upstairs. If it's okay, toot your horn and I'll come down. If not, just forget it."

Verita and I went into the building as he was picking up the phone. She followed me up the flight of stairs and into the apartment. I opened the door and stared in astonishment. The apartment had never looked like this.

It had been cleaned so thoroughly that even the windows and the crummy furniture shone. And when I went into the bedroom, I found that my clothes had been pressed, all my shirts washed and neatly ironed.

"You're quite a housekeeper," she said. "I wouldn't have guessed."

Before I could answer, the boy came out of the bathroom. He was nude except for an apron around his middle. In one hand he held a bottle of Clorox, in the other a cleaning brush. He stared at us. "Who are you?" he asked.

"I'm Gareth," I said. "I live here."

His face broke into a sudden smile. "Oh, Gareth, I love you," he said. "I want to cook and clean and wash and press for you. I want to be your slave."

Just then I heard the horn blast from the Jaguar outside in the street. I looked from one to the other. Nothing made sense anymore.

There was a hint of laughter in Verita's voice. "I think you'd better send him down to the clinic and get him a shot, but not until after he finishes in the bathroom."

Chapter Four

The offices of the *Hollywood Express* were located in a dingy store on Santa Monica Boulevard about a block from the Goldwyn Studios. The Collector pulled his car to a stop in front of the store in a no-parking zone. With a fine disregard for the rules of the road he managed also to take up half the bus stop.

The windows of the store were painted over with dirty white paint so that you could not see inside, and smeared black lettering spelled out the newspaper's name.

The Collector opened the door and walked in. Along the walls of the store were eight or nine empty desks. At the back of the room was a large wallboard filled with papers pinned up with red, yellow and blue tacks.

"Anybody here?" the Collector called out.

There was the sound of a door creaking from a back room and a tired-looking, middle-aged man came out, drying his hands on a paper towel. He dropped it on the floor as he came toward us. "You're an hour late," he said in a complaining voice.

"I wasn't late, you were early," the Collector said flatly.

"Lonergan said—" The man's voice faded as the Collector looked at him.

The Collector gestured to me. "Gareth Brendan, Joe Persky."

The man shook my hand unenthusiastically. Even his fingers felt tired. "Nice to meet you."

I nodded. "This is Verita Velasquez, my accountant."

He shook hands with her, then turned back to me. "Lonergan says you're interested in buying the paper."

"I'm glad he told you. I didn't hear about it until last night."

Persky turned back to the Collector. For the first time a note of emotion came into his voice. "What the hell is Lonergan trying to pull? He told me he had a bona fide customer."

The Collector just looked at him.

Persky turned back to me. "Are you interested or not?"

"Maybe. That depends. I'd like to look over your operation before I make up my mind."

"There's nothing to look over. It's all here."

"You don't sound as if you want to sell. Maybe we'd better forget the whole thing."

"He don't have any choice," the Collector said. "Lonergan says he wants to sell."

There was a moment's silence; then the anger seemed to seep out of the man. "What do you want to know?" he asked.

"The usual things. Circulation, sales, advertising revenue, costs. If you'll show your books to Miss Velasquez, I'm sure we can find out everything we want to know."

The man was sullen. "We never kept any formal books."

"You must have records of some kind. How else would you know how you were doing?"

"I operated mostly on a cash basis. The money came in. I paid it out. That's all."

I turned to the Collector. "Does Lonergan know that?"

The Collector shrugged. I should have known better than to ask. Of course Lonergan knew. I turned back to Persky. "You must have some figures. You had to file tax returns."

"I don't have any copies."

"Somebody must have. Your accountant?"

"I didn't use an accountant. I did everything myself. And that included stuffing the paper into mailboxes."

I'd had it. If Lonergan thought I was going to stick my neck into this mess, he was crazier than I was. I turned to the Collector. "Let's go."

The Collector moved so fast I hardly saw his hand. Suddenly Persky was thrown back against a desk. His hands clutched at his stomach and he was bent over and almost retching. The Collector's voice was empty. "You give the man the information he asks for."

Persky's voice rasped in his throat. "How do I know this guy an' this dame ain't some kind of revenue dicks? There's nothing in the law that says I got to incriminate myself."

"Fuckhead! Internal Revenue ain't goin' to get Lonergan's money back for him."

Slowly Persky straightened up. His face returned to its normal colour. "I don't keep the books here. They're in my apartment."

"We'll go over there and look at them then," I said. "Where is your apartment?"

"Upstairs," he said. "Over the store."

Verita spread the ledgers and the pile of forms across the kitchen table. "It's going to take me some time to sort this out," she said.

"How long?" I asked.

"Maybe the rest of the day. It's a mess." She turned to Persky. "Do you have a four-column pad?"

"What you see is what I got."

"I'll run down to a stationery store and get one," she said.

Persky looked at me after she had gone out. "Would you like a beer?"

"Thanks," I said.

I followed him into the kitchen and he took two beers from the refrigerator. We drank from the cans. "Ever run a paper?" he asked.

"No." I let the beer run down my throat. It was cool, not cold.

He saw the expression on my face. "There's something wrong with the damn refrigerator. Sometimes it works; sometimes it doesn't. If you've never run a paper, what makes you interested in this one?"

"I didn't say I was. It was Lonergan's idea."

"What makes him think you can do it?"

"I don't know. Maybe because I used to write and worked on some magazines."

"It's not the same thing," he said. He looked at me shrewdly. "Lonergan got you, too?"

"No. I'm straight with him." That was the truth. At the moment I owed him nothing.

He was silent for a moment. "Be careful. Lonergan's got half the world by the balls now and he's looking to get the other half."

I didn't say anything.

For the first time an expression of interest came over his face. "Write, you said? What kind of material?"

"Articles, commentary, poetry, fiction. I tried them all."

"Any good at it?"

"Not very."

"I'd settle if I could be even a half-assed writer, but I know now I can't get enough words together to make a decent sentence. Once I thought I could. That's how I got into this paper."

"What did you do before?" I asked.

"I was circulation manager for several papers like this around the state. They all did pretty good and it seemed easy, so when I got the chance, I grabbed this one." He paused heavily. "It wasn't easy."

"How'd you get in with Lonergan?"

"How does anybody get involved with Lonergan? You run a little short. Next thing you know you're a lot short."

"You had a business. What about the banks?"

"Zilch. I tapped out with them the first time around."

"What do you owe Lonergan?"

"I don't the fuck know. How does anybody know with that crazy six-for-five bookkeeping mushrooming week after week? I wouldn't be surprised if it turned out to be a million dollars by now."

By the time Verita finished at six o'clock that evening it turned out that he owed Lonergan nineteen thousand dollars. Plus about eight thousand dollars to the printers and suppliers and thirty-seven thousand dollars in withholding taxes to the state and federal governments. And no assets except a couple of lousy old desks.

"You hit the jackpot. Sixty-four thousand dollars," I said.

His voice was a whisper as he stared down at the yellow sheet covered with Verita's neat little accountant's figures. "Jesus! I knew it was a lot, but seeing it like that – it's scary."

Verita's voice was gentle. "You have nothing really to sell. What you should do is go bankrupt."

He stared down at her. "Does bankruptcy get me out of the taxes?"

She shook her head. "No, taxes are not forgiven."

"Nobody busts out on Lonergan either. Not if you want to keep your head attached to your neck." His voice was dull. He turned to me. "What do we do now?"

I felt sorry for him. Then I got angry at myself. I was feeling sorry for too many people. I had even been sorry for the gooks I lined up in my rifle sights in Vietnam. The first time it happened I couldn't squeeze the trigger until I saw the bullets tearing into the shrubbery around me and realised that he was my enemy and wasn't feeling sorry for anybody. Then I squeezed the trigger and saw the automatic fire hemstitch across his middle until he almost broke in half. I had had no business feeling sorry then and I had no business feeling sorry now. Not for the kid who tried to hit me last night or for this asshole who was willing to go along while Lonergan ripped me off.

I turned to Verita. "Let's go. We're not catching the Hollywood Express."

She began to get up. Persky grabbed my arm. "But Lonergan said—"

Roughly I shook my arm free. "I don't give a damn what Lonergan said. Lonergan wants your paper, let him buy it. With his money, not with mine."

"The Collector's coming baek for you at seven. What should I tell him?"

"You can tell him what I told you. He can give Lonergan the message. I'm going home."

Chapter Five

Verita had left her car at my place, so we walked home. It took us about an hour.

"I'll go home now," she said as we reached the apartment.

"No, come upstairs. I have a bottle of wine. We can have a drink. I want to thank you for what you've done."

She laughed. "It was fun. I had six years of training for this kind of work and today was the first time I ever got a chance to use it."

Something hit me. "You're not talking Chicano."

She laughed. "That's for the unemployment office. Accountants speak another language."

I found myself with a new respect for her. "Come on up," I said. "I promise we'll talk American."

She looked up at me out of the corner of her slightly slanted eyes. "But – the boy?"

I smiled at her. "He's probably gone by now."

But I was wrong.

The delicious odour of roast beef greeted us as we came through the door. The table was set for two – china, crystal, linen napkins and heavy silver flatware and candlesticks.

"You live pretty good," Verita said, looking at me.

"None of those things are mine. I never saw them before."

I went into the kitchen. The boy was standing in front of the oven. He was dressed in a light plaid jacket and white linen slacks, a St. Laurent foulard tied casually inside the collar of his silk shirt. He turned as I came in. "Dinner will be ready in about twenty minutes." He smiled. "Go back inside and relax. I'll be right out to fix you a drink."

Without answering, I turned back to the living room. "He says he'll be right in to fix us a drink," I said in a stunned voice.

She laughed. "Looks like you came up with a winner."

The boy came in from the kitchen, went over to the small hutch on the wall and opened it. The bottles were neatly arranged on the shelf – vodka, gin, scotch, vermouth. Without saying anything, he took some ice from a golden bucket, put it in a glass and poured scotch over it. He turned to me, holding it out. "You drink scotch if I remember?"

I nodded as I took the drink. He turned to Verita. "What would you like?"

"Vodka tonic?" Her voice was questioning.

He nodded and came up with a bottle of tonic from a lower shelf. Quickly he fixed her drink. She took it and we both stood there staring at him. He gestured toward the couch. "I rolled a few joints," he said. "They're with the cigarettes in the box on the coffee table. Why don't you just have a few tokes? It will help you relax. You both look a little uptight."

"Hey—" I called as he went through the door to the kitchen.

He turned. "Yes?"

"Where did all this come from?"

"I just called up and ordered it."

"You called up and ordered it?" I repeated. "Just like that?"

He nodded. "They were very nice. I told them to rush because I needed everything for dinner."

I looked at him suspiciously. "They didn't ask you for money or anything?"

"Why should they? I just charged it."

I was getty punchy. "You ever stop to think how I'm going to pay for it? I haven't any money."

"That's nothing. I told you I'm rich."

"When did you tell me?"

"Last night. Don't you remember?"

I shook my head. "I don't remember anything about last night."

"You were reading your poetry, the window was open and it began to rain. You were naked and you said that the Lord was washing away your sins. It was beautiful. Then you began to cry and said the world was all fucked up because of money and that if everyone had been born rich, there wouldn't be any problems. That's when I told you I was rich and I had problems. And you felt sorry for me. That's when I fell in love with you. No one had ever felt sorry for me before."

"Oh, shit," I said. "I must have been stoned out of my head."

"No," he said quickly. "You were really cool. You made me see things more clearly than I had ever seen them before."

"I did?"

He nodded. "I called my father and told him I forgave him."

I hadn't the faintest notion of what he was talking about. He saw the expression on my face. "You really don't remember anything, do you?"

I shook my head.

"You were on Hollywood Boulevard hitching a ride—"

I had a sudden flash of memory. "The silver-blue Rolls convertible?"

"Yes. I stopped to pick you up and we began to talk. I said I would drive you home, but you said a car like that in this neighbourhood would get ripped off. So we put it in a garage a few blocks away."

It was beginning to come back to me. We'd stopped in a liquor store and he'd paid for a few bottles of wine; then we'd come to my place and talked. Mostly about his father and how his father could not accept the fact that his son was gay. And how he constantly tried to keep the boy hidden from his congregation. After all, the Reverend Sam Gannon was almost as famous as Billy Graham, Oral Roberts and Kathryn Kuhlman combined. You could see him almost every week on television, preaching to the world that God cures all. Yet even God couldn't straighten out his son. Jesus did His own thing and look at all the trouble He'd got himself into. I remembered telling the boy to tell that to his father. I also remembered something else. We just talked.

"Okay, Bobby," I said, finally remembering the boy's name. "I just got it together."

"Good," he said, smiling. "Now, relax while I finish dinner."

"We're going to have to talk," I said.

He nodded. "After dinner."

I turned to Verita, who had been watching us. "We got a shot for nothing."

She looked at me, relief in her eyes. "That proves one thing, Lonergan doesn't know as much as he thinks he does."

I slumped onto the couch and reached for a cigarette.

She stood looking down at me. "Lonergan isn't going to like it."

"Fuck him."

"Not that easy. He's tough. He usualy gets what he wants."

"Not this time."

A shadow came into her eyes. "You'll hear from him."

She was right about that. The knock came just as we were finishing dinner. I started to get up.

"Finish your coffee," Bobby said, opening the door. Over his shoulder I could see the Collector.

He pushed past the boy, his eyes taking in the room before looking down at me. "Got the best of both worlds, haven't you?"

"I'm trying."

"Lonergan wants to see you."

"Okay. Tell him I'll be over later."

"He wants to see you now."

"There's no rush. We've got nothing to talk about. Besides, I haven't finished dinner."

I sensed rather than saw his movement. I was a lot slower than I had been in the Green Berets seven years ago, but a lot faster than he could have expected. My knee and elbow came up, the knee catching him in the balls, my elbow jammed into his Adam's apple. He gave a weird kind of grunt and fell onto his knees. Then slowly he rolled over on his back. His eyes bulged in a face that had turned a strange shade, pale grey-blue, his mouth was open, gasping for air, and his hands clutched at his genitals.

I looked down at him and, after a moment, saw the natural black colour begin to return to his face. Without getting out of my chair, I picked up the steak knife and held the point to his throat while I opened his jacket and took the heater from his belt holster. I waited until his caught his breath. "I don't like being pushed. I said I would come over later."

His eyes crossed as he looked down at the knife held to his throat. Lonergan's voice came from the still-open doorway. "Feel better now, Gareth?"

He was slim and pale and his eyes were narrowed behind the gold-rimmed spectacles. He stepped into the room, his bodyguard on his heels. "You've proved yourself. Now you can let him up."

I straightened up and put the knife back on the table. I met his eyes. "You got my message?"

He nodded.

"I'm not interested in the paper. It's like buying my way into bankruptcy."

"You're right."

I was silent.

"If you had gone for that deal, I wouldn't have made it. I can't stand stupidity."

"Then what do you want?"

"Would you take the paper if it were free and clear of all attachments?"

I glanced at Verita. She nodded almost imperceptibly. I turned back to him. "Yes."

"You'll still have to get a loan to carry the operating expenses."

Verita spoke before I had a chance to answer. "The only way he can afford that is if he gets to keep twenty-five per cent of the classified advertising revenue."

"Your accountant's pretty sharp," he said. "Twenty per cent."

I looked at Verita. "With twenty per cent we could just make it," she said. "But it would be tight."

"Let me think about it. I'll let you know in the morning."

Lonergan's voice turned hard. "You'll let me know now."

I was silent while I thought. What the hell did I know about running a newspaper even if it was just an advertising freebie?

"Afraid you can't cut it, Gareth? All the big talk about writing and publishing is different now that you might have to put your money where your mouth is."

I still didn't say anything.

"At least your father tried, even if he didn't have the guts to carry it through. You haven't even got the guts to begin." His voice had taken on an icy edge.

I remembered that voice from when I was a kid and knew that it reflected a controlled contempt for the rest of the world. I was suddenly angry. I wasn't going to let him or the sound of his voice push me into doing anything I wasn't ready to do.

"I'll need help," I said. "Experienced help. Will Persky still be around?"

"If you want him."

"I'll need an art director, reporters, photographers."

"There are services that supply all that. You don't need them on your payroll," he said.

"Have you figured out how many copies I would have to sell at a quarter each to break even?" I asked Verita.

"About fifteen thousand," she said. "But nobody ever paid for the paper before."

"I know that, but that's not the kind of paper I want to run. I want a chance to make some real money."

Lonergan smiled suddenly. For a moment I almost suspected he had a sense of humour. "Gareth," he said, "I'm beginning to think you're growing up. This is the first time I've ever heard you express an interest in money."

"What's wrong with that, Uncle John? Being rich hasn't seemed to cramp your lifestyle."

"It might cramp yours."

"I'll take that chance."

"Then we have a deal?"

I nodded. I leaned forward and helped the Collector to his feet. I held out his gun. He took it. "I'm sorry," I said. "I get nervous when people make sudden moves toward me."

He growled something roughly in his throat.

"Your throat might be sore for a few days," I said. "But don't worry about it. Just gargle with warm salt water and it'll be all right."

"Come on, Bill," Lonergan said, moving toward the door. "Let's leave these good people to finish their dinner."

In the doorway he looked back at me. "Eleven o'clock tomorrow morning in my office in Beverly Hills."

"I'll be there."

"Good night, Gareth."

"Good night, Uncle John."

The door closed behind him and I turned to Verita. "I guess we're in the publishing business," I said.

She didn't speak.

"You'll come with me, of course."

"But my job."

"I'm offering you a better one. A chance to do what you trained for. Besides, I need you. You know I'm not a businessman."

She looked at me for a moment. "I can take a leave of absence while we see how it works out."

"That's okay with me. At least that way if I go on my ass, you won't get hurt."

"I've got the strangest feeling," she said in a hushed voice.

"What's that?"

"Your stars have crossed. And the path of your life will change."

"I don't know what that means. Is it good or bad?"

She hesitated. "Good, I think."

There was a knock at the door. I started to open it, but Bobby got there first. The bodyguard looked over the boy's head. "Mr. Lonergan asked if you wanted a car sent for you."

"Please thank him," I answered. "But tell him I have transportation."

The door closed. Bobby came back toward me, his eyes wide. "Are you really buying a newspaper?"

"Yes," I said. "Not much of a paper, but it's something."

"I was art director of my college paper," he said.

I laughed. "Okay. You got a job. You're now the art director of the *Hollywood Express.*"

Suddenly we all were laughing and none of us really knew why. Except that maybe Verita was right. Our stars had crossed and somehow the world had changed.

Chapter Six

Bobby's eyes were shining. "Did you mean what you said?"

'What did I say?"

"About my being art director on your paper?"

"Sure, but I can't pay a big salary."

"That's not imortant. It's the opportunity I want. Nobody ever offered me a real job before."

"Well, you've got it now."

"What kind of paper is it?"

Right now it's an advertising throwaway. But that's not what it's going to be when I get through with it."

"What will it be then?"

"A cross between the underground papers and *Playboy*. We're going to hit people where they live. In the balls."

"I don't understand," he said.

"*Playboy* fudges," I said. "They airbrush their articles just like they airbrush the pussies off their girls. The underground press shovels the shit so hard your fingers smell from just holding one of their rags. I think there's a balance, a way of telling it how it is and at the same time not make the reader feel he's covered with dirt."

"But that's not what Lonergan wants," Verita said. "He wants the kind of paper that it is."

"What Lonergan is buying is a laundry. Four pages of advertising to convert his cash. He doesn't give a damn about the rest of it. You can print it on toilet paper for all he cares."

"I don't know," Verita said doubtfully.

"I do, I've known him all my life. Money is his only passion."

"You called him Uncle John," she said.

"He's my uncle, my mother's brother."

She took a deep breath. Now she understood. "You don't like him?"

"I don't feel one way or the other," I said. But it wasn't true. If anything, I felt too much. There was not one area in my life that Uncle John did not seem to touch. And that began even before I was born. First, with my mother, then, my father.

"I'm tired," I said abruptly. "I'm going to bed."

"I'd better be going home then," Verita said quickly.

"No," Bobby said. "You don't have to go. I'll sleep on the couch."

"Shit, Verita, it's too late for you to go," I said.

"You sure?"

"Of course I'm sure," I snapped. "You always make me horny. Come to bed. I want to fuck the ass off you." I started for the bedroom. When I saw the tears suddenly well up in Bobby's eyes, I stopped. "What's with you?"

"I love you, Gareth," he wailed. "I want to be your slave. I want you to love me."

I put an arm around his shoulders and kissed his cheek, "I love you, Bobby, but not that way. I feel like a big brother to you."

He wiped at his eyes. "I never had a brother."

"Neither did I."

He smiled. "I like that. It's pure."

"Superpure. Like the scotch. Now I'm going to bed."

Verita followed me into the bedroom about ten minutes later. I couldn't wait until I got her clothes off. My cock felt as if it were made out of stone. We fucked until I collapsed with exhaustion. But I still didn't come. Scotch did that to me. She was asleep almost before I rolled off her. I closed my eyes and zonked.

It seemed as if I had been asleep for hours when I felt a nuzzling at my balls. Still in the twilight zone, I put my hands in her hair and guided my cock into her mouth. Her mouth was warm and expert. At times I felt as if she were going to swallow me alive. "Oh, baby, you do that so good," I murmured. Then I exploded. The orgasm seemed to drain all the fluids from my body, leaving me empty and exhausted. A few second later I dropped back into a deep sleep.

I woke up with the sun streaming into my eyes. I began to sit up. She opened her eyes. I bent over and kissed her forehead. "I never knew you could give head like that," I said. "You blew everything, including my mind."

Her eyes widened. "What are you talking about?"

"Last night."

She shook her head.

I swung my feet off the bed and stepped on his back. He moved away without waking up. Then I put it all together. At first I was angry; then I began to laugh.

Verita was puzzled. "What is it?"

"Damn!" I said.

"What are you complaining about?" she asked. "You got the best of both worlds."

Bobby drove us into Beverly Hills in his Rolls convertible. I felt like one of the Beverly Hillbillies driving past Nate n' Al's and seeing all the New York refugees standing on line, waiting to get in for the Sunday service of lox, cream cheese and bagels.

When we got to my uncle's office down the street, we found the building locked. I pressed the call button. A uniformed guard peered through the glass window.

"Lonergan," I shouted.

He nodded and opened the door. "Mr. Brendan?"

"Yes."

"Mr. Lonergan's expecting you. Penthouse floor."

"I'm hungry," Bobby said. "I'll be over at the deli."

"Okay," I said and with Verita followed the guard to the elevator. My uncle's bodyguard was waiting for us. Silently he led us through the corridor to Lonergan's office and opened the door.

My uncle was behind his desk and Persky was with him. This was nothing like the Hollywood office. This one smelled of money – silk drapes, thick carpets and a Louis Quinze desk.

"Good morning," I said.

My uncle waved us to chairs in front of his desk and pressed a button. A moment later a man came in the side door, carrying a folder of papers.

"My attorney, Mark Coler," my uncle said. "He has all the papers ready. Purchase agreements, loan applications, everything."

Looking at him, I thought, he really was kind of fantastic. Although I knew he couldn't possibly have gone to bed before five in the morning, he looked as fresh as if he had twelve hours' sleep. I also realized that he must have been very sure of this deal because there was no way he could have had all the papers prepared between last night and this morning.

Coler spread the documents on the desk in front of me. "You want to look them over?"

I pushed them toward Verita. "Miss Velasquez will check them for me."

Coler glanced at her, then back at me. "Is she an attorney?"

Verita answered for herself. "I've graduated UCLA law school, but I haven't taken the bar. I am a certified public accountant, however."

He seemed impressed and fell silent while she looked at the papers.

I turned to Persky. "Did Mr. Lonergan tell you I would like you to stay on?"

"Yes," Persky answered. "But I can't afford it. I gotta make some bread. I'm six months behind on my child support and alimony."

"I didn't expect you to work for nothing."

"What you plan on paying?"

I didn't know what the going rates were, so I took a stab. "A buck and half a week, plus a ride on the profits."

"I can't cut it. I got an offer of two-fifty from the *Valley Times*."

I didn't need anyone to tell me that two hundred and fifty dollars was way over my head. "A buck and a half is my top."

"He'll take it," my uncle said before he could answer.

Persky started to object, but the expression on my uncle's face stopped him. "I can't cover my bills on that kind of money, Mr. Lonergan," he said in a mild tone.

My uncle's voice was cold. "You'll cover less bills from a hospital bed, Persky. The only reason you're getting off this easily is because I want this deal made."

Persky looked at me. He knew when he was licked. "I'm working for you," he said.

"Good." I smiled. "We get lucky you'll get more bread."

"I got your word," he said, holding out his hand. "Shake."

"Everything seems okay," Verita said. "But there's one more thing that I think is necessary – an indemnification guarantee against the past debts and taxes of the company signed by Mr. Lonergan."

Coler sounded annoyed. "Mr. Lonergan is not a principal in this deal. There's no reason for him to sign a paper like that. Besides, you already have Mr. Persky's signature."

Verita looked at me for support. "Mr. Coler," I said, "I can't pay Mr. Persky enough money to make his signature worth the paper it's written on. Mr. Lonergan told me I would have the paper free and clear. If I don't get it that way, I don't want it."

"Mr. Lonergan never—" Coler began.

My uncle interrupted him. "Prepare the guarantee, Mr. Coler. I'll sign it."

"I can't have it until tomorrow. There's no one in my office today."

"You'll have it tomorrow, Gareth. Will my word do?"

"Yes, Uncle John."

My uncle smiled. "Good. Then let's sign the rest of the papers."

I arranged to meet Persky at the office the next morning and by the time I left I owned a newspaper. We pushed our way through the crowd at Nate n' Al's and sat down at Bobby's table.

"How'd it go?" he asked.

"We're in business," I said.

Chapter Seven

It was a little more than two weeks later that Lonergan came down to the store, the first edition of the new *Hollywood Express* clutched in his hand. He pushed his way past the crowd of kids who were busy cleaning and painting to my desk at the back of the room.

He threw the paper down in front of me. "What the hell are you trying to pull?"

"You wanted the paper in a hurry. I got it out."

"You call this a paper?" he stormed. "There's nothing in it but my ads. Who the hell do you think's going to look at that?"

"Who the hell looked at the others?"

"And your headline, 'This edition was published solely in order not to disappoint the readers who had come to depend on us for a superior brand of toilet paper.' I don't think that's funny."

"I do."

"It's vulgar and in bad taste."

"That's right," I agreed.

"You can't expect me to pay you thirty-two hundred dollars a week for that. If you do, you have another think coming."

"You'll pay me, Uncle John," I said quietly. "We have a firm contract which you signed. It says we publish four pages of classified in every issue. There's nothing in the contract that says we have to print anything else."

"I'm not going to pay."

"Then you're going to get sued. It's a perfectly valid contract."

Suddenly he began to smile. "Okay, I'll pay. Now will you tell me what this is all about?"

"It's going to take me eight to ten weeks to put together the kind of paper I want to publish. Until then I need the bread that your ads give me."

"You could have told me that. I would have given you the time."

"But not the money. Thirty-two grand is a lot of bread."

"We still can't put out a paper like this. It's like waving a red flag in front of the IRS."

"That's not my problem."

"If I advance you the money, will you hold up until the paper is ready?"

"No. Advances have to be earned out or repaid."

He was silent for a moment. "If I give you twenty-five thousand cash free and clear, will you hold up?"

"No payback, no strings?"

"No strings."

"Deal."

He took a checkbook out of his inside pocket, wrote the check and handed it to me.

"Thanks, Uncle John."

"I have only one consolation, Gareth," he said. "If I had to get stung, at least it was all in the family."

I laughed. "I've got the best example in the world, Uncle John."

He looked around the store. "What are all these kids doing?"

"We're dressing up the place. The kind of paper I want can't be published from a shithouse."

"Where'd they all come from?"

"The Reverend Gannon's Youth Workshop. They work in their spare time for fifty cents an hour and contribute it to the church."

"Your boyfriend's father has better business sense than either of us."

"You can't beat Jesus Christ," I said.

He looked back at the paper. "Do you have many of these left?"

"No."

"Too bad. If I had known in time, we could have stopped them from going out."

"Don't worry about it, Uncle John. Nobody else will see them."

"How can you be sure?"

I smiled. "I printed only twenty-five copies. And all of them were delivered to you."

"Mr. Brendan." The voice was soft. "I'm sorry to bother you, Mr. Brendan."

I looked up. It was one of the girls from Reverend Sam's Youth Workshop. She stood in front of me almost apologetically, the tight jeans hugging her ass, the loose boy's shirt accentuating the curve of her breasts. Her arms and face were smudged with paint.

"I'm sorry to bother you, Mr. Brendan," she repeated. "But we're ready to begin work back here."

"Of course. Let me get my papers off the desk and I'll be out of your way."

"Can I help, Mr. Brendan?"

"Thanks. If you'll carry these, I can manage the rest."

She took a stack of folders from my hands. I picked up the typewriter and we went up the back stairs to the apartment. I spread out on one of the tables we had set up in what used to be the living room.

"Is there anything else I can do for you, Mr. Brendan?"

"I don't think so."

She made no move to leave.

"Is there something else?" I asked.

"Bobby said that you were looking for a secretary but that you couldn't afford to pay very much."

"That's right."

"I'm a secretary. I graduated from Sawyer Business College."

"You take shorthand?"

"Not too well. But I'm a very fast typist. Eighty words a minute." She brushed her long brown hair back from her face. "And I know filing, too."

"What's your name?"

"Denise Brace."

"Where do you live, Denise?"

"At the workshop."

"How old are you?"

"Seventeen. I'll be eighteen next month."

"How come you're not living at home?"

Her dark eyes met mine. "I got pregnant. My father threw me out. Reverend Sam took me in and looked after me."

"What about the baby?"

"Reverend Sam arranged for it to be adopted. It was the best thing. I was only sixteen when it happened."

"And you've been at the workshop ever since?"

She nodded. "Reverend Sam is wonderful to me, to all of us. All he wants for us is to be happy and to serve the Lord."

"And when you work, you give all your salary to him?"

"No. To the workshop."

"Don't you keep any for yourself?" I asked curiously.

"Why?" There was an earnest look on her face. "I don't need anything. The workshop gives us everything we need."

"Are there many like you in the workshop?"

"About sixty or seventy. More girls than boys."

"And they all do the same thing that you do? Turn their money over to the workshop?"

She nodded.

"What do you do when you're not working?"

"We spread God's love. We sell tracts and pamphlets. We keep busy."

"And all the money goes to Reverend Sam?"

"Not to him. Reverend Sam isn't interested in money. It goes to the church and the workshop to help in the good work."

Lonergan was right. Reverend Sam had a better thing going than either of us. I looked at her clear, guileless face. "You know you're a very pretty girl," I said.

"Thank you." She smiled. But there was no coquettishness in her smile.

"I don't know whether I could have you work for me," I said. "It would be too tempting. I might want to make love to you."

"I'd like that," she said simply.

"I mean real love, not just petting and kissing."

"I know what you mean."

"What about Reverend Sam? Isn't that considered sinful?"

"Not to Reverend Sam. He preaches that our bodies have

needs as much as our souls and that love can be expressed with both."

I thought that over for a moment. "Is there a great deal of sex in the workshop?"

"Not much. Just between those that like each other."

"Aren't you afraid you'll become pregnant again?"

She laughed. "No chance. The head nurse makes sure we take our pill at breakfast every day and those of us that can't take it are fitted with an IUD."

"And Reverend Sam? Does he go with any of the girls?"

"No. Reverend Sam is above all that. He lives on a higher plane."

"You mean he doesn't have any sex?"

"I didn't say that. We all live on different planes. I'm on the fifth plane. I'm allowed to relate to people as high as the third plane. Only those on the first and second planes can relate physically to the Reverend."

"I see. What does it take to move up to the other planes?"

"Good work. Devotion to the church. Complete honesty in your relations with others."

"That's all?"

She nodded.

"But you have to turn your money over to the workshop?"

"No," she said quickly. "We don't have to. We do it because we want to."

"Would you still do that if you came to work for me?"

"Yes," she said. Her eyes looked down into mine. "May I ask you a question?"

"Sure."

"I know Bobby's in love with you. And I think that girl Verita is too. Are you in love with them?"

"I love them," I said. "I'm not in love with them."

"But you have sex with them?"

"Yes."

"I would like to have sex with you. Do you think I might join you sometime?"

I didn't answer.

"You wouldn't have to give me the job," she said quickly.

"That's not it."

"What is it then?"

"You're way ahead of me. For one thing, you're on a higher plane; for another, you're not eighteen yet."

She smiled suddenly. "That's honest," she said approvingly. "And honesty puts you on the fifth plane automatically." She went to the door and looked back at me. "Wait for me," she said. "I'll be back next month on my birthday."

Chapter Eight

"The distributors want to see a mock-up before they even talk to me," Persky said. "And they said if you don't come up with good pictures, not to bother coming in."

"What do they mean, good pictures?" I asked.

"Girls," he said flatly. "Tits and ass they already got. They want cunt pictures."

"Did you tell them about the editorial policy?"

"They don't give a damn. Words is something they read after they buy the paper. Pictures is what grabs them."

"Okay, we'll get pictures then."

"It ain't that easy. The agencies and the photographers will break you. We can't compete for the exclusives. We haven't that kind of bread."

"Then we'll shoot our own."

"You know some photographers?" he asked.

"We'll find them. Meanwhile, get in touch with the movie studios. I want to get on their press lists. They're always sending out pictures of starlets."

"That's not the kind of pictures they're talking about."

"I know, but it's a beginning. There may be some we can use.'

"I got an idea," he said.

He went to his desk and returned with his attaché case. He took out some small magazines and spread them on the desk.

The titles blew my mind. *Anal Sex*, *Oral Sex*, *Lesbian Love*, *Fuck Party*. I picked up one and riffled through the pages. It was exactly what the title said it was. "Where'd you get these?"

"From Ronzi Distributors. They got them under the counters all over town at five bucks a pop. They got a proposition for us. We give them an exclusive distribution deal and they'll look the other way if we lift a few pictures. Of course, we'll have to crop them carefully so that nobody can trace them."

"We'd be off the stands in a minute if we printed pictures like these."

"We crop them to show only the girls."

"Who's behind Ronzi?" I asked.

He looked uncomfortable. "I don't know. Some guys from back East, I hear."

"Mafia?"

"Like I said, I don't know."

"What else do they want besides exclusive?"

"We didn't go into that."

"Set up a meeting, I'd like to talk to them."

"Sure. I'll get right on . . ." His voice trailed off and I followed his gaze out the front door.

A black Mercedes stretch-out 600 limousine was rolling to a stop. A uniformed chauffeur leaped out and opened the rear door.

I immediately recognized the man who got out of the car. I had often seen him on television. What I hadn't realized was how large he was in person. Over six-four and with shoulders so broad that he had to turn sideways to come through the doorway.

The kids stopped working. Their voices were filled with hushed respect. "Peace and love, Reverend Sam."

He held up a benevolent hand. "God is love, my children," he rumbled with a warm smile.

"God is love," they answered in unison.

He came through the store toward my desk. I rose to my feet as he approached, making everything in the store look dwarfed beside him. "Mr. Brendan?"

"Yes, Reverend Sam."

He held out a hand. "God is love. It's a pleasure to meet you, boy."

I took his hand and felt not only his tremendous strength but a flow of energy that seemed electrically charged. "My pleasure, sir. What can I do for you?"

He glanced sideways at Persky. "Is there some place we can talk privately?"

"Of course. Follow me." I led him up the back stairs to the apartment and closed the door behind us. "This okay?"

He nodded. I waved him to a chair at the small kitchen table. "Care for coffee or something?"

"No, thank you." His eyes were appraising. "I came to thank you in person."

"For what?"

"My son, Bobby," he answered. "You did something I've never been able to do: You straightened him out."

I looked puzzled and he chuckled. "In some ways, I mean."

I laughed. "I don't want you giving me too much credit."

He was still smiling. "For the first time in his life somebody got him to work."

"Maybe nobody ever offered him a job before."

"I offered many times. But he wasn't interested."

"You're his father," I said. "As far as he was concerned that didn't count."

"Maybe that's it. Anyway he's a different person now. He's not just drifting anymore."

I was silent. I had nothing more to say about Bobby. But I could tell that he wasn't finished.

"You know Bobby's homosexual?"

I nodded.

"Are you?"

I smiled. "I don't think so."

"You're not sure?"

I shrugged. "There was a time when I was sure of everything. Now I know better."

He glanced around the small apartment. "You live here?"

"I will after Bobby gets through fixing it up. Right now he's scouring the secondhand stores for furniture."

"He tells me that you will need advertising to stay in business."

"That's right."

"Do you have any now?"

"I'm guaranteed four pages an issue."

"Could you use more?"

"Of course."

"My church advertises regularly in the papers and on radio and television. I can take some space and ask businessmen in my congregation to do the same."

"I'd appreciate that," I said. "But wouldn't it be better if you see the kind of paper we put out first?"

"You object to religious advertising?"

"No. But you might not like what we do."

"Bobby already told me. You're going to print pictures of naked women and write about sex and drugs. I have no objections to that. It's part of life. I'm a preacher, not a saint or a moralist. I want to help people find themselves and lead happy lives. Isn't that what you're trying to do in your own way?"

"I used to. But the ideals are gone. Now all I want to do is make a lot of money."

"Nothing the matter with that either." He chuckled deep in his throat. "I've managed to do pretty well combining the two."

He didn't have to tell me how successful he'd been. I had heard how the money poured in.

"I'd like to buy a piece of your paper," he said.

"Sorry, I made a rule when I went into this. No partners."

His eyes were shrewd. "I hear Lonergan has a piece."

"You heard wrong. He has a contract guaranteeing four pages of advertising an issue, which he subcontracts out of his own advertising agency. He has nothing to do with the ownership or the running of the paper."

"That's smart of him." By the way he said it, I knew he had figured out Lonergan's interest.

"We should be getting out our first issue in two three weeks. Why don't you look at it and then let me know what you want to do?"

"I already know what I want to do. How much for a full page?"

"I don't know yet. We haven't worked out a rate sheet."

"How much is Lonergan guaranteeing you a page?"

"Eight hundred."

"You think that's fair?"

I nodded.

"I'll take one page a week for a year," he said. He reached into his pocket, came out with a roll of money and began counting thousand-dollar bills onto the table.

When he got to forty, he pushed the pile of bills towards me. "I think buying a year in advance entitles me to two weeks free."

"You're entitled to more than that."

"I'm satisfied."

"You don't have to pay in advance. What if the paper doesn't last a year?"

He smiled. "That advance should increase your odds on staying in business. You can use the money to put out a better paper."

"There are still no guarantees."

He got to his feet. "Then I'll play the devil. I'll deal for your soul. If you fold before the year is out, you can come to one of my services and consider the bill paid."

Chapter Nine

Ronzi Distributors was located in an old one-storey warehouse in Anaheim. I followed Persky up the loading platform and into the long, narrow building. Racks of books and magazines ran throughout the building seemingly without any kind of system. We walked past the shipping tables, at which a few men were busy packing and filling orders, and down the dirty aisles to the back of the warehouse, where there was an office of sorts behind a glass partition.

It was an open area with several desks scattered around and one large desk off by itself in a corner. Two women and a man were at the smaller desks. Both women were on the phone taking orders; the man seemed to be making up invoices. He looked up. "Ronzi's expecting you," he said, picking up the phone. "I'll call him."

A few minutes later a burly-looking Italian with thick black curly hair and heavy eyebrows came barreling in. He didn't waste any words. "I'm Giuseppe Ronzi," he said. "Come over here and sit down."

We followed him to the big desk. He threw some books and magazines off the chairs and onto the floor. One of the girls silently left her desk and picked them up as we sat down.

"You got a mock-up?" he asked me.

"No. But—"

He cut me off. He stared at Persky belligerently. "I tol' yuh not to come out here without a mock-up. I got no time to waste with amateurs." He got to his feet. "Goddammit! It's tough enough tryin' to run a business without—"

"Mr. Ronzi," I said softly, "how would you like exclusive distribution of *Playboy* in the LA area?"

He looked at me with an expression of disbelief. "What'd you say?"

I made my voice a little louder. "Didn't you hear me?"

"I heard something about *Playboy*."

"You heard me," I said, still louder. "You interested?"

"I gotta be crazy not to be."

"Is that what you told Hefner when he came around the first time?"

"You know fucking well I never got a chance at it. He never asked me."

"Then don't make the same mistake twice."

"How can I make the same mistake twiice when I never made it the first time?" he yelled. He turned to Joe. "What's a matter with this guy? He crazy or something?"

"He's crazy," Joe said, smiling.

I got to my feet. "Okay, Joe, let's go."

Joe got out of his chair. So did Ronzi. "Where the hell are you going?" Ronzi shouted. "I thought you guys came out here for a meeting."

"You said you wanted a mock-up. Since I don't have one, I won't waste your time."

"Sit down, sit down," he said. "You're here. We might as well talk."

I returned to my seat. "Okay."

"Who's behind you? Lonergan?"

"Who's behind you? The Mafia?"

"Don't be a smart ass. You want us to distribute your paper or don't you?"

"I don't know yet. You haven't made me an offer."

"How the hell do I know what to offer until I know what you got to sell?"

"That's a good question."

"If it's the same throwaway rag it used to be, I don't want it at any price."

"Neither do I."

"I got eight thousand racks spread around."

"That's good."

"You give me a raunchy paper an' I get you into two thousand of them. Ten in each. That's twenty thousand copies. At a dime a pop for you, that's two grand clear. That's not bad."

"Not for you, it isn't," I said. "But the kind of quality I plan to put into the paper, I have to net at least five thousand an issue to get whole."

"You are crazy. There ain't a garage paper in town that's good for fifty thousand copies a week."

"That's what you told Hefner," I said.

"How many times do I have to tell you, I never spoke to the man?" he shouted.

I laughed. "Just a figure of speech. You would have told him exactly what you're telling me."

"You ain't Hugh Hefner yet."

"That's right," I agreed. "But how do you know who I'll be tomorrow?"

He turned to Joe. "How come you bring me all the crazies?"

Joe smiled. "If he were sane, he wouldn't go into this business."

Ronzi turned back to me. "Thirty-thousand-copy guarantee. Cash in advance. I'll eat the returns for an exclusive."

"Not enough. Forty thousand copies at twelve and half cents on the same basis and you're exclusive for the first year only."

"My partners won't go for it. I got no protection. What if the fucking thing takes off? I get left holding my cock while you grab the brass ring."

"You can always give me more money."

He scowled. "I'd feel better if you give just one idea of what I'm buying."

I had him and I knew it. By now he was convinced that he was turning down Hugh Hefner. But I still had to come up with the clincher. "Who buys these magazines and papers?" I asked, stalling for time.

"Guys buy them. Who else?"

"And why do they buy them?"

"Pussy. They get their rocks off on the pictures. They're always lookin' for somethin' new."

He didn't know it, but he had just given me the idea. "Now, you're getting warm."

"I am?" He was puzzled.

I looked at Joe. I wanted to think the expression on his face was one of respect, but it was probably simply wonder about what I was going to come up with next. The idea was shaping up, but I needed a few seconds more to get it together. I lobbed the ball at Persky. "Okay, Joe, do you want to tell him, or should I?"

"You're the boss. You tell him." He sounded uncomfortable, not wanting to get caught off base.

I lowered my voice. "It's got to be confidential. Not a word outside this office. I don't want anybody stealing this one."

"I'm like a priest at confession. I don't tell nobody," Ronzi said solemnly.

I smiled. Somehow he didn't fit the role. "New pussy," I said.

"New pussy?" he repeated questioningly.

I nodded. "Lead feature, front page. Banner headline. NEW GIRL IN TOWN! A beautiful chick in micro-mini or hot pants. Carrying a small valise. At a bus or train station or an airport. Streamer headline right across her cunt in bold white letters. SEE HER NAKED IN OUR CENTERFOLD!. And there's a new girl each and every week. Fifty-two weeks a year."

Ronzi's mouth was open. "That's fucking genius! Why didn't you tell me before, Joe?"

I got Joe off the hook. "He was bound to secrecy."

"It's great. You know what I like about it? She's naked inside the paper, not outside. That means they got to buy it to see her."

"You got the idea."

"I'll take the forty, but you gotta give me an overrun of ten thousand on consignment and a free page of advertising in each issue."

"Consignment okay at fifteen cents a copy. No freebie advertising. You pay eight hundred bucks a page just like everybody else."

Ronzi appealed to Joe. "Explain the facts of life to this nut. What I'm askin' is only normal."

"What he says is true, Gareth."

"Okay, I'm considerate. I'll give him a fifty per cent trade discount on the advertising. That'll make it only four hundred a page."

"What about the consignment? Fifteen cents a copy is shafting me for doing a good job and selling more," Ronzi said. "I want to hit the newsstands with those. That means I split my money with the dealer and it costs me a nickel a copy to get them out there against only two cents in the boxes."

"You're making me cry," I said.

"You're a crazy prick," he said.

"Thanks. I'll have my lawyer draw up an agreement."

"Who needs a lawyer? My word is good."

"Mine isn't," I said. "You need a lawyer."

Persky didn't speak until we were on the freeway heading back to Los Angeles. "I don't understand you," he said finally.

I lit a cigarette. "There's nothing to understand."

"You don't play with guys like him. He'll kill you if you don't deliver."

"We'll deliver."

"When?" he asked. "We've been cocking around for four weeks now and I haven't even got the smell of the paper yet."

"Two weeks," I said.

"Now I know you're crazy. You just sold a photo layout we haven't even thought through and on top of that not one word of copy has been prepared. Where do you think that's coming from? Heaven?"

I looked at him and smiled. "In a way. Meanwhile, I got another job for you."

"What is it?" he asked disgustedly.

"Advertising sales manager."

"Oh, no. You're not going to stick me with that. There isn't a legitimate advertiser that would spend a nickel in our paper."

"Right on," I said. "What about illegitimate advertisers? There's got to be thousands of topless bars, discos and massage parlours that can't get into the regular papers. We set up a special entertainment section and sell them an eighth of a page at discount rates for seventy-five bucks. I want four pages like that."

"You'll never get 'em. Joints like that want out of the papers, not in. They're afraid of getting busted."

"Everybody likes to see his name in print. They'll buy."

He shook his head. "I don't know."

"'I don't know' gets you a fifty-dollar raise for dawning intelligence. 'Can do' get you a hundred more on top of that."

"Can do," he said with sudden enthusiasm. A moment later he was worried again. "But what about the paper?"

"You do your job, Joe. I'll do mine."

Chapter Ten

"You're spending a lot of money," Verita said.

I put down the piece of copy I was checking. "We short?"

"No. But you've run the cost of this issue up to eleven thousand dollars already. That's as much as we're taking in. If we keep it up, we won't be making a profit."

"First issues always cost more. We needed a lot of things. Give me a breakdown."

She picked up a sheet of paper. "Printer and paper for first issue, seven thousand. We can save a thousand if you don't use glossy for the cover pages."

"Glossy is classy. We keep it. Otherwise, we look like every other rag on the racks."

"Photos, art and layout, twenty-five hundred. Bobby has expensive tastes; he doesn't have a clue to the value of money."

"I told him to go first cabin. That's ninety-five hundred. What's the rest of it?"

"Salary, expenses, et cetera."

"Not much we can do about that. People have to get paid." I lit a cigarette. "What do you think we ought to do?"

"Tighten up on the next issue. Skip the glossy paper and cut Bobby's budget in half."

I smiled. "Spoken like a true accountant. I have a better idea. How much do we have in the bank right now?"

"About eighty thousand dollars."

"Why don't we grab the money and jump over the border to Mexico? We can live pretty good down there for that."

She looked to see if I was kidding. I played it straight. "That would be dishonest."

"So what? We'd have a ball."

She shook her head seriously. "If I wanted to live down there, I could have gone years ago. But I'm American. I like it here."

I laughed. "So do I."

A look of relief came into her eyes. " Iwas beginning to think you meant it."

"Look, it's not so bad," I said. "Bobby's shot enough girls to carry us for six issues. He also has the forms worked out for the layout. All we have to do now is slot them in. He doesn't expect his costs to run over a grand a week from now on."

"That makes me feel better. What about the glossy?"

"It stays. We're asking thirty-five cents a copy. That's a dime more than the other papers and it's the first thing a customer sees. It's gotta look like he's getting more for his money."

"Okay," she said. She took an invoice from her folder. "This bill just came in."

It was from Acme Photo Supplies. Three thousand dollars for cameras and equipment. I tossed it back to her. "Pay it."

"He bought the most expensive cameras. A Rollei and a motor-driven Nikon plus lenses and tripod."

"He could have gone more expensive. It's used equipment. New, they would have cost ten grand. But it doesn't matter. He's going to shoot all the photos himself. That saves us a hundred an hour off the top for the photographer."

"I give up," she said.

I grinned. "You worry too much. How long's it been since you got laid?"

She finally smiled. "You ought to know. Unless you have been grabbing some little chickees from the mission that I don't know about."

"Workshop, not mission," I said. I put down my pencil. The last ten days had been a bitch. There wasn't a night that I had gotten out of the office before two in the morning. That was the trouble with writing everything yourself. There were only so many puff handouts from the film companies that you could use to fill space; then you had to go to work. I made up my mind that if we made money, the first thing I would do was hire a couple of reporter-writers. I hadn't been made for this kind of grind. I checked my watch. It was almost midnight and we were the only two left in the office.

"What do you say we go up to Sneaky Pete's on the Strip and get us a steak then go home and fuck?"

"I have a better idea."

"I'm open."

"You have steaks in the fridge. I can throw them on the broiler and ball while they're cooking."

"Your idea is better." I got to my feet. "What's taking you so long?"

I was really into sleeping. That deep black nothing kind of sleep that is forever and only happens when you've blown your balls out the head of your cock. I didn't hear the telephone. But Verita did.

She shook me awake and put the phone on the pillow next to my ear. "Your mother," she said.

"Hello, Mother," I mumbled.

"Who was that girl?" My mother's voice echoed in the receiver.

"What girl?" I was still fuzzy.

"The one that answered the phone."

"That was no girl. That's my accountant."

"She sounds Mexican," my mother said.

I opened my eyes. My mother always knew how to wake me up. "She's black, too," I said.

"Why are you avoiding me?" my mother asked.

"I'm not avoiding you. I just don't play tennis anymore."

"That's not funny. Do you know what day this is?"

"Christ, Mother, how should I know? At this time of the morning I don't even know what year it is."

"It's ten o'clock in the morning. You haven't changed a bit. I knew what Uncle John was telling me couldn't be true."

"What did he tell you?"

"He said you had really straightened out and were working very hard. He should know better. You'll probably lose all that money he gave you."

"Shit, Mother. Come to the point, why the call?"

"It's the fourth anniversary of your father's death. I thought it might be nice if we had dinner together. You, John and me."

"It won't bring him back, Mother."

"I know that," she said. "But it would be nice if we did something that showed we remember him. Eight o'clock all right?"

"Okay."

"Wear a tie if you still have one. I have a new butler and I don't want him to think that my son is a bum." With that she clicked off.

"That was my mother," I said to Verita as I reached for a cigarette.

"I know." She held a match to my cigarette. "You looked like a baby, you were so fast asleep. I hated to wake you."

"What's that?" I asked, hearing sounds from the kitchen.

"I don't know. Did you expect Bobby to come back last night?"

I shook my head and got out of bed. The moment I opened the bedroom door I could smell the frying bacon. I went to the kitchen.

Bobby, at the stove, spoke without turning his head. "Go back to bed. I'll bring breakfast."

"He's cooking," I told Verita as I returned to the bedroom.

"Better him than me." She laughed. "I'd better get something on."

The door opened just as she got out of bed. Quickly she jumped back in and pulled the sheet over her breasts. Bobby, dressed in a butler's outfit – striped pants, wing collar and bow tie – had a broad smile on his face. In his hands he held a white breakfast tray.

"Breakfast is served, sir," he said, stepping through the doorway.

I heard a giggle and Denise followed him into the room, dressed in a French maid's uniform – shiny black micro-mini dress, long black opera-length nylons, tiny white apron and cap. She, too, carried a breakfast tray. "Breakfast is served, madame," she giggled.

Solemnly each of them placed the trays on our laps. "What the hell's going on, Bobby?" I asked.

He laughed. "Drink your orange juice and champagne. This is a very important day."

He grinned broadly, reached under his jacket and came out with a neatly folded paper. "Morning paper, sir. First copy off the press."

I looked down at the bold black heading. THE HOLLYWOOD

EXPRESS. Beneath it was the bold two-colour picture of Denise getting off the bus at the Greyhound station and the streamer running through the photo read NEW GIRL IN TOWN!

"You got it!" I yelled.

He was laughing. "We were down at the printers at six this morning."

"Jesus," I said, turning the pages. There was something about it that was different. Even though I had seen everything in proofs, I got what felt like an electric charge from holding the actual paper in my hands.

"Like it?" Bobby asked.

"Hey," I said in answer to his question, "call Persky, tell him to get down there and start the distribution."

"He's down there already. The first five thousand are on their way to Ronzi." He came up with two more glasses of orange juice and champagne and gave one to Denise. "To the *Hollywood Express*," he said. "May it never get derailed."

In a strange way I still couldn't believe it was real. I flipped through the pages again and stopped at the centerfold. There Denise was – naked and beautiful. The photographs had a fresh country-fed sensuality that leaped off the pages. It was a kind of innocent sexual awareness that spoke a language all its own.

I could see that Verita felt the same way I did. "What do you think?" I asked her.

"I'll pay the bills this morning," she answered simply.

"The pictures are sensational, Bobby. And I can't believe how beautiful you look, Denise."

She smiled artlessly. "Thank you. I was nervous about them."

"She was worried about showing too much pussy. I told her I would take care of it."

"Airbrush?"

He shook his head. "You said no airbrush, remember? I gave her a trim. It came out sensationally, don't you think?"

I grinned at him. "You can put a sign out as a cunt coiffeur. You'll wind up making a mint." Suddenly I was starved and started attacking the bacon and eggs. "What about you two?" I asked between bites. "Have you had any breakfast?"

"I thought you'd never ask," Bobby said, leaving the room. He was back a moment later with another tray. He put it across the bed and they both climbed on and sat cross-legged facing us. Suddenly a thought crossed my mind.

"Your father's ad," I said to Bobby. "I never saw it."

"We got it down there last night. It's on the back cover."

I turned over the paper. There was the usual picture of Reverend Sam's smiling face that I had seen many times before in other papers. But the copy was different. Under the banner heading, THE CHURCH OF SEVEN PLANES, there were two simple lines: "What you do with your bodies is your business. What you do with your soul is ours. Let us help you find God on your own terms."

"Does he really mean that, Bobby?"

"Yes," Denise said, answering for him. "I told him I was doing the photographs. He didn't say anything. I also told him how I felt about you."

"What's that got to do with it?"

She smiled. "I thought you might have forgotten." She leaned across the tray and kissed me on the mouth. "I'm eighteen today."

Chapter Eleven

The distance between Hollywood and Bel Air was a million dollars. When I went past the Bel Air patrol at the main gate, they didn't give me a second glance. I was driving Bobby's Rolls and that meant automatic approval. I would have been flagged down in anything less than a Caddy or a Lincoln Continental. I turned onto Stone Canyon Drive, which led to my mother's house.

The streets were dark and deserted. Lights shone in the houses on either side, but there was no sound coming from them. Lonergan's car was already in my mother's driveway. His chauffeur was leaning up against the big black Caddy limousine. I pulled to a stop behind him. He looked at me curiously as I got out. I think the car or the straight suit and tie I was wearing must have thrown him because he gave no sign of recognition.

As I pressed the doorbell, I could hear the soft tinkle of the chimes. A butler whom I didn't know opened the door. "I'm Gareth," I said, walking past him into the foyer.

His face was devoid of expression. "Mr. Lonergan is in the library. Your mother will be down in a minute."

That was par for the course. Eight o'clock sharp meant that mother would be ready by eight-thirty.

Lonergan was standing at the library window with a drink in his hand, looking out at the lighted swimming pool and tennis court.

"May I serve you a drink, sir?" the butler asked, as Lonergan turned toward me.

"What are you drinking?' I asked Lonergan.

"Dry martini."

"I'll have the same."

"The house is just as beautiful as the day you moved in. Do you remember that, Gareth?"

"I don't think so. After all, I was only about a year old at the time."

The butler vanished after handing me the drink. I took a sip and it exploded in my stomach. Too late I remembered that I couldn't handle martinis. I put the drink down carefully.

Lonergan studied me. "I had forgotten. Time moves too quickly sometimes."

I didn't answer.

"You look different,' he said.

"It's the threads. Mother wanted me to show up straight."

"You ought to wear them more often. You look good."

"Thank you." I went to the bar and fixed myself a scotch and water. "Martinis are too much for me," I said.

He smiled. "One before dinner gives me an appetite." He came and sat down on one of the couches. "Don't you miss living here?"

"No."

"Why?"

"It's a ghetto."

"Ghetto?"

I sat down on the couch opposite him, the cocktail table between us. "The walls outside separate this place from the rest of the world. It may be rich, but it's still a ghetto. Only the people here don't want to get out."

"I never thought of it like that," he said. He took another sip of his martini. "I don't like your paper. I'm withdrawing my advertising," he said in the same conversational tone.

"You do and I'll sue your ass off,' I said quietly. "We have a firm contract."

"It's an immoral paper. Pictures of naked girls and articles dealing with explicit sex. There isn't a court in the land that would uphold that contract if I showed them a copy of the paper."

I laughed. "I don't advise you to try it. You have too many business interests that can't stand examination. At least not on the basis of morality."

"You mean that?"

I met his eyes. "You better believe it. You were the one who pushed me into this paper. What did you expect me to do? Follow Persky's footsteps into bankruptcy? I went into this to make money, not to act as a Chinese laundry, giving you silk shirts for cotton."

"How many copies did you put out?"

"Fifty thousand. That's thirty-five more than Persky ever got out before. With a circulation like that, you'll buy two more pages if you're smart. Based on those figures, there's no question in my mind that you can justify it."

"How do you know they'll stick?"

"They'll stick. Ronzi's nobody's fool. He's pulled out all the stops on this one."

"Ronzi's Mafia," he said disapprovingly.

"So?"

"You don't want to get involved with people like that."

I laughed. "He warned me about people like you."

We heard Mother's footsteps coming down the staircase. "Come to my office Monday. We'll talk about it then," he said.

"There's nothing to talk about. Besides, I'm busy. I've got the next issue to get out."

We rose to our feet as Mother came in the room. I had to admit that she was quite something. At fifty-two, she didn't look a day over thirty-five. Her face was tanned and unlined, her hair as blond as it had been when I was a kid, and her body lithe from the tennis she played every day. She came toward me and turned a cheek to be kissed.

"You look thin," she said.

She could do it every time. Suddenly I was fifteen years old again. All arms and legs and no tongue.

She didn't wait for me to answer. "Don't you think he looks thin, John?"

A faint smile curved his lips. "I wouldn't worry about him if I were you," he said dryly. "He seems quite capable of taking care of himself."

"He knows nothing about proper diet. I'll bet he hasn't eaten a green salad in months. Have you?"

"I didn't know green salads were fattening."

"Don't be sarcastic, Gareth. You know perfectly well what I mean."

"Mother," I said sharply.

A sudden nervous tremor came into her voice. "What?"

I swallowed my irritation, realizing that it was as difficult for her to communicate with me as it was for me to reach her.

There was no mutual ground on which we could walk. Sad. Down deep sad. I kept my voice light. "You look beautiful, Mother."

She smiled. "Do you mean that?"

"You know I do."

This was safe ground. Her ground. Her voice relaxed. "I have to. Youth is such a cult these days."

Not with the young, I thought to myself. "Let me fix you a drink," I said.

"I'll have a glass of white wine. Less calories."

I went around behind the bar and was taking the wine from the refrigerator when the doorbell chimed. I opened the bottle and looked quizzically at my mother. I had thought there were just going to be the three of us.

My mother read the question in my eyes. "I thought it would be nice if we had just one more person. To balance the table. A girl," she said, taking the glass I offered her. You remember her. Eileen Sheridan. She was really quite fond of your father."

This was no time to argue, but I remembered that Eileen had still had braces on her teeth when my father died. Mother greeted her at the door of the library. Eileen had changed since I'd seen her last. A lot.

She held out her hand to me across the bar and smiled. Her teeth were California white and even. "Hello, Gareth. Nice to see you again."

"Eileen," I said. Her hand had the Bel Air touch – a cross between the effusiveness of the Beverly Hills girls and the limp politeness of the girls from Holmsby Hills. Sincere, polite, cool warmth, I thought. "What are you drinking?"

"What are you drinking?" she asked. Right on. Find out what's going in the establishment. Don't make waves. Then I reminded myself that I'd done the same thing a few minutes before.

"I'm on scotch; Uncle John's into dry martinis; Mother's having low-cal white wine."

"I'll go along with the low-cal."

There was a pause. "That's a beautiful Rolls you have out there," she continued, making conversation.

"Rolls? What Rolls?" Mother was annoyed. "You didn't tell me you had a Rolls."

"You asked me to wear a tie, Mother," I said. "How would it look if I thumb-tripped my way up here?"

"If it's not your car, whose is it?" My mother was not to be put off. Rich friends were okay.

"A friend's."

"That Mexican girl that answered your phone this morning?" she asked suspiciously.

"No, Mother." I laughed. "She's got a beat-up old Valiant that would never get past the guards at the main gate."

"You don't want to tell me," she accused.

"Okay, Mother. If you really want to know, it belongs to a boy who's living with me. He wants to be my slave."

She didn't have a clue to what I was talking about. "Slave?"

"Yes. You know, cook, clean everything."

"And he has a Rolls-Royce? Where did he get it?"

"He also has a rich father."

The light suddenly dawned. "Is he – uh?"

I supplied the word for her. "Homosexual? Yes, Mother, he's gay."

She stared at me, her glass of wine frozen halfway to her lips.

"Dinner is served," the butler announced from the doorway.

I smiled at my mother. "Shall we dine?"

Silently we went into the dining room. Mother had pulled out all the stops – the gold flatware, the Coalport china and the Baccarat crystal. The candles were glowing in the tall candelabra, the bases of which were covered with flowers.

"The table is just beautiful, Mrs. Brendan," Eileen said.

"Thank you," Mother answered absently. We didn't exchange another word until the butler had placed the salad in front of us and left the room. Then Mother broke the silence. "I don't understand you, Gareth. How can you do such a thing?"

"I'm not doing anything, Mother. All I said was that he is living with me."

Mother stood up suddenly. "I think I'm going to be sick."

"Margaret!" My uncle's voice was sharp. "Sit down."

She stared at him for a moment, then sank back into her chair.

"You invited him for a quiet family dinner," Uncle John said mildly. "And you've been on his back from the moment he came in the door."

"But – but, John."

Uncle John didn't let her continue. "Now we're going to have a nice quiet dinner just as you said. And if you need any testimonial to your son's manhood, let me tell you that he is more of a man than his father ever was."

"May his soul rest in peace," I said, putting on a slight brogue. I turned to Eileen. "It's really been nice seeing you again." Then I got to my feet. "Thanks for the vote of confidence, Uncle John, but it doesn't help. I don't belong here and I haven't for a long time. I'm sorry, Mother."

Uncle John caught up with me at the front door. "Gareth, don't be a child.'.

My voice was bitter. "I'm not being a child. A child would sit there and take that shit."

His voice was patient. 'She's upset. You know how important this dinner is to her. Please come back to the table."

I stared at him. I don't think I had ever heard him say "please" before.

"Let it slide," he said. "Being angry with her won't make things better. For either of you."

I nodded my head. He was right. I was acting like a child. Exactly the way I had always acted toward her. When it would get to be too much, I would go off and sulk. I went back to the table.

"I'm sorry, Mother," I said again and sat down.

We had the rest of the meal without further bloodshed.

Chapter Twelve

After dinner we went back into the library for coffee. The coffee was served in demitasse cups, and the cognac in preheated giant brandy snifters.

"Your father loved to have coffee in here," Mother said. "He liked to sit on this couch and look out at the fountain and the lights in the pool." Suddenly she began to cry.

Eileen put her arm around her shoulders. "You mustn't cry, Mrs. Brendan," she said. "It's all in the past."

"Not for me," Mother said in a tight, almost angry voice. "Not until I know why he did this to me."

"He didn't do it to you, Mother," I said. "He did it to himself."

"I still don't understand why he did it. All they wanted him to do was to answer some questions. The investigation afterward proved he had done nothing wrong."

That was her opinion. But the facts were that the government recognized that they couldn't put a corpse in jail. So they wrapped up the case and put it away. I looked at my uncle. His face was impassive.

"Maybe you could explain it to her, Uncle John," I said.

"I already have. I told your mother that he was a fool. There was nothing they could do to him."

I didn't believe that and neither did he. He had one story for me and another for my mother. "Then what was he afraid of?" I asked. "He couldn't be held responsible for the collapse of that school building."

My uncle's voice was expressionless. "Perhaps he was afraid that the politicians would lay the blame on him for their negligence in not placing stricter quality controls in their contracts."

"Could it be that someone got to the politicians and made them ease up?" I asked.

His eyes were unblinking. "I wouldn't know."

"Uncle John is right," I said. "Father lived up to the contract. If the contract wasn't good, he was not to blame. But unfortunately, Father couldn't convince himself of that. He knew the specs were substandard. So he did what he did and the only thing you can do is accept it. Once you do that, you can put it away and go back to living a normal life."

"There's no such thing as a normal life for me," she said.

"Don't give me that crap, Mother," I said. "You haven't stopped playing tennis, have you?"

Her eyes dropped. She knew what I meant. She had a thing about tennis pros and I knew that several of them had serviced her with more than just tennis balls.

"Have you ever thought about getting married again, Mother?" I asked.

"Who would want to marry an old woman like me?"

I laughed. "You're not old and you know it. Besides, you're a beautiful lady and you've got a few million in the bank. It's an unbeatable combination. All you have to do is loosen up a little and stop dropping ice cubes if some guy wants to make it with you."

She was torn, liking the flattery but wanting to assume the proper attitude. "Gareth, try to remember that you're talking to your mother."

"I remember, Mother." I laughed. "And since I'm not the product of an immaculate conception, I want to remind you that it's still fun."

She shook her head. "There's no talking to you, is there? Isn't there anything you respect, Gareth?"

"No, Mother. Not anymore. There was a time I used to believe in a lot of things. Honesty, decency, goodness. But if you get dumped on enough, you get cured. I've been dumped on enough."

"Then what is it you're looking for?"

"I want to be rich. Not just simple rich like Father was, not even rich rich like Uncle John, but superrich. When you're supperich, you've got the world by the balls. Money buys everything – society, politicians, property, power. All you have to do is have the money to pay for it. And the irony is when you have the money, you don't have to pay for anything. People tumble all over themselves to give it to you for free."

"And you think this paper will do it for you?" Uncle John asked, with mild curiosity in his voice.

"No, Uncle John. But it's a beginning." I got to my feet. "It's after ten, Mother," I said. "I've got some work to do."

"What kind of work?"

"The paper has been on the stands in Hollywood since this morning. I'd like to check and see how they're doing."

"I haven't seen a copy of the paper. Would you send me one?"

"Of course."

Uncle John cleared his throat. "I realy don't think you'd be interested in that sort of paper, Margaret."

"Why not?"

"Well – it's sort of, uh, pornographic."

Mother turned to me. "Is it?"

"That's Uncle John's opinion. I don't think it is. You read it for yourself and make up your own mind."

"I will," she said firmly. "You send it to me."

"I'll be leaving, too," Eileen said, getting up. "I have some early classes tomorrow."

We exchanged goodnights. I kissed Mother on the cheek and left her there with Uncle John. Eileen and I went out together. The Rolls and the big Caddy were the only cars in the driveway. Where's your car?" I asked.

"I walked over. It's only two houses down the road, remember?"

I remembered. "Hop in," I said. "I'll drop you off."

We got into the car and she opened her purse. "Want a smoke?"

"You got one?"

"I'm always prepared. I didn't know what kind of night it would be." She lit the joint as I pulled the car out of the driveway. She took a deep toke and passed it to me.

When we arrived at her driveway, she touched my arm to keep me from turning in. "Can I go downtown with you?"

I gave the joint back to her and kept on going. "Sure." I glanced at her face in the glow of the dashboard lights. "What made you come tonight?"

"I was curious about you. I heard so many stories." She turned to me. "You're not really gay, are you?"

I met her glance. "Sometimes."

"Most guys who say they're bi are really only one way."

"Want proof?" I asked. I took her hand and put it down on my hard. All it took to get me there was good grass and the right company.

She pulled her hand away. "I believe you."

"Want me to take you home now?"

"No. Besides, I want to get a copy of your paper to see for myself what it's like."

I pulled the Rolls into a parking-meter space across the street from the newsstand in front of the Ranch Market on La Brea. We sat in the car and watched the action. The usual night crawlers were hanging out. They wore a look of bored patience. It was still early for them. The crunch would come about midnight. If they didn't score by 1 a.m. the ball game would be called off for the night.

We got out of the car, locked it and crossed the street. I started at the corner and walked down past the rows of paperback books and magazines, looking for the paper. I found it near the cash register.

While Eileen hung in back of me, I pretended to be a customer and picked up a copy. I started to open it, but there was a small piece of Scotch tape that bound the edges closed.

The man at the register scarcely looked at me as he spoke. His eyes kept darting up and down the newsstand. "Costs you fifty cents to look at the pussy."

"How do I know it's not a rip-off?"

He gestured with his thumb. I looked at the back of the stand. The paper's centerfold was tacked along the backboard. "Fifty cents," he said in a rasping voice.

"I never saw this paper before," I said, handing him the change.

"Just out today."

"How's it going?"

"I started out this afternoon with fifty. I got maybe five left." For the first time his eyes focused on me. "You the law?"

"No, the publisher."

His weather-beaten face cracked in a smile. "You got a hot number there, sonny. You gotta make a lotta money if they don't hassle you."

"Thanks."

"Maybe you can help me out. I called Ronzi and asked him for a hundred more. I got a big weekend coming up."

"What'd he say?"

"No dice. He says there ain't no more. Now I'm sorry I didn't take the hundred he tried to lay on me."

"I'll see what I can do."

It was the same everywhere we went – Hollywood Boulevard, Sunset, Western Avenue. On the way back to Eileen's house we stopped in at MFK's drugstore in the Beverly Wilshire Hotel. The paper wasn't on the small stand there. It was in a vending machine. While we watched, a man threw two quarters in the slot and took the last copy.

At the counter I ordered a coffee for her and an all-black soda with an extra seltzer for me. As I sucked up the bitter sweetness, I watched her go through the paper. Finally, she looked at me. "Not bad."

I lit a cigarette. "Thanks."

"I can make a few sugggestions if they won't trip over your ego."

"Suggest away."

"The paper's got a lot of guts and vitality," she said, taking the cigarette from my hand. "But there's a lot you don't know."

I nodded for her to go on and lit another cigarette.

"First, the writing is all the same style. It looks as if one man did it all."

"One man did," I said. "Me."

"Not bad," she said. "But you could use a change-up pitcher. Another thing, you have the lead article on page seven. The lead article should always be on page three, so that the reader catches it the minute he opens the paper."

I said nothing.

"Want me to continue?"

I nodded.

The typography should be cleaned up. Whoever sets it hasn't the faintest idea of the content of the story. It'll make the paper look crisper. Who's in charge of typesetting?"

"The printer takes care of that."

"He must charge you plenty for it. You ought to be able to get your own machine for about three thousand. You'll get a better job and the machine should pay for itself in a couple of months."

"You sound like an expert."

"Journalism major for four years. I've got my BA and I'm working on my Master's. For the past two years I've been editor-in-chief of the *Trojan*."

"You are an expert. I appreciate your comments. They make a lot of sense."

"If you like, I'll come down to the paper and see if I can help out."

"That would be nice, but why the interest?"

"I guess maybe it's because you've got something new. I don't quite understand it yet, but I have the feeling that you've come up with a new kind of communication. An interpersonal thing. The paper seems to be talking to people, saying things that maybe they thought about but never put into words."

"I take that as a compliment."

Her eyes were level. "That's the way I meant it."

I reached for the check. "Thank you. I'll take you home now. You give me a call when you're ready to come down."

She smiled. "Tomorrow afternoon okay?"

Chapter Thirteen

The lights were on in the office when I pulled up. The door was unlocked. Persky was at his desk. "I've been waiting for you," he said.

"What's up?"

"Ronzi's been on my back since seven o'clock tonight. He wants another five thousand copies in the morning. He's getting calls from dealers all over town."

"Good. Tell him no."

"He said he'll pay cash."

"He can increase the order for next week's issue. Let their tongues hang out a little. It'll give them an appetite. He can afford it. We agreed on a thirty-five-cent newsstand price and he's been getting fifty. He's been ripipng us off for fifteen cents a copy. Fuck him."

"I think I can push him up to ten thousand. That's another fifteen hundred, Gareth."

"If he runs out, he'll go for twenty thousand more next week. Tell him I don't want to do it."

"I been in this business a long time, Gareth. You gotta grab it when you can get it."

"We're going to be in business for a long time. Let's not run until we learn to walk." I started for the stairs. "How much would it cost to get a typesetting machine?"

"A good one – used, about three grand, new, eight."

"Tomorrow start looking for a good used machine," I said, thinking that Eileen knew what she was talking about. "Bobby still around? I brought his car back."

Persky gave me a funny look. "He left in a cab about an hour ago. He said he was going to a costume party or somethin'."

"Costume party?"

Persky laughed. "I never seen him like that. He was all made up. Rouge, lipstick, eyebrow pencil, and dressed in shiny black leather with pants so tight it was like they were glued on."

"Did he say where he was going?"

"Not a word. Just took off like a bat outta hell."

"Shit." I knew I should put the Rolls in the garage, but it was four blocks away and I didn't feel like it. "Good night," I called as I went up the stairs.

I let myself into the apartment. The bedroom door opened and Denise came out, still in the French Maid's costume she had had on in the morning.

"May I take your coat, sir?"

"What are you doing here?"

"Bobby left me on duty, sir," she said, straight-faced.

"On duty?"

"Yes, sir. He went to a party."

"Where's Verita?"

"She went home. She said she had a whole week's laundry to catch up on." She came around behind me and helped me off with my jacket. "Can I fix you a drink?"

"I need one," I said, sprawling on the couch. I watched her as she bent over the bar. She had a beautiful ass. I took a healthy slug of the drink she gave me. "What did the three of you do? Draw lots to see who got me tonight?"

"No, sir."

"For Christ's sake, stop calling me sir. You know my name."

"But I'm on duty, sir. Bobby asked me to stay when he got the phone call. He said you don't like to be alone."

"When did he get the call?"

"About ten o'clock. He was really excited about it. I never saw him take so much time dressing. He was really up. He laid down two big lines of coke."

With that much coke in him he had to be bouncing off the moon. "Must be a hell of a party. Did he say who was giving it?"

"No, but I heard him talking to someone named Kitty." I felt my face tighten. She saw my expression change. "Is there anything wrong?"

"I don't know," I said grimly. If this was the Kitty I had heard about, Bobby had really got himself into the shit. Kitty, straight name James Hutchinson, headed up the meanest leather and S/M queens in town. He came from an old Pasadena family with nothing but money and upstate political clout. Rumour had it that he ran what they called a Chicken of the

Month party and that some of the boys chosen for the honour had ended up in the hospital. If it weren't for his connections, he probably would have been put away a long time ago. "Did Bobby say where they were holding the party?"

She shook her head.

I picked up the phone book. No Hutchinson. I tried directory assistance, but there was no number listed. "What cab company did he call, Denise?"

"Yellow."

I called, but they wouldn't give me any information. The only people they were allowed to give information to was the police. I pressed down the button and dialed again.

A gruff voice answered. "Silver Stud."

"Mr. Lonergan, please. Gareth Brendan calling."

A moment later my uncle's voice came on the phone. "Yes, Gareth?"

"I need your help, Uncle John. I think my young friend may have gotten himself into trouble."

"What kind of trouble?"

"I think he got himself elected Chicken of the Month at a James Hutchinson party."

"What do you want me to do?"

"He took a Yellow Cab to the party. I want to know where it is."

"Hold on a minute." I heard the click of the phone as he went off the line. Less than a minute later he was back. There weren't many people in town who said no to him. The address was right in the middle of the fashionable residential strip on Mulholland Drive.

"Thanks, Uncle John."

"Wait a minute," he said quickly. "What are you going to do?"

"Go up there and get him."

"Alone?"

"There's nobody else."

"You could get yourself killed."

"They told me that in Vietnam. I'm still here."

"You won't get a medal for this one. Where are you now?"

"At my apartment over the office."

"You wait there. I'll have some help for you in ten minutes."

"You don't have to, Uncle John. It's not your problem."

His voice grew testy. "You're my nephew, aren't you?"

"Yes."

"Then wait there. You're my problem."

The line went dead in my hand.

"Is everything all right?" Denise asked in an anxious voice.

"It will be," I said. "Where'd Bobby put the coke?"

"In the middle drawer over the bar."

I laid down two lines for myself. I might need the energy. Lonergan was as good as his word. Within ten minutes I heard a horn outside my window. The Collector's Jag was right behind the Rolls. I started for the door.

Denise's voice was anxious. "You'll be all right?"

"Just relax. I won't be long."

I went downstairs and stuck my head in the window of the Jag. "Lock your car," I said. "We'll take the Rolls."

"Lonergan told me you would fill me in," he said as I pulled away from the curb.

"My little friend got himself elected Chicken of the Month at one of Hutchinson's parties."

"And we're goin' to get him?'

"Right."

"Jealous?"

"No."

"Then why bother? Little boys like him are a dime a dozen. Sooner or later they all wind up there." He reached for a cigarette. "They love that kind of thing. They're always askin' for it."

"He's romantic. He doesn't know he can get hurt bad."

"They want that, too."

"If I thought that was his thing, we wouldn't be going up there." By this time we were on Coldwater, climbing up the hill.

He reached into his coat pocket, took out a pair of leather gloves and began to slip them on. "I have another pair for you," he said, giving them to me. "I don't like to hurt my hands."

They felt heavy and a little stiff. I looked at him questioningly.

"They got a steel wire lining. Put 'em on. I know that crowd."

The house was set back far off the road behind a high wall and steel gates. I saw the lights and the closed-circuit TV monitor as we pulled up to the call box. "Get down on the seat," I said as I reached for the phone through the car window.

The floodlights came on as soon as I picked up the phone and the monitor observed me with its glass eye. There was a click in the receiver and I heard loud music in the background. The voice sounded tinny. "Who is it?"

I looked into the monitor. "Gareth Brendan. Bobby Gannon told me to meet him here."

There was another click. I could see the monitor change focus to examine the car. I was glad I had taken the Rolls. The tin voice echoed in my ear. "Just a minute."

It was almost five minutes before the voice came back on. "There's no one here by that name."

I made myself sound shrill and angry. "You tell Kitty that if he doesn't let me in, I'm going to take this car through the fucking gate."

"Just a minute."

There was a pause. "Okay. Put the car in the parking area just inside the gate and walk up the driveway."

The gates began to open slowly. Floodlights went on in the driveway. That meant more TV monitors. "You stay down," I told the Collector. "Wait until I get into the house and the lights go out; then bring the car up to the front door and wait for me."

"What if you need me?"

"I'll holler."

"Okay."

As I walked up the driveway to the house, I could feel the monitors on me. The front door opened before I could press the bell.

A burly butch queen looked out at me. He jerked his thumb over his shoulder toward the living-room. "The party's in there."

Music was blasting from a built-in sound system and the room was filled with the smell of hash and amies. The lights were down low and it took a moment for my eyes to adjust. There were about five or six queens in the room, two of them in drag, the others in freaked-out leather outfits. I didn't see Bobby anywhere.

One of the drag queens came toward me. He looked like Mae West – overblown and wearing a teased blond wig. His mouth was garish with purplish lipstick and he had dark rhinestone-flecked shadow above thick, artificially lashed eyes. The voice was a rasping baritone trying to be soprano. "I'm Kitty," he said. "Have a drink."

Chapter Fourteen

I followed him to the bar. "Scotch rocks," I said to the white-jacketed little Filipino. I watched him pour the drink from the bottle and took the glass from his hand. There was no point in taking chances. I wasn't in the mood for a mickey.

"Cheers," I said, turning back to Kitty. The whisky tasted clean. "Where's Bobby?"

Kitty smiled. "You are stubborn. You can see for yourself, he's not here."

I played dumb. "I don't get it. He told me to meet him here."

"When did he tell you?"

"There was a message for me when I got home. I was having dinner with my mother."

"A boy's best friend is his mother," he said.

I raised my glass. "I'll drink to that."

Kitty's eyes were on my hands. "Why don't you take your gloves off?"

"I have a contagious fungus," I said. "Sort of vaginitis of the hands."

Kitty laughed. "Now I've heard everything. Come join the party." He turned toward the room. "Girls, this is Gareth. He's come here looking for his slave."

They giggled and one of the leather boys came over. "He's cute," he lisped. "I wouldn't mind being his slave."

"You're too big. I'd be afraid of you. I like the delicate, gentle kind."

"I can be gentle," he lisped. He put a hand on my arm, his fingers digging in like steel claws. "I won't hurt you too much."

Smiling, I gripped his throat, squeezing his Adam's apple between my thumb and forefinger. "I won't hurt you too much either," I said, watching him turn purple, trying to breathe, his hand falling from my arm.

Kitty's voice was matter-of-fact. "He's choking."

"Yeah," I said in the same tone. But I didn't let go.

"Be careful. He's got a weak heart."

I let him go. The leather queen sank to his knees, gasping. "People with weak hearts shouldn't play strenuous games," I said.

The leather boy looked up at me. "That was beautiful," he rasped. "I had the most fantastic orgasm. I thought I was going to die."

I didn't answer.

"I want to suck you," he said.

I grinned down at him. "I told you. You're not my type."

I turned back to Kitty. "You've got a beautiful place here."

"Thank you," he simpered.

I walked over to a delicate table, near the couch. "This is a lovely piece."

"It's priceless, genuine Chippendale." I could hear the pride in his voice. "I have two of them. One on either side of the couch."

"Really?" I brought my hand down in a karate chop. The table splintered and I started moving toward the other one.

Kitty's voice was a scream. "What are you doing?"

"Didn't Bobby tell you? My thing is breaking furniture." I raised my hand.

"Stop him, somebody!" Kitty screamed. "Those tables are worth thirty thousand dollars each."

The butch from the doorway came barreling into the room. He paused for a moment to figure out what was happening, then charged toward me. I kicked him in the face without moving from the table. He tumbled backward to the floor, blood gushing from his nose and mouth.

"My white carpets!" Kitty screamed. "I'm going to faint!"

"Better not," I said. "Because when you wake up, you won't have a whole piece of furniture in the house."

"You really must love that boy."

"You better believe it," I said grimly.

"Okay. Come with me. I'll take you to him."

"Open the front door first."

Kitty nodded. The other drag queen minced to the door and opened it.

"Bill!" I hollered.

The Collector's massive frame appeared in the doorway almost before his name was out of my mouth. His white teeth gleamed in his black face when he saw the butch on the floor. "You been havin' a party," he said.

"You keep an eye on the others. I'm going with Kitty to get the boy."

A .357 Magnum suddenly appeared in his hand. "Okay, you guys, or ladies, whichever you are. On the floor facedown an' put your hands behin' your heads."

A moment later they all were stretched out on the rug. He nodded approvingly. "That's cool."

I followed Kitty down the corridor to a staircase which led to the basement. At the foot of the stairs there was a room – a special room.

The walls were covered with padded brown leather. Fixed to the wall were racks, and hanging from the racks was the largest assortment of whips, handcuffs and leg chains I had ever seen. In the center of the room were two things I had heard about but never seen before. One was a stocks, similar to the one the Puritans once used. But with this one the victim was forced to kneel in order to place his arms and legs through the holes. The base was covered with torn pieces of leather clothing and a pair of shoes lay next to the platform.

The other instrument was a wheel rack, on which Bobby was spread-eagled, his hips thrust obscenely forward over the center spoke. His head was lolling on his chest and his eyes were closed.

"Bobby," I said.

He raised his head and tried to open his eyes. "Gareth," he mumbled through swollen lips, "you came to the party." Then his head fell forward.

I looked at the wall rack and saw what I wanted – a wide-choke leather dog collar with studs and a short leash. "Against the wall," I said.

For the first time I heard the sound of fear in Kitty's voice. "What are you going to do?"

With an open palm between his shoulder blades, I slammed him into the wall and held him there. With my free hand I took down the choke collar, pulled it around his neck and then tightened it with a jerk.

He screamed in pain, his fingers clawing at his throat.

Bobby attempted a smile. "Good, you're playing, too," he whispered.

I tugged at the leash, dragging Kitty over to the rack. "Get him down."

Frantically, Kitty worked at the clamps. I moved next to him and caught Bobby as he came down from the wheel rack. He hung limply across my shoulder.

I tugged at the leash again. "Upstairs."

The Collector grinned when he saw Kitty on the leash. "Got yourself a new dog."

"Let's go," I said. We moved to the open door. I pulled Kitty with me. "Open the gates."

He picked up a telephone near the door and pressed two buttons. A television screen came to life in the wall above the phone. I could see the gates opening slowly. I took the gun from the Collector.

"Put Bobby in the car," I said.

He took Bobby as if he were a fragile piece of glass and I turned back to the drag queen. "What did you give him?"

"Nothing. He wanted to do it all himself."

I jerked on the leash. He gave a choking cough. "Don't lie to me!" I snarled. "I saw his eyes."

He pulled the collar loose. "Angel dust and acid."

I looked at him for a moment, then dropped the leash and started out.

Kitty called behind me. "You're welcome to him. He really isn't very much. We've all had him, you know."

Not bothering to turn around, I caught him with a back kick. I felt the heel of my shoe crunch into his jawbone. When I glanced back, his chin was somewhere up under his nose and the blood was beginning to spill out of his mouth. "Bitch!" I said.

The Collector was at the wheel of the car. I got in beside him. "Did you see that kid's back?" he asked.

I turned and looked into the back seat. Bobby was sprawled on his stomach. From his shoulders to his buttocks he was nothing but raw meat. They had done everything but flay him alive.

"Take him to UCLA emergency, Bill."

We were through the gate. "That'll bring the police down on you. And they'll ask questions."

"The kid needs a doctor."

"I know a place where they don't ask no questions."

It was a small private hospital in West Los Angeles, but they knew what they were doing. I hung around until the doctor came out of the emergency room.

"How's he doing?"

"He's going to be all right. But he's going to have to stay in here at least three weeks."

"I didn't think it was that bad."

"Even the back isn't as bad as it looks. It's inside."

For a moment I thought I was going to be sick. "I'll get in touch with his father," I said.

The doctor nodded solemnly. "You can assure Reverend Sam that we'll be very discreet."

"You know the boy?" I asked in surprise.

"No, but Mr. Lonergan called and said you might be stopping by."

Lonergan had thought of everything. Now maybe he could think of a way I could tell a father who trusted me to look after his son that I failed him.

Chapter Fifteen

The Collector was on the pay phone when I went into the waiting room. "Lonergan wants to talk with you," he said.

My uncle's voice was flat. "How is the boy?"

"Hurt bad. But he'll make it. I was just going to call his father."

"I've already done that. He's on his way over there now. I'm sending a car to take you home."

"I have the Rolls here."

"The police are looking for it. Leave the keys for Reverend Sam and get out of there."

"I didn't figure they were stupid enough to call the cops."

"You put two men in the hospital," he said dryly. "And the police ask questions. But you're in the clear for now. Nobody gave them your name."

My uncle always managed to surprise me. He seemed to have ears everywhere.

"When you get home, stay there until you hear from me. I'll have a better line on this in the morning."

"I have to talk to Reverend Sam and explain to him what happened."

"You can do that tomorrow. Right now get your ass out of there."

The phone went dead. I think it was the first time I ever heard my uncle swear.

The Collector held out his hand. "The car keys."

I dropped them in his hand and followed him to the reception desk, where he gave the keys to the nurse, and then out the front door.

"There's an all-night coffee shop on the next corner," he said. "The car is pickin' us up there."

We walked the street in silence, the only sound our footsteps and an occasional automobile passing. The clock behind the counter in the restaurant read four-fifteen.

The waiter put steaming cups of coffee in front of us. "What'll it be, gents?"

"Ham 'n' aig sandwich on kaiser roll," the Collector said. He looked at me.

I shook my head. "Nothing."

The coffee was scalding hot. I searched my pocket for a cigarette. The Collector held out a pack. I took one and lit it.

The Collector took a big bite from the sandwich the counterman put in front of him. He spoke with his mouth full. "You learn all that shit in the army?"

"What shit?"

"That judo stuff. The kicks an' all that." There was a note of admiration in his voice.

"That's not judo. And they don't teach it in the army."

"What is it then?"

"Savate. It's French. I took lessons from an old Foreign Legion sergeant who stayed in Saigon after the French pulled out."

He took another bite of his sandwich and chuckled. "Man, I wish't I could do that. It was graceful like a ballet dancer. Lonergan tol' me that it'll take 'em three hours just to wire up his jaw. He'll be eating through a straw for three months."

"The son of a bitch is lucky I didn't kill him."

The Collector looked into my eyes. "You're a strange one, Gareth. I don' understand you at all. All this time I got you figured for a nothin'. I never understood why Lonergan took such a personal interest in you."

"Now you know. I'm his nephew."

"It ain't just that. Lonergan's too smart to go for the family crap. You're somethin' else." His eyes went to the window. He got to his feet, pulled out two dollars and dropped it on the table. "The car is here. Let's go."

By the time I reached the apartment door the coke had burned out of my system and I was dragging. I reached for my key, but the door was open. The lights were on in the living room.

Denise, still wearing the maid's uniform, was asleep on the couch, one arm thrown over her eyes to shield them from the light.

I went to the bedroom, pulled an extra blanket from the bed and covered her. She didn't move. I shook my head. The innocents. They thought they were so wise. Yet they knew nothing.

Denise was eighteen, Bobby nineteen. For them life was still a dream, an ideal, filled with beauty and goodness.

Shit. I returned to the bedroom, kicked off my shoes and fell across the bed. I used to be an innocent. Used to be. Used to – be. I closed my eyes and dreamt.

I felt a hand on my shoulder. "Gareth! Gareth! Wake up!"

This was not a voice from a dream. I opened my eyes. Denise was shaking me. "What? What?" I mumbled.

"You were shouting and screaming."

I shook my head groggily. "No."

"You were having a bad dream."

"I'm sorry." I sat up and reached for a cigarette. My hands were shaking.

"Are you all right?"

"Yes."

"Did you find Bobby?"

"Yes." The cigarette steadied me. "He was hurt. I took him to a hospital." I saw the look of concern on her face. "He'll be okay," I said quickly.

"What did they do to him?"

"They drugged him, then assaulted him." I felt the tears in my eyes. I tried to hold them back but couldn't. Suddenly I was crying.

She straightened up. "I'll make you a cup of warm milk."

I stopped her at the door. "I'm old enough for a whisky."

"We'll put it in milk. Meanwhile, get out of your clothes and into bed."

The bottle of scotch was on the tray next to the cup of warm milk. She looked disapprovingly at my shirt and jeans, lying on the floor next to the bed. "You're not neat," she said as she put the tray down.

"I never said I was."

She picked up my clothes and took them to the closet. I took a sip of the milk that I had laced with the scotch. It was awful. I put down the cup and took a swig of whiskey from the bottle.

"That's cheating," she said over her shoulder. "Drink the milk."

I watched her crossing the room. The maid's uniform was crumpled now. "You going to wear that stupid outfit the rest of your life?" I asked.

"Don't change the subject. Drink the milk."

I drained the cup. "Okay. Now get out of that uniform and come to bed."

She hesitated a moment, then sat down in the chair near the foot of the bed. With her eyes fixed steadily on mine, she leaned forward, unbuckled the patent leather pumps and kicked them off, then slowly rolled down the black silk hose and hung them neatly over the back of the chair. She got to her feet and her hand went behind her back to the zipper. "Turn off the light," she said. "I don't want you to get excited. I want you to sleep."

"Too late. If you'd taken off one more stocking, I would have come."

"Turn out the light," she said, not moving.

I turned it out. I heard the rustle of her dress, then felt the weight of her body on the bed and reached for her.

Her hands caught mine. "No," she said firmly. "You're too uptight. I want to make love to you, not just be something you pour your tensions into."

"What's wrong with that? You know a better way to unwind?"

"Yes. The fifth-plane exercise."

"What the hell is that? Some kind of mumbo jumbo you learned at the workshop?"

"Do what I say," she said, placing my hands at my sides. "Lie back flat and close your eyes. Let your body go loose and open your mind. I'm going to touch you in different places with both hands at the same time. My right hand will be the ying contact, the left hand, the yang. Your body currents will flow through me and be restored to their natural balance. Every time I touch you I will ask if you feel me; when you feel both hands, say yes. Understand?"

"Yes."

She placed an open hand on my chest and gently pressed me

back. When I was flat, she took the pillow from behind my head, pulled down the sheet and placed it under my feet. "Comfortable?"

"Yes."

"Close your eyes and we'll begin."

Her fingers were soft and light as a feather's touch at my temples. "Feel me?"

"Yes."

At my cheeks. At my ankles. At my knees. At my shoulders. At my nipples. At my arms. "Feel me?"

"Yes."

At my ribs. At my hips. At my chin. At my calves. At my thighs. I giggled.

Her voice was patient. "What are you laughing at?"

"I'm waiting for you to touch my balls."

She didn't answer. I felt her hands at my temples again and then the warmth of her breasts on my face as she bent over me. "Feel me?"

"Yes." I had an idea. "If your hands are ying and yang, wouldn't your breasts be ying and yang also?"

She thought for a moment. "It's possible."

"Well?"

"You're a difficult case," she said. She slipped down on the bed beside me. Her arm circled my head and drew me to her breasts. "That better?"

"Yes." They were warm, so warm. I buried my face between them.

"Try to sleep," she said softly.

I closed my eyes. I had a feeling of total security. The knots in my stomach were untangling and my bones were turning soft. I pressed my lips to the side of her breast. I was so tired it was an effort for me to talk. "Do you know you have beautiful breasts?"

I thought I heard her whisper, "Thank you." But I couldn't be sure. I was fast asleep.

Chapter Sixteen

There was a knock at the door. I struggled up through the darkness. "Come in."

Sunlight flooded through the open door. I blinked. Denise came in with a tray of orange juice and coffee. Silently she put it on the bed. Verita followed.

"I am sorry to wake you, Gareth," Verita said, her faint accent more noticeable because of her excitement. "But Persky said it was very important."

My eyes adjusted to the light. "What time is it?"

"Eleven o'clock."

I got out of bed and padded to the bathroom on my bare feet. I flipped the seat back on the toilet. "What did he want?" I shouted.

"Mr. Ronzi is downstairs. He says he has to see you."

"Tell him I'll be there in ten minutes." I stepped into the shower and turned it on full blast. When I went back into the bedroom, Verita had gone, but Denise was still there.

She picked up the glass of orange juice. "Drink it."

I sipped at the juice. It was freshly squeezed and ice cold. "How long are you going to keep wearing that silly outfit?"

"Don't you like it?"

"That's got nothing to do with it. I like it fine. But it keeps turning me on. I've got a French maid fetish."

She didn't understand. "How do you get a thing like that?"

I laughed. "We had one when I was a kid. I used to stand at the foot of the stairs, trying to get a peek up her dress. Then I would go to my room and beat off."

She didn't smile. "That's stupid."

"Maybe. But it's quite common." I had an idea. "Remind me to use that for one of the future layouts."

She exchanged the orange juice for coffee. "You've had some phone calls." She held out some slips of paper.

I sat down on the bed, sipping the coffee. "Read them to me. I don't think my eyes are up to it yet."

She looked down. "Miss Sheridan wants to know if two o'clock is still okay for today. Mr. Lonergan will call you back. Your mother. Call her this evening."

"Nothing from Reverend Sam?"

She shook her head.

I didn't like it. "Try to get him for me." I put down the coffee and began to dress while she dialed. I had my shoes and jeans on by the time she put down the phone.

"He's not at home, at the church or at the workshop," she said.

"Try the hospital."

I had just finished buttoning my shirt when she held the phone toward me. "He's coming to the phone."

All the strength seemed to have gone from his voice. "Gareth?"

"Yes, sir. How's Bobby?"

"He just went back into surgery."

"I thought—"

He interrupted. "The bleeding wouldn't stop. And they can't find the source without going inside."

"I'll be right over."

"No." His voice was stronger. "There's nothing you can do. He'll be in there for a couple of hours. I'll be here. I'll call you as soon as I know something."

"I'm sorry. I didn't know what he was going to do. If I had, I would have stopped him."

His voice was gentle. "Don't blame yourself. You did all you could do. In the end each person has to accept the responsibility for himself."

I couldn't entirely shake my feelings of guilt, but Reverend Sam had a point. I knew Bobby was submissive, and it wasn't a long jump from his kind of passivity to heavy masochism. He was just naïve enough to think it would all be fun and games.

"How is he?" Denise asked.

"He just went back into surgery," I said heavily. "They have to find what's causing the bleeding before they can stop it."

She reached for my hand. "I'll pray for him."

I looked into her earnest eyes. "Do that," I said, starting for the door.

Her voice stopped me. "You don't believe in God, do you?"

I thought of all the savagery, death and destruction I had seen in my life. "No," I answered.

Her voice was soft. "I feel a great sorrow for you."

I saw the tears in her eyes. Only the innocent can believe in God.

"Don't feel sorry for me. I'm not the one who was hurt."

Her eyes seemed to look into my soul. "Don't lie to me, Gareth. You hurt all the time. More than anyone I know."

"Give me another ten thousand copies and I can move them out by Monday," Ronzi said.

"No way."

"Don't be a schmuck. You got a hot issue. Ride it. How do you know the next one will be as good?"

"It will be better. If you're smart, you'll go to seventy-five thousand on your next order."

"You're crazy. There's never been a paper that topped fifty thousand."

"If I printed ten more, this issue would."

He was silent.

I pressed. "This would have been sixty thousand. With what I'm laying on for next week, seventy-five will be a cake."

"What are you doing?"

"Four-colour cover and centerfold."

"You'll go broke. You can't afford that at thirty-five cents."

"Don't shit me, you hiked the price to fifty cents already. That's my new price."

He turned to Persky. "This guy is crazy."

Persky didn't answer.

I signaled to Verita. "Bring me the eight-by-ten color prints of next week's girl."

A moment later she spread the photographs on my desk. It was an airport layout. A beautiful Eurasian girl with hair down to her ass. I pushed the pictures toward him in sequence from the time she came down the ramp of the plane until she lay naked on the bed in her room, hugging her knees to her chest.

"You won't be able to print that," Ronzi said. "You can see her slit."

"It's already on the presses."

"You'll get busted."

"That's my problem."

"It's my problem, too. I'm the distributor. And I got enough troubles without this."

"You want out?"

"I didn't say that," he said quickly.

"I'm not pushing you. Take your time. Think about it. I'm sure I can get Ace or Curtis if you want out."

He stared at me balefully. "Fuck you, I'll take it."

"Seventy-five thousand," I said.

He nodded. "Seventy-five thousand." He glanced at Persky, then back at me. "Is there someplace we can talk alone?"

"You can say anything you want to right here."

"This ain't business. It's personal."

He followed me up the stairs to the apartment. Denise let us in. The crazy uniform was gone and she was back in shirt and jeans. She looked better. I took him into the bedroom and closed the door behind us.

I waved him to the chair and sat on the edge of the bed. "Okay. What's personal?"

"I was on the wire to my contacts back East. We think you got a big future in this business."

"Thanks for the vote. What does that mean?"

"It means we want in. Lonergan's small potatoes. We can take you national. That means real money. Big bucks."

"No partners. I like being alone."

"Come off it, Gareth. We know Lonergan's in with you."

"All I got with him is a space contract. Nothing else. Maybe I didn't make that clear to you."

"Okay then, that makes it easy. We'll give you a hundred grand for fifty per cent of your action. You still run the paper like before and we take it all over the country."

"No."

"You're a fool. We'll make you a millionaire."

"Give me a million now for half the paper and you'll convince me."

He exploded. "You are crazy. What makes you think that stinking rag is worth a million?"

"You did."

"Only if you go national."

"I'll go national."

"Not without us, you won't. We're your exclusive distributor and if we don't take you out, nobody does."

"Our deal is only for one year."

"By that time your paper will be ripped off all over the country. It won't mean nothing nationally."

I was silent. He was right. I couldn't go anywhere without him. I was locked in. "I'll have to think about it."

"How much time do you want?"

"A month."

"You got two weeks. That's as long as I can hold them off." He got out of the chair and went to the door. He looked back at me his hand on the doorknob. "You're a strange man, Gareth. Just a few weeks ago you were on your ass scrounging unemployment checks. Now I'm offering you a clean hundred grand and you want to think about it. What's the matter with you? Don't you want to be rich?"

"You're forgetting one important thing, Ronzi."

"What's that?"

I smiled at him. "Money doesn't mean that much to me. I was born rich."

Chapter Seventeen

"We're in trouble," Persky said. "The printer just told me we're short four pages of copy."

"How the hell did that happen? How much time do we have to do it?"

"One day. He needs it by Monday morning if he's going to run seventy-five thousand copies."

"Damn." I stared down at the desk. The schedule for the next two issues had only about half the copy needed.

"He wants an answer now. It's the only way he can get the issue out in time."

"Tell him he'll have his copy Monday morning."

Persky went back to his desk. I looked over at Eileen, who'd come in a few minutes earlier and was sitting opposite me, a faint smile on her face. "You have this trouble at your paper, too?"

"No, we're locked in by the school schedule." She got to her feet. "Maybe I'd better go. You're up to your head. We can talk some other time."

"You don't have to go," I said quickly. "It's not so bad. I have thirty-six hours."

"You need some writers, Gareth. You can't do it all yourself."

"I'll get to that next week. Right now I'm in trouble." I looked up at her. "Maybe you can help me. I have an idea, but I think a woman should write it."

"I don't have much time, I'm pretty busy at school."

"Okay. It was just a thought. You probably wouldn't be interested."

She sank back into the chair. "Tell me anyway."

"Right now all the magazines cater to men and their sexual fantasies. I think an article on women's fantasies would make good reading."

She thought for a moment. "It might."

"Do you think you could write it?"

"Wait a minute. What do I know about the subject? I'm no expert."

"That makes two of us. I don't know anything about publishing either. But I am going to be getting a paper out everyweek."

"It's not the same thing."

I smiled. "Do you have any sexual fantasies?"

"That's a silly question. Of course I do. Everyone has."

"Then you're an expert. Especially if you write about your own."

"But that's personal," she protested.

"We won't tell anyone. We'll change the names. We'll lay it on Mary X, Jane Doe and Susan A."

She laughed. "You make it sound so easy."

"It could be fun."

"You might find out I have a very dirty mind."

"Giving mental head isn't bad either. How about it?"

"I could try. But I'm not promising anything."

"There's an empty desk and typewriter over there."

"Do you want me to start right now?"

"We've only got thirty-six hours." As I looked down at the layouts for the next few issues, I realized that this was just the beginning of what would be a continuing battle against deadlines. I turned back to her. "You're absolutely right. I need more writers. Will you take over as features editor for me?"

"Aren't you jumping too quickly? You don't even know if I'm any good."

"If your mind is as dirty as you think, you're good enough for me."

She laughed. I could see she was pleased. "Let's wait until I finish the article. Then we'll decide."

"It's a deal." I held out my hand.

"I still don't know how you talked me into it," she said as we shook hands.

"Virgin's last words," I said. I left her huddled over the typewriter, staring at a blank sheet of paper, and went upstairs. A cold shower would help. I hadn't had much sleep last night and I was beginning to fade.

*

Verita was waiting for me when I came out of the shower. "I have some checks for you to sign."

"Okay."

She followed me into the kitchen and placed the folder in front of me on the table.

"How are we doing?" I asked as I signed the checks.

Verita sounded pleased. "We're okay. Seventy-five thousand copies next week gives us a net of eleven thousand two hundred and fifty dollars on circulation alone. Add advertising to that and we could come up with fifteen thousand dollars."

"Net?"

"Net." She smiled.

Ronzi was no fool, I thought. A hundred grand for three-quarters to a million dollars a year was not a bad deal. For him. He had been way ahead of me. I glanced back at her. "Now maybe you'll quit your job at the unemployment office."

"I gave notice yesterday."

"Good. Beginning next week, you get a hundred-dollar raise."

"You don't have to do that."

"Without you none of this would ever have happened. If I'm going to make it, so are you."

"It's not the money, Gareth. You know that," she said earnestly."

"I know it." I leaned across the table and kissed her cheek. "Tonight we celebrate. I'll take you to La Cantina for the best Mexican dinner in town. Then we'll come back here and turn on."

"I would like that very much."

"So would I."

But it didn't work out that way at all. Half an hour later I got a call from the hospital. Bobby wanted to see me. I grabbed the keys to Verita's car and ran.

The Rolls was still in the lot where I had left it. I pulled the little Valiant into the next parking space. Reverend Sam was waiting just inside the doors.

"How's he going?" I asked.

His face was grey and weary. "They finally stopped the bleeding."

"Good."

"It was touch and go for a while. He was losing blood faster than they could get it into him." He took my hand. "Now he won't let himself go to sleep until he sees you."

"I'm here."

Reverend Sam opened the door to Bobby's room and I followed him inside. Bobby was lying on his back with saline solution dripping into one arm and a tube running into his nose.

The nurse rose from her chair. She looked at me disapprovingly. "Don't be too long," she said and went out the door.

We moved to the side of the bed. "Bobby," Reverend Sam said.

He didn't move.

"Bobby, Gareth is here."

Slowly Bobby opened his eyes. He found me. A faint smile came to his white lips, then disappeared. His voice was a whisper. "Gareth, you're not angry with me?"

"Of course I'm not angry."

"I was afraid . . . you were." He blinked his eyes. "I love you, Gareth. Truly I do."

I pressed his hand. "I love you, too."

"I—I didn't mean anything. I thought it would be fun."

"It's over," I said. "Forget it."

"My job. I don't want to lose it."

"You're not going to lose it. Just get well. It will be there when you get out."

"I just don't want you to be mad at me."

"I'm not mad. You concentrate on getting better. We need you back on the paper. Your photo layout sold out our first edition."

The faint smile came back. "Really?"

"Really. Ronzi wants us to print seventy-five thousand next week."

"I'm glad." He turned toward his father. "I'm sorry, Dad."

"It's all right, son. Just do as Gareth says and get well. That's all I want."

"I love you, Father. I've always loved you. You know that."

"And I love you. Do you know that, son?"

"I know, Father. But I never was what you wanted."

Reverend Sam looked at me. I could see the anguish and tears in his eyes; then he turned back to Bobby and, bending forward, kissed his cheek. "You're my son. We love each other. That's all I want."

The nurse came bustling back into the room. "That's enough time," she said sternly. "Now he must rest."

Out in the corridor I turned to the Reverend. "Now you'd better get some rest before we have to take another room in here."

A weary smile crossed his lips. "I don't know how to thank you."

"You don't have to. That's what friends are for. Besides, Bobby's a very special boy."

"You really believe that, don't you?"

"Yes. What he needs is time. He'll find himself."

He shook his head wearily. "I still don't understand it. What kind of people can do a thing like that?"

"Sick," I said.

"I never knew things like that existed. Something ought to be done about them. Bobby can't be the only one they've done it to."

"Probably not."

He gave me a peculiar look. "Lonergan asked me not to go to the police. He said that it would get you into trouble."

"I put two of them into the hospital and they filed charges," I said. "The police are looking for me right now and if you called, it would lead them right to me."

"There isn't a court in the land that would hold you when they hear the real story."

"Maybe. But Bobby went there of his own free will and I am guilty of illegal entry and assault. The courts don't have much sympathy for a gay boy."

Reverend Sam was silent for a moment. "Then it has happened before?"

"Like maybe ten thousand times a year in this city alone."

"God." He took a deep breath.

I put a hand on his shoulder. "You go home to sleep. We can talk some more tomorrow."

We walked toward the entrance and were almost at the door when the receptionist called after us. "Mr. Brendan."

"Yes?"

"I have a call for you."

"You go ahead, Reverend Sam. I'll see you tomorrow."

I saw his stretch-out Mercedes pull away as I took the phone. "Hello," I said.

"I have Mr. Lonergan for you," a girl's voice said.

There was a click, then his voice. "Gareth, where are you?"

"I'm at the hospital, where your girl reached me."

"Good. Don't go back to the paper."

"I've got work to do. I've got to get next week's paper out."

"There's no way you can publish a paper from the cemetery," he said in his flat, expressionless voice. "I just learned they shopped a contract on you."

"You've got to be kidding."

His voice was annoyed. "I don't joke about things like that. You get out of town until I can straighten this out."

"How the hell can they get away with something like that?"

"Your fag friends carry a lot of muscle. I'll get it put away, but it might take some time. And I don't want you to get killed in the meantime."

"Shit."

"I don't want anyone to know where you've gone. People have a way of talking whether they want to or not. One wrong word and you get buried."

Suddenly I was angry. "I don't like being pushed around. I'll go up to Mulholland Drive and kill the son of a bitch."

"That would make it easy for them. They'd cut you down before you got to the door. You do as I say."

I was silent.

"Did you hear me?"

"Yes."

"Are you going to do as I say?"

"Do I have any choice?"

"No."

"Then I'll do it."

I heard his faint sigh but couldn't tell whether it was relief or not. "Now you get your ass out of there in a hurry and call me tomorrow evening at six o'clock. I'll bring you up to date."

"Okay."

"And be careful," he warned. "He's got professionals. They don't play around. They're all business."

The phone went dead in my hand. "Everything all right?" the receptionist asked.

"Just lovely, thank you," I said and went out the door.

Chapter Eighteen

I knew I'd made a mistake the minute I walked into the parking lot and saw the two men standing next to the Rolls. The next time I would pay more attention when Lonergan told me to be careful. I would have cut and run, but they saw me at the same moment I saw them. Running would have meant a bullet in the back. I continued toward the Valiant as if there were nothing unusual going down. They watched me get into the small car, put the key into the ignition and start the engine.

The taller of the two men walked around the Rolls and put a hand on the window, which was rolled halfway down. "Do you know who that Rolls belongs to?"

"No."

"We're looking for a tall guy about your size who was driving this car. See anybody like that in the hospital?"

"You guys cops?"

"Private. The guy's behind on his payments."

I looked at the Rolls, then back at him. "For twenty bucks I can hot wire the car for you."

The man's face turned ugly. "Don't be a wise guy," he snarled. "Did you see him or didn't you?"

"Nope. I didn't see anybody like that."

He took his hand away. "Okay then. Blow out of here."

I put the Valiant in reverse and started to back out. "Wait a minute!" the man on the other side of the Rolls called out.

For a brief second I toyed with the idea of hitting the accelerator and jamming out. The glint of light off the barrel of a silver-blue silencer-equipped .357 Magnum changed my mind. There was no way I could outrun a bullet from that gun. I stopped the car.

For the first time I noticed the sedan parked on the other side of the Rolls. He pulled open the rear door. For the first time I could see someone lying on the floor in front of the rear seat. "You!" he snapped. "Get out here!"

Slowly the figure got up. When I saw who it was, I remained impassive as I stared into Denise's face and prayed.

"Do you know this guy?" he snapped.

There was a big black bruise on her cheek and she looked at me through swollen eyes. I gripped the steering wheel so that my hands wouldn't shake. She blinked. "No," she mumbled through puffed lips.

The man turned back to me. I held my breath. Then he nodded. "Get outta here!"

I put the car into gear again and began backing out as he pushed Denise back into the sedan and slammed the door on her. The two men walked behind the Rolls and leaned against the trunk.

In my rearview mirror I could see them watching me until I reached the far end of the parking lot and turned into the exit lane. Then they turned their backs. I think I would have kept on going, but then I saw Denise's face, staring out the back window of the sedan.

That did it. I felt the bitter gall rise in my throat. The innocents. Why did it always have to be the innocents? I felt just as I had that day in 'Nam when we went into the village and I saw the torn and broken bodies of women and children lying in the rubble after we had finished shelling.

I was almost at the exit when I did it. It was all reflex. Without thinking, I swung the car back into the entrance lane, threw the lever into low gear and pushed the accelerator to the floor. The little Valiant almost leaped off the road.

The man with the gun began to straighten up and raise his hand. I could see his startled face in the windshield as I spun the wheel, sideswiping them with the little car, pinning them to the Rolls.

I felt the crunch and the shock and heard the scream of pain as the little Valiant bounced off the heavy Rolls like a Dodgem in an amusement park. I twisted the wheel, turning the little car completely around, then stopped it and jumped out.

They were sprawled on the ground. Their legs, twisted and broken, were spread out at awkward angles to their bodies. The man with the gun was out cold, his head under the bumper of the Rolls. The other man was half sitting, hanging onto the bumper. His face was white and he was sweating with pain. His gun was on the ground next to him.

I scooped it up as Denise came out of the sedan. She was crying. I didn't give her time to talk. "Get into the car!"

She seemed frozen. I pushed her roughly. "It's all right. Get into the car!"

She still didn't move. I bent over the man. "Who are you working for?"

"Fuck you, you crazy bastard!"

I pulled the safety on the gun and put a bullet into the ground between his legs. "You get the next one in the balls."

His lips tightened.

I shoved the muzzle of the gun into his crotch. He almost screamed. "I don't know!"

"You're lying!" I made as if I were going to squeeze the trigger.

"No!" he screamed. "We got the contract from back East. A grand to take you out."

I stared into his face. There wasn't a man alive who could lie with a gun in his balls.

"Johnny wanted to hit you the minute you came into the lot. I was the one that said, 'Wait'."

"He's telling the truth, Gareth," Denise said suddenly. "I heard him."

"You get in the car," I said, still looking down at him.

"I saved your life," he almost screamed. "Hers, too."

I straightened up, putting the safety on. "I'll send you a thank-you note."

I took her arm and shoved her toward the Valiant. The doors on the passenger side were all bashed in, so I pushed her across the seat and got in after her. We were out of the parking lot before the first man out of the hospital came around the corner.

We were four blocks away before we spoke. "How did they get you?" I asked.

"They were parked in front of the office when I came out. The big man got out and asked if you were inside. I told them that you had gone to the hospital. Then he asked if you still had the Rolls. Something made me say you did. Then he asked what hospital. I said I didn't know. That's when he pulled me into the car and hit me." She began to cry. "I didn't want to tell them, but he kept on hitting me."

I put an arm around her shoulder and pulled her head against me. "It's all right. It's all right."

After a few moments she stopped crying. "Who are those men? Why are they after you?"

"Bobby's ex-friends play rough. They don't like what I did last night."

"They're not going to like what you did tonight either."

I looked at her quickly to see if she was joking. But she wasn't, she was straight. I smiled. "I think you're right."

"What are you going to do now?"

"I'll have to leave town for a while. Lonergan said he needs time to straighten this out. I haven't made up my mind exactly where to go yet."

"I have a place," she said quickly. "They'll never find us there."

"Us?"

"Yes. You won't be able to get in without me. They won't take anyone unless a member brings them."

"What place?"

"Reverend Sam's farm in Fullerton."

"Don't some of the boys who worked at the store live there?"

"Yes."

"Then I can't go. I have to go someplace where nobody knows me."

She looked up into my face. "If you dyed your hair black, not even your own mother would recognize you."

About seven o'clock that evening I was sitting in a motel room off the freeway with quick tan on my face and a plastic cap tied over my dyed hair. I put in a call to the office and Verita answered.

"Where are you?" she asked. "We called the hospital, but they said you left almost two hours ago."

"A problem came up. Lonergan said I should leave town for a few days. I can't go into it on the phone, but everything will be all right."

"Are you sure?"

"Yes. But you're going to have to see that the paper gets out on time. Persky and Eileen there?"

"Yes."

"All of you pick up extensions and listen." I heard the clicks in the phone. "Eileen, I'm going to have to ask a special favor. You're going to have to supply the copy for the next issue."

"Gareth, I don't know what to write."

"I don't care what you do. Print anything. Letters from the readers, publicity releases, anything to fill the pages until I get back. It's very important that we don't miss an issue. Understand?"

"I understand."

"Thank you. How's the article coming?"

"There's a lot more to it than I thought."

"Good. Stretch it. Maybe we can turn it into a weekly feature. Persky?"

"Yes, Gareth."

"Stay on top of the printer. Make sure that Ronzi gets the seventy-five thousand copies."

"I just heard from him. He wants you to call him right away. I think he's worried about his print order."

"I'll call him as soon as we're finished here. The important thing is to keep rolling. If we miss an issue, we've blown it."

"Can I get some writers from the school?" Eileen asked.

"You do what you have to do. You're the editor while I'm away. It's your baby."

"What about the bills?" Verita asked.

"You pay them. The bank has your signature." I looked up. Denise was making motions. It was time for me to rinse out the dye. "By the way, you'd better shop around for another car. I bust this one up pretty good."

"You weren't hurt?" she asked quickly.

"I'm fine. Don't worry. If we get the next issue out, we can afford to get you a new car." Denise was dancing up and down in front of me, pointing to her head. "I've got to go now. I'll call you in a few days."

I pressed the button to disconnect. "One more call," I said to Denise. I dialed Ronzi.

"Gareth," I said when he answered. "What's up?"

"I got the word from back East. You got some very important people mad at you."

"So?"

"There's a contract out on you."

"I know that, but Lonergan's straightening it out. It's all a mistake."

"Mistakes don't matter if you're dead."

"What are you getting at?"

"My friends tell me that if we're partners, ain't nothing going to happen to you. Nobody fucks around with the family."

"How much time do I get to give you an answer?"

"Twenty-four hours."

"I'll get back to you. Meanwhile, we have a deal for seventy-five thousand copies, right?"

"Right. We don't welsh on deals."

"That's what I wanted to hear," I said and hung up the phone. I looked at Denise. "Now what do we do?"

"We shampoo out the excess," she said, slipping on a pair of plastic gloves.

I went into the bathroom and put my head over the sink. She shampooed my hair twice and when I finally straightened up and looked at myself in the mirror, I had to admit she was right.

Forget about my mother not recognizing me. I didn't even recognize myself.

Chapter Nineteen

It was after midnight when we finally bounced to a stop on the dirt road in front of the farmhouse. The windows were dark; the night was silent. I cut the switch and turned off the headlights. I turned to Denise. "Looks like everyone's asleep."

"That's okay," she said, getting out of the car. "The visitors' rooms are always unlocked."

I followed her up the steps to the veranda and in the door. The only sound was the creaking floorboards beneath our feet. I stumbled against a chair.

"Take my hand," she said.

It was like playing blindman's bluff. I couldn't see where she was leading me, but she seemed to know exactly where she was going. I didn't walk into any walls or stumble over any more furniture.

We stopped in front of a door and she knocked softly. "Just in case there is someone already inside," she whispered.

There was no answer. She opened the door and led me into the room, then closed it softly behind us. "Do you have a match?" she asked.

I found a package in my pocket. She struck the match. I looked quickly around the small room. Against the far wall was a narrow bed and a chest of drawers, on top of which was a porcelain basin and pitcher. A mirror hung over the chest. Against the other wall was a wooden closet and above it was a small casement window. The match sputtered out.

In the dark I heard her cross the room and open one of the drawers. A moment later she lit another match. She took a candle from the drawer and touched the flame to its wick. The yellow light flickered in the room as she placed it on the holder next to the basin.

I looked up and saw the electric light fixture in the ceiling. "Why don't you just turn on the light?" I asked.

"The power is on an automatic switch. It goes off after nine o'clock to save electricity. Besides, we begin early here. By five o'clock in the morning we're up and ready to work. Very few of us are up later than nine."

"Many people up here?"

"Thirty, sometimes forty. It depends."

"On what?"

"Whether they want to be here or not. It's mostly kids who are trying to kick one habit or another."

"Drugs."

"And alcohol."

"What do they do?"

"Work on the farm. Pray. Get counsel."

"What do you grow here?"

"Reverend Sam says people."

I was silent for a moment. Then I nodded. Maybe he was right. At least he was trying. I fished a cigarette out of my pocket and lit it from the candle. When I turned back to her, she had kicked off her shoes and stretched out on the bed. "Tired?" I asked.

She nodded, looking up at me.

"I am, too," I said, taking off my jacket. "Think both of us can fit in there without one of us falling off?"

She stared at me without answering. Suddenly she began to tremble, the tears coming to her eyes.

"What's the matter?" I asked. Then I realized she had seen the gun I had shoved into my belt. I took it out and put it on top of the chest.

"I'm afraid," she whispered through chattering teeth.

I sat down on the edge of the bed and pulled her head to my chest. "It's over. There's nothing to be afraid of now."

"They were going to kill you."

"They didn't."

"They'll try again."

"Lonergan will straighten it out in a few days. Then we'll go back to normal."

She looked up into my face. "Would you have killed that man if I hadn't stopped you?"

"I don't know. When I came back from Vietnam, I hated the thought of violence. I was sick of it. But then, when I saw your face, I didn't think anymore. I was just angry." I raised her face and traced her cheek with my finger. "You know, tomorrow you're going to have one of the great shiners of all time."

She looked puzzled.

"A black eye," I explained.

She was off the bed and at the mirror almost before the words were out of my mouth. "Wow! It looks awful!"

I smiled. "I've seen worse."

"Is there anything we can do about it?"

"They used to hold a beefsteak against it."

"We don't have any."

"Cold compress. Ice."

"We don't have that either."

"Then you have a black eye."

"I guess so. Do I look funny?"

I kept the smile from my lips. "No."

She turned suddenly and blew out the candle. "Now you don't have to look at it."

"I didn't mind."

"I did. I don't like looking funny."

I dragged on the cigarette. The tip glowed in the dark and I could see her begin to unbutton her shirt. There was a rustle of clothing; then she scrambled past me into the bed. I turned to touch her. She was already under the blanket.

I got to my feet, put the cigarette out in the candleholder and began to take off my shirt.

"Gareth."

"Yes?"

"Would you let me undress you?" Not waiting for my answer, she rose to her knees and unbuttoned my shirt, sliding the sleeves down my arms. She dropped the shirt on the floor. Her fingers touched my nipples lightly. "Are you cold?"

"No." I reached for her.

She put my arms gently back at my sides. "Not yet." Her mouth, tongue and teeth licked, laved, sucked and nipped at my chest while her hands unbuckled my belt and opened the zipper. My jeans fell to the floor around my legs and her hands cupped my balls.

"Your balls are so big and swollen," she whispered as she slid her cheek down across my belly, seeking my cock with her mouth. I felt her teeth gently rake my engorged glans.

"Okay. That's enough," I said, lifting her away from me.

There was hurt in her voice. "What's the matter, Gareth? Don't you like it?"

"I love it." I laughed. "But if I don't get these jeans off my legs, I'm going to fall on my face."

It was a great bed for balling, narrow and firm, but the only way we could sleep on it together was spoon fashion. I put my back against the wall and my arm under her head while she snuggled backward against me. "Comfortable?" I asked.

"Mm-hmm."

I closed my eyes.

"Was it good for you?" she whispered.

The generation gap didn't exist in that respect. It was the one question every woman asked. "It was beautiful."

She was silent a moment, then she said, "You're getting hard again. I can feel it."

"Let's try to sleep. It'll go away."

She rubbed her buttocks against me.

"Jesus. That's no way to do it."

"Put it inside me," she whispered, excitedly. "I want to sleep with you inside me." She moved slightly and I entered her as easily as a hot knife slips into butter. She put a hand down between her legs and cupped my testicles. "That feels so good. I wish you could shove your balls into me, too."

We lay quietly for a moment. I began to doze.

"Gareth, which do you like better, boys or girls?"

"Girls. Now go back to sleep."

"I want you to do everything with me that you've ever done with anybody."

"Let's start with sleeping."

"I want to be everything you've ever wanted. I love you, Gareth. You're a beautiful man. You care more about people than anyone I've ever known."

That was the end of it. A moment later she was fast asleep, but I was wide awake. I slipped out of bed quietly, dressed, put the gun back in my belt and stumbled through the dark until I found the door to the veranda.

I opened the door and stepped out. The faint light of dawn shone in the east. I stepped to the railing and lit a cigarette. The morning was cold and I pulled my jacket tight around me. A floorboard behind me creaked. I whirled around, the gun already in my hand.

The man was big and bearded. He was wearing a checked lumberjack shirt tucked into faded Levi's. His dark eyes looked down at the gun. His voice was calm. "You can put the gun away. You're welcome here. I'm Brother Jonathan."

He smiled. And the warmth of his smile took the edge from his words. "By the way, the next time you colour your hair, colour your eyebrows to match."

Chapter Twenty

I shoved the gun back into my belt and he came and stood at my side. "That your car?"

"Yes."

"It looks as if you were sideswiped by a truck."

I didn't answer.

"You'd better put it around back in the barn. The highway patrol comes by here every morning about eight o'clock." He looked at me. "Are you hiding from the police?"

"No." At least that was the truth.

"But you are hiding from someone?"

"Yes." I threw the cigarette into the dirt in front of the house and watched the ashes scatter and die. I made up my mind. This was no place to hang out. Now that daylight was here it all looked too wide open. "Would you give Denise a message for me?"

"A message?" His voice was puzzled.

"Tell her I think it's better if I leave. Ask her to keep in touch with the office. I'll be back as soon as everything is okay." I started down the steps.

"You don't have to leave, Gareth. You'll be safe here."

His words stopped me. "How do you know my name?"

He chuckled. "Don't worry. I can't read your mind. Denise called from a motel on the way up here. She said she was bringing you and that no one was supposed to know who you were."

"She shouldn't have done that."

"Don't be angry with her. One way or another she would have to tell me the truth. We don't believe in lying to each other."

"The more people who know who I am, the more dangerous it gets. For everybody. I'd better go."

"The only name you have to give anyone here is Brother. We'll keep your secret."

I didn't answer.

"Where are you going to go? You look beat. Did you get any sleep at all last night?"

I looked up at him. "In that narrow bed?"

"Narrow bed?" He looked puzzled for a moment; then a broad smile came to his lips. "You were in a very small room? Just a chest of drawers and a closet?"

I nodded. He began to laugh. "What's so funny?"

"The little fox." He chuckled. "I told her to take the big room. The one with two beds."

I stared at him for a moment; then I began to laugh. It seemed that in any generation a woman is a girl is a woman.

"Come," he said. "Let me give you a cup of coffee and get you to bed. I think I'm beginning to understand why you look so tired."

I put the car in the barn, then followed him to the kitchen. It was a large room in the rear of the house with an old-fashioned restaurant stove. A kettle of water was already boiling. He made two cups of instant coffee and we sat down at the wooden table.

"You'll have to get into our routine," he said, "or else you'll stick out like a sore thumb."

"Okay. I don't want to make waves."

"Reveille at five, services at five-thirty. We're in the fields working by six o'clock. Lunch is at eleven, then back to work until three-thirty. You'll have free time until six o'clock dinner and be free again until lights out at nine."

"Sounds like a healthy life."

"It is. How long do you plan to stay?"

"I don't know. A couple of weeks at the outside, maybe only a day or two."

"I'll have to ask you to leave the gun with me. I'll return it when you leave."

I gave it to him and he checked to see if the safety was on, then put it on the table. "That's an ugly little toy."

"You know guns?"

"I was a retired cop, wandering around with no purpose in life, until I met Reverend Sam and got religion. Now it's all worthwhile again." He looked at me. "Do you believe in God?"

I met his gaze. "Not really."

A faint sorrow tinged his voice. "Too bad. You're missing out on something good."

I didn't answer.

He looked at his watch. "It's almost five. I'd better get you to your room before reveille or you'll never get any sleep. When you wake up, look for me. I'll be around."

It was past three-thirty in the afternoon when I awakened. My own clothes were gone. A checked woollen lumberjack shirt and a pair of Levi's similar to those worn by Brother Jonathan were draped over a chair. Barefoot, I went into the bathroom and stepped under the shower. There was no hot water and the cold really woke me up. I came out with chattering teeth, rubbing myself vigorously with the rough towel. I had just put on the jeans when the door opened.

Denise came in, smiling. "You're awake already?"

I nodded.

"I was in about an hour ago. You were still asleep. Brother Jonathan sent this razor for you and an eyebrow pencil."

I still didn't speak.

"Are you angry with me?"

"No."

"You're not talking."

"There's nothing to say." I took the razor and pencil from her and went back to the bathroom. She came to the door and watched me shave. I saw her face in the mirror. "Your black eye isn't as bad as I thought it would be."

"Makeup," she said. "It's horrible." She came toward me. "You want me to do your eyebrows?"

I nodded. I followed her into the bedroom and sat down on the edge of the bed. She stood in front of me and began to brush the pencil lightly across my brow. I felt the warmth of her and put my hands on her waist. "Why didn't you bring us to this room?"

She paused and looked down into my face. "I was beginning to feel afraid that you would never make love to me, that you thought I was too much of a child."

"Are you like that with everyone you want?"

"I never felt like that about anyone else."

"Why me?"

She moistened the pencil with her tongue and continued brushing. "I don't know. But every time I'm near you I get so turned on I'm soaking wet."

"Even now?"

She nodded. "Do you think I'm terrible?"

"No. I just don't understand, that's all."

"Then maybe you never really loved anybody." She put the pencil down. "I think we've done it. Go look in the mirror."

"We've done it," I said, staring at my strange reflection.

"Brother Jonathan would like you to join him at the fifth-plane meeting this afternoon."

"When is that?"

"Four o'clock."

"How long does it last? I have to call Lonergan at six."

"About an hour."

"Okay."

She smiled suddenly. "I'm glad. Now let me get you something to eat. Then we'll go to the meeting together."

The windowless room was no more than fourteen feet square with a high, beamed ceiling sloping from a central ridge. Six others – three men and three women – were already in the room when we got there. They were seated in pairs, each pair facing a wall on which there was a tall wooden bas-relief of Christ on the cross. The only light came from altar candles in front of each carving.

Following Denise's example, I took off my shoes outside the door, then went to a spot opposite the far wall and sat down with her on the bare floor. No one looked at us. A moment later I heard a sound at the door. I peeked over my shoulder. It was Brother Jonathan. He was barefoot and wearing a brown cassock that reached his ankles. Silently he closed and locked the door, then crossed to the center of the room and sank to the floor beneath the apex of the ceiling. There was a moment's silence; then he began speaking.

"Two thousand years ago He walked among us. A man among men. But he was also the Son of God and He came to this earth to expiate our sins and free us of our fears. And it was for our sins and because of our fears that He gave His life on the cross. His tomb was in a small pyramid which had been built by the Jews in their flight from Egypt many thousands of years before. And it was through the apex of this pyramid that God returned life to His only Son and so Jesus arose from his grave, bringing us this message: 'I have died for you so that you may have the gift of eternal life with me. Give unto me your sins and your faith and you will be with me forever in the kingdom of heaven.' "

There was a soft chorus of "Amens." Then Brother Jonathan spoke again. "Since that time man has attempted to climb the steps of the pyramid to heaven, but he has fallen by the wayside because of his own weaknesses. It was not until Reverend Sam discovered the Principle of the Seven Planes, that the truth became evident. Man could not reach God until he had rid himself of the seven deadly sins – pride, covetousness, lust anger, gluttony, envy and sloth. The more sins a man has, the lower the level of his existence and the farther his distance from God; the less he has, the higher the level of his existence, the closer he is to God. And it is only from the highest level that man can climb to the apex of the pyramid and stand in God's pure light. Reverend Sam has shown us that this goal is within reach of all of us. He reaches down to raise us up into God's pure light. May he continue to shine with God's blessing. Praise the Lord, Jesus Christ. Amen."

There was a faint rustle of movement, another chorus of "Amens", then silence.

Brother Jonathan's voice was gentle. "All of us come here standing on the fifth plane of the stairway to heaven. There are still five planes to climb before you can reach for the pure light of the apex. We will begin by confessing to ourselves and each other the sin that troubles us most. Who will be the first to confess?"

Denise's voice broke the momentary silence. "I will, Brother."

"And the sin you confess, Sister?"

I glanced around the room. No one had turned to look at her. They all sat quietly, hands clasped in their laps, their eyes on the cross in front of them. Denise, too, was focusing on the crucifix.

"I confess to the sin of lust, Brother."

She closed her eyes and spoke in a hushed voice. "Several weeks ago I met a man. Since I met this man, my body has been on fire, my mind filled with lustful images and desire. When I think of him, my legs become weak and my sex overflows. I lie in bed and masturbate, his image constantly in my mind. In my lust for him I have lain with other men and used their bodies to assuage the desire in my own. Now that I have lain with him I am still not satisfied. My lust for him continues unabated. My only thoughts are of sex. I am a slave to my lust, unable to think of anything else."

Her voice faded away and she bowed her head. I could see that she was weeping. After a moment she added in a small voice. "I confess to my sin and pray to God for His guidance."

"We will join in a moment of prayer with our sister," Brother Jonathan said. For a moment there was the hushed murmur of voices; then Brother Jonathan spoke again. "In the eyes of God there is only love, Sister, and love takes many forms, love of the body as well as of the spirit. There are times that there is no other way to express this love except with the body. Examine your heart carefully, Sister. Is it possible that you truly love this man?"

Her voice was low. "I don't know, Brother. Until now all that I have felt has been physical. I know that he does not desire me as much as I desire him, but that does not dampen my desire. Even now, as I speak of it, my sex overflows and I am burning with desire."

"Are you ready to communicate these desires to the kinetic conductor?"

"Yes, Brother."

"Then come to me, Sister."

Denise rose to her feet slowly, her eyes half closed as if she were almost asleep. She turned and moved toward Brother Jonathan, unbuttoning her shirt as she walked. When she reached him, she took off her shirt and a moment later her jeans. Then she lay down naked in front of him.

"Sister Mary and Sister Jean will take Sister Denise's hands and feet. The others will turn toward us and join in our prayers."

Two of the girls rose and went to Denise. Each of them kissed her on the mouth. Then one sat cross-legged at her head, holding her hands; the other sat at her feet, holding her ankles. I glanced at the others. Their faces were thoughtful, not curious. Apparently this was something they had all been through before.

Brother Jonathan moved and next to him I saw what looked like a small transformer. In his hand he was holding something that resembled a glass wand a little less than a foot long. A black cable ran from the wand to the transformer, which he was now adjusting. There was a crackle, then a spark of blue light in the wand. A moment later there was a faint odor of ozone in the air. The light in the wand grew steady and cast a strange pale color over their faces. The crackling sound was somewhat louder.

Brother Jonathan held the wand high over his head. "O Lord! In the name of thy son, Jesus Christ, I beg of you. Listen to the communication of our sister in sin as she speaks to you through the force of the energy with which you give us life."

"Amen." The chorus of voices was stronger now.

Brother Jonathan brought the wand down slowly. Denise's eyes were closed; she didn't move. "Are you ready, Sister?"

"I am ready, Brother," she whispered.

He touched her right arm with the wand. The crackling noise increased, her arm twitched for a moment, but then she was still. Slowly he traced her arm to the shoulder, then her other arm. It wasn't until the wand began to approach her breasts that she started to move. Squirming slightly, at first, then thrusting her body upward toward the wand almost orgastically. Finally, she began to moan and I knew what she was feeling. I had heard the same moans coming from her last night while we were in bed.

The nipples burst forth as the wand touched her breasts, and she was thrashing around wildly. Now I knew why the two girls were there. If it weren't for them, there would have been no way to hold her down.

"Oh, God!" she screamed. The wand was moving across her

stomach now and she was thrusting her hips up at it if it were a live force. "I can't stop!" She cried. It was at her pubis now. "Stick it in me!" she yelled.

Brother Jonathan's face was impassive as he held the wand over her pubis. She kept turning and screaming.

"Oh, God, I can't stop! I can't stop!" Her face was contorted in agony as she threw her head from side to side. "Jesus! It's too much! It's too much!" Her voice turned into a high-pitched scream; then suddenly she slumped back, her face pale, her eyes closed.

Silently Brother Jonathan moved the wand down her legs until he reached her feet. Then he touched the transformer. Slowly the light faded from the wand and he put it down. She lay quietly. The only sound in the room was that of our breathing.

Brother Jonathan looked at the two girls and they went back to their places in the circle.

Denise opened her eyes. "Is it over?"

He nodded. "Yes. Do you need help to your room?"

She sat up, reaching for her shirt. "I think I'm all right." He held out a steadying hand as she put on her jeans. "Thank you, Brother Jonathan," she said. "And thank you, Brothers and Sisters. I love you all."

"We love you, Sister," they chorused.

Brother Jonathan rose to his feet and placed his hands on her shoulders and kissed her mouth. "Remember, Sister, the body is nothing but flesh. It is the soul that gives it life and love that fuses the two."

She nodded, then turned and, without looking at me, quietly let herself out of the room.

Brother Jonathan regarded me with sympathetic eyes." "Thank you, Brothers and Sisters. The meeting is ended. Peace and Love."

"Peace and love," they answered and began to file out.

I rose to my feet and waited until the others had left. Brother Jonathan knelt beside the transformer and placed a cover over it. "Does that thing really work?"

"Moses spoke to God through a burning bush."

"This isn't the same thing."

His voice was patient. "Anything that helps a man communicate with God works."

"Thank you, Brother Jonathan."

"Peace and love," he said.

I glanced at my watch as I left. It was almost six o'clock. Right now it wasn't as important to me to talk to God as it was to talk to Lonergan.

Chapter Twenty One

Lonergan's voice was a weary whisper in my ear. "Have you ever thought of living in Mexico?"

"Can't drink the water. It gives me the trots."

"You're not making it easy for me. They don't like having their boys messed with."

"Then we're even. I don't like the idea of getting killed. Level with me, Uncle John. Can you get them off my back or can't you?"

I heard his faint sigh and realized that he was no longer the Uncle John of my childhood. He was close to seventy and for him the clock ticked twenty-four hours a day. "I don't know," he answered. "Before it was just a contract; now it's personal. One of those men will never walk again."

"That's real tough."

"I need a handle. Something to trade off with them." He chuckled dryly. "Besides you, that is."

"Ronzi said they'd lay off if I took them in as partners."

"That was last night, before they knew what happened in the parking lot. Ronzi called this morning to tell me to let you know that deal is off now."

"I was supposed to call him tonight."

"Don't. He probably has an electronic bug on his line. They could be on your back before you got off the phone."

"Then what do I do?"

"Nothing. Just keep out of sight. Maybe they'll cool off in a week or two and I can get them to talk."

"What about the paper? After this issue, it's all going to fall apart."

"So it falls apart. You can always ask them to wrap you in it before they bury you."

I was silent.

"Gareth."

"Yes?"

"Don't do anything foolish. Just give me some time."

"You've got all the time you want, Uncle John. I haven't. If that paper doesn't come out for two weeks, I'm back on the street again."

"At least you'll be alive. You'll find other games to play."

"Sure." I hung up the phone and listened to the coins drop in the box. I turned to find Denise standing a few feet away.

"I came to take you to dinner."

I nodded and fell into step beside her.

"I'm sorry," she said.

"What for?"

"I made it worse for you. I shouldn't have told them where you were."

"It's not your fault."

She put a hand on my arm and stopped me. "I'm really making a fool of myself, aren't I?"

I looked at her without speaking.

"The kinetic conductor didn't help this time. This was the first time it didn't work for me. Brother Jonathan said I might need a few more sessions before I can be free of this sin."

"Are you sure it's a sin?"

"I don't understand."

"Doesn't Reverend Sam teach that love is not a sin? That to love each other is good? Love can also be a very physical thing."

"That's what Brother Jonathan said. But I don't know. I never felt like this before. I want you all the time. That's all I can think about." We stopped at the entrance to the dining room. "All this time I've been talking about how I felt. How do you feel about me?"

"I think you're beautiful."

"That's not what I mean," she said quickly. "What should I do about the way I feel?"

I smiled down at her. "Groove with it, baby. It only happens when you're young. You'll grow out of it soon enough."

There was hurt in her voice. "Is that what you really think?"

I didn't answer.

"I want you to tell me the truth," she said insistently.

The truth was what she got. "I've got more things on my mind right now than I can handle. And that is the least of them."

Abruptly she turned and ran off down the hall, leaving me standing in the doorway. I looked in the room and saw Brother Jonathan watching me. He gestured to an empty seat next to him.

There were six other young men at the table. They nodded but did not speak. They were too busy eating.

"We serve ourselves," Brother Jonathan said, pointing to a large casserole in the middle of the table.

The beef stew, stretched out with carrots and potatoes, was plain but good. I dipped the bread in the gravy because there was no butter. I filled my glass from the pitcher of milk and found it cold and surprisingly refreshing. No one spoke until the meal was over. Then one by one they got up, said, "Peace and love," and left the table.

I glanced around the room. There had been thirty-five or forty people there when I'd come in. Now there were only the few who were cleaning the tables.

"I have coffee in my office," Brother Jonathan said. "Would you like some?"

"That would be fine."

His office was a small room just off the entrance hallway. He closed the door behind us and in a few minutes placed a cup of instant in front of me.

"I also have some scotch," he said.

"I thought it was against the rules."

He smiled. "Strictly for medicinal purposes."

I nodded. "I don't feel too good."

He poured two shot glasses. "Peace and love," he said.

"Peace and love," I answered.

He threw back the whisky like a professional and refilled his glass when I was still only halfway through mine. He met my eyes. "You can't stay here," he said. "You know that."

"Why? Because of Denise?"

"No, we can handle that. It's you. You've got a price on your head. It will only be a few days before they come here looking for you."

"Denise tell you that?"

"No."

"Then how did you find out?"

"I told you I was an ex-cop. I still have contacts. The word is out that you ran off with Denise. It's just a matter of time before they figure out where she might have gone."

I was silent.

"I'm sorry, but I just can't take the chance. Too many people might be hurt."

"But even if I'm not here, they'll find Denise."

"They won't find her. I'm sending her away. By tomorrow night she'll be a thousand miles from here."

I finished the scotch. "When do you want me to leave?"

"Tonight when everyone's asleep. I'll come and get you. Use the small room that Denise took you to last night. Your own clothes are there already."

I got to my feet. "Thank you, Brother Jonathan."

"How are you fixed for cash?" he asked.

"I'm okay."

"Peace and love."

"Peace and love," I said and left the office.

My clothes, neatly pressed, were on a hanger on the back of the door. I stripped quickly and went into the bathroom. The lights went out in the middle of my shower. I swore for a moment, then remembered that they were on an automatic switch. I wrapped a coarse towel around me and went in search of the candle. I didn't know she was there until I lit it.

She was sitting, small and forlorn, on the edge of the narrow bed. Some of the makeup had come off her eye and it still looked dark and swollen. "You're going away," she said.

I rubbed the towel over my head without answering.

"I knew that when Brother Jonathan had your clothes returned."

I finished drying myself and reached for my shirt.

"I want to go with you."

"You can't," I said bluntly.

"Why?" she asked much like a child.

"Because you might get yourself killed, that's why. Brother Jonathan doesn't want that to happen to either of us."

"I don't care. I want to be with you."

I pulled on my trousers and sat in a chair to put on my shoes and socks.

She came off the bed and knelt in front of me. "Please take me with you. I love you."

"I can't. I'm sorry."

She hid her face in her hands and began to cry. Her voice was a faint wail. "I never do anything right. I thought it would be good here. We would be safe."

I touched her hair. She caught my hand and pressed it to her lips. "If I stay here, nobody would be safe. Not you, not Brother Jonathan, not any of the kids. And they had nothing to do with it."

"I'm not asking for forever," she whispered against my fingers. "I know I'm not enough for you. All I want is to be with you for a little bit. Then, when you want me to go, I will."

I put my hand under her chin and turned her face up. "That's not it, baby. Not it at all. Enough people have been hurt already. I don't want to bring that shit up here."

She was silent for a moment, staring into the palm of my hand. "Do you know you have two lifelines?" she asked.

My mind leaped to follow her chain of thought. "No."

With her finger she traced a line from the heel of my palm to the bottom of my index finger. "Nothing's going to happen to you. You're going to live a long time."

"That makes me feel better."

"But right now your lifelines are running parallel to each other." Her finger touched the center of my palm. "And the first one stops about here."

"Is that good or bad?"

Her eyes were serious. "I don't know. But it means that one of your lives is going to come to an end soon."

"I hope it's not the one that has to do with my breathing."

"I'm not being funny," she snapped.

I didn't answer.

"I'm very into palm reading. I'm good at it."

"I believe you."

"No, you don't," she said petulantly.

I smiled down at her. "Will starting a quarrel make you feel better?"

Her lips trembled. "I don't want to quarrel with you. Not on our last night together."

"Then stay cool."

"When are you leaving?"

"Brother Jonathan said he would come for me."

"That would be around midnight, when he makes his final rounds. We have time for a farewell fuck."

I laughed aloud. "You've got to be kidding."

"Unh-unh." She got to her feet and began to unbutton her shirt. "Just holding your hand made me get soaking wet."

I put a hand over hers. "I'll never make it, baby. With what I got going in my head there's no way I can think of getting it up."

"I can think of lots of ways."

I was right and she was wrong. But it didn't matter. She made it so many times grooving on the game that it didn't matter who won or who lost. By the time Brother Jonathan knocked on the door we both were dressed again.

His eyes took in the scene, rumpled bed and all.

I turned to Denise. "It's time."

"I'll walk out to the car with you," she said.

Silently we went around back to the barn. Brother Jonathan swung open the doors. They creaked loudly in the night. We went inside and I got into the car. The old Valiant lived up to its name. The motor turned over without protest.

Brother Jonathan stuck his hand through the open window. "Good luck, Gareth. Peace and love."

He turned and walked out of the barn, leaving Denise. She leaned into the window and kissed me. "Will you call me when you come back?"

"You know I will."

"I'll be waiting here for you."

It wasn't until then that I realized that she didn't know Brother Jonathan was sending her away. I wasn't going to be the one who told her, so I just nodded.

"I love you," she said, kissing me again. She stepped back. "Peace and love."

"Peace and love," I said, putting the car into gear and backing out of the barn. As I started down the dirt driveway, I saw in the rearview mirror that Brother Jonathan had put his arm around her shoulder and was walking her back to the house. Then I turned a curve and there was nothing behind me but night.

Chapter Twenty Two

It wasn't until I pulled into a gas station on the freeway to San Francisco that I noticed the brown manila envelope on the seat beside me. The attendant stuck his head in the window. "Fill it up," I said.

He went behind the car and I opened the envelope. Inside was a thousand dollars in one-hundred-dollar bills and a folded note: "I dumped the gun for you. Go to Reverend Sam's Peace and Love Mission on North Beach in San Francisco and ask for Brother Harry. He will have a ticket for a flight to Honolulu tomorrow and information about your contact there. Peace and love."

There was no signature. It wasn't needed. I stuffed the money in my pocket, read the note again, then tore it up. I got out of the car and dropped the pieces in the trash can.

"Check under the hood?" the attendant asked.

"Everything," I said and headed for the john.

The attendant was waiting for me with a slip of paper in his hand. "You needed a quart of oil and I topped up your radiator and battery water. Six-fifteen."

I gave him seven dollars and got back in the car.

It was five-thirty in the morning and the day was coming up as I cruised past the mission at the end of North Beach. It was an old grey building, more like a warehouse than a hostel. There was a sign over the vacant lot! NO PARKING EXCEPT MISSION VISITORS. I pulled into a spot right up against the building. Then I got out of the car and started toward the door.

Before I could knock, it was opened by a medium-sized man in a brown suit. "Brother Gareth?" he asked in a thin voice.

I nodded.

"I'm Brother Harry," he said, extending his hand. "Peace and love."

"Peace and love," I replied. His hand was soft.

"Come inside. I've been waiting for you since four o'clock. I was beginning to worry."

I smiled at him. "That Valiant is not exactly the fastest car in the world."

"You're here. That's all that matters," he said, leading the way down a corridor. "I've got a room ready for you. You can crash there until your plane leaves."

"What time is that?"

"Three-forty-five. But don't worry about it. I'll get you there on time." He opened a door and I followed him into the room. "Can I have your car keys?"

I stared at him.

I was told the car is hot. It will stick out like a sore thumb on our lot."

I gave him the keys. "What are you going to do with it?"

"I was told to put it into a compacter."

There was nothing to say. If you have to get rid of a car, that was the way to do it. No trace left. All the same I felt a twinge. The little old car and I had done a lot together.

I looked around the plainly furnished room. There was a narrow bed, a narrow chair, a narrow closet and a narrow window on the wall. It was a perfect room for a thin man. Suddenly I was totally exhausted. I couldn't think. All I wanted to do was sleep.

"I'll be back in a few hours with your breakfast. I think it's a good idea if you stay in the room. We don't want anybody to spot you."

I nodded. Speaking was too much effort. He closed the door behind him and I stretched out on the bed with my clothes on. I had just enough strength to kick off my shoes before I went out like a light.

I slept through breakfast, but Brother Harry woke me for lunch. "You have to be at the aiprort an hour before departure," he said almost apologetically as he placed the tray on a chair before me.

"That's okay." I looked down at the tray. Beef stew. I might have guessed. "I'm not really hungry right now. I'll get something at the airport later."

"The bathroom's over there. You'd better shave. Blond

beards don't go with black hair." He gestured to the other door. "You'll find a razor in the medicine cabinet."

The shave and shower helped. I began to feel alive again. I came out of the bathroom. He was waiting and so was the beef stew. I still wasn't up to it. "Any objection to getting out to the airport early?" I asked.

"I don't think so. Do you want to leave now?"

"Yes." Suddenly I had had enough of small rooms and narrow beds.

He pulled his old Ford Fairlane to a stop in front of the United Airlines terminal, reached into his coat pocket and handed me an envelope. "Your ticket's in there," he said. "Brother Robert will be waiting for you in Honolulu. He'll take you to the mission."

"How will I recognize him?"

"He'll find you."

"Thanks."

"You're welcome," he said. "Peace and love."

"Peace and—" I stopped. "Can I ask you a question?"

"Of course."

"Why are you going to all this trouble for me? I'm not even a member of your church. And yet all it took was a word from Brother Jonathan."

"Oh, no," he said quickly. "It wasn't Brother Jonathan. He hasn't got that kind of authority."

"Then who has?" But I knew the answer almost before the question passed my lips.

"Reverend Sam," he said in a hushed voice. "There isn't a thing that happens in the church without his knowledge. He takes care of all of us. God bless him. Peace and love."

"Peace and love." I got out of the car and watched him drive off into the traffic heading toward the city. Inside the terminal I checked the departure board. It was only two-thirty, which meant that I had an hour and a quarter to wait. I headed for the nearest cocktail lounge.

The bar was crowded, so I sat down at one of the small tables. The waitress came with my order – a double scotch on the rocks.

The way I figured it Brother Jonathan must have called Reverend Sam almost as soon as I got to his mission. Jonathan wouldn't have made these arrangements on his own. It was organization all the way.

But what had made Reverend Sam decide that I needed protection?

"Another double, sir?"

I looked up with surprise. I hadn't realized I had emptied my glass. They had to be watering their whiskey because I didn't even feel it. I nodded.

She put down the drink. I glanced at the clock behind the bar. Two-forty-five. "Is there a phone here?" I asked.

"Just outside the entrance, sir."

I paid the tab. "I'll be back," I said, leaving the drink on the table. I got a stack of quarters from the cashier and put in a call to Reverend Sam.

I caught him at home. "How is Bobby?" I asked.

"Much better. The doctors expect to have him on normal foods by the end of the week." His voice lowered. "Where are you?"

"San Francisco International."

I could hear the relief in his voice. "Then you are going to Honolulu?"

"The plane leaves in an hour."

"Good. When Lonergan told me how bad things were, I knew I had to do something."

"Was it Lonergan's idea that I ship out?"

"No. But when I told him what we could do, he thought it was a good solution. I owe you too much not to help out."

I was silent.

"I've made all the arrangements. You'll be well looked after."

"Thank you," I said.

"You don't have to thank me. After all, you wouldn't be in this trouble if it weren't for Bobby." He hesitated a moment. "If you need anything, you call me."

"I'm all right."

"Then don't worry. I'm sure Lonergan will have everything straightened out in a short time; then you'll be able to come back."

"Sure."

"Have a good flight. God be with you."

"Peace and love," I said, hanging up the phone.

I made a series of calls trying to track down Lonergan, but he was nowhere to be found. No one at his home, his office or the Silver Stud knew where he was. I couldn't even get an answer on the mobile telephone in his car.

I was bothered. It was all too pat. Lonergan knew I didn't want to go away. Yet I was moving farther and farther away from where I wanted to be. I didn't even know whether the copy for the paper had made it to the printers on time. I put another quarter in the phone and called the paper.

"*Hollywood Express.*" I recognized Verita's voice.

I knew she would know who it was, so I didn't identify myself. "You okay?"

"Yes. You?"

"Fine. Can you talk? Anyone around?"

"I'm alone. Everyone's gone."

"The copy make it to the printers?"

"It's all done. Your friend is very good. She worked all night to have everything ready."

"Good."

"Are you coming back?"

"That's a strange question. Of course I'm coming back. What makes you ask?"

"Lonergan says you're not. He was here with Ronzi. They took Persky upstairs for a meeting. When they came down, Lonergan said you were selling the paper to Ronzi and that Persky was taking over for you. When Lonergan and Ronzi left, Persky told me that I wouldn't be needed after this week."

I felt the rush of cold anger. My uncle was doing his usual number. Playing God. "No way," I said. "It's not going to happen."

"What can you do? If you come back, they will find you and kill you. They are evil, those men."

"You go home and wait there until you hear from me." I put down the phone and walked over to the departure board. There was a flight to Los Angeles at 3.30.

I was on it.

Chapter Twenty Three

Honest John, the used-car man, squinted against the late afternoon sun. "This here's our special for the week. Jes goin' on TV with it today."

I looked at the Corvair convertible. The black top and vinyl seats had been freshly polished and the yellow body gleamed from a recent wax job. "What are you asking for it?"

"Eight hundred including T and L. It's a steal at that money. Twenty-three hundred new in sixty-five. Practically no mileage on it at all, considerin'."

"How much?"

"Look at the speedometer fer yerself."

I opened the door and looked. Sixteen thousand miles. I turned back to him.

He nodded. "Sixteen. That's right. Nothin'. That car's good for a hundred.

"Not according to Ralph Nader."

"What the hell does he know? He's jes makin' a name fer hisself scarin' hell outta people. I drove that car myself. Handles like a baby carriage and jes as safe as one in the hands of a mother."

I opened the lid. The engine looked good. At least it had been steam cleaned. The treads on the tires were not bad. Didn't look like sixteen thousand miles. I went to the front of the car and opened the trunk. In the Corvair everything was back to front. The engine in the rear, the trunk in the front. There was no tread at all on the spare tire. There were even some bald spots showing through the black rubber. I looked at Honest John.

He had an answer waiting. "You know how some people are. Cheap. Wo'nt buy a new tire for a spare."

"Sure. Can I take it around the block for a test?"

"You don't have to. With our money-back guarantee, if you're not happy, jes bring her back within ninety days an' we give you the full credit fer the price against any other car you pick."

"I'd like to try it. Just to see if I'm comfortable in it."

"You put the top down on that sweetie an' you'll be more comfortable than you've ever been in yer life. You'll be floatin' in tail. That there car is a natural pussy catcher."

"That's great. Right now I want to know if it runs."

He stared at me for a moment, then noded. "Okay." He turned and called to one of the men. "Hey, Chico, go out with this guy."

The Mexican dropped the rag on the hood of the car he had been polishing and came over. I got into the car and started the motor. It turned over easily enough. I switched on the radio. Rock music blared out. I reached and unsnapped the catches and pressed the switch. The top went down smoothly. I turned on the wipers and hit the washer button. Water sprayed on the windshield and the wipers took it away. Then I put on the headlights, got out of the car and walked around it. All the lights were on. I went to the front of the car. "Put on the brights," I called.

The Mexican touched the floor button. The brights worked.

"Now the directionals."

Right, then left. They worked, too. I got back into the car. Honest John was watching me with a strange expression on his face. "I just like to check," I said.

"That's okay."

I took the car out and drove it a few blocks. The brakes were good, all the gears including reverse were solid, and the steering was okay, considering the car weighed nothing. He was waiting for me when we drove back on the lot.

The Mexican got out and went back to his polishing. I remained seated. Honest John came up and leaned against the door. "What do you think?" he asked.

"It's okay," I said. "Six hundred."

He laughed.

I took out the roll and let him smell the money. "All cash."

He looked at the money, then at me. "Seven-fifty."

I riffled the bills. "Six and a quarter."

"Seven."

"Six-seventy-five and we close."

"You jes bought yerself a car. Come into the office and we'll fill out the papers."

"Okay." I switched off the engine. When I turned back to him, he had that strange expression on his face again.

"You a rock musician?"

"What makes you ask?"

"They have all kinds of weird getups. I never seen nobody with orange hair before."

I looked at myself in the rearview mirror. My hair had turned a peculiar orange color. Shit. I wondered what was in that dye Denise used on me.

"Yer mother have orange hair?"

"No."

"Yer father?"

I smiled at him. "I don't know. I never saw him without a hat on."

"It's strange all right."

"It sure is," I agreed. I had the registration made out in Lonergan's name, using his office address. After we'd taped the registration to the windshield, I drove to the nearest office supply store and bought four quart cans of rubber cement. Then I went to a phone and called Verita at home.

"Hello." She sounded nervous. When she heard my voice, she sighed with relief. "Oh, Gary, I was so worried about you. Where are you?"

"I'm in town."

"Two men in a black Buick followed me home from the office. They're parked across the street from my apartment now."

It figured. Sooner or later they would cover everyone they thought I might contact. The big question was who they were. "They look like cops?"

"I don't know. The car has Nevada plates."

That was a help. They weren't cops. Whoever they were, it was better than having the whole Los Angeles police force looking for me. "Don't worry," I said. "They won't bother you. They're looking for me."

"I know that. But I want to see you."

"You will. Can you contact your cousin Julio Vasquez for me? He might help. We were in Vietnam together."

"He is a dangerous man, Gary."

"I know that." Julio Vasquez was the king of the barrio. Nothing went on down there that he didn't know about. "But the men we are playing with are dangerous, too."

"I will call him."

"Try to get a meeting for me." I checked my watch. It was almost six-thirty. "Nine o'clock, if you can."

"I will try."

"Good. I'll call you back in an hour." I almost said, "Peace and love." It was catching. Then I went over to the nearest Norm's and had steak and fries for dinner.

"He say he cannot meet with you until ten o'clock." I could tell from Verita's accent that she was anxious.

"That's fine. Where?"

"He say that I should bring you to the garage."

"Tell me where it is. I can go there myself."

"I cannot. He made me promise to tell no one, not even you."

"Did you tell him about the two men in front of your house?"

"No."

"Call him back and tell him. I'll call you again in fifteen minutes."

I put down the phone and had another cup of coffee, then called her back. "What did he say?"

"He said not to worry. He take care."

"Okay."

"He say for you to bring your car to my house and stop around the corner. At nine-thirty I leave to meet you. He wants to know what kind of car you drive."

"A yellow Corvair convertible with a black top."

"You rent it?"

"I bought it."

"Big mistake," she said. "Ralph Nader say car is not safe."

I laughed. "I'm getting used to living dangerously."

*

There was a tall Chicano in a leather jacket leaning against the lamp-post when I pulled the car into the curb around the corner from her house. It was exactly nine-twenty-five. He came toward me. The shiny studs over his breast pocket spelled out J. V. KINGS.

"Señor Brendan?" he asked.

"Yes."

"Get in the back seat. I will drive."

I got into the back seat and he climbed behind the wheel. "Get down on the floor," he said without turning around.

With the engine in the rear there was no floorboard hump, but it was still a tight fit. I moved the cans of rubber cement onto the seat.

A minute later I heard Verita's voice. "*Qué pasa?*"

He said something rapidly in Spanish. The passenger door opened. I felt the pressure against the back of the seat as she sat down. She spoke to him in Spanish. The only word I got was "Buick."

"Okay," he said, starting the engine. He moved away from the curb. We couldn't have gone more than a quarter of a block when I heard a loud crash behind me. Unthinkingly I raised my head to glance through the rear window.

A Buick was wrapped around the corner lamppost held there by a two-ton truck.

"Get down!" the Chicano snapped.

I turned and saw Verita staring down at me. "Hi, baby." I grinned, lying back on the floor.

"Gary!" she exclaimed in a shocked voice. "What have you done to your hair? It's orange."

Chapter Twenty Four

There was no way I could tell where we were. From the floor all I could see was the streetlights flashing by. About ten minutes later he turned the car onto a ramp and I could tell by the overhead fluorescents that we were in a parking facility. The car kept going up and up and finally came to a stop.

The Chicano got out of the car. "You can get up now."

I pulled myself onto the seat and sat for a moment to ease my cramped muscles; then I got out. Verita threw herself into my arms.

"I was worried about you," she said.

I kissed her cheek. "I'm okay. You okay?"

"I'm okay. I feel better now that I see you."

"Follow me," the Chicano said.

He led us to the elevator. The sign next to the door read "Park Level 5." We boarded the elevator and he pressed the SB button. The elevator took us down to the sub basement. We followed him through a dimly lit corridor to a door which opened into a brightly lit room.

Several Chicanos, all wearing leather jackets like our driver, were watching a colour television set with rapt attention. They glanced at us without interest, then turned back to the set.

Our driver crossed to the other door and opened it. He said something rapidly in Spanish. A voice answered and he stepped back. "Julio says for you to go in."

We went through the door and the driver closed it behind us, remaining outside. Julio was sitting behind a desk. On the desk in front of him were some papers and an ugly-looking blue 9mm automatic. He came from behind his desk and held out his hand. He wasn't a big man, but his grip was strong. "Hello, Lieutenant."

"Hello, Sergeant," I said, returning his grip.

His teeth were white under his moustache. "You look different." A note of wonder came into his voice. "Your hair is orange!"

"Shit," I said.

He turned to Verita and embraced her. They exchanged a few rapid words in Spanish; then he sat down behind his desk and waved us to the chairs in front of him.

"We are cousins, but I do not see the family very much. It's a very big family. Sometimes I think we are all cousins down here."

I nodded without speaking.

"We are very proud of her. She has graduated very many colleges and universities."

"Julio!" she exclaimed, then spoke in Spanish.

Julio smiled. 'My cousin is modest. She does not like me brag about her." The smile disappeared. "You in big trouble, man."

"The story of my life. If it isn't one screwup, it's another."

"This is a good one."

I stared at him. There were no secrets in this town. Everybody knew everything. "Yeah."

The telephone rang and he answered it. He listened a few moments, then put it down. "These two men in the Buick," he said. "They are both in the prison hospital. The police found two blasters and an automatic rifle in their car. They're syndicate men from Vegas." He lit a small *cigarro*. "They must want you real bad to send in all that heavy artillery."

I smiled. "They're not going to like it very much when they find out it was your truck that took them out."

"They have no right to come into my town unless they ask me first."

"Would you have given them an okay if they had asked?"

His eyes met mine. "To get you, yes. With Verita, no."

I was silent. He knew what I was thinking. Both of us knew what a blaster could do. We had seen that in Vietnam. If she were within two feet of me, she would have been cut in half along with me.

"Why do you want to see me?" he asked.

"I think you know."

He was silent for a moment. "It's not my war."

"It wasn't our war in 'Nam either. But we were both there."

He knew what I was talking about. The Vietcong had had him nailed in a murderous crossfire. His only shelter was under the dead bodies of the other men in his squad. It was simply a matter of time before the bullets chewed them up and found their way to him. I got him out.

"I owe you one, Lieutenant," he'd said as I dragged him back to the first-aid station with a bullet in his thigh. They shipped him back to Saigon, where he promoted himself a job in the supply section at the hospital. By the time I saw him a few months later he had already become the biggest dope dealer in the army.

He'd heard I was on leave and came looking for me. For the next four days I felt as if I were living in a fantasy world. He moved me out of the dump I was in to a suite in the best hotel in Saigon. From then on it was party time – liquor, champagne, all kinds of dope from grass to angel dust, cocaine to acid, plus unlimited supplies of food and girls. He'd even had papers cut for me to stay in Saigon, but I was still stupid then. I went back.

I remembered standing on the airstrip just before boarding the plane. "Man, this is too much," I had said. "How're you going to get used to it when you go back home?"

His face had been serious behind his smile. "I'm rich, Lieutenant, and I learned a lot out here. When I go back, I'm going to own that town. It's about time the Mexicans took it back."

I heard later that not only did he come back with money in a Swiss bank but he also weighed about ten kilos more when he got off the plane in Los Angeles than he normally weighed. He had pure, uncut snow, in cellophane bags wrapped around his body from his armpits to his hips. Cut twenty times, it had a street value of ten million dollars in the cities back East.

And someone told me that's where he'd shipped it. "Let the niggers and the spics have it," he'd said. "The Mexicans ain't into it. They sniff, snort, smoke, drink and eat, but when it comes to sticking needles in themselves, they're all cowards. They can't stand the sight of their own blood."

At least that was one version. Another version was that he used it to make a deal with the syndicate, that he'd given it to them for a dime on the dollar, provided they left him his town.

I didn't know which, if either, was true, but one thing was sure: It was his town. Everything had been quieter in the barrio since he'd taken charge. I'd even heard that school attendance had picked up.

I turned to Verita. "I'm going to talk to your cousin about certain matters. I don't want you involved."

"I am involved. I brought you here."

"You're a lawyer. You know what I mean. You're not party to anything you don't know about."

She sat there with a stubborn expression on her face.

Julio spoke rapidly in Spanish. His voice was sharp and commanding. Without a word she got out of her chair and left the room. "Now," he said.

"I want you to put a blanket on her."

"I already did that. The minute she called and told me about the two men."

"Good. I need about six of your boys for the next twelve hours."

"Pistoleros?"

"No. There won't be any shooting. I just want to be sure they're bright and tough and know how to handle themselves."

He thought for a moment. "Why me? Why don't you go to Lonergan? He's your partner."

"He's not my partner, he's my uncle, and I don't trust him. He had me on my way to Hawaii while he was busy selling me out. I'd be on the balls of my ass broke again by the time he got through with me."

"You'd be alive."

"I've had enough of that shit. I decided it's time I got a taste of the good life. I should have learned that from you that weekend in Vietnam, but I was stupid."

His eyes were unsmiling. "What do you expect to get out of it? You can't win. They're going to take over and you know it."

"It's Vietnam all over again, only this time it's my war, not theirs. By the time I get through they'll think six men is an army. I'm looking to negotiate a better peace. I don't give a damn about the paper. They can have it. All I want to do is come out of it with enough money to start something else."

"Like what?"

"A magazine. Right now *Playboy's* got the market all to itself. I can do better. I'll make so much money it'll be unbelievable."

"Money shouldn't be any problem. Lonergan would come up with it. So would I. There's got to be a hundred places you could get it."

"I don't want any partners. It's got to be all mine."

"Everybody has partners."

"Do you?"

He was silent for a moment. "I don't want my boys to get hurt."

"They won't get hurt."

"What if somebody shoots at them?"

I was silent.

He picked up the 9mm from the desk and got to his feet. "Come with me," he said.

I followed him through another door and into a corridor. He hit a switch and the lights flooded on. At the end of the corridor was a soundproofed target range. "You used to be pretty good with this," he said, handing me the gun.

I hefted the gun, then threw the safety and emptied it into the target. I lowered the gun while he walked down the range and came back with the sheet. The bull's-eye was completely obliterated, nothing but a gaping hole.

"All bull's-eyes," he said. "You're still good."

I didn't answer.

"You're the pistolero. I'll hold you responsible for my boys."

"Okay."

We went back to his office, where he gave me a fresh clip of cartridges. After reloading, I checked to make sure the safety was on and stuck the gun in my belt.

"Now we get down to business," he said. "What's in it for me?"

I smiled at him. "I'll take you back to Saigon for a four-day weekend and we'll be even."

He stared at me for a moment, then burst into laughter. "That was one crazy weekend," he said.

Chapter Twenty Five

I watched them put the last sandbag in the front trunk of the Corvair. Three of the bags were propped on their sides against the grille and each of them had two more bags behind them for support. I knelt and looked under the car to see if the wheels had clearance. It seemed okay. The heavy-duty shocks we'd put under the front end carried the load. I got behind the wheel and started the engine. I drove the car around the garage. It turned easily and there was no problem with the steering. I turned off the engine and got out.

The Chicano who had driven me to the garage came up to me. "We have the crash helmet and shoulder pads."

"Let me try 'em," I said.

I put the helmet on, snapped the chin guard in place and pulled down the visor. It fitted perfectly. I took it off and threw it in the front seat of the car. Then I took off my shirt and put on the shoulder pads. I kept them on and put my shirt over them. The shirt split the moment I moved.

"There's a bigger shirt in the mechanic's locker," the Chicano said.

"Thanks. I'll be down in the office."

"The sign painters are finished. Want to see them before you go down?"

"Okay." I followed him across the garage to where the sign painters had been working. The thin white canvas sheets were stretched taut across the boards.

The Chicano gestured to the painters. "Hold it against the side of the van so he can see it."

The painters lifted it and quickly fastened it into place on the panels of the delivery van. The lettering was in shiny black. In an arc, THE FLOWER FARM, and beneath it, in smaller letters, "beverly hills." It looked phoney enough to be real Beverly Hills.

"Good," I said. "Put them in the van. I'll tell you when to put them on."

I went downstairs. Julio was talking to Verita. He looked at me. "Everything okay, Lieutenant?"

"Couldn't be better."

"Your shirt is split," Verita said.

"I'm getting another one."

"When are you going to do something about your hair?"

"I should be back here by ten-thirty. We'll fix it then."

"I'll get some stuff. Meet me at my apartment."

"No, you'll stay here. We're not playing with children. I don't want them coming back for you after they hear what happened to their men."

"I will take her to my house," Julio said. "My mother will be glad to see her."

The Chicano came in with a faded blue mechanic's shirt, which I exchanged for mine. It was big enough for two of me. I let it hang out over my jeans.

I checked my watch. It was 2.45 am. "Time to go," I said.

Verita got to her feet. "Be careful."

I kissed her cheek. "Always." I turned to Julio. "Thanks."

His face was serious. "It's okay. I always pick up my markers."

"Thanks anyway."

"Just take care of my boys."

"I will."

I went up into the garage and walked toward the car. "Did you get the mattress?" I asked the Chicano.

"In the back seat of the car like you said."

"Good." I looked in. Even folded over, the mattress took up the whole back seat. "One of you come with me. The others will follow in the van."

"I'll come with you," he said.

There was no traffic either in town or on the freeway. I pulled to a stop in front of Ronzi's warehouse in Encino at twenty minutes after three. The van pulled in behind me.

The nearest building was another warehouse at the end of the block. The street seemed deserted. I got out of the car. The Chicano followed me out and one of the boys from the van joined us.

"Wait here," I said. "I'm going to check for the night watchman. If you hear any noise, don't hang around. Just get out of here."

The Chicano nodded.

I cut across the street, climbed up on the truck-loading platform and looked in the window. There was a light coming from the office at the back of the warehouse, but I couldn't see if anyone was in there. I jumped off the platform, went to the back of the building and up the steps to the back entrance. Through the window I could see into the office. It was empty.

I had counted on that. Ronzi had to feel damn secure. With his connections he figured that no one would rip him off.

I came down the steps, cut around the side of the building to the parking lot and counted the delivery trucks. There were fourteen. I went back across the street.

"It's clear," I said. I took the cans of rubber cement from the floor in the back. The boys gathered around me. "I want you to put about a quarter of a can of this stuff in the gas tank of each one of those delivery trucks."

"What'll it do?" one of the boys asked. "Blow them up?"

"No. It'll just fuck up the engines."

"You mean they won't start?"

"They'll start okay, but they'll croak when they get about five or ten miles from here."

They laughed. "Jesus! They'll all be going crazy."

"Get moving," I said, opening a can. "I want to be out of here in ten minutes." I turned to the Chicano. "I want one of the boys behind the wheel of both cars so that we can take off as soon as we get back."

He nodded and said something quickly in Spanish. One boy walked disconsolately back to the van. He turned back to me. "You wait here with the car."

"No, I go with the boys. Someone else waits here."

He nodded and gestured to another boy, who got behind the wheel of my car. We raced across the street to the parking lot. "We work in teams," I whispered. "One opens the tank. One pours."

The boys acted as if they had been doing it all their lives. We were finished and away from there in less than fifteen minutes.

By four o'clock we were back in Los Angeles and in front of the Silver Stud. I turned the car up the side street and the van followed. Halfway up the block I stopped.

"Okay," I said to the Chicano.

He nodded, knowing what he had to do. He got out of the car while I reached for the crash helmet and put it on. He climbed in the van and they moved down the block and parked across the street next to the Silver Stud. The front of the van was facing me.

I pulled the mattress from the back seat, propped it up in front of the passenger seat, then slid behind it. I reached behind me, pulled the safety harness across my chest and locked it into place. I leaned across the wheel and signaled with my lights.

The van signaled back. One flash. They were ready. I put my left foot on the brake and pressed the shift lever into low; then, leaning sideways so I could hold the wheel, I waited.

It seemed like an hour, but it couldn't have been more than fifteen minutes. Finally, the signal came. The brights went on and off twice in rapid succession. The street was clear enough for me to make it across. I took my foot off the brake and hit the gas pedal.

I crossed the street and jumped the curb at almost thirty miles an hour. I had just enough time to pull the mattress down over me when the car hit the front doors and crashed through with an explosive sound. The hood buckled and the sound of breaking glass mixed with the screaming of a burglar alarm. The little car plowed into the saloon, through the bar and into the wall mirror before it came to a stop.

I sat there stunned for a moment, then automatically reached for the key to switch off the engine. The saloon was a shambles. Furniture had been thrown all over the place. Quickly I pulled off the harness. I kicked open the jammed door with both feet and got out. I took a last look at the car before I left it.

Nader couldn't have been right. The windshield hadn't even cracked. I ran out. The van was already moving as I climbed into it.

"Hey, man!"

"Some driving!"

"He's a real *bracero!*"

"*Silencio!*" the Chicano shouted from behind the wheel. He turned to me. "Now what do we do?"

I looked at my watch. It was four-thirty. We had to wait four hours for the next project. "Let's find a restaurant and get some food," I said.

It was ten minutes to nine when I pulled the van in front of the house on Mulholland. I leaned out and hit the signal button.

I heard the whir of the closed-circuit camera, then the voice. "Who is it?"

"Flower delivery."

I saw the camera move and survey the truck. I knew they were reading the sign on the panels. "Okay."

The gates swung open and I drove up to the front of the house. I got out of the van, went to the back and opened the rear doors. The boys watched me as I picked up the giant basket of flowers and went up to the front door.

The door was opened by a heavyset man before I had a chance to ring the bell. I pushed the flowers toward him. He took them automatically in both hands. His mouth opened in surprise when he saw my gun.

"Not a word!" I said in a low voice, shoving the muzzle in his face. I pushed him back into the house. A moment later the boys were all behind me with baseball bats in their hands. The Chicano gave me my crash helmet and I put it on.

The man's face was white with fear. I guess the sight of all of us in crash helmets with the visors down was not very reassuring.

"If you put the flowers down and don't make any noise, nothing will happen to you," I said.

He set the flowers on the floor.

"Where's the master bedroom?" I asked.

"Upstairs."

"Okay. Face down on the floor."

He stretched out and in less than a few seconds he was taped hand, mouth and foot.

I turned to the Chicano. "One of you wait here; the others come with me."

He nodded and I went up the steps two at a time. There were only two doors on the upper floor. I opened the first door. It was a combination office and study. Empty.

I found him in the next room. He was sitting up in bed, sipping orange juice through a straw that was stuck through an opening in his still-bandaged face. "What the hell?" he mumbled, reaching for the button next to him.

I pointed the 9mm at him. "The only thing that button will do for you is open the gates of hell."

He pulled back from the button as if it were a snake. "What do you want?" he asked in a trembling voice.

Without answering, I nodded to the Chicano. The boys knew what to do. One went into the bathroom; the others except for the Chicano scattered through the house. A moment later we heard the sounds of destruction.

I walked over to the bed, took the panic button and put it out of his reach.

"There's no money or jewelry here," he said.

"That's not what we're after."

"Then what?"

I saw the scissors lying on the table beside the bed. I gave the gun to the Chicano. "Hold it on him," I said, picking up the scissors. I leaned over him and began to snip the bandage away from his face.

"What are you doing?" His voice became shrill.

"I just want to see the kind of job they did on your face, Kitty."

For the first time he seemed to recognize what was happening. "You?"

I flipped up the visor. "Hello again. Surprised?"

He stared at me, unable to speak.

I had all the bandages off now. I looked at his jaw. "I wonder what would happen now if someone should decide to pull out those wires?"

He shrank away from me. The Chicano turned to me as the boys began to come back into the room. "They're finished."

I took the gun from him. "Okay. Leave me alone with him. I'll meet you downstairs."

"Gonna blast him?" one of the boys asked.

I didn't answer.

"*Vamos!*" the Chicano said.

I waited until they were gone; then I spoke. "This was just to convince you that I have friends. You have until six o'clock tonight to let me hear you canceled the contract. After that you're a dead man. And if anything should happen to me before that, you're dead, too. So you'd better start praying that I stay healthy."

I raised the gun and put a bullet into the headboard over his head. "Understand?"

There was no point in my waiting around for him to answer. He had fainted when I pulled the trigger.

I left the room and made my way through the mess. There wasn't a piece of furniture in the place that had been left unbroken.

They followed me out to the van. On the road into town the boys were quiet. Finally, one of them couldn't keep it in any longer. "Did you kill him?"

"No. But I scared him a lot."

He was silent for a moment. "You know, I never seen a house like that. It was so pretty that I kind of hated to break it up."

Chapter Twenty Six

I fell onto the couch in Julio's office and didn't open my eyes until two-thirty in the afternoon. Julio was sitting behind his desk, watching me, I rolled over and sat up.

Silently he got to his feet and opened a closet door. From an electric coffeepot on top of a small refrigerator he filled a coffee mug and brought it to me.

I took a sip of the scalding black liquid and began to come alive. "Thanks."

"*De nada*," he said, going back to his desk. "Lonergan's turning the town upside down for you."

"What does he want?"

He shrugged. "*Quién sabe?* Lonergan doesn't talk."

I took another belt of the coffee. "I think it's time I gave him a call. Mind if I use your phone?"

"Be my guest."

The girl who answered told me he was unavailable until she heard my name. A few seconds later he was on the phone.

"Where are you?" he asked.

"Not in Hawaii, that's for sure. I hear you're looking for me."

His voice didn't change tone. "Have you gone crazy? What are you trying to pull?"

"One thing I learned in Vietnam – if you turn and run in battle, the only thing you get is a bullet in your back."

"Is that why you put me on the list last night?"

"You made a deal for the paper the minute you thought I was on my way out of the country."

"I made a deal for your life."

"It wasn't good enough. Those blasters and the MI waiting for me outside my girl's apartment didn't do much to convince me that they had pulled out."

He was silent for a moment. "I didn't know about that."

"You're slipping, Uncle John. I thought you made it your business to know everything."

"The queen canceled his contract, but they're still angry with you back East and Ronzi says he'll personally tear you apart when he sees you."

"You can tell Ronzi that he got off easy last night. If I had wanted to, I could have blown the whole place sky high. They have a million-dollar business to protect and if he and those moustaches still want to play, it'll cost them. If they do the arithmetic, they might figure I'm not worth the hassle."

"You sound pretty cocky," Lonergan said.

"They're out in the open, easy to find. I'm the Vietcong. I can hit and run before they even know I'm there."

"What makes you so sure you can get away with it?"

"I learned something in the time I spent at Reverend Sam's mission. The swords of the righteous are mighty. And I'm on God's side."

"The mission backing you up?"

I laughed. "You know better than that, Uncle John. Their motto is 'Peace and love.' "

"What will you setttle for?"

"Tell Ronzi I'll take the last deal he offered me. One hundred thousand dollars and he can have the paper, lock, stock and barrel. I'll go away quietly."

"Call me back in an hour."

I put down the telephone and looked at Julio.

"You got *cojones*, Lieutenant," he said. "The minute you walk out of here, you're a dead man."

"How much time do I have?"

"When are you calling him back?"

"In an hour."

"Until then."

The door opened and a boy came in, carrying a large covered tray. He placed it on the desk and went out. Julio removed the cover from the tray, which was filled with tortillas, enchiladas, hamburgitas and bowls of hot, sweet smelling chilli. "Hungry?" he asked.

I nodded, my mouth watering. He turned the tray toward me as I pulled up a chair. The condemned man ate a hearty meal.

"Ronzi says no deal unless you meet first," Lonergan said.

I thought for a moment. He could be setting me up. But I

had no choice. I had run out my string. Julio had picked up his marker. "Okay," I said. "At the newspaper office, ten o'clock tonight."

"We'll see you then," he said, clicking off.

I looked at Julio. "I'll be going now. Thanks for everything."

He nodded expressionlessly. "It's okay."

"Just one more favour. Keep Verita under the blanket until you hear either from me or about me."

"I planned on doing that."

I started for the door. He called after me. "Lieutenant."

I glanced back at him.

"You ought to do something about that orange hair. I'd hate to see you laid out like that. Everybody would think you were a faggot."

I laughed. "I'll take care of it."

He smiled and came out from behind his desk, his hand outstretched. "Good luck, Lieutenant."

His grip was firm. "Thanks. I'll need it."

"If you should change your mind when this is over, I've got all the money you need."

"I'll remember that, Julio." I opened the door.

"*Vaya con Dios*, Lieutenant."

The street was crowded with afternoon shoppers – women with loaded shopping bags and their kids dragging along behind them. Very quickly I became aware of how they were staring at my hair. It was as if I were the newest freak in town.

I caught a glimpse of myself in a store window. Julio was right. My hair was no longer orange; it was tangerine and it looked ridiculous. Another day with hair like this and I could be the Queen of Los Angeles.

I noticed a Unisex beauty parlour across the street and decided to go in. The store was divided in half by a panel, women on one side, men on the other.

A gay boy in a mauve jacket minced up to me. "What can I do for you, sir?"

"Can you get my hair back to its own colour?"

"What colour is that?"

I opened my shirt and let him see the hair on my chest.

His voice rose almost to a shrill scream. "You're a natural blond! How could you do such a thing to yourself?"

"It wasn't easy."

"It will take some time. We'll have to strip it, condition it—"

I cut him short. "I have the time."

He led me to a chair. He put his fingers in my hair to check the texture. "You came to me just in time," he lisped. "Your hair is burned. It breaks off in my hand. A few more days and it would begin falling out. I should cut it real short so I can really work on your scalp and give your hair a chance to breathe and grow."

"You do whatever you have to."

"It will be expensive."

"How much?"

"Thirty dollars."

"Okay."

"Cash. No checks."

I laughed and took out the money. "You want it in advance?"

"It won't be necessary. I knew you were good for it the minute you walked in. You're nothing like those types down here." He pulled out a sheet and began to wrap it around me. "Would you care for a manicure as well?"

"The works."

"The works" took three hours. It was seven o'clock by the time I got out of the chair and by then I'd heard the whole story of his life. His latest boyfriend had just left him for some rich Santa Barbara queen and he had been completely shattered.

"I almost had a nervous breakdown." Snip, snip. "You can believe that. After all I did for the little bitch. She didn't even know which fork to use for the salad when I found her." Snip, snip. "Now she's living off the fat of the land. Cartier watch, diamond rings and a Cadillac convertible. But I'm strong. You can't imagine how strong I am. I pulled myself together and said to myself, 'Charles, this is ridiculous. She's not the only fish in the sea. You'll find someone else. You always have. You always will.' The little bitch never even wanted to work. Never. I'm a worker. I go out and break my ass to make money, money, money and she lays around the house, watching television and playing with herself. And she knew how much I loved that big tool sticking out a half mile in front of her. The first thing she'd do when I came home from work, absolutely exhausted, was take it out and wave it in front of my face and the next thing I knew I was down on my knees in front of her worshipping that thing."

He pulled the comb through my hair and gently patted the side. "That should do it. How do you like it?"

I looked in the mirror. My hair hadn't been this short since I graduated from public school. But the colour seemed much like my own. "Fine."

"Makes you look younger, don't you think?"

I nodded.

"You should use conditioner on your hair, at least twice a week until it grows in. The best thing to do would be to come in at least once a week for a treatment. That way the hair will grow back strong and healthy."

"Sure."

He began unwrapping the towel from around my neck. "I'm really glad to be rid of her. I'm much better off now. I'm even saving money again. I didn't know how much she was costing me until she was gone. She ate enough for six people."

I got to my feet. "How much?"

"Thirty for the hair. Two for the shave and two for the manicure. Thirty-four dollars."

I gave him two twenty-dollar bills. "Keep five for yourself give a buck to the manicurist."

"Thank you." He followed me to the door. "Next time give me a call before you come. Ask for Charles. I'll make time for you."

"I'll do that. Thanks, Charles."

"If you're not tied up, maybe we could have some dinner. I know a darling Mexican restaurant down here."

Lunch had done me in. "I'm not big on Mexican food," I said. "Besides, I have to meet some people at ten o'clock."

"They have great steaks. And the service is quick. Besides, I enjoy talking to you."

That didn't surprise me. He never stopped. But I had two and a half hours to kill and it was better than moping around alone.

"Okay, but only if it's my treat. I insist." He didn't give me an argument.

The street was deserted. I put the key in the lock and began to turn it. The night light cast the diagonal shadow of a wire across the glass door. Instinct suddenly raised the short hairs on my neck. Without thinking, I threw myself out of the doorway, facedown on the sidewalk, just as the whole storefront blew out with a thunderous roar.

I was still lying on the sidewalk, my hands over the back of my head when out of the corner of my eye I saw Lonergan's car roll up to the curb. The door opened as I scrambled to my feet.

He leaned through the door without getting out. "You all right, Gareth?"

I turned to look at the storefront. It was gone. "Fine."

"You don't want to be here when the police come," he said. "Get in."

I got into the car and pulled the door closed. It moved away from the curb and around the corner. I leaned back and looked at Lonergan. There was a faint smile on his lips. "What's so funny?" I snapped.

"Children shouldn't try to play grown-ups' games."

"But I might have been killed!" I said angrily.

"Then you wouldn't have been as smart as I thought you were," he said calmly. "But you still have a lot to learn."

I stared at him sullenly.

His voice turned thin and cold. "How long do you think you would have lasted if I hadn't protected you? First with Reverend Sam, then with Julio Vasquez. Two minutes after your girl called him, he checked with me. If I hadn't okayed you, you would have been fed to the wolves."

I stared at him for a moment, then nodded. "Okay, Uncle John, I apologize. Now what do we do?"

"That's better, Gareth." He smiled and leaned back against the seat cushion. "First, we go to see Ronzi and get rid of the paper. I never really cared for that cheap sheet anyway, but it served to get you off the streets."

"And then what do I do, Uncle John?"

His eyes met mine steadily. "That will be entirely up to you. From now on you're on your own."

I didn't say anything.

"Of course, it would please me if you came in with me."

"It's not my game, Uncle John," I said gently. "You just told me that yourself."

His eyes grew thoughtful. "Do you know what you'd like to do?"

"Yes, Uncle John. I think I do."

BOOK TWO

The Up Side

The [illegible] brought the [illegible] three thousand feet and put the [illegible] could see the [illegible]

[illegible]

[illegible] on the beach [illegible] with the game fishing boats [illegible] one after the other like balls riding the waves, and I [illegible] that the boat was part of a [illegible]

[illegible] would the [illegible]

[illegible] off the [illegible] Vegas.

[illegible] the boat [illegible] the small [illegible]

[illegible] Across the cabin [illegible] and Bobby were [illegible] their belts. Behind them Bobby's four models were chattering and his two [illegible] were [illegible] to gather their gear.

Bobby got out of his seat. "If we move fast, we can get in at least one set before night falls. We should be able to get some great shots with the sunset on the beach."

Chapter One

The pilot brought the Lear down to three thousand feet and put the plane into a long, sweeping turn so that we could see the whole coast of Mazatlán. The blue-green water of the Pacific spilled over the sparkling white sand beaches. Murtagh leaned across the table, his finger touching the window. "We're coming up on it now, Mr. Brendan."

I followed the direction of his finger. At first I saw nothing but green jungle. Then, suddenly, there was the airstrip, a clean narrow cut through the trees, and beyond it, the hotel.

At first glance the eleven-storey concrete-and-metal structure seemed out of place in this untamed place. But then I saw the thatched roofs of the cottages with their individual pools, the tennis courts and golf courses, the Olympic-size pool and cabanas on the beach, the marina with the game fishing boats moored one after the other like gulls riding the waves, and I realized that the hotel was part of a separate world.

"Where would the casino be?" I asked.

"Just off the hotel lobby," Murtagh answered. "Exactly like in Las Vegas."

Now the hotel was far behind us. In the distance we could see the homes of Puerto Vallarta and behind us the flat sandy haze of La Paz. The turn completed, the pilot began his descent to the airstrip. I felt the shudder as the landing wheels went down and locked into position. A moment later we touched down. The pilot hit the brakes; we pushed against the seat belts for a moment, then eased off as the plane rolled toward the small building.

Lonergan was sitting next to me, his face expressionless. Across the cabin Verita and Bobby were unbuckling their belts. Behind them Bobby's four models were chattering and his two assistants were beginning to gather their gear.

Bobby got out of his seat. "If we move fast, we can get in at least one set before night falls. We should be able to get some great shots with the sunset on the beach."

"We'll be ready," one of the assistants answered.

Bobby turned to me. "What are your plans?"

"I've got meetings. You go ahead. We'll all get together at dinner."

They were off the plane and on their way to the beach before Murtagh finished introducing us to the officials who were waiting to greet us.

There were six of them, including the mayor of the town. All of them were short except one. He was six feet tall, blond and blue-eyed, with a tanned face and white flashing teeth. His name was Dieter von Halsbach. He was Mexican born like the others, but his parents had been Germans who'd emigrated after the war. He was the *jefe.* And the moment we shook hands I knew something else about him that I hadn't read in the background reports. He was gay.

Lonergan and I followed Dieter into the white Cadillac limousine. Verita, Murtagh and the others followed in another car.

"I have reserved three bungalows for you, Mr. Brendan," Dieter said.

"Thank you," I said. He needn't have gone to the trouble. From what I had heard we'd probably be the only guests. I glanced out the window at the manicured gardens through which we approached the hotel. "You have done a beautiful job here."

"We have spared no expense. My father and I believe in doing things right."

I glanced at Lonergan. If he was impressed, there was no way I could tell. The car swung past the entrance to the hotel and went down a side road toward the beach, coming to a stop in front of the bungalow.

We followed Dieter through the wrought-iron gates to the patio and swimming pool in front of the cottage. Fruit trees laden with oranges and limes cast their perfume on the warm, mildly salted air. A liveried butler and maid opened the door for us.

A bar was already set up in the living room. "Make yourselves comfortable, gentlemen," Dieter said. "We appreciate you might be fatigued from your journey, so my father and I thought you might want to rest. We can meet you at dinner at ten o'clock."

We watched him drive off in the limousine. The servants were busy with our luggage. I turned to Lonergan. "What do you think?"

"Eighteen million is too much." His words were flat.

"They've got thirty million in the place."

"That's their tough luck. I notice he didn't take us into the hotel. He probably didn't want us to see them shooting pigeons in the lobby."

I laughed. "Uncle John, I'm beginning to think you're a very suspicious man."

"They dropped six million in their first year of operation. Four million last year. That's ten million and they've only been open two years."

"They had the wrong approach. They tried to make this a jet setters' paradise. But the jet never set."

He permitted himself a faint smile. "You think you can do better?"

"If I didn't, I wouldn't be here."

"Eighteen million is still too much."

"I won't be talking dollars."

"We're jumping the gun. We haven't even started looking around."

I started for the bar. "Care for a drink?"

"No, thanks. I think I'll follow the young man's advice. I'm going to lie down and rest a bit."

Lonergan went to his room and I fixed myself a scotch on the rocks. I looked out the window at the beach. The sand was white, the water blue and inviting. I walked out to the edge of the beach and stood sipping my drink. The water looked great. I looked up and down the beach. There was no one in sight. I put down the drink, took off my clothes and went into the water naked.

The water was as soft and warm as it looked. I swam a good distance, then turned to look back at the shore, treading water. I could see the whole beach all the way past the hotel until the land curved away.

About five hundred yards down the beach I saw Bobby and his crew setting up for the shooting. Already the big silver reflectors were in place and as I watched, the parasol filters began to open up. They weren't wasting time. Bobby meant it when he said he was going to get his first set in before sunset.

I turned, put my head in the water and began to swim back to the shore in a slow, easy crawl. I could feel the heat of the sun warming my back and was awash in contentment. There was no doubt about it. They had something here. The good life. The only thing they didn't understand was that it had to be available to all the people, not just a chosen few.

When I came out of the water, there was a girl standing near my clothing, a giant beach towel outstretched in her hands. I stepped into it silently and she folded it around me.

"I'm Marissa," she said. "Count Dieter assigned me to be your translator."

Her long black hair, dark eyes and high cheekbones belied her name. So did the loose peasant blouse and soft Mexican skirt. "That's not a Mexican name," I said.

She smiled, showing white, even teeth. "My mother is Mexican; my father is Austrian. I was named after his mother."

"Are you related to Dieter?"

"We're cousins." She picked up my clothes from the sand. "Shall we go back to the cottage? The servants speak no English. If there's anything you want from them, I'll be glad to tell them for you."

"I'm okay," I said, starting up the beach. At the doorway to the cottage I turned and took the clothing from her arms. "I don't need a translator. My executive assistant speaks Spanish."

She hesitated a moment, then nodded. There was disappointment in her voice. "As you wish. But if there is anything else you should want, I am at your disposal. I'm in the guest relations office in the hotel."

"Thank you."

"Just one thing Count Dieter wanted me to show you. May I?"

I nodded and followed her into the cottage. A faint scent of verbena floated past me. She bent over the coffee table to press a small button on the side and a drawer rolled out. I looked over her shoulder.

It was all there. A wooden cigarette box of machine-rolled joints with filter tips, a plastic jar of cocaine with four tiny Mexican silver spoons and another box of crushed herbs. "Mescaline?" I asked.

She nodded.

"Thank you."

She closed the drawer. "I can go now?"

I smiled. "Will you be at dinner?"

"If you want me to be."

"I think it would be nice."

"I will see you then."

After she had gone, I opened the drawer and took out a joint. Then I went into the bathroom and filled the tub with warm water. I smoked the joint while lying in the tub. It was lovely.

Afterward I took a nap.

Chapter Two

The telephone woke me. It was Bobby. "Can I see you for a minute? I've got a great idea."

"Come on down," I said. I got out of bed and slipped into a bathrobe. The living room was empty and the door to Lonergan's room was open. I looked in. He was nowhere around. It was still daylight, even though it was after eight o'clock.

A butler came in, his white teeth flashing. "*Sí, señor?*"

"Scotch on the rocks," I tried.

He nodded and went behind the bar. I watched him fix the drink. At least, he spoke that much English. I took the glass and went out to the patio. The air was still warm even though the sun had gone.

I felt good. Very relaxed and low-key. There was something about this place. Not like Los Angeles, where the world kept screaming in my ears. This was really out of it.

Bobby came through the wrought-iron gates. "They really know how to do things here," he said. "We've all got separate bungalows. My boys and I in one, the girls right next door."

"How did the session go?"

"It was okay. I got a few good shots, but the girls weren't ready."

"What went wrong?"

"My fault. I forgot to prep them."

I laughed.

"You'd think that was the first thing they would do," he said in an aggrieved voice. "They know they're coming down here to show pink. You'd think the least they could do is to give themselves a little trim. Except for the blonde, it's like trying to shoot through a forest."

"What are you doing about it?"

"I turned them over to the cunt coiffeur. They'll be ready tomorrow.."

"They'd better be," Bobby said darkly. "I told him if he screws this one up, I'll kill him."

"What's your great idea?" I asked.

"I'd like to bring King Dong down here for a jungle layout with some of the girls. I got this whole scam where the girls dressed as white hunters come upon him in just a loincloth with his cock hanging out below. They get turned on and try to civilise him. He turns the tables on them and winds up the number one pimp in town."

"It's a funny idea, but it won't be easy to do," I said. "We caught a lot of flak the last time we used him in a layout."

"It was all from jerks who were jealous. But the issue sold a hundred thousand more than any other and is still the biggest copy of the backlist."

"Circulation said that the gays are all buying it."

"Sure they are, but so are a lot of women. I've seen them go absolutely glassy-eyed and come right in their pants the minute he takes out his tool. Even the most hard-bitten models get turned on no matter how many fuck layouts they've done."

"I don't know. We've got the racist shit to contend with. The blacks say we're putting them down by playing on the old fear. The red-necks say we're demeaning white womanhood."

"Let me get the set. You can always make up your mind when we have the pictures."

"Okay." I laughed. "This should be fun. Let me know when you shoot it. I'd like to see what happens."

"You've got to wind up with an inferiority complex. He's the closest thing to a bull I can imagine. Twelve inches long and he had six orgasms in four hours at our last session."

"I'll wear my wet suit," I said.

"What time is dinner?" he asked.

"Ten o'clock."

"I'll grab a shower and change."

"No rush," I said. I went back inside, took a joint from the drawer and gave it to him. "This is dynamite shit. Skip the shower and smoke this in the bath. It's beautiful."

He took the joint and sniffed it. "Thanks. I'll call the office first and make sure they get him down here on the morning flight."

Lonergan and Verita came back a few moments after he'd left. "Care for a drink?" I asked as the butler appeared.

"Dry martini," Lonergan said.

"Tequila,' Verita ordered.

I looked at her. "I thought you were a scotch drinker."

"We're in Mexico." She smiled. "I'm home now."

The butler brought the drinks and disappeared. Lonergan sat down opposite me; Verita took the lounge chair next to him. "We just strolled around the place," Lonergan said.

"What do you think?"

"They spent the money all right," he answered. "There's no doubt about it. But Verita came up with something interesting I thought you should hear."

I turned toward her. "Yes?"

"I spent all afternoon talking to the personnel. You learn a lot more that way. They know things even the owners don't."

I nodded.

"They have an opinion on why the place didn't make it."

"I'm interested."

"The gays put it away."

"I don't understand."

"Dieter brought his international crowd down. They really took over the place. So much so that when he asked them to cool it, they turned on him and laid a heavy rap on the hotel. And you know that crowd. They practically run the jet set. If they approve, society comes running, like Capri, like Acapulco, like the South of France. If they say it's *de mode*, you drop dead. Like Patino's place down the coast and Porto Cervo, Aga Khan's resort in Sardinia."

"It doesn't make sense," I said. "Why should Dieter sit on them? After all, they were his friends."

"One of the stories I heard was that some rich queen stole his steady and that it made him angry." She licked some salt from the back of her hand and took a sip of the tequila. "Another story is that his father made him push them out. He wants Dieter to marry and carry on the family name. He's got the girl picked out, a second cousin or something."

"Is her name Marissa?"

Verita nodded. "That's the name they mentioned. She works up in the office. You met her?"

"Yes. Dieter assigned her to be my translator. I told her that you were with me and that I wouldn't need her. But I asked her to join us for dinner."

"I thought you were sleeping," Lonergan said.

I laughed. "That was before I took a nap. I went for a swim. When I came out of the water, there she was."

"You'll never get the money crowd back now," Lonergan said.

"That's good," I replied. "Because it means von Halsbach has no place else to go. We're the only game in town and if they lose us, they go into the sewer." I went behind the bar and refilled my glass. "The deal I was going to offer them just went down by fifty per cent."

"You were going to offer them nine million?"

"No. That's half of what they were asking. I was going to offer them twelve. Now it's six."

"Something else I think you ought to know," Lonergan said.

"What's that?"

"I just heard from my office. There's some talk around that Julio has a big part of the action down here."

"Any proof?"

He shrugged. "That airstrip is just a short hop from Culiacán."

I knew what he meant. Culiacán was the drug center of Mexico. Almost every shipment of dope that came into the United States from Mexico either originated there or was trans-shipped from that point. "Any chance our hosts are in on it?"

"I have no way of knowing."

I pulled at my drink and looked at Verita. "You're going over the books tomorrow?"

"Murtagh said everything would be ready for me."

"Okay. Keep your eyes and ears open. If there is anything that doesn't make sense, no matter how trivial it may seem, let me know."

Dieter and his father were waiting at the bar when we came up to the main building. Slim and only slightly shorter than his son, the count was in his early sixties, with crew-cut, iron-grey hair, sharp, hard blue eyes and a dueling scar on his left cheek. If he'd had a monocle, he would have been straight out of a 1940s Warner Brothers movie.

"I have been looking forward to our meeting, Mr. Brendan," he said in soft Mayfair English. "I have heard a great deal about you."

"Good, I hope."

He smiled. "Of course. Here we listen to nothing but good about people."

"It's the only way to live," I said. My remark didn't seem to register. "Thank you for the accommodations. They're lovely."

"It is our pleasure. I only hope you will be able to spend enough time with us really to enjoy it."

"I'll try."

His eyes brightened as Marissa came toward us. The Indian-looking girl I had met that afternoon had disappeared. In her place was a tall, aristocratic lady in a long, clinging white dress that set off the tanned skin of her body and the black hair that fell below her shoulders. She kissed him on the cheek. "My niece, the Baroness Marissa," he said proudly.

"We've already met," she informed him, holding her hand out to me. "Mr. Brendan."

"Baroness," I said, smiling.

She let go of my hand as she turned to the others. A moment later we followed the count to the patio, where our table had been set up under a large tree. Marissa sat between the count and me and I could not tell whether the perfume I smelled came from her or from the scented air of the garden.

Dinner was European, very formal and very dull. All the right things were spoken, but nothing was said. In contrast with our table, Bobby, the models and his assistants were having a ball. I could tell from the shouts of laughter that they had managed to find their own source of supply. They all were stoned.

Lonergan and the old count seemed to find common ground. Maybe it was their age, but my uncle seemed genuinely to enjoy the dinner and the stories the count had to tell. I was so bored I couldn't take it any longer and finally pleaded a bad headache and retreated to the bungalow.

The first thing I did was light up a joint. Then I sat down on the patio and stared up into the night sky. There seemed to be more stars than I had ever seen before. I wondered if anyone out there in that limitless night was getting stoned and thinking the same thoughts.

I heard the creak of the wrought-iron gate. Marissa's white dress floated like a soft cloud in the darkness. "I came to see how you were," she said.

"I didn't know you were a baroness."

"I'm not really. But my uncle takes great pleasure in introducing me that way."

"Here, have a toke," I said, holding out the joint.

"No, thanks. That stuff makes me crazy."

I laughed. "If I had to stay down here, I'd go crazy without it."

"My uncle is very old-fashioned."

"Whatever got him into this? It seems so out of character."

He felt he had to do something. He owns all the land. And the government kept complaining that if something wasn't done they would break up his holdings and distribute them among the *campesinos*."

"That's no excuse to blow thirty million dollars."

"He put in the land and about six million. The government put in ten and the rest came from private investors."

"Who are they?"

"I don't know."

"Are they Mexican or foreign?"

"I don't know."

"He would have been better off if he had brought some people down from Las Vegas."

She didn't answer.

I took another toke and patted the chair beside me. "Come, sit down."

She didn't move.

"Did you come up here on your own or did Dieter send you?"

She hesitated a moment. "Dieter."

"Did he also happen to tell you that fucking me is part of your job?"

Again she didn't answer.

"What happens if they don't make a deal with me?"

"The government has threatened to forclose on them. They will lose everything."

"Thirty million dollars is a heavy trip to lay on you. It's really not fair."

She raised her arms behind her neck under her long black hair. When she put them down, the dress slipped from her body. She stepped out of it and stood naked in front of me. Now I knew the source of the perfume I had smelled in the garden.

I looked at her without moving. "You're beautiful," I said. And she was.

"What do you want me to do?"

I leaned forward, picked up the dress from the ground and held it out to her. "You could find me two aspirin. I really have a headache."

She took the dress from my hands and held it against her breasts. There was a puzzled sound in her voice. "You don't want to—"

I laughed. "I want to, all right. But that would be like taking money under false pretences. I haven't made up my mind about this place yet. So if we made love and I didn't buy, you would have wasted it."

For the first time she laughed. She let go of the dress. "What's a fuck between friends?" she asked.

Chapter Three

The telephone rang at eight o'clock in the morning. I reached for the telephone. Through the door leading to the bathroom, I could see Marissa's shadow on the glass shower door and hear the splashing of the water. "Unh," I grunted into the phone.

"Sounds like you had a big night," Eileen said.

"Yeah. What's up?"

"While you're down there having a good time, I want you to know that some people in the organisation are working."

"We'll have to correct that. It's ruining our image. The world thinks we do nothing but party."

"I'll be on the next plane," she said teasingly. "But meanwhile, I thought you'd like some good news."

"Tell me."

"We just got the circulation figures for January, February. We broke the three and a half million mark."

"How about that?"

"That isn't all. *Lifestyle Digest* went to a million one. That's not bad."

"What are we doing wrong?"

"I don't know, but we'd beter make sure we keep on doing it."

I laughed.

"What's it like down there?"

"I don't know yet. Verita's getting into the books today and I'm taking the grand tour."

"I don't understand why you're thinking of taking on a resort complex. The two magazines are making nothing but money."

"I remember people saying that when I went into the clubs. Meanwhile, the London club alone is throwing off six million a year."

"That's because it has gambling. New York, Chicago and Los Angeles are lucky to break even."

"We need them for our image. We'll have gambling in Atlantic City and this place has a gambling license."

"If that's what you want, why don't you go into Vegas?"

"I'm waiting for an opening. Meanwhile, the travel agency and packaged tours are getting a lot of action. I can fill this place right out of our own agency."

"How are you going to get the people there with only two commercial flights a day?"

"I'll have a charter service from LA. Plus which, the Princess Lines will make it a stop on their cruise."

"Put it all together and it's still chicken shit compared to what the magazines bring in. They're netting almost three million a month."

"Eileen. Such language."

"I'm serious. Why?"

I thought for a moment. "It's the action."

"I don't think that's it," she said. "Maybe someday, when you have some time, we'll go into it." Her voice grew soft. "I miss you."

The phone went dead in my hand before I could answer. The lady was very good. She knew exactly where it was at. There was no heat, no pressure. She let it happen in its own time. And time was on her side. We both knew that. Sooner or later I would be there.

Marissa came out of the bathroom, wrapped in a big turkish towel sarong. "Good morning."

"Good morning."

"Sleep well?"

"I think so."

"That's good." She crossed to the dresser and opened the small purse she'd brought with her. A moment later she was wearing a tiny bikini. She saw me watching her in the mirror. "It would look silly if I went up to the main building in my evening gown."

I nodded.

"Can I get you something?"

"I could use some coffee."

"Right away." She pressed a button near the door. "Anything else?"

I got out of bed and started for the bathroom. At the door I turned and looked back at her. "Don't be so formal, Baroness.

I thought we were supposed to be friends. I'd hate to think you were just doing your job."

When I came out of the bathroom, I saw that a small table had been rolled onto the terrace beyond the sliding glass doors. It was set with yellow linen napkins and tablecloth and there was a single yellow rose in a silver bud vase. The breakfast was continental – orange juice, coffee, hot rolls and croissants.

Marissa heard my footsteps and turned from the railing, where she had been looking out at the sea. "I owe you an apology," she said.

"It's okay."

"No. I didn't mean to be so stiff. It's just that – I've never done anything like this before. I felt awkward. I didn't know what to say?"

"You've said all the right things. Just as long as we're still friends."

She smiled. "We're friends. Coffee?"

"Black, please."

I took the cup from her hand. It was thick and strong. "What's on the program for today?"

"Dieter will be waiting in the main building at ten o'clock to show you around."

"Will you be with us?"

"I don't think so. I have work to do. But there's a cocktail reception for you at seven this evening. All the local officials are coming to meet you. I'll be there."

"What about dinner?"

"I'll be there if you want me."

"I want," I said. "And this time bring something else to wear back to the hotel in the morning. I think it's just as silly to show up in the office in a bikini as in an evening gown."

The grand tour lasted until noon. By then the sun was so hot that even the ocean breeze coming through the open canvas-topped jeep gave no relief. Dieter did the driving and I sat next to him. Lonergan was in the back. Several times I glanced back at my uncle. If he was uncomfortable, he gave no sign of it in spite of the fact that he was the only one wearing a suit and tie.

Still, I could sense that he was glad to get into the air-conditioned hotel.

We headed toward the bar. Lonergan ordered his usual dry martini. I decided on a gin and tonic and Dieter took tequila. We had covered two golf courses – one eighteen holes, the other nine – twelve tennis courts, a forty-horse riding stable and seventeen bungalows. All that was left to see was the main building.

"There are one hundred and eighty suites in this building," Dieter said. "Each with a bedroom, living room, bar, kitchen and two baths. They were designed with every luxury in mind. At an average of two hundred dollars a day per suite we estimated break-even at forty percent occupancy."

Lonergan nodded. "According to your figures, you averaged no better than fifteen percent."

"Truthfully," Dieter said, "we averaged less."

"What's capacity?" I asked.

"At two persons per suite and four per bungalow, four hundred twenty-eight."

"Then at an average rate of one hundred dollars a day per guest you figured break-even at sixteen thousand a day?"

Dieter nodded. "That included all meals."

"And if meals were not included?"

"Ten thousand, but you have to give them a continental breakfast. It's part of our licence with the government. That's figured in the ten thousand."

"Can the suites be converted into individual double rooms?"

"Yes. We thought about doing it, but we were not in a position to invest another million dollars in the changeover."

"I see." I signaled the bartender for another drink. "Why do you think the hotel didn't make it?"

"There are two reasons," Dieter said quickly. "The first is that the airlines did not keep their promise to increase the number of flights down here. The second is that the government won't let us open the casino until after the elections, despite having issued us the gambling license last year."

"What makes you so sure they'll give their permission now?"

"They don't want us to close. They have too much money invested."

"Do you have the commitment in writing?"

He smiled. "This is Mexico. Nothing is ever in writing And even if it were, it would mean nothing."

"Then they could still withhold it?"

"Anything is possible, though I doubt it. But you will be able to judge for yourself. The governor of the state will be at the cocktail party this evening. So will the *jefe* of the treasury department from Mexico City. They are the ones who will decide."

The telephone at the end of the bar rang. The barman nodded to Dieter. "*Para usted, excelencia.*"

Dieter took the telephone, said a few words, then put it down. "The official plane from Mexico City is arriving at the airstrip and I must go to meet them. If you gentlemen will excuse me?"

"No problem," I said.

"I have reserved a table in the garden for luncheon."

"Thank you."

He looked at me. "The baroness will be here in a moment to accompany you and see to your comfort."

"Thank you again."

"I don't like it. Something isn't right," Lonergan said as he walked away.

"Tell me."

"I don't think there will be gambling. If it were a sure thing, the boys would be here in a minute offering more money than you can come up with."

"You may be right. But let's run the game out. We'll know more tomorrow than we do today." I saw Marissa come into the bar. "Right now it's time for lunch."

Chapter Four

The luncheon was as beautifully served as the dinner had been the evening before. There was fish, freshly caught from the waters in front of the hotel, a lovely Montrachet, which was completely wasted on me but which my uncle savoured, followed by fresh lime ice and coffee. The soft breeze through the overhanging trees kept the sun from being too hot on our backs.

When we had finished, Marissa got to her feet. "I have some work to attend to in the office. Is there anything I can do for you this afternoon?"

I glanced at my uncle. He shook his head slightly. "No, thank you. I think we'll just go back to our cottage and rest awhile before the cocktail party."

"Okay. But if there is anything you should want, you know where to reach me."

We got to our feet as she left. My uncle looked after her approvingly. "A fine figure of a woman," he said. "Quality."

I looked at him sceptically. It might have been the sun, but I thought I saw him flush. He changed the subject quickly. "Walk back along the beach?"

"I'm with you."

When we got to the water's edge, my uncle suddenly bent down, took off his shoes and socks and rolled up his trouser cuffs. Holding the shoes in his hand, he stepped gingerly into the surf. He looked back at me. "Do you mind?"

"Not at all."

He was like a kid, kicking at the water and skipping away from the surf as it threatened to climb his legs. There was a faint smile on his lips and an oddly distant look in his eyes. "I've always wanted to do this ever since I was a kid."

"You never—"

"No," he said quickly. "I was eleven years old when I went to work. Your mother was a baby, your grandfather was dead and your grandmother was taking in washing to keep the family together."

"What did you do?"

"I got a job sweeping up and cleaning out the spittoons in Clancy's Saloon opposite the railroad station in Los Angeles."

I was silent. This was something I had never heard. No one in my family had ever talked about where he had begun.

"Your grandfather and Clancy had worked on the railroad together. That's how I got the job." He stopped and looked out over the water. "I can still remember watching the Union Pacific freight train coming down the center of Santa Monica Boulevard and running alongside the tracks, waving to my father and Clancy in the cab of the big steam locomotive."

"We're a long way from Santa Monica Boulevard right now."

"We both are. I remember that you began there, too."

I nodded. It was hard for me to believe that it was only five years since I stood in the store on Santa Monica Boulevard and watched Persky direct the moving men as they took out the last pieces of furniture from the office of the *Hollywood Express.*

Persky glanced around, trying not to look at me. The store was empty except for scraps of paper and litter on the floor. "I guess that's all of it."

He went out the door followed by the moving men. Outside, in the street, the carpenter finished boarding up the shattered storefront. He tried the door to see that it worked, then turned to me. "That'll be a hundred bucks," he said.

I gestured to Verita, who was standing next to me. "Give him a check."

"No checks. Cash."

For a moment I began to get angry; then I realized how foolish it was. If I were in his place and saw all the furniture going out, I would feel the same way. I stuck my hand in my pocket and came up with a roll. I paid him with a hundred-dollar bill that I peeled off the top.

"Thank you," he said, obviously impressed. "If you need anything else, give me a holler."

I locked the door behind me and turned to Vertita. "I should have known it was too good to last."

"Could have been worse. You might be dead. But you're not.

You might be broke. But you're not. With the twenty-five thousand you got from Ronzi in settlement, you have eighty-one thousand in the bank."

"Let's see how much is left after I pay my bills."

We went upstairs and sat down at the kitchen table, where she had set up the account books. "Let's take the big ones first," I said. "How much of Reverend Sam's advance is left?"

She flipped the pages of the ledger. "He gave you forty thousand. You ran six pages. That leaves thirty-four thousand in his account."

"Write the check." I waited until she pushed the signed check over to me. "Lonergan next."

"You don't owe him anything. He called me this morning and told me he wrote it all off as an investment."

"Fuck him. I don't need his charity."

She was silent.

"Did we pay his share of the ads in the last issue?"

"No."

"How much did it come to?"

"Three thousand one hundred," she said, glancing at the ledger.

"Add the twenty-five thousand advance and draw the check."

Silently she wrote the check and gave it to me. Unpaid printers' bills and other miscellaneous expenses came to twelve thousand. Salaries came to seventeen hundred. "Now what have we got left?"

"Five thousand three hundred,' she said without looking at the ledger.

"You're right. I'm not broke."

The tears began to roll down her cheeks.

"Hey, didn't you tell me it could have been worse? Just a few months ago I had absolutely zero. Now I have five grand."

"I'm – I'm sorry, Gary."

I took her hand across the table. "Don't be. It was fun while it lasted and it sure beat hell out of standing in the unemployment line."

She drew her hand away. Her eyes fell. "I spoke to the office yesterday. The supervisor said that I could start again on Monday morning."

"Am I eligible for benefits?"

"No."

"Then you're not going back. If I can't be in the line at your window, what good is it?"

"But I have to work Gareth."

"You are working. I didn't tell you you weren't, did I?"

"No – but." She hesitated. "I thought it was all finished."

"Finished?" I got out of the chair and took a can of beer from the refrigerator. I pulled the tab and drank from the can. "I'm just beginning. Before all this started, I was wandering around like a bum, pissed off with the world. But no more. That's over. Now I know how to get it I'm going to fuck the whole world."

Without thinking she spoke in Spanish. "*Usted está muy macho.*"

"That's it." I crushed the empty beer can in my hand and dropped it in the wastebasket. I pulled her to her feet and hugged her. "That's what I was looking for."

"*No comprendo.*"

I laughed. "*Macho.* The name of our new magazine."

Chapter Five

It took us six months to get the first issue on the stands and it was a disaster. *Penthouse* had come into the States just before we started publishing and began to tear up the market. Comparing *Macho* to *Playboy* and *Penthouse* was like comparing the *Hollywood Express* to the *New York Times.* The soft-focus photographs of beaver that *Penthouse* was using had every man in America sprouting a mustache. *Playboy* fought back by going full frontal, but they still airbrushed their girls. We laughed when we saw it. The neatest pussies in the country. But it wasn't funny to us. We were really hurting. And there was no way we could top either magazine – with words or pictures. They just had too much talent going for them. And the talent went where the money showed. All we had were promises.

We put out the second issue a month late in order to give the newsstands a chance to dispose of more of the first issue. The third issue was also a month late. By that time we knew it was all over but the shouting. The national distributor sent us a termination notice which meant that if we wanted our magazine on the stands, we had to deliver it ourselves. But that was academic. I was almost fifty grand in hock and there was no way I could hope to get the money to publish even another issue.

We sat around the kitchen table, staring glumly at the piles of bills in front of us. "Is that all of it?" I asked.

Verita nodded. "Forty-nine thousand three hundred fifty-seven dollars and sixteen cents exclusive of payroll."

"How much is that?"

She looked at Bobby and Eileen. "The staff took a vote. We pass."

That made the tenth week in a row they had passed. "Thank you," I said. "How much have we got in the bank?"

Verita glanced at the ledger. "About seven hundred."

"Shit. It'll take the rest of my life to pay off."

"You don't have to," Verita said. "You can file for bankruptcy. Both for yourself and the company. Then you'll be clean. You can start all over again if you want."

"What happens to the name?"

"*Macho?*"

I nodded.

"It belongs to the company. You lose it together with whatever other assets they turn up."

"What other assets? Some secondhand pictures and articles that nobody wants?"

"My father says he'll lend you the money to go on," Bobby said.

"Thank him for me, but that would be like throwing the money down the sewer. We haven't cut it."

"Maybe one more issue would turn the corner," Bobby said.

"No way. Not when we're trying to do what the others are already doing better." I reached for a cigarette. "Unless we come with a new approach, we're nothing more than a third-rate imitation."

"What new approach is there?" Bobby asked. "There are only so many ways you can shoot girls and we're down to beaver already."

I stared at him. It wasn't what he said but the way in which he said it. Somewhere in my head a wheel started turning.

"And between the *Playboy* Advisor and *Penthouse* Forum, they've covered almost every sexual idea you can think of in writing," Eileen said. "There's not much more we can do in that area."

Another wheel began to turn. "Maybe what we did was play the game by their rules. Maybe we were on the right track with the *Express* because we didn't know the rules and made up our own as we went along."

"A national magazine isn't the same as a local paper," she said.

"Isn't it? Do you think the rest of the people in America are different from the people in Los Angeles? They're all interested in the same thing."

"LA has a more liberal lifstyle than Squeedunk. They're more open about things."

"They don't fuck in Squeedunk?"

"Maybe they do, but they don't talk about it as much."

"I don't care whether they're talking about it. What I'm interested in is whether they're thinking about it and reading about it."

"They have to be. They're buying *Playboy* and *Penthouse* even if they don't understand some of the words."

"They're looking at the pictures, too," Bobby said. "*Penthouse* grabbed almost three million copies by the end of their first year. All beaver shots and raunch. Hefner feels the pinch in his circulation and he's coming up with a new magazine to compete with Guccione. He made a deal with the French magazine Lui to share photos and other material. He's calling it *Oui.* A friend of mine saw an advance copy. He says it's class raunch."

"What does that mean?" I asked.

"No airbrushed beavers," Bobby answered. "The girls comb it."

We all laughed.

"But they're still pushing the same old line. Both of them. It's called everyman's instant expertise. The right French wines, the 'in' fashions. Clothes, holidays, sports, movies, books, food. You name it. Mr. Blue Collar can now order a sixty-seven Pommard to go with his Big Mac or he can jump into his Aston Martin to take his old lady to the local drive-in movie."

The girls laughed, but I didn't. I didn't think it was funny. Fifty thousand dollars unfunny. I got to my feet. "We're not going to settle anything tonight. I'm going to lie around over the weekend and do some heavy thinking. I have the strangest feeling I fucked up by missing the obvious."

"If it's so obvious, what is it?" Bobby asked.

"It sounds stupid, doesn't it? But that's the honest truth. I just don't know."

The telephone rang just after they left. Lonergan's voice was cool. "Gareth?"

"Yes, Uncle John."

"I'd like to see you."

We had neither seen nor spoken to each other for more than four months, but there was no "How are you?" or "What's new?" Just "I'd like to see you." I'd eaten enough shit for that day; I didn't need him to lay any more on me. "You know where I am," I said truculently.

"Can you meet me at the Silver Stud at midnight?"

"What the hell for?" I snapped.

He was unruffled. "I have an interesting proposition for you."

"The last time I went for one of your interesting propositions I almost got myself killed."

"That was your fault. You insisted on doing things your own way instead of letting me handle it. Midnight. Be there."

I hesitated a moment. "Okay."

"Gareth."

"Yes, Uncle John?"

There was the hint of a chuckle in his voice. "This time do me a favour and park your car in the street, will you?"

He hung up before I could answer. He didn't have to worry. I'd never got around to buying a car of my own. And it was just as well because if I had, the finance company would have picked it up a long time ago.

I almost didn't recognize the place when I got there. The windows were all silvered over except for two small white ovals through which the neon sign was visible. There was no way that anyone from the street could see in. There were even more changes in the interior.

The old wood and mahogany bar and tables had been replaced by chrome and black plastic. Four silent film projectors hung from the ceiling in the center of the room and threw their pictures on the screens which were set up in different corners of the room. Toward the rear of the bar a wild-looking black girl sat on a small platform, playing the piano and singing in a hoarse voice. There was no way I could make out what she was singing over the noise until I got close. They were all dipstick songs with gay lyrics.

I managed to get through the crowd to the rear of the saloon after having my cock and balls cupped once, my ass grabbed twice and turning down an offer of a hundred dollars from some old queen who wanted me to spend the night at his house in the

Hollywood Hills. As usual, the Collector was seated at the table beside the staircase.

"What are they giving away?" I asked.

"It's been like this ever since they remodeled. Every night is New Year's Eve." He gestured to the seat opposite him. There was a bottle of scotch on the table. He filled a glass with ice cubes from a plastic bucket and pushed it toward me. "I got your drink here. Help yourself."

I splashed the whisky over the rocks. "When did they remodel?"

"Right after you parked your car at the bar." He grinned. "I figured you did Lonergan a favour. The insurance company paid for the whole thing."

"Shit. Maybe I ought to ask Lonergan for a commission."

The Collector laughed. "You kin ask." He poured himself another drink. "How you been keepin'?"

"Usual."

"Lonergan will be a little late." His eyes went over my shoulder. "Did you see the chick at the piano?"

"Yeah."

"Wild-lookin', isn't she?"

"Yeah."

His voice dropped almost as if he were talking to himself. "Man, would I like to put it to her. She's got me climbin' a wall."

"Why don't you just ask her?"

"I did. She just ain't interested. No way."

"Maybe she's a dyke."

"She's no dyke," he said quickly. "She wants to be a star. Shirley Bassey. Aretha. Like that. She's out to make a big score."

"She's not going to find it here."

"You can't tell. The night people really dig her. And some of those queens carry a lot of weight." He got to his feet. "She's 'bout due for her break. I'll introduce you."

"What for?"

"How the hell do I know. Shee-it," he added, "if I didn't have an excuse, she wouldn't even come here and sit with me."

"Okay." He was really hurting. "I'll tell her what a big man you are."

He was right about one thing. She was out to make a score. Almost before she sat down, the words were out of her mouth. "Bill tells me you're a publisher. I wrote some songs I'd like you to look at."

"I'm not that kind of publisher."

"What kind are you?"

"I publish a magazine. *Macho.*"

Her face went blank. "Never heard of it. What's it like?"

"*Playboy. Penthouse.* Like that."

"I don't do nude layouts," she said flatly.

I was annoyed. "Don't worry. I won't ask you. You're too skinny."

She turned to the Collector. "What are you wasting my time with creeps like this for?" she complained. "I thought you said he could do me some good."

"Maybe I can," I said in a mild voice.

Her voice changed instantly, became almost civil. "Yes?"

"If your cunt is as big as your mouth, I'll pay you a thousand dollars for a centerfold."

She stared at me for a second, then got up angrily. "Motherfucker!" she snapped and marched off.

I looked at the Collector. He was the picture of dejection. "I don't think I did you any good," I said.

He nodded heavily. "You didn't help, that's for sure." He picked up the bottle of scotch and refilled our glasses. We threw the drinks back and he poured again. "Do you think her cunt is as big as her mouth?" he asked in a wondering voice.

"Why do you ask?"

A broad smile cracked his face. "If it is, I'd sure like to put my whole face in it."

I laughed and raised my glass to him. That was true love if I ever saw it. By the time Lonergan got there at one-thirty in the morning I was so drunk I could hardly make it up the stairs to his office.

Chapter Six

"You're drunk," he said in a tone of disapproval.

"So what else is new?" I slurred.

"You can't talk business in that condition."

"That's right." I fixed my eyes on him. "You really want me to sober up, Uncle John?"

"This is important."

"Okay. Order some black coffee for me. I'll be back in a minute." I went into his private bathroom and stuck two fingers down my throat. The liquor burned twice as much coming up as it had going down. Afterward I held my head under the cold-water tap until the pain behind my temples stopped. Then I dried myself with a towel and went back into the office.

Lonergan pushed a mug of steaming black coffee toward me. "You look like a drowned rat."

I swallowed half the cup of coffee and put it down on the desk. "But a sober drowned rat. Now what is it you want to talk about?"

"How are you doing with the magazine?"

"You know. Why ask me?"

"I want you to tell me."

"I'm folding. Tapped out. Busted. Anything more you want to know?"

"Yes. Why?"

I finished the mug of coffee before I answered. I had been giving that a lot of thought. "You want an excuse or the truth?"

"The truth."

"Because I was stupid. I finaly figured it out. I tried to publish *Playboy* and *Penthouse*. But that's not my game."

"What is your game?"

"I'm a street publisher. That's why the *Hollywood Express* worked. I can hit the guy on the street with the things I do. I can't hit the middle-crust white-collar guy with social pretensions the way Hefner and Guccione can. My best shot is to the gut, not the head."

He was silent for a moment. "Do you think you can still make a magazine pay off?"

"Yes."

"What does it take?"

"To start with, money. After that, distribution. That wouldn't be easy because of my track record. I'd have to try to find one who was willing to take a chance on me."

"If you had the money and the magazine, would you go back to Ronzi?"

"I don't like the prick. Besides, he's local. I need a national distributor for the magazine."

"What if he comes up with a national distributor?"

I was sober now. Lonergan never did anything without a reason. "You're not leveling with me, Uncle John. What's with Ronzi?"

"Persky took the *Express* down the tube and Ronzi went for a bundle. Now he wants to come up with something good so he can prove himself with his associates in the East."

"He tell you to contact me?"

"Not in so many words. But he managed to give me the feeling he wouldn't be averse to a deal."

"I'm not going back to publishing the *Express*."

"That's not what I asked. I'm talking about the magazine. Your magazine. *Macho*. That's something the Italians would understand."

"I won't go with the moustaches. No pieces. No partners."

"The magazine is yours. They would just be the distributors."

I thought for a moment. "I would still have to come with enough money to get the magazine out. I owe fifty grand now and my creditors won't carry me."

"I might be able to talk them into a hundred big ones as an advance for exclusive distribution for two years."

"One year. And no personal liability if the magazine drops dead. They lose their money. Period."

"You're taking a hard line for a man who's on his ass."

"Why not?" I smiled. "What more have I got to lose?"

"I should have let you stay drunk. You would have been easier to deal with."

"Why?" I had a thought. "Do you have a piece of Ronzi's action?"

"No. But he still thinks I have a piece of yours. He doesn't believe anyone but the Italians think that blood is thicker than water."

I had a sudden burst of understanding. All Lonergan had ever taken from me was what had been his. He had never taken anything of mine. He had used me. But I had used him in return. And in the end, if he hadn't kept his arm around me, I would have been dead. I met his eyes. "Uncle John, I've just changed my mind."

"About what?"

"I do want a partner. You."

I saw his Adam's apple move as he swallowed a deep gulp of air. He blinked his eyes, polished his gold-rimmed glasses, then put them back on his nose. "I'm flattered," he said huskily. "How much will it cost me?"

"I owe fifty. Even after I pay it off, I will still need a hundred to get the magazine the way I want it. Ronzi's advance leaves me short. Fifty gets you ten per cent."

"Ten per cent is nothing," he said. "A finder's fee is that much without any investment."

"That's my deal."

He looked at me for a moment. "I'll make you a better offer. I'll give you a hundred for twenty per cent. You run the whole show. That will give you a real shot."

"What if it goes into the sewer?"

"Then I'll cry a lot. But you won't owe me anything."

I stared at him. It was something I thought I would never do. Not after what had happened to my father. They had been partners and my father had blown his brains out because Uncle John wouldn't help him.

He responded as if he'd been reading my mind. "Your father was a weak man. He did something he shouldn't have done. When he was caught, he compounded it by involving other people, people who were innocent of any wrongdoing. By the time he came to me there was nothing I could do, nothing anyone could do. I advised him to tell the truth and take his fall. I told him that when he got out, I would help him start all over again. But he couldn't face the truth. He thought more of his image than he did about your mother or you. So he wrote the note blaming everything on me. It made newspaper headlines and there were enough people who didn't like me to give it credence. But didn't you ever wonder why, if the charges that he made were true, no one ever brought me into court?"

I let him talk.

"They were all investigated. By every authority, local and federal. And not one of them was true. Because if they had found one, they would have cheerfully hanged me from the nearest tree." He took off his glasses and wiped them again. "I'm sorry. I don't know what brought that on. I never meant to talk to you about your father like that. But it was always there between us. You were a child when it happened and you grew up with it. It even affected your attitude toward your mother because you did not understand why our relationship continued as if nothing had happened."

I looked at him without speaking. I had nothing to say. It was all in the past and nothing could change that. Again he seemed to pick up my thoughts.

"It's over. And it has nothing to do with what we were talking about."

I nodded.

"Do we have a deal?" he asked somewhat hesitantly as if fearing rejection.

I held out my hand to him. "Yes, partner."

He took my hand in both of his and held on tigntly. His eyes blinked behind his glasses. "We'll do all right. You'll see."

Even I had to blink. "I know we will. And I'll do my damnedest not to let you down."

"Now that we're partners, son, the first thing I'm going to do is tell that Guinea bastard he's got to come up with at least two hundred if he wants a national exclusive."

"Uncle John, remember our deal? You said that I run the show."

"I'm not interfering," he said quickly. "But you'll have enough to do getting out the magazine. And besides, I can handle that bastard better than anybody. He knows damn well that I can fix it so he won't have a truck left on the streets of Los Angeles."

There was no arguing with that. He could speak the only language the moustaches understood. "Okay, Uncle John. You started with Ronzi, you finish with him." Suddenly I was hungry. I got to my feet.

"Where are you going?"

"I'm starved. It's past two in the morning and I haven't eaten since lunch."

He put his hand in his pocket. "You haven't any money?"

I laughed. "I have money. I just haven't had the time. I've been too busy."

"Where are you going?"

"The Bagel Delicatessen on Fairfax. They're open late."

"Have Bill drive you over and wait for you. Then he can take you home. I don't want you walking around the streets at night.

"I'm a big boy, Uncle John, and you've never worried about me before."

"We weren't partners then," he said. "Now I have more than blood invested in you."

Chapter Seven

MACHO

Giant block letters on royal blue velvet background.

In smaller white letters on the left: "For the Masculine Mystique." Same type on the right: Volume 2, Number 1.

Completely nude girl, white cowboy hat on head, standing in classic aggressive gunfighter's pose, holding gun in each hand, pointing at reader. Cellophane layover on which has been imprinted white lace bikini, covering breasts and genitalia of girl. Through the lace can be seen the faint colouring of girl's breasts and pubic hair. Lettering running down left side of photograph: "Are you man enough?" On the right side running parallel: "To tear off my bikini?"

Absolutely no other copy. Except the price in the upper right-hand corner: $1.25.

Inside front cover in black letters: "Our new symbol—" Giant Red Letters: THE FIGHTING COCK! Artwork. A pop drawing of a phallus, erect and angry, over which is imposed a fighting cock, complete with red comb, thrusting beak and sharp, angry claws fitted with knives below swollen testicles which constitute the body. The fighting cock seems to be hanging in the air about to pounce on the nude body of a girl lying supine beneath him. Copy: "For the Masculine Mystique. The man who is willing to fight for what he wants is the man who gets what he wants."

Facing page. The publisher's statement:

DON'T BUY THIS MAGAZINE IF—
You like bunnies—buy a rabbit.
You want a pet—buy a poodle.

BUY THIS MAGAZINE IF—

YOU LIKE GIRLS—We have six in this issue. Thirty pages of naked beauties. All shapes, sizes and colours. Just to please you and turn you on to the possibilities of life.

YOU LIKE SEX—We have stories, articles, jokes, cartoons, fantasies, fetishes, all dealing with the one subject that men talk more about, think more about and want more of than any other thing, including money. Sixty pages of nothing but sex. We won't tell you what car, what stereo or what camera to buy or what you should wear. Who can afford those things anyway? But there is one thing you can afford. PLEASURE. And sex is pleasure. And for a buck and a quarter a month we're going to give you more pleasure than you ever dreamed of.

THIS, I PROMISE YOU.

[signed] Gareth Brendan,
Publisher

P.S. PUBLISHER'S SPECIAL NOTE!

In this issue, and in every monthly issue to follow, you will find a life-size pullout centerfold, 22 inches by 34 inches, featuring the girl we select as—

SUPERCUNT OF THE MONTH!

This one giant life-size photograph of nothing but beautiful inviting pink pussy is guaranteed to make the FIGHTING COCK in each of you rise to do battle and make your mouth water to see more of the girl to whom it belongs. So turn the pages and you will find ten other turn-on photographs of this month's SUPERCUNT.

And if that doesn't work, you have the option to do one or both of the following:

1. SEE YOUR DOCTOR.
2. Place the pullout centerfold together with your name and return address in an envelope and mail it to us for a complete refund of the cost of the magazine. You may keep the rest of the magazine with our compliments.

[signed] G. B.
Publisher

It was three months after Lonergan and I had made our deal that we stood looking at the mock-up of the magazine. It was spread out, page by page, on the wall and we watched as the production estimator from the printer went down the line, making his notes. At last he finished and came back to us.

"Can you do it?" I asked.

"We can do anything. It'll just cost."

"How much?"

"How many copies you thinkin' of?"

"I haven't made up my mind yet. What's the base price?"

"You have two special jobs: cellophane wrapper and the centerfold. We'll need special machinery to handle that." He turned and looked at the wall. "That's thirty thousand for openers whether you print a hundred copies or a million. I figure colour press time and paper for two hundred thousand will bring you up to about eighty thousand."

"The production cost comes to forty cents a copy," Verita said. "Ronzi gets twelve and a half cents per copy distribution commission and withholds fifteen cents per copy for returns. Out of the sixty-two and a half cents dealer's price, that leaves us with thirty-five cents and a deficit for openers of a nickel a copy."

I glanced at Lonergan. He was silent.

"That doesn't take into account our costs and overheads, which amount to about twenty thousand to date. That brings our loss to fifteen cents a copy."

I went back to the production man. "What if we run a million copies?"

He made some pencil calculations on his scratch pad. "We could bring it in for about one hundred and forty thousand, give or take a few dollars."

Verita didn't need a scratch pad. "Even with a forty per cent return, we make a profit of ninety thousand dollars."

"And if we sell out one hundred per cent?"

"Then we're in gravy. We pick up an additional quarter of a million dollars making our net three hundred and forty thousand."

I turned to Ronzi, who up to now hadn't said a word. "What do you think? Can we sell a million copies?"

"I don't know."

"I'll ask you another question then. Can you get a million copies on the stands for me?"

"I can do that, but I won't guarantee that they'll stick."

"Would you lay fifty grand on top of my one-fifty in a co-operative advertising campaign to introduce the magazine to the market?"

"What's in it for me if I do?"

"First, you pick up an extra hundred grand for selling the eight hundred thousand copies, plus which I'll give you a five per cent override, and that'll net you another thirty."

"I wouldn't do it for less than a ten per cent override."

"You got it."

"Wait a minute. Not so fast. I didn't say I'd do it. Nobody ever advertised a magazine like this before."

I smiled. "That doesn't mean it can't be done."

"Where you gonna advertise?"

"The usual places. Newspaper, radio, TV."

"They won't take your ads."

"What if I told you I already have the campaign placed?"

"I'll believe that when I see it."

"Come upstairs then."

They followed me up to the apartment. There on an easel was the newspaper ad. The illustration was a simple line drawing. A woman in a discreet sexy negligee, a bored expression on her face, standing next to a chair in which her husband was sitting, his eyes glued on the television set. The copy was simple. "MACHO. A new magazine. For the Masculine Mystique. Attention, ladies! Get your husband a copy today. It will do more for him than vitamins. At your newsdealer now."

"The TV spots run ten seconds voice-over the same illustration, using the same copy you just read. The radio spots are exactly the same. They're timed to go out the first week we hit the stands. Everything is cleared. All it takes now is my signature on the contract."

"I think you're crazy."

"You're in for two hundred grand now. What's another fifty? It could make you a big man with the moustaches back East."

"And if I'm wrong, it could get me a very nice cement overcoat."

"Grey is a good colour for you."

He studied the ad again. "One million copies," he murmured, half to himself. "What if we don't sell the million? Will you give me the override on the first million sold whenever we reach it?"

"That's fair enough."

"Okay, I'll go. When do you think we can be on the stands?"

"How long will it take you?" I asked the production manager.

"We can be ready in six weeks if the colour tests work out."

"You heard the man. Two months."

But we were both wrong. It was more than four months before the magazine was ready for the press and we weren't on the stands until April of the following year. We encountered all kinds of reproduction problems – the pink wasn't pink enough and the pussies tended to resemble wrinkled prunes when photographed. Like everything else about a woman, they looked better with makeup and a coiffure. And that was why we developed a whole new line of beauty care. For the cunt.

Chapter Eight

We could hear Bobby screaming at the models. Lonergan stepped from the water onto the sand, then jumped back quickly. "My God! It's burning hot."

"Wait a minute. I'll have them send down a towel so you can dry your feet and get back into your shoes." I cuped my mouth with my hands and called up to the camera crew to send down a towel.

A moment later one of the models came running toward us, completely nude, with the towel flapping in her hands. "Is this what you wanted, Mr. Brendan?"

"That's right." I saw my uncle turn away from the girl and look out at the ocean. I smiled to myself. "What's your name?"

"Samantha Jones."

"Samantha, would you be kind enough to dry Mr. Lonergan's feet and help him on with his shoes?"

My uncle spoke quickly. "That's all right. I can do it."

"Don't be silly. Samantha doesn't mind."

She knelt at my uncle's feet. He fixed his eyes steadfastly on the horizon as she picked up one foot and began to dry it. Lonergan almost lost his balance. "Maybe it will be easier if you put a hand on my shoulder," Samantha said.

"No, I'll be all right." Then he almost lost his balance again.

She caught his arm to steady him and guided it to her shoulder. "There, isn't that better?"

Lonergan didn't answer but remained standing on one leg, his face turned towards the sea.

"You're in good hands," I said to him. "I'm going up there to see what's happening."

Bobby was still screaming at the model when I got there. "You stupid cow! You're supposed to be conscious of it, not self-conscious about it. Make it look as if you can't wait to get pronged."

The girl was near tears. "But, Bobby, it feels so funny. I never saw it before. Not like that. All trimmed and shaved so that everything sticks out."

"It's supposed to, you idiot," Bobby shouted. "What did you think we were going to take pictures of? Your eyeballs? He turned away in disgust. "Oh, shit." He saw me. "We'll never get through."

"Take five," I said. "And come with me."

"Take five," he called over his shoulder and followed me up the beach. "What is it?"

I looked at him. His face was flushed with the heat, and the perspiration was dripping down his forehead. "How long you been out there in that sun?"

"Two hours maybe."

"How do you feel?"

"Hot. I've never been so hot in my life."

"How do you think the girls feel?"

He stared at me silently for a moment. "But we need the sun."

"If you keep them out in it much longer, you'll all wind up in the hospital."

"I'll never finish the set."

"You can always get them in the studio. When's King Dong coming in?"

"This afternoon's flight."

"You can shoot that tomorrow. That's something you can't do in the studio. Have you made arrangements for the costumes?"

"He's bringing them down with him."

"You're all set then."

"Yes. We leave at seven tomorrow morning for the Retreat."

"The Retreat?" I didn't know what he was talking about.

"My father's mission. It's about seventeen miles from here on the edge of the jungle."

"That's a strange place for a mission. Who do they convert? The Indians?"

He laughed. "It's not that kind of mission. It's more like a school. This is where candidates for the second plane take instruction to qualify as teachers. It's called the Retreat because it has absolutely no communication with the outside world, no radio, no telephone. Only the supply trucks that go back and forth."

His expression changed. A troubled look crossed his face. "Was I terribly awful, Gareth?"

"You've just had too much sun."

"I'm sorry. I just get so involved."

"That's all right. Just remember. People aren't cameras, and models aren't just pieces of equipment."

He nodded and went back to the setup. His voice floated back to me. "Wrap it up. We're finished for the day. Seven o'clock call tomorrow morning."

Lonergan caught up with me as I walked on to the cottage. "You didn't have to do that," he said.

I played innocent. "Do what?"

"You know. Have that naked girl wipe my feet. It was very embarrassing. What if someone had taken a picture?"

"Damn! I knew I forgot something," I said in mock chagrin.

"I don't know why I bother with you."

"I do." I held the cottage door open for him. "Do you know of anyone else who would make it possible for you to fulfill a childhood dream and walk barefoot in the surf?"

Verita was waiting for me, a margarita in her hand. "You took the long way back from lunch."

"Lonergan wanted to walk in the surf," I said. "You're finished early."

"It was simple. Murtagh was right. Everything was laid out for me. No tricks. Everything open. The books verify their claim. Both as to cost and losses."

"But you still look uncertain."

"It just doesn't make sense. Everything in order like that. It's not Mexican." She took a sip of the cocktail. "After I finished the books, I took a stroll down to the airstrip and talked to some of the mechanics."

The butler came in. I ordered a scotch on the rocks, Lonergan his usual dry martini. When the butler had gone, she went on. "Do you know that about thirty private planes use that airstrip every week?"

"No."

"About half of them belong to landowners around here."

"The other half?"

"Transient. Land, refuel and take off. They rarely stay on the ground more than an hour."

"Any idea of where they come from?"

"The Baja Peninsula, the mechanics say. But that doesn't make sense. La Paz is closer for them. This is two hundred miles farther away. Another thing, they're all flying one way. North. None of them ever lands on their way down."

"They keep records down at the airstrip?" I asked.

"No. They do it the Mexican way. They keep a cashbox and just throw whatever money they collect into it. Landing fees, fuel, things like that."

"Is there a Mexican customs officer there?"

"No. Only a local policeman. And he was sleeping all the time I was there."

I turned to Lonergan. "What do you think?"

"Dope, probably. But that doesn't mean that the von Halsbachs are in on it. If they were, they wouldn't be so eager to unload. There has to be more money in that than there is in running the hotel. More than enough to cover any losses."

"How do we find out?"

He looked at Verita. "They had private investors. Do the books give us any information on them?"

"No. They put up part of the money themselves. The rest came from a syndicate."

"Can we get any information on who is in the syndicate?" I asked.

Lonergan shrugged. "Swiss banks."

I looked at Verita. "Do you think Julio might know?"

She finished her drink. "You can ask him when we get back to Los Angeles."

But I didn't have to wait that long. He was there for the reception that afternoon. And so was Eileen.

The cocktail party was almost over when they arrived. I had just finished thanking the governor for his interest and for taking time from his busy schedule to see me.

"No, Señor Brendan," he protested in almost accent-free

English. "It is we who are indebted to you for your interest. We feel we have one of the most beautiful vacation lands in the world here and with the efforts of you and people like you it can become a veritable paradise. I pledge you our cooperation."

"Thank you, Excellency. At the moment my only concern is when the casino will be permitted to open. Without it, it would be impossible for my kind of operation to succeed."

"All the local approvals have been obtained. Now we must wait for approval from the federal government."

"How long do you think that will take?"

"We are bringing all the pressure we can to bring it about."

I wouldn't let him off the hook. "Without a definite date, Excellency, there is no way I can undertake an investment of this magnitude."

"I will do all I can to give you a quick answer," he said smoothly. "Now, unfortunately, I must go. I am due in La Paz for an important dinner."

"Thank you again, Excellency."

He bowed and held out his hand. "*Hasta la vista*, Señor Brendan." It was a politician's handshake and had a certain kind of phony warmth. He bowed again, then made his way through the room, saying goodbye to the others. He was followed by his two silent bodyguards, whose tight suits didn't hide the bulges made by the guns under their arms.

I walked over to Lonergan. "No commitments," I said in answer to his unspoken question. "But lots of promises."

He didn't answer. His eyes went to the door. I followed his gaze and saw Eileen and Julio, who were just entering.

The governor stopped in apparent surprise; then the two men embraced and shook hands. They spoke a few words to each other; then Julio continued on into the room as the governor turned down the corridor.

Julio seemed to know everyone there. I watched as he stopped to chat on his way through the room. And there was something else: the way they reacted to him. It was as if he were a king. They were deferential and wanted to be sure that he saw them. It was more of a fuss than they had made over the governor.

Eileen reached me. She leaned forward so that I could kiss her cheek. "Surprise!" she whispered.

I laughed.

She turned to Lonergan. "Hello, Uncle John."

He smiled and kissed her cheek. "My dear."

Her eyes zeroed in on Marissa, who was talking to Dieter and two other Mexicans. "Is that the one?" she whispered to me.

"Hey!" I said. "You know the rules. You don't ask me, I don't ask you."

"She's beautiful."

I knew the look on her face. Every now and then a girl would come along. This was one of those times. She was hooked. I groaned. "Not again? Why does it always have to be one of my chicks?"

She smiled. "I told you before. We have the same tastes."

I gestured toward Julio, who was stuck in the middle of the room. "When did you find out he was coming down?"

"Not until I got on the plane. I thought I would able to play pilot with King Dong's joystick all the way down here, but it didn't work out that way. Julio was in the seat next to me."

"What did he have to say?"

"Nothing much. Did you know that he came from here? That his whole family still lives here?"

"No."

"That's strange. I thought Verita might have mentioned it."

"It never came up."

She took me by the arm. "Your girlfriend is looking at us. Don't you think it's time we met?"

Chapter Nine

I was sitting in a warm bathtub with bubbles up to my nose, smoking a joint and thinking lovely thoughts when Eileen came into the bathroom. I looked up at her. "It can't be time for dinner. We just finished the cocktail party."

"You have company. Julio and the von Halsbachs, *père et fils.*"

"Shit. I'm too stoned to talk to them." I slid further into the tub. "Tell them I'll see them at dinner."

She nodded and went out. A moment later she was back. "Julio says it's very important."

"Damn." I got to my feet. "Find out if Uncle John can join us. I'll be out in a minute."

I stepped under a cold shower. It took five minutes before I felt my head clear. I dried myself. Then, wrapped in one of those European-style terry towel robes, I went out into the living room.

Uncle John was completely dressed and was sipping his martini when I entered. The others were drinking tequila. I went behind the bar and got myself a glass of ice water. Eileen had disappeared. I leaned on the bar. "Okay, Julio, what's so important?"

"Verita told me she is already finished with her examination of the books and that she is satisfied that everything is straight."

"That's right."

"What do you think?"

"Of what?"

"The proposition."

"I'm still thinking about it."

"You have all the information. What more do you need to know?"

I glanced at Lonergan. His face was impassive. "Nothing else really. But I must admit to a little curiosity. How do you fit into this?"

Julio's voice was bland. "I'm the Swiss bank."

I nodded.

"You don't seem surprised."

"It figured. I just didn't realize you had that kind of money."

"I work very hard."

I met his eyes. "Then why did you piss it away down here?"

He flushed. "My family comes from here. All poor *campesinos.* This was a chance to bring business down here and do them some good."

"It would have been cheaper to send them each a hundred bucks a month."

"We are a very proud people," he said stiffly. "We don't want charity."

"Family isn't charity," I said. I took a sip of the ice water. "I'm beginning to feel this is too rich for my blood."

"It will be a gold mine when gambling comes."

"Julio, we've known each other a long time. Did I ever shit you?"

"No, Lieutenant, never."

"Then don't shit me. We both know that gambling is not going to come here. At least not before it comes to all Mexico. Do you think Acapulco is going to let you grab it off before they do?"

"But we have promises. From the highest officials."

"Those are promises. I'll believe them when I see them. The governor himself told me that he was awaiting approval from the federal government." The grass had left my mouth dry. I took another sip of ice water. "Without gambling, this place isn't worth burning down."

Julio was silent.

The old count spoke for the first time since the meeting. "It could pay with all the tourist plans you told me about."

"If they all worked. But not with the cost as it stands now. And at best, I would be lucky to just cover expenses."

"Are you saying that you're not interested?"

"I'm saying that I'm still thinking about it. Meanwhile, if you have another interested party, please feel free to talk to them."

The count rose to his feet. "Thank you for speaking so honestly, Mr. Brendan. We will meet again when you have come to a decision."

"Yes."

Dieter got up and followed his father to the door. Julio didn't move from his chair. "I'll stay a few more minutes," he said. He waited until the door closed behind him, then turned to me. "Okay, Lieutenant, we can talk."

"I don't buy that family shit, Julio. You got to have a better reason than that to lay down four million."

"Like what?"

"Like fifteen private planes a week. All moving north."

He was silent. He lifted his glass and took another belt of tequila. There was a smile on his lips, but his eyes were cold. "Where did you hear that?"

"You can't stop people from talking. You know that."

"Talk like that can get people killed."

"Talk like that can put me out of business if I buy into this place."

"The hotel hasn't anything to do with the traffic on the airstrip. They don't even own it."

"Who does?"

"The local government."

I laughed. "Then the von Halsbachs aren't even in on the gravy? You really let them go down the path."

"They built the hotel. I didn't."

"Who led them to believe that they would get gambling? You have a lot of friends here. I could see that at the party."

"There would have been none of this if Dieter hadn't let his fag friends bum rap the place. It would have worked out fine."

"There's nothing you can do about that now."

Julio turned to my uncle. His voice was very respectful. "What is your interest in this, Mr. Lonergan?"

"I'm just an observer. I'm not interested in your business. You know I don't deal."

Julio turned back to me. "If you do buy into this place, where do I fit in?"

"You don't. The Swiss bank can stay in, but those private planes can't come anywhere near here."

"That means a lot of money to me."

"That's a decision you'll have to make before I make mine."

Julio got to his feet. "We both have a lot of thinking to do."

"That's right." When he had gone, I turned to my uncle. "Well?"

"I don't know. He's got to be dealing with a million a week wholesale. He's not going to give it up that easily."

"Julio is very upset," Verita said at the dinner table. "He feels you do not like him."

"I like him fine. I just don't want any part of his business around me."

"You did not invite him to dinner."

Suddenly I understood. Face. It all had to do with face. After all, we were old friends, we'd been in the army together. "Where is he?"

"In his room."

"Call him and ask him to come down. Tell him I assumed that he would be joining us and that's why I didn't say anything."

She nodded and left the table.

Eileen looked at me. "What's going on?"

"Nothing."

She looked at Lonergan. "Why don't you tell him to stick to the magazines, Uncle John? He really doesn't need all this."

"He never listened to anyone when he was young. Why should he begin now?"

Verita came back. "He'll be right down. He's very happy."

He showed up five minutes later, resplendent in a white tropical suit, all smiles. "Forgive me for being late," he said.

A few minutes later Dieter and Marissa joined us and we had another superb dinner, from which we all rose sated.

"There is a mariachi show and native dances on the beach tonight if you care to attend," Dieter said.

"I'm not as young as all of you," Lonergan said. "I'll just go back to my bed."

I looked at him. In Los Angeles he never went to bed before five in the morning and it was now only midnight. "Are you feeling all right?" I asked.

"Just fine. I'm just not used to all this sunshine and fresh air." He said his goodnights and went back down the path.

Dieter led the way and we followed him to the beach. A bonfire was blazing and there were blankets scattered on the sand. Next to the fire a five-piece group was playing "La Cucaracha". We grabbed a few blankets, pulled them together and sat down. Other guests filtered onto the beach.

Dieter took out a gold cigarette case and offered it around. "Smoke?"

It was dynamite shit and in no time at all I was flying. I looked at the girls. They felt it, too. So did Dieter. But Julio just puffed at his joint. It seemed to have no effect on him at all.

The dancers began. They were amateur, mostly staff from the hotel, but they obviously loved it. We hit on the rhythm. Suddenly Marissa was on her feet, dancing with them, then Verita and, after a moment's hesitation, Eileen. Julio watched them, smiling. Verita leaned over and pulled him to his feet.

Julio and Verita were so good that after a while everyone stopped dancing to watch them. I leaned back on the blanket.

Dieter sat facing me. "You must think us stupid, Mr. Brendan, that we do not know what is happening here."

I looked at him without speaking.

"But there is nothing we can do about it. You must remember that we are newcomers here and a wrong word from them would strip us of everything we own."

"If it could happen to you who are now Mexican citizens, imagine what they could do to me."

"It's not the same thing. You are a gringo. And even if they don't like gringos, they respect the money and business you can bring. They would not dare alienate you. Besides, there is your uncle."

"What about him?"

"He is a very important man in Los Angeles, is he not? He is the only man I think Julio has respect for." He lit another joint. "Julio is a very important man down here, but your uncle is even more important. We have heard that without your uncle's permission, Julio could not exist in Los Angeles."

Julio was smiling and happy now, dancing with Verita. The other men standing around and watching all looked like Julio. He was really home.

But Lonergan had gone to bed. Suddenly I realized that he had changed the moment that Julio had appeared. He'd withdrawn into himself, like the boss who does not want to associate with the hired help. I remembered that once he had said, "How long do you think Julio would have protected you if I didn't okay it?"

I looked back at Dieter. "How much do you really know?" I asked.

"Enough to tell you that Julio would never stop the planes from using the airstrip for you. The only man who could make him do that is your uncle."

Chapter Ten

I lay back on the blanket, letting the music swirl around me while I floated on the stars. The night sky was purple-black, the stars tiny Christmas-tree lights flickering on and off. I threaded my way through them, wondering if there really was a Santa Claus.

Marissa's voice was soft in my ear. "Your girlfriend is very pretty."

I rolled over onto my stomach. "She says the same thing about you." I held my cigarette toward her.

She took several tokes, then gave it back to me. "I'm sad," she said.

"Why? It's a beautiful life down here."

"Nothing is what it seems to be, is it?"

"Reality is whatever you see. Even if no one else in the world sees what you see, it doesn't make it any less real."

She smiled. "You have an answer for everything."

"I wish I did." I sat up. "Life would be simpler."

A burst of laughter caught our attention. The models, Bobby, the crew and King Dong had joined the party. Now they were really jumping around the fire.

Bobby fell onto the blanket beside me. "I couldn't keep them away once they heard the music."

"That's okay. Let them have fun."

"I'll never get them up for a seven o'clock call tomorrow morning."

"Relax." I passed him the joint.

He dragged deeply. "How's it going?"

"Okay?"

"Make up your mind yet?"

"Not yet."

"If it's money, my father told me to tell you he's interested."

"It's not money."

He turned to Marissa. "I'd like to do a set with you."

She looked bewildered.

"Photographs," I explained.

"Oh." She smiled. "I don't think so."

"You've got a great body," he said. "You'd look beautiful."

"I'm not the type. It would be too embarrassing."

"Tell her we're very cool about it," Bobby said to me.

"I'm sure she knows that."

"As a publisher you're not much help. She'd make a dynamite centerfold."

"If I did your job as well as mine," I said, "I'd be Bob Guccione."

He dragged on the cigarette again, then gave it back to me as he got to his feet. "If you can't lick 'em, join 'em. The music's fantastic."

They were into mean salsa now. I held my hand out to Marissa. "Come," I said.

"Wait a minute." Dieter held a coke spoon and vial in his hand. "This will get the motor running."

Even before we finished, we were surrounded by the others and the spoon and vial moved quickly from hand to hand. By the time it got back to Dieter it was empty and everybody was high. Dieter sent for more coke and the party began to rock.

The musicians played at a faster pace and in addition to the coke and grass, Bobby had come up with a box of poppers. An hour later we were soaking wet all strung out. I went back to the blanket and sat down. Age was catching up on me.

Samantha, the model, started it first. She ripped off her bra and skirt. "I can't stand it," she yelled, running toward the water. "Last one in is a stinker!"

A moment later the other models were getting out of their clothes and then we all joined in a mad scramble to shed our clothing and run for the water. In the midst of all the noise the band suddenly stopped playing. The silence was shocking.

I looked up. All of them, men and women alike, were staring at King Dong. Slowly he stepped out of his trousers. You could hear the collective gasp as they reacted to his nakedness.

Dieter's eyes glazed over. Julio's mouth hung open. The girls, too, were silent, fascinated, unable to turn away. I glanced around. Anyone who said that women didn't respond to a big cock was crazy.

Julio's voice broke the stillness. "*El toro.*"

Everybody laughed. "I don't believe it," Dieter said almost worshipfully. He started toward him, but King Dong had already begun to run into the water. He cut into the surf in a clean dive. We could see the girls clustering around him and hear their screams of laughter as he broke the surface.

Eileen dropped to the blanket beside me. "My knees went weak."

I laughed. "He got to you?"

"I'm soaking wet. I almost came just looking at it. And I thought I'd seen everything."

"Those were just pictures. This was the real thing."

"I wonder what it's like hard," she said.

"You'll never see it."

"Why not?"

"Before it gets halfway hard, it's drawn all the blood from his body and he faints," I said with a straight face.

"Funny," she said, raising her hand as if to hit me. Then she laughed.

I saw Marissa watching us with a strange expression on her face. I held my hand out to her. She took it and I drew her down on my other side. She seemed very stiff. So I bent over and kissed her. Her mouth was soft and moist.

After a moment she pulled back. "I think I'd better go to my room."

"I thought you were with me."

She looked across at Eileen. "Not now that your girlfriend is here."

"Nothing has changed. After all, aren't we all friends?"

"That's right," Eileen said softly. "Friends." She touched Marissa's face tenderly with her fingers. "Friends share. Friends love."

Marissa's eyes were wide. "I don't know. I never—" She hesitated, then shivered suddenly. "I'm stoned." Abruptly she got to her feet. She stood there, weaving slightly. "I'm going to my room." She managed two steps before she swayed and began to fall.

I caught her before she hit the sand and put her gently on the blanket. Her face was pale and there were faint beads of perspiration on her upper lip. I checked her pulse. It was all right.

Eileen looked frightened. "She just passed out," I said reassuringly.

"Is there anything I can do?"

"A wet compress on her forehead wouldn't hurt."

Eileen ran toward the surf, untying the kerchief from around her neck. It wouldn't do much good, but at least it would make Eileen feel better. The only thing that would really help Marissa was sleep.

Between us we managed to get her to the cottage. I put her on the couch. A note on the coffee table caught my eye. I picked it up.

Gareth—

I thought we'd all be more comfortable if I moved up to the main building. See you in the morning.

'We can put her in the other bedroom," I said. "Uncle John's moved out."

I left Eileen in the bedroom to undress her and went out into the living room and made myself a drink. The junk had all worn off. I had come down from the high and felt strangely sober and wide-awake. Coke did that to me.

I took the drink out into the garden and sank into a chaise. I could hear the sounds of laughter as the models made their way back to the cottage and Bobby's voice giving instructions to the crew for the morning session. Then silence again. I took a sip of the drink. The party was over.

Eileen came out and stood beside the chaise. "She's sleeping."

I didn't answer.

"I'll go back on the morning plane."

I looked up at her.

"I shouldn't have come down. I have no business being here. I work on the magazine."

"Hey, there's no reason to feel like that."

"I was jealous. I can cope with the girls in Los Angeles, but when you're away, I get paranoid, thinking that you'll find someone you really flip out over."

"You shouldn't feel like that," I said lightly. "If I find someone, you'll be the first to know."

She wasn't in the mood for jokes. "Fuck you!" she said angrily. "I don't want to be the first to know. Tell your mother! She's the one who's always after me about your getting married. Thirty-seven, she says, and time you settled down."

I was surprised. "She really lays that on you?"

"Yes," she snapped bitterly.

"Why doesn't she say anything to me?"

"How the hell do I know?" she retorted. "Your mother's afraid of you. She says she never could talk to you. Next time she hits me with it, I'm going to tell her that it's none of my business what the fuck you do!"

I grabbed her hand. "Easy," I said.

She suddenly softened and I pulled her down on to the chaise with me. I stroked her face gently and felt the tears on her cheeks. "It's not that bad," I said.

"Yes, it is," she said, straightening up. "I really did it this time, didn't I? I broke all the rules. Went way out of line."

I put a finger on her lips. "Hush, child. I didn't know there were rules that governed how people should love each other."

She stared at me for a moment, then rested her head on my chest. "Gareth," she whispered in a small voice, "how did things become so complicated? Why can't it be simple the way it used to be?"

I didn't answer.

Her voice was low. "Remember how it was when we first started the magazine? How there just weren't enough hours in the day for us and I came down to live with you in that little apartment over the store? There was just you and me."

"Yes," I said, still stroking her cheek. But I thought memories are funny things. Private things. Each of us remembers only what we want to. We discard as extraneous those things that are not important to us.

As far as she was concerned, she was right. There were just the two of us. But she had forgotten. There was also Denise.

Chapter Eleven

Eileen's voice was weary as she placed a folder on the kitchen table in front of me. "That's 'Head Trips' for the May issue. A thousand words for his Trip, twelve hundred more for her Trip."

"How come she gets more words than he does?" I asked. "I know women talk more but—"

She was too tired to rise to the bait. "Women's sexual fantasies are easier for me than men's. But either way I don't think I can do it anymore. I'm all fantasied out. We need help."

I opened the folder. With illustrations the article could be stretched to six pages. I looked up at her. "Hang in there, baby. We'll be on the stands next week. If things go the way I hope they will, you can hire half the town to help you." I checked my watch. It was past two in the morning. "Go home and get some sleep. We'll pick up again tomorrow."

"Tomorrow's Sunday."

I looked at my watch again. She was right. Seiko said so. And the Japanese were never wrong. Not since World War Two anyway. "Stay in bed tomorrow and catch up on your sleep," I said.

"I still have four features to write and the third episode of Modern Fanny Hill," she said.

"It'll keep till Monday."

"What are you going to do?"

"Bobby left me six layouts. I have to select the photos, decide which one will be Supercunt and then write the commentary and captions. I'm having the same trouble you are. I'm running out of ideas for nymphomaniacs."

"Do they all have to be?" she asked.

I smiled at her. "When every picture shows her playing with herself, what's she supposed to be thinking of – going to church on Sunday?"

"It's such a put-down. Sometimes I think—" She stopped and got to her feet.

"What do you think?"

"It's not important. I'm just tired, I guess."

"Say it. If you think it, say it."

"We make everything seem so cheap. As if nothing in the world existed except cocks and cunts. I didn't have to take my master's in journalism to turn this out."

"You have options. You don't have to do it if you don't want to."

"Do you have options, Gareth?"

"Not anymore. I used to think I did, but I know better now. I had big dreams when I came back from 'Nam. I was going to tell them what a downer we were on. But nobody listened; nobody even really cared, except a few politicians who wanted to make points. The people didn't give a damn. The dreams are gone now. I'm going to give them what they really want. And it will be just as filled with their own illusions as their cars, their beer and their television."

"Do you really believe that?"

"No. I'm justifying myself." I got out of the chair. "But I think somehow I've grown up. I'm never going to be able to make society over in my image, so I might as well go along and make the best of it. And the name of the game is money. If this works, I'll make a lot of it."

"Will that make you happy?"

"I don't know. But I wasn't happy when I was broke. It will certainly be a lot more comfortable being unhappy when I'm rich."

She nodded thoughtfully. "Maybe you're right." A weary sigh escaped her. "I will take your advice and stay in bed tomorrow."

"Good. I'll walk you to your car."

The streets were almost deserted. Only an occasional auto went by, as we walked to the corner where her car was parked.

She unlocked the door, got in and rolled down the window. "I'm beginning to feel it's awfully silly to be going home every night and coming back again early the next morning."

I was silent.

"Gareth, why didn't you ever ask me to stay over?"

"In that apartment? You know what it's like. A real shit-house with papers scattered all over the place.'

"You've had girls there. Boys, too. Why not me?"

"You're different."

"How?" she asked. "I like to fuck, too."

I shook my head. "That's not it."

"You still think of me as a child, but I'm not. I know exactly where your head is at and I understand it. I've made it with girls, too. So what? It's not really important, but relationships are. And I care about you."

"I know that. But you're something else. You're a commitment."

"And you don't want commitments?"

"Not until I know where I'm at and who I am."

She turned the key in the ignition and started the engine. She stuck her head out the window and I kissed her. "I know who you are, Gareth," she said softly. "Why don't you?"

I watched the car speed off toward Beverly Hills, then turned and started to walk slowly back to the store.

"Hey, Gareth." The voice called from across the street. I turned and saw the thin leather-jacketed boy come toward me. The streetlight fell across his face. I recognized him as a hustler who had been working the Silver Stud for years.

We slapped hands. "Hey, Danny," I said. "What are you doing up this way?"

"I'm headin' for Hollywood Boulevard to see if I can find me a trick." He looked into my face. "What are you doing?"

"Not me. I've got to go back to work."

He couldn't help the slightly bitchy tone. "The chick leave you dry?"

I laughed. "I told you straight."

"Man," he said, "the world's a downer."

"No action at the Silver Stud tonight?"

"There's action all right, but the kids are acing me out!"

"I guess I'm an old man to them."

"That's rough, but you got a long way to go before you're old."

"Twenty-five is old in my business."

"You just had a run of bad luck; things will turn."

He shook his head despondently. "I gotta score tonight. My girl is bitchin'. He says I haven't bought him a present in weeks."

"Belt him."

"You gotta be kidding. He's six-two and thirty pounds heavier than me. If things keep up like this, I'll have to find another line of work. I may go into dealing full time." He looked into my face, his voice lowered to a whisper. "Can you use a gram of pure rock crystal?"

"How much?"

"Sixty-five." He saw the expression on my face. "For you fifty," he added quickly.

He palmed the fifty and slipped me the cellophane envelope, which I put into my pocket. "Thanks," he said. "That'll help."

"Okay."

We began walking toward the store. "Nobody appreciates style anymore," he said. "All they want is young juice."

I didn't answer.

"Christ, I could put any of those kids away. If those queens only knew. I can do more than one of those kids could with a two-foot cock."

We were at my door. "Don't get discouraged," I said. "Class will tell."

"Yeah." He nodded. "That's right." He looked at me. "The word on the street is very good about you. They think you're goin' to make it. Especially now that Lonergan's behind you. He picks nothin' but winners." We slapped hands again. "Good luck," he said. "See ya around."

"Good luck to you, too." I watched him hurry to the corner and turn up the side street, then reached for my keys. I didn't need them. The door opened as soon as I touched the knob. Then I remembered I hadn't set the latch. I went inside, locked the door, then went up to the apartment.

I stared at the papers strewn all over the kitchen table. The *Hollywood Express* was child's play compared with the magazine. Everything had been easier with the paper – production, typography, pictures, printing. With the magazine everything was important, even the staples that held it together.

I thought about the coke I had just bought. A snort wouldn't hurt. If it was any good, it would energize me enough to get in a few more hours' work. I took a single-edge razor blade from the artist's easel and a glass plate from the closet and placed the crystal on it. It looked like a white jagged rock slightly smaller than my thumb and the light reflected from it just as it would bounce from a clump of snow. I wet my index finger, then rubbed it on the crystal and licked it. The slightly saline taste and tingling of my tongue told me it was okay. Carefully I began to shave the crystal so that the little flakes fell to the plate. I had a small mound and there was still a large crystal left. It was solidly packed.

I put the rock back in the cellophane bag and chopped the flakes into a fine powder. Then I separated it into thin lines. There was enough for four good snorts. I rolled a ten-dollar bill into a make-shift straw, snorted one line into each nostril, then put the rest aside for later.

It was good coke. It hit me almost immediately. I could feel my head clear and my eyes open at the same time the inside of my nostrils began to tingle and go slightly numb as if my sinuses were clogging. "Yeah," I said aloud.

I made myself a cup of instant coffee, sat down and opened the first folder. I laughed aloud at the title. AN ASS MAN'S GUIDE TO CHARACTER. The thrust of the article was that a girl's ass told you as much about her character as her face. It had all sorts of detail about the meaning of characteristics such as high, low, broad, tight, hard, soft, bouncy, flabby, droopy, wiggly, big, small, stuck out, stuck in, even what it meant when one buttock was a different size from the other. We had paid a college kid that Eileen knew twenty-five dollars for the piece. The kid was worth every penny of it. He had really made a study of the subject. The more I read, the more I laughed until I realized I was having too good a time. Nothing could be that funny. I was as high as a kite.

I finished the coffee. There was no use trying to read. I decided to check out some of the photographs. I turned off the ceiling light and went over to the slide projector. I switched it on and the white light filled the screen. I pressed the button, the slide fell into place and I was staring into the biggest, funniest cunt I had ever seen in my life. A picture of a train going into the Holland Tunnel flashed through my mind. I pressed the button again. This time I got a rear shot. Two trains, I thought, laughing aloud.

I switched off the projector and sank back in the chair. It was too much. I couldn't handle it. I was too high on the ladder and couldn't come down enough even to make sense to myself.

I thought I heard the bedroom door behind me creak. I shook my head. Come on now, I was beginning to hear things. I was alone in the apartment. Then I heard the door creak again and I got out of the chair.

Now I knew I was gone. Somebody had cut that coke with acid. I was beginning to hallucinate. Denise was standing in the bedroom doorway, dressed in the French maid's costume she hadn't worn for almost a year. "Oh, shit," I said.

She came into the room slowly, her eyes wide. "Gareth," she asked in a hushed, hesitant voice, "can I have my old job back?"

For a moment I didn't speak. Then I realized that she was not a hallucination. I held out my arms to her. She came into them and rested her face against my chest. "Hey, baby," I said, "where you been?"

I could feel her trembling against me. Her voice was muffled against my shirt. "Gareth, Gareth," she said in a hurt voice, "you never sent for me like you promised."

Chapter Twelve

She straddled me like a jockey, her knees bent, thighs pressing against my hips, using her legs as leverage to raise and lower herself gently onto me. My cock felt as if it were floating in warm oil. She leaned forward so that her breasts touched mine and kissed me. Now she was sliding across me, the pressure of her pubis harder against me. I felt her go over the wall as another orgasm shuddered through her. "Oh, lover," she said.

I held her face tightly. After a moment she sat up and looked at me. I was still inside her, but she made no move to let me go. She looked down at me. "Your energy particles are diffused," she said.

I smiled. "They should be." Over her shoulders, daylight was coming through the window. "We've been balling for hours."

"That's not the reason. I feel I came a thousand times, but you didn't even come once."

"That's the coke. It gives me a hard that won't quit. But if I overdo it, I can't come."

"It's not the coke. I'm on the third plane now. I know about those things."

"I forgot," I said. "Peace and love."

"Peace and love," she replied automatically. "I know a lot more now than when we were together the last time." She rose to her knees and moved up until she was over my face. "Drink me," she said.

I put a hand on each buttock and brought her down to me. She was honey and myrrh, pomegranates and tangerines, mulled wine and mountain dew and all the sweet tastes of love. I felt the muscles in her buttocks strain as she shuddered again and I bathed in her sweetness.

This time she rolled on her back, her chest rising and falling heavily. "I can't stop coming," she said. "My cunt feels like I've had the kinetic conductor on it for a week."

I didn't say anything.

After a moment she sat up and leaned over me. She closed

her hand over my cock and looked at it. "It's beautiful," she said, kissing it. Then she took the glans in her mouth and gently flicked her tongue across the tip. Afterward she held it close to her cheek, her eyes closed. "I wish you could come," she said.

"I told you. It's the coke."

She opened her eyes and looked at me. "No, it's not the coke."

"What is it then?"

"You're in love with her," she said.

"In love?" I was surprised. "With who?"

"Eileen."

"You're crazy."

"No, I'm not," she said seriously. "I told you I'm on the third plane. I see things more clearly now. I was across the street when you came out with her. I saw your auras as you walked to the car. They merged into each other with love and when you kissed her, there was enough light to turn the night into day."

"What else did you see?" I asked.

"There was a man in a doorway across the street from the car. He was waiting to see you. I didn't see him, but I felt his aura and I new he meant you no harm, so I came upstairs."

I didn't speak.

"There's one thing I don't understand," she said in a puzzled voice. "Why isn't she here with you?"

I looked at her.

"I wouldn't mind," she said. "I love you and you love each other and so, of course, I love her too."

It was late afternoon when I awoke; the sun was beginning to move down in the west. I sat up and reached for a cigarette. The bedroom door was closed, but I could hear music from the radio. I lit the cigarette and went into the bathroom. When I came out, she was waiting for me with a tray in her hand.

"Get back into bed," she said.

"I have work to do."

"Get back into bed and eat your breakfast," she said firmly. "You're not working today. You have to allow your energy particles to regroup."

The smell of the freshly brewed coffee and the steak and eggs made my mouth water. I hadn't known I was so hungry. I got back into bed and she put the tray across my legs.

I picked up the glass of orange juice while she poured the coffee. "I didn't know we had food in the refrigerator."

"I went to the store while you were sleeping," she said. "You had absolutely nothing."

I finished the juice and began to eat. She watched me for a moment, then went back to the door. "Call me when you've finished and I'll come get the tray. Then you're going back to sleep."

"What are you going to be doing?"

"Getting things straight out there. I can't believe the mess. The place hasn't been cleaned in months."

She closed the door behind her and I cut into the steak. It was perfect, pink and rare, and the eggs were just as I liked them, the yolks hot but still soft. I cleaned the plate as if I hadn't eaten for months.

She seemed to have a built-in sensor because she came in just as I finished and poured the second cup of coffee. She picked up the tray.

"Leave the coffeepot," I said.

"No more than two cups. I want you to go back to sleep."

"But I'm not sleepy."

I was wrong. I leaned back for just a moment to rest my eyes and the next thing I knew it was nine o'clock at night. Again the built-in sensor seemed to be working because she came into the bedroom just as I woke up.

"What did you feed me?" I asked. "I went out like a light."

"Nothing. You were just making up for a sleep deficiency. Now take a nice hot bath and relax while I put fresh linen on the bed. Afterward you can slip into a comfortable robe and you come out for dinner. I have a nice roast chicken in the oven."

I had no arguments. I was feeling better than I had in a long time. I got out of bed and kissed her nose. "Hey, why are you so good to me?"

"I told you. I love you," she said in a matter-of-fact voice. "Now go in and take your bath."

I found an already-rolled joint on the night table and took it into the bathroom with me. I loved to smoke in a hot tub. I knew of no better way to relax and feel good. High, but not too high. Up and easy. By the time I got out of the tub a half hour later the whole world glowed. I finished brushing my hair, but when I looked for my robe, it wasn't there. I went into the bedroom and found it, freshly washed and neatly ironed, lying across the bed. I put it on and went into the living room. I stood there frozen with surprise.

The furniture had been moved, and the room completely rearranged. It was as if it suddenly had become twice its previous size. Now the work area was just inside the entrance door in a neatly compact arrangement, instead of scattered throughout the room, as it had been. The couch had been moved to the wall on the far end of the room. There was a cocktail table in front of it and an easy chair at right angles to it, so that it created a warm conversation corner. The small round dining table had been moved from the kitchen to a place in front of the window. It was beautifully set with pink linen, dinner plates, wineglasses and silverware. In the center of the table was a combined crystal candlestick and flower vase, which held a single rose and a glowing red candle. Next to it was a bottle of Château Mouton Rothschild, already opened and breathing.

But it was the sight of Eileen coming toward me, a tremulous smile on her lips, offering a scotch on the rocks that really blew my mind. "Like it?" she asked. "We've been working all afternoon."

I stared at her like a dummy.

Denise came toward us, carrying a valise. "Sit down and enjoy your drinks while I unpack Eileen's bag."

I found my voice. "What made you come?" I asked Eileen.

"I called her and told her about your auras," Denise said.

"That's gotta be crazy," I said.

"Is it? Just look at the two of you now. Your incandescence is lighting up the whole room."

She went into the bedroom and I looked at Eileen. "Do you believe that shit?"

"I have to. I'm here, aren't I?"

I put down the drink and she moved into my arms. Her lips

were soft, her mouth warm and sweet and the press of her body against mine was like a counterimage of my own that had been missing all the time.

The table had been set for just the two of us and when I asked Denise to join us, she refused. "Your auras aren't ready for me yet," she said.

I don't know what Eileen and I talked about. The dinner was delicious, but I don't remember eating it. Then sudddenly it was midnight and Denise had vanished. Neither of us had seen her leave.

"Where did she go?"

"I don't know."

I sipped the wine. "Do you think she might be Cinderella?"

Eileen laughed. "No. I am. And you're Prince Charming."

I picked up the bottle of wine. "Come into the bedroom."

I opened the door and stood there for a moment. Denise had worked her little magic in there, too. The bed was turned down a candle was glowing on the night table and there was a note lying on the pillow.

Eileen went to the bed and picked up the note.

"What does it say?" I asked.

"Peace and love," she said.

I put the wine on the night table. "You never told me what she said that made you come here."

"She said that you couldn't come unless you were with me. That I was the only one who could get your energy particles to regroup and become whole again."

"Do you believe that?"

"Of course I do," she said. "She told me you made love all night and never came. Not even once." She came toward me and began to open my robe. She bent forward, pressing her lips to my nipples. "It's not going to be like that tonight," she said, her fingers tracing a gentle line down the center of my body.

I didn't know then how right she was. But I found out. Being inside her was not screwing – it was going home. Drinking her was not drinking – it was swallowing the juices of life. Sucking breasts, I was her child feeding on the milk she'd made for me and each time she gave to me, she took from me because she was the eternal fountain of my life.

I lay back against the pillow, her head resting on my shoulder. She turned her face toward me. "I love you," she said.

I started to answer her.

She placed a silencing finger against my lips. "Don't say anything. Not now. It's not time yet."

I was silent. I knew there was still a lot I had to learn about myself.

"Kiss me goodnight, my love. And let's go to sleep."

I woke with the first hint of daylight. I looked across the pillow at Eileen. She was in deep sleep, her face soft and vulnerable. I wanted to touch her and stroke her, but instead, I slipped out of bed, drew the window drapes quietly and went out of the darkened room into the living room. I walked to the kitchen, turned on the light and began to fill the coffee percolator.

"I'll take care of that." Denise's voice came from behind me.

I turned around. She was standing naked in the doorway. "Where did you come from?"

"There," she said, pointing.

I followed her finger and saw the sheet, blanket and pillow on the couch. "I thought you'd left," I said.

"How could I?" she asked, taking the percolator from my hand. "I work here, don't I?" She began to spoon coffee into the pot. "I thought it would be nice if the two of you were alone for a while."

"That's nice of you," I said. "When did you come back?"

"Right after you turned out the living-room light."

"Then you were here all night?"

"Yes." She smiled. "It was beautiful. I was right, you know. She regrouped your energy particles. You came four times."

"I wasn't keeping score," I said sarcastically. "What were you doing? Peeking through the keyhole?"

"I don't have to," she said seriously. "I'm tuned into your aura. I came with you kinetically each time."

"Oh, shit," I said disgustedly. "Now I've got no privacy at all. Look, this just isn't going to work."

"Don't be so negative. We're all good for each other. Everything will work out fine." She stepped closer and touched me.

"See? I know what I'm talking about. You've got a hard-on. I felt it in your aura when you came into the room."

I stared at her speechlessly.

"Would you like a little fuck while the coffee is perking?" she asked seriously.

I broke up. A puzzled look came over her face. I kissed the top of her head. "You know you're beautiful," I said. "But right now I've got to take a piss."

Chapter Thirteen

Macho hit the newsstands the third week in April. The following Monday the advertising campaign went into full gear. Our ads appeared on fifty-five independent television stations, on four hundred and nine radio stations and in one hundred and sixty newspapers in key cities all over the country. It was a heavy saturation campaign designed to run a full week, but it didn't turn out that way.

By Wednesday we were off television completely. Only twenty-one newspapers were continuing to accept our advertising and only about one hundred and forty radio stations were still airing our commercials. By Friday police in various cities had confiscated the magazine from ninety-three newsstands and had arrested forty-two newsdealers. The Hearst newspapers across the country ran an editorial decrying the fact that such a magazine could be advertised, without making any mention of the fact that they had run the ads themselves on Monday and Tuesday. On Sunday two detectives from LAPD served me with a warrant to appear in court the following Friday on charges of breaching the peace and committing a public nuisance. The story was picked up by the wire service and went out over the national media, TV, radio and newspapers. By Wednesday, two days before I was due to appear in court, Ronzi was screaming at me to go back to press. We were sold out. One million copies. Sold out.

On Thursday night Phyllis Diller, substituting for Johnny Carson on *The Tonight Show*, came out for her opening monologue wearing a giant white cowboy hat and over her dress a plastic dry cleaning bag on which had been painted a yellow polka-dotted bikini. She carried a six-gun in each hand. Strutting belligerently into a close-up, she challenged the camera in a harsh, strident voice, "Are you man enough – to tear my bikini off?" The audience went wild as Doc Severinsen played "Pistol Packin' Mama" in the background.

We'd all gathered together to watch the program, having

heard about it from one of the distributors in the East, who had seen it three hours ahead of us.

"You gotta go back to press after this," Ronzi said. "We can sell another five hundred thousand copies."

"No way. I just ordered them to run the next issue."

"That means we'll have nothing on the stands for more than two weeks."

"That's right."

He turned to Lonergan. "Can't you make him listen?"

Lonergan smiled. "He's the publisher."

"Christ," Ronzi complained, "we got another three hundred grand in our hands and you're letting it slip through our fingers."

"I don't think so. I think it will only whet their appetites. They'll go for the next issue just to see what they missed."

"I can't win," Ronzi said in disgust.

"You already have. You made yourself a five per cent bonus on the first issue."

"Gimme the same deal on the next issue and I'll get another million copies out for you."

I laughed at him. "That was a one-shot just to show you it could be done. No bonus. But I am going to give you a break. I ordered a print run of one million two-fifty."

"Now I know you're nuts. What makes you think we can sell that many?"

"You do. You wouldn't be asking for the bonus again if you hadn't figured it was a sure thing."

"What have you got on the cover?"

"I'm staying with the same idea basically. Only this time the girl has her back to us; she's bent over with her hands on her knees. She's got a cheerleader's pompom on her head as she's looking back over her shoulder at us. She's wearing a red mini-skirt that just covers her ass. The skirt is held on with an easy-off glue that can be removed by just peeling it away. The copy is practically the same. 'Are you man enough – to tear my skirt off?'"

He nodded his head approvingly. "I like it."

"Thanks. What's the latest on the news dealers who were arrested?"

"All except two have either had the charges dismissed or got-off with a small fine. It's cost us about eleven grand so far, including legal fees."

"What about the remaining two?"

"Their hearings aren't until next week. We don't expect any trouble."

"Good. Send each of the arrested dealers a hundred dollars as a token of my appreciation for their support."

"That's nuts. Word gets out, you'll have dealers all over the country running to the cops and begging to get busted."

I laughed. "Do it anyway."

"Okay. It's your money."

After he had gone, I said to Lonergan, "I hope I get off tomorrow as easily as the dealers."

"You have nothing to worry about," he said calmly. "The charges will be dismissed."

And that was exactly what happened.

I went into court with an attorney, but I could have gone alone. He never had a chance to say a word. After the charges were read and even before I was asked to enter my plea, the judge called the attorneys to the bench.

I leaned forward to try to hear what was being said. The prosecuting attorney murmured something about publishing and causing the distribution of pornography. The judge responded. I could only catch a few words. "Does not apply under the statutes . . .. breach of the peace and . . . public nuisance." He gestured to the attorneys to leave the bench and banged the gavel even before they'd reached their tables. "The charges against the defendant are hereby dismissed on the grounds of being improperly drawn."

The reporters and TV camera crews were waiting in the corridor when I came out. They clustered around me.

"Are you pleased with the judge's decision?"

"Of course," I answered.

"On what basis do you think the judge came to his decision?"

I looked to my attorney. At last he had a chance to speak. "I think the judge dismissed the charges against Mr. Brendan because he realied that they were nothing but a harassment since they could not bring a successful action against Mr. Brendan in any other manner."

"Does this mean that your magazine will be back on sale at the newsstands?"

"It was never off," I said.

"I tried to buy a copy on a number of stands, but there weren't any," the reporter said.

"That's because the issue has been sold out."

"If we should want a copy, where might we buy it?"

"Try your neighbour. If he won't sell it, maybe he'll lend it to you."

"Do you intend to keep publishing the magazine?"

"Yes. The next issue is on the presses now and should be at the news dealers in about two weeks."

"Will the cover of your next issue be as provocative as the last?"

"I'll let you judge for yourself," I said. I opened my leather folder and took out the mock-up of the cover. I held it up so that they could all see it. The flashbulbs began popping and I could see the news cameras zooming in.

That was how the cover of the next issue got on television. It sold out within the first week and every month after that we added fifty to a hundred thousand copies more to our circulation. Six months later *Macho* was selling an average of a million five hundred thousand copies a month and we were netting better than a half million dollars' profit on each issue.

By August I realized that we were big business. We outgrew the store downstairs and rented other vacant stores on the block and finally, we were forced to rent still another store a few blocks away. The original store was where the accounting and editorial offices were located. Verita had seven clerks and two secretaries in her department; Eileen had twelve readers and writers and four secretaries. We fixed up another of the stores as a photographic studio for Bobby, who now had a staff of four photographers and three assistants, plus a propman, a set designer, a costumer, a photographic editor and two secretaries.

Production and mechanicals with twelve employees went into still another store. The most recently acquired space housed the mail and cartoon and illustration departments. Including the two telephone operators, who were hidden at a switchboard under the staircase in the main store, we had a total of sixty-four employees.

There was no way now that Denise could keep the apartment in order. There were meetings all day and into the night. It was in a continual shambles, even with the help of the cleaning crew that came in at night.

The heat of the August day had spilled over into the night and the air in the apartment was warm, even with the labouring of the air conditioners in the windows. The editorial meeting was drawing to a close. It was after midnight and the meeting had begun about nine. "Is there anything more before we wrap it up?" I asked.

The young black man who ran the mail department spoke up. "I have something, Mr. Brendan," he said hesitantly.

This was the first time he had opened his mouth in the three months he had been atttending the meetings. "Yes, Jack."

He glanced around at the others self-consciously. "I don't know whether this is pertinent or not, but do you remember the series of articles we ran on marital aids and aphrodisiacs a few months back?"

"Yes."

"Since they began, we have been receiving approximately five, six hundred letters a week asking where they can be bought."

"Write up a form letter telling them to go to their nearest sex shop," I said.

"Almost all the letters come from small towns and places where they don't have anything like a sex shop. They wouldn't know what it was if they stumbled over it and even if they did, I have the feeling they would be too embarrassed to go inside."

I saw that he was leading up to something. "That makes sense," I said encouragingly.

"I started thinking about it," he continued more confidently. "So I took me over to the sex shop down near the Pussycat Theater and had a little talk with the owner. He got real excited and offered to buy two full pages of advertising in each issue. When I told him that it was not our policy to accept advertising, he offered to set up a mail-order department and pay us a twenty per cent commisison on gross sales."

"That's interesting." I had a feeling, however, that he wasn't finished.

"That's what I thought," he said. "So I did some more checking. I found out where most of the stuff can be bought. I also found out there's a hell of a markup – anywhere from two hundred per cent to a thousand per cent. So the twenty per cent of the gross he's offering us is like nothing."

"You have an idea?"

"Yes, sir," he said. "We've got a big cellar in the store on the next block. I can stock it with the most popular items and if we just fill the orders based on our letters, we can gross thirty or forty thousand a month and at least fifty per cent of that would be net profit."

I nodded. Whether we went into the mail-order business or not, Jack wasn't going to stay in his present job for long. He had something going in his head. "Good thinking," I said. "You go into it with Verita and get a line on what the operation would cost. As soon as we have the facts on paper, I'll make a decision."

"Thank you," he said.

I looked around the room. "Anything else?"

That was it and the meeting broke up. Only Bobby, Verita, Eileen, Denise and I were left. Eileen and Denise got busy removing the glasses and emptying the ashtray. "What do you think of Jack's idea?" I asked Verita.

"It's interesting. He mentioned it to me about two weeks ago. I told him to follow it up."

"You never said anything to me."

She smiled. "It was his idea."

Eileen and Denise came back and sank into two chairs. "You all look like wrecks," Bobby said.

"The days never stop," Eileen said.

He put his hand in his pocket and came up with a vial of coke and a gold spoon. "I think we could all use a snort. Our trouble is we're all too busy to have fun anymore."

I spooned a hit into each nostril and passed the vial to Eileen. She took a spoon, so did Denise and Bobby, but Verita passed.

I felt a small lift but not much. The coke had been cut all the way down. "What are you shooting tomorrow?" I asked Bobby.

He grinned. "I think I have a goodie this time."

"Yeah?"

"Have you seen the twins over at Paul Gitlin's office? The new legal secretaries. Dynamite-looking kids, about nineteen, twenty. I talked them into trying a session."

"Does Paul know about it?"

"Hell, no." Bobby laughed. "You know how straight he is. He'd kill me if he found out what I was doing. As it is, he's got the twins so buffaloed that I had to promise to shoot them in disguise."

"How are you going to manage that?"

"I've got a wild idea for the layout," he said. "Wrap around sunglasses and wild wigs. And for the centerfold I shoot them together, one up on her knees, the other on her back with her legs spread. The first twin Supercunts."

I began to laugh. "It would be funny if Paul recognized them anyway."

He smiled. "If he does, then maybe he's not as straight as we think he is. But I don't think so. I had to promise the kids we'd give them a job if he cans them."

"Are they good secretaries?" I asked.

"Paul says they're the best he's ever had."

"No problem then. We could use some good help. Maybe you ought to see to it that he does find out."

Bobby got to his feet. "I'm going to take off now. I want to drop into the Silver Stud and see what the action is like. Want to come along?"

"No, thanks. I've about had it for the day."

"Me too," Verita said. "I'm going home to bed. The auditors are coming in early tomorrow to complete the statement for our first six months' operation."

"How does it look?" I asked.

"I'm afraid to tell you. It's too good. I don't believe it myself."

"Give me a hint."

"Would you believe that your tax liability is over a million and a half right now? And there's no place to bury it. We might just have to turn it over to the government."

"Maybe we won't have to." I smiled.

"Then you know something I don't. Tell me."

"I have an idea for another magazine."

"Goddammit! That does it!" Eileen exploded. "I'm packing and getting out of here tonight."

"What's eating you?"

"You, you asshole!" she snapped. "We're living in this shitty little place like pigs without a minute to ourselves and you haven't got it through your head yet that you're rich and can live any way you want. You haven't even bought yourself a car. You're still bumming rides and cigarettes from everyone around you!"

She stormed into the bedroom and slammed the door behind her. A moment later Denise got to her feet and followed her. I turned to Verita. I really had never thought about it before. "Is it true what she said? Am I rich?"

Verita nodded. "You're rich."

"How rich?"

She took a deep breath. "You've got about two million dollars net after tax obligations and by the end of the year, the way we're going, you'll be worth at least double that."

"Jesus," I said. I lit a cigarette and sat there for a long time after they left. Then I poured myself a scotch on the rocks and went to the bedroom.

The closet door was open and Eileen's clothes were scattered all over the floor. They were sitting on the edge of the bed, Eileen sobbing against Denise's breast.

"Hey, baby, I'm sorry," I said.

"Go away," Eileen cried. "We hate you."

The next day we moved into a bungalow in the Beverly Hills Hotel.

Chapter Fourteen

Lifestyle Digest came out the day Denise left us.

The first issue had a press run of two hundred and fifty thousand. Physically the magazine was more like *Coronet* than *Reader's Digest*, but that was the only resemblance.

There were ten pages of colour photographs in the middle, equally divided between girls, men and love sets, both heterosexual and homosexual. The articles were culled from magazines all around the world. Not until I got into it did I realize how widespread the men's megazine business had become. Every country and every language had at least one of its own. And we found that the articles which were designed to appeal to their own market had a peculiar fascination in translation. We also included pieces on subjects we did not touch in *Macho*. *Lifestyle Digest* made it a point to extol the values of the impossible dream – expensive cars, out-of-sight stereos, cameras and unusual vacations. Pure snob and easy to collect. The specialty magazines provided us with the features at almost no cost. In addition to this, we had a rap column where men and women could air their grievances, sexual and otherwise, advice and how-to columns that covered every subject from birth control to premature ejaculation. One hundred and fifty pages, all for seventy-five cents.

The logo was simple. LIFESTYLE DIGEST. A MAGAZINE FOR PEOPLE WHO ENJOY LIFE. The first cover was a simple black silhouette on a white circle of the heads of a man and a woman in profile, their lips touching gently.

On the day the first issue came out, Eileen went home early, but I had to stay late. I still had some checks to sign and papers to clear up. My office was in the apartment where we used to live. It had been completely redecorated. The bedroom was now my private office, all wood paneling and expensive white leather. The living room was divided in two by a floor-to-ceiling glass wall. The secretaries' office was just inside the front door. Behind the glass panel was the conference room, furnished with round table, directors' chairs and drapes that could be closed when meetings were in session. The kitchen had been hidden by sliding room dividers and the whole apartment was cooled and heated by a large central unit.

I was begininng to get writer's cramp when one of the Bobbsey twins came in with the last batch of checks. "This is the end of them, Mr. Brendan," she said.

"Thank you, Dana."

She smiled. "I'm Shana."

The twins had been working for me for six months. Paul Gitlin called the moment he found out the girls had posed for the centerfold against his wishes.

"If you print one word about the fact that those two girls worked in my office, I'll sue you," he said in a flat tone.

"Did you say 'worked'?" I asked.

"That's what I said."

I put down the phone and called Bobby. The next day the twins reported to my office. But even now I still couldn't tell them apart.

"You're going to have to do something about that. From now on you have to wear a pin with your initial on it."

"Yes, Mr. Brendan," she answered as she left.

I knew she wouldn't do it. This wasn't the first time I'd asked them. But they took a perverse pleasure in putting me on. I would have fired them, but they were just too good. And too beautiful. Blond, blue-eyed mirror images of each other, they gave the office a great look.

I finished signing the last check and pressed the buzzer. She came back in. I pushed the checks toward her. "You can send these back to accounting, Shana."

She picked up the checks and smiled. "I'm Dana."

It was no use. They had done it again. "How do you girls know which one is which when you wake up in the morning?" I asked sarcastically.

"It's easy, Mr. Brendan," she said with a straight face. "I sleep on the left side of the bed."

"What happens if you should happen to sleep on the right side?"

"Then I'm Shana that day," she said seriously.

That was the first thing I'd heard that made sense. They were interchangeable. I dropped the subject. "Are we caught up on everything?"

"Yes, Mr. Brendan."

"Then get me a scotch on the rocks and find out if Bobby can give me a lift back to the hotel." She got the drink from the built-in bar and left the office. I sipped the drink. The phone buzzed and I picked it up.

"Mr. Ronzi on the first line," she said.

I punched the button. "Yes?"

"Just called to let you know the early reports sound good. The dealers racked *Lifestyle* right next to the *Reader's Digest*."

"That's not bad," I said.

"We'll have a better line on it by the end of the week. I'll keep you up to date, though."

"Good." I pressed another button and dialed Verita's number. "How much are we into for this issue of the *Digest*?" I asked.

"Fifty-five thousand. We have to sell one hundred and seventy thousand to come out."

"We'll do it," I said. "Got time for a drink?"

"Sorry, but thanks anyway. I have to dash. I have a date."

"The judge again?"

"Yes."

"I like him. Give him my best." I put down the phone and returned to my drink. Things weren't the same now that I was here in a private office. I felt out of touch. People just didn't walk in anymore. They called for an appointment.

The phone buzzed again. Bobby would pick me up in ten minutes. I was getting edgy sitting in the office, so I left my drink and went downstairs into the store.

Almost everyone had gone, but I saw that Jack was still there, talking to one of the bookkeepers. He straightened up as I approached them. "Good evening, Mr. Brendan."

"How's it going, Jack?" I asked.

"Real fine, Mr. Brendan. We grossed almost seventy thousand last month, net fifty."

"That's fantastic. Good work, Jack."

"Thank you, Mr. Brendan." He looked at me hesitantly. "Do

you think you might have some time soon to come over and take a look at our operation?"

"Of course. Just give me a few days to get out from under the new magazine." An automobile horn sounded outside. "My transportation. Gotta run."

"I understand. Good luck with the *Digest*."

I started out the door, then stopped and turned back to him. Suddenly I knew what had been missing. He was the first person that day who'd wished me luck with the magazine. No one else had thought of it. "Thanks, Jack," I said. "I'll try to make it over there tomorrow."

I got into the Rolls and Bobby rolled into the traffic. "Got a cigarette?" I asked

"In the glove compartment," he said. "I have some great thai stick if you want."

"I'll take a Lucky," I said, helping myself. I lit the cigarette and looked out the window.

"There's this guy I'd like you to meet," he said. "I know you'll like him. He's really a beautiful person."

"Yeah."

He looked at me. "Anything wrong?"

"No, nothing. Why?"

"You seem down."

"I'm just tired, I guess."

"You should be. You have a lot on your plate."

"Do I seem any different to you?"

"No," he said quickly. Then he stopped. "Yes."

"In what way?"

"You seem more distant somehow." He seemed to be searching for the words. "Far away. Unreachable. Apart."

"I don't feel different. I haven't changed."

"You have. But it was not something you did. It had to happen. It was a gradual thing, but I think I knew it the night that Eileen got angry with you. Suddenly you reminded me of my father. You had all the power. It wasn't like that when we started. We all were working together then. Now we're all working for you. That's the difference."

"But, Bobby, I still love you."

"And I still love you. But my father explained it to me. People have to follow their own paths. And we all grow in different ways, that's all."

He pulled the car to a stop. "Here we are."

I looked up in surprise. We were at the hotel entrance. Smitty opened the door for me and I got out. I leaned back into the car. "Want to come in for a drink?"

"No, thanks," he said. "I've got to change. I have a big party tonight. I'm bucking for queen of the year."

I laughed. "Have fun. Thanks for the lift."

He waved and drove off. I watched the car move out of the driveway and then went into the hotel. I stopped in the Polo Lounge, thinking that I would have a drink before going to the bungalow, but it took three drinks before I put it all together.

It wasn't I who had changed. I was still the same. It was they who had changed in the way they thought about me. And there was nothing I could do about it.

It didn't make me feel any better but, at least, I knew where I was at. I signed the check and went to the bungalow. After knocking on the door, I opened it with my key.

Eileen was slumped on the couch, her eyes filled with tears. "What happened?" I asked.

"Denise is gone."

"Gone?"

"Yes." She held a piece of paper toward me. "She left this note for you. She said you would understand."

I looked down and read it.

> Dear Gareth,
>
> There comes a time in everyone's life when they have to disconnect. I have just been summoned for second-plane instruction. When it is completed, I will be a teacher and later, when I enter the first plane, I'll be eligible for sisterhood. But to do that, I can have no other ties except to God and my work. So I must disconnect you from my inner being in order to free my body from its physical need of you. I will always remember and love you both.
>
> Peace and love—
>
> Denise

"Shit," I said. "Couldn't you stop her?"

"You know better than that," Eileen said. "I tried, but she wouldn't budge. I love her, too. I'll miss her."

I sat down beside her. She put her head on my shoulder. "She had only one regret about leaving, she said."

"What's that?"

She turned away with a strange smile on her face. "I can't tell you," she said. Then suddenly she began to laugh.

"If it's so goddamn funny, you can tell me," I snapped.

She caught her breath and wiped at her eyes. "Her only regret was that she would never know what it was like to be fucked completely by you."

Chapter Fifteen

The Mexican sun woke me early. I slipped into my jeans and went up to the main building to have breakfast with Lonergan. Eileen was still asleep and Marissa hadn't moved from her bed. I called Lonergan from the house phone in the lobby.

There was no answer. I checked my watch. Eight o'clock. He was probably having breakfast in the coffee shop. He wasn't there either, but Verita was sitting at a table alone.

I went over to her. "Good morning. What are you doing up so early?"

"I'm finished here. I thought I'd catch the morning flight back. The auditors have completed their report on the clubs. I want to go over it."

"What's the rush?" I asked, sitting down opposite her. A waiter came and put a cup of coffee in front of me. "It's beautiful here. Why don't you just stay and get some sun? The auditors can wait."

"That's easy for you to say. You don't have to go through all those figures."

I sipped at the coffee. It was hot and black and bitter. I made a face. "This coffee alone would chase customers away."

"The Mexicans like it that way."

"The Mexicans don't stay at this hotel." I looked at her. "What do you think of the place?"

"It's beautiful. But we don't need it. Even if we do make money, it would be a big headache."

"Do you think we can make money?"

"*Quién sabe?*" She shrugged. "Maybe, if all your ideas work."

"Do you think we would lose money?"

"If you can keep your investment under four million dollars, no. Anything over that is a big question mark." She sipped at her coffee. "The changes you want to make could cost more than a million dollars. That means you shouldn't offer them more than three."

"They won't go for that."

"Then I'd pass."

"You're getting conservative in your old age."

"You're not paying me to take chances. Gambling with your money is your privilege, not mine. All I can do is answer your questions honestly."

"Hey, don't get touchy," I said. "I know that."

She didn't answer.

"Have you seen Lonergan around?"

"He left a few minutes before you came in."

"Do you know where he went?"

"No. Though I did see him get into a car with Julio."

I stared down at my coffee. Verita saw the expression on my face and called the waiter. "*Café americano por el señor.*"

"You know, I think Lonergan's beginning to like me," she said.

"What makes you say that?"

"He actually sat down and had coffee with me. He asked what I thought about the hotel and I told him."

"Did he have anything to say?"

She shook her head. "You know him. He doesn't say anything. He just sat there and nodded. I had the feeling that he agreed with me. And when he left, he actually smiled and wished me a pleasant flight."

The waiter came back with a pot of hot water and a jar of American instant coffee. I fixed myself a cup and tasted it. This was better.

"What are you going to do?" she asked.

"I don't know yet." I fished in my pockets for cigarettes. She held a pack out to me. "Did Lonergan happen to mention where he was going?"

She struck a match and held it for me. "No."

I remembered what Dieter had said yesterday. That Lonergan was the only man who could make Julio stop using the airstrip. I wondered what they were talking about.

"Did you have a chance to talk to Julio?" I asked.

"Not really. But I know that he is very excited about your taking over the hotel. He feels that you will make a big success with it."

I laughed. "I'll bet. Is it true that he has a big family down here?"

"*Es vero.*" She nodedd. "I think in one way or the other he is related to everyone. And they all are benefiting from the hotel, by either working here or supplying food. They all are farmers, you know. The hotel buys everything they grow."

"Are you related to them, too?"

"No. They are all *campesinos.* I am related to Julio through marriage. My father was a teacher at the university in Mexico City. I didn't meet Julio until we moved to Los Angeles."

Murtagh came into the dining room and saw us. He waved and threaded his way through the room to our table. "How's it going?" he asked in his hearty real estate agent manner.

"Fine," I answered.

"Getting all the information you want?"

"Yes."

"Well, if there's anything more you need, just let me know and I'll get it for you."

"I think I'm covered," I said.

"When do you think you'll be ready to have a meeting with the von Halsbachs?"

"I'll let you know this evening." I wanted to hear about Lonergan's meeting with Julio before I did anything.

"Fine," he said. "Dieter just took off for the day, but he told me to tell you he'll be back this evening and at your disposal."

I was curious. "Where did he go?"

"He mentioned something about going up to the Retreat. He's quite an amateur photographer himself. I guess he wants to see how the professionals do it."

He left the coffee shop and when I turned back to Verita, she was smiling. She knew what I was thinking. Bobby had been shooting for two days right here at the hotel and Dieter hadn't even looked out the window. "King Dong scores again," I said. "Do you think Dieter might be in love?"

She laughed and got to her feet. "I have to go upstairs and finish packing if I want to make the plane."

"I'll wait and go down to the airstrip with you."

"But what about Eileen and Marissa?" she asked sweetly.

I knew a dig when I heard one but chose to ignore it. "The judge meeting you at the airport?" I asked.

She blushed.

I smiled. "It's that serious?"

"Gareth," she said, "we're just very good friends, that's all. I respect him for what he's accomplished. There aren't many Chicanos that have gone as far as he has."

"Sure," I teased. "And he respects you for your mind."

"That's right."

"Well, give him a taste of that sweet pussy and he'll fall in love with you," I said.

"Is that all you ever think of, Gareth?"

I laughed. "Yes. After all, I'm in the business, aren't I?"

We turned onto a dirt road about fifteen miles from the hotel "The Retreat is about two miles from here," Marissa said. "Just on the other side of the small forest."

"Pretty isolated." We had seen no signs of life for the past ten miles.

She looked at me from behind the wheel as she negotiated a tight turn. "They want it that way. In the rainy season you cannot even drive this road."

I could believe that. The car bumped over the hard-packed ruts. I held onto the door and looked back at Eileen. She didn't look too happy.

She saw my glance and grimaced. "This is no way to treat a hangover."

I laughed. "You can't win 'em all."

The road cut through the forest and we came out on the other side into bright glaring sunlight. The Retreat spread out in front of us. The low American ranch-style buildings seemed familiar. Then I remembered. It was almost a duplicate of Reverend Sam's farm in Fullerton. It had the same central building and, surrounding it, the wooden barracks that served as dormitories. There was a weathered split rail fence with a gate to the driveway that led to the main building of the compound.

We saw no sign of life as we pulled to a stop. I looked at my watch as I got out of the car. It was just after eleven o'clock. "I wonder where everybody is?"

"Everybody goes to work in the fields," Marissa explained, coming around the car. "I think they take lunch there, too."

Eileen got out of the car. She dabbed at her face with a Kleenex. "It's hot."

I went up the steps of the veranda and tried the door. It was open. We went inside. It was cooler there. And also familiar. It was very much the same layout as that of the Fullerton farm. I led the way to the office. That door, too, was unlocked. I opened it. The man sitting at the desk raised his head.

"Peace and love, Brother Jonathan," I said.

"Peace and love," he answered automatically. Then a look of recognition came over his face. He got to his feet. "Gareth!" He smiled.

I held out my hand. His grip was firm and warm.

"You manage to turn up in the strangest places," he said.

"So do you." I introduced the girls. He already knew Marissa.

"What brings you out here?" he asked.

I explained to him that I was down at the hotel and had come out here to check on Bobby's photo session.

"Oh, yes. I saw them this morning. They're shooting near the old Indian village."

"I know where that is," Marissa said.

"May I offer you a cool drink or a coffee?" Brother Jonathan asked.

"We don't want to put you to any trouble. We'll just run up to the village."

"No trouble at all. We'll just go over to the commissary."

We followed him down the corridor to the dining room. We could hear sounds of people working in the kitchen. No sooner did we sit down than a bearded young man appeared. We all asked for coffee.

"You're doing very well, I understand," Brother Jonathan said. "I'm really pleased for you."

"Thank you." The young man came back with the coffee. "How long have you been out here?"

"Two years now. I helped build the place. Most of it was

built with leftover material from the hotel construction."

"Don't you miss home?"

"No. My home is where my work takes me. If Reverend Sam feels I can serve him better here, then I am content."

I tasted the coffee. One sip was enough. I put it down without saying anything. "This is a school?"

"Not really. It is more of a seminary. We bring members to the second plane, so that they can go forward and teach."

"How long does that take?"

"It varies. Some have more problems disconnecting than others. Two years, three years, who knows? When they are ready, they move out. We have no formal time limit."

"What about Denise?"

He hesitated a moment before answering. "Yes. She's here."

"Can we see her?"

"You can. But I would prefer that you do not. For her sake," he adedd quickly. "As you know, she felt very strongly about you. It has been extremely difficult for her to disconnect and I am afraid that if she saw you, she would have a severe setback."

"You make it sound as if I were a communicable disease."

"I'm sorry. I didn't mean it like that. It's just that she has come a long way. I would not like to see her lose the ground she has gained. She is just beginning to achieve tranquillity."

"I understand. But when the time is right, could you tell her that we asked for her?"

I thought a look of relief crossed his face. "Of course, I will do that."

"I think we'll get on to the session. Thank you for the coffee."

He rose. "My pleasure."

"If there is anything I can do for you back home, just drop me a line and it will be done."

"Thank you. But Reverend Sam provides us with all we need."

He followed us out to the car. I waved to him through the open window. "Peace and love."

He raised his hand in a kind of benediction. "Peace and love."

He was still there as the car went out the gate and turned up the road toward the Indian village.

Chapter Sixteen

The road wound through the fields that belonged to the Retreat. In each of the fields we could see four or five men and women at work tending the crops. They did not seem under any great pressure and moved almost languidly in the heat. They wore tan cotton khaki shirts and pants, and native wide-brimmed straw hats shielded their faces. They did not look up as we drove by, although they must have heard the sound of the car We passed the last field about a mile and a half from the Retreat and entered a small forest glade.

"We are now on the property of Señor Carillo," Marissa said. "You met him at the reception. He is the largest landowner in the area and a first cousin to the governor. His brother is the mayor."

"What does he do?"

"Nothing," Marissa said. "He is rich.".

"I mean, is he in farming? Cattle?"

"A little of both. But mostly it is his tenants that do those things. He collects rents. The Indian village is also on his property. He is from the oldest family in the state." She continued in a faintly bitter tone. "They do not threaten him with expropriation of his lands as they did my cousin and he owns four times as much as they do."

The village, just on the other side of the glade, consisted of a collection of timeworn adobe and wooden shacks. It seemed completely deserted.

"Where is everybody?" I asked.

"No one has lived here for twenty years," Marissa answered. "The last of the Indians are supposed to have moved into the hills. But no one really knows for sure."

"That doesn't make sense. People just don't vanish. They must have some contacts."

"There are none." She hesitated a moment. "It has been whispered that Carillo has done away with them. But they are only Indians. No one seems to care."

We drove through the dusty street of the village, entered still another small forest on the far side and a moment later came into an open field, where the photo session was taking place.

The first thing I noticed were the uniformed armed guards standing about nonchalantly with M1 rifles in the crooks of their arms. I saw them glance at our car and just as quickly, glance away. There were at least thirty or forty of them.

"Policemen?" I asked Marissa.

"No. They are Carillo's private guards."

"What are they doing here?"

"They are protecting the visitors. There are many bandits in these parts. It is not wise to travel alone here."

She stopped the car and we walked over to the group. Bobby looked up and saw us. He checked his watch and held up his hand. "Okay. Break for lunch."

"How's it coming?" I asked.

"Pretty good. I got four setups done already. If I can get five in this afternoon, we've got it made. We brought box lunches from the hotel if you'd like to join us."

"You're on," I said. I turned in time to catch Eileen and Marissa staring at King Dong slipping into his pants. It wasn't easy for him. It took some care to arrange the pants so that they fitted over his bulge. I laughed. "You girls want to join us for lunch?"

We sat in the shade under some trees, eating the box lunch of cold beer and wine, chicken, roast beef, fish in aspic, tortillas and French bread.

"We did three setups in the village," Bobby said. "Great backgrounds. We have one more here. Then we go on to Carillo's place. He's given us special permission to photograph in his gardens. They told me he has acres and acres of flowers."

"Sounds good," I said, popping open another Carta Blanca. "Has Dieter been around?"

Bobby shook his head. "Haven't seen him."

"I heard he was coming up here."

"Never showed."

"How about Lonergan and Julio?"

"Nope."

Bobby's assistant came up to us. "We're ready to go."

Bobby got to his feet and looked down at me. "Back to work."

I checked Marissa and Eileen. "You girls want to stay and watch?"

That was a stupid question. They followed Bobby down to the set. I watched for a few minutes while the models got set for the next shot. King Dong was nude again and lying spread-eagled on the ground with his hands and feet fastened to stakes. This frame supposedly represented his capture and the girls presumably teasing and torturing him while making up their minds what to do with him. From the way they were acting it looked as if it could turn into reality at any moment. They could not keep their hands off him and it was getting to be more than he could take. He was almost totally erect when Bobby began to yell at him.

"For Christ's sake, be professional! You know goddamn well that we can't print pictures showing full erections. Soften it up, you dumb bastard!"

"I cain't help it, Mr. Bobby," King Dong said in a plaintive voice. "Make them girls stop foolin'. I'm only human."

"All right, girls, quit horsin' around!" Bobby said. "This is serious business."

"You want me to throw some cold water on it?" Bobby's assistant asked.

"We tried that the last time," Bobby said disgustedly. "It didn't work."

"I don't know what you're all upset about, Bobby," Samantha Jones said soothingly. "I can take care of it."

"Oh, shit. We haven't got time for that."

"Really. I used to be a nurse and there was a trick we used in the hospital. Works every time."

"Okay," Bobby said.

Samantha knelt on the ground beside him. Delicately she raised it, holding it straight up in the air between three fingers. "How does that feel?" she asked, smiling sweetly.

King Dong's grin was broad. "Real fine."

Her other hand moved quickly and then there was a sound of a sharp slap. It snapped against his hip.

"Ow!" he yelled.

Samantha got to her feet and looked down. The erection had gone. "Never fails," she said smiling.

King Dong scowled at her. "Bitch!"

"Okay," Bobby shouted. "Let's get back to work."

I watched for a few minutes, then walked back toward the village. I didn't mind seeing the pictures, but I had no interest in the taking of them. I noticed two of the armed guards fall in step about twenty yards behind me.

The windows in the little shacks were all gone and the doors hung on broken hinges. I stopped and looked in one of them. There was nothing inside except a few pieces of broken furniture and layers of dust and sand. When I glanced back, the guards were standing at the edge of the street.

The voice came from a building at the corner. "Gareth!"

I looked around but saw nothing.

"Up here!"

Denise was sitting on a windowsill, her legs dangling out of the building's second storey. "Catch me!" she cried.

Automatically I caught her as she jumped. "Are you nuts?" I asked angrily.

She grabbed my hand. "Quick. Follow me!"

We ran up the street, around another corner, then across the field into the forest. It took almost five minutes to reach the trees on the far side of a barbed-wire fence. We sat down at the base of a giant tree that concealed us from view.

"What's this all about?" I asked, catching my breath.

"We're not supposed to go on Carillo's property," she said.

"For Christ's sake!"

"No," she said seriously. "That's why he has the guards."

"All they can do is throw you out. They can't shoot you."

"They can do anything they want. It's his property."

"That's crazy."

"This is Mexico." She looked up at me. "I didn't want to leave you. You know that."

I was silent for a moment. "Nobody pushed."

"I had to. But I didn't know it would be like this."

"Is it bad?"

"I miss you so much. That's what's bad."

"Then come back."

"I can't do that. If I do, I'll never reach the second plane."

"What the hell is so important about that? It's more important that you're happy."

"Brother Jonathan says that I will be happy when I can disconnect. He says it's harder for some than others."

"He didn't want me to see you."

"He was protecting me."

"From whom? He knows I wouldn't hurt you."

"From myself. But he didn't have to say anything. Nobody had to. I knew you were here."

"How'd you know that?"

"I felt your aura," she said.

"Keep that up and you'll have me believing it."

"It's true," she said. "But I wasn't sure. Three days ago he assigned me to an awareness trip."

"What's that?"

"Mescaline. To expand the consciousness." She reached out and touched my face lightly. The pupils of her eyes were dilated. "Even now I'm not sure that it's really you and that I'm not tripping."

"It's really me."

"I'm not sure." She began to cry. "I'm not sure of anything anymore."

I pulled her head down to my chest. "It's real."

She was silent for a moment. "Bobby and Eileen are here with you, too?"

"Yes."

"I thought so. I felt them, too." She moved away from me. "But it was you that drew me. I followed your aura from the Retreat."

I was silent.

She fished in her shirt pocket and came up with a machine-rolled yellow-papered joint and lit it. She took two heavy tokes, then passed it to me. I dragged deeply. It zapped me like an explosion. I'd never had grass like this.

"Where did this come from?" I asked. "It's dynamite."

"It grows all over the place. This is doper's paradise. Mescaline, peyote, marijuana and a hundred others that I don't even know the names of. All you have to do is go out into the field and pick them." She took the joint from my fingers and pinched it out. Carefully she put it back into her pocket.

She got to her feet and looked down at me. "I'll have to go back now. Before the people in the fields report that they saw me come down here."

I felt very relaxed. "What difference does it make? They probably never even noticed. They didn't even look up when we drove by in the car."

"They saw you. But it didn't matter. They were all stoned."

"Stoned? Then how could they work?"

She laughed. "They don't work."

"But the crops—"

"That's a big joke. We really don't grow anything out there. We just go out to meditate. Carillo sends in all the food that we need. We don't have to do anything except prepare ourselves for the second plane."

"Is everybody on shit?"

"Almost everybody. Some aren't. But they're already second plane and they can achieve without help. Brother Jonathan is first plane. He doesn't need anything."

I remembered the whiskey he had hidden in the office at Fullerton. Maybe he wasn't quite as cool as Denise thought.

"Come home with me," I said.

"I can't. I'm just beginning to be able to deal with the desires of my flesh. I know I can go all the way."

"All what way?"

"Toward freedom, Gareth. To a point where I can soar far above the earth without my body and communicate my spirit to everyone I want. I will dwell on many planets and on many levels of consciousness. I will be one with the universe."

I was silent.

She bent down over me. "You won't tell anyone that we met?"

"I won't."

A faint smile came to her lips. "Goodbye, Gareth. Peace and love."

"Peace and love," I answered.

But she was already gone. Slowly I got to my feet. I felt dizzy and put a hand against the tree to steady myself. The whole thing felt unreal. I began to wonder whether it had ever happened or whether I was hallucinating from the grass or too much heat and sun. Then the dizziness passed and I made my way back to the village. The armed guards were waiting for me. They let me pass without speaking and then, maintaining a discreet distance, followed me back to the car.

Chapter Seventeen

The bus had moved onto the field and the equipment was being loaded for the move to the next location. King Dong and the models were already aboard as I came up. Bobby turned toward me. "Coming with us?"

I shook my head. "I think I'll go back." I looked at Eileen and Marissa. "I can find my way if you want to go back with them."

Eileen answered for both of them. "We'll go back with you."

Bobby climbed into the bus. "Okay. See you tonight then."

We walked back to our car. Marissa turned it around and we started back the way we had come. They were still working in the fields as we drove by. I looked at them more carefully this time. They had to be high. There was a languor about them that did not suggest heavy work.

As we came to the gate of the Retreat, I impulsively told Marissa to turn in. I asked them to wait in the car for a moment while I went inside.

Brother Jonathan wasn't in his office. I went down to the commissary. The dining room was empty, so I went back to the kitchen, where a few men and women were working.

"Peace and love," I said. "Is Brother Jonathan around?"

"Peace and love," they chorused.

The man nearest me answered. "He's not in the office?"

"No."

They glanced at each other; then the young man stepped forward. "I'll find him for you."

"I don't want to disturb your work. Just tell me where to find him."

"No trouble. He's probably in the laboratory."

"Laboratory?"

He smiled. "That's what we call the chapel down here." I followed him into the dining room. "If you wait here, I'll be back in a moment," he said.

I fished a cigarette from my pocket. He returned alone a few minutes later.

"Brother Jonathan apologizes for not being able to see you," he said. "But he is conducting a supplicant through transition and cannot leave."

"How long will it take?"

"One never knows," the young man answered. "Supplicants in transit can take anywhere from ten minutes to three days to disconnect."

I thought for a moment. "Would you answer a question?"

"Of course." The young man smiled. "We are all here to help and serve."

"What happens if a candidate for the second plane can't cut it?"

"Nothing. But it hasn't happened yet. We are all very determined to reach our goal."

"But if a candidate should change his mind, can he go home?"

He smiled again. "We're not prisoners here. We came of our own free will. We can leave the same way." He reached into his shirt pocket and came out with an airline ticket. He handed it to me. "On arrival all of us are given a return ticket home. One of the rules is that we always carry it on us as a reminder that we can leave if we want to."

I looked at the ticket. It was an open return to Chicago. Prepaid. I gave it back to him without comment.

He put it back in his pocket. "Not one of us has ever used the ticket," he said proudly.

"Thank you," I said. "Peace and love."

"Peace and love," he answered.

I was almost at the door when I turned back. "I'm sorry," I said. "I almost forgot. I meant to ask Brother Jonathan for a few of those Js you roll here. The ones in the yellow paper."

"Sure thing." He fished in his breast pocket and came up with three cigarettes, which he held out to me. "Will that be enough?"

"I don't want to take your last," I said.

"I can always get more. We get four a day."

I put them in my pocket. "Thank you again."

"You're welcome. Peace and love."

"Peace and love." I went outside to the car. No wonder no one ever left. With four of those sticks a day they were walking on clouds. And who in their right mind would want to leave heaven?

Marissa's voice broke into my thoughts. "Where to now?"

"Back to the hotel." The first thing I planned to do when I got back to Los Angeles was to send these sticks to a laboratory for analysis. I was dead certain that there was something more than marijuana in them. And if I was right, I was going to see Reverend Sam about it. He was entitled to know what was going on in his own Retreat.

It was past four o'clock by the time we got back to the hotel and Lonergan had not yet returned. We stood at the desk in the lobby. "Want to join us for a drink?" I asked Marissa.

"I think I'd better get up to the office," she said. "I've been out all day and things have a way of piling up."

I nodded. "Dinner tonight?"

She smiled. "Of course."

I had an idea. "Can I have dinner served in the cottage? I'm getting a little tired of eating with all those people around."

"You can have anything you want. Just tell me what time and how many people."

"Just the three of us," I said.

"It is done."

"Another thing. Could you have the plane stand by to take me back to LA at two o'clock tomorrow afternoon?"

"No problem. Do you want me to drive you down to the bungalow before I go upstairs?"

"That's okay. We'll walk. I could use the exercise."

The sun was still hot and by the time Eileen and I reached the cottage I was soaking wet. The small patio pool looked inviting. "Swim?" I asked.

We stripped right there and jumped in. The water was warm but refreshing. I held onto the side of the pool and yelled for the butler.

"*Sí, señor?*" His expression didn't change when he saw our nudity.

"Planter's punch?" I asked Eileen. She nodded. I held up two fingers. "*Dos.*"

He grinned. "*Sí, señor. Dos* planter's punch."

I swam over to Eileen. "It's not a bad life."

"You have something on your mind."

"What makes you say that?"

"I know you," she said flatly. "What is it?"

"I don't know," I said truthfully. "I really don't know."

She watched me silently.

I did a slow crawl up and down the pool, then stopped in front of her. "I wish I did know. But thinking doesn't seem to help. It's jungle instinct. Something I picked up in 'Nam. Nothing I can put my finger on. But everything seems just a beat off center."

She leaned over and kissed me. "I have faith. You'll figure it out."

The butler came out with the drinks on a silver tray. He put it down at the edge of the pool and went back inside. We picked up our glasses.

"To the good life," I said.

"The good life."

We sipped our drink. It was potent. He must have used four different kinds of rum to create this explosive combination. "Whoo-oo," she said huskily. "It feels like liquid fire."

I laughed. She was right. It was instant high. I put my drink down. "Did you ever have your pussy eaten under water?"

She giggled, already a little drunk. "Can't say that I have."

I took the glass from her hand and put it down next to mine. "Brace yourself then," I said. And dived.

Bobby came back around eight o'clock. He sprawled in the living-room chair. "I've had it," he said. "The next time I get a brilliant idea don't let me do it."

"Finish?"

He nodded. "Just made it before we lost the light." He leaned toward me. "Do you know how big that guy's cock really is?"

"I really don't care," I said.

"He told us twelve inches, but it's really fourteen and a half."

"Why would he say it's smaller than it really is?"

"That's what I asked him," Bobby replied. "He looked at me with his sad brown eyes and said in a hurt voice, 'Ah don' want people to think I'm a freak.' "

I laughed. "How'd you happen to find out?"

"Samantha. She got him up, then sprang a tape measure on him."

He got to his feet. "What are you doing for dinner?"

"Quiet. Just Eileen, Marissa and me."

"Why don't you come over to our cottage afterward?" he said. "We might have some fun. Danny and the girls each threw two hundred dollars into a prong poker pool. It all started when Danny said that he could take more of King Dong than any of them."

"I think the heat's gotten to all of you."

"It was bound to happen," he said. "King Dong got to all of them. The same thing happened the last time I did a session with him."

"He's got to be the eighth wonder of the world," I said.

"He doesn't think so. He says his kid brother is bigger."

"Now that would make a layout. Why don't you shoot both of them together?"

"Can't," he answered. "The kid's only fifteen." He started for the door, then stopped. "Incidentally, you know who's got the real hots for him?"

I looked at him.

"Dieter," he said. "He came by at the end of our session. He volunteered to be the judge tonight."

"What was he doing out there?"

"I don't know. We were shooting in a flower field in back of the house. He came from there. When we were finished, he went back inside."

I lit a cigarette and got to my feet. "I've asked the plane to stand by to take me back tomorrow afternoon. Want to stay down and finish the set here or come back with me?"

Bobby didn't hesitate. "I've had it here. I'll go back with you."

Chapter Eighteen

I leaned back in the tub. The soft fragrance of the perfumed bubbles and the grass was better than the greatest incense in the world. I watched Eileen go from the makeup table to the closet door. "Hey, you're looking good," I said.

I meant it. Standing there naked, she was like a vision out of a wet dream. "I don't know what to wear," she said.

"What difference does it make?" "It's just the three of us."

She threw me a look which said I was stupid. She took a long black dress and held it against her. "What do you think?"

"That's fine."

She replaced it and took out another. A flowing pink-beige chiffon. "How about this one?"

"That's good, too."

"You're no help," she said in a disgusted tone and turned back to the closet. "I should have brought the white Loris Azzaro."

I took another toke as the telephone rang. "Will you get that?" I asked.

She picked up the receiver. "Yes?" She listened for a moment, then brought the phone over to the side of the tub. "It's Uncle John," she said, handing it to me.

"What are you doing?" he asked.

"Right now I'm stoned and sitting in the bathtub watching a fashion show."

There was disapproval in his voice. "I'm serious."

"You asked what I was doing."

"I think we ought to meet."

"Okay. How about breakfast?"

"Tonight." His voice was flat. "I think I've come up with an answer to our problem. How long will it take you to get straight?"

"Half an hour all right?"

"Meet me in my room."

I put down the phone, climbed out of the tub and headed for

the shower stall. "Dinner might be a little late," I told Eileen. "I've got to go up to the hotel and see Lonergan." Then I went into the shower and turned on the cold water full blast.

"Come, have a drink," he said as he let me in. "I just fixed myself a martini."

I followed him to the bar and climbed up on a stool while he poured a scotch on the rocks for me. I tasted the whisky. "Cheers."

"Cheers." He came right to the point. "Julio agreed to move his operation away from here."

"What made him agree to that?"

"Eight-three relatives who are either on the payroll or working for the hotel in other ways."

"That's good enough reason," I said thoughtfully. I took another sip of the drink. "What makes you so sure that he'll do what he promised?"

"He gave me his word," he answered coldly.

That was the end of it. Final. Period. Lonergan's face was impassive. Even if I were Julio, I would think a long time before I crossed him.

"I'm still not sure. I don't think we're going to get gambling down here. At least not in the foreseeable future. And without gambling, the costs are too high."

"I've taken care of that, too," Lonergan said.

"You've been busy."

He didn't smile. "They'll take a lease with a purchase option."

"That's interesting. How much?"

"Two hundred fifty thousand a year plus twenty per cent of the operating profit from the hotel and fifty per cent of the casino profits if we get gambling. The term of the lease is five years. You can buy the hotel at any time during the lease period for ten million dollars cash. The only thing you have to guarantee is to spend one million dollars for changes and improvements which you would have to do anyway."

I did some quick mental arithmetic. Rent, staff, overhead and amortization of the improvements added up to a base cost of about eight hundred thousand a year.

He was right with me. "You could break even at about a thirty-five or forty per cent occupancy."

"It's still a big nut."

"That's right."

"I'll have to think about it. I wonder what made them go for a deal like this?"

"They had an attack of realism. And no place else to go."

I stabbed. "What about Señor Carillo?"

He shot me a sharp look. "You know about him?"

"Only what I read in the newspapers."

"We saw him this afternoon. He guaranteed government approval of the deal."

"He's got that much power?"

"He owns practically everything in the state."

"Where are the Indians?" I asked.

Lonergan was puzzled. "I don't know what you're talking about."

"It's nothing." I laughed. "When do they expect an answer?"

"As soon as possible."

"Let me sleep on it. I'll have an answer for them before I get on the plane tomorrow."

"Okay." He took another sip of the martini.

"One thing you haven't told me, Uncle John."

"What's that?"

"How do you feel about it? Do you think it's a good deal?"

"I think it's as good a deal as you can get. But you're the one that has to decide whether you want to take the shot or not. It's your money."

"Your money, too. You're a partner."

"I haven't done too badly going along with you so far. Whatever you decide now is all right with me." He walked me to the door. "Either way I haven't lost anything."

"What do you mean?"

A smile came to his lips. "I managed to take a walk barefoot in the surf."

Eileen had chosen the black dress and her eyes were shining as she let me in. I glanced over at the cocktail table.

"That's not fair," I said. "You got a head start."

"I was going down. I needed a boost. What happened with Uncle John?"

"I've got a deal if I want it."

"Going to take it?"

"I haven't made up my mind yet."

She came toward me, her face serious. "Don't do it. I have bad vibes about the whole thing."

"You may be right. But if it works, it could mean a lot of money."

"Do you need the money, Gareth?"

"Not the money. But the game is fun."

"It won't be fun if you lose."

"I can afford it."

Her eyes grew dark. "Maybe, if all you lose is what this costs you. But that's not what I'm talking about."

"Then what are you talking about?"

"I don't know." She shook her head as if to clear it. "Maybe I'm just on a down trip."

The butler came in with hors d'oeuvres, tiny enchiladas, delicately thin tortillas rolled around chilli and beef, crackers and avocado dip. He fixed a scotch on the rocks for me and a margarita for Eileen. He gestured toward the dining table, seeking our approval.

The table was beautifully set for three with candles, linen, crystal glasses and Dom Pérignon in the wine bucket. I called on my limited Spanish. "*Muy hermosa.*"

He smiled, bowing, a grin of pleasure on his face. "*Muchas gracias, señor.*"

There was a knock at the door and he went to answer it. Marissa was wearing the white gown she had worn the first night.

"You look absolutely beautiful," Eileen said.

Marissa smiled with pleasure. "And so do you," she said.

Without asking, the butler brought her a margarita.

"Wait a minute," I said, picking up the coke. "We're two spoons up on you."

Marissa looked at us doubtfully. "I don't know. After last night—"

I laughed. "It was the mixture that got to you. I won't let that happen tonight."

"Okay." She took two good hits.

I held up my glass. "To happiness."

We drank.

"There's one thing missing," Eileen said. "If you take over this place, I'm going to insist that there be music in every room."

"There is music," Marissa said. "I guess I forgot to show you." She walked over to the bar and pressed a button on the wall beside it. Mexican music poured into the room. "We also have American music," she added, pressing the button again. It was Frank Sinatra singing "Night and Day."

"I like that," I said. "Dance?"

"Which one of us?" Marissa asked.

"Silly questions get silly answers," I said, holding my arms wide. "Both of you, of course."

They moved close to me and I put an arm around each of them. Eileen laid her head on my left shoulder; Marissa rested her face against my right cheek. Their perfumes intermingled. We moved slowly; our bodies pressed closer and closer together. It was beautiful.

And so was dinner. We all fell in love.

The golden light from the fireplace played on their naked bodies as they lay sleeping, entwined in each other's arms, on the zebra rug. I sat on the floor, leaned back against the couch and swirled the cognac in the crystal snifter. I sipped it slowly, savouring its tart warmth.

They were double Goyas, two Naked Majas. The fire turned Eileen's pale flesh to gold and Marissa's already tanned body to copper. Marissa's nipples were like purple grapes compared to Eileen's which were more cherry pink. They slept facing each other, each had an arm under the other's shoulder and one hand cupping and shielding the other's sex.

At first, Marissa had been shy, but when she felt the warmth and love and heightened sexuality brought on by the combination of music, drink, dancing and dope, she opened like a flower.

And in the end she was the most sensual of all of us, demanding, taking, tasting and loving until we were drained and exhausted.

Now they were asleep and I was wide-awake. Coke did it every time. I watched them for a moment more, then got to my feet. I slipped into my slacks and went into the jasmine-filled night air.

There were still screams and shouts of laughter coming from Bobby's cottage. They had been going strong all night, although after a while we hadn't heard them.

Holding the drink in my hand, I padded down the walk to the other cottage. I opened the door and stepped into the middle of an argument.

Samantha was staring at Bobby and Dieter, her naked breasts heaving with anger. "It's not fair!" she yelled. "You fags always stick together." She turned and saw me. "They screwed us!" she shouted. "They had it rigged so that Danny would win."

"I could have told you that." I smiled. "He's president of the Los Angeles chapter of the FFA."

"I wouldn't give a damn if he were the president of the DAR!" she snapped.

"Okay," I said. "What was unfair?"

"All of us girls used KY jelly. He used Crisco."

"I don't see what's wrong with that."

"Of course it's wrong," she shouted. "Everybody knows that Crisco is shortening!"

I broke up. I hadn't known that Samantha had that kind of humour. When I caught my breath, I said, "Okay, just so that you girls have no beefs, I'll give you each the two hundred you put into the pot. But next time make sure you spell out the rules first."

She seemed satisfied. "Okay, but right now I want to get laid and there are no men around here."

I gestured toward King Dong, who was stretched out on the floor, with his head in one of the girl's laps. "What about him?"

"He's all shagged out," she said in a disgusted tone. "It took us over an hour to get him up for the last one."

"Don't look at me," I said quickly and ducked out the door. I went back to my cottage. My two Naked Majas were sleeping exactly as I had left them. I went into the bedroom, pulled a blanket from the bed and covered them. They didn't stir. I had just started for the bedroom when there was a heavy knock at the door. Angrily I pulled it open.

Denise's face was scratched and swollen and her khaki shirt and pants were torn. She took a stumbling step toward me, her eyes dilated with terror. I caught her before she fell.

"Take me home, Gareth, please take me home," she said in a hoarse, frightened voice. "They're after me. Don't let them take me back. I want to go home!"

Chapter Nineteen

I carried her into the bedroom and placed her on the bed. Her eyes were tightly closed and she was shivering with fear. I threw a blanket over her and knelt beside the bed. Her lips were moving in a hoarse whisper. "No, please . . . I don't want to go back into transit . . . No more . . . I did see him. I swear it. I wasn't hallucinating . . . Please. No."

Eileen's voice came from the doorway behind me. "What is it?"

"Denise. She's hurt. See if you find a doctor."

Marissa appeared behind Eileen's shoulder. "I'll call," she said.

Eileen put on a shirt and jeans and came over to look at Denise. "My God!" she exclaimed. "What happened to her?"

"I don't know. Get a towel and some warm water. See if you can clean up some of those scratches."

"Gareth." Denise reached up for me.

I sat on the side of the bed and took her hand.

She held it tightly. "They said you weren't real. That I was hallucinating."

"I'm real," I said. "Who are 'they'?"

"Brother Jonathan. The others. He was angry. I broke the rule against connections. He made me go into transit. I didn't want to go. But he made me. The others helped him. They dragged me into the laboratory."

She was growing hysterical again. "It's all right now," I said soothingly. "You're safe now. You're here with me."

Her fingers tightened around my hand. "I'm not hallucinating, am I, Gareth?"

"No. You told me not to tell him I saw you. How did he find out?"

"I told him. We must tell the truth. Always. That's the first rule. Then he got angry and said that I was lying. That you weren't anywhere near here and that I was hallucinating." She began to shiver again. "You won't let them take me back, will you?"

"I won't. You'll stay with me. And come home with me."

"Promise?"

"Promise."

Eileen came with a towel and a basin of hot water. She put it down and began to clean Denise's face.

"Eileen?" Denise's voice was questioning.

"Yes, dear."

"Is it really you?"

"Yes, dear."

She reached up and touched Eileen's cheek. "I've always loved you. You know that?"

Eileen's voice was as gentle as her touch. "I know that. And we love you."

"I was frightened," she whispered. "I was running in the forest all night. And there were animals."

"You're safe now. Don't think about it."

Denise suddenly tensed. "Don't let them take me back! Please!"

Eileen held her close. "We won't, baby. I promise you we won't."

Marissa came into the doorway. "The doctor will be here in a few minutes."

"Good," I said.

"I have extra shirts and jeans in the closet," Eileen called over her shoulder.

Marissa dressed, then joined us around the bed. "Is there anything I can do?"

"Who's that?" Denise asked in a frightened voice.

"Marissa," I said. "She's our friend."

"Let me touch her," Denise said, reaching out a hand.

Marissa took it and Denise held it for a long moment, then let it go with a gentle sigh. "She is a good person," Denise whispered. "Her aura is filled with love."

"Help me undress her," Eileen said to Marissa.

They bent over Denise, carefully removed the torn shirt and slacks and began to wash her scratch-covered body.

"The guards!" Denise exclaimed suddenly. "They told Brother Jonathan about us. They saw us running from the village."

"Why would they do that? They have nothing to do with the Retreat."

"They do!" Denise became vehement. "Every day they come in a truck and take about twenty people to work on Carillo's property."

"That doesn't make sense," I said.

But she was already off on another track. "That's why when I came in, the first thing he said to me was that I didn't see you. That it was an hallucination. Even before I told him the truth." She sat up suddenly. "You mustn't let them take me back! No matter what they say to you."

"I won't."

"They'll keep me in transit for days." Her voice began to rise to a scream. "I'll go crazy if they do that. I can't take any more!"

The doorbell rang and she leaped from the bed. I caught her just before she went out the window. Hysterically she fought me. "I won't go back! " she screamed.

Over my shoulder I caught a glimpse of the doctor, a small man with a neatly trimmed mustache and the standard black bag. "No one's come for you," I said soothingly. "It's only the doctor."

She stopped fighting. I led her back to the bed and she got in and pulled the sheet up around her. The doctor came toward the bed. He put a hand under Denise's chin and looked into her eyes. He said something to Marissa in Spanish.

"The doctor wants you to lie down," she said.

Denise looked at me. I nodded. She lay back against the pillows.

Slowly the doctor lifted the sheet and looked at her. He spoke again and Marissa translated. "He says that she will need a shot against infection and he will give her a salve for her cuts. He says also that she needs rest. She is on the verge of hysterical exhaustion."

"I don't want a shot," Denise said. "They'll take me away while I'm sleeping."

"No one will take you," I said. "I'll be with you every minute."

She looked at Eileen. "You too?"

Eileen nodded. "Yes, baby. Me too."

"I don't want to go back into transit."

"The only place you're going is home with me," I said.

Denise looked at the doctor. "Okay."

"Roll over on your stomach," Marissa said, translating the doctor's instructions.

She got an injection in each buttock. Then the doctor took a tube of ointment out of the little black bag. By the time he finished putting the ointment on her she was fast asleep.

"The doctor says she will sleep for six to eight hours. He says that she needs the rest and that we should not wake her up," Marissa said. "He also thinks she's had a bad reaction to mescaline and that she may be suffering from a toxic psychosis. She may need further specialized treatment because some forms of this drug get into the system and have a long-term effect even without additional use."

"Tell the doctor I will see to it that she is properly taken care of," I said.

"He says that he will come around noon tomorrow to see her," Marissa translated.

"Thank you. *Muchas gracias*," I said to the doctor.

The doctor bowed quickly and walked out of the room. Marissa saw him to the front door, then returned to the bedroom.

Eileen straightened the covers over Denise. Then she turned off the bedside lights and we went into the other room.

"The doctor says there have been several other cases like this at the Retreat," Marissa said. "Twice he has had to put them into a hospital."

"What does he think causes it?"

"He says that everyone out there is on drugs. And some of them do not know how to handle it. They take too much."

But, I thought to myself, maybe they didn't take it. Maybe it was given to them without their knowledge. The boy had told me they were given four sticks a day. "Any chance of getting a cup of coffee at this hour?" I asked.

Marissa smiled. "Easy. There's American instant coffee in the kitchen. I'll boil some water."

Eileen waited until she had left the room. "What do you think is happening out there?"

"I don't know," I said. "But you can be sure I'm going to see Reverend Sam about it when I get back."

We had almost finished our coffee when we heard the sound of cars drawing up outside. A moment later the doorbell rang.

Brother Jonathan was standing on the threshold with two young men in the khaki garb of the Retreat. Behind them I saw several of Carillo's guards; two of them had Dobermans on leashes.

"Brother Jonathan," I said. "Peace and love."

He started through the doorway, but I stepped in his path, blocking his entrance. He paused. "Peace and love, Gareth," he said. "We're looking for Denise. Have you seen her?"

"Yes."

"Thank God!" he exclaimed. "We were so worried about her. She's been missing since eight o'clock this evening. Is she with you?"

"Yes."

"Good," he said. "Now we can take her back."

"No," I said.

There was an edge of surprise in his voice. "But she's very ill. She needs help. She's on a bad trip. I have a doctor standing by at the Retreat to help her."

"I've already had a doctor here. He advised me not to move her under any circumstances."

He fell silent for a moment, then asked, "May I see her?"

"She's asleep."

"I'll leave my two men here to help take care of her."

"It won't be necessary. I have help."

He made a gesture with his hands. "Okay then. You seem to have everything under control. We'll be back for her in the morning."

"You can save yourself the trip. She's not going back. She's coming home with me."

"She can't do that!"

"Why not, Brother Jonathan?" I asked politely. "As I understand it, anyone can leave anytime." I recognized one of the young men standing behind him. "Wasn't it you who told me that each of you always carries a return ticket?"

The boy didn't speak. Brother Jonathan's voice grew harsh. "Now you're making it very difficult for me. I'm personally responsible to Reverend Sam for everyone here. And I can't allow her to leave until I get an okay from our doctors."

I saw Bobby and Dieter coming toward us. They were at the door in time to hear me say, "Then I'll put in a call to Reverend Sam right now and get an okay."

"What's happening?" Bobby asked.

"Brother Jonathan says I need an okay from your father to bring Denise home."

"Is she here?" he asked in surprise.

"Yes. She said she wants to come home with us."

Bobby looked at Brother Jonathan. "She has the right to go home and she doesn't need anyone's permission. Not even my father's. You know that."

"But she's ill. She doesn't know what she's doing," he protested.

"You know the rules. A free choice made by a free will. My father wouldn't like it if that rule were broken."

Brother Jonathan back down. "We'll return in the morning. I want to talk to her."

"What if she doesn't want to speak to you?" I asked.

"She'll talk to me," he said grimly.

"Brother Jonathan, you're beginning to sound more and more like the cop you used to be."

He glared at me and turned away. He spoke to the armed guards in Spanish. They nodded and went back to their cars.

"Brother Jonathan," I called, "haven't you forgotten something?"

He turned to look at me.

"Peace and love," I said.

Chapter Twenty

I couldn't sleep. I sat outside in the patio, watching the sun come up. The butler arrived at seven o'clock. He smiled. "*Desayuno?* Breakfast?"

Suddenly I was starved. "*Sí.*"

I was in the middle of ham steak and eggs when a shadow fell across the table.

Lonergan smiled. "You had a busy night."

I swallowed a mouthful of food. "You heard?"

He nodded. "I saw Dieter this morning."

"What do you think?"

"You haven't really changed. You're still playing Sir Galahad. Chasing lost causes."

"What makes you say that?"

"The girl's a doper," he said flatly. "Dieter told me it's not the first time she's freaked out."

"She wasn't a doper when she came down here. Whatever happened happened since she got here."

He dropped into the chair opposite me. The butler brought him a cup of coffee. "I suppose you haven't had much time to think about the proposition?"

"Not really."

"May I offer an opinion?"

"I would appreciate it,' I said, taking another piece of the ham steak.

"I don't see how you can lose on the deal. If you just break even, you make money."

"How's that?"

"Your investment comes out of the States and is deducted from federal income taxes so that the net cost to you is only about fifty cents on the dollar. If you break even on the operation and leave the money here, you've already got a fifty per cent profit. And if the operation makes a profit, you're way ahead."

"You make it sound easy. What if we don't break even?"

"You can't lose that much," he replied. "What's fifty per cent of fifty per cent?"

I finished the eggs and picked up my coffee. "I have another problem. Personnel. There's no one in my organization who knows anything about hotel operation."

"Dieter says he will stay on. And I found out that the general manager of the Princess in the Bahamas wants to make a move."

"Is he good?"

"Very good. In case we do get gambling, he's got casino experience. He once worked at the Mayfair in London. He'll come for sixty thousand a year and one-quarter of one per cent of the hotel profit."

"How do you know?"

"I had him on the phone this morning."

"You're not wasting time."

"Can't afford to," he said. "I'm not getting any younger."

I got to my feet and walked to the edge of the patio, my coffee cup in hand. I looked out over the ocean, then back at the hotel and the mountains behind it. It was really beautiful. I came back to the table. "You really like it?"

"Yes," he answered. "I wasn't wrong when I urged you to go into the clubs, was I?"

"No."

"You're putting together experience. The clubs, this hotel, Atlantic City when it opens. Who knows? Maybe even Vegas. Never can tell when something might break there. Then it becomes real money."

"Uncle John, you're a greedy man. I think all you want is for me to make you rich."

He smiled. "There's nothing wrong with that."

My mind was made up. "Okay. Let's give it a spin."

"You mean you'll take it?"

I nodded. "You convinced me. You can tell them we've got a deal."

He held out his hand. "Good luck."

I took it. "To both of us."

Eileen came out of the cottage. She paused when she saw Uncle John and pulled the robe closer around her. "Gareth."

"Congratulate us," I said. "We're in the hotel business."

It didn't register. There was concern in her voice. "I just went in to look at Denise. She's burning up with fever."

We went into the bedroom. Denise's face was white and there were beads of perspiration running down her forehead. Her cheeks were flushed and her body was shivering under the blanket. I sat down on the bed beside her. "Get me a washcloth and some rubbing alcohol."

"We don't have any alcohol," Eileen said.

"Toilet water then. And while I'm sponging her down, get on the phone and call the doctor."

I worked quickly. In 'Nam I had seen soldiers come down with fevers like this. Sometimes it was malaria, sometimes paratyphoid. I heard Eileen talking to Marissa in the other room, then Marissa's voice on the phone.

Eileen came back into the room. "Anything I can do?"

"Yes," I said, pulling down the sheets. "Tell the maid to bring dry sheets."

I lifted her from the bed and covered her with a blanket while they changed the sheets. She weighed almost nothing. I hadn't noticed how much weight she had lost. I put her back on the bed when they had finished.

I turned to see Lonergan watching me with an inscrutable expression. "I'll go up to the hotel and let them know of your decision."

"Okay." I followed him into the living room.

Marissa came toward us. "The doctor is on his way."

I sprawled in an easy chair and leaned my head back. The lack of sleep had finally caught up with me.

"What time would you like to meet with them?" Lonergan asked.

I shook my head to clear it. Everything seemed an effort. "You handle it. I'll try to see them before I leave."

He nodded and went out. I closed my eyes and slept. I couldn't have been out for long when I felt a gentle hand on my shoulder.

"Gareth." Eileen's voice was soft. "Wake up. The doctor wants to talk with you."

I fought my way out of the fog. "Get me a cup of coffee." The butler brought it immediately. It helped but not enough. I opened the small drawer and snorted two spoons. My head cleared immediately. I went into the bedroom.

Denise was still sleeping. The doctor's face was very serious. He spoke rapidly and Marissa translated for him.

"She is a very sick girl. She is suffering from malnutrition, as well as some form of viral dysentery which has caused her to lose considerable fluids. It is possible that she is also running a fever from an infection, either traumatic or viral or both. He recommends that she be hospitalised immediately."

"Where is the nearest hospital?" I asked.

"La Paz," Marissa answered. "He can call for the ambulance plane."

La Paz was two hundred miles away. "How long would it take?"

"The plane could be here this afternoon," she said.

"Call the airstrip and find out if my plane is ready to take off now."

I sat down on the edge of the bed while Marissa phoned. "Is there anything you can do now?" I asked the doctor.

He looked blank. He didn't understand a word I was saying. Marissa came back. "They can be ready to leave within the hour."

"Tell them to be ready," I said.

Marissa nodded and went back to the phone. "They'll be ready," she said.

"Good. Now ask the doctor if there is anything he can do for her now?"

"The only thing he suggests is getting some saline solution into her. He doesn't want to use any medication until he runs some tests."

I nodded.

"The doctor asks if there is room for him to accompany her on the plane. He would like to make sure that her condition remains stable."

"Tell him I would be grateful."

"May I come, too?" she asked.

"Of course."

The doctor spoke to Marissa, then turned and left. "He's going to his pharmacy and get some bottles of saline solution.

He'll be back in time to go to the airstrip with us."

"Get the big limo for us. I want Denise to be able to stretch out on the back seat."

"Okay. Do I have time to run up to the hotel and get a change of clothes? I'm still wearing Eileen's jeans."

"Don't be too long," I said. I waited until she was gone; then I turned to Eileen. "You're coming with us."

She looked at me silently for a moment, then at Denise. "What do you think is wrong with her?"

"I don't know. But we'll find out."

"The doctor said she's running a temperature of a hundred and three. I don't like it. That's too high."

"I've seen them go higher with paratyphoid in Vietnam," I said. "They get over it."

"I don't trust Mexican hospitals."

Neither did I. I waited until the pilot switched off the no-smoking sign and the doctor had rigged up the saline drip. Then I got out of my seat, went forward and told the pilot to change course for Los Angeles and to radio ahead to have an ambulance meet us at the airport.

When I got back to my seat, the doctor was visibly upset. He looked out the window and spoke rapidly to Marissa.

"The doctor says that La Paz is to the east and that we have changed course and are flying north," she said.

"That's right. I changed my mind. We're going to Los Angeles."

Marissa's voice was surprised. "Why?"

"I promised her I would take her home," I said.

We were in the waiting room in the private pavilion of the UCLA medical center for almost an hour before Dr. Aldor came down. The clock on the wall read one o'clock. Marissa and the doctor were probably already back in Mazatlán. I had asked the pilot to take them back as soon as he refueled.

Ed gestured from the doorway. "Let's find a quiet place to talk," he said.

Eileen and I followed him through the crowded corridors until we came to a door marked PRIVATE—DOCTORS ONLY.

We sat down at the table and he looked at us with sad brown eyes. "She's a very sick young lady."

"What's the matter with her?"

"We're not sure yet," he answered. "I suspect infectious hepatitis complicated by malnutrition and heavy drug abuse. There are evidences of some kidney and liver malfunction. I have her in intensive care and we're watching her very carefully."

"She seems heavily sedated," he went on. "I tried to speak to her, but she couldn't respond. She managed to come out of it long enough to ask me where she was and when I told her she was here, she went back to sleep."

"She wanted to come home," I said.

"I need a little information on her. Do you know what sedative the doctor gave her on the plane?"

"None that I know of," I answered. "He rigged up some kind of temporary saline drip, but the only sedative I know of was the shot he gave her last night. He said that would last about six to eight hours, so that should have worn off by now."

Ed thought for a moment. "That's strange. Sure there wasn't anything else in that bottle besides saline solution?"

Eileen spoke up. "He did change the original bottle once on the way up."

"When you went forward to the pilot's cabin to telephone Dr Aldor. He said something about that bottle not working properly."

"What time was that?" Ed asked.

"About halfway through the flight. We were an hour and fifteen minutes out of Los Angeles."

Ed nodded. "An hour and fifteen minutes on Thorazine could account for the way she is reacting. Do you have any idea of what drugs she was on?" he asked, looking at me.

"You name them. Grass, mescaline . . ." I remembered something and fished in my pocket. I put the yellow-papered joint on the table. "How about four a day of those for starters?"

He picked it up gingerly and sniffed at it. "What is it?"

"Grass and something else. I don't know what. Maybe the lab can find out. All I know is that I took just two tokes from one that she gave me and it almost put me away. I was dizzy when I got to my feet."

"I'll have it analyzed. Is there anything else you can tell me?"

"You know as much as I do."

"One more question. Any idea how long she's been on this stuff?"

"It's been more than two years since we last saw her. Maybe all that time."

He got to his feet. "You two look pretty beat. Go home and get some rest. And don't worry, we'll take good care of her."

"Thanks, Ed." I held out my hand. He gave me a reassuring grip. I smiled. "Just get her straight. She's a good girl."

"It may take some time, but I think we can do it. She's young enough and strong enough."

We started for the door. In the hallway I paused. "Don't spare the expenses. I want her to have everything. Private nurses around the clock. Just tell them to send all the bills to my office."

"Okay. I'll check with you tonight and let you know how she's doing."

"Can we visit her?"

"Better hold off until tomorrow. She should be in shape to talk by then." He pressed my hand again and went off down the hall.

Lonergan's car was waiting at the entrance when we came out. The chauffer was behind the wheel and the Collector was leaning against the door. The Collector opened the back door when he saw us. "Welcome home," he said.

"How'd you know where to find us?" I asked.

"Your office. Lonergan called and asked us to pick you up. He figured you'd be too cheap to get a car." He closed the door and climbed into the front seat next to the chauffeur. "He asked us to take you to his place for a meeting."

"Not this time, Bill," I said. "We're going home to sleep. Business can wait until morning."

Chapter Twenty One

The elevators in the new Century City office buildings boasted that they were the fastest in California. Even so, they were nothing compared to New York and Chicago. Californians just aren't vertically oriented.

The floor lights flashed as we went up.

17—GARETH BRENDAN PUBLICATIONS LTD.
Production
18—GARETH BRENDAN PUBLICATIONS LTD.
Sales and Accounting
19—GARETH BRENDAN PUBLICATIONS LTD.
Executive Offices

The door opened and I stepped into the nineteenth-floor reception area. A large lucite panel listed the corporate divisions in burnished gold lettering.

GARETH BRENDAN PUBLICATIONS LIMITED
MAGAZINES

MACHO
NIGHT PEOPLE
GIRLS OF THE WORLD QUARTERLY
LIFESTYLE DIGEST
MACHO BOOK CLUB
LIFESTYLE PRODUCT SALES
LIFESTYLE RECORD CLUB
LIFESTYLE PRESS INC.

LIFESTYLE CLUBS AND HOTELS

NEW YORK LIFESTYLE CLUB
CHICAGO LIFESTYLE CLUB
LOS ANGELES LIFESTYLE CLUB
LONDON LIFESTYLE CLUB
MAZATLÁN LIFESTYLE HOTEL
LIFESTYLE TOURS AND TRAVEL
LIFESTYLE CHARTER AIRLINES
LIFESTYLE MEDIA PRODUCTIONS

As I walked toward the crescent-shaped reception desk, I could see the snow glistening at the top of Mount Baldy forty miles to the east. It was one of those freaky smog-free days that happen in Los Angeles more than Eastern propaganda admits. There were places for three call directors at the fourteen-foot desk, but only one chair was occupied at the moment.

I glanced up at the clock on the wall. Nine-twenty. The office did not open officially until nine-thirty. There were three girls at the desk at all times from then on. No visitor was ever sent into an office alone. They were always escorted by one of the receptionists. And they were dynamite-looking chicks, a girl who had modeled for one of our magazines or a recruit from one of our clubs. It was a matter of image. Once a visitor saw our receptionists there was no doubt about our business.

There were already eight people waiting for appointments. They were seated in various conversational groupings which allowed them privacy for conversation or perusal of the magazines on the small coffee tables in front of them. The walls were covered with paintings, blowups of our magazine covers and centerfold girls all carefully toned down for obvious reasons. To those who wanted it a pretty girl in a maid's uniform served coffee or tea from a rolling lucite wagon.

The girl behind the reception desk was new. It was clear from her tone of voice that she did not recognize me, despite the fact that there were a number of photographs of me among others on the walls. "Good morning. May I help you?"

"Is Denise in yet?" I asked.

"If you'll take a seat, she should be here in a few minutes."

"No, thank you," I said, taking the gift box from under my arm. "Would you mind giving this to her, please?"

"Not at all." She picked up the package and put it on the floor behind the desk.

"Thank you." Fishing in my pocket for my special key, I crossed the reception area to the private elevator that would take me to my office in the penthouse on the floor above.

"Pardon me, sir," the receptionist called after me. "The down elevators are behind the screen."

I glanced back at her. Her finger was already on the panic button. One touch and two special guards would be there in less than a minute. "I know that," I said.

"That elevator is for company executives only," she said.

I smiled and held the key up so that she could see it. "Young lady," I said, turning the key in the lock, "I am the company."

I stepped into the elevator and, before the doors closed, caught a glimpse of her staring at me with an open mouth. I hit the button and went up to the penthouse floor.

The special police were waiting as I stepped from the elevator into my secretaries' office. They relaxed when they saw me. "The new girl didn't recognize you."

"I gathered that. At least we know she's on the job."

The Bobbsey twins were at their desks which flanked the door to my office. "Good morning, Mr. Brendan," they chorused as I went by.

"Good morning," I said closing the door behind me. I crossed the room and sat down behind my desk. I looked around at the Chippendale furniture with which the office was decorated and shook my head in disgust. Some decorator had talked Eileen out of two hundred grand for all this. I hated it, but she said it had dignity.

I spun the chair around and looked out the window to the west. As I said, it was one of those freaky days in Los Angeles. The sun was already hanging like a fiery yellow globe in the blue sky. It would be hot as hell today. The water of the Pacific was sparkling, out beyond the airport, and a big jet was coming in for a landing.

I turned back to the desk and punched out the airport code for our charter airline. The screen lit up, giving me arrival and departure times for all our charter flights for the next twelve hours. Our Lifestyle Tour from Hawaii wasn't due into LAX until eleven o'clock. I turned it off, got up and peered at the airport through the telescope which was mounted on a tripod near the window. The plane was a Pan Am 747 and I followed it in until it disappeared just before touchdown. It didn't matter that it wasn't one of ours. I got a big thrill out of just watching them.

I returned to my chair just as one of the twins came in with a silver coffee service. Carefuly she poured a cup of coffee, added one cube of sugar, then stirred and placed it in front of me.

"Good morning, Dana," I said.

"Good morning, Mr. Brendan." She laughed. "I'm—"

"Don't tell me. I know. You're Shana."

"That's right, Mr. Brendan."

I picked up the coffee and sipped at it. Four years and I still couldn't tell them apart. I was convinced now that they were playing games with me.

"Dana's coming in with the mail and messages," she said. "And the meeting with the underwriters is at ten o'clock in your conference room."

I nodded.

She took a folded newspaper from under her arm and opened it on the desk in front of me. "We thought you'd get a kick out of this headline in today's *Wall Street Journal*."

It was a featured story in the first column on the front page. The headline was in bold type: SEX MAKES IT BIG ON THE STREET. A smaller headline followed: "Brendan Publications First Public Offering 1000% Oversubscribed."

The intercom buzzed. I pressed the button. "Denise on the inside line for you."

I picked up the phone. "Happy anniversary," I said.

Denise was bubbling. You remembered."

"How could I forget? You're my special baby."

"I can't believe that it's been two years," she said. "It seems like only yesterday that I came back."

"May the next two years pass just as quickly and as happily," I said.

"Thank you," she said. "I'd come up there and kiss you if I didn't know how busy you were."

"How is she?" Shana asked as I hung up.

"She's doing just fine. But everything takes time. She sees the psychoanalyst three times a week. They shoveled a lot of shit into her head down there and it's not that easy to get out."

Shana nodded sympathetically. "Shall I have Dana come in now?"

"No. Save everything until after the meeting with the underwriters."

She left the office, closing the door quietly behind her. Denise's voice echoed in my ear. "I could come up there and kiss you if I didn't know how busy you were."

Shit. I never had it so good. But why, when I was sitting right here on the top of the world, did I feel so cut off from it?

The intercom buzzed again. "Verita on the inside line."

"*Buenos dias,*" I said.

She laughed. "If you're not too busy, I'd like to see you for a moment before the meeting."

"Come on up."

She came in, carrying her usual folder. I watched her as she walked toward the desk. This poised, assured woman was completely different from the girl at the unemployment window I'd once known. She wore a black, smartly tailored dress that accented her femininity and at the same time let you know she was totally businesslike.

"You're lookin' good," I said.

"Thank you." She came right to the point. "I thought you might like to see the first-quarter results before the meeting. There's a summary on the first page if you won't want to go through the whole report."

The heading of the report was simple. Net profits before taxes I read down the column.

Publishing Group	$ 7,900,000
Lifestyle Group	2,600,000
All Others	1,500,000
Total	$12,000,000

"We're selling out too cheap," I said.

She smiled. "*Macho*'s circulation for the three months averaged out at four million one hundred and fifty thousand copies. *Girls of the World Quarterly* made another big profit contribution. Even at the six dollar new price, we sold almost seven million copies."

"I'm not complaining," I smiled.

"Our net after taxes should be about seven million," she added.

"Leave this to me. I think the underwriters might be interested in knowing about it."

"I've already prepared copies for them."

She was way ahead of me. There was really nothing I had to

do anymore. Everything had already been thought of. "Good," I said.

"Two more things if you have the time," she said quickly.

There was that phrase again – "If you have the time." It was beginning to seem to me that this was the opening line in almost every conversation I'd had for the last year. I managed to contain my annoyance. "I have the time."

"The auditors reported that the personnel in the supply divisions of the club has increased between seventeen and twenty men per club during the last two years."

"So?"

"It doesn't make sense. At most they only need two men."

"With profits like that what difference does it make?"

"That's no way to run a business," she said disapprovingly. "If you let that happen in other areas of the company, there won't be any profits to talk about."

"Okay. Look into it."

"I already am."

Again she was ahead of me. I couldn't keep the annoyance from creeping into my voice this time. "Then why bother me if you're already doing something about it?"

"I think you should be kept informed," she said evenly.

"You said there were two things. What's the other?"

"The second is personal. I'm getting marired next month."

I stared at her in surprise. "The judge?"

She smiled, blushing slightly. "Yes."

I came out from behind the desk and kissed her. "Congratulations. He's a hell of a guy. I know you'll both be very happy."

"He's planing to run for Congress next year," she said. "And this is the right time to do it."

"Hey, anytime is the right time if you love the guy."

"I love him," she said. "He's a fine man."

I kissed her again and looked down into her face. She was radiant. "That's beautiful," I said.

Chapter Twenty Two

The underwriters were jubilant. The sweet smell of success hung heavy in the air. I looked around the table. They all were there. The big brokers. Merrill Lynch, Kuhn Loeb, Citibank, Bank of America.

Martin Courtland, chairman of the underwriters' group, smiled at me. "This is the most successful offering to hit the street since the Ford Motor Company. We could have doubled our per-share asking price and it still would have been oversubscribed."

"I'm not complaining," I said. "One hundred million dollars is still a lot of money."

"I have word that the day after it comes out it will open on the Exchange at fifty per cent above the asking price."

The price was fifty dollars a share. That meant it should appear on the board the very first day at seventy-five. "You guys are going to get rich just on trading alone," I said.

"Maybe you'd like to place some of your private shares with us." He laughed.

"No, thanks. I'm not greedy."

They all laughed. Two million shares went out to the public. One million remained in the treasury. I retained three million shares for myself. "I have some interesting figures," I said, refering them to the first-quarter report.

They had already seen it. "At this rate, even at fifteen or twenty times earnings, the shareholders are getting the biggest bargain of their lives," Courtland said.

I didn't say anything.

He looked around the table. "I trust, gentlemen, that you all realize this is the first time a major financing has been undertaken to build a hotel and casino in Las Vegas without a mortgage commitment by any of the usual sources."

I knew what he meant. It had all started when Lonergan had come to me with the land in Vegas, along with seventy million dollars' worth of financing commitments from various unions and insurance companies. I liked the idea, but I didn't like having partners. Their terms reminded me too much of the moustaches back East. It was then I decided to go public. *Playboy* had done it with even less. I added the ten million dollars that I needed to exercise my option on Mazatlán Lifestyle and took it to the Street. There was scepticism at first, but that changed when they saw the profit figures. This underwriting was the net result.

"Let's not get carried away prematurely, gentlemen," I said. "We still have two more weeks before the stock is issued."

"A mere technicality," Courtland said. "There's nothing that could go wrong now."

"It'd better not. I've signed the contracts and I'm already on the line for the money. If this doesn't go through, I'm in big trouble."

"That will never happen," Courtland said. "Right now you can put the money in the bank. The day the market opens your stock will be worth two hundred and twenty-five million dollars."

A small round of applause greeted his statement. At first I thought it was a put-on. But when I looked around the table, I saw that it wasn't. They were deadly serious. I had forgotten that money was a living thing for them. Too bad it couldn't get up and take a bow. I remained silent.

"Since this will be our last meeting before the underwriting, I have been asked by the board of governors of the Stock Exchange to extend an invitation for lunch on the day the stock is placed on the board."

"It will be my pleasure."

"Good," he said obviously pleased. "That will be on Monday. I would also like to confirm your speech before the Security Analysts Club on the preceding Friday."

"I have that scheduled. Now I'll plan to remain in New York over that weekend."

"Marvelous." He looked around the table. "Any further questions before we close the meeting?"

"Just one." One of the bankers got to his feet. "When are we going to get an invitation to one of those fabulous parties at your mansion that we've heard so much about?"

I smiled at him. "I'm afraid you've got me confused with Hefner. I don't give parties and I don't have a mansion. I live in a bungalow at the Beverly Hills Hotel."

He flushed with embarrassment.

"But I thank you for asking," I added quickly. "It's a good idea and maybe now I'll be able to afford to do things like that."

They all laughed and the meeting ended on a note of mutual respect, even love. I went back to my office wondering if an equation could be developed to reflect the ratio of money to love. Obviously the more money you had, the more love you received.

It was a few minutes after twelve when I got back to my office. The messages were piled neatly on my desk. I glanced through them. There was nothing important, no one I really had to call back. I stared out the window. It really was a beautiful day.

I picked up the phone and dialed Eileen. "How did the meeting go?" she asked.

"All sweetness and light."

"I'm glad."

"I got an idea. What do you say we take the afternoon off and go out to the beach?"

"I'm sorry. But I can't. I have two editorial meetings and four writers scheduled this afternoon."

"Tell them to fuck off."

"I can't do that." She laughed. "These meetings were set up in advance. If I don't settle some of these things, we'll have a lot of blank pages in the magazine three months from now."

"Shit," I said.

"Don't feel bad. After all, we are having dinner at your mother's tonight."

I tried Bobby next, but he was socked in. Production was on his back to aprpove some layouts. Three photographers were there for thematic assignments and nine models were waiting in his outer office for his okay.

Marissa, who was now running the tour and travel division, was also tied up. Dieter was on his way up to her office and they were scheduled to meet with representatives of the Los Angeles

Dental Association regarding a convention of six hundred people at the Mazatlán Lifestyle.

Finally, I called Denise. "It's your anniversary," I said. "Get a replacement from the pool to cover your desk and we'll spend the afternoon at the beach."

There was genuine regret in her voice. "Oh, Gareth, I can't."

"What do you mean you can't?"

"A bunch of girls are giving me a cocktail party at La Cantina when the office closes.'

That was the last straw. I slammed down the telephone. Everybody in the fucking place had something to do except me. Now I knew what being boss meant. It meant having nothing to do.

I pressed down the intercom. "Get me a car right away."

"Yes, Mr. Brendan. Do you want Tony to drive you?"

"I don't want anybody to drive me I'll drive myself."

There was astonishment in her voice. "You'll drive yourself?"

"You heard me," I snapped, flicking the switch.

They got me an Eldo convertible. I put the top down and twenty minutes later I was tooling out Sunset Boulevard toward the beach. I picked up a basket of the Colonel's chicken and a six-pack of beer and continued up the Pacic Coast Highway past Paradise Cove to a little beach that I remembered as being fairly deserted.

It was about one-thirty when I got there and the sun was high in the sky. I parked on the þluff, took the basket of chicken and the six-pack and trudged down to the sand. I found a partially shaded spot where it would not be too hot, then stripped off my shirt and spread it on the sand.

Except for one surfer who was trying to catch the big wave, I was alone on the beach. I slipped off my slacks and sat down in my black Jockey briefs. I leaned my head back against the bluff and snapped open a beer can. It was nice and cold and felt good going down. Idly I watched the surfer.

He was riding a crest. There wasn't enough force in the wave to carry him and he sank into the water. A moment later he reappeared on his surfboard, paddling out to sea to catch the next wave.

The wheeling gulls were chasing fish, the sandpipers chasing their shadows. I took my shades out of my shirt pocket and put them on to shield my eyes against the sun's glare. The surfer was riding a good one. I watched him come almost to the edge of the sand, then step off. I wondered if I could still do it. When I was a kid I used to spend a lot of time looking for the big wave.

"Just one more wave, Uncle John," I pleaded. "Please."

He hesitated, then nodded. "Just one more. Then we go home. The beach is empty and your mother will begin to worry about you."

I ran into the water, carrying my junior-sized surfboard. I swam out as far as I dared, waited for what I thought was the big one, then got on the board with a pounding heart and stood up. It was a beautiful curler and I screamed at the top of my seven-year-old lungs all the way in.

Uncle John was waiting with a big bath towel as I came out of the water. "Now get out of your trunks and let me dry you off," he said.

He knelt in front of me, rubibng me with the towel. My father's voice came from behind me. "Can't you even manage to keep your hands off your own nephew, you perverted bastard?"

I saw my uncle's eyes turn to ice behind his rimless glasses. Slowly he rose to his feet. Then he moved so quickly I didn't see what happened. By the time I turned around my father was sprawled on the sand, blood streaming from his mouth and nose. My uncle was standing over him with fists clenched.

I ran and knelt at my father's side. He moved his head weakly, trying to speak. I could see the broken tooth hanging below his lip and the look of terror on his face.

I screamed at my uncle in pure anger. "Don't you dare hit my father no more, you mean, terrible man!"

My uncle stood looking down at us silently with an expression of sorrow on his face.

I tried to lift my father's head. "Get up, Daddy, get up."

My father struggled to a sitting position. When I looked up, Uncle John was walking down the beach toward his car.

For a long time after that Uncle John didn't come to our house. And when he finally did, the closeness that had existed between us was gone.

Maybe it was the surfer that aroused the memory. I couldn't recall ever having thought about it before. I pulled the tab on another can of beer and dipped into the Colonel's basket. The chicken was still hot and moist.

The surfer had come out of the water and was walking up the beach, with his board under his arm when he saw me watching him. He tightened his ass and thrust his pelvis forward so that the bulge in his bikini stood out more prominently.

I grinned at the obvious hustle. He saw my smile and took it as an invitation. He turned up the beach and stopped in front of me. Jamming the surfboard nose first into the sand, he leaned over it with one arm. With legs spread and hips thrust forward, he was practically shoving his prick in my face.

"Hi," he said.

At close range, he was older than he looked from a distance. I had figured him for fifteen, sixteen. Nineteen or twenty was more like it. "Hi."

"Nice day," he said. "But the surf ain't worth a damn."

"Yeah."

"Alone?"

He hooked a thumb into the front of his bikini and pushed it down so that half his cock and the top of his balls were showing. He smiled at me. "How about that?"

I grinned up at him. "Half a flash is better than none."

The humour didn't faze him. He was all business. "Twenty for French, thirty for Greek, forty for the round trip."

"You're stupid, buster," I said pleasantly. "For all you know I could be a vice cop."

His face turned white under his tan and he pulled his bikini up so quickly I could hear it snap against his gut. "You're not—"

"No, I'm not."

He sighed with relief. "Jesus! You had me going there for a minute."

I reached for another piece of chicken.

"Man, I usually don't do this sort of thing," he said. "But I need the bread. My landlady is hollering for the room rent."

"I'll give you twenty for the loan of your surboard for a few minutes," I said.

"You're on."

I got to my feet, took my money out of my pocket, peeled off a twenty and stuck the rest in my Jockeys. "Help yourself to a beer and some chicken," I said, picking up the board. "I won't be too long."

The surf was colder than I remembered its being when I was a kid. I paddled out to where the breakers were forming and waited for the wave. I wiped out four times before I caught one that I managed to ride almost to shore. That was enough for me. I quit and came out.

"How was it?" he asked. "You didn't look bad out there."

"I think I'll leave it to you kids. I'm getting too old for that sort of thing."

"You're okay for an old guy. I like you. What do you say we get it on? No charge."

I guess from where he was thirty-six was a long way. "No, thanks. I've just made up my mind. I'm giving up boys."

"Why?"

"Because they spoil you for girls."

"That's stupid," he said. "You'll be missing half the fun."

"Where do you live?" I asked.

"Half a mile down the beach."

I never made it to my mother's for dinner.

It was four o'clock in the morning when I let myself into the bungalow at the hotel. I peeked into our bedroom. In the faint light I could see Eileen, sleeping. Softly I closed the door and went to the other bathroom to shower.

I saw her shadow through the glass of the shower stall. "Are you all right?" she called over the noise of the water.

"I'm fine."

"Your mother was worried about you."

I didn't answer.

"So was I," she added.

"I'm sorry," I said, coming out of the shower. She handed me a towel and I began to rub myself dry.

"She made me promise that I'd have you call her in the morning."

"I'll do that."

She went back to our bedroom and when I got into bed a few minutes later, she moved close to me. I drew her head down to my shoulder. I felt the tears on her cheeks. "Hey, why are you crying?"

"I love you. And I can't bear to see the way you are. You've got everything you've ever wanted. I just don't understand why you're unhappy."

I kissed her hair and brushed the tears from her cheeks. But there was nothing I could say to her. I didn't know why any more than she did.

Her fingers reached up and touched my cheek lightly. "Poor Gareth," she whispered with sleepy tenderness. "So many wars."

Chapter Twenty Three

There's a difference between old money and new money. New money buys antiques and restores them to pristine condition so that one might almost imagine Louis Quinze sweeping through the door and putting his royal ass on the couch. Old money buys antiques and leaves them the way they are with wood unpolished, material faded and cushions so lumpy that your ass feels as if it's perching on a pile of cobblestones.

Martin Courtland was old money. But sitting behind his desk in his office on one of the upper storeys of 70 Wall Street, he didn't have to worry about cobblestones. His chair was the only new piece of furniture in the room. He smiled as I sat on the edge of my chair and signed the last of the papers. Then he pressed a button to have a flunky take the papers away.

Courtland leaned back in his chair and smiled at us. "That finishes it," he said in a satisfied tone. "From now on everything's automatic."

I shifted on my chair and glanced at Eileen. She didn't seem any more comfortable than I was. "What does that mean?"

"Your signature on those papers are irrevocable orders to the underwriters to transfer the moneys they collected from the sale of the stock to your company," he explained. "That's why I asked you to come into New York early so that we could get it out of the way. Now when you appear before the analysts luncheon the day after tomorrow you know the money is in your pocket. And there's nothing that anyone can do about it except you."

"Me?"

He nodded. "You are the only one with the power to revoke this order." He got to his feet. "Is there anything I can do to make your stay in town more comfortable?"

The meeting was obviously over. It was just like the magazine business. We were already last month's issue. "We're okay," I said.

"I'm sorry we couldn't have lunch. But we have time for a

quick drink." Without waiting for an answer, he picked up the phone. "Bring in the bottle of Glen Morangie." He looked over the desk at me. "That's my special occasion scotch."

Then he saw us to the door of his office and we went down to the street where the limo was waiting. The car pulled away before we even told the driver where we were going.

The sidewalks were jammed with people. Nothing like California. Here everybody moved. It was a bright sunny day, but with the tall buildings surrounding us, the street looked as if it were in the twilight zone. "Fun City," I said. "The Big Apple. What do you say we go out and turn it on?"

"Can't we go back to the hotel and get some sleep first?" she asked plaintively. "That red-eye from California wore me out."

We had arrived at the airport at six-forty-five in the morning and we'd just had time to make it to the hotel, shower, change and get down to Wall Street by nine. I looked at my watch. It was ten o'clock. A couple of hours' sleep wouldn't hurt before lunch.

I lowered the window that separated us from the driver. "Back to the hotel, please."

The answer was typically New York. "We're on the way," he said. "I figured that's where you were going."

It seemed as if I had just closed my eyes when the telephone began banging in my ear. I reached over and picked it up. "Yes?"

"Gareth?"

"Yes?"

"Martin Courtland here." His voice crackled with tension. "Have you been watching the twelve o'clock news?"

"I've been asleep," I said.

"There's a news teletype in the lobby," he said. "Take a look at it and call me back."

He clicked off abruptly. I put down the receiver. Eileen hadn't moved. Silently I got out of bed, dressed and went downstairs. I got out of the elevator and walked to the teletype near the Park Avenue entrance.

The machine chattered away, largely ignored by the people

who hurried back and forth, apparently more interested in their own world than the one outside. The machine was pouring out figures on the Federal Reserve Bank. I picked up the long sheet hanging over the back and read it. The story hit me between the eyes.

FROM UPI * NEW YORK 12 NOON
TREASURY DEPARTMENT OFFICIALS ANNOUNCED AT NOON TODAY SEIZURE OF WHAT MAY TURN OUT TO BE THE BIGGEST HAUL OF ILLEGAL NARCOTICS IN THE HISTORY OF THE DEPARTMENT. IN A MASSIVE OPERATION REMINISCENT OF MILITARY OPERATIONS DURING WORLD WAR TWO, RAIDS WERE CONDUCTED IN THREE MAJOR CITIES IN THE UNITED STATES AND TWO FOREIGN COUNTRIES. THE FBI AND THE NARCOTICS DIVISION OF THE TREASURY DEPARTMENT IN COOPERATION WITH SCOTLAND YARD AND THE NEWLY FORMED OPERATION CONDOR GROUP OF THE MEXICAN NATIONAL POLICE TIMED THE RAIDS FOR EXACTLY ELEVEN A.M. E.S.T. PREMISES RAIDED WERER THE LIFESTYLE CLUBS IN NEW YORK, CHICAGO, LOS ANGELES AND LONDON, THE LIFESTYLE HOTEL IN MAZATLAN, MEXICO, THE RETREAT, A RELIGIOUS MISSION IN MAZATLAN, AND THE PRIVATE ESTATE OF SENOR ESTEBAN CARILLO, A FIRST COUSIN OF THE GOVERNOR OF MAZATLAN. THE LIFESTYLE CLUBS AND HOTEL ARE OWNED BY GARETH BRENDAN PUBLICATIONS, PUBLISHERS OF MACHO MAGAZINE AND OTHERS. NUMEROUS ARRESTS WERE MADE AND OTHERS ARE EXPECTED MOMENTARILY. DRUGS SEIZED WERE LARGE AMOUNTS OF HEROIN, COCAINE, MARIJUANA, AMPHETAMINES AND QUAALUDES WITH A STREET VALUE ESTIMATED AT BETWEEN TWO AND THREE HUNDRED MILLION DOLLARS. POLICE IN EACH OF THE MAJOR CITIES ORDERED THE PREMISES OF THE LIFESTYLE CLUBS CLOSED PENDING FURTHER INVESTIGATION.

FOLLOW-UP *** MEXICO CITY
MEXICAN POLICE REPORT THREE DEAD AND TWO WOUNDED IN GUN BATTLE AT SCENE OF DRUG RAID. A HEATED GUN BATTLE IN WHICH MORE THAN TWO HUNDRED ROUNDS WERE EXCHANGED RESULTED IN THE DEATH OF TWO PRIVATE GUARDS IN THE EMPLOY OF SENOR CARILLO AND BROTHER JONATHAN, A MISSIONARY AT

THE RETREAT. TWO MEXICAN POLICEMEN WERE WOUNDED. BROTHER JONATHAN WAS IDENTIFIED AS JOHN SINGER, A FORMER SERGEANT OF THE LOS ANGELES POLICE FORCE WHO RETIRED WHILE UNDER INVESTIGATION BY THE LAPD ON CHARGES OF SHAKEDOWN OF DRUG PUSHERS. THE CHARGES WERE LATER DROPPED.

FOLLOW-UP *** NEW YORK AND WASHINGTON
JUSTICE DEPARTMENT OFFICIALS PROMISE SPEEDY ARRAIGNMENT OF MANAGERS OF LIFESTYLE CLUBS AND OTHERS ARRESTED IN THIS MORNING'S DRUG RAID WHICH RESULTED IN THE CONFISCATION OF THREE HUNDRED MILLION DOLLARS OF NARCOTICS. A HIGH DEPARTMENT OFFICIAL CLAIMS THAT THE BACK OF THE SO-CALLED MEXICAN CONNECTION MAY BE PERMANENTLY BROKEN. THE MEXICAN CONNECTION REPLACED THE FRENCH CONNECTION BROKEN MORE THAN THREE YEARS AGO IN A CRACKDOWN IN FRANCE AS THE PRINCIPAL SOURCE AND SUPPLY OF DRUGS IN THE UNITED STATES.

FOLLOW-UP *** NEW YORK
GARETH BRENDAN PUBLICATIONS LTD., OWNERS OF THE LIFESTYLE CLUBS AND HOTEL CLOSED TODAY AFTER MASSIVE DRUG RAID, IN ONE OF THE MOST SUCCESSFUL STOCK OFFERINGS IN RECENT HISTORY HAS SOLD TWO MILLION SHARES TO THE PUBLIC FOR ONE HUNDRED MILLON DOLLARS. MR. BRENDAN, WITH THREE MILLION SHARES OF THE COMPANY STILL IN HIS PERSONAL POSSESSION, IS PRESIDENT AND CHIEF EXECUTIVE OFFICER OF THE COMPANY. THE STOCK WILL BE POSTED ON THE BIG BOARD FOR THE FIRST TIME NEXT MONDAY.

I tore the sheets from the teletype and went back upstairs. Eileen was awake when I came into the suite. "What's happening?" she asked. "The telephones have gone crazy. It seems like everybody in the world is trying to reach you."

I handed her the teletypes. "Read that."

"Verita wants you to call her right back," she said. "It's urgent."

I nodded, went to the phone and punched out Verita's direct line. "Gareth," I said.

"You know what happen?" It was the first time in a long while I'd heard her lapse into an accent.

"Yes. I just found out."

"You better come back real quick. All hell is breaking loose."

"I'll be there on the next plane." I thought for a moment. Her fiancé had been one of the hottest criminal attorneys in California before he was elected to the bench. "Your friend the judge. Do you think he can arrange to meet me at the airport when I come in?"

"I theenk so."

"Good. I'll let you know what flight as soon as I make the reservations." I couldn't keep the bitterness from my voice. "Julio fucked us."

"You haven't heard the news?" Surprise was in her voice.

I was up to my ass in news. "What news?"

"Julio was machine-gunned to death when he came out of his garage less than an hour ago by two men in a car. The police were on their way to arrest him and they say he was killed to keep him from talking."

"Oh, shit." That had to mean that Julio wasn't the loner he led the Chicanos to believe. There must have been some ties to the moustaches. This was a gangland-style killing. "Okay. I'll call you back in a few minutes as soon as I have flight confirmation."

I put down the telephone. It began to ring the moment the receiver touched the cradle. I picked it up and put it down, disconnecting the call without answering it. Then I dialed the hotel operator. "Hold all calls on twenty-one, two and three until further notice. I don't want to talk to anyone."

As soon as she hung up, I dialed Courtland. While waiting for him to get on the phone, I told Eileen to book us on the next flight to LA and to let Verita know.

"How can a thing like this happen?" Courtland asked.

"I don't know. But I'm on my way back to the Coast to find out."

"If this isn't cleared up to everyone's satisfaction by the time the stock is posted on the board, the board of governors will have no alternative but to suspend the stock from trading."

"Does that mean we have to give the money back?" I asked.

He sounded horrified. "We don't do things like that on the Street. We honour our commitments."

Like their seventeen million dollars' worth of commissions, I was thinking but didn't say anything.

"But it is very embarrassing," he added.

"I'll keep you posted," I said and hung up.

Eileen came back into the room. "There's a three o'clock and a five o'clock. But we'll never make the three o'clock. We have to pack."

"Fuck packing," I said. "We'll make the three o'clock."

ETA Los Angeles was 5.52 pm. Not 5.50, not 5.55. Airlines had their own ways of calculating time. They always took off on the five-minute unit, but they always landed on the five-minute unit plus two. I guess they had their reasons, but on this flight it didn't matter. We ran into heavy headwinds and pulled up to the gate at 6.41. I looked at my watch and wondered what that did to their computers.

I was met at the gate by a crowd of newspaper, radio and TV reporters and two process servers. One was a subpoena to appear before the federal grand jury in Los Angeles, the other to appear before the Congressional committee on organized crime in Washington. Both were on the same day and almost at the same time.

Judge Alfonso Moreno was just behind the process servers. Verita's fiancé was a tall, lean Mexican with a lantern jaw and sandy brown hair. Actually, he looked like a Texas cowboy, which was, in fact, what he was. He'd been born in El Paso and played football for Texas State.

He didn't waste time. "My advice is to answer every question with a 'no comment' until we have had time to talk."

I met his eyes. "I would like to make a short statement which I wrote on the plane if you agree."

"Let me see it." He took the note from my hand, studied it, then gave it back to me. "Okay," he said. "But not one word more."

"Thank you."

"Give me the subpoenas," he said.

I gave them to him. He stuck them in an inside jacket pocket, turned to the reporters and held up his hands. They fell into momentary silence. "Mr. Brendan has a statement that he would like to make."

I read from the note. "I have returned to Los Angeles to aid and assist the authorities in their investigation of this affair. It is my firm belief that when the investigation is completed, they will find that no officer of the company or the company itself has been involved in the matter."

There was a babble of shouted questions from the crowd. I heard one reporter's voice above the others. "Are you aware that the Nevada Gaming Commission withdrew the gambling licence for your proposed hotel and casino pending further investigation?"

I answered without even glancing at the judge. "No comment."

Another reporter. "Is it true that you spent several days at the Mazatlán Lifestyle Hotel in the company of Julio Valdez, who was shot to death this morning?"

"No comment."

The judge took me by the arm. I held onto Eileen and we began to push our way through the crush of reporters. To each of their shouted questions, I gave the same answer: "No comment."

We finally reached the limo at the curb outside the terminal. Tony took off as soon as the door had closed. "Where to, boss?" he asked as we moved into the airport traffic.

"Verita said that we should come to her apartment. It would be quieter there and we would be able to talk," the judge said.

"Okay." I gave Tony the address and turned back to the judge. "Is that statement about the Nevada Gaming Commission true?"

"Verita told me that she received the telegram from them at three-thirty this afternoon."

I shook my head. It wasn't getting any better. "Verita was anxious for me to get back here in a hurry. Did she have anything special to tell me?"

"She didn't confide in me. She said she wanted to talk to you first."

But that never happened. Because when we pulled up to the new high-rise apartment on Wilshire Boulevard where Verita had moved in order to be near the office, the ambulance and four police cars were already there. A body, covered with a blanket, lay half on and half off the curb.

The judge and I were out of the car almost before it stopped. We pushed through the small crowd toward the police. A boy with a little dog in his arms was talking to a policeman, who was taking notes.

"I was just taking Schnapsi for her evening walk when I heard this scream and I looked up and saw this woman come flying over the railing up there on the fifteenth floor falling down on me."

"Did you see anybody else up there?" the policeman asked.

"Hell, no," the boy said. "I was too busy getting out of the way."

"My God!" The judge's voice was a strangled sob in his throat. I followed his gaze to a small hand that was not covered by the blanket. A diamond twinkled on the ring finger. "I just gave that to her last week!"

Then his face turned a peculiar green and he lurched toward the curb. I grabbed him by the shoulders to keep him from falling and held him while he cried and vomited his guts into the street.

Chapter Twenty Four

The next day was another slice of hell. The *LA Times* ran a screaming banner across the top of the front page. WOMAN VP BRENDAN PUBLICATIONS SUICIDE, POLICE SAY.

The subhead wasn't much better. "Verita Velasquez, first cousin to Mexican Crime King, who was shot to death yesterday." The story itself was a masterful construction of facts that added up to a totally false impression and left the reader thinking that Verita was Mrs. Inside while Julio was Mr. Outside.

It took us two hours to clear the reception area of reporters and work out a system that would keep them out. We did it by closing off all but two of the six elevators and screening all visitors in the downstairs lobby.

Finally, the office was quiet, although it was more like a mausoleum than a place of business with everyone walking around on tiptoe and speaking in hushed whispers.

Even Shana and Dana were subdued. They weren't playing their usual game. Today I seemed to get their names right every time. "Mr. Saunders of circulation on the line."

"Thank you, Shana," I said picking up the phone. "Yes, Charlie."

"We have some real problems, Mr. Brendan," he said in an upset tone.

I didn't need him to tell me. I kept my voice calm. "Yes?"

"Many wholesalers and distributors are refusing to accept our shipments of the new issue of *Macho* and others are returning them in unopened bundles."

This was a real problem. These were the people who got our magazines on the stands and racks where they could be bought by the public. "How many did we print?"

"Four million five hundred thousand."

"How many do you think will stick?"

"According to our computer, between five and seven hundred thousand."

There went two million dollars in real money and didn't take into account possible profits. It didn't take long for the story to dig in and hurt. I took a deep breath. There was nothing that could be done about it, at least for the moment. There was an old saying that a lie could travel halfway around the world while the truth was putting on its boots to go after it. Maybe if I were in their place, I would feel the same way. I wouldn't want to be doing business with what looked like the biggest drug pusher in the world.

"Sit tight, Charlie," I said. "Things will get back to normal once we get this business straightened out."

I put down the telephone. The intercom buzzed again. "Bobby is here to see you."

"Send him in."

Bobby came in with his eyes red from weeping. "Oh, Gareth! " he cried. "I can't believe she's dead."

I got out of my chair and put my arms around him. He leaned his face against my chest, sobbing like a child. Gently I stroked his head. "Easy," I said.

"Why did she kill herself? I'll never understand it. She was going to get married next month."

"She didn't kill herself."

He stepped back. "But the police said that she did. They said there was no sign that anyone had been in the apartment with her."

"I don't give a damn what they said." I went back to my chair.

"If she didn't kill herself, then who killed her?"

"I think it was the same people who killed Julio. I have a feeling that they thought that she and Julio were closer than they really were."

His eyes were wide. "The Mafia?"

"I don't know," I said. "But I'm damn well going to try to find out." I took a cigarette from the box on the desk and lit it. "Is your father in town?"

"He's at home."

I pressed down the intercom. "Get Reverend Sam for me. He's at home." I released the switch. "I thought he got rid of Brother Jonathan two years ago."

"You know father. He sees only the good in people. Brother

Jonathan managed to convince him that Denise was a doper and that he tried to get her straight but couldn't."

The intercom buzzed. "Reverend Sam on the line."

Reverend Sam's voice was genuinely sympathetic. "A terrible business, Gareth, a terrible business. She was a lovely girl."

"Yes, Reverend Sam. But I'm calling about Brother Jonathan."

"Shocking. I couldn't believe that the man was capable of such duplicity."

"How long did you know him?"

There was a moment's pause. "Let me see . . . seven, maybe eight years . . . He joined the mission right after he left the police force."

"How did you happen to meet him?"

"Your Uncle John sent him to me. There had been some threats against my life at that time and he came to work for me as a bodyguard. But then God shone His light on him and he began to devote himself to the mission. By the time we decided that the threats were no longer a problem he had already reached the second level."

"I see. Thank you, Reverend Sam."

"You're quite welcome, Gareth. If there is anything I can do to ease your burden, don't hesitate to come to me."

"Thank you again. Goodbye, Reverend Sam."

"Goodbye, Gareth."

"You're right about your father, Bobby. He sees only the good in everyone."

He managed a smile. "The last of the innocents."

"Not the last," I said. "The first."

After he had gone, I sat alone for a while, just thinking. Brother Jonathan still bothered me. On an impulse I sent for Denise.

She, too, had been weeping. "Poor Verita. I really loved her. Her aura was so pure."

"She was a good lady," I said. "Look, I need help. If what I ask you hurts too much, just tell me. I didn't want to disturb you."

"I love you, Gareth. I'll do anything I can to help you."

"When Brother Jonathan had you in transit at the Retreat, was it really me that he was exorcising from your mind?"

"It seemed like that." She hesitated. "We always started the transit that way. The first thing he told me was that I had to get you out of my mind and my body."

"Did he ever talk about anything else?"

"I think so. But I don't remember too well. After the question about you, everything always seemed to go fuzzy."

"That's because he gave you a shot of Pentothal," I said. "There were still traces of it in your blood when I brought you to the hospital. And it was from one of those injections with an unsterilized needle that you got hepatitis."

"That's the truth serum, isn't it?"

"Yes. But it can also be used as a hypnotic. Perhaps there was something he wanted you to disconnect, to forget completely without being conscious of it."

"I don't know what that could be. After all, I was his secretary for the first year I was down there and it was my job to keep track of everything. I even used to type all his reports."

"Reports? To whom?"

"There were a lot of people. The religious ones to Reverend Sam, of course. The others to . . . the others . . ." A puzzled look came into her eyes. "Funny, but I can't seem to remember."

"What were the other reports about?"

She thought for a moment, then shook her head. "I can't remember that either."

I look at her silently.

"I'm sorry."

I smiled. "That's okay."

"I'd better go back to work now."

I waited until she was halfway to the door before playing my hunch. "Lonergan!" I said sharply.

She didn't turn around. "I know. He always gets the top copy," she said automatically, then continued on to the door as if she hadn't spoken. She looked back. "Goodbye, Gareth."

"Goodbye, Denise."

I waited until the door closed behind her before calling personnel. A man answered. "Erikson speaking."

"Do you have copies of the personnel forms of the club and hotel employees, Mr. Erikson?"

"They're on the computer, sir."

"Can I get the readout?"

"Yes, sir, but you have to know the code."

"I need some information. Can you come up to my office?"

"I'll be right there, Mr. Brendan."

Two minutes later he was standing beside my desk with a code book in his hand. Ten minutes later I had all the information that I sought.

Each employee was required to give three personal references before being placed on the payroll. One of the three references provided by all the general managers and supply managers of the clubs and the hotel was always John Lonergan.

It all began to fall into place.

When I'd gotten into his car after the explosion outside the little store on Santa Monica Boulevard, he had all but spelled it out for me. If he hadn't protected me, Julio would have fed me to the wolves.

And Dieter had implied it again in Mexico when he told me that without my uncle's permission Julio could not exist in Los Angeles and that Lonergan was the only man who could stop Julio from using the airstrip.

Julio had probably never stopped using the airstrip at all. Not even for one day. And when I'd made the deal for the hotel, Lonergan had it all together. It had to be the most profitable one-man cartel in history. Three hundred million dollars a year with built-in profits at every stage from manufacture to distribution.

And it hadn't cost him one penny. He'd done it all with my money.

Chapter Twenty Five

It was six o'clock and Lonergan was nowhere to be found. He wasn't at home, at his Beverly Hills office or at the Silver Stud. My mother had gone to visit some friends at Newport Beach for the day, so she was of no help to me right then. She was expected to be home for dinner, however, so I left word with the butler to have her call when she came in.

The intercom buzzed. "Mr. Courtland on the line from New York."

"You're working late," I said. "It's nine o'clock there."

"Our office doesn't close with the market despite what people think," he said humorlessly. "Any new developments?"

"Some."

"Anything I can report to the board of governors?"

"I don't think so."

"What about that girl who killed herself? Logic says she could have been the Trojan Horse in your organization."

"She wasn't."

"I hear they're shipping your magazine back by the thousands," he said.

"Millions."

He was shocked into silence for a moment. "Would you like me to cancel your appearance at the analysts' luncheon tomorrow?"

"Have they withdrawn their invitation?"

"No."

"Then I'll be there."

"I'm just trying to save you some embarrassment," he said. "Many of them touted your stock to the sky and they feel you took them. They can get pretty rough and they're not in a happy frame of mind."

"Neither am I. See you tomorrow." I put down the phone and pressed the intercom.

"Yes, Mr Brendan?"

"Charter a plane to take me to New York tonight. I expect

to leave sometime between midnight and three in the morning."

"Yes, Mr. Brendan," she said. "Your mother's on the line, returning your call."

"Hello, Mother."

"Gareth, I feel so bad for you." She seemed to mean it.

"I'm all right, Mother."

"How could those Mexicans do such terrible things to you? And after you were so good to her, too. Taking her out of a menial clerk's position and giving her such an important job. I knew you couldn't trust her the first time I heard her voice over the telephone. We were just talking about it on the Fischer's yacht at lunch today. They have such a beautiful yacht. Seventy—"

"Mother," I interrupted, "who was talking about it?"

"We all were. But then Uncle John explained what really happened and we all felt so badly for you."

"Uncle John was with you?"

"Yes."

"Is he with you now?"

"No. He had an appointment for dinner."

"With whom?"

"I thought I heard him mention the name of that nice young man, Dieter von Halsbach."

"Thank you, Mother." I put down the telephone without even saying goodbye and pressed the intercom. "See if Marissa is still in her office."

She wasn't, so I told them to keep trying her at home. They reached her a half hour later. "Do you know where Dieter might be having dinner?" I asked.

"No. I saw him in the office about five-thirty. Then he rushed off for a very important appointment."

"Where could he be?"

"If I hear from him, I'll have him call you."

"Thanks."

"Gareth, I'm sorry about Verita. I hope you don't believe what the papers are saying."

"I don't."

"I'm glad. I don't either."

I decided to call Bobby at home. Since there were no secrets in the gay world, I thought he might be able to help. "Do you think you can find out where Dieter is tonight?" I asked.

"I'll try," he said. "It may take some time. Where can I reach you if I do?"

"I'll be in the office."

He called back at ten-fifteen. "Dieter had a reservation at the Greek Chorus."

"The Greek Chorus?" I echoed.

"That's right. He took a suite for the whole night. Dinner and everything. Our friend must be flush."

I put down the telephone. It didn't make sense. The Greek Chorus was the most expensive gay brothel in the world. Appointments were by reservation only and the minimum charge was five hundred dollars. I've heard of tabs that ran as high as ten thousand for one evening. But that was an Arab who had flown in especially for the night and bought everything and everyone in sight.

The Greek Chorus was in an old movie star's mansion high in the Hollywood Hills. Tony pulled the car into the driveway and stopped in front of the entrance. "Wait for me," I said as I rang the bell.

A burly man in a dinner jacket opened the door. Another man in a dinner jacket stood just behind him. "Do you have a reservation?" the first man asked.

"No, but I only have a few hours in town and I heard so much about this place."

"Sorry," the man said, stepping back. "Reservations only." He began to close the door.

I stopped it with my foot and showed him a hundred-dollar bill.

He looked at it impassively.

I added another hundred to it. Then another, and another and another. I stopped at five hundred. Too much and I would blow it.

"What's your name?" he asked.

"Gareth."

"Just a moment, sir. I may have overlooked your name in the book."

He stepped inside and spoke to the other man. A moment

later he was back. "I'm sorry to have kept you waiting, sir," he said, pocketing the five bills. "But an ink smudge partly covered your name."

I followed him through the door. "This is just a precaution, sir," he said, stopping me. "Would you please hold out your arms."

I did as he asked and he patted me down very professionally. He straightened up. "We don't allow guns or knives in here," he said apologetically. "It's for your own protection as well as that of the other clientele."

We passed through the grand entrance hall. The elegant old twenties' mansion had been re-created as a gays' paradise. "Do you prefer any particular type, sir?" he asked.

"I'm open. I'd like to see them all."

"Yes sir," he said, opening a door. When I heard the buzz of conversation I realized how thoroughly soundproofed the place was. "This is the salon, sir. The fees depend on the person you choose. There is a five-hundred dollar minimum. Drinks and food are on the house."

"Thank you." I stood for a moment to let my eyes get used to the soft light, then headed for the semicircular bar at the end of the room.

Groups of men, many of them nude, were sprawled around the room on couches and chaise-longues.

A man in a dinner jacket leaned across the bar. "Your pleasure, sir."

"Scotch on the rocks." I threw down a five-dollar bill as tip.

"Sorry, sir," he said, pushing the bill toward me. "No tipping allowed. You are our guest, sir."

"Thank you." I leaned back against the bar, looked around the room and took a healthy slug of my drink. Then I saw someone I knew and smiled to myself.

With drink in hand I crossed the room and stopped in front of the naked black man who was stretched out on the chaise with his eyes closed. "Jack," I said in a low voice.

King Dong opened his eyes in surprise.

"Sleeping on the job?" I smiled.

He sat up slowly. "What are you doin' here, Mistuh Gareth? I never expected to find you in a place like this."

"How about you?" I retorted.

"I work here one night a week. Sometimes I pick up as much as a grand. It pays the rent. There ain't much work in modelin' no more."

"Are you interested in a grand clear?"

"Money's my middle name."

"Remember the Mexican man, the blond one?" I sat down on the couch next to him. "Is he here tonight?"

A man walked by in a dinner jacket. "Pretend," King Dong said. "That's one of the spotters."

I lifted it. I swear it weighed as much as a boa constrictor. The spotter retraced his steps and went out the door.

"Yes, he's here," King Dong said.

"Do you know what room he's in?"

He nodded.

"Can you get me in to see him?"

"To do that you go upstairs. An' the only way you gits upstairs is with one of the boys."

"I'll go up with you."

"I don't know," he said doubtfully. "If'n these guys fin' out, I'm dead. They killers."

"Nobody will find out. There won't be any trouble."

"It'll cost you five hundred for the house."

"Okay."

His low voice rumbled through the room. "You in an awful hurry, man." He laughed.

"I've got a plane to catch," I said, playing along.

I followed him to the bar..

"I got me an eager beaver," he said to the bartender.

The bartender didn't smile. "Five hundred dollars, please."

I laid five bills on the bar.

"Thank you." He reached under the bar and came up with a gold-plated room key. "Room sixteen."

"Six or seven open?" King Dong asked. "You know I don't do my best work in a room with a low ceiling."

The bartender checked again. He changed the keys. "Six."

"Thanks," King Dong said.

In the far corner of the room he parted some drapes, revealing a staircase.

"We lucked in," he whispered. "He's right next door in Room Five."

"Will I need a key to get in?" I asked.

He shook his head. "The doors are never locked when the room is in use. Sometimes there's trouble an' they have to get in there in a hurry."

We reached the first landing. He stopped in front of the door that was emblazoned with a brass number six. He looked up and down the hall. It was empty. "You kin go in there now," he whispered. "But be careful comin' out."

I opened the next door and slipped into the room. At the same time I saw King Dong disappear into number six.

All the lights were on. Across the room Dieter lay facedown on the bed. On the floor next to him was an empty hypodermic syringe and a twisted rubber cord. I saw the needle marks on Dieter's outstretched arm. The future Count von Halsbach was nothing but a junkie.

I knelt over him and shook his shoulder. He moved but didn't open his eyes. I heard a sound coming from behind the curtain at the other end of the room. I moved toward it quickly and pulled the curtain back.

Three pairs of dark eyes looked up at me from around a table, laden with food. I stared down at their grubby faces.

They looked at me and then resumed eating as if they had never been interrupted. I let the curtain drop and went back to the bed.

I shook Dieter harder. He finally opened his eyes and after a moment showed a sign of recognition.

"Where's Lonergan?" I asked.

He shook his head, then groaned. "He's gone."

"How long?"

"An hour, a half hour. I don't know. I was asleep."

"Go back to sleep," I said.

He closed his eyes again. I went to the door, opened it a crack and peered out. The hall was empty. Quickly I went next door.

King Dong was sitting on the edge of the bed.

"Okay," I said. "Let's go."

"Just a minute," he said, reaching for a towel. He closed his eyes. "Ahh," he sighed.

After a moment, he stood up. He reached across the bed, pulling down the cover and mussing the sheets. "That's still my favorite way," he said over his shoulder pleasantly.

After wrinkling the bed, he threw the towel into the middle of it. "Okay, now we kin go. I was jus' takin' no chances. They might git suspicious if'n evvything was too neat and tidy."

"You can pick up your grand at the office tomorrow," I said, following him down the stairs.

The man at the door bowed. "I trust everything was to your pleasure, sir."

"Just fine," I said.

"Thank you, sir. Please come again."

Tony started the engine as I got into the car. I looked at the digital clock on the dash. Twelve-ten. I knew exactly where to find Lonergan at this time of the night.

Chapter Twenty Six

The Silver Stud was as crowded and as noisy as it had always been. Everything seemed the same. Only the chick banging away at the piano was different.

But a few minutes later I noticed that there was something else that was different. I made it all the way across the room and not once did anyone make a grab at me. Now I knew I was getting older.

I stopped in front of the Collector. As usual, there was a bottle of scotch on the table in front of him. He looked at me with a smile. "Hey, man, it's been a long time." We slapped hands. "Sit down an' have a drink," he invited. "We been expectin' you."

He poured me a drink. "Lonergan in?" I asked.

He nodded. "He's finishin' a meeting. He'll see you in a few minutes."

I had a taste. The liquor helped.

"What do you think of that chick at the piano?" he asked enthusiastically.

"It seems to me I've heard that song before."

He laughed, showing all his teeth and slapping his thigh. "Can I he'p it if I'm a freak for chick piano players?" A buzzer sounded under the table. "You can go up now."

Lonergan, seated behind his desk, regarded me with cool eyes. "I hear you've been looking for me."

"All day."

"Any special reason?" he asked mildly.

"I think you know."

"You tell me."

"You set me up. You killed Julio and Verita and God only knows how many others."

His voice was calm. "You can't prove that."

"That's right. I just wanted you to know."

"I saved your ass. I gave you a perfect setup. Now you can get up in front of your analysts' lunch on Wall Street and lay everything out for them. In a few days everything opens up again and you're home free."

"Is that all there is to it?"

"What more do you want?"

"I want Verita back. Alive and well and happy. The way she was the last time I saw her."

"Only God can do that. Ask me for something I can do."

"Shit. You and I will never understand each other."

"I think I understand you. You're like your father. You think tough, but inside you're all mush. Neither of you was strong enough to be real men."

"But you are?"

He nodded. "Nobody takes anything from me."

"You mean you give nothing to nobody."

"Semantics."

"Love," I said.

His voice was cool. "What's that?"

"If you have to ask, you'll never know."

"Do you have anything more to say?"

I shook my head.

"Then you'd better go. It's twenty-four hundred miles to New York and if you don't make your luncheon on time, you're finished."

I started for the door. A picture of the grubby faces and three pairs of staring eyes flashed through my mind and I had a sudden jolt of memory. I stopped. "There is one thing you can tell me, Uncle John," I said.

"What's that?"

"You were playing with my baby prick that day my father found us on the beach, weren't you?"

He didn't blink, but I saw him turn pale. It was enough. I went out of his office and down the stairs without loooking back. I fought back the tears that burned my eyes. I had really wanted to love him.

The Collector had enticed the piano player to his table. He gave me a wave as I went by. I pushed my way through the crowded bar. There was a gang of leather boys standing near the door. The tears blurred my vision and I stumbled into one of them.

I stepped back. "Pardon me," I said.

"*De nada*," he said, averting his face quickly. But not before I recognized him. I saw the shining stud lettering over his breast pocket. J. V. KINGS. It was the same boy who had picked me up near Verita's apartment a thousand years ago. I hesitated for a moment, thinking of going back and warning Lonergan. But it was his war, not mine. And I'd had enough of fighting other people's wars.

I went outside and got into the car. "Okay, Tony," I said. "The airport."

I called Eileen from a pay station in the terminal. "I'm on my way to New York. Don't wait up for me. I'll be back tomorrow night."

"Good luck," she said. "I love you."

"I love you," I said and put the phone back on the hook.

The advantage of a charter plane was that it had a beautiful comfortable bed. I slept all the way to New York and when I got off the plane, I saw the headline in the *New York Daily News*. Lonergan was dead. I didn't even buy the newspaper to read the story.

I arrived at the luncheon just as they were serving the dessert. I heard the surprised buzz as I came into the room. I kept my eyes straight ahead, and went directly to the dais. There was an empty seat with my name on a place card near the center of the long table.

A moment later the man next to me rose to his feet and rapped the gavel for attention. The room grew quiet. "Ladies and gentlemen," he said tersely, "Mr. Gareth Brendan."

There was no polite applause. A sea of faces stared at me in deadly silence as I made my way to the microphone.

"Mr. Chairman, ladies and gentlemen, I will be brief. As you know, Gareth Brendan Publication Limited's first public stock offering is a tremendous success. And I wish to express my appreciation to all of you who worked so hard to make that success. Thank you."

I paused. The silence was deafening.

"But unfortunately, certain factors have arisen which becloud the value of that offering. I am a naïve man in many ways. I like to feel that there are those among you who care even more for your client's welfare than for your own commisssions.

"I was told by Mr. Courtland that the offering is irrevocable and can only be canceled by one man. Me. As of this moment, it is still my stock and my company. So I take this opportunity to inform you that this offering is hereby officially withdrawn from sale."

A hum spread through the room, forcing me to raise my voice to be heard over it. "So that no one suffers any financial losses in connection with this offering I also offer to reimburse any and all legitimate expenses incurred by the underwriters in connection with it. Thank you."

I turned from the dais and started to make my way to the exit. The mum rose to a roar. I caught a glimpse of Courtland. He was stunned; a seventeen-million-dollar pallor suffused his face.

Reporters crowded around, grabbing at my coat and shouting questions. I pushed through them and made my way out the door without comment.

The telephone was ringing when I got to the hotel. It was Eileen. "I heard some of your speech on the newscast," she said. "I'm very proud of you."

"I don't know. Maybe I'm stupid."

"No. You're beautiful." Her voice changed. "You heard about your uncle?"

"Yes."

"It's terrible."

"No, it's not," I said and meant it. "Lonergan screwed up enough lives, including mine. But no more."

She was silent.

"I'll be leaving in about an hour. How about meeting in Vegas and we'll have a little fun?"

"Haven't you lost enough money for one day?"

"That's not the kind of fun I'm talking about. I mean like getting married."

There was a moment of startled silence. "You mean it?" she asked incredulously.

"Of course I mean it. I love you."